W9-BUA-581

THE NIGHT BELONGS TO CHARLIE

Movement stirred in the brush to Baxter's right, between him and the river, where a man-sized shape crouched among the leaves and ferns. He was raising a weapon . . .

There was no telling how many others might be in the area who would hear gunfire. Letting his AK dangle on its strap, Baxter pulled his knife as he lunged at the Vietnamese, who was training a Russian-made SKS rifle at the SEALs in the water. Baxter grabbed the man from behind, smothering his mouth with one hand, yanking the rifle up and back, bringing the black blade of the knife up and across the man's throat just below the angle of his jaw. The man thrashed once, gurgling and struggling as Baxter continued to clamp his mouth shut. Warm blood spilled across Baxter's arm.

At almost the same instant, a second VC rose from cover a few yards away, the AK in his hands swinging to aim at Baxter and his dying victim. For a horrible instant, Baxter knew the other soldier was going to pull the trigger . . .

SEALS
THE
WARRIOR BREED
— BOOK THREE —

BRONZE STAR

H. JAY RIKER

AVON BOOKS ◆ NEW YORK

SEALS, THE WARRIOR BREED: BRONZE STAR is an original publication of Avon Books. This work has never before appeared in book form. This is a work of fiction. Characters and organizations in this novel are either the product of the author's imagnation, or, if real, used fictitiously without any intent to describe their actual conduct.

AVON BOOKS
A division of
The Hearst Corporation
1350 Avenue of the Americas
New York, New York 10019

Copyright © 1995 by Bill Fawcett & Associates
Published by arrangement with the author
Library of Congress Catalog Card Number: 95-94482
ISBN: 0-380-76970-0

First Avon Books Printing: December 1995

AVON TRADEMARK REG. U.S. PAT. OFF. AND IN OTHER COUNTRIES, MARCA REGISTRADA, HECHO EN U.S.A.

Printed in the U.S.A.

RA 10 9 8 7 6 5 4

Author's Note

This is a work of fiction, but the story is closely based on real men, on what they said and did, and on events that actually took place during the early years of the U.S. Navy SEALS. Names and the specifics of various incidents have been changed for dramatic purposes, and also for dramatic purposes, some of the characters are completely fictitious or are composites based on the exploits of several real people. These changes, however, should in no way be misconstrued as disrespect for the real heroes of the SEAL story, the men—living and dead—who put everything they had and everything they were on the line for something in which they believed.

In particular, it should be noted that the accounts of those SEALS killed in Vietnam, though based closely on fact, have been fictionalized, at least in part because their living comrades and families would not care to see their names or their memories used in a work of fiction.

It is to those brave men who gave everything they had, in a war where genuine heroes were despised or, at best, ignored and forgotten by their own countrymen, that this work is respectfully dedicated.

—H. Jay Riker
December 1994

Chapter 1

"Christ on a crutch. It's hot!"

"C'mon, c'mon, people. Let's move it."

"I don't like the service on this airline. Who do I see to complain?"

The line of men in green Marine-style fatigues filed down the sloping deck of the aircraft's passenger compartment and out through the narrow aft doorway. As he stepped into full daylight, the first thing to hit Lieutenant j.g. Edward Charles Baxter was the heat. It struck him full in the face as he stepped through the open cabin door of the C-118 Liftmaster, embraced him with a clinging familiarity, raising beads of sweat on his forehead in seconds. By the time he reached the bottom of the rickety metal boarding ladder, his fatigues were soaked beneath his arms and down the center of his back.

The second thing he noticed was the incredible flatness of his surroundings. Baxter had been watching the ground through his window aboard the Liftmaster on the way in, of course, with an eager attention to detail, as though he could memorize each shade of green, each checkerboard square of rice paddy or field, but flying always seemed to flatten out the landscape somewhat. Now that he was on the ground, though, he could compare the landscape encircling the air base to the sere, brown hills of southern California, and he realized that this place was as flat and as mechanically precise as the deck

1

of an aircraft carrier. From here there was little to see except tarmac. The base was huge and sprawling, with one horizon taken up by an endless line of low, concrete block buildings, Quonset huts, and revetments of corrugated steel and sandbags, the skyline unrelieved by even a single palm tree.

"Man, it's hot!" Machinist's Mate First Class Terrance A. Connors said, stepping off the ladder at Baxter's side. His dark face glistened with sweat.

"Ah, it ain't the heat, it's the fuckin' humidity," Torpedoman Third Class Christopher Luciano said, swinging his green nylon seabag off of his shoulder and letting it thump on the tarmac.

An olive-drab helicopter, a big "fore-and-aft" rotor Chinook, clattered noisily past a couple of hundred yards away. A jet engine roar in the distance spooled up to thunderous proportions. Noise, Baxter decided, was the third aspect of this place to impress itself on him, though other sensations were crowding in now too quickly to be categorized. He'd expected the place to smell like jungle, but here, at least, the stink was of kerosene, aviation fuel, and hot metal. The sky, perhaps in contrast to the flatness of the surroundings, was as blue and as deep as any sky he'd ever seen, with the clouds assuming a stark three-dimensionality that gave them an almost ponderous weight and mass.

Baxter glanced at the others, filing off the aircraft's boarding ladder with their seabags balanced on their shoulders or slung from their backs by their canvas straps. "Well, gentlemen," he said with a grin. "Welcome to the Republic of Vietnam!"

There was an air of unreality about it all, even as he said the words. Just thirty hours earlier he and the seventeen men with him had been stateside, boarding the C-118 at North Island Naval Air Station for the first of four legs to a journey that brought them halfway around the world. It had been cool and partly cloudy in San Diego, with the temperature in the fifties—seasonable for late February in southern California. The temperature here had to be thirty degrees higher, beneath a brassy hot sun that cast long shadows across the tarmac. Despite Connors's assessment of the humidity, Baxter thought it was probably drier here than it had been in California, but the heat made it seem stickier and far more unpleasant.

"So, Lieutenant," Radioman Second Class Paul Weaver said. "Where to next?"

"Yeah," Ensign Ronald H. Hanrahan added in his nasal, somewhat annoying squeak of a voice. "When do we start killing things?"

The third of the three officers in the group, another j.g. named Gilbert Chalker, shaded his eyes against the glare from the sky, then pointed. "Just maybe," he said in his easy Texas drawl, "these folks have the answer to that."

The vehicle looked as though it might have begun life as a school bus in the United States, but that obviously had been a few years ago. Its sides were dinged and battered over a more or less uniform coat of olive-drab paint. It pulled up in front of the waiting men with a wheeze, the door folded open, and a short man in green fatigues stepped off. U.S. Army was emblazoned in yellow block letters stitched to a black patch above his shirt pocket, and he wore the silver railroad tracks of an Army captain on his collar.

The man consulted the clipboard he carried. "Lieutenant junior grade, uh, Baxter?"

Baxter saluted. "That's me, sir."

"Captain George Maxwell," the other said, returning the gesture with a careless touch to the corner of his fatigue cap. "Welcome to the Nam. Have your men fall in."

"All right, people," Baxter called. "You heard the man! Fall in!"

"Adams!" The captain called.

"Yo!"

"Alvarez!"

"Here!"

He made a check on his list. "Baxter, I have you. Bosniak!"

"Here!"

As the captain ran down the rest of the list, Baxter groaned inwardly. They'd warned him about this back in Coronado . . . that when he got to Vietnam he'd be in with the *real* military again, and the Mickey Mouse would start in earnest. They'd been right. Two minutes off the damned aircraft, and it was fall in, sound off, and listen up, the litany of human beings reduced to ticks on a checklist, or numbers in a file.

How long, he wondered, before one of the seventeen rugged

individualists in his tiny command sounded off the wrong way? It would happen, he was certain. The only question was when. U.S. Navy SEALs, Baxter had learned, could adapt well to almost any dirty, wet, uncomfortable, or dangerous situation imaginable. What they had trouble adapting to was the starched shirts and rule books of the bureaucracy.

"Woj—uh, Wojciechowski!"

"Here, sir!"

Maxwell checked off the final name, then lowered the clipboard to his side.

"Okay, men," he said. "I still don't know what the hell you Navy types are supposed to be doing here, but the bus here'll take you in to a hotel in Saigon. Tomorrow morning at 0900 hours, you'll be brought back out here. A helo'll take you to your new post down at Nha Be."

"Excuse me, Captain," Chalker drawled. "But the way I heard it, Nha Be's only about eight-nine miles from Saigon." He jerked his thumb over his shoulder, toward the south. "Seems to me we could just head on out."

"Shit," Ordnanceman Second Class John Adams said with a shrug. "We could *walk* that far and be there in time for chow."

"Quiet in the ranks!" Maxwell growled. He turned on Chalker. "For your information, Navy, this outfit isn't run for your convenience. You're laying over in Saigon because that's what these orders say you're going to do, and if you don't like it, you can take it up with CO-MACV, you read me?"

"Loud and clear, sir," Chalker said.

"Same old shit," said Luciano, a Southside Chicago boy who bore the obvious sobriquet of "Lucky." He made an expression that wavered uncertainly somewhere between a grin and a sneer. "Hurry up and fuckin' wait!"

Maxwell had certainly heard the comment but apparently chose to ignore it. "C'mon, c'mon, people," he called. "Grab your duffels and get your asses on the bus. Snap it up!"

As Baxter climbed up the steps of the bus behind Maxwell, he heard the captain mutter something to the vehicle's driver. "Damned Navy pukes" was all he caught, but it seemed to sum up nicely the Army's attitude about the new U.S. Navy special warfare unit in Vietnam.

This, Baxter thought to himself, *is going to be interesting.*

The U.S. Navy SEALs. Baxter was fiercely proud to be a part of the unit, still only a few years old, "still getting its sea legs," as one SEAL officer had described it to him, back in San Diego. He was proud, too, to be one of the first three officers and fifteen SEALs assigned to actual combat operations—"direct action," as the stateside planners called it—in the rapidly expanding war in Southeast Asia. Unfortunately, most military officers, department heads, and strategic planners that Baxter had talked with so far still had absolutely no idea as to how the SEALs were to be used.

Nobody, not even the SEALs themselves, knew the unit's capabilities.

The SEALs had been commissioned by direct presidential order on January 1, 1962, and it was well known that Kennedy himself had taken a hand in their creation, calling for all of the services to increase their capabilities in the fields of unconventional and guerrilla warfare. Raised from the ranks of the Navy's Underwater Demolition Teams, the SEALs were something entirely new. Members of the UDTs had become known as "naked warriors" during World War II and the so-called police action in Korea, because they carried out dangerous beach reconnaissance or demolition missions—often in full view of the enemy and under constant fire—equipped with nothing but mask, fins, swim trunks, and a knife. By direct order, the UDT's area of responsibility ended at the high-tide line on the beach, a logical but impractical division of authority that had killed a lot of good men in the past. At Peleliu, in the Pacific in World War II, a UDT's beach recon could easily have revealed the stronger-than-expected defenses the Japanese had placed *behind* the beach, but didn't . . . and the Marines had walked into hellfire. There'd even been cases of military intelligence that the Teams had gathered being deliberately ignored, simply because it was not the UDT's designated job to gather it.

That had been a large part of the reasoning behind the creation of the SEALs. Naked warriors no longer, they were trained in the use of a wide variety of weapons—including those likely to be used by their enemies. They could freefall from an aircraft at thirty thousand feet, pop their chutes at six hundred feet, and glide to a silent insertion far behind enemy lines in a technique called "HALO," for High-Altitude, Low-Opening, or they could lock out of a submarine's escape trunk for an undetected swim to the beach. They had the UDT's expertise in high explosives and the Marines' skill at quick and silent killing. Most important, they were no longer restricted by the high-tide line; they could go *anywhere* their mission orders sent them, an operational flexibility reflected by their name, an acronym drawn from the words Sea, Air, and Land.

All of the SEALs had started off as UDT in the beginning, though more and more recruits were being drawn from other Navy specialties lately as well. Kennedy had not wanted to lose the UDT's very special skills in beach reconnaissance and mine clearing, so the two sister units were being kept carefully compartmentalized, operating under separate command structures, though the two units still shared much of the same training, a course already widely regarded as the toughest military training program in the world. Kennedy's order had established two SEAL commands. SEAL Team 1 operated out of the newly established facility at the Navy's Amphibious Warfare Base at Coronado, just across the bay from San Diego, California. SEAL Team 2, the East Coast SEALs, worked out of their headquarters near the amphibious base at Little Creek, Virginia.

Baxter's unit, designated Detachment Delta, had been tapped from Team 1.

The trouble was, not many people knew about SEALs yet. Much about the new unit was still highly classified, with unit commanders briefed only on a need-to-know basis. Many in Washington felt that the SEALs would be invaluable on covert missions and therefore the less that was publicly known about them, the better. There was already a bureaucratic tug-of-war underway with the Teams squarely in the middle. Were SEAL ops to be primarily information-gathering, like the Army's LRRP units created with NATO in Europe a few years ago? Or would they be more useful deployed on missions of sabotage, demolition, and ambush? No one knew, and the unit retained its blanket of secrecy. Baxter had heard rumors back in training of SEAL ops going down a few years ago in Castro's Cuba, but those were so highly classified the whole story might never come out. In the meantime, the usual response by officers or administrative personnel Baxter had to deal with was, "SEALs? What's that?"

And, of course, there were always the jokes by those not fully in the know, usually involving clapping the hands together and barking like a circus seal.

In fact, SEALs had been in Vietnam for four years now. Two SEAL Team 1 officers had arrived in Nam in January of 1962 to survey the situation and report on how the new unit might be used in support of the South Vietnamese government against the growing insurgency. On 10 March of the same year, two more SEALs had arrived to begin training South Vietnamese commandos in the gentle arts of maritime reconnaissance and demolition, and a handful of SEALs had been here ever since, in advisory or training roles, working with the Vietnamese military.

Everyone took it for granted that Kennedy's advisors had had Vietnam in mind when they began discussing the design and the mission of the new unit. The United States was finding, as had France before her, that the Vietnamese were masters at unconventional warfare. No one seriously expected the Communist insurgents of South Vietnam, the Vietcong as they were called, to be able to stand for long against the full might of the American military . . . but the idea was to defeat them *without* throwing that full might against them. Ideally, the ARVN, the Army of the Republic of Vietnam—American trained, American equipped, and American advised—ought to be able to win South Vietnam's war by itself. Unfortunately, that simply wasn't possible yet. Advisors and training cadres had been coming to South Vietnam for years now, but the war had continued getting bigger and bigger and more out of hand. The first major commitment of U.S. ground troops to Vietnam had begun last year, with the 8 March amphibious landings by the Third Marine Regiment, Third Marine Division, near Da Nang.

And no one could guess where it was going to end.

Baxter smiled at the thought of the Marine landings and glanced across the aisle of the bus. Gunner's Mate First Class Toby Bosniak, tall, with pale-blond hair and a deep, California tan, had joined the SEALs out of UDT 12. He liked to tell the story of how he'd been one of the Team 12 men who'd reconned the beach ahead of the Marine landings and left behind what had become a long-standing tradition for the UDTs, a sign stretched between two oars facing out to sea:

WELCOME U.S. MARINES
UDT 12

Calling cards like that one had been left behind on nearly
every beach since Guam in World War II, a not-so-subtle dig
at the Marines' claim to always be the first ashore. Bosniak
was one of only two men in the unit who'd been to Vietnam
already. The other was Hospitalman Second Class John Randolph, though in another long-standing tradition, he was simply known as "Doc." Randolph had served a six-month tour
in Vietnam as a SEAL, working as an advisor with the Vietnamese naval commandos. That experience made him invaluable to the team; he not only knew the people, but he spoke
a fair amount of both French and Vietnamese.

They would need his skills if they were to work closely
with the Vietnamese people.

Baxter looked out the bus window and realized with a start
that they'd already entered the northern reaches of Saigon. The
open country around Tan Son Nhut had ended, and the city
proper begun, with an almost bewildering suddenness. One
moment, they'd been driving down a macadam road through
country, open fields, and the endless drabness of tank farms
and sheet-metal storage buildings; the next, the bustle of Saigon exploded around the rattletrap bus in an insistent, demanding clamor.

Though he looked hard for it, there was little evidence that
Saigon was the capital of a nation at war. Much of the city
was cluttered and dirty, with bright spots of Western-style ad-
vertising and shop signs, but there were many imposing ex-
amples of colonial French architecture rising from among the
smaller, shabbier buildings and storefronts. As the bus turned
onto To Do Street, Baxter's eye was caught by the large, English lettering on the face of a modern office building: BANK
OF AMERICA.

The city was crowded. Some of the people wore black pajamas, sandals, and coolie hats, but most were clad in Western
dress that wouldn't have been out of place in any city back in
the States. Bright, pastel-colored shirts were everywhere, as
were blue jeans. Vehicular traffic ranged from buses and jit-
neys to American- or French-made cars, trucks, and—as was

inevitable anywhere in the Orient—whole fleets of motor scooters, cyclos, pedicabs, and bicycles. He saw a few ARVN soldiers and lots of police, but no weapons were in evidence and all the people appeared to be going about their business with a complete and unhurried calm that made Baxter wonder where the war was.

Perhaps most surprising to Baxter was the large number of obviously Western businessmen and workers. He'd read reports back at Coronado about the boom that had begun in South Vietnam last year—the U.S. Department of Defense had reportedly contracted with various American construction firms to build over three hundred million dollars worth of air bases, hospitals, docks, warehouses, and military installations, with another two hundred million allocated for 1966 and 1967 alone. The result had been an economic boom in this small nation that had attracted a small army of Western contractors, builders, speculators, bankers, and businessmen. And yet, many Americans had barely even heard of South Vietnam and could not have found it on a map.

The bus pulled to a halt at a red light, and Ensign Hanrahan leaned over the back of Baxter's seat. "Hey, Lieutenant," he said. "How's it feel to finally be here, huh?"

"It's not quite what I expected, Ron," Baxter replied. He wasn't sure what he *had* been expecting. His briefings had included descriptions and photographs of Saigon, so the Western buildings and Western dress shouldn't have surprised him. Possibly it was simply that his American prejudices had emphasized the water buffalo and rice paddies and ignorant peasants.

"I'm just glad we're finally here," Hanrahan said. "Hey, you have any idea how close the enemy is?"

Baxter looked down from the window of the bus and briefly locked eyes with a young Vietnamese civilian sitting astride a motor scooter, waiting for the light to change. He wore a white shirt, dark slacks, and what looked like U.S.-issue boots. His eyes were black and utterly without revealed emotion, his face impassive. Baxter had no way of judging the man's age. He could have been in his mid-twenties . . . or as young as fifteen.

A civilian.

And yet, there were stories. . . .

"All I know is what we were briefed on," he told Hanrahan. "The Vietcong often mingle with the rest of the people, and it's hard to tell sometimes who the enemy is."

"She-it," Bosniak said with a wide grin. "Ain't no problem there, Lieutenant. See, the ones that are shootin' at you, they're the bad guys. The ones shootin' *with* you, why, they're the good guys. Couldn't be simpler!"

The traffic light changed, and the motor scooter drew ahead of the bus, engine gunning in a cloud of swirling, blue-white exhaust. None of the SEALs expected that it would be quite as easy as Bosniak had described it, of course, least of all Bosniak himself, who'd served two terms in the Nam already. Still, all of the SEALs possessed a good-natured cockiness about their mission in Vietnam that would have done credit to John Wayne.

They wanted to be here, all of them, and with good reason. Det Delta was the first Navy SEAL team assigned to Vietnam with the express purpose of engaging the enemy in combat.

Combat! That was what the SEALs were all about, and it set Baxter's spine tingling when he thought about it. Every one of the men in Det Delta was a volunteer, and every one was excited about the prospect of combat.

Baxter had thought a lot about that on the flight over the Pacific. It wasn't as though any of them possessed a death wish, and all of them, he was pretty sure, had as realistic an understanding of what combat was like as it was possible to get through a training program. All of the others seemed like normal, healthy, and reasonably well-balanced individuals, if you accepted the hotdog in them . . . that peculiarly American touch of innocent madness born in the worship of war heroes and John Wayne, of jet fighter pilots and heroic last stands, of astronauts, fast cars, and fast women. *Cowboys . . .*

Baxter wondered what was in store for them. For the first time in his life, the future seemed a complete blank, exciting . . . and not a little scary.

For himself, though, he'd never cared much for the idea of *predictability. . . .*

Chapter 2

Saigon
1730 hours

For Edward Charles Baxter, the future had always been predictable. The son of a building contractor and a dental assistant, he'd been born and raised in a suburb of Dayton, Ohio, not far from the sprawl of Wright-Patterson Air Force Base. School had been tedious and boring; a summer's job at a hardware store had been tedious and boring. He wanted excitement and something different, and for a kid about to graduate from high school in a town next to a big military base, the obvious career choice involved military service. As a kid he'd watched the military jets coming and going in the skies above Dayton and known that one day he would be flying one of them. In the mid-1950s, *every* kid in the Dayton area wanted to be an Air Force jet pilot. He'd attended Kent State College through the ROTC program, sure that the Air Force was where he would end up.

When the time had finally come, however, to actually sign the paper and raise his hand for the swearing in, he'd hesitated a long time before choosing the Navy instead of the Air Force. Even now he wasn't entirely sure why he'd made that decision, other than the rather irrational notion that he disliked the bland predictability of having known for years that he was going to join the Air Force. It might have had something to do with the fact that many of his friends had fathers in the Air Force . . . and he'd begun to realize that only a tiny fraction

11

of the men who wanted to fly jets ever got to realize that dream. His father had been in the Army Air Corps in World War II, but as ground crew, not air crew, based throughout the war at Lakenheath, England. Baxter could imagine few things worse than spending an entire enlistment watching the aircraft lift from the tarmac and vanish beyond the horizon without having the chance to actually fly them.

But the Navy, *that* was different. No matter what happened, with the Navy he would get to see something of the world, whether it was aboard ship or at some foreign duty station. Baxter wanted excitement, something different, something more exotic and colorful than the drab sameness of the checkerboard farms and the prairie-flat expanses of southwestern Ohio. That lust for excitement had led him to apply for the new Navy SEAL school while he was still attending OCS.

Be careful what you wish for, the ancient dictum ran. *You just might get it. . . .*

Baxter was twenty-four years old now and had been in the Navy for just over two years. He'd had plenty of the excitement he craved already, certainly, with the brutal SEAL training course at Coronado, from races on his back in thick, black mud to leaping out of a C-130 with nothing between his life and the ground twenty thousand feet below but a lightweight sheet of paneled nylon. He'd never even *seen* the ocean until he'd reported for Officer's Candidate School at Newport, Rhode Island; he'd not swum in it until his assignment to BUD/S—the Basic Underwater Demolition/SEAL training program at Coronado, just across the bay from San Diego. For months now, though, he'd been toughening mind and body by swimming or paddling for mile upon mile in the open Pacific.

Now, at last, all of the work, all of the preparation, was about to pay off. Vietnam was a new country, a new culture, a whole new *world* that he was eager to experience, and he didn't want to miss a second of it.

Saigon grew more and more crowded as they got closer to downtown, with crowds thronging the sidewalks and streets. At times, it seemed that the motor scooters and cycles were battling with the bus for right of way . . . and that they might actually win through sheer weight of numbers.

''Y'know,'' Bosniak said, grinning as the bus lurched to a stop to avoid hitting a daredevil cyclist, ''that it's already been conclusively proven that the VC can never take Saigon."

"Oh, yeah?" Hanrahan said, knowingly playing the straight man with a broad smile. "How come?"

"They'd get caught in the traffic coming into town. They'd never make it as far as the Presidential Palace!"

The hotel chosen for them, Baxter was told, was fast becoming a favorite with all Navy SEALs when they visited Saigon. It was called the Victoria, and from the outside, at least, it looked secure if not particularly inviting. The massive walls still showed the grooves left by the wooden forms used when the concrete was poured, and there were chinks, here and there, that looked as though they could have been gouged by stray bullets in some long-ago battle. Vietnam, Baxter reminded himself as he walked into the dingy lobby, had been at war now for a long, long time, fighting the Vietcong insurgency now, the French before that, the Japanese before *that*. . . .

Baxter, Chalker, and Hanrahan would share a large room on the sixth floor, while the enlisted men divided three smaller rooms among themselves on the fifth. Since they would only be staying the night, Baxter elected to leave all of his gear in his single, small travel bag rather than trusting it to the rather dubious-looking interior of the room's single, small chest of drawers. At Chalker's urging, though, he changed into one of his two sets of civilian clothes for drinks before dinner.

Before leaving, he sat on the edge of the ominously creaking bed and pulled out once more the thumb-worn white card that had been issued to him before he'd left the States. Beneath the sword-on-shield emblem of the MACV were the words NINE RULES in large, black type, followed by smaller letters, reading "for personnel of U.S. Military Assistance Command, Vietnam."

"The Vietnamese have paid a heavy price in suffering for their long fight against the Communists," it read. "We military men are in Vietnam now because their government has asked us to help its soldiers and people in winning their struggle. The Vietcong will attempt to turn the Vietnamese people against you. You can defeat them at every turn by the strength, understanding, and generosity you display with the people. Here are nine simple rules."

Flipping the card over, Baxter ran his eye down the now-familiar paragraphs.

1. Remember we are guests here: We make no demands and seek no special treatment.
2. Join with the people! Understand their life, use phrases from their language, and honor their customs and laws.
3. Treat women with politeness and respect.
4. Make personal friends among the soldiers and common people.
5. Always give the Vietnamese the right of way.
6. Be alert to security and ready to react with your military skill.
7. Don't attract attention by loud, rude, or unusual behavior.
8. Avoid separating yourself from the people by a display of wealth or privilege.
9. Above all else you are members of the U.S. Military Forces on a difficult mission, responsible for all your official and personal actions. Reflect honor upon yourself and the United States of America.

"Reading the propaganda again, huh?"

Slipping the card back inside his wallet, Baxter turned to study the speaker. Hanrahan was small, tough, and feisty, with what often seemed like an inborn disrespect for authority. Baxter wasn't sure yet whether he liked the guy or not . . . though the training they'd endured together at Coronado had certainly forged the bond of shared misery. Baxter shrugged. He wanted to say something about how the card made sense, or maybe to challenge Hanrahan's assumption that it was propaganda, but he didn't want to appear foolish. "Fuck you."

For Baxter, the vulgarity was fast becoming an all-purpose and utilitarian response for any social occasion, at least among Navy personnel, a means of saving face and a way to look cool at the same time.

"Hey, thanks for the offer, Lieutenant," Hanrahan said breezily. "But I think I'll have more fun with the B-babes upstairs. You comin'?"

"What B-babes?"

"B-girls," Chalker said with a wink. "Bar girls. This joint

has a bar up on the roof, complete with pool and hot and cold running chicks.''

"Sounds good," Baxter said. "Let's check it out."

The bar was under an awning just outside of the Victoria's rooftop restaurant. There *was* a pool, but the slime of algae ringing the concrete right at water level and the cloudy greenish water made it look less than inviting.

"Hey!" Hanrahan said. "You guys want to go for a swim?"

"Looks like something our instructors back at BUD/S would've come up with," Baxter said.

"Yeah," Chalker added. "Sadistic bastards, all of 'em. Now *that's* more my idea of a good time!"

That was a bevy of young women standing at the bar, watching the newcomers with veiled expressions. Actually, they didn't look all that good to Baxter. His girlfriend back in the States, Jeanie Nalder, was a tall, long-legged blond he'd met at Kent State; these women were small, no more than chest-high on the big Americans, with black hair and expressionless black eyes and far too much pancake makeup and lurid green or blue eye shadow. Their thick, heavy lipstick looked like bright scarlet paint, though they did possess a dark-eyed exoticism he found pleasantly alluring.

Baxter, Chalker, and Hanrahan sat down at a round table comfortably removed from the faint stink lingering above the pool. Three of the women joined them, their blank faces magically transforming as they switched on sunny smiles. "Hey, G.I." A woman in a tight red dress as bright as her lipstick leaned forward, deliberately angling her exposed cleavage in Baxter's direction. "You buy me drink, okay?" She leaned over further, and he caught a glimpse of one large, red-brown nipple.

Faintly embarrassed, Baxter shrugged and smiled. "Uh, sure. Why not?" Part of him was realizing that nothing like this had ever happened to him before. Another part was wondering what Jeanie would say, what she would *think. . . .*

But mostly he was thinking that this was his first evening in a strange, new country, and that he would never get to know these people if he didn't relax and enjoy the experience. *Let go! . . .*

Besides, he was here to fight for these people, right?

"Hey, you all right, G.I. I *like* you!"

As the women sat down at the table with the three of them, he ordered a scotch for himself, while Hanrahan ordered gin and Chalker asked for a beer. He wasn't sure what the women were having, though he'd heard stories of places that served bar girls tea while charging the buyer the cost of a real drink. He didn't really care. He had money, and he would be spending the next few months in a place where he wouldn't have much opportunity to spend it. Hell, it was all in a good cause. . . .

"What's your name?" he asked the woman in red. The more he looked at her, the prettier she seemed.

"My-le," she told him and giggled.

"And I am Hoa," the one snuggling up next to Hanrahan said. She wore a tight-fitting blue dress that sparkled as she moved.

"I am Long Lay," the third said.

"Hey, I like the sound of that name," Chalker said. The men laughed; the women giggled, though Baxter wasn't sure how well they understood English.

They talked about America—a mystical land that filled the women with wide-eyed wonder. They talked about the war—and the certain knowledge that, with the help of the Americans, the VC would be crushed. Baxter finished one drink and ordered another. My-le was definitely starting to look more appealing . . . especially when she leaned over to give him a glimpse of her breasts. At one point, he was startled by a sudden pressure high on the inside of his thigh and realized that she was gently rubbing him with her bare foot, while smiling at him across the top of her glass of tea.

More customers drifted into the bar area as the afternoon wore on. Most appeared to be American servicemen, though some, he supposed, might have been businessmen. There weren't too many uniforms in sight, so it was hard to tell, sometimes, whether that scrawny-looking kid with coke-bottle glasses on the far side of the pool, say, was an Army corporal or an accountant.

As they talked and drank, Baxter became increasingly aware of the woman across from him. He could scarcely help it. Her bare foot was becoming more insistent, more rhythmic in its movements against his crotch. He was at once embarrassed and entranced, unwilling to ask her to stop, afraid that someone might see . . . and wondering where this chance encounter might be leading. . . .

"Ladies?" a man said, walking up to stand beside the table. "I wonder if you would excuse us?"

"Aw, *shit*!" Hanrahan said.

Giggling, the women stood up and left. Glancing back over her shoulder, My-le gave Baxter a dark look filled with promise and walked back to the bar with an exaggerated roll to her buttocks.

"Lieutenant Baxter?"

The man was wearing civilian clothing, a yellow shirt and dark slacks, but he had the clean-cut and boyish look of an American, with the authoritative voice of an officer used to giving orders.

"I'm Baxter."

"Lieutenant Frank Kellerman. I'm gonna be your NILO down at Nha Be."

Baxter rose and shook the man's extended hand. NILO was the military acronym for Navy Intelligence Liaison Officer. This was the man who would be bringing Det Delta its missions, and the military intelligence they would need to carry them out. "Pleased to meet you, sir."

Kellerman glanced briefly at the women sitting at the bar nearby, then joined them at the table. "Can the 'sir' crap. Frank."

"Okay . . . Frank."

"Buy you something?"

He held up his empty glass. "Sure. How about another scotch?"

"Well, the hooch in this joint's never been within twelve thousand miles of Scotland, but it'll do." He signaled one of the girls, ordering more drinks. "Sorry to interrupt you gents," he continued, "but I thought this would be a good chance to get acquainted."

"Fair enough," Chalker said. "Maybe you can tell us something about where we're going."

Kellerman chuckled as he pulled out a cigarette. "There's not that much to tell," he said. "What can you say about hell?" He offered cigarettes to Chalker and Hanrahan, who accepted, and then to Baxter.

"No thanks." He'd tried smoking in college but never quite gotten the hang of it. The instructors had discouraged the habit at BUD/S, claiming it cut down lung capacity during SCUBA ops, and Baxter saw no reason to doubt them. "Aw, it can't be that bad, Frank. I mean, Nha Be's right outside of Saigon, right? It'll be like commuting to the suburbs."

"Hmm. You've been briefed on the Rung Sat?"

"Sure. Rung Sat Special Zone."

" 'The Forest of Assassins,' " Chalker added with a dramatic quaver to his voice.

"Part of the Mekong Delta, right?" Hanrahan said.

"Better hit your geography books, kid," Kellerman said. "The Mekong, the eight mouths of the Mekong, I should say, are farther southeast, down the coast." He jerked his thumb across his shoulder. "The Sai Gon River, out there, makes a hard right just a few miles from here." He stopped, reached into his pocket for a pen, then began sketching lines on a cocktail napkin, laying out the confused tangle of waterways south of Saigon. "Now, depending on what map you happen to be looking at, it flows into either the Soi Rap or the Dong Hai, or else it stays the Sai Gon. Just a little farther south, it splits up, right here at Nha Be. The Soi Rap/Sai Gon goes south and the Long Tau heads southeast, smack through the most godawful maze of rivers and canals and mangrove swamps, a thousand square kilometers of mud, trees, snakes, insects, and VC stretching all the way from Nha Be to the South China Sea. That, gentlemen, is the RSSZ.

"The Rung Sat's been a hidey-hole for pirates, rebels, fugitives, bandits, and renegades for centuries. That's how it got its name, in fact, Forest of Assassins. Nowadays, though, it's Victor Charlie. Charlie's real strong, back there in the swamps, with hidden bases, bunkers, supply depots, the works, and it's getting to be a real tough problem for MACV. You see, Saigon's main shipping channel, coming up from the coast, runs right up the Long Tau to the Soi Rap and the Sai Gon. Charlie's been launching mortar and rocket attacks on freighters moving on the river, and MACV is afraid he's going to get enough of a stranglehold on that region that all of our supplies and equipment coming into Saigon are going to have to come in by air. Some of us've convinced the high command that you SEALs might be useful down there, clearing out the VC nests."

"Sounds great," Hanrahan said, his eyes glowing.

"That close to the capital," Chalker mused. "Damn, can't the locals keep their own shipping channel clear?"

Kellerman laughed, an unpleasant sound. "Who, Marvin ARVN? Are you shitting me?"

"I take it," Baxter said, "you don't have a real high opinion of the Vietnamese military." He was frankly suspicious of Kellerman. The man sounded bitter, as though he had some unknown axe to grind, and Baxter had the feeling that the man was trying deliberately to infect the three SEAL officers with his attitude.

The NILO chuckled again, then seemed to think about the question. "I'll tell you something, Baxter," he said. "Some of the enlisted guys and lower-ranking officers, they're okay. Most of the locals I work with do the best they can under really shitty conditions. The trouble is in the Vietnamese officer corps, the high-ranking brass. Sometimes I get the feeling they don't care whether they win this war or not. Others are probably on the take. Some are probably VC themselves."

"You're shitting me!" Hanrahan said, outraged.

"Nope. Hell, I've got an aide on my staff who's probably VC."

"In *Intelligence*?" Baxter was genuinely shocked.

Kellerman shrugged. "It's easier, knowing who the plants are. But I'll tell you gentlemen something, a word of advice. Get any crap you may have floating around in your heads about helping the Vietnamese fight their war flushed right now. Uncle Sam's been 'helping them fight their war' for ten or twelve years, now, ever since the French bailed out, and things have been going steadily from bad to worse. Your Vietnamese counterparts, the guys you're going to be working with every day, half of them are either VC, or they're not VC themselves, but they happily pass information along to cousins or fathers or brothers or girlfriends who are." He cocked his head slightly, indicating the women clustered at the bar with a shifting of his eyes and a lift to his eyebrows. "Those girls you were being friendly with? You boys better be careful, and I'm not talking about wearing your rubbers. Chances are, you're going to be hunting for their brothers down in the Rung Sat . . . or their brothers are going to be hunting you."

"That's crazy," Baxter said.

"So? This is a crazy damned war. Where do you think those VC hiding out in the Rung Sat go for liberty, huh? Right here to Saigon, the Paris of the Orient. Hey, why not? They need nookie too, every so often. You've probably bumped into a few already, right here in the hotel.''

"Man,'' Chalker said, shaking his head. "What a way to run a war!''

"Gentlemen,'' Kellerman said, raising his glass to his lips. "You ain't seen fuckin' *nothing* yet!''

"So where do we come into the picture, Frank?'' Baxter said, leaning back with his arms folded. "You guys must have some ideas about how the SEALs are going to help.''

"Oh, there are plenty of ideas. No clear consensus, just yet. Lots of the brass back at headquarters still aren't quite sure what to do with Navy personnel.''

"I gathered that already.''

"There's a special boat squadron stationed at Nha Be. You'll be working closely with them, and probably with a contingent of LDNN.''

"Of what?'' Hanrahan asked.

"*Lien Doc Nguoi Nhia*,'' Chalker said, rattling the alien words off his tongue with a singsong confidence. "That's the Vietnamese frogmen, the counterparts of the SEALs.''

"Right,'' Kellerman added, smiling. "The 'Soldiers Who Fight Under the Water,' or, at least that's what the name means. Some of them are pretty good. Others . . .'' He held his hand above the table, palm down, and waggled it back and forth. "In any case, I expect you'll be doing a fair amount of patrolling on the rivers. Maybe some foot patrols, looking for bunkers, trails, rice stores, shit like that. Headquarters isn't real sure, yet.''

"Way I heard it,'' Chalker said, lowering his voice, "there was a big op coming up soon. . . .''

Kellerman's eyes shifted in his face, as he checked for anyone who might be within earshot of the table. "Let's not, ah, speculate about that, shall we? At least, not here. We'll talk again in a few days, at Nha Be.''

"Fair enough,'' Baxter said. The op Chalker had been obliquely referring to was Operation Jackstay. Det Delta hadn't been briefed on the scope of Jackstay, but it was supposed to include both SEALs and the UDT, Vietnamese forces, and the United States Marines. That, together with the fact that Det Delta had been doing a lot of extra training back at Coronado on beach surveys before they'd left for Vietnam, suggested to Baxter that it probably involved a major amphibious landing.

He could certainly understand why Kellerman didn't want to talk about such things in public.

But damn, if one of his own staff officers was VC . . . where *could* you talk about it?

Conversation fell then to generalities, about how nobody stateside even seemed to know there was a war on yet, and about how effective the U.S. Marines had been this past year up near Da Nang. It was almost as if, Baxter thought to himself, the Navy Intelligence officer needed some point of contact with the newcomers from CONUS—the continental United States. Two rounds of drinks later, Kellerman bid them all a good evening and left, weaving ever so slightly as he navigated his way between tables and pool.

"Shit!" Hanrahan said, watching him go. "The guy's half-plastered! And he's supposed to be our NILO?"

"He must've been working up a real head of steam before he found us," Baxter said. He took another swallow of his scotch. "Hell, this stuff hasn't given me more than a light buzz."

"Aw, you know those intel types," Chalker said. "Can't hold their liquor worth a damn. *Hello*, there!"

"We join, now?" the girl in blue asked. Baxter couldn't remember her name. "Officer gone now."

"He short," My-le said with a disapproving frown. "We like *tall* men. . . ."

This time My-le took the chair next to him instead of across the table. As she sat down, he smelled her strange mingling of some sweet, heavy perfume, sweat, and the musky odor of a woman. As they talked, she leaned against him at every opportunity, resting her head against his shoulder, and occasionally pressing her breast against his arm. Within five minutes, he felt her hand rubbing against his thigh, and he could feel the intense, growing warmth of his reaction concentrating in his groin.

"Hey, G.I.," his companion said, grinning mischievously. "You like, eh?" Her hand was on his erection now, kneading it through the material of his pants. "You get nice hard!"

Across the table, Hanrahan had just raised a glass of gin to his mouth. The woman's observation triggered a spray of liquid and hoots of laughter from both Hanrahan and Chalker. "I think she likes you!" Chalker gasped.

"That's okay," Baxter said, putting his arm around My-le's shoulders and giving her a hug. He didn't care what Kellerman had said. "I like her too."

He'd never known a girl like this, direct and inviting and openly sexy. He liked it, liked the attention she was giving him, and he wasn't about to turn her away. Hell, so what if her brothers *were* VC? It wasn't as though he was going to tell her any deep, dark secrets, right?

Baxter remembered little of that evening, or of the night that followed. What he did remember was waking up early the next morning in a strange hotel room—My-le had taken him to her room on the third floor—with a thundering headache and his clothes and wallet gone. When the full realization of what had happened hit him, he didn't know whether to ram his fist through one of the hotel's paper-thin walls, or sit on the edge of the rumpled bed and cry. He'd been warned that My-le might be a communist sympathizer; no one had bothered to tell him that she could also be a thief. *Shit!* He should have known. He should have *known*, damn it, when he, clumsy and unsure of himself, had asked her how much . . . and she'd turned that dazzling smile on him and told him, no, this was for free, because she really, *really* liked him. . . .

He made it more or less modestly back to his sixth-floor room by wrapping himself in a sweat-soaked sheet, though he collected more than his share of strange looks from hotel staff and other guests along the way. Minutes later, dressed and furiously angry, he confronted the bland-faced clerks at the front desk, only to be told that there was no record of a "My-le" working at the Victoria, ever, and that the room he'd taken the night before had been rented in his name, and would he now please pay the charges, six dollar, American? My-le, in fact, wasn't a regular name. It was Vietnamese for "Beautiful" and might have been either the equivalent of a stage name or simply a joke played on a naive and gullible American.

Both Chalker and Hanrahan still possessed both their wallets and their clothes, thank God, and both men chipped in to cover the bill for the extra room. They arrived at Tan Son Nhut late to find a helicopter waiting for them, but Captain

Maxwell wasn't around to say anything about it. More time was spent at the base administrative office, reporting the stolen ID and filling out the forms necessary to get a new one. He spent some time with a security officer assuring the man that there'd been nothing compromising or classified in his wallet and being assured in return that this sort of thing happened all the time. "Don't let it get to you, Mac," the officer said at the end of the interview. "The gooks around here are damned pickpockets, sneak thieves, and worse, every fuckin' one of them."

It seemed a rather dismal philosophy to live by in this country. Was it possible to live here, never trusting *anyone* who wasn't an American?

An hour later, the SEALs of Det Delta were aboard an Army UH-1, flying down the pale-brown ribbon of the Soi Rap River on their way to Nha Be.

It was, Baxter thought, with just a trace of festering bitterness, not at all an auspicious beginning for his tour of duty in South Vietnam.

Chapter 3

Saturday, 26 March 1966

Long Tau River
Fifteen miles southeast of Nha Be
1330 hours

All of that training in the mud flats at Coronado is sure as hell paying off now. . . .

If he leaned forward into the muck, spreading his arms to distribute his weight, Lieutenant j.g. Baxter found that he could almost swim in the stuff . . . but not quite. Any movement at all was difficult, and after hours of wading through soft, clinging mud that was at times chest-deep, all four SEALs in the Det Delta interdiction team were nearing total exhaustion.

They'd been dropped off on the shores of the Long Tau that morning by an LCM, a gray-painted landing craft identical to the Landing Craft, Mechanized used in World War II amphibious operations from Normandy to Okinawa. Their path, navigated by map and compass through some of the most difficult terrain Baxter had ever seen, had taken them across part of the island bordered to east and west by the Soi Rap and Long Tau, through stinking mangrove swamps, across a relatively dry rise covered by nipa palms and jungle, then back into the swamps again. Now they were following a narrow creek upstream; passage here was marginally easier in the water than among the massive boles and tangled, dripping roots of the mangrove trees . . . or it had been until the water had turned into mud. The tide was going out, draining many of the Rung Sat's smaller waterways and leaving behind mud flats that were nearly identical in consistency and difficulty to the flats in the inside stretches of Coronado, where SEAL recruits played and exercised throughout their BUD/S training. For most of the stretch of legalized torture known as Hell Week, the recruits lived in mud like this, and for the first time, Baxter found he truly appreciated the edge that experience had given him.

The Rung Sat, Baxter was now convinced, consisted of some of the most miserable real estate on the planet. Travel of any sort was treacherously slow. Tides in this area could fall eight feet, exposing vast stretches of greasy, fetid mud flats. Roads were nonexistent, and the numerous paths were to be avoided at all costs.

This was Charlie's country.

Ahead of him, some ten meters in the lead, Connors had point, wading forward in the mud with his M-16 held above his head. Spread out behind him, he knew, Toby Bosniak and Doc Randolph were bringing up the rear. As was usual for SEAL patrols, they carried a miscellany of weapons. Baxter was packing an AK-47, one of the Russian-made Kalashnikov assault rifles favored by the communist forces in Vietnam,

when they could get them. Doc carried an M45 Carl Gustaf
Swedish K submachine gun, one of the special-issue weapons
with an integral suppresser over the muzzle. Bosniak was lugging an M-14, an automatic rifle considered obsolete now that
the M-16 was available, but still favored for its durability and
heavy punch. The weapon's main drawback was its size; thirteen centimeters longer than an M-16 and over a kilo heavier,
it was in Baxter's opinion too long and too bulky to serve well
on a patrol where the SEALs would be spending much of their
time wading around in neck-deep water.

Choice of weapon, however, was very much a personal matter for SEALs, and Baxter had already decided not to intervene
unless one of his men decided to try something really out-
landish. In addition to their primary weapons, Connors was
also carrying an M79 grenade launcher, while Doc carried an
extremely unofficial and unsanctioned Ithaca combat shotgun
slung muzzle-down across his back. All of them packed 9-mm
Smith & Wesson M39 pistols as backup, plus hand grenades,
and, of course, all carried their Mark I diving knives in scab-
bards strapped to belts or legs or combat vests.

He wondered again if four men would be enough on this
op, no matter how well armed they might be.

Operation Jackstay was under way . . . or at least, it *should*
be, though so far the SEAL patrol had seen no evidence that
anything at all unusual or violent was happening in the thousand square kilometers of the Rung Sat. UDT-11 had kicked
things off at 0300 hours that morning, going ashore at the
mouth of the Soi Rap River in a drizzling rain to plant beacons
marking shallow spots and mud flats for the U.S. Marine landing craft following on behind, then sweeping the beach areas
for mines.

Baxter was disappointed in the SEALs' assignment for
Jackstay. For much of the past month, ever since Det Delta
had arrived in Nha Be, in fact, he'd been going round after
round with MACV headquarters in Saigon, arguing that the
SEALs should be essentially turned loose, allowed to patrol—
to ''prowl and growl,'' as they liked to call it—on their own.
The idea that Det Delta was to be the first direct action SEAL
unit in Vietnam had led them to expect a certain amount of
freedom in their operational parameters.

But apparently the SEALs were not to be given that free-

dom. In fact, Baxter's orders for Jackstay, signed by MACV's
General McAllister himself, directed the SEALs to "operate
in support of U.S. Marine and UDT operations within the
Rung Sat Special Zone," but that "under no circumstances
are you to initiate hostilities against communist forces in your
assigned sector."

Jackstay was an enormous, sprawling operation, one involving thousands of men from Saigon to the South China
Sea. While the Marines and UDT were coming ashore at the
mouth of the Soi Rap River, the SEALs of Det Delta were to
work closely with U.S. Marine Recon forces, inserting at various points within the Rung Sat well north of the landing areas.
As the Marines came ashore, it was expected that either the
VC would flee . . . running smack into the SEAL and Marine
ambush positions inland, or they would be reinforced from the
north, and again the SEALs and Marines would be there to
block them.

As Baxter waded through the ooze, he glanced at the towering mangrove trees left and right and thought once more
that this whole plan had a terribly makeshift feel to it.
Chalker and Bosniak and the rest of the SEALs in Det Delta
shared his opinion. Twenty-four SEALs and Recon Marines,
scattered across the vastness of the Rung Sat in four-man
teams, simply could not block all movement north and south
among these miles upon miles of waterways, jungle, and
swamp. Bosniak had suggested—and Baxter agreed with
him—that it looked as though some bright boy had been
playing with colored thumbtacks and a map back in his air-
conditioned office in Saigon: put four men *here* . . . and *here*
. . . and four more over *here* . . .

. . . all with absolutely no concept of how fucking *big* these
swamps really were.

Intelligence estimated that "something in excess" of one
thousand VC or VC sympathizers were currently hiding in the
Rung Sat. If that guess was anywhere near accurate, twenty-
four men were going to have a hell of a time stopping them
from going anywhere.

It was, Baxter thought, a criminal waste of a valuable asset—the SEALs and their training. They'd spent months
crawling through mud and swamps back in Coronado during
BUD/S. The SEALs should be out here as hunters, tracking

down the VC on the basis of various pieces of intel. To simply send them in to preselected points on a map and have them sit there, with orders not to initiate hostilities, yet . . .

A shrill cry split the air, and a large, brightly colored bird flapped out of the trees to the right, flew across the muddy stream, and vanished among the trees on the other side. Insects continued their raucous keeking, a good indication that the SEALs were alone, for now. As they made their way farther up the stream, the mosquitoes and tiny, stinging gnats that had been dogging them ever since they'd left the LCM turned into veritable clouds swarming about their faces and hands.

What are these bastards eating when they can't get SEAL? Baxter wondered to himself.

The rigid thinking that used the SEALs as pieces on a chess-board, part of a static defense, was probably an aspect of the greatest weakness Baxter had noted so far during the SEAL deployment to Nha Be—the problem of intelligence. Some wag—probably at about the time of the Trojan War—had observed that military intelligence was an oxymoron, self-contradictory, and that seemed more than usually apt in Vietnam.

Lieutenant Kellerman was competent enough, if a little hung-over some mornings during the daily intel briefs. His superiors, though, appeared to be rather rigidly set in their ways, willing to accept any information from sources they considered reliable, and at the same time unwilling to even consider information that did not conform to their theories of how things were really working. Baxter was beginning to think that the SEALs would be better served in their field operations if they started gathering their own intel . . . and their own sources.

Sources like Nguyen Manh Quon.

Lieutenant Nguyen was a member of the LDNN, the South Vietnamese version of the SEALs He was a good man, all hard-chiseled angles and cold, black eyes until a sudden smile transformed his features. He smoked a lot, enjoyed joking with the Americans about Vietnamese politics, and hated the VC with a cold-blooded dedication and completeness that Baxter found amazing. He'd been assigned as a Vietnamese liaison between the LDNN and Det Delta, and he believed strongly that the way to win the war was to forget politics and concentrate on training elite ARVN units for hunter-killer ops against the VC in their home territories. In their attitudes and feelings about how the war should be fought, the two frogmen, one American and one Vietnamese, had more in common with each other than they had with their own respective senior commands. Baxter liked him.

And it was a friendship that might well prove useful, if Baxter could just find a way to get past the barriers of red tape erected around MACV and the tightly structured fortress of U.S. military intelligence in Saigon. Ong Quon—Doc Randolph had explained to the other SEALs that in Vietnam, people were called by their given name rather than their family name, with an honorific such as *ong* or "Mister"—had numerous contacts with villagers throughout the Rung Sat. Often, the intelligence he'd been able to provide—about VC movements or the locations of supply and weapons caches—had been more accurate than anything coming down the pipeline from MACV.

Unfortunately, MACV didn't trust information provided by indigenous sources . . . unless, of course, that source was an approved one, which usually meant one with political connections. Though Nguyen's LDNN unit had been brought south to participate in Operation Jackstay, the unit was to be held in reserve, kept out of the major fighting.

So far as Baxter was concerned, that was just one more bond that he and Nguyen shared as comrades-in-arms.

He'd relied a lot already on the outgoing Vietnamese's voluminous knowledge of the area and the local VC during the team's preparations for Jackstay. Quon had friends living in the Rung Sat and a knowledge of the Vietcong organizational structure that was both detailed and, insofar as Baxter had been able to test it so far, accurate. He hadn't been encouraging when he'd seen where Baxter's team was being deployed. "You watch yourself in there, Lieutenant Edward," Quon had told him the evening before. "My sources say there's something big in your zone. Maybe bunker. Maybe storehouse. Maybe many VC."

"Why hasn't anybody gone in after it?" Baxter had asked.

Quon had shrugged, impassive. "Maybe information not confirmed. Maybe somebody think VC be gone by time we get there. But, VC there now. I *know*. . . ."

"*Sat Cong*," Baxter had said, smiling and clenching his fist for emphasis. *Kill the VC!*

"*Sat Cong*!" Quon had replied, grinning back. The exchange

was fast becoming a kind of password between the SEALs and the South Vietnamese commandos they worked with.

But right now, the idea was to avoid *sat SEAL*. As Baxter moved slowly, step by painful step through the mud, he could imagine two thousand VC eyes watching each movement he and his men were making.

Connors stopped up ahead, one hand raised. The muddy inlet they'd been following jogged sharply left ahead, away from the navigational line they'd been following.

Baxter clenched his fist in answer, then flicked his hand up and to the side. They would leave the stream here and travel overland for a time. Often, waterways—even mudways as difficult as this one—provided easier access to the waypoints of a march than did tangled jungle and mangrove thickets, but it wasn't good to stick to such obvious trails for very long; to do so invited ambush.

In any case, Baxter wanted out of the mud. His legs were starting to burn with the effort of walking in that stuff; any time now, he expected to wake up . . . and find himself back with thirty other BUD/S recruits enduring the hell of Hell Week. Ahead, Connors's mud-soaked body slowly eased up onto a spreading platform of mangrove roots, pausing as though testing the air, then slipping quietly ahead and into the underbrush beyond.

Baxter followed. Clambering free of the mud's tenacious grip, he moved inland through tangled brush and swamp weed, following the faint traces Connors left behind on mossy rocks or the soft ground. He sighted the other SEAL just ahead, crouched beside a stream gurgling among the rocks on its way to join the broader mud inlet nearby.

The two SEALs crouched at the edge of the clearing for a time, weapons at the ready, searching for any sign of the enemy. Nothing. Insects continued to swarm and buzz, as unseen chirpers continued their droning symphony in the surrounding forest. If there were VC nearby, they were as still and as stealthy as the SEALs themselves.

Moments later, they were joined by Randolph and Bosniak. Silently, still without a word being spoken, the SEALs circled the area, checking for any sign of the enemy, for anything at all out of the ordinary. Satisfied at last, Baxter signaled a halt to the march. After a brief exchange of hand signs, Connors and Randolph took security, vanishing into the brush to keep eyes and ears out for the enemy. Baxter and Bosniak sat down beside the small crystal stream.

First on the agenda was their weapons. Carefully and quickly, they stripped them down, washing off the mud in the stream, taking the time even to remove all the rounds from the magazines, rinsing them off individually so they wouldn't foul the weapons' receivers. An oily rag returned a faint, lubricated sheen to receivers and slides. One virtue was stressed almost above all others during BUD/S and was very much a part of SEAL philosophy: taking care of your weapon could save your ass.

After the weapons came the radio Bosniak was carrying in a backpack harness, the team's twenty-two-pound PRC-25, a "Prick-twenty-five" when pronounced by SEALs. Batteries were checked and the watertight case inspected for leakage. Weapons and radio seen to, the two men took a moment to check themselves and each other for unwanted guests. Rolling up the legs of his fatigue pants, Baxter cupped water enough from the stream to rinse some of the green-black muck from his skin, revealing the glistening black bodies of several fat leeches happily attached to his legs. A quick mutual inspection proved that both men were carrying a number of two- to four-inch-long bloodsuckers on their legs, stomachs, and lower backs. Cigarette lighters burned the slimy horrors off one by one easily enough, though the SEALs could only take the time to get those that were easily accessible. Some, no doubt, were attached to more private places beneath their clothing than shins or back—the blind creatures showed an almost magical propensity for somehow penetrating even multiple layers of clothing to get at the tender bare skin beneath—but those would have to wait until after the mission before they could be removed. He could distinctly feel something soft and heavy nestled against the inside of his right foot, somehow riding inside both his combat boot and two layers of socks.

But this was no time to start removing his footgear, just to track down a leech or three.

Finally, Baxter and Bosniak took a moment more to down mouthfuls of water from their canteens. It seemed strange to have to worry about dehydration with so much water about, but the SEALs had been sweating heavily for hours in the hot and humid forest, and by now dehydration was as big a problem as exhaustion . . . perhaps more so. After a few minutes more of rest, Bosniak slipped away into the trees to relieve Connors and Randolph. Baxter remained in the clearing, studying his plastic-covered map of the Rung Sat.

They were, he estimated, within two kilometers of their objective, a waypoint in an otherwise completely trackless forest overlooking a small clearing and a village called Phu Tho. It still seemed strange to think that anything could live in this dripping, stinking wilderness—anything, that is, save crocodiles, mosquitoes, leeches, and SEALs. Still, the Rung Sat Special Zone was fairly heavily populated. The last census, taken in the early sixties, had counted some sixteen thousand Vietnamese living in the various villages among the twisting brown rivers of the Rung Sat, in villages like Phu Tho and Quang Xuyen and Can Gio, and in Nha Be, which served as the gateway to the region. Since the escalation of the war during the past year or two, however, the population of the district had swelled ominously with refugees from elsewhere in the war-torn country . . . and with the refugees had come the Vietcong, ready to exploit the population's unrest.

From here, though, the place seemed as deserted as the far side of the moon.

Within another ten minutes, Randolph and Connors had finished stripping and cleaning their weapons, and killed the leeches they could reach. All four men checked the area carefully for telltale signs they might have accidentally left—a dropped .223 round for the ARs, say, or a button from someone's shirt. Baxter consulted his compass, getting a bearing on the next waypoint on their march and indicating it with a silent, up-and-down chopping motion of his right hand: three-five-five degrees . . . *that* way.

He wished they could take the time to wash some of the mud out of their clothing. All four SEALs were wearing camouflaged combat fatigues, but it was almost impossible to see the pattern now. At the moment, the mud actually helped the camouflage scheme, letting the SEALs blend into the background of the swamp better than any manmade textile pattern possibly could, but in a few hours, when the mud started to dry, Baxter knew from experience that it would turn lighter in color and chalky in consistency, with contrast enough, possibly, to give a man away if he wasn't damned careful.

But washing off their clothing would take time they didn't

have. Worse, it would leave the quiet pools of that crystal-clear stream muddied, muddier than was likely for any animal smaller than a water buffalo. That mud might cloud the water for hours, and Baxter wanted to leave no such clue behind to the SEALs' passage. They would have to make do by staying wet. *That,* at least, shouldn't be a major problem in this dripping forest. The early morning rain had given way to a dreary, humid overcast that promised more rain to come.

They moved more slowly now, during this final leg of their approach to their assigned position. Connors had the point again, with the other three scattered behind in a diamond formation that gave the team an all-round view of their surroundings, Baxter on the right, Randolph on the left, and Bosniak as the tail-gunner, keeping an eye out to the rear.

Thirty minutes after they'd set out, Connors froze, every line of his body betraying his tension . . . and an alertness of the senses keyed to the highest possible pitch. Turning slightly so that Baxter could see, Connors held up his hand in warning, then touched his nose. *I smell something.* Baxter inhaled, testing the air. It was hard to get past the stink of the mud and the jungle, but . . . yes. He caught it as well. A sour hint of something like overripe fish.

The smell was unmistakable. Once you'd experienced that particular odor, you never forgot it. *Nuoc mam,* "nuke mom," as Americans in Vietnam sometimes called it, was a kind of fermented fish sauce that was as much a part of any Vietnamese meal as soy sauce was for Japanese. Quon had told Baxter once that the stuff was made by letting highly salted fish ferment in large ceramic vats for anywhere from four months to a year. The stuff smelled to high heaven, so much so that some Americans in-country had taken to calling the stuff "armpit sauce." The only thing stronger was a shrimp sauce called *mam tom,* a pyrotechnic concoction that American G.I.s referred to as "VC tear gas."

The distinctive odor of *nuoc mam* permeated all Vietnamese cooking. In the cities and villages, it was a part of the background, always present, usually forgotten once the visitor had gotten used to it. You could nearly always smell it on the clothing and breath of the Vietnamese, though, the way a nonsmoker could smell cigarettes on a smoker.

Baxter lay absolutely still, testing the air. The scent *could* be from the village up ahead, but he didn't think so. The SEALs were still a good klick or so from Phu Tho, and there was almost no wind. He stayed in place, straining with every sense to pierce the wall of greenery surrounding him.

Suddenly, giving warning, Connors brought his splayed fingers up in front of his face, like a mask. *Enemy in sight!*

The waiting went on and on. There were no sounds but the insects and frogs, nothing to see but green and Connors's prone body five meters ahead. The vegetation here was so thick Baxter couldn't see farther than that.

Then Connors relaxed, turning once more to give another set of hand signals: *VC. Three of them. Armed. That way.*

To his left, Randolph moved his head, questioning. *Follow them?*

Baxter shook his head, then pointed. *Negative. Stay on course.*

Had this been a hunt-and-kill op, the SEALs could have taken down three VC in short order, possibly capturing one or more for interrogation back at Nha Be. *Initiate no hostilities. . . .*

They would play by the rules, this time at least.

Phu Tho was little more than a collection of twelve hootches, all bamboo and palm thatch and corrugated sheet tin. The SEALs reached the edge of the clearing, looking down from a slight, thickly overgrown rise into the village, with Bosniak, Connors, and Baxter observing the town, and Randolph staying behind as rear security. From this vantage point, Baxter could see a well, a pile of what might be burlap rice bags stacked up outside one of the huts, and several chickens . . . but no sign of any human occupants at all. There were no cooking fires going, no movement visible within any of the buildings' dark windows.

Baxter signaled the others silently, circling his finger in the air. They would move around the clearing, checking it from different angles.

Ten minutes later, they spotted the bunker.

It was not large as such things went, little more than a green, flat-topped mound of earth with squared-off sides, and a single opening in the east side that was probably a door. It was made of earth, not concrete, and there were no firing slits; instead, it appeared to be an open-topped, hundred-square-meter enclosure, probably with tunnels and storerooms underneath. It was located inside the forest, in a position overlooking the village but hidden from view from the air by the trees. What was it Quon had said last night? *Maybe bunker. Maybe storehouse. Maybe many VC.*

Bingo. *Right on, Quon, old buddy. If I get out of this, I'm buying you a drink.*

The SEALs selected positions for their observation post, then settled down to wait.

For Baxter, this was the most frustrating part of the op. The bunker might be inhabited, or it might not. What the SEAL patrol *ought* to be doing was finding out. If there were VC inside, the SEALs could use their radio to direct air strikes against it; if it was abandoned, they could search it for arms caches and documents, then do a bit of quick-and-dirty interior redecorating with a couple of fair-sized satchel charges.

But their orders were specific. VC routed by the Marine landings to the south might flee this way, and the SEALs were in a good position to observe them. At that, though, they weren't supposed to do anything but watch . . . and call in coordinates on the PRC-25.

He would have preferred setting up an ambush . . . though he wouldn't have chosen this site for it, not with the possibility that that bunker over there was filled with VC troops.

But damn it all! He couldn't carry out a decent ambush with four men!

Hours passed. As the sky had promised, it started raining again in mid-afternoon, but the shower quickly let up without more than moistening the ground. Baxter had found a position behind a two-foot-thick log near the edge of the village clearing.

He heard them first, a singsong of voices in the distance and the clink of something that might possibly have been metal shackles or snapping swivels. Then he saw them, two men walking through the village. One wore the black pajamas characteristic of Vietnamese peasants; the other seemed to be wearing jeans or light blue slacks and an olive-drab shirt. Baxter couldn't tell immediately whether they were carrying weapons or not, but they *were* walking directly toward his hiding place. Carefully, carefully, with no sudden motion that might be detected by the approaching Vietnamese, he eased himself down behind the log, reaching at the same time to the SEAL knife sheathed to the front of his combat vest, unhooking the strap, and drawing steel. He lay on his back, looking up at the overhang of the log and the tree canopy beyond. If they stepped over the log, they might not see him; if they did spot him, he'd have to try to take them out with his knife, since shots would alert every VC soldier in the area. *Do not initiate hostilities. . . .*

Fuck that. If they see me, I'm going to initiate hostilities right down their throats. . . .

Baxter couldn't see the approaching men, but he could hear them . . . *feel* them as they walked toward the log, now scant feet from where he lay. He could smell the fish-stink of *nuoc mam* strongly now. He tensed, knife ready. . . .

Suddenly, the log groaned, shifting slightly. He still couldn't see the VC . . . but from the sounds they were making, from the creaking of the fallen tree trunk, he realized that they were standing or sitting on it, probably less than a yard from his hiding place.

"Phong qua nong," one voice said.

"Rat nong!" Another voice answered.

"Xin loi." There was a rustling of paper. *"Ong co lua khong?"*

"Di nhien."

There was the scratch-snick of a cigarette lighter striking, the rasp of an indrawn breath.

"Ong qua tu-te doi voi toi."

Baxter lay there, listening to the incomprehensible conversation going on just a few feet away. The speakers did not sound rushed or panicked. One of them exhaled sharply, and he caught the acrid stink of cigarette smoke; they'd stopped for a light and a friendly chat.

"Ah," one of the voices said. *"Xin moi anh di."*

A cigarette flew past Baxter's upward line of sight, trailing sparks. It struck the ground a couple of yards away.

"Dan don!" The voice was sharp. *"Cam xa rac!"*

"Xin loi ong!"

A man in black pajamas leaped off the log, his bare feet slapping in the mud inches from Baxter's knee. He took three steps, stooped, and retrieved the offending cigarette butt.

It all happened so suddenly that Baxter didn't have time to

think anything through. He was squarely between the two men; if he rose to attack one, the other would see, and Baxter couldn't kill them both quickly enough to make sure no alarm was given. The man with the cigarette turned, took several steps directly toward Baxter, stepped on his right shin, and vaulted back over the log.

He hadn't seen him.

The SEAL lay there for several moments more, knife ready, listening as the two picked up clinking pieces of gear. The log shifted again, rolling slightly and pressing hard against Baxter's shoulder. And then the two VC were gone.

Had they been VC? He still couldn't be sure since he'd never actually seen any weapons . . . but that clink of metal could have been the strap swivels for a rifle. And the field discipline—not wanting to leave cigarette butts on the ground for an enemy to discover—that *had* to mean VC.

Carefully, weapon at the ready, Baxter sat up behind the log, peering past it rather than over it as he scanned the clearing beyond. Empty. The strangers were gone . . . *that* way, he thought, down the trail leading away from the town and the bunker.

The other SEALs emerged from the sheltering jungle a moment later. *You see them?* Baxter asked, signing.

Connors replied, using his fingers to frame two letters: *VC.* Then he tapped two fingers against the back of his hand, numbering them. Two VC wasn't enough to warrant calling in a report. HQ wanted to hear about platoons, companies, whole regiments of VC . . . not two individuals who might well be isolated stragglers.

They saw nothing more of the VC that day. They remained in position as the jungle grew dark and night finally descended over the tiny, empty hamlet of Phu Tho. The night dragged on, hour after hour, with a hard rain beginning to fall just before midnight. The SEALs remained in place, deliberately crouched in uncomfortable positions in order to stay awaké. By this time, all four men were tired enough that mistakes—a thoughtless word, an unconscious movement—were definite possibilities, but Baxter was becoming more and more convinced that there was nothing in Phu Tho to watch.

The night belongs to Charlie was a popular expression among U.S. servicemen in Vietnam, an almost superstitious vocalization of their fear of the dark and what the dark held. Charlie was always active at night . . . but he sure as hell wasn't active around here. Baxter thought that those two who'd come through during the afternoon must be stragglers, that any retreat through Phu Tho had already been completed before the SEALs reached their position.

He'd argued that the SEAL and Marine recon teams should have gone in when the UDT beach surveys had begun, at 0300 hours the day before, but he'd been overruled. Sending in the interdiction teams too early might have tipped off Charlie that something big was happening.

Well, Charlie had known anyway. There was nothing here to interdict.

As the rain began letting up around 0400 hours, Baxter finally pulled back from his position, stretching kinked and chill-stiffened arms and legs. The other SEALs watched him with the impassivity of stark exhaustion as he signaled to them. *Police the area. Move out!* They'd put in the requisite hours, without result. It was time to pack up and get the hell out.

At that, he thought as they started to move through the pre-dawn darkness, what they were going through now wasn't as bad as BUD/S. All of them had been without sleep for long periods before. During the six days of Hell Week, trainees counted themselves lucky if they managed three hours of sleep total. Somehow, it was good to know that there'd been a reason behind that BUD/S torture.

Eighteen hours after their insertion, Baxter, Bosniak, Connors, and Randolph neared their recovery point, a nameless bend in the Long Tau River, upstream from where they'd gone in and six kilometers from Phu Tho. It was growing light with the speed typical of the tropics. Motoring slowly back and forth offshore were two converted LCPLs, looking like thirty-six-foot gray speed boats with small forward enclosures. Gaping sharks' mouths and eyes had been painted on the bows. American sailors in dungarees and life jackets were visible in their well decks, studying the shore or manning the .50-caliber machine guns mounted fore and aft.

The SEALs started forward, with Baxter and Connors covering Bosniak and Randolph as they waded out into the water. Movement stirred in the brush to Baxter's right, between him and the river, where a man-sized shape crouched among the leaves and ferns. He was raising a weapon. . . .

There was no telling how many others might be in the area who would hear gunfire. Letting his AK dangle on its strap, Baxter pulled his knife as he lunged at the Vietnamese, grabbing the man from behind as he trained a Russian-made SKS rifle at the SEALs in the water, smothering his mouth with one hand, yanking the rifle up and back, bringing the black blade of the knife slashing up and across his throat just below the angle of his jaw. The man thrashed once, gurgling and struggling as Baxter continued to clamp his mouth shut. Warm blood spilled across Baxter's arm.

At almost the same instant, a second VC rose from cover a few yards away, the AK in his hands swinging to aim at Baxter and his dying victim. For a horrible instant, Baxter knew the other soldier was going to pull the trigger . . . and then he sagged, eyes going blank as Connors snagged him from the rear and drove his knife hilt-deep up into the man's skull just below the ear.

Baxter's victim gave a final kick, then went completely limp, eyes staring, blood still spilling from the ugly, ear-to-ear gash in his throat. The SEALs carefully reconnoitered the area and searched the two bodies. Besides the AK-47 and the SKS, they found a small packet of maps and papers on Connors's man and a radio in the weeds nearby. Chances were, the two VC had been observing the Navy LCPLs, possibly waiting to call in mortar or rocket fire, possibly waiting for the men they obviously had been sent to pick up.

Leaving the bodies where they were but bringing along the weapons, documents, and radio, the two SEALs slipped into the water, backing away from the shore as they kept the silent shoreside covered. Together, Baxter and Connors waded to the pickup boat. Minutes later, they were aboard, motoring back toward Nha Be as sailors offered them coffee from a small, jury-rigged hotplate next to the boat's helm.

Now that it was over, Baxter allowed himself the luxury of a shiver. Eighteen hours of misery for two dead VC, a few documents, and a no-show at the interdiction site. What a perfect, grade-A clusterfuck. . . .

It wasn't until they were halfway back to Nha Be when

another fact finally worked its way through Baxter's skull and lodged in his exhaustion-fogged mind.

He'd never killed a man before. All of his training, all of his preparation for more than a year now had been aimed at this one exercise—the taking of an enemy's life. He'd *done* it, done it without hesitation, without even immediately realizing or thinking about what he'd done. Now that he thought about it, though, he wasn't entirely sure he liked the feeling. . . .

Chapter 4

Thursday, 31 March 1966

U.S. Navy Amphibious Base
Coronado, California
1343 hours

Lieutenant Steven Vincent Tangretti tapped the brakes of the jeep lightly to slow down as he overtook the double line of running men trotting along the side of the road. Their T-shirts were soaked with sweat as they labored to keep pace with the burly chief urging them forward, and they had the familiar look of men who had been pushed to the very limits of their endurance—and beyond—by the toughest training course known to the United States Navy.

Tangretti knew that look and smiled as he passed the all-but-exhausted sailors. SEALs nearing the end of Hell Week . . . there was no mistaking them.

He watched them in his side mirror for a moment longer, envying them a little. Steve Tangretti had been the very first Navy SEAL, four years back. He had helped establish the training program, sweated through it alongside his first team-mates, and he still missed the straightforward sense of being a part of the Navy's elite commando force.

A sign ahead indicated his turnoff, the compound that housed the headquarters for the Navy's Pacific Amphibious Forces, and Tangretti pulled into the large parking lot off the Silver Strand Highway that ran along the western side of North Island. He climbed out of the jeep and looked up at the long, low, one-story building that frowned over the half-empty lot. A lifetime of service had brought Tangretti to plenty of new duty stations over the years, but this one made him feel par-ticularly uncomfortable. For nearly three years he'd been working overseas, shuttling from one assignment to another as an advisor to the South Vietnamese navy, a series of jobs that had at least kept him near the action of the growing war in Southeast Asia. But now, when American military forces were finally starting to see direct action in the field—including his beloved SEALs themselves—he had been reassigned State-side, to a rear-echelon job where he'd probably end up com-manding a desk instead of a unit of commandos out in the field.

For a man like Steve Tangretti, a man who had seen action from Kwajalein to Normandy to Okinawa to Korea, the man who had led a top-secret raid into Cuban waters in the dark days of the Missile Crisis, being condemned to a staff job was something like a sentence of exile.

He paused beside the jeep and adjusted the mirror to study his reflection. A lot of years had passed since Steve Tangretti had joined the Navy, back in the days after Pearl Harbor. He was pushing fifty now, and although he'd put on some weight over the years his tall, solid body was still muscle, not fat. But his hair was going gray and his face was lined, and the eyes that looked back at him out of the mirror had seen a lot of things he preferred not to dwell on too long or often.

A forty-seven-year-old mustang lieutenant . . . was there still room for his kind in a Navy that really belonged to the youngsters he'd seen sweating out there on the road? Tangretti could still keep up with the best of them, physically. But at-titudes in the service were changing, and he often found him-self wondering if he could do as well meeting the demands of those kinds of changes.

He shook his head, dismissing the thought. Maybe he was a dinosaur in the new Navy . . . but he still couldn't imagine any other life. Even a staff post would be better than giving it all up and retiring.

Straightening up, he turned away from the jeep and walked briskly toward the front of the building, shoulders squared, back straight.

The petty officer at the reception desk inside directed him down a long hall toward his destination. The sign beside the open door read HEADQUARTERS—NAVAL OPERATIONS SUPPORT GROUP, PACIFIC, and inside he could see all the typical bustle of a small, overworked Navy office. Enlisted men in crisp whites were working at and around a double row of desks behind a counter manned by a bored-looking second class. The man looked up as Tangretti approached and gave him a half-nod.

"May I help you, Lieutenant?" he asked.

"Lieutenant Steve Tangretti. I'm supposed to check in with Captain Bucklew."

The petty officer indicated the rear of the room with a curt gesture. "In the back, sir," he said. "His aide will take care of you."

Tangretti rounded the counter and headed for the rear of the office. After years of working at the edge of civilization, there was something unnerving about the bilious green walls, the clacking typewriters, the men pushing papers and filing reports, that put him on edge. Even though his liaison jobs in Vietnam had been theoretically rear-echelon duty, there'd been little room for bureaucracy and the sterile environment of an office. It was going to take some getting used to, he decided.

As he reached the back of the room, he saw the door to the captain's office, guarded by a desk set apart from the others. A khaki-clad officer was bending over a filing cabinet in the corner as he reached the desk. Tangretti waited a moment, then cleared his throat.

"One more minute, please," the man said without looking up. Tangretti had heard the voice before, the heavy upper-class Bostonian accent, though he couldn't quite place it. . . .

Then the officer straightened up and turned to face him, and Tangretti remembered.

"Well, well, Lieutenant Tangretti." The younger man

looked less than pleased to see him. The feeling was entirely mutual. Lieutenant Peter Howell was someone Tangretti had hoped he'd never run across again. It seemed those hopes had been in vain. "Still in the procurement business, Lieutenant? Or did you finally learn your lesson after all?"

Tangretti ignored the barb. "I'm under orders to report to Captain Bucklew," he said stiffly. "Is he in?"

"I'll have to see what his schedule looks like," the other officer responded. "Wait over there." His gesture took in a row of chairs opposite his desk.

As Tangretti settled into one of them, Howell crossed to the door and rapped softly on it, then went inside. Tangretti was left alone to stare at the door and remember.

He had last crossed swords with Howell back in the summer of 1962, in those heady days after President Kennedy had first tapped Tangretti to be part of the initial SEAL contingent. As executive officer of UDT-21 in Virginia, Tangretti had bombarded the Pentagon with suggestions on the topic of a Navy counterpart to the new Army Special Forces, and on the first day of January, 1962, Kennedy had signed the final authorization creating a SEAL team on each coast. Tangretti had been called in to see the President to receive those orders in person. He was slated to become the exec of the East Coast SEALs, Team Two, but because the team's new commander had commitments that tied him up for several months, the responsibility of organizing Team Two had fallen squarely on Tangretti's shoulders.

Tangretti often suspected that the brass in Washington had deliberately arranged things to make him the effective CO of the unit in those critical early days. He'd come up through the ranks in World War II and was awarded a commission during the Korean War, but in 1962 he had still been a mere lieutenant junior grade. A junior officer—especially a mustang who had risen to the job from the enlisted ranks—might have been expected to be overawed by the responsibility or the frowns of those set above him.

If that had been their plan, though, the brass had badly miscalculated. Steven Tangretti had been bucking the high command almost from the very start of his long and checkered career. And because he'd believed so passionately in the possibilities of a unit like the SEALs he had turned all of his energy, and all of his considerable talents, to making the new team work.

His most pressing problem in those early days had been obtaining the equipment the SEALs would need to fulfill their job. Tangretti had reverted to his roots. Back in World War II, before joining the UDT, Tangretti had been a Seabee in the Pacific with a reputation as a cumshaw king. In fact, his penchant for unauthorized trades and scrounging had led his superiors to suggest a career in demolition—with the unspoken threat that it was a choice between that and the stockade. The young Tangretti had continued to use his talents after joining the demolition teams and had built up quite a reputation among his comrades as a man who could get things done outside of official channels. Even the officers over him came to look the other way when Tangretti started to work his magic.

So when procurement for the new teams became a problem, Tangretti came up with a typically straightforward solution. If the ponderous Pentagon bureaucracy wouldn't come through for him, he'd find less official but more effective ways to get things done.

The first test had been in the area of weapons. After a commander in the Navy supply office had intervened in Tangretti's attempts to purchase a .357 Smith & Wesson Model 19 Combat Magnum revolver, replacing it with the Model 15 Combat Masterpiece that used .38 Special ammo instead—this despite the fact that Team Two already had .357 Magnum ammo in stock—Tangretti decided not to waste his time trying to persuade bureaucrats to cooperate. For a combat rifle, the SEALs were interested in trying out the new AR-15, a lightweight weapon that had only recently appeared on the market. With some of his teammates in tow, Tangretti had gone to the Colt factory in Baltimore and conducted his own weapons trials with the AR-15, exposing the weapons to surf and sand and determining that it was, indeed, a superb weapon that would take plenty of punishment with minimal maintenance. So Tangretti had issued an open purchase order for 132 of the weapons, sending half of them to his opposite number on the West Coast. He'd gone on to do the same sort of thing to solve other problems, too, buying aqualungs from commercial dealers and then modifying them to SEAL specifications, and pick-

ing up used parachutes at low prices and having them cut and
sewn into steerable airfoil shapes.

He'd cut corners, of course, with both supply procedures
and safety standards, but with trouble threatening from Castro's Cuba he'd been in a hurry to make the unit combat-ready.
Nonetheless, the hidebound bureaucracy had frowned on his
initiative, and by summer Tangretti had been threatened with
no less than five separate investigations into irregularities in
his fledgling command. Any one of them could have put an
end to his career, and in combination they might have landed
him in prison for years.

Lieutenant Peter Howell had been one of the investigators
assigned to look into the case. His zeal in going after Tangretti
had taken on the proportions of a witch hunt; and even though
he had a Presidential Priority Two authorization and the support of senior officers from the UDT, Tangretti had been very
close to a court martial. Luck had fallen his way, though. The
president had paid a visit to the SEALs in Norfolk, and during
a weapons demonstration he'd asked a SEAL how he liked
his rifle. The SEAL, typical of the breed, had been blunt, de-
claring that the AR-15 was the weapon the SEALs wanted and
needed, that everything else in the arsenal was garbage, and
that in his opinion the persecution of Tangretti was a horrible
miscarriage of justice.

Within a matter of weeks, the outspoken SEAL had received
an autographed picture of Kennedy, and Steve Tangretti's legal problems had vanished as if they'd never been. Eventually,
the AR-15 had been chosen by the DOD as the standard combat rifle of the American military and redesignated the M-16.
As for Howell, he had quietly packed up and moved on.

But now, it seemed, Tangretti had fallen in with the man
once more. If he was part of Bucklew's staff, Howell was
likely to make life miserable for Tangretti.

He was jerked out of his reverie by the office door opening
again. Howell stood there, frowning at him. "The captain will
see you now," he said curtly.

Tangretti gave Howell a sour smile as he passed. The door
closed behind him, and he paused to take in the office and its
sole occupant.

The room was a reflection of the man, he decided, decorated
with souvenirs of old exploits and a few football mementos.

Captain Philip Bucklew had been a football star before joining the Navy in World War II. He still had an athlete's build, tall, big-shouldered, putting on weight but still managing to look fit. He looked up from his desk. "Ah, Lieutenant Tangretti. Have a seat, won't you?"

As Tangretti sat down he noticed a framed page from a newspaper comic section. He hid a derisive smile. That, too, was somehow entirely in character for Phil Bucklew.

Bucklew had created the Navy/Marine Scouts and Raiders, a unit designed to do beach reconnaissance work in World War II. Men from Bucklew's outfit had been among the first trainers for the units that ultimately became the UDT; Tangretti still remembered an S&R man named Rand who had started out as one of his instructors but after Normandy had transferred to Underwater Demolition and served side by side with Tangretti at Okinawa. Bucklew's Scouts and Raiders had probed the beaches in Sicily, Italy, and Normandy, but they'd never been quite as versatile as the UDT.

Late in the war Bucklew had gone to the Pacific and operated among guerrilla fighters in China, earning the nickname "Big Stoop" from the posture he'd been forced to adopt to disguise his height among the Chinese peasants. His exploits as "Big Stoop" had later become the basis for a story in the popular comic *Terry and the Pirates*. The framed comic page was from the strip, another trophy from Bucklew's long and varied career.

In Tangretti's eyes, though, Bucklew simply didn't measure up to the men he'd known in UDT and SEALs. He'd always seemed most interested in relentless self-promotion and career advancement. Perhaps the fact that he'd never gone through UDT training, never served in an outfit like the SEALs, accounted for Bucklew's approach to life. An old UDT man placed nothing higher than the duty to the rest of the Teams, and Tangretti could not conceive of seeking personal recognition at the expense of the men who served with him. As far as Tangretti was concerned, even Bucklew's medals were suspect. The man had been in a position to write himself up for some of those awards, especially the Silver Star from the China operations.

Friends of Tangretti's, even a few UDT men, had tried to tell him that Bucklew was one of the good guys, but he had never really bought it. The man claimed to be the real founder of Navy special warfare, but Tangretti had been there, and he knew there were plenty of others with a better claim. Studying the man and his surroundings, his doubts were stronger than ever now.

"Well, Lieutenant," Bucklew said slowly, leaning back in his chair with a smile. "Welcome to Coronado."

"Thank you, sir," Tangretti replied formally. Though he had strong opinions of the man, this was the first time they'd actually met, and there was no use showing hostility to the man who was supposed to be his new commanding officer. "It's . . . a little bit different from what I've been used to."

Bucklew picked up a paper from an open file folder on his desk and studied it for a moment. "So I see," he said. "Advisor to the LDNN in Vietnam . . . two different tours, in fact. Last assignment setting up riverine forces." Bucklew put down the paper, obviously something from Tangretti's personnel file. "There seems to have been some controversy attached to some of your work over there . . ."

"I did my job, sir," Tangretti told him stiffly.

"Indeed." Bucklew straightened up. "Your job, then, included going out in the field with South Vietnamese troops, although American advisors were explicitly forbidden to engage in active combat operations?"

"They were training exercises, sir," Tangretti said, wearing his best poker face. "Unfortunately, from time to time we ran into opposition and were forced to fight . . ."

Bucklew chuckled. "Right. And it was a training mission when you took command of a raid on a VC-held island, I suppose. A U.S. Navy officer commanding Vietnamese troops in the field . . . and, as I understand it, going out wounded."

"Lieutenant Ninh was . . . indisposed that day, sir," Tangretti said. "I felt it necessary to go out . . . to supervise the training." In his mind's eye he could picture the day. The South Vietnamese officer in command of the force of *Lien Doc Nguoi Nhia* commandos, the local counterpart to the UDT/SEAL teams, had opted out of the mission at the last possible moment, afraid of taking his men in against the VC forces known to be based on Ilo Ilo island. So Tangretti, officially attached to the LDNN as an American advisor in charge of their training program, had taken command and led the paradrop, although he'd been wearing a cast from an earlier injury at the time.

Perhaps it had been foolish, but Tangretti had hated the inactivity of the advisor's life around Saigon. He was a SEAL first and foremost, and he found it all but impossible to sit on the sidelines while other men fought. In Vietnam, in an all but independent command, he'd been free to evade the restrictions put on him by the high command. Now, it seemed, his free-wheeling approach to his job was catching up with him once more.

"Look, Lieutenant," Bucklew said. "I know how it is out there. When I went in to get sand samples from the beaches before Normandy, I didn't let the brass breathe down my neck either. Same when I was in China. You see a job, you do a job. That's the way it ought to be when you're out in the field. But here, things are different. NOSG was set up to oversee naval special warfare, to coordinate UDT and SEALs and beach jumpers and the brown-water sailors. With things starting to heat up in Nam, we're going to be a very visible part of the service. We've got our first direct-action SEAL unit in-country now, along with the UDT men and your buddies in the riverine forces." He paused, tapping Tangretti's file. "There's no room in a staff job in a command like this one for someone who's going to make up the rules as he goes along. Washington's going to be watching how we handle our responsibilities, and the kind of stunts you've pulled over the years won't help us under that kind of scrutiny. Do I make myself clear?"

"Crystal clear, Captain," Tangretti said. "But . . . if I may speak freely? . . ."

"Go ahead."

"I didn't ask to be assigned here, sir. I would've preferred to stay in Vietnam as an advisor . . . or to get active duty with the SEALs again. Just about anything. I don't belong behind a desk, and I don't always get along with the bureaucrats who put their precious regulations up on some kind of damned pedestal to be worshipped by all the rest of us swabbies." He didn't add that he'd file for a transfer as soon as he could manage it. Tangretti had no more desire to work for Bucklew and Howell than they had to have someone like Tangretti spoiling their pleasant little Navy fiefdom.

"Who would have guessed it?" Bucklew said, voice heavy with irony. "Well, the fact is that we didn't ask for you, either. Evidently somebody at the five-sided squirrel cage decided we needed someone on our staff with Vietnam experience and firsthand knowledge of SEAL capabilities. Captain Galloway, I believe it was. He seems to feel you'd be an asset to NOSG. I hope he's right in that assessment."

That made Tangretti reconsider his feelings about the assignment. He'd first met Joseph Galloway years ago, before Normandy, when the man had been a liaison officer at the Pentagon overseeing the operations of the early UDTs. And Galloway had been with him that fateful day when he met the president, still promoting the need for naval special warfare. Galloway never did anything without a good reason, and he'd never worked against the best interests of the Teams. If he wanted Tangretti as part of Bucklew's staff, there was probably something behind the decision.

Bucklew's command was intended to shape the role of naval special warfare as the American commitment in Vietnam grew broader and deeper. "Big Stoop" had already been the head of a junket two years earlier sent to explore the role the SEALs and others might play in Southeast Asia, and now he was in charge of implementing many of the policies he'd recommended back then. Perhaps Galloway felt that Bucklew, who had never been part of the close-knit UDT or SEAL communities, needed someone with that sort of experience on his staff. Someone who had proven, over the years, that he was blunt and outspoken enough to put up a fight if he didn't think his CO was heading in the right direction. Someone who wasn't intimidated by high rank or concerned over his own future career prospects.

Someone like Steven Tangretti.

"I'm glad to hear Captain Galloway wanted me here, sir," Tangretti said slowly. "I'll do my best to live up to his expectations of me."

Bucklew met his eye with a probing look. "So . . . I guess the real question is, can I count on you to maintain a proper respect for the lines of command?"

"Captain," Tangretti told him. "The biggest mistake the Navy ever made was making me an officer. I've never been very good at fitting in with the whole 'officer and gentleman' thing. And after all these years I'm pretty well set in my ways. But I don't go out of my way to cause trouble. I do what I think needs to be done. A lot of people over the years have thought that was a pretty damned good idea, all things considered. I hope you'll find it that way too.'' He paused. ''Maybe I take shortcuts now and then, but that's only when people push me into it. Don't judge me on what those papers say about me. I'd rather you judged me on who I am and what I do. I think you'll find I've got the good of the service in mind, no matter what.''

The captain studied him for a long moment, as if not quite satisfied with the answer. ''You talk a good game, Tangretti, I'll give you that,'' he said at last. ''But be very, very sure of this. If you do anything—*anything*—to screw up this command, you'll bounce so hard they'll have to send a space capsule up to bring you back to Earth. You could contribute a hell of a lot to this command . . . but I'll be keeping an eye on you, too. Just remember that, and we'll get along just fine. Understood?''

''Aye-aye, sir,'' Tangretti said slowly.

''Good.'' Bucklew smiled again. ''All right, then. You'll have a desk out in the bullpen Monday morning. Your primary job's going to be handling the reports out of the SEALs in Nam and helping to translate them into recommendations we can turn into NOSG policy. We're pretty short on accommodations on the base, so until Housing can get you something permanent you'll get a billet at the Hotel de Coronado. You have family?''

''Yes, sir,'' Tangretti said. ''A wife. One kid still at home . . . the other's in the SEALs, at Little Creek.''

''Hmmph.'' Bucklew didn't seem interested. ''Well, your best bet would probably be across the harbor, over in San Diego. Might be a little pricey, but . . . well, let Housing sort it out for you. You'll have the weekend to get settled in at the hotel and take care of your personal business. Be here at 0800 Monday, and we'll get your nose to the grindstone. Any questions?''

''No, sir,'' he said.

''Then you're dismissed.'' Bucklew's tone was curt.

Lieutenant Howell didn't even look up as Tangretti left the room. Walking stiffly through the outer office, Tangretti turned over the implications of the conversation with Bucklew in his mind. If he really did have an important function to carry out here on behalf of Galloway and the Teams, he'd have to watch his step. Bucklew seemed most concerned about not letting him make waves, from the sound of things, but Howell would most likely be all too eager to pounce on the slightest misstep.

On the whole, Tangretti would have been far happier surveying an enemy-held beach. At least there he would have known exactly what he was up against. . . .

He was so distracted that he bumped into another officer halfway to the front door. "Excuse me, Commander," he muttered, taking in the man's insignia without really registering anything else about him.

"No harm done," the other man said. As Tangretti started to turn away he went on. "Hold on a minute . . . I know you, Lieutenant . . . Tangretti, wasn't it?" He paused. "Of course, of course, Steve Tangretti. The SEAL officer. You might not remember me, but I sure remember you and that bunch of cutthroats from Little Creek. I'm Pembroke . . . Dr. Pembroke, from the *Sea Lion*. Back in '62 . . . that little cruise to play tag with Uncle Fidel. Last time I saw you, you were half-drowned and swearing a blue streak because the captain almost missed your pickup."

Tangretti didn't answer right away. He studied the officer closely for the first time, registering the caduceus insignia and a face that looked vaguely familiar. The words took him back across nearly four years, to the spring of 1962 and the first SEAL mission. Tangretti had led a six-man unit on a clandestine swim from the submarine *Sea Lion* to survey the beaches near Havana and determine if they were suitable for an amphibious landing. They'd carried out their mission but almost missed finding the sub on their way back. And Komar patrol boats had complicated things. Tangretti had been forced to swim down thirty-five feet to the sub's escape hatch so that he could use the intercom inside to demand that the captain surface long enough for the other swimmers to get aboard. Now that he thought about it, the sub's doctor had been named Pembroke, at that . . .

He almost returned the man's greeting but checked his first enthusiastic response. The mission to Cuba had been carried out in the strictest secrecy, and as far as he knew it hadn't been declassified. Admitting to it would be a violation of orders . . . just the kind of thing someone like Howell would be eager to use against him.

Tangretti called upon his poker face again. ''I'm sorry, Doctor,'' he said evenly. ''I've never seen you before.''

''Oh, come on, man,'' Pembroke said. ''I know it was you. I'm not likely to forget that Cuban cruise . . .''

He shook his head slowly. ''I was never there, Doctor,'' he told the man, more forceful this time. ''You must have me confused with someone else.'' Tangretti did turn away this time, walking off with his shoulders set.

As he left the office, he was already regretting having to lie to the man. Ignoring an old shipmate, however brief an acquaintance it might have been, was something that just wasn't done in the Navy. No doubt Pembroke had been sincerely glad to see him, and the rebuff made Tangretti feel like Peter denying his Master.

But the SEALs stood apart from the rest of the Navy, their work largely clandestine, their very existence something the Navy rarely talked about. Tangretti had learned how to keep his mouth shut when it counted . . . and he wasn't about to let a slip of the tongue get him in hot water with Bucklew or Howell this early in the game.

He left the building feeling like a man who had just come back from a recon mission deep in the Mekong jungles. Tangretti had survived his first contact with the enemy. Now all he had to do was keep surviving, until he found out just what his real mission might be.

Hotel de Coronado
Coronado, California
1926 hours

The hotel had the opulent look of a resort built in the twenties, back in the expansive days before the Depression. Perched high above the Pacific, it was a large and attractive old building decorated in a Spanish motif, with white stucco walls and a red tile roof. A verandah commanded a view of the ocean and a jumble of slippery, seaweed-coated rocks on shore. From the window of his temporary room Tangretti could see a party of men—UDT or SEALs, he wasn't sure which—going through exercises among those treacherous rocks. The Hotel de Coronado was separate from the North Island facility, but close by the base, and it housed a number of transient or newly arrived officers in addition to the wealthy guests who were the hotel's bread and butter.

Tangretti had rarely had such luxurious accommodations on any Navy assignment.

The base Housing Office had assigned him this third-floor hotel room, and he would remain here until the rest of the family was ready to join him and a more permanent arrangement was necessary. For now, though, he was as well settled as he was likely to be. Tangretti traveled light, and it had taken almost no time to unpack and stow his gear.

He sat on the edge of his bed and contemplated the battered old tape recorder he'd set up on the bedside table. It was just about the only item in Tangretti's effects that wasn't Navy issue. Tangretti had never been very good at writing letters, and for a long time he'd found it hard to keep in touch with his family as much as he should have. The old recorder had changed all that, though. He found talking a lot easier than writing.

Tangretti switched on the machine and picked up the microphone. "Well, here I am, gang," he began. "Old Dad's back in the good old U.S. of A. at last. Like I told you in my last letter, the powers that be have decided to send me to a headquarters job in Coronado. California's not changed a whole lot since we were here back in '54. A little more crowded, maybe, but after Vietnam anything looks crowded to me. I've already put in to have you guys moved out here, and they're looking for off-base housing. The guy at the Housing Office said we'll probably be able to get something decent in San Diego, but don't count on it being a tight-knit Navy community like Little Creek. The base here is crowded onto North Island, and there isn't much room. So the Navy families live where they can, instead of bunching together like they do back home. Right now they've got me roosting in a fancy hotel room, of all things. Government money at work, I guess. I feel like they're going to assign me a body servant and a chauffeur just so I fit in around here!"

He stopped the tape and stood up, pacing back and forth in the small space beside the window. As a rule Tangretti tried not to unload any of his personal problems on his family, but that made it difficult to talk much about his new assignment. It was probably best to gloss over the whole thing, though Veronica would probably see right through it all. Somehow she always knew when he was trying to keep things from her.

Veronica . . .

After all his time overseas, with only a few brief leaves to visit home, it might be good to have a tour or two Stateside. Tangretti had seen precious little of his family since starting work with the SEALs. Now the strain of too much time apart was starting to show in his marriage. Veronica's last few letters had been shorter, colder than before. She had to deal with more than her share of problems at home, and Tangretti hadn't been there lately to help her. But he couldn't seem to make her understand how much he needed to be a part of the Navy, or why he felt compelled to be wherever the action was. Now that the Navy had decided he was more useful in a stateside job, maybe he and Veronica could try to rebuild the bridges across the gaps that had come between them of late.

He sat down again and turned the machine back on. "It'll be great to see both of you again, and if Hank can get a spell of leave this summer maybe we can take a vacation together . . . drive up the coast or go camping in the mountains, something like that. Just the family . . . it's been a long time since all four of us could do something together." The thought made him smile, remembering the last time they'd all camped out together. That had been a long time ago. . . .

"I was happy to hear about Bill making the Honor Roll again last semester. He must take after you, Ronnie, that's all I can figure. Nobody could've expected *my* son to be the academic type, that much is certain. My dad would sure be proud to know that a Tangretti stood a chance at getting in to a good college and really making something of himself.

"And speaking of the kids, I had a tape from Junior just before I left Saigon. Wasn't it great, him winning the judo tournament? That young man is going to do the SEALs proud . . . and I just know old Hank would be feeling damned good about the way his son turned out."

He switched off the tape again and cleared his throat. It always choked him up a little bit, even after all these years, to talk about Hank Richardson. They'd been swim buddies

from the first day of training together back at Fort Pierce in
Florida, a mismatched pair who had been drawn together by
bonds of shared hardship that had transcended differences in
rank, background, and social class. Tangretti, the tall, lanky
petty officer who always made the Navy dance to his tune,
had found a damned good friend in Henry Elliot Richardson,
short, slender, refined, an officer and a gentleman who had
seemingly ignored the Navy and its strictures as somehow beneath his notice. Mutt and Jeff, someone had called them back
in those early days, but they'd discovered they had a lot in
common despite the obvious contrasts between them. Fort
Pierce had taught them the value of teamwork; the beaches of
Kwajalein had united them with the ties only men who had
been under fire together could understand.

Richardson was the one who had first met and fallen in love
with Veronica Stevens, a young WAC stationed in England
when they arrived there together to join the preparations for
Operation Overlord. Tangretti had used all of his talents to
help the two of them get hitched just a few weeks before D-
Day. But Hank hadn't come home from the blood-soaked
beaches of Normandy. He'd left Veronica alone, pregnant with
a son. Tangretti had loved him like a brother, and their common love for Hank Richardson had brought him and Veronica
together when the war finally ended.

Yeah, old Hank would've been proud of the kid, he thought.
Tangretti had raised Hank Junior as his own son, and as the
years went by he'd seen a lot of his old buddy in the boy.
The boy's grandparents had been scandalized when he'd gone
into the Navy as an enlisted man. That was one battle they
hadn't won. When he and Veronica had first married, the elder
Richardsons had insisted that Steve not adopt the boy or make
him change his name; they wanted a Richardson to carry on
the line. Hank Junior had a sizable trust fund set aside in his
name and could have gone to an expensive Eastern college or
wangled an Annapolis appointment if he'd so desired. But the
boy had decided to join the Navy straight out of high school.
He'd wanted to be an enlisted man . . . and a SEAL. That had
been the proudest day of Steve Tangretti's life, when Hank
Junior had been picked for training as a SEAL. He was with
Seal Team Two in Little Creek, the unit Tangretti had set up,
and it was good to know he was carrying on the family tra-

dition now that Tangretti himself was no longer part of the
rank and file of the SEAL teams himself.

Tangretti only wished every aspect of being a family man
was as easy as raising Hank Junior had turned out to be. But
though Veronica had been a good Navy wife for years, she
wasn't as patient with him as she'd been in years gone by.
And sometimes he wondered if she wasn't right when she
accused him of neglecting the family, especially their son Bill.
He would be graduating from high school soon, a quiet, stu-
dious teenager. Tangretti hadn't been around enough over the
past few years to really get to know the younger boy, not like
he knew Hank Junior. But it was too late now to undo any of
that. All he could do now was try to make a fresh start with
all of them.

Tangretti reached for the machine again. This tape was the
first step toward that fresh start. He hoped it would do the job.

Chapter 5

Tuesday, 5 April 1966

**Soi Rap River
Ten miles south of Nha Be
1910 hours**

The two U.S. Navy PBRs made their way slowly up the Soi
Rap River, one trailing the other by nearly four hundred yards.
It was almost dark, though an orange glow lingered behind
the trees on the river's west bank and the sky overhead remained a rich and bottomless blue. Besides the second PBR's
regular four-man crew, the small craft's well deck was
crowded with Baxter and three of his SEALs, plus Mineman

Chief Devereaux of UDT-11 and Lieutenant Nguyen of the LDNN.

Four more UDT men and Adams, another SEAL, were on the lead boat. It had been Baxter's idea to insert this afternoon on the new PBRs, but he wasn't convinced yet that it was a good idea. The well decks on the tiny speedsters were cramped, and the men huddled together shoulder to shoulder. The riverine craft could have handled a single SEAL squad easily enough, but not the SEALs and a UDT demo squad and their equipment as well.

They'd spent much of the afternoon ashore with Devereaux and his men, providing security for the UDT people as they placed explosives inside a Vietcong bunker overlooking the Soi Rap just a few miles inland from the South China Sea. It was demanding, delicate, and supremely boring work, and the SEALs were all becoming heartily sick of it. When, Baxter wondered, were they going to start some halfway decent *aggressive* patrolling of the Rung Sat? This joint-command stuff was make-work nonsense, a waste of time and talent.

Baxter wondered if there was someone he could write, someone he could talk to in order to convince the brass that the SEALs could be better used as an independent unit.

"So I hear you SEALies're some kind of really hot commandos," a young sailor said, grinning as he leaned against the port-side M60 machine-gun mount. He was a seaman, an E3, and couldn't have been more than nineteen years old.

Baxter looked up at the sailor, mildly annoyed. His first thought was to put the kid down, possibly by pointing out that he was an officer and enlisted personnel should call him *sir*, but he dismissed the thought almost at once. In the first place, Baxter wasn't wearing any emblems of rank. None of the SEALs were. In the second, none of the SEALs cared that much for rank anyway, and it seemed silly to carp about it, even to brush someone off.

Besides, Baxter recognized that glow in the SN's eyes. Hero worship . . . with perhaps a touch of John Wayne and last stands, of astronauts, fast cars, and fast women.

"Something like that" was what he said.

The sailor nodded. "Yeah, so why do they gotcha pulling demo details out here, huh?"

Connors was sitting on the well-deck bench, squeezed in

between Baxter and Lieutenant Nguyen. "Maybe," Connors said darkly, " 'cause the demolition detail is just a *cover* story, see? And we're really here to assassinate high-ranking VC party members . . . and anyone else who finds out about our mission . . . even our own boat crews and any snot-nosed pus-gutted pukes who accidentally find out what we're doing. If you find out too much, we have to kill you, see?"

The seaman's eyes had been getting wider and wider as Connors spoke, and now he took an uncertain step backward, nodding hard. "Uh, sure. Sir. Uh, look, I don't know nothin', okay? I'll just, uh, go up and help the Skipper. . . . "

He retreated in disorder, with several nervous glances back over his shoulder. Gilbert Chalker, seated across the well deck from Baxter, laughed and shook his head. "She-it, Connie. You didn't have to scare the kid to death."

"Easier'n gettin' your leg talked off."

"Don't be too rough on these guys," Baxter told Connors. "We're going to be seeing a lot of these PBR boys from now on. Let's not make their job any harder than we have to, okay?"

Connors shrugged and looked off at the shoreline, drifting slowly past a few dozen yards away. "Yeah. I guess."

"These PBRs," Nguyen said, "are going to do much to help us win the war for these rivers. I think both the SEALs and the LDNN will benefit, if we can learn how to work with one another."

The Patrol Boat, River was a brand new addition to the Navy's inventory, and one of the strangest. Thirty-one feet long, with a lightweight fiberglass hull, the dark-green craft was propelled by Jacuzzi water-jet pumps that could rocket the craft along at high speeds. The manuals claimed a speed of better than thirty knots, and Baxter believed that for an unloaded, stripped-down boat. With six passengers and all of their arms and equipment, with three 60-guns aft and the big twin .50 in its open-topped turret forward, the PBR would be lucky to top twenty-five knots.

Even so, it was a hell of a lot better than those converted LCPLs.

These two particular boats were part of River Squadron Five, working under the direction of Task Group 116.2. They were among the very first of the new vessels to arrive in-country, and both their crews and the officers in command of the operation were obviously still trying to figure out how best to apply this new weapon to the peculiar conditions of warfare among the rivers, waterways, and swamps south of Saigon.

The river patrol force had been created the previous December under the code name Operation Game Warden, and under the direction of CHNAVADVGRU, the Chief of the Naval Advisory Group in South Vietnam. The small American flotilla of gun boats and riverine vessels were responsible for patrolling the waters both of the Rung Sat and of the Mekong Delta to the west; stopping and searching suspicious Vietnamese boats, enforcing the curfew intended to keep all civilian craft off the water at night, and attempting to block the veritable flood of weapons, ammunition, and supplies coming in to the Vietcong near Saigon from across the Cambodian border.

The new PBRs represented a tremendous technological advance over the first battered and antiquated LCPLs to arrive in South Vietnam. Converted by the diligent efforts of Lieutenant Kenneth MacLeod and his crew—"MacLeod's Navy," as they called themselves, after "*McHale's Navy*," the popular television program in the States about a WWII PT boat skipper—those former landing craft had been effective in their patrols despite the fact that they were too slow and too deep-drafted to effectively operate in the Rung Sat. The first of over a hundred PBRs to be shipped to South Vietnam had arrived in March. With an unloaded draft at speed of only nine inches, they were expected—as Nguyen had suggested—to radically transform the art of river warfare in South Vietnam . . . *if*, of course, they were allowed to fight it. Standing orders permitted the four-man crews of the PBRs to open fire if and *only* if they received fire from the enemy.

Baxter knew how the PBR crews felt about those orders and could sympathize. The SEALs, too, continued to operate under sharp operational constraints dictated by the brass back in Saigon. They were like those PBRs, race horses ready and raring to go . . . but handicapped by the load they were forced to bear.

It was eleven days since the commencement of Operation Jackstay. To hear the SEAL team's NILO tell the story, Jackstay was the most spectacular military success since the war in Vietnam had begun, though facts and figures backing that claim were scanty, scattered, and often contradictory. Every day at the morning briefing, Kellerman passed down intel reports telling of so many tons of rice captured, so many VC sympathizers picked up, so many bunkers or storehouses or VC buildings burned or demolished. The trouble was Baxter had only been in-country for a month now and already he was convinced that the war was never going to be won by tallying up numbers, like the score in some huge and complicated game. It would be people like Nguyen Quon who would win the war, win their own war . . . with American help, to be sure.

"So what's your angle on things, Ong Quon?" Baxter asked the Vietnamese special forces man. "Is Jackstay a hit or not?"

Quon was quietly assembling his weapon, an M-1 carbine of WWII vintage. "It is beginning, Lieutenant," Quon said, his voice just loud enough to carry above the rumble of the PBR's diesels. "But is *only* beginning. Americans kill some Cong, but there are many, many more."

Nguyen Quon was being polite, Baxter thought. On the day of the landings, SEAL forces had killed exactly four VC in different encounters, all in situations where VC had stumbled accidentally across SEAL team members and had to be killed to allow the SEALs to extract. Four kills in eleven days. All in all, it wasn't a very good showing for the SEALs, especially given that they were supposed to be here for direct action.

"Killing VC is what I thought we were brought here for," Baxter said. "But somebody sure as hell better figure out what 'direct action' means."

"I'll tell you what," Lucky Luciano said. "I think it's this way, see? There's this one bunch of admirals and captains in San Diego, and they've got this dictionary, see? It says, 'direct action' means 'kill lots of VC.' And they wrote our orders.

"But then you got this bunch of dickhead admirals in Washington, and they have a dictionary that says 'direct action' means 'Hey! Don't make anybody mad!' "

The others chuckled at that. "Yeah," Connors said. "And there's more dickhead admirals up in Saigon. Their dictionary says it means 'Go bury your fuckin' head in the mud. . . .' "

"Aw, admit it, you guys!" Devereaux said. "You guys're

still just jealous because the UDT made the big score.''

Chalker dragged a life vest out from under the PBR's bench and whacked Devereaux over his helmet.

"Go catch flies, frogman!" Luciano said, laughing.

The most dramatic kill of the whole operation had also taken place on that first day, when a UDT force blocking the flank of the Marine landing had ambushed a junk in the river. A fierce firefight had broken out, and five VC on the junk had been killed, while a sixth had leaped overboard and swum to safety. The SEALs' UDT buddies had been rubbing in the fact that they were ahead in the count ever since.

"Damn it," Baxter said as the good-natured roughhouse subsided. "It just doesn't make sense. There are supposed to be over a thousand VC in the Rung Sat! Where the hell are they?"

"Yeah, Mister Quon," Luciano said. "The way we heard it, these swamps're crawlin' with VC. You got any scuttlebutt on where they're hiding?"

"With all the mammoth preparation and planning for Jackstay," Connors said, "you'd think we could've caught and pinned 'em for a stand-up fight."

"Much as I hate to say," the LDNN officer said slowly, "Charlie is Vietnamese. And much as some American deskwarmers in Saigon not want to believe, Vietnamese are *not* stupid. Charlie knows he can't take on Americans in stand-up fight. So he wait."

"We know he *was* here," Baxter put in. Certainly, there'd been plenty of evidence of that—field hospitals and storehouses, bunkers and weapons caches, and even a rest camp. He knew because the SEALs had been doing little for the past week and a half save helping the UDT blow up or burn the captured—and empty—structures.

"I'll tell you what I think," Chalker said. "I think that Charlie knew we were coming and pulled a *di di mau.*" He used the Vietnamese phrase meaning to get out or leave quickly, which Americans in Nam were already adopting as their own.

"Negative, Lieutenant," Quon said. He was watching the shoreline drifting slowly past to the east. "Probably many VC moved out of Rung Sat, but there are plenty still here. Watching us."

"Man, Lieutenant," Luciano said. "You give me the willies."

"*Sat Cong!*" Quon said.

"*Sat Cong!*" the others replied, a verbal ritual.

Now if they could just find some Cong to *sat*. . . .

It was nearly full dark now, as the PBRs continued their slow cruise up the river. The sky continued to glow a brilliant, deepening blue overhead, but the trees along the river banks were lost in their own ink-black shadows. As the PBR rounded a bend in the river, Baxter glanced aft over the fantail just in time to catch the wink of a single yellow light among the trees on the east bank, perhaps a hundred yards astern.

Briefly, a second light switched on across the stream, on the west bank, flashed twice, then vanished.

Baxter got up and made his way forward to the PBR's small pilot house. "Say, Boats?"

Boatswain's Mate Chief Nathan Broderick was at the PBR's helm. He turned at Baxter's call. "What's up, Lieutenant?"

"I just saw a couple of lights aft. Like signals. We're not close to any villages here, are we?"

"That's a negative." Broderick motioned to a gunner's mate to take the conn, then joined Baxter in the crowded well deck. "Where?" he said, looking aft. "I don't see anything."

Baxter pointed. "East side. It was just on for a second or two. Then it was answered from over there, on-off, on-off, on-off. We may be too far around the bend now to see where they were."

"A VC signal, you think, Lieutenant?" Connors asked.

"Um." Broderick rubbed his chin. "You SEALs in the mood for a little detour?"

"Sounds good to me, Chief," Chalker said. "Maybe it'll give us a chance to see the *real* war."

"Could be. Probably just some fisherman out violating the curfew." Moving forward, he picked up the radio. "Gold Star Two, Gold Star Two, this is One. C'mon in."

There was a hiss of static. "Copy, One. Two. Over."

"We might have a crosser aft. I'm giving him five, then coming about. Over."

"We copy that, One. We'll take the shooter position. Over."

"Roger that. Keep alert, and watch your target. One out."

He replaced the radio handset, then glanced at Baxter. "Better have your men get their weapons ready, Lieutenant. This gets . . . interesting, sometimes."

"You heard the man," Baxter told the SEALs. "Lock and load!"

PBR-1 continued her slow, steady cruise toward the north for several minutes more. Then, with Broderick again at the helm, they came about one hundred eighty degrees. By this time, Baxter couldn't see PBR-2 in the darkness ahead, but he knew she, too, had come about and was following them down the river.

It seemed as though they were barely moving, the PBR's two hundred-horsepower GM diesels throttled back to a muffled growl. Broderick stood at the helm; the other three sailors manned three of the craft's machine guns, while Connors took a fourth, the M60 on its standing pedestal on the fantail. The young seaman, Baxter noticed, was manning the twin-fifty mount in its forward deck housing just in front of the PBR's pilot house, while the other two sailors stood by the M60s in their pintel mounts port and starboard. The SEALs and the lone UDT man all carried their personal weapons, ranging from M-16s to an Ithaca combat shotgun.

As they rounded the bend once more, Broderick brought the throttle all the way back, so that the PBR was barely gliding along with the river's current. He was leaning forward, peering into the pitch blackness ahead.

Baxter stood beside him. "What do you think, Boats? Gun runners?"

"Curfew violators, that's for damned sure. They lie low until they see us pass, then cross the river in our wake. We just might be able to . . . uh-oh."

"What is it?" Baxter couldn't see anything but night, blackness and shadows, and a faint, phosphorescent sparkle of the water.

"This might be it." He turned, speaking in urgent, hushed tones to the starboard-side gunner. "Greg! I think we got a live 'un up there. Light 'em!"

A spotlight switched on, its glare dazzling and sudden. Eighty feet ahead, pinned in the light like a moth in a display case, was a sampan, a small one, half the PBR's length and with a freeboard only inches above the surface of the river.

Two men, one wearing a flat, broad coolie hat, the other bare-headed, blinked into the light. "Hey, Mr. Quon?" Broderick called back. "You want to hail 'em?"

"Sure, Chief." Quon leaned closer to the PBR's control panel, reaching between Broderick and Baxter to pick up a microphone and switch on the boat's PA. "*Nghe di! Nghe di! Dung lai!*"

There was no immediate response from the sampan, which continued slowly moving across the river from west to east.

"This is fuckin' crazy," Broderick told Baxter. "We can't do a damned thing but ask 'em to heave to. Can't shoot 'em unless they shoot first."

"Are they VC?" Devereaux wanted to know.

"Hell, how the fuck should I know? Ask Mr. Quon!"

Nguyen, still holding the microphone, reared up above the PBR's cockpit, raised his carbine one-handed to point into the sky, and pulled the trigger. The gunshot was terrifically loud, the muzzle flash a brief flare of yellow almost lost in the glare from the searchlight.

"*Nghe di!*" he ordered again. "*Dung lai!*"

Ahead, the bare-headed man suddenly leaned over, grabbing something from the bottom of the sampan. "Watch out!" Broderick yelled.

Then the man in the sampan had a rifle. A second shot barked in the night, and Baxter heard the *thunk* of the bullet plowing through fiberglass.

Broderick kicked the throttle full-forward. "*Hit* 'em, damn it!" he shouted. "Hit 'em!"

Machine gun fire lit up the night, streams of yellow tracers, interlacing one another in intricate patterns sweeping across the sampan and the river. Another rifle shot cracked from the water, but it seemed like nearly everybody in the PBR was firing back, slashing the tiny sampan with a steady, thunderous barrage. Broderick brought the patrol boat hard to the left, circling away, as the men at the various gun mounts danced around their weapons, keeping them trained on the target. As the spotlight swept across the sampan, Baxter could see geysers of water erupting all around the craft, as round after round shredded the wicker canopy near its center in a hailstorm of whispering, snapping lead. Upriver, the second PBR was bearing down on the skirmish, its own machine guns already flickering in the near-darkness as they probed for the sampan. Gunfire thundered as tracer rounds flashed and flamed in the darkness, lashing the water about the stricken sampan.

Still caught in the searchlight's glare, the sampan was riddled in seconds. Baxter had an instant's glimpse of the man in the hat standing near the center of the small boat, arms spread wide as if in supplication, before he toppled backward into the water. The machine guns continued to shred the sampan, which was constructed of such lightweight materials that it stubbornly refused to sink.

There was now no sign of the man with the rifle. Baxter wondered if he'd been hit, if anyone had seen him go in.

Circling back, PBR-1 pulled up alongside the floating wreckage, while PBR-2 kept overwatch a hundred yards upriver. Setting his weapon aside, Connors jumped into the dark water and swam to the sampan, which was drifting broadside with the current and was now so full of water and riding so low in the river that there was almost no freeboard at all. The SEAL checked the sampan from both sides, then secured a line tossed down from the PBR so that the others could haul the craft in close aboard and examine their catch. Connors, meanwhile, swam to the floating body and dragged it back.

A careful search of the bullet-riddled native boat turned up nothing, no rice or other supplies, no documents, no weapons. The dead man was old; leaning over the PBR's railing, Baxter looked down into his age-wrinkled face and guessed that the man must have been sixty at least, though he still wasn't very good at guessing the age of the people here.

Of the younger, bare-headed man, the one who'd snatched up a rifle and fired it at the Americans, there was no trace. He could have been hit and killed, his body swept away by the river's current, but Baxter didn't think so. More likely, he'd dived overboard in the confusion and swam away under water. Hell, he might be ashore now, taking aim at the PBRs floating motionless in the river just a few tens of meters away. . . .

The hair at the back of his neck prickled as he scanned both the east and west shores of the river. "Boats? Maybe we should get the hell out of here."

"I'm with you, sir. No telling how many of his little brown buddies our friend Victor Charlie's gonna bring back. Those guys just *love* to party." Spinning the wheel, he urged the patrol boat forward, carefully ramming the half-sunken sampan in the center and smashing what was left of it beneath the surface. Illuminated in a pool of light from the spot, the old man's body continued floating face-up in the muddy water. The young guy had certainly been VC . . . but what about him? Maybe he'd been VC or a sympathizer. But maybe the young guy had paid him five thousand dong to ferry him across the river. Maybe he'd been threatened. Maybe he was just doing the guy a favor. . . .

"What a miserable way to fight a war," Baxter said, half-aloud, half to himself, his fist closing and coming down hard on the PBR's gunwale. "What a damned, stupid, *fucking* way to fight a war. . . ."

Chapter 6

Friday, 8 April 1966

Hotel de Coronado
Coronado, California
1948 hours

Steve Tangretti stared at the telephone for a long time after he'd hung the receiver up, his mind a whirl of conflicting emotions. Pain, confusion, frustration . . . anger. They were all there. He'd known Veronica was upset as soon as he heard her voice on the other end of the line. She hadn't even waited to make a tape back to him; she'd called instead, her voice choked and on the edge of tears.

Veronica's words continued to echo through his thoughts over and over again. "If you'd bothered to think about it, Steve, you'd see what a mistake it would be to pull Bill out of school now," she had said. "His graduation's coming up in June, and you can't just expect us to uproot and move now."

Later, she'd been even blunter. "To tell you the truth, I don't even know if it would be a good idea for us to come this summer. After all, by August or September they could be cutting you new orders again, and if you go overseas again I'd just as soon be here, with my friends, than stuck in California again. When we were younger, I was willing to follow you from one duty station to another, but I'm too old to settle in to a new home every time you're transferred." And she'd finished up in a choked voice. "Think about it, at least, between now and June. We won't make a final decision until then, after Bill's out of school, but don't take it for granted that I'm just going to drop my whole life and move because you've stopped over for a few months and you're *only* three thousand miles away!"

The hell of it was, she was *right*. He should have given thought to Bill's last semester in high school. Uprooting him less than three months before graduation would cause problems. And Tangretti's past record was working against him, too. Veronica knew him well enough by now to know he wouldn't be happy holding down a staff job for very long. Before the year was out, if the Navy hadn't decided to ship him somewhere else he'd probably bombard them with transfer requests of his own. It wasn't fair to Ronnie to make her move and then to turn around and abandon her again . . .

But, damn it all, it wasn't fair to *him* to have his own wife holding an ultimatum over his head like this, either! Twenty years of marriage had taught Tangretti all of Veronica's codes, all the unspoken meanings and hidden signals behind the most innocuous phrases. What she was really telling him was that he was getting close to retirement age. If he'd been an enlisted man he probably would have been forced out of the service already, and the Navy didn't have much use for a lieutenant who was nearly fifty. For years now he'd been putting off even thinking about the day when he had to leave the Navy, but it wasn't far off now. And Veronica was looking for a chance to put down roots and settle into a comfortable retirement. Little Creek had been home for nearly twelve years now, and perhaps she figured it should stay that way.

Tangretti could understand her wanting to stay in Virginia. Hell, most of his best buddies from UDT and SEALs were there. But he still had a few good years in him yet, and he didn't like Veronica blackmailing him this way!

It was easy to see how a young Navy wife could get upset at having to move from place to place at the whim of the service. But Veronica had adjusted to all that years ago. She'd been a WAC in World War II, for that matter, so she couldn't claim not to understand how the system worked. And the least she could do would be to try to meet him part way. He'd been looking forward to having his family with him while he wrestled with his job on Bucklew's staff. God knew his morale needed boosting *somehow*.

A knock on the door interrupted his bleak train of thought, and Tangretti stood up and clumped across the room, glowering. If this was another messenger with more paperwork from Howell, like that batch he'd sent over last week . . .

He opened the door, already starting to frame a suitably profane and withering attack, but the man at the door, though wearing Navy whites, was no messenger. It took Tangretti a few tries before he finally was able to greet his visitor properly.

"Spence! My God, how long's it been? How're they hanging, you old son-of-a-bitch?"

Chief Machinist's Mate Michael Spencer gave him a grin and clasped his hand with a solid, powerful grip. "Hey, Gator . . . sorry, *Lieutenant* Gator! I heard you were hanging around with the rest of the paper-pushers over at PHIBPAC, but it was damned hard tracking you down. What's the matter, Gator, you couldn't look any of the old gang up? Or are you just too good for your buddies these days?"

"Ah, shit, Spence, you know how it is," Tangretti told him. It was strange having somebody use his old UDT nickname. He'd picked it up back at Fort Pierce, but since he'd been in Nam he'd gotten used to everyone calling him "Lieutenant Steve," the name his Vietnamese charges had hung on him. "I was going to drop in on you a couple of weeks back, but somebody told me your bunch was out on San Clemente nursing some trainees." He stood back from the door. "Haul your ass inside and make yourself at home."

Spencer looked around the hotel room as he walked in.

"Nice place, Gator. Reminds me of that high-class whorehouse in Frisco. You remember? 'Hey, wait a minute, sailor...'"

"...'I only do one at a time!'" Tangretti chimed in. "Guess she didn't know swim buddies share *everything*, huh?"

The brawny CPO perched on the edge of the bed, grinning. Tangretti pulled a chair over and sat across from him, his mind going back to the days when he'd first known Mike Spencer. That had been in Korea, back when Tangretti was still an enlisted man and Spencer had been new to UDT-3. They'd been swim buddies through most of the war, a friendship that had grown even tighter when they returned stateside despite Tangretti's brand-new commission. When Tangretti had transferred to the East Coast he'd lost touch with Spencer, except for the occasional card or quick note. They'd seen each other only once since then, when SEAL Team One moved from Coronado to Little Creek during the alert in October of '62, when the SEALs were getting ready for a possible invasion of Cuba. There hadn't been much of a chance to socialize, though, and when the Missile Crisis fizzled out and Team One headed back to California the two still hadn't been able to get together for a real reunion.

It was good to see the big man again. More than a decade younger than Tangretti, he was taller and broader, with a wrestler's build. But his rugged looks hid a keen mind, and he could move on a night op quicker and more quietly than a man half his size.

"So... a staff job, huh?" Spencer looked him over critically. "Funny... you're still breathing. I thought you always said you'd drop dead before you got your fat ass stuck in some swivel chair at headquarters."

"Just a temporary setback," Tangretti said. "I'll get back in the field. I'm allergic to pencil lead, you know."

The chief chuckled. "Yeah. I still remember the look on that commander's face when you told him that's why you couldn't keep up with all the paperwork they said you owed them!" Spencer waited until Tangretti finished laughing and leaned forward. "How're Veronica and the kids?"

Tangretti looked away. "Good enough, I guess. Stuck in Little Creek. Bill doesn't graduate high school until June, so it'll be a while before we can get together again . . ."

"High school! Good God, that makes me feel like a fossil! I wasn't much out of high school when we met."

"I've got news for you, Spencer . . . you *are* a fossil," Tangretti shot back, happy to have something else to talk about. "Hey, did you hear about Hank Junior?"

"No . . . what?"

"He's a SEAL now. Team Two, of course, the only *real* SEAL team. He enlisted . . . oh, it was almost three years back, I guess. Got accepted into UDT straight out of boot camp, then went on to the SEALs last year."

"Well, I'll be damned. I remember when he was too small to join Little League! Of course, we could've made a real man out of him here at Coronado, but I guess he'll do okay with the rest of the East Coast pukes."

"Yeah . . . a lot better than with all you surfer-boys." Tangretti paused. "How 'bout you, Mike? Still baching it? Any kids turn up claiming you're their daddy?"

Spencer grinned, shaking his head. "Nah, I'm too fast for 'em. And you know I ain't ever settling down with one woman, Gator. Not as long as there's still some wild beaver out there to hunt down and trap!"

"Same old Spence, all right," Tangretti said. "Hey, man, this talking's pretty dry work, you know? You can't catch up on old times without a couple of pitchers of beer and some loud music on the jukebox. What say we head out and find ourselves a place we can really unwind in, huh?"

"Good idea, Gator," the CPO said with a grin. "But this time let's try to stick to drinking, okay? I'm getting too old and creaky to go around bashing up the beer joints like in the old days."

"Old and creaky. Right. I bet you can still run rings around the new kids and then stay out all night boozing it up afterwards. Tell you what, Spence . . . how close are your quarters?"

"Oh, only about five minutes' drive. Why? Camouflage?"

"Yeah. Why don't you go home and change, and pick me up out front in . . . call it fifteen minutes. Then we'll show 'em what a genuine night on the town is all about."

Spencer left while Tangretti took a shower, shaved, and put on a sports shirt and blazer. Tangretti always preferred to do his bar-hopping in civvies. Wearing a uniform would have emphasized his officer's rank, and that could make things uncomfortable. Most of Tangretti's preferred drinking partners were enlisted men, and he liked to blend in.

The thought reminded him of the night he and Richardson had first met Veronica. Hank, a brand-new junior grade lieutenant, had shed his rank bars so that Corporal Veronica Stevens, WAC, would stop deferring to him as an officer. In England before D-Day that was something Richardson could get away with. Tangretti wasn't so sure how it would have gone over in an uptight stateside Navy town like San Diego.

By the time he had finished and gone downstairs, through the hotel lobby, and out the front door, the fifteen minutes were up. Spencer had returned, driving a beat-up red '64 Mustang convertible. He pulled up in front of the hotel and honked the horn as Tangretti was looking around, eyeing the rich tourists and the handful of other Navy men near the hotel's front entrance. The CPO was now wearing a sports shirt and dungaree trousers, but he still managed to look like a sailor getting ready for a night on the town.

They drove past the Main Gate and down to the ferry landing that overlooked San Diego harbor. After a twenty-minute wait, the ferry arrived and Spencer guided the car up onto the boat's main deck. The two men were busy catching each other up on twelve years worth of Navy life, and neither one of them paid much heed to the wait for the boat or for the trip across the harbor.

Once ashore, Spencer headed for the waterfront. The area around the foot of Broadway had been a favorite haunt of theirs when they'd last been stationed at Coronado together, and according to Spencer things hadn't changed there much. Unlike the East Coast, where the SEALs had a few favorite hangouts, there was no one bar that Team One considered its own. Tangretti knew that Mike Spencer was the sort who could be counted on to know the best places for a good time, and he was more than willing to place himself in the CPO's hands for the evening.

The Anchorage was a dimly lit, smoke-filled bar that got a lot of Navy traffic. As they walked in, the babble of conversation threatened to drown out the jukebox that was blaring a Hank Williams number in the corner. They stood by the entrance for a moment with Spencer scanning the dark interior. Halfway across the room, a trio of sailors in whites caught sight of them and waved.

"You'll like these guys," he bawled in Tangretti's ear as he guided him toward the table.

"Hey, Chief!" one of them said as they approached. "Just in time. It's your turn to buy a round!"

"Is that so?" Spencer grinned at him. "How do you figure that, huh?"

"Simple enough, Chief. I bought the last round, and Billy-boy got the one before that, so it *must* be your turn!"

"Looks like our timing's off, Spence," Tangretti said, sitting down. "We should have got started earlier."

"Nah . . . these deadbeats would still have found a way to stick us with the bill," Spencer told him. "Gator, meet three of my teammates from Golf Platoon. The big motherfucker who's so free with my money is Harvey Stewart. He's another plank owner in Team One. The redhead next to him in Tom Herrick, and the kid, here, is Willy Marshall. This here's Gator Tangretti, who's been kicking around ever since WW Two . . . goes back even further than I do, and that's saying something. He's not bad . . . for an East Coast puke."

"You still a SEAL, Gator?" Herrick asked. He was a big man whose insignia identified him as a first class torpedoman. "Or have you retired?"

Tangretti shrugged. "Haven't really been with the Teams for a couple of years. They had me over in Nam as an advisor. But I'm still a SEAL down where it counts."

"Nam? Damn, I sure wish we were over there. Delta Platoon got the first shot, though." RD/2 Willy Marshall looked wistful. He was the youngest man at the table, and junior in rank. "But we're up to relieve them this summer. What's it like over there?"

As Tangretti started telling them about Vietnam, Spencer signaled to a waitress and ordered beers for all of them. When she returned to the table with their drinks, Tangretti couldn't help noticing her, a petite, dark-haired woman with small but well-shaped breasts accentuated by a tight, low-cut blouse. She reminded him of Veronica as she'd been back in the days after Korea.

The waitress noticed his eyes on her and gave him a wink, and when she leaned over him to put his beer on the table she let one breast brush against his arm. "You boys let me know if there's anything else you need," she told them as Spencer fished the money for the drinks from his wallet. She tucked the bills into her cleavage and gave them all a smile. "Nothing's too good for the USN."

As she was leaving Spencer leaned over. "There's a hot one, huh, Gator? I think she was giving you the eye."

Tangretti shrugged and took a swig from his bottle. "Probably has a husband and six kids at home," he said gruffly. "And gets her kicks being a prick tease." He wasn't going to admit any interest in the woman, not to Spencer. In the past, he'd strayed from time to time, cheated on Veronica, especially when he was away from home and out on the town with a bunch of Navy buddies. He wasn't proud of it, but temptation could be hard to resist.

After the phone call from Veronica, he was feeling just perverse enough to go out looking for a conquest, but another part of his mind held him back. Despite all the strains in his marriage these last few years, Tangretti still loved his wife and didn't want to hurt her, not even to get back at her for trying to use emotional blackmail to get her way. He wanted to put the marriage back together, not tear it down more, and a one-night stand with some bimbo wouldn't make things any better between them.

So he tried to put the waitress out of his mind, while making it clear to Spencer and the others that he wasn't interested. "Encouragement" from Mike Spencer had resulted in more than one of his lapses in years past, but he wasn't going to let it happen again tonight.

"So . . . what was I telling you?" he asked. "Oh . . . yeah. The Vietnamese. I want to tell you guys, don't listen to the crap they hand you about gooks and gomers and all that. There's some damned good people over there, people who feel just as strongly about their country and their lives as we do about ours."

"Well, yeah, maybe so," Stewart said. "But you gotta admit, they've been doing a pretty poor job keeping the Commies out. There's a buddy of mine from Delta who wrote me a letter, says the VC are everywhere . . . even working on our bases. How can you trust anybody if you don't know who's side they're really on?"

"Let me tell you something, man," Tangretti said, taking another drink. "When I was over there, I knew a VC battalion commander. He fed me info now and then. I liked him a whole lot better than I liked my supply officer!"

They all laughed. "Well, shit, who wouldn't? I mean, supply officers are always the *real* enemy, huh, Gator?" Spencer grinned as he signaled the waitress. "Hey, sweetheart, bring us another round. Look, seriously, Gator, you don't really mean the Vietnamese can do the job better than we can, do you?"

"That's exactly what I mean," Tangretti told them. "Okay, I'll admit it, some of the Vietnamese officers are pretty corrupt, and I knew one guy who chickened out when he was supposed to lead a mission. You get those kinds everywhere. But I worked with their navy commandos, their versions of UDT and SEALs, and properly trained and led I'd stand them up man for man against anything but a SEAL team of our own. They *want* to keep their homes safe, they *want* to live free . . . not just of the Commies, but from everybody who wants to interfere with them. The French and the Japs and the Americans . . . especially the big corporations that go over there and act like the whole damned country's just another entry in the old ledger book. We were just starting to get their level of training up to the point where they were really starting to get the job done when Uncle Sugar decided to start pumping in the regular troops and take over the war from them. Biggest mistake we'll ever make."

"You don't think we should be over there, Gator?" Marshall asked as the waitress brought their beers again. Tangretti paid for the round this time, adding a hefty tip.

"Oh, *we* should be there," Tangretti said. "The SEALs. The Brown Water gang . . . Green Berets . . . all the special warfare boys. We can work *with* the Vietnamese troops, training, raiding, patrolling, ambushing . . . all the shit we really know how to do. But the Marines? The Army? *They* were trained to fight a real war, you know, like Korea or WW Two. And that's not the kind of fighting that's going to settle anything in Vietnam. The VC can melt away into the jungle and blend in with the local population. How the hell are you going to stop that with a tank?"

"Sounds like you're not too fond of the brass hats, Gator,"

Herrick said. "You think you know more about strategy than they do?"

"You listen to me, friend. Back in '44 me and my buddy Hank Richardson hit the beaches at Normandy with the old NCDU. That's what they called the UDT back in the very beginning— Naval Combat Demolitions Units. They gave us a whole shitload of training . . . shit, we went through Hell Week back before it was even called Hell Week, y'know? Set us up to blow obstacles on the beaches and clear the way for the troops on Omaha. Then they turned around and started screwing around with us. Loaded us down with these silly antichemical suits that were too bulky to move around in. Wouldn't give us any weapons except knives. Sent us in with the first wave of the invasion instead of letting us go in ahead of time and get the job done before a bunch of seasick dogfaces started crowding in around the obstacles *we* were trying to blow up! If you can think of a way to screw up a beach clearing op, our orders included it. Our casualties ran better'n sixty percent on D-Day, and Hank Richardson was one of the guys who bought the farm."

Tangretti paused to take a long drink from his bottle. "And the thing is, that wasn't the only time the boys in charge screwed us over. Oh, they learned some things from Omaha . . . but they turned right around and thought up new ways to get us in deep shit. Back in those days they wouldn't let UDT men work past the high-water mark when we went in on a Jap island. In Korea they had us stealing fishing nets from the North Koreans when they couldn't think how else to use us. And it seemed like they never could get their intelligence straight before they sent us in. I remember a time we were supposed to deliver a bunch of Korean guerrillas to a Buddhist monastery to organize it as a base for resistance ops behind enemy lines . . . only when we got there we didn't find any damned monastery." He fixed Herrick with a probing look. "Do I know more about strategy than the brass? Not hardly. But I sure as hell know more about how to use commandos than any of them."

They were all looking at him now with a mixture of surprise and concern, even Spencer. Tangretti drank again, finishing the bottle off, and shrugged. "Yeah, yeah, I know, the old man's running off at the mouth again. I didn't dredge up all that just because I'm getting senile and living in the past, though. You guys've got to be ready for anything when you get out in the field. Trust your teammates and your instincts over there . . . but don't you ever trust to luck or headquarters. It ain't healthy.'' He paused. ''Hell with it. Where's that waitress? It's time to get down to some *serious* drinking!''

As the evening went on the talk at their table turned away from weighty matters. They swapped stories about UDT and SEAL life, and Spencer and Tangretti vied with one another recounting embarrassing situations each remembered about the other from their time together in Korea. The beers kept coming, and eventually Tangretti lost count of them. That didn't matter, though. Most SEALs, Tangretti among them, took pride in their ability to hold their liquor.

After a while Marshall drifted off, joining some other sailors who had gone through UDT training with him. Then Herrick set his sights on a woman sitting alone at the bar and moved in on her. The two of them left together a few minutes later, with Herrick flashing Spencer a thumb's up signal behind her back on the way out. Stewart stayed long enough to finish one more drink and then headed for home with a grumbled comment about having to get back to the wife and kids. That left Spencer and Tangretti alone, nursing their beers as they continued to swap anecdotes and catch each other up on their lives since Korea.

''I gotta ask you, buddy,'' Spencer said suddenly. ''Seems to me like you've been dodging every time I ask about the family. Are things okay with you and Ronnie?''

Tangretti looked down at the table top. ''Wish to hell I knew, Spence,'' he said. ''Wish to hell I knew.''

The chief pried the story out of him little by little. ''Trouble is,'' Tangretti said at last. ''Trouble is, I don't really know when things started goin' wrong. She never griped when we were over in Korea, y'know? But after I went over to Nam, suddenly every time I turn around I'm hearin' all about how it's time to let the younger guys take over. She seems to think I'd be happy putterin' around the house all day, takin' it easy. How can I take it easy. I've spent most of my life *doin'* things, Spence . . . big things, things that make a difference. If they put me out to pasture now, I'll go crazy in a year. Probably end up blowin' my brains out or something.''

Spencer didn't respond right away. Finally he put down his beer bottle and looked Tangretti in the eye. ''You know you're not going to be in much longer, whether you like it or not,'' he said seriously. ''Sooner or later you're going to *have* to learn how to deal with retiring. But you're not even fifty yet. You can still find something to do with your life after you leave the Navy.''

''Yeah? What would I do? I'm a SEAL, Spence. A fuckin' *frogman*. I led the swim into Havana harbor and took the LDNN through Ilo Ilo. What does that qualify me to do in civilian life, huh? Answer me that.''

''Didn't you tell me one of your old buddies from Okinawa has his own business?''

''Frank Rand? Yeah. He's building boats in Michigan, or he was the last time I heard. So what? His father-in-law left it to him. Am I supposed to beg Frank for work designing boats? I still ain't qualified.''

''The point is, Gator, you could find *something* to do. Get a job selling weapons for Colt. Open a school for SCUBA divers. Write your memoirs.'' Spencer cracked a smile. ''Hell, with some of the shit you've lived through, there'd be people who'd pay you *not* to write your memoirs.''

''More likely they'd just have me quietly bumped off,'' Tangretti countered. ''Look, Spence, thanks for all the suggestions, but it still ain't the same as bein' a SEAL. If I had my druthers, I'd keep on doing what I do best . . . maybe be a merc in Africa, like that guy Hoare. But that wouldn't change anything with Ronnie. She wants to tame me, Spence, and I don't think I can live with that.''

''So what's left? Sounds to me like Ronnie still means something to you.''

''*Of course* she does!'' Tangretti exploded. ''Damn it, Spence, I wouldn't be so fucked up if I didn't still want things to work out with Ronnie. She turned a lot of things around for me, after the war, y'know. If it hadn't been for her . . . God, I don't know what would've happened to me.'' He fumbled for a moment and pulled off his wedding ring, holding it up. ''We *needed* each other back then, Spence. We'd both loved Hank, in our own ways. He was like a brother to me . . . and then Ronnie and me found out we loved each other, too. And I still do love her, even with all this other shit getting in the way. This ring . . . it means everything to me, man. I just don't know if I can be the man Ronnie wants now. And if I can't . . . Christ, I don't know. I feel like I'm gonna go crazy whichever way I go.''

"Sounds to me like you've got some thinking to do, Gator,"
Spencer told him. "If you really can't give up the kind of life
you've been leading, then you'd better be ready to let go of
Ronnie. It just ain't fair to either of you to just keep drifting
along like this, buddy. Better a clean break . . . with her, or with
your SEAL life, one or the other. 'Cause I don't see how you
can have both."

"Yeah . . . Yeah, I know." Tangretti looked away. "But I
tell you what, Spence. I'm screwed either way."

"You'll work it out, Gator. You always had your shit together before. You're a SEAL, by God, a gen-u-wine, shock-
proof, waterproof, rootin', tootin', parachutin', fightin',
fuckin' frogman." Spencer pushed his chair back from the
table. "Time we were heading for home, buddy."

"You go ahead, Spence. I'll catch a cab back to the ferry
later on."

The chief gave him a worried look. "You sure, Gator?
Look, I can stick around . . ."

Tangretti shook his head, though the motion made him
dizzy. "Nah, you go on. I figure I'll have a couple more belts.
Try to think things through, y'know? I've been getting sick
of the inside of that damned hotel room, and you know I've
always thought better with a bottle in one hand and a cigarette
in the other. You head on back . . . or go chase up some kind
of action. Ain't too late to find a date, like old Poet Perry used
to say."

Spencer chuckled and stood up, a little unsteady. "You
know what you want, Gator," he said. "But just remember,
don't go busting up the joint or picking fights with jarheads
without your old buddy Spence around to back you up. And
if you call me to come post bail . . ."

"You never heard of me," he finished the old joke, mus-
tering a feeble grin. "I've heard it all before. Just remember
who got you out of the brig, that time in Tokyo."

Spencer just grinned at him and turned away, making his
way toward the door. Tangretti stared after him for a few
minutes. When the chief had disappeared through the front
door he held his ring in his palm, staring at the plain gold
circlet as if it held the secrets of life. After a few moments
Tangretti tried to slip it back on, but he almost dropped it.
Finally he shrugged, slipped it into his blazer pocket, and signaled the waitress to bring him another beer.

There was comfort—temporary comfort, at least—in the bottom of a bottle.

Saturday, 9 April 1966

San Diego, California
0837 hours

Tangretti woke up with the grandfather of all hangovers and a taste in his mouth that reminded him of the bottom of a bird cage. He stifled a groan and tried to ignore the pounding in his head while he tried to decide where he was. It didn't feel like his bed at the Hotel de Coronado. The mattress was thinner, and there was a spring prodding him in the ribs. He shifted uncomfortably to avoid it, though the motion didn't do his head or his stomach any good at all.

Slowly, he opened his eyes and looked around him. He was in a small, plain room, sparsely furnished but with a homey look. Some of the details were a little fuzzy. The light slanting through the window above him made it hard to focus his eyes.

It took him a few minutes to realize he was naked under the sheet, though he was wearing the chain around his neck that held a Japanese rifle bullet, a souvenir of the first combat dive he and Hank Richardson had pulled at Kwajalein. A few more minutes passed before he recognized his clothes folded neatly on a chair by the bed. Then he noticed the bra hanging over the back of the chair.

Oh, God, he thought. *I didn't?* . . .

"Are you finally awake, lover?" A woman stood in a doorway that looked like it opened onto a bathroom. She was naked and making no attempt to cover up. In fact, she struck a sexy pose leaning against the door frame and gave him a seductive smile. "Maybe you want to take up where you left off earlier, huh?"

For a muddled moment he thought she was Ronnie. She had her build, the same dark hair tumbling over her shoulders, the same small but firm breasts . . . but she was the Veronica of ten years ago, somewhere in her thirties, without any gray hairs mingling with the black. Tangretti was sure he'd seen her before, but the memory wasn't clear.

Then something clicked. The waitress from the Anchorage. He remembered the look she'd given him when she brought the first round of drinks to the table, the feel of her body brushing against his when she leaned past him. And he remembered coming back to his table after a trip to the bathroom, sometime after Spencer had left, to find her sitting there and waiting for him. She'd just got off her shift, and she had said she was worried he didn't have a way to get home. Apparently she'd heard enough of the talk at the table to know he was a Navy man despite his civvies, and he'd stayed at the bar too long, missed the last ferry of the night back to North Island. So she'd offered to drop him off at a hotel if he needed a place to stay overnight.

Tangretti couldn't remember much beyond that, though. But he could fill in the blanks. No doubt he'd turned on the charm, handed her some of his best lines. This didn't look like a hotel room at all. Was it her place? Probably . . .

He wished he could remember her name.

"Look, ahhh . . . Look." His voice was a bullfrog's croak. "I was . . . pretty drunk last night . . ."

"You seemed lively enough to me, honey," she said, still smiling at him. Then she seemed to take in his perplexed frown, and the smile went away. She took a few steps toward him, then stopped in the middle of the room. She didn't look seductive any more, nude or not. Now she was starting to look angry. "You don't remember, do you, Steve? That's real flattering . . ."

Tangretti sat up in the bed and swung his legs to the floor. A moment's embarrassment passed quickly. If she wasn't going to be concerned with modesty, he didn't see any reason to worry about it. "I'm sorry, er . . ."

"Sheila," she supplied the name, sounding unhappy. "Sheila Martin. Don't you remember *anything?*"

"Bits and pieces," he admitted. "You offered me a lift at the bar . . ."

"And *you* said the party was just getting started," she said. "You didn't seem too drunk then."

He shrugged. "I can usually carry my liquor pretty well. But it catches up with you after a while . . ." He trailed off. "Look, Sheila, last night was a mistake. A big mistake . . . I shouldn't have . . ."

Her brow clouded. "A mistake, was it? Just what's that supposed to mean? What are you, married or something?"

"Yeah . . . married."

"You . . . you *bastard*!" Her voice was shrill, and it made him feel like there was an ice pick working its way in behind his eyes. She advanced on him and gave him a backhanded slap across the face. "All that shit about being alone and having no place to go . . . God *damn* you!"

"God . . . look, Sheila, I'm sorry . . ."

"Shut the fuck up and get out of here!" She gave a sob and turned away, rushing back into the bathroom and slamming the door behind her.

Tangretti stood up, ignoring the stabbing pain in his head, his churning stomach, the stinging on his cheek where she'd struck him. Moving slowly, he gathered up his clothes and dressed. As he finished buttoning his shirt he tried to think of something he could say or do to mollify Sheila, but finally he just gave a shrug and left.

Outside, he studied his surroundings and tried to get his bearings. Sheila lived in a run-down little apartment building in one of the poorer sections of town. As he stood in the foyer of the building, he took a quick inventory of his pockets. His wallet was where it belonged, and he still had a few bills in it even after all the drinks he'd paid for at the Anchorage. Keys, change . . . everything was where it should be.

He found his wedding ring in his blazer pocket, vaguely remembering having put it there when he'd been fumbling with it in the bar. Tangretti slipped it back on his finger, feeling guilty and ashamed.

Never again, he told himself as he stepped out onto the sidewalk. *I swear I won't cheat on Ronnie again. . . .*

Trouble was, he'd sworn that oath to himself time and again. But somehow he never managed to keep it. His good intentions never lasted. . . .

He spotted a phone booth at the end of the block and started for it, but his grim thoughts followed him all the way. Why couldn't he do right by Ronnie?

Maybe it really would be for the best if he and Veronica went their separate ways after all. God knew she deserved better than Steve Tangretti.

Chapter 7

Vam Sat River
Twenty-four miles southeast of Nha Be
0305 hours

Edward Baxter lay flat on his belly in several inches of water that had been tepid when he reached this position several hours ago, but which had by now soaked his camo fatigues and left him chilled. Iron control kept him from shivering; he wanted not the slightest trace of movement or vibration in the still water to give him away. As he shifted very slowly to relieve a cramp in his leg, the ground gave slightly, neither wholly mud nor entirely solid beneath his weight. The reeds growing thickly around him swayed with his movement; he paused, moved again, then paused once more, breaking up his motions with unequal hesitations to keep them from appearing rhythmic.

Not that there was anyone out there to see, he thought with a sarcastic lift to the corner of his mouth. He was beginning to think that Charlie always knew exactly where the SEALs were going to be next. Baxter's greatest concern lately was the possibility that, one day, Charlie would decide to *really* use his knowledge of SEAL movements, not to avoid an ambush, but to set up an ambush of his own. Despite everything, despite all of the official interference and the bad intel and the distrust MACV had for the new Navy unit, the SEALs had been getting results. One of these days, they would hurt the VC badly enough, make them *mad* enough, that the bad guys were going to try to hit the SEALs back.

The SEALs had discussed that possibility quite a bit during the past couple of weeks. All of them agreed that they were eager to get into a *real* fight with Charlie, a stand-up, ass-kicking set-to at knife-fighting range. The trouble was, when that fight started, it would be Charlie who was calling the shots. The SEALs were going to have to be very careful—and very, *very* good—or they were never going to know what had hit them.

This was a war with no front lines, and no way to keep your own movements screened from the enemy. In South Vietnam, the enemy was everywhere, his eyes were everywhere, and he was generally aware of your movements as soon as you made them. Baxter had already given a lot of consideration to the fact that Nha Be, perched at the apex of the Rung Sat triangle, was almost certainly under observation twenty-four hours a day . . . which meant that as soon as a PBR or LCM carrying SEALs pulled away from the Nha Be docks, the Vietcong in the jungle a few miles downriver knew it too.

Baxter had discussed the problem at length both with Lieutenant Kellerman and with Commander George White, who was on the MACV staff for ops planning in the Rung Sat. He wanted to try something new but was meeting with considerable bureaucratic resistance. Why couldn't the SEALs load out their patrol boats at the Nha Be docks, then pile into a truck and drive to the Saigon waterfront? The VC watchers would see the PBRs pull away from the Nha Be pier and head north. They might assume the boats were off to patrol portions of the river usually patrolled by the Vietnamese Navy, along the approaches to Saigon, or further east, along the Dong Hai River below Bien Hoa. An hour or so later, the SEALs would climb aboard in Saigon, the PBRs would open up, and they would hit the Rung Sat at twenty-five knots, catching the VC flat-footed and red-handed.

The plan had attracted some interest at headquarters, but for the most part Baxter had been hearing problems: there were VC in Saigon, too; the PBRs would still have to pass Nha Be on their way south; the VC would catch on after a few runs. And what the hell difference did any of that make, Baxter wondered? Even if it only worked once, at last they would bag some Victor Charlies . . . and wasn't that why they were here in the first place?

A mosquito whined in his ear, then settled on his paint-smeared face, but Baxter didn't move. The insect apparently had trouble drilling through the layers of black and green grease paint on his skin, because after a moment it gave up and tried the back of his hand. Baxter continued watching the river beyond the thin curtain of reeds. The whine of the tiny flying pest was lost in the vaster chorus of peeping and chirruping coming from the trees and reeds all around the SEALs' hiding place.

SEALs were well-trained in the gentle art of ambush, and in the skills and discipline needed for remaining motionless for hour after hour after soul-grinding hour, waiting for the prey to enter the kill zone. Tonight, he was part of a four-man squad that included Connors, Luciano, and Wojciechowski. That morning, Kellerman had passed on an intelligence report that sampans were crossing in this general area late at night, after curfew, and so an ambush had been planned in hopes of putting a dent in the traffic. Kellerman had rated the intel on this one as "reliable."

Intelligence. That was the weak link in SEAL operations in the Rung Sat time after time after time. Intel came down the chain of command, but by the time the NILO passed it on to the team it was old, old and starting to smell. Charlie played things smart in these swamps, changing his movement patterns, shifting his supply caches and headquarters and even his hospitals every few days. Baxter had by now completely lost track of the number of times the SEALs of Det Delta had deployed during Operation Jackstay, wading for miles through chest-deep mud and impenetrable mangrove forest, sneaking up on the reported site of a major VC center . . . only to find abandoned huts, empty dugouts and trenches, cold cookfire sites, buried garbage pits, plenty of evidence that Charlie *had* been there a few days or weeks or months ago.

Operation Jackstay had been officially declared ended a week ago, on 7 April. The word from on high was that Jackstay had been a major success, that Vietcong influence throughout the Rung Sat had been rolled back, that the entire VC infrastructure had been seriously hurt. So far as Baxter could tell, all three statements were flat-out lies. Oh, the VC were more cautious, certainly, and it was likely that a lot of them had pulled out of the Rung Sat operational area during

Jackstay; hell, lots of them had probably left before Jackstay, warned ahead of time by sympathizers in Saigon who seemed to know everything the Americans and the South Vietnamese government were planning. But what were the American forces supposed to do, now that the Rung Sat had been "pacified," to use the official language? Post Marines along every few yards of every stream and river? Garrison each one of the hundreds of nameless islands? Plow the entire thousand square kilometers of the Rung Sat under, pour on concrete, and turn the whole region into a colossal parking lot? It would take something just about that drastic to keep Charlie out now, assuming he'd really left in the first place.

Hell, even assuming the Rung Sat had been cleared out during Jackstay, that only meant that Charlie had packed up his marbles and gone someplace else. If there was one thing that was already clear to Baxter and the other SEALs about this war, it was that territory controlled counted for precious little. What mattered was the enemy's will to resist, to keep on fighting . . . and from all he'd heard, it sounded as though the Vietcong had plenty of will.

To beat the Vietcong, the SEALs needed fresher information and the freedom to use it, and that was all there was to it. Ideally, the SEALs needed to gather their own information . . . and have the freedom to act on it at once, without this endless shuffling of paperwork, plans, proposals, and counterproposals up and down the chain of command between Nha Be and Saigon and, in some cases, even as far as Washington. As it was, each time Baxter suggested an op and sent it up the chain of command, it was several days before a reply came back down. Usually the reply was negative; the people at MACV didn't have much imagination when it came to field operations, and they tended to think in terms of large numbers of men, large amounts of equipment, and massive, overwhelming striking power, rather than of four or six or seven men who knew how to make themselves invisible. Occasionally, the reply was positive . . . but nine times out of ten it had taken so long to clear channels that the object of the original plan was already lost.

Especially if the communists had somehow gotten a complete copy of the plan in the meantime, packed up, and moved elsewhere.

So far, the most reliable information Baxter and the other SEALs had seen had come by way of Lieutenant Nguyen Quon. Quon was as frustrated as the SEALs—possibly more so, if that were possible—because though his unit had been brought into the Rung Sat region for Jackstay, the American planners in Saigon had never used him. As a result, he often fed bits and pieces of his own intel to Baxter with the hope that the SEALs would be able to use them, somehow. Quon had corroborated the idea, for instance, that VC were watching Nha Be now, to alert their comrades downstream when the SEALs were going out on an op. Part of the problem, of course, was the fact that Quon was Vietnamese. Some of the planners back at HQ automatically discounted as unreliable any intel that came from a Vietnamese source; most others would accept Vietnamese sources—there were few other ways to get any firsthand information, after all—but insist that they be verified several times over.

The intelligence the SEALs were operating on tonight had not come initially from Quon, but the LDNN lieutenant had been able to corroborate at least part of it. Military intelligence specialists in Saigon, working out of MACV G2, had collected a number of reports that a lone man had frequently been seen up the Vam Sat in this area, and that he was probably smuggling weapons out from Co Gong Province, to the west. The suspect appeared alone and at night, moving along the Vam Sat in a motorized sampan without lights.

There was the possibility, of course, that he was simply a local fisherman who chose to disregard the government's orders not to travel on the river at night; after all, many of the people in the Rung Sat were fishermen, many lived a marginal existence at best, and working at night, when you could attract fish with a light on your boat, had been a common and profitable practice in the region for countless generations. Still, Nguyen Quon, when Baxter had questioned him about it earlier, had said that *his* contacts in the area knew nothing about this mysterious late-night fisherman.

Baxter had decided not to tell Kellerman about Quon's piece of negative intel. Why complicate things? The ambush had been carefully planned, submitted through the NILO for approval, and cleared. The SEALs had left Nha Be in a pair of PBRs just after sunset, and Baxter wondered how many sets of eyes, in Nha Be and across the river in the northern reaches of the Rung Sat, had noted that departure. Baxter had deliberately ordered the PBR crews to stage several fake insertions along the way, slowing to a crawl while several of the SEALs splashed in the water alongside. After the SEALs had made their real insertion at about 1045 hours, the PBRs had continued downstream a ways, leaving Baxter and his men with the promise that they would continue the false inserts for at least another half hour.

It was a cheap trick, but it might confuse those VC watchers as to what the SEALs' real target was. Of course, if someone in MACV itself was an informant, then all of the fake insertions in the world wouldn't do a damned bit of good. The VC gun runner would not make his regular delivery tonight . . . or he would make his rendezvous by some devious, alternate route.

Or the SEALs themselves would be ambushed. That disturbing possibility was becoming more and more possible with each new SEAL raid.

Come on, come on, he thought, scanning the quiet water in front of him. Insects peeped and chirped, a cacophony of jungle noises. *Show yourself!*

This could so easily be another dry well. How much was really known about this mysterious sampan driver, anyway? It was believed he crossed the Soi Rap somewhere between Nha Be and the mouth of the Vam Co River, entered the Vam Sat, and slipped downstream to the junction with the Rach Cat Lai River. Somewhere in that maze of swamps and marshes, he must make contact with the VC, bringing them guns, ammo, and possible money as well. Hell, even the VC liked an occasional shopping spree, and as Kellerman had pointed out an age or two ago, Saigon had everything they needed, including nookie.

Baxter hoped this turkey had the pay chest for the whole damned VC Rung Sat operation. The VC were supposed to be so great at living in the swamps? Fine! Let 'em stay there!

For the SEALs, this was more and more becoming an intensely *personal* war, with individual SEALs against individual VC. Baxter found himself hating this nameless individual with the intensity that until now he'd reserved for his tenth-grade algebra teacher and, just possibly, a few of the more self-important of the gold-braid bastards back in Saigon.

He heard a rippling splash off to his left. Turning his head, he tried to pierce the near total blackness of the shadows smothering the river. Had one of the other SEALs shifted, disturbing the water? Or had a fish jumped? His men were good . . . too good to give themselves away with carelessness.

Movement caught his eye, a black shape silhouetted by the scarcely lighter gray of the river. The moon was just beginning to clear the treetops, making the shadows deeper, the water brighter. Whatever it was was too small for a sampan; for a moment, Baxter thought that it was a swimming man. Then he revised his first estimate. It was a log, moss-covered and gnarled, floating slowly down the river with the current.

Then the tail flicked, splashing the water as the creature dived. A crocodile . . . a fairly good-sized one, too, six feet long at least. *God I hate this place,* Baxter thought to himself with heartfelt sincerity. Crocodiles. What the hell was a SEAL supposed to do if he was lying out on an ambush somewhere in the swamp, and one of those reptiles got curious? Baxter was pretty damned sure he knew what *he* would do in such circumstances: shoot first, and worry about VC later. The VC might shoot him, but at least they weren't likely to take a bite out of his leg. . . .

He checked the luminous hands on his watch. Nearly 0330 hours . . . "zero-dark-thirty" in Navy parlance. After their insertion near the mouth of the Vam Sat River, they'd moved overland east from the Soi Rap, crossing the northern tip of an island defined by the snakelike twistings of the Vam Sat. The trek had only been three kilometers, but it had been made slow by mud, jungle, and the ever-present possibility of a VC ambush. They'd only reached this position at 0030 hours, after almost two hours of painstaking movement through swamp and mangrove thicket. And they'd been lying in the water ever since . . . two hours. If something didn't start shaking within, say, another hour . . .

Movement again, and the ripple of moving water. The outboard motor was quiet, purring just loud enough to be audible above the incessant racket of the frogs and insects. In another moment, Baxter could make out the shape moving out of the marsh ahead. It was a sampan, even smaller than the one he'd seen sunk by the PBR two weeks before. A single Vietnamese crouched in the stern, his black pajamas giving him almost perfect invisibility in the night.

This was it. It *had* to be.

It would be perfect if they could capture the man, taking him back for interrogation. That sampan was no speedboat; once a warning was given, the target wouldn't be going anywhere, at least, not with any speed. As planned, Baxter aimed his M-16 at the bow of the sampan, checked the selector switch to make sure it was on single shot, then squeezed the trigger. The single shot was startlingly loud, loud enough to silence the crickets, frogs, and other choristers of the night.

"*Dung lai!*" Baxter yelled into the sudden silence, using the command for "halt" that Lieutenant Quon had taught him.

The man in the sampan started, looking toward the wall of reeds where Baxter was hiding, then reached into the bottom of the boat. When he straightened again, he was holding an AK-47.

Shit! Baxter had really been hoping for a prisoner, but if this guy wanted to do it the hard way, the SEALs were happy to accommodate him. Baxter was not going to risk the life of a single one of his people. He snapped the selector switch on his weapon to full auto and squeezed off a burst as the other hidden SEALs opened up as well. The man in the sampan twisted, his face contorted, and then fell over the side of his boat with a loud splash. He never even got off one shot in reply.

"Connie! Lucky! Woj!" Baxter yelled. "Cease fire! Cease fire!"

The gunfire stopped as suddenly as it had begun. The sampan, its motor stalled, drifted slowly with the current ten yards out from the shore.

"Heads up, people," he called. "I'm moving into the kill zone."

"Fire zone's clear!" Connors called back from the right.

"Clear!" Tom Wojciechowski added.

"We got you covered, Lieutenant," Luciano's voice came back from the left. "Go ahead!"

Gratefully stretching cramped muscles, Baxter stood up and, after a last careful check up and down the river to make certain there were no other sampans, he waded out into the water, which was only a few feet deep.

Inside the sampan, hidden beneath a layer of palm fronds, were three more AK-47s and a green metal box holding perhaps five hundred rounds of ammo. This ambush, at least, had brought up something positive. The little bastard must have been sneaking arms across the Vam Sat, just like Intelligence had said.

Carefully, they placed the body back inside the sampan, fished the AK out of the mud where it had been dropped, then started wading back upstream. The sampan would be quite a nice prize to submit to the MACV boys, and Intelligence had insisted that if the SEALs couldn't capture the gun runner, it would help a lot if they could bring back his body.

Happy to oblige, boys! . . .

Hell, this was the first op in a month that had gone even halfway right. Baxter was happy as he led his team upriver toward the extraction site. Maybe now the SEALs' luck in Nam was finally starting to turn. . . .

Chapter 8

Saturday, 16 April 1966

**Hoa Bien Bar
To Do Street, Saigon
2110 hours**

Baxter walked into the dimly lit bar, glanced left and right, then began making his way past the clusters of round tables toward a line of booths in the back. On a small stage to the left, a girl in blue-spangled bikini and short white boots gyrated beneath a glaring spotlight, as the Rolling Stones' *"I Can't Get No Satisfaction"* pounded out the beat.

The Hoa Bien was a favorite watering hole for American servicemen, especially Navy, though Army and Marines could be found there as well. It was one of several places in the capital favored by SEALs, and the manager of the place knew most of them by sight.

Was that a good idea, Baxter wondered? Suppose the VC decided to cap a few SEALs. Suppose someone in the Hoa Bien was VC? . . .

Baxter knew he was becoming more and more paranoid, especially on matters of security and intelligence, but there didn't seem to be any way around it. Only keeping a low profile, he thought now, would give the SEALs much of a chance of coming through this tour alive.

The trouble was, he couldn't just order the SEALs of Det Delta to stay on base and rot, not if he wanted to have something like decent unit discipline and order. It was Saturday night, and most of the SEALs were on forty-eight-hour liberty. Officers, of course, could come and go pretty much as they pleased without worrying about passes, but Baxter had been left more or less at loose ends when the enlisted men had vanished into Saigon that morning. Though he had an enormous stack of paperwork awaiting him in the in basket on his desk back at Nha Be, he'd decided at last to shuck it all tonight and come into town this evening for a drink or three.

After his latest encounter with the brass from MACV, he needed to get drunk.

"Hey, Lieutenant!" a familiar voice called from a table three over from the one he was passing. "Yo! Lieutenant Baxter! Here!"

It was hard to see in the near darkness, but he recognized the lanky frame of Toby Bosniak, the short, fireplug shape of Lucky Luciano, and the slender form of Doc Randolph. Bosniak was the one waving him over.

"Good evening, gentlemen," he said, walking up to the table.

"'Gentlemen!'" Bosniak said, looking around the bar wildly. "Where? Where?"

"Don't tell us there's been a recall," Luciano said. "Man, I don't think I could take that right now. See?" He held out his hands, palms down and trembling. "See? My nerves are shot the fuck t'hell, Lieutenant."

"Right," Baxter said. "I believe that one. Don't worry, people. I'm here to get gassed like the rest of you." He started to pass on by.

"Hey, don't go so fast," Bosniak said.

"Yeah, pull up a chair, Lieutenant," Doc said.

"I don't want to, ah . . ."

"Don't give it a thought, Mr. Baxter," Bosniak said, grinning. "We're all equal when we're shit-faced. Right, guys?"

"Hear, hear!" Randolph said, holding up his half-empty glass.

"Abso-damn-lutely," Luciano added. He stifled a belch with his fist. "You're a reg'lar guy, Mr. Baxter. Shit, we hardly even know you're an officer, most of the time."

"Okay," Baxter said. "But lay off the mister shit. For tonight, I'm E. C." That had been his nickname in college, a handle he'd always been secretly proud of.

" 'Easy,' huh?" Bosniak said, slurring the sounds deliberately. "Easy it is!"

A waitress came by and took his order: a bottle of bourbon, Johnny Walker, and a glass with ice. For a moment, Baxter simply leaned back in his chair and watched the dancer on the floodlit stage.

He could be disciplined for what he was doing right now, taken aside by his CO and dressed down for "undue familiarization with his men." There were various regulations, written and unwritten, about fraternization between the ranks . . . and telling his men to call him by anything other than his rank or his last name preceded by the honorific "mister" was breaking at least half of them. He knew all of the warnings against that sort of behavior. Officers couldn't afford to be friends with the men they might have to order into danger; enlisted men wouldn't take a friend's orders seriously; it was necessary to maintain a social barrier between the ranks and the fraternity of officers; familiarity bred contempt . . . yeah, he knew all the reasons why he shouldn't.

Bullshit, all of them. Out in the field, wading through the mud in the Rung Sat, rank just didn't matter the way it did back in the "real Navy."

One very good thing about the SEALs, Baxter was now

convinced, was the fact that there wasn't the usual yawning gulf between the officers and the men they commanded. The simple fact that SEAL and UDT officers went through every phase of BUD/S, including Hell Week, was enough to make them accepted by the enlisteds in a way that simply wasn't possible in any other branch of the service.

And the respect was decidedly mutual. Baxter felt he had far more in common with Luciano and Bosniak and Randolph than he did with any of the fat-assed captains and admirals cluttering up the offices and passageways of MACV's Saigon headquarters. A new term was beginning to make itself known throughout Vietnam, a term of savage and mocking disrespect applied by anyone who'd been in combat to all of the bastards, enlisted and officer alike, who stayed nice and clean and safe in their air-conditioned offices in Saigon or San Diego or the Pentagon: *REMF*.

The acronym, and the foul sentiments it gave euphemistic voice to, expressed Baxter's feelings about MACV and the Naval Command, Vietnam perfectly.

"So, Easy," Bosniak said as the waitress brought Baxter's order. "What's the word? Those idiots at HQ making any more sense today?"

"Ha!" Baxter poured himself a drink, drained the glass in one gulp, and poured another one. "You believe in the tooth fairy, too? Our beloved Commander White is of the opinion that we're coming up dry out in the field because we are, I quote, harboring a security risk, end quote."

"Security risk?" Luciano scratched his head. "Who? One of our gooks?"

"That seems to be the general idea," Baxter told him. "He says there must be someone working at Nha Be who's passing our plans on to Charlie."

"But, fuck, man, that's a load of shit!" Bosniak said. "It's plain as the fat asses planted in their swivel chairs how the Cong are spotting us. I mean, we load up all our gear and pile into one of the boats. It goes chugging down the river in full view of anybody bothering to watch. Why drag our gooks into it?"

Baxter nodded. He'd tried arguing that very point with Commander White pushing his notion of trucking the men up to Saigon and boarding the craft there. That would at least confuse the VC enough to restore an element of surprise to their missions that had been missing since the early days of Jackstay. But the REMFs at MACV were convinced they were dealing with leaks from inside the SEAL base. They had told Baxter he could do what he wanted about river patrols but insisted on new security precautions to deal with their suspicions.

He shrugged and took another slug of bourbon. "The brass have their reasons, I guess," he told Bosniak morosely. He hesitated before going on. "Fact is, there's a rumor going around that our LDNN friend Quon might be VC. They don't have any direct evidence, and they're not taking any action yet, but he's the one they're trying to pin the blame on. So we're being told to freeze him out."

"Shit," Luciano said. "I don't believe it. Quon's no Charlie. I'd bet my shot at an air-conditioned seat in hell on that."

"Well, don't tell me," Baxter said. "Tell HQ, for Christ's sake. The way they're talking, it's about two steps short of treason to even talk to the guy. Even though he's been about the best damned source of information we've had since we got over here."

"If he is Charlie, he sure hides it," Bosniak commented. "He's a good guy . . . for a gook."

"You know," Doc Randolph said. "I knew a SEAL officer when I was here a couple of years back. Crazy guy, in some ways. He was one of the old hands. Joined the UDT back in World War II and had a hand in most every UDT action since. Okinawa. Korea. You name it.

"Anyway, I served with him a bit during my first tour in-country. We weren't allowed to go on hot missions, of course. We were just advisors. Didn't have the luxury of this 'direct action' stuff."

The others laughed, and Baxter relaxed a bit.

"Like I said, this guy was crazy. He'd lead his LDNNs on a training patrol? Always seemed to run into VC and get into a firefight."

"What, deliberately?"

"Sure, deliberately. Thing was, he had this buddy who was also VC."

"You're shittin' me," Luciano said.

"Nope. Mostly, when he went out on those patrols, he was

out alone. No other SEALs along, I mean. He had his LDNNs, of course. But I heard about it from some other SEALs and some of the Viets, and, well, knowing this guy, I could believe just about anything. Sometimes, right in the middle of a fire-fight, he'd hoist a flag up so the enemy could see it. After a while, a flag would go up on the other side, and the shooting would stop. Then he'd walk out and meet this buddy of his. Of course, he had his people aiming at the guy, and he was in the crosshairs of some VC sniper, of course, but they'd exchange some pleasantries, maybe say, 'Okay, see you at the usual bar in town tonight, twenty-hundred.' Then they'd get together for drinks.''

"How the hell did they meet in the first place?" Baxter wanted to know.

"The way I heard it," Randolph replied, "this SEAL was always going out on weekends to visit villages east of Saigon. He'd hold sick call for the people . . . you know, dispense antibiotics, bandage wounds. He met his Cong buddy that way first. Then it turned out the guy drove a cab in Saigon when he wasn't off doing his VC thing.''

"That's weird, man," Luciano said.

"It could be interpreted as treason," Baxter added.

"Shit," Randolph said. "It was all part of the game. I don't know. Maybe the war was more relaxed in those days.''

"Maybe he pumped the guy for intel," Bosniak suggested. "Y'know, something like that might be worth a shot.''

"I don't know. Could be. He always said he'd learned a lot about how Charlie thought by having dinner with this guy, learned to respect him. He told me once that he had more respect for that VC buddy of his, an enemy, than he did for some of the guys who were giving him orders. At least the VC guy knew what the hell he was fighting for!''

"I dig it," Luciano said, grinning. "Me, I hate that new personnel officer at Nha Be more than I hate the Cong.''

"What was this guy's name?" Baxter wanted to know.

"Tangretti," Randolph replied. "Lieutenant Steve Tangretti.''

"Never heard of him.''

Randolph shrugged. "It's a big Navy.''

"Not so big," Bosniak pointed out. "You stay in long enough, you meet *everybody* sooner or later.''

"Great," Baxter said. "So we can't even talk to a guy we all know has been straight with us. But here's a guy you knew, a SEAL, no less, who routinely had drinks and dinner with the VC." He shook his head. "Man, I just don't get it!"

The hoots, whistles, shouts, and gleeful table-poundings of the Hoa Bien's American patrons made them look up from their table. On the stage, the dancer had taken off her bra, and was dancing now to the Temptations singing "*My Girl*" wearing nothing but blue panties and white boots. The regulations in Saigon restricting nude and seminude dancing were pretty strict, but the Hoa Bien's owner either knew when the M.P.s and the Vietnamese police weren't looking ... or he had a private arrangement with someone. Every so often his girls managed to bend the rules a bit, which was one reason the place was so popular, especially on the weekends.

There wasn't a lot to see, actually. The girl was almost flat-chested and looked an immature fifteen, with a face as dead and unerotic as any burned-out whore's. As he started to look away, however, his eye was caught by a lone man sitting at another table. A Vietnamese in civilian clothes.

Nguyen Manh Quon.

"Excuse me, gents," Baxter said, rising from the table. "I've got to see somebody over there."

Bosniak followed his look. "You sure that's a good idea, Easy?" he asked. "If he really is Charlie ..."

"Fuck that," Baxter said bluntly. "He's pretty near part of the outfit ... and SEALs don't let down their own."

As he walked over to Quon's table, the LDNN lieutenant frowned at him. "I'm sure you have been told to stay clear of me, Lieutenant Edward," he said. "I seem to be in disgrace."

"Hello, Ong Quon." He wondered how to say it. "I, I've been ordered to be careful about what I say to you. Seems there are some folks, my bosses included, who think you're a Communist, that you've been passing intel on to the VC."

"Nothing new about that," Quon said. His voice was low, lacking any emotion whatsoever.

"Quon, you and I haven't known each other all that long. Six weeks, maybe. But in a war, six weeks can be forever, and I think I know you pretty well by now. I would never have thought you were working for the VC . . . but, well, this is way over my head.''

"And you believe the stories about me?''

"Shit, I don't know what to think anymore. Look, this is a crazy kind of war. I've heard stories about guys, Americans, who were drinking buddies with VC, for God's sake. I've heard of Vietnamese who were working both sides of the fence. Quon, if you're one of those, I've got to hear it from you, and hear it straight. If I'm putting my boys at risk because someone inside Det Delta is telling the VC what we're going to do, I've got to know about it.'' He was thinking about Tangretti . . . and about Garland's lecture on the VC threat. "Maybe we could even pull some kind of deal. I sure as hell won't squeal on you. But I'm not going to get my boys killed in some kind of stupid, asshole game dreamed up to amuse the REMFs in Saigon!''

Quon sat at the table, staring into his drink for a long time. "I am no Communist,'' he said.

Baxter was already ashamed of his outburst and was afraid that he'd gone too far. "Ong Quon,'' he said. "I'm sorry. I probably shouldn't have said it that way. I didn't mean that—''

"You needn't apologize,'' the Vietnamese said. "I know what they say about me. I do not have the, the *respect* for my leaders that I should.'' He shrugged. "Sometimes I make jokes. The jokes get back to people in important positions. It is bad, sometimes, how political this war is.''

"Tell me about it.''

He'd meant the words as ironic agreement, a way of telling Quon that the two of them faced many of the same problems. Quon, however, appeared to misunderstand, to take the statement literally.

"I have not told anyone, Lieutenant Edward. But you . . . yes. Perhaps I should. You have the right to know, since you have risked your own position, your rank, your career, by openly remaining friends with me.''

"Quon, you don't have to tell me a damned thing if you don't want to.''

"I came from a small village in Song Bay,'' Quon said. "Xom Gia. You can find the records at MACV-SOG headquarters, to verify what I say. My father was Nguyen Dinh

Kiet, and he was . . . you would probably say 'chief' of the village.'' He smiled. ''I dislike that way of saying it. It makes it sound as though I am one of your Wild West Indians, a savage.''

''How about 'mayor'?''

''Very well, then. My father was mayor of Xom Gia. The village is not large. You would probably think it a very primitive place. But my family had money enough and political connections enough to send me to Saigon to school and to buy an opportunity for me to join the army as an officer, rather than as an enlisted man. It . . . gave him great status, you see.''

Baxter wasn't sure he did see, but he said nothing, listening as Quon told the story.

''One day two years ago, not long after I'd joined LDNN, in fact, the Vietcong came to our village. There were twenty or thirty of them, and a VC tax collector. They demanded, as usual, a tax amounting to several bags of rice, some chickens and pigs, the usual . . . how do you say? Extortion. They demanded the young men, also, all those between fourteen and twenty years. The VC too, have a draft, you see, though it is not as organized as what you have in America. They simply show up in a town, say 'you, you, and you will now join the fight against the Imperialists,' and take the young men with them into the forest.''

Quon was silent for a moment, and Baxter wondered where the story was going. Then Quon added in a voice so low that Baxter could hardly hear, ''And they also demanded me.''

''You?''

''As I said, I had recently joined LDNN. The VC commander had information that I was in Xom Gia at that time. In fact, I had been there only the day before. His informant had made a mistake.'' Quon gave a grim smile. ''It is comforting, is it not, that the VC have trouble with their intelligence too?

''I think they planned to execute me in front of the village, an object lesson to any who would help the Saigon government or military, or the Americans, in any way. However, I had already left. My father gave them the pigs and chickens and rice. We were used to paying taxes to both sides, you see. It was simply the price of staying alive and being left alone, usually. The young men were gone, hiding in the rice paddies.

It is a small village, and there were only four or five.

"And as for me, well, my father was a proud man, stiff-necked, I think you would say. He told them that he would tell me that they were looking for me. He told them that I would bring the entire *Lien Doc Nguoi Nhia* and feed the VC commander and the tax collector their balls, and that he would watch. This is, in our language . . . an impolite thing to say to someone."

"It's impolite in anyone's language."

"Yes. My father thought they would not hurt him, because I was LDNN. My position did not impress the VC, however. Worse, my father had challenged the Vietcong commander, in front of his men, and in front of the village. So my father became the lesson these people wanted to teach."

"Oh, God."

"They stripped him of his clothing and nailed him to a three-meter-tall post in the center of the village. *Nailed* him, with his hands stretched up above his head. The VC, you see, learned something from the French missionaries, yes? They brought out my mother, and my younger brother, who was ten, and my two sisters, who were fourteen and seventeen. And they forced everyone in Xom Gia to gather around and watch.

"They began by . . . what is the word, Edward? When they cut your belly open and pull out what's inside?"

The words, spoken in an innocent and matter-of-fact turn, shocked Baxter. He felt an icy lump rising in his throat, and fought to swallow it. "Disemboweling."

"Yes. That is it. They disemboweled my brother with a bayonet and left him on the ground to die. Next they stripped and beat and raped my sisters and my mother, all of the VC soldiers taking turns, and then they killed them in front of my father and the village, very, very slowly. I am told it took nearly all day. And when they were done, they cut off my father's balls, put them in his mouth, and sewed his mouth shut with needle and thread, after which they told the villagers that the same would happen to any of them who tried to take him down off that post. They vanished into the forest, and so terrified were the people that not one helped either my father or my brother, who both were still alive. They must have finally died sometime during the night. They would probably still be there in the middle of the village if an Army patrol hadn't come by the following afternoon.''

Quon fell silent, and Baxter said nothing, letting the silence drag on for several painful moments. At last, Quon downed the last of his drink, then met Baxter's eyes. ''It is *that* kind of war, Edward, my friend.''

''Ong Quon. I had no idea. . . .''

''Of course not. And I do not tell you to win sympathy or pity. It is . . . the evil of this war. And I will go on hunting VC and killing VC, and maybe some day I will meet the men who took my family, and then I will kill them.'' The cold way Quon said the words left little doubt in Baxter's mind that those people would not enjoy an easy death. ''In the meantime, perhaps you will understand that I am not the double agent you seek. If details of an operation were leaked to the VC, it was not me who leaked them.'' Carefully, he picked up the bottle on the table and poured three fingers of liquid into his empty glass. Setting the bottle down again, he lifted the glass, stared into Baxter's eyes across the rim. ''*Sat Cong!*''

With equal ceremony, Baxter lifted his glass and touched it gently to Quon's with a tiny, crystal *ping*. ''*Sat Cong!*''

Chapter 9

Tuesday, 26 April 1966

**HQ, Naval Operations
Support Group, Pacific
Coronado, California
1130 hours**

''The Old Man asked me to remind you about the meeting this morning, Lieutenant. In his office . . . right away.'' The

yeoman delivering the message seemed too young to be a
Navy man, and Tangretti wondered for a moment how a kid
who looked that helpless and vulnerable had ever gotten
through boot camp. He probably had been careful to list "typ-
ing" as one of his job skills when he enlisted, to make sure
he'd end up in a nice safe stateside office instead of manning
a Swift boat somewhere in the Mekong Delta.

Then he pictured some of the younger men who had gone
through training at Fort Pierce with the NCDU and thought
better of his evaluation. Nobody would have pegged Ensign
Hank Richardson as tough enough for the job he'd done, not
back then. But Richardson had turned out to be a real hero on
the beaches of Normandy.

"Thanks, kid," he growled, standing up from his desk and
stretching to get a few of the kinks out. Tangretti was starting
to feel like this office work was rotting his whole body away.
He made a silent vow to start working out again, just to stay
in shape. And, maybe, to work off some of the frustration and
aggression that built up a little more each day he was stuck at
NOSG.

He gathered up a stack of folders from one side of the desk,
a collection of reports and studies on Operation Jackstay. The
material had been trickling into the office over the past two
weeks, making its way slowly up the chain of command from
the men in the field, growing in size and complexity as each
new office got hold of the information and put their own in-
terpretation on it. Tangretti was considering getting an ink
stamp with the word CRAP on it, to make his job of evaluating
the material and adding comments thereto easier. He doubted,
though, that Bucklew or Howell would appreciate the suggestion.

In point of fact, though, it was easy to see that the Navy
was up to its old tricks again. Not only were the SEALs in
Vietnam being completely mishandled, but on top of that the
higher echelons who had studied Det Delta's reports were, as
usual, completely missing the problems that were all too clear
to Tangretti. And they persisted in making suggestions that
would only hamper the SEAL unit further if they were put
into effect.

Maybe Captain Galloway had been right to stick him in this
post after all. If Bucklew took even some of the advice regular

Navy men and faceless bureaucrats were starting to offer regarding the best ways to use SEALs in Southeast Asia, the whole concept of naval special warfare would quickly wither on the vine.

Perhaps, Tangretti thought grimly, that was just what some of the regular Navy men were hoping for.

Howell wasn't at his desk, so Tangretti went straight to the office door and knocked. Bucklew's voice answered, inviting him in, so Tangretti slipped the small stack under one arm, opened the door, and entered. The captain and his aide were both there, apparently comparing notes on yet another set of reports.

"Meeting was scheduled for 1130 hours, Tangretti," Howell told him. "Try to make it on time in future."

Tangretti didn't answer. Instead he put his reports down on Bucklew's desk and pulled up a chair. "Here're the Jackstay files, Captain," he said, sitting down. "Can't say they're worth much, though."

"Really?" Bucklew raised his eyebrows. "I thought they raised some interesting points we're going to have to consider, Lieutenant." He raised his hand to forestall an explosive response from Tangretti. "All in good time, Mr. Tangretti. You're here because we value your input. You probably know as much about UDT and SEAL operations as any man in the service. But Lieutenant Howell has the floor for the moment."

"Thank you, sir," Howell said smoothly. "As I was saying, I think SEALs can be a very effective force, so long as they are properly employed. Unfortunately, from what I've seen of the Jackstay reports, they haven't really found their niche yet."

The words came as a pleasant surprise to Tangretti. Maybe Howell wasn't as blind and hidebound as he'd thought. "I'm surprised, Lieutenant," he said aloud, offering a tentative smile. "It sounds like we might agree on something, for a change."

Howell shrugged. "If you say so, Tangretti," he answered. "Captain, Det Delta performed very well during Jackstay. All the reports make that clear enough. But I have to say I can't really see that they did anything that the UDT and Marine Force Recon couldn't do just as well . . . maybe even better, in the final analysis. After all, they worked with the Marines for the first day of the op and then went on to do demo work alongside the UDT. If that's all there is to SEALs, we've made a bad investment . . ."

"Oh, come on, Howell!" Tangretti burst out. "And to think I actually got the idea you might know what you were talking about!"

"*If* I could finish, Captain . . ." Howell grated.

"Please, Mr. Tangretti, let the lieutenant make his point," Bucklew said. "You'll get your own chance."

"Thank you, Captain," Howell said with a disdainful glance at Tangretti. "Now as I see it, the most promising reports we've had are the ones involving the sorties aboard riverine craft. This operation on the fifth, for instance. Combining SEALs with the regular riverine crews gives our boats a lot more striking power. They can put men ashore to check suspected enemy positions, set up ambushes, whatever. And it's definitely something set apart from the UDT or Marine Recon . . . different from what the Special Forces boys do, too, when you come right down to it. I think we should start concentrating our efforts in that direction."

"Hmph." Bucklew was frowning. "Didn't a couple of the reports suggest the VC could probably monitor our operations just by watching when the boats left their docks? We don't want to be too predictable."

Howell held up a manila folder. "This is our most recent update from Det Delta, Captain. From last week. Seems Lieutenant Baxter was having the same doubts himself. He's started sending the boats out at irregular intervals up the river to Saigon. Has his gear and men flown up there to meet up with them. First time out, they killed three VC in a sampan . . . caught 'em right out in the open, completely by surprise. If this holds up, I think we've got a real winner on our hands."

Bucklew glanced over at Tangretti. "You still disagree, I take it, Lieutenant?" he asked mildly.

"You'd better believe I disagree," he answered. "Howell here is talking about taking a bunch of prize racehorses and hitching them to a plow. That's not what the SEALs are all about. It's the same fucking idiocy that said the UDT shouldn't do recon above the high-water mark on Okinawa, for Christ's sake!"

"Easy, Lieutenant," Bucklew said, wincing a little. He

could trade profanity with the best of them, but in his new position as a rising star of the Navy establishment he frowned on anyone swearing in the office. Tangretti knew it well enough and "forgot" any time he wanted to make a strong point. "Go on . . . but try to keep the language under control, if you please."

"Look, the SEALs were put together as an all-purpose Navy commando unit. Sea, Air, Land . . . they get cross-trained six ways from Sunday, and they go through some of the toughest physical and mental preparation you can think of. You can't just decree they put all that aside and sit on Swift boats all the time, only going ashore when the brown water boys run into something they can't handle. It's a waste, pure and simple."

"Well, what's your take on it, then?" the captain asked. "You said you agreed with Lieutenant Howell when he said the SEALs weren't being used properly."

"That's right, they're not." Tangretti leaned forward in his seat. "Look, the SEALs were trained as commandos. Everything we've been grooming them for involved sending them out against specific targets, with a specific mission. Like what the LDNN has been doing out of Da Nang. They go north by sea, swim ashore, blow a radar station or take out a bridge, then pull out again. Blundering around through the swamps with no clear-cut objective . . . that's as stupid as letting them rot aboard Swift boats!"

"Conditions in the Rung Sat aren't conducive to commando ops," Howell said quietly. "There's no infrastructure to wipe out, no hard targets to mount raids against. The VC move their camps and their caches around. By your arguments, Tangretti, we might as well pull the SEALs out entirely."

"No!" Tangretti and Bucklew said it almost together.

"You're still thinking too much like a regular Navy man, Lieutenant," Tangretti went on. "I've been in Nam, for Christ's sake. I probably know more about how the VC operate than all your reports and all your analyses will ever tell you. Don't you get it? We can keep right on mounting the very same kinds of operations we're doing right now. The problem so far isn't that the ops aren't right, not by a long shot. The problem is that the SEALs aren't being given enough freedom of action."

"Explain what you mean, Mr. Tangretti," Bucklew said.

"Two things. The first is a matter of training." Tangretti stood up and walked over to Bucklew's window. It looked out across the parking lot and the Silver Strand Highway toward the entrance to the SEAL compound, where trainees were being put through their paces out on the grinder. "Det Delta wasn't given much time prepping for Nam. They went over there not knowing what to expect. I think in future we'd better start picking our units early and giving them some extra training before we ship 'em out."

"What kind of training?"

"Mostly, I think we need to teach them all about mud. Swamps. Marshes. Rivers. Far as I can tell, a good chunk of the problem with our boys right now is that they went over there expecting to do the kind of ops we did back in Korea with the UDT. Instead they have to slog through the jungle on narrow tracks, looking out for booby traps and hoping the VC don't see them first. The way I figure it, we should start hunting for some place enough like Nam to give our guys a taste of it in advance. Over the long haul it'll save lives, I guarantee it."

"We've already got the Jungle Warfare School down in Panama. Don't some of the SEALs already train there?" At least Howell wasn't stubborn enough to deny the sense of Tangretti's suggestion.

"I knew some of the first guys who went there," Tangretti said. "They said it was a load of shit . . ." He glanced at Bucklew. "Beg your pardon, sir. Crap. Look, the terrain in Panama isn't much like Nam anyway. What we're looking for is a place like the Rung Sat or the Mekong Delta. Preferably close by. Two places, really, 'cause sooner or later I bet we'll be wanting the East Coast to do the same thing, if they start getting involved in Nam. I'll bet you we can find suitable stretches somewhere . . . a Louisiana bayou, if need be. Point is, we need to start getting the men acclimated *before* they get over there . . . not just to the terrain, but to the kinds of ops and situations they'll be facing, too."

"That'll be like putting together a whole new training school," Bucklew said.

"Maybe so, sir, but it's a good investment. And we already have the basis for the curriculum." He crossed back over to the desk and fished a stack of papers out of one of his folders. "They call them barn dance cards . . . Lieutenant Baxter is having every one of his men fill them out every time they go out on patrol. Right here, Captain, is where you'll find the best recommendations for how to improve our ops over in Nam. From the men who really know what's going on, instead of the rear-echelon wonders who only think they know what it's like in the field." He glanced at Howell, who flushed.

"I've seen them," Bucklew said, nodding. "You're right, Mr. Tangretti. They'll be very useful for getting firsthand experience distilled into a useful form." He cleared his throat. "I think your suggestions are worth pursuing, although it's going to take time to get a new training program set up. I doubt we can do anything for Golf Platoon before they go over this summer, for instance."

"Maybe not," Tangretti said. "But maybe we can get them in-country a little early, before the end of Delta's tour. Have the old hands show them the ropes for a week or two."

Bucklew jotted down a note. "That might be worth pursuing. All right, that's one area for improvement. You said there were two things you wanted to suggest?"

"Yes, sir, I did." Tangretti sat down again, still holding the barn dance cards. He rifled through the papers absently as he spoke. "Look, the thing that strikes me about all the reports that came out of Jackstay, and the follow-up stuff since then, is the way our guys are getting screwed by bad intelligence. Everything they're getting is being filtered through God knows how many layers of bureaucrats and staffers. It's no wonder a lot of their leads have been coming up cold . . . it takes weeks for supposedly hot intel to get to Nha Be for Baxter to act on it."

"Come on, Tangretti, it can't be that bad," Howell protested. "You're exaggerating the problem just to make your point. We-'ve got plenty of intelligence sources over there . . . and they're not *that* slow."

"No?" Tangretti pulled out a report on the first stage of Operation Jackstay. "If our data was so good, how come a bunch of SEALs got posted to an ambush point right on top of a VC bunker that none of the maps showed? I'm telling you, if you're as much as a week behind in your intel over in Nam, you might as well give it up."

"I suppose we can try to speed up the flow of information," Bucklew said. "Though I don't really see how we can eliminate the delays entirely . . ."

"It won't work," Tangretti told him flatly. "Not just because bureaucrats will screw up anything they touch. You're also seeing the results of having too damn many fingers in the pie over there."

"How so?" the captain asked.

"Nobody tells anybody else anything," Tangretti told him. "Assuming our people even know who the SEALs are and what they're doing, they probably think they should stay classified. Especially the way the brass over there treats our so-called allies. . . ."

"If you're proposing that we wave a magic wand and suddenly make interagency rivalry and all the rest disappear, Lieutenant, I'm afraid we're going to have to send you away for a long rest." Bucklew was smiling as he shook his head. "I imagine Washington had the same kind of problems in the Continental Army. We're not going to fix the system now."

"Amen to that," Tangretti said. "That's my whole point. We've got to stop relying on outside agencies. If the SEALs are going to be effective, Captain, they have to be able to function on their own. No strings. I know what those guys can do if they're just turned loose with a mission and enough resources to carry it out. And the most important resource of all is intelligence they can rely on . . . intelligence they gather and evaluate for *themselves*."

"So you want to add to the confusion over there, is that it?" Howell looked disgusted. "If you thought there were too many people holding out on each other before, how's it going to help to add another batch?"

"Ah, but this is different," Tangretti said. "This is *our* group gathering *our* information for *our* use." He paused. "Look, I know what I'm talking about here. When I was advising the LDNN, we were having the same kind of problems. American intelligence sources weren't very eager to share with the Vietnamese, and we couldn't always rely on what we got from the government, either. So we cultivated our own sources of information."

"Such as?" Howell asked.

"Well . . . you know, people accused me of being too

friendly with known VC. Like Thanh . . . he was the CO of a VC battalion that operated east of Saigon, along the edge of the Rung Sat. When I was with a patrol that ran into Thanh, we used to call a ceasefire and go out and meet. And sometimes we'd set up get-togethers in town. He drove a cab in Saigon, and he'd pick me up and take me into the Chinese district, where Americans didn't usually go. While we were out, we'd talk. I picked up a hell of a lot of useful information that way and passed it on to the LDNN.''

''And no doubt he picked up plenty from you, too,'' Howell said with a frown. ''I'd seen reports about you and your gook friend, but I never thought you'd be brazen enough to boast about it. There's a word for consorting with the enemy that way, Tangretti . . . treason.''

Tangretti held up a hand. ''Whoa, there, Lieutenant,'' he said. Under the bantering tone he was angry at Howell's instant assumption of his guilt. ''I never told Thanh a damned thing he didn't already know. Never even confirmed something that was common knowledge. *He* was helping *me*. Had some relatives with the government side, so his sympathies were divided. My point in bringing him up is that we didn't let limits imposed from outside keep us from being effective. And that's what I think our guys should be doing now.''

''Consorting with the enemy?'' Bucklew asked, his voice laced with heavy irony.

''Gathering information, for Christ's sake!'' Tangretti said loudly. ''However they can do it. I'd suggest we start making prisoners and documents a high priority when our people get out on patrol. And don't have them just turn the shit over to somebody else, either. We've got liaison people, NILOs and Vietnamese scouts and what not. Sit down with them and go through the documents, or interrogate the prisoners, or go over every scrap of information all of our boys have seen. And, yes, cultivate local informants, too. What we want to do is make SEAL operations self-supporting whenever we can. I'll bet you any amount you want to name that we can start doing some serious damage inside of a few weeks once we start using the information we generate from one raid to lead us right into the next.''

''Tactical units in the field are not supposed to process information," Howell said stubbornly. "They're not trained to interpret intelligence data, and they don't have access to a bigger picture so that they can put the material they do have access to into context."

"We're not talking about gathering intel that'll tell us when Uncle Ho is planning the next big push," Tangretti countered. "You're right, that stuff's for the brass hats behind the lines. We can pass on everything we've got up the chain of command so they can see what our boys find. But in the meantime *we* can get the stuff we need. Locations and movements of individual VC units. Where are they storing weapons or rice? What's the schedule for their tax collectors to make the rounds in a given neighborhood? With that kind of information, the SEALs can start to make a real difference. They'll have a much more current picture of what the hell's going on around them, and that can only make them more effective when the time comes to mount an ambush or strike at a specific target."

Bucklew was frowning. "You make some good points, Lieutenant, I'll give you that," he said slowly. "But it's a pretty ambitious program for a unit the size of Det Delta."

"Then get more SEALs on the ground over there," Tangretti said bluntly. "Det Delta's too damned small as it is. We need the manpower and the resources to start doing something more than just sit on our asses and hope that the VC blunder into us somewhere."

"Hmmm . . . maybe so." Bucklew didn't sound convinced. "I'm a little worried about just what direction naval special warfare ends up going, though. It sounds to me like you're trying to duplicate the Green Berets, and I really don't think that should be our function. We need to find our own niche, something we do that nobody else does. And don't forget, Lieutenant, the SEALs are only one component of our overall responsibility. NOSG handles UDT, SEALs, riverine units, beach jumpers . . . we've got to keep in mind the need to balance all these elements within our command and use each of them wisely."

"That's my point exactly, sir," Howell said quickly. "All this talk about gathering intelligence and working independently doesn't take into account the overall divisions of responsibility. I mean, let's face it, a lot of our own people don't know that much about any of the Navy's special warfare units, and they don't really know how to use them. Unless we define clear roles for our people to fill, how are we ever going to be more than a fifth wheel?''

"Exactly,'' Bucklew said, nodding. "Mr. Tangretti, you've brought up some excellent ideas here. I intend to get right on top of the training program you suggested, and I intend to recommend we expand the intelligence-gathering capabilities of the SEALs in the field. I think both of these ideas will make our people considerably more effective. At the same time, though, I like Mr. Howell's point about linking the SEALs more closely to the riverine operations. The more we can integrate the various components of naval special warfare under our control, the better. So I'm going to start promoting the idea of mounting river patrols using SEAL and riverine units in combination. The SEALs can insert ashore from the boats to gather information or carry out limited operations.''

"I still say that's wasting a hell of a lot of potential,'' Tangretti said. "I thought the job we were trying to do in the Rung Sat was to shut down the VC once and for all. How are we going to accomplish that if we're tied to patrol boats all the time? Let the guys off the leash, and they'll have the zone secured before you can say Ho Chi Minh . . .''

Bucklew shook his head. "We're in no position to try to play cowboy, Lieutenant,'' he said. "The fighting over in Nam has to be a team effort. Special Warfare people are useful for small, highly selective strikes, ambushes and raids and, yes, as you suggested, gathering information. But in the long run it will be up to the Marines and the Army to do the actual work of clearing areas of organized opposition. That's their job. You surely don't advocate turning the SEALs into ordinary ground-pounders, do you?''

"No, sir,'' Tangretti said. "The day someone tries to use a SEAL platoon like a Marine rifle unit we'll know we've been screwed but good. But I know Vietnam, Captain. This war is going to be won or lost by small units, squads or platoons, not by overwhelming firepower. Pumping hundreds of thousands of men into the country isn't going to be worth a damned thing if we don't find a way to deal with the small guerrilla units . . . and the best way to deal with them is to go after them on their own terms, with elite troops who can match them in every way, go where they go, hit 'em where it hurts and then disappear just the way they do."

Bucklew gave him an unfathomable look. "I know how dedicated you are to your SEALs, Lieutenant," he said quietly. "But I really do think you've got to keep your feet on the ground. When I was in charge of the Scouts and Raiders, I always kept in mind the fact that it was only one cog in a big machine. Some of my boys used to go overboard with playing at being rough, tough commandos . . . I remember having to chew some of them out after the Sicily landings because they took unnecessary risks. Our job back then was to gather beach information before a landing and then guide the invasion force into those beaches when the big day finally came. There wasn't any room for trying to single-handedly take out German bunkers or any of that nonsense. It's the same with your SEALs today. You can't just close your eyes and wish that they could do everything on their own. Even if it was practical, you've still got to deal with the realities of national policy . . . and service politics. The Army, the Air Force, the Marines . . . they all have a stake in things too. We're damned lucky the Navy even has a look-in over there, all things considered. That's one reason why I want to emphasize the riverine connection for now." He grinned. "We're the Navy . . . we're in charge of stuff that floats. That's a lot less threatening than trying to move in on Army and Marine turf . . . and it keeps us in line for our fair share of the funding we need to keep our operation going. *That's* reality."

"So the primary role of naval special warfare is to receive funding so that we can promote the role of Navy special warfare?" Tangretti didn't bother to hide his scorn. "I thought we were trying to win a war over there, not score points off the other services and make sure we kept our big fat paychecks coming—"

"That'll be enough, Lieutenant," Bucklew said, his smile turning to an angry frown. "We'll win the war, sure enough . . . but we'll do it working *with* the system, not against it. That may not be something you're very familiar with, but it's the way things are going to be here on out. Do I make myself clear?"

"Yes, sir," Tangretti said. "Crystal clear."

"Good. I want you to write up detailed proposals on the

ideas you've outlined here today. . . . Please make sure, though, that they conform to our overall policy goals. No going off on wild tangents about how much more we could be doing, for instance. Have the material on my desk first thing in the morning, if you please. Mr. Howell, the same goes for your riverine plan. Understood?''

"Aye-aye, sir," the two lieutenants said.

"Good. Then you're both dismissed." Bucklew hesitated. "And . . . thank you both, gentlemen. In spite of your obvious . . . deep feelings on various matters, this has been a very productive session. I feel good about our prospects for making this team work well together."

Tangretti bit back a retort and followed Howell out of the office. The aide turned on Tangretti as he was closing the door behind them.

"The captain went pretty easy on you in there, Tangretti," Howell told him. "He put up with a hell of a lot of shit I certainly wouldn't have stood for."

Tangretti just smiled at him. "Now, now, Thurston. Language . . . watch your language." As usual, Howell winced at Tangretti's contemptuous nickname for him. It had caught on—behind the aide's back, mostly—among the rest of the NOSG-Pacific staff. Howell's thick Harvard accent and superior attitude reminded everybody of Jim Backus playing Thurston Howell III on "Gilligan's Island."

Howell stepped toward him, flushing. "Listen to me, Tangretti. You may think you're a clever fellow, always playing games and flaunting higher authority. It worked for you back at Little Creek . . . once you got the president to intervene. Somehow I don't think that's too likely out here in Coronado. So just keep in mind this simple little fact, Lieutenant . . . I'm watching you. Every move you make, every word you say, I'm keeping track of it all. And if you screw up, if you cause problems for this office, I'll take great pride in being the one to file formal charges against you. A court martial should have been convened on you years ago . . . but it's never too late."

Tangretti shrugged. "If you say so, Lieutenant," he said quietly. "But I was under the impression that we were supposed to be on the same team, here. And that Captain Bucklew, misguided though he may be in some areas, thought that I was making some worthwhile contributions today."

"Worthwhile contributions." Howell sounded disgusted. "All you managed to do today, Tangretti, was cloud the issue. And as for being a part of the team . . . that's something you'll never be. As far as I'm concerned you're a cocky, incompetent idiot in way over your head because you never should have been made an officer in the first place. That's at best . . . if you're not a traitor who's conspired with the enemy in Vietnam . . . and maybe here at home, for that matter. So don't talk about being on *my* team!"

Howell turned and strode stiffly toward his desk. Tangretti shook his head, looking after him for a moment, and then shrugged and walked away.

It seemed he wasn't going to have much of an impact here, no matter what Captain Galloway may have hoped for. A few of his ideas might be picked up from time to time, but not his overall vision for the SEALs and what they could do. Left in the hands of men like Howell and Bucklew, the SEALs would wind up being so completely hamstrung by procedures and protocols that they'd be worse than useless.

Chapter 10

Wednesday, 27 April 1966

HQ, Military Assistance Command, Vietnam
Saigon 1439 hours

"What the hell was he doing traveling in that area at night, without a light?" Baxter protested, suppressing a small shiver as he spoke. The air conditioning in the office kept the atmosphere damned near icy, but it was more than the cool air that sent chills down Baxter's spine. Another week of long and arduous effort with few solid returns had already taken its toll on the SEALs and their commanding officer, but the news he'd been summoned to headquarters to hear had cut right to the quick.

One of their most solid successes to date had come back to haunt them. The fight on the Vam Sat River in mid-April had been an unqualified success . . . or so it had seemed at the time. But there was a problem. That VC that Baxter's team had ambushed on the night of April 13, it turned out, had been no VC at all, but a Tong Huy Minh, an agent working for South Vietnamese military intelligence. Apparently the dead man had actually infiltrated the VC's Rung Sat network, convincing them of his Communist sympathies by smuggling in AK-47s and passing them on to VC units. For almost two months, Minh had been the best eyes and ears in the Rung Sat anyone in Saigon headquarters had had; his reports had helped in the final planning of Jackstay, and *everybody* knew what a resounding success *that* operation had been. It had taken nearly two weeks for the tangled web of Vietnamese and American military bureaucrats to pass on the information, but now that it was known the reaction from MACV was swift and uncompromising.

The whole sordid story had left Baxter feeling sick in the pit of his stomach. *How* could such a screw-up have happened? And why had his SEALs been singled out to take the blame? Surely there was plenty to go around? . . . "Hell, sir," he continued. "Why did he grab a weapon?"

"Possibly because somebody shouted at him in Vietnamese?" Commander George White's voice was loud and sarcastic. "Possibly because he felt threatened? Tell me, Lieutenant. What would you do if someone shouted at you to stop, in a situation like that?"

"Not reach for a gun and get myself killed! Sir."

"Well perhaps, Mr. Baxter, not everyone is possessed of your native intelligence, logic, and cool-headed powers of reason. Damn it, Lieutenant, what am I supposed to tell Captain Garland? Or Admiral Hargreaves? We're getting messages from the Vietnamese military command, from SEPES, even from the Presidential Palace! MACV-SOG is in an uproar from here to Cambodia! I would have to say, Mr. Baxter, that you and your SEALs have just about worn out your welcome in South Vietnam!''

''Sir. The ambush was logged and approved through Det Delta's NILO. MACV G2 knew we were going to be operating in that district on that night. Hell, if they'd bothered to check, they would have found out that it was their own people who passed down the word that there were a lot of weapons moving down the Vam Sat in that area. Shit, they *knew* we were going into that area. They could've warned the guy.''

''Lieutenant, you've been in-country long enough to know that it's not a good idea to share sensitive information with our counterparts. You've heard of SEPES?''

''Yes, sir.'' Baxter nodded. The *Service des Etudes Politique et Sociologique* was a Vietnamese civilian intelligence agency—a mini-CIA.

''Even they're riddled with communist informants. And you're suggesting that we should start clearing our covert operations with them?''

''Then someone could have told *us*, sir. Told *me*.''

''The reason you screwed up, Lieutenant, was that you were operating without full clearance or authority.''

''Sir! I—''

''Shut up! I'm doing the talking now, Lieutenant! I know you people came over here with some romantic, James Bond notions of direct action. What did you think, you had a license to kill or some bullshit like that? Ever since you people got here you've been grousing about the role you're expected to play. I've been hearing too damned many ideas, from you and from others, about what you SEALs could do over here, crazy stuff off in the boondocks somewhere, and not one shred of thought to how any of that would fit into the big picture. *That's* your trouble, Lieutenant. You're not a team player. You're a loner, your men are loners, and there's no place in this war for a unit that can't work together with the rest of us. You follow me?''

''Yes, sir. I do.''

''You're not wanted in Vietnam. Not if you can't play the game by the rules.''

''I was not aware, sir, that war had any rules.''

''Then wake up and look around! Modern warfare is loaded

with rules, and the people in my command are going to follow them to the letter. Do you read me, mister?"

"Yes, sir."

So the SEALs weren't wanted in Vietnam. That suited Baxter just fine. Ever since he'd heard the direct action scuttlebutt, hell, ever since he'd volunteered for the SEALs in the first place, he'd assumed that the unit would be operating more or less independently. Covert ops to take out VC leaders. Prisoner snatches to get valuable intelligence. Commando raids on Hanoi. During the let-down after Hell Week, while the BUD/S trainees were still recovering, Baxter had exercised his exhaustion-numbed brain by coming up with various schemes that he could try out once he was in command of a SEAL team of his own. His favorite involved going ashore in North Vietnam near Haiphong, moving overland to Hanoi, and penetrating the defenses of either the National Assembly Building or the Presidential Palace. Hell, it would be easy for SEALs. No one in their right minds would expect such a wild-ass idea. . . .

"Now," White said, relaxing somewhat as he pulled a cigarette from a pack and lit it with a silver lighter bearing the Annapolis crest in gold. "I'm sure you're upset over Minh's death. I want you to know that I know it was accident. It was regrettable, but this is war and accidents happen in war. Understand?"

"Yes, sir."

"As a matter of fact, it may not actually have been your fault, except indirectly. That Viet liaison man of yours, Nguyen. This Vam Sat op went down before we warned you about his possible VC ties. It's possible he fed you some bad intel deliberately."

"Sir," Baxter said slowly. "I have every reason to believe Lieutenant Quon is loyal. I really don't think this is his fault at all. He's not to blame for the screw-ups in passing information back and forth with the ARVN and their crowd. . . ."

"That may be your opinion, Lieutenant," White told him harshly. "But it isn't likely to be very popular. I've had reports that you've continued to fraternize with Nguyen off duty and still involved him in your operations despite the warnings we gave you last month. So I'm repeating them now. In the future, you will be careful about what you say in front of him. And

. . . as a word to the wise, Lieutenant. I would stay clear of Nguyen all together. When he goes down, he's going to take others down with him. Understand me?''

"I just can't believe it, sir," Baxter protested. "Not Quon . . ."

"Shit, Lieutenant. You haven't learned a damned thing about this country yet, have you?" White looked disgusted. "First off, you should know by now that the VC are everywhere, even in positions of trust. We're trying to change that, but it's slow going. And in this case, whatever your *personal* opinion of Nguyen might be, it would be a hell of a lot smarter of you to get with the program. We have a major strain in our relations with the Vietnamese government right now, thanks to this little exploit. If unmasking a VC sympathizer can set it right, then that's the option we have to follow."

"Even if the man's not guilty, sir?" Baxter asked pointedly. "Because he isn't. . . ."

"All we have right now are suspicions, Lieutenant. Nothing certain. This is a matter for the local government to deal with, from here on out." White looked down at his desk. "I only warned you to keep clear of the man until his guilt . . . or innocence . . . can be established. It's the wisest course all the way around."

Baxter didn't respond, and after a long moment White gave him a hard look. "All right, Lieutenant. That will be all. Try to keep your nose clean . . . and your head down. You're dismissed."

He left the chill air of the office in something like shock. It seemed that a lot of the things he had thought he was fighting for over here in Vietnam were being sacrificed on the altar of expediency. . . .

And Charles Edward Baxter didn't like the idea at all.

Sunday, 8 May 1966

SEAL Compound, U.S. Naval Base
Nha Be
0145 hours

Baxter was not drunk when he staggered off the bus that had brought him down from Saigon to the stinging rathole of Nha Be. Not quite. He was feeling a buzz, though, and enjoying a thin, alcohol-induced haze that went a long way to cutting some of the pain he was feeling just now. Pausing outside the hootch that served as the SEALs' officers' quarters at the base, he worked for a moment at focusing on his wristwatch. Mickey's big hand was on the eight . . . his little hand halfway between the eleven and the twelve: 2340 hours? Close enough.

Stepping inside the hootch, he stood there for a moment and stared at the cluttered, ramshackle room. In the past few months, the place had taken on a decidedly nonmilitary air. Gil's six-string folk guitar, purchased a few weeks back in Saigon, hung from the corner of his rack; Baxter had given up on his rack with its thin mattress in favor of a hammock slung beneath a window. Sheet upon sheet of mosquito netting gave the place the atmosphere of the set of some grade-B horror movie, complete with thickly draped curtains of spider web. Miss February smiled down from a wall next to the door, a lovingly dog-eared copy of a four-month-old *Playboy* pin-up. Automatically, he reached out and gave the centerfold's bared left nipple a light caress, a gesture the SEAL officers had adopted early on for good luck but which long ago had lost any meaning.

Gil and Hanrahan were both out . . . Gil still in town, Hanrahan standing the duty for the weekend over at the Nha Be admin office.

He stood for a moment by the door, torn between looking for the bottle Hanrahan stashed in his foot locker or just collapsing in his hammock to sleep it off. Baxter hadn't felt this miserable in a long, long time. He felt betrayed by his own high command. Worse he felt like he'd been a party to the betrayal of another, a man he'd come to regard as a friend. The vague suspicions about Nguyen Quon had coalesced all too suddenly into action, and Baxter hadn't even been around to defend the man from his accusers when they'd finally decided to strike.

It was over a week since he'd last seen Lieutenant Quon. For a few days after the meeting with White the LDNN officer had continued to perform his duties with the SEALs. But then, one morning, Det Delta had returned to the base from a patrol in the Rung Sat to discover that Quon was no longer anywhere on the base. After several inquiries through Kellerman and through contacts in Saigon, Baxter had been curtly told that Quon had been "reassigned."

Okay. It happened, especially in war . . . but the circumstances of that "reassignment" had left Baxter extremely suspicious of the whole situation. Ultimately, he'd had to call in a marker with a lieutenant j.g. working in the Naval Intelligence Office at NAVADVGRU to get a look at a brief he really wasn't supposed to be able to see. On the direct orders of General Kim of the ARVN, Lieutenant Nguyen Quon had been arrested and taken into custody. There was no charge listed, but the suspicion was treason.

This filthy, stinking, fucking, son of a bitch war. . . .

For Baxter, this was the final, camel-breaking straw. For months now, he'd been struggling against the entrenched, do-it-this-way-or-else narrow-mindedness of MACV; against intelligence that was politically slanted or wrong or, most often, both; against the intense prejudice his superiors had toward anything as innovative or as different as the SEALs; against a bureaucracy as tangled and as impenetrable as any jungle in the Rung Sat. Lately, he'd been fighting Kellerman and White and Garland far more often than he fought the Vietcong. The Vietcong were a *lot* harder to find than desk-bound REMFs.

And now, to put the finishing touches on this black-comic farce, the one Vietnamese in this whole damned country that Baxter had admired, respected, and trusted had just been purged by his own commanding officers.

What a fucking stupid way to run a war. . . .

More than anything else, he thought, the problem lay in the way the SEALs were being used . . . misused, rather. They should be operating independently, not working with half a dozen different military commands. They should be responsible for their own intel, their own equipment, their own weapons.

Stationery. He needed stationery. Gil had a pad of Navy stationery, white paper with blue lines printed across a faint, faint screened image of an aircraft carrier. He found a ballpoint pen that actually worked, pulled out the folding metal chair, and set himself up on the ancient and well-worn dark green card table that served as a desk in the small and cluttered room.

He sat there, staring at Miss February. She stared back with a coy and empty-headed smile, unhelpful as always.

Then he started to write.

An old, old saying—ancient, no doubt, when the sailors of Carthage put to sea against the Romans—held that there were exactly three ways to do anything: the right way, the wrong way, and the Navy way. He wasn't entirely sure whether what he was doing now was right or wrong, but he knew damned well that it wasn't the Navy's way. He was letting himself in for a hell of a lot of trouble.

The Navy had a rigidly established way of doing things, a chain of command through which everything got done. To pull an end-run around that structure wasn't quite considered treason, but it could come close in certain quarters. If you complained to the guy who was in command of the guy over you, you were as much as saying your commanding officer couldn't do his job; worse, you identified yourself as a whiner, as a complainer, as someone who was both disloyal and unable or unwilling to play by the rules.

But, what the hell? They already knew he couldn't play by the rules, so one more infraction wasn't going to matter. The problem was who to complain to.

Randolph's talk in the bar a few weeks back about an old veteran of the UDT had gotten him thinking about one of the best-known characters in Navy Special Warfare . . . Captain Phillip Bucklew. Now *there* was a legend. Old Big Stoop was running the Navy Special Operations Group back at Coronado, though to date the instructions and advice coming out of Bucklew's office tended to be directly contradicted by orders that came out of MACV. Take the question of intelligence data, for instance. NOSG said the SEALs should be developing their own sources and aggressively patrolling in search of documents and prisoners who could put them on the track of real targets in the Rung Sat. But Kellerman, the NILO, wanted everything turned directly over to MACV and refused to approve any mission plan that hadn't originated with the REMFs in Saigon. . . .

Baxter wasn't certain that Bucklew was even in the direct chain of command between Det Delta and the Pentagon, a question that depended on how you looked at the tangled web of interconnected authorities and responsibilities that was the Military Assistance Command, Vietnam. Possibly he couldn't even help . . . but if anyone in the whole damned U.S. Navy should know what a clusterfuck the brass was making of things out here, it was Bucklew.

Shit, this letter could spell the end of his career, Baxter knew, but he simply did not care anymore. He'd entered the

SEAL program convinced that the SEALs could do great things, *wonderful* things, expanding the Navy's abilities in unconventional warfare, fighting Communism, creating a genuine democracy in Southeast Asia. But if no one allowed them to do what they'd been trained to do . . .

It would be better by far if the SEALs were simply withdrawn from Vietnam. He remembered those rumors he'd heard once of SEAL ops a few years back in Cuba. Maybe *that* was where the SEAL story ought to be written, in places where they could operate on their own, and at their own discretion. Trying to fight a war run by people who didn't understand them, didn't even *want* them, made SEAL ops in Nam a waste of everyone's time and talents.

He left a space at the top of the paper for the address. He would have to get that from O'Reilley over in Admin, after he was finished writing the thing.

"Dear Sir," he began.

For a long time, the tiny room was silent save for the scratching of Baxter's pen.

Monday, 23 May 1966

HQ, Naval Operations Support Group, Pacific Coronado, California 1445 hours

"Have a seat, Lieutenant. We've got a problem."

Tangretti sat down across the desk from Bucklew. He glanced at Howell, sitting in the other chair, but the man's expression was unreadable. What sort of problem had prompted Bucklew to call this meeting? Something Tangretti had done—or been accused of doing?

"Sir?" His query was cautious.

Bucklew pushed a paper across the desk. "Take a look at this. See what you make of it."

Tangretti scanned it quickly. Then, his attention caught, he read it through more slowly. There was silence in the office until he finally put it down, frowning. "This is one very unhappy SEAL," he said quietly.

"An understatement if I ever heard one," Bucklew com-

mented. "This Lieutenant Baxter makes it sound as if everything's coming apart over there. Do you think it's really as bad as
he makes out, Mr. Tangretti? Or is the strain too much for him?"

"He's a SEAL, by God," Tangretti exploded. "I can't believe
he can't handle a little stress. Since you're asking for my opinion,
sir, I'd have to say he's not exaggerating a damned thing. I know
what it's like, trying to conform to MACV and the rest of the
brass and still get some kind of decent job done. If you're willing
to just say 'fuck it' and do what you have to do, you'll get things
done . . . but if you try to please the powers-that-be at the same
time you're bound to run into trouble."

"The kind of answer I'd expect from you," Howell commented. "Have you *ever* tried looking at a problem from the
point of view of the officers in charge?"

"Damn it, Howell, even a blind man can see this kid's in
over his head!" Tangretti shot back. "I'd like to see you try
to handle life in the field, you—"

Bucklew held up his hands. "Gentlemen, please! This is
too important for us to get bogged down in petty arguments."

"Sorry, sir," Howell said. "I guess in the heat of the moment . . ."

"You're right, Captain," Tangretti overrode him. "This is
important." He picked up the paper again and read the phrase
that had first caught his eye. " 'This is not for us.' Baxter
thinks there's no place for SEAL operations in Vietnam at all.
If the CO on the spot feels that way . . ."

"It's intolerable!" Bucklew said sharply. "This is the only
war in town, people. If special warfare is going to have a
future in the Navy, we have to make a showing in Nam. That's
all there is to it."

Tangretti nodded grimly. "It looks to me like Baxter's still
mired down in the same kind of problems we saw with Jackstay. Spotty intelligence work, too many restrictions from
higher up, no clear-cut objectives . . . that would make anybody crazy. It's like I've said before, sir . . . we need to cut
the SEALs loose from headquarters' apron strings. They've
got the ability to make a real impact on the war, but you can't
keep them in a straitjacket and still expect them to do the job."

"From the sounds of this," Howell said, gesturing toward
the letter from Baxter, "I'd say a straitjacket is about what we
need right now. What could have possessed the man to go

outside channels and write to you this way, Captain? What kind of people are we turning out in the SEALs, anyhow?''

"Real go-getters who know what needs to be done and how they can get there," Tangretti put in before Bucklew could respond. "I've seen Baxter's service record. The man's a top-notch officer. Damned fine SEAL, too. That's why it's getting to him over there, I guarantee it. When I was over in Nam, I felt like cutting loose and letting HQ know what was wrong too, a time or ten. Difference is, Baxter doesn't think he can push the envelope. I did . . . and I got results, too."

"Maybe so," Bucklew said. "But we can't just operate independently of the chain of command over there. MACV has their own notions of how to run the war, and we can't just go thumbing our noses at them. I'll say it again . . . this is the only war in town. If we wear out our welcome with the folks who are running it, they won't invite us back."

"And if our own SEALs are so screwed up they want to chuck it all and pull out, how much of a future do we have then?" Tangretti countered. "Look, we may not be able to go against MACV directives *officially*, but we sure as hell ought to let our people know there are things they could do . . . shall we say when nobody's looking? Turn 'em loose for the kind of patrol and ambush work they do best, the way we were talking a few weeks back. Tell Baxter to quit worrying so much what MACV thinks. If he starts producing results, *real* results, the brass will have to let him have his head."

"You can't be serious," Howell said. "We can't go on record with a suggestion like that! Anyway, you're just looking for an excuse to let those maniacs of yours off their leash. I swear, you're trying to turn these SEALs into a whole separate army!"

"What I want is to see them used for what President Kennedy created them for in the first place," Tangretti grated. "Special warfare doesn't operate under the same rules as the regular Navy. It can't. We have to be able to play to our own strengths: independence, creativity, surprise, stealth. You don't get that operating under a bunch of fat-assed bureaucrats who wouldn't know a battlefield from a barroom brawl."

"But where does it all end?" the aide demanded. "You skim off the best men from the Navy and puff them up about how great they are. You give them a chance to choose their own weapons and gear, even if it means going outside normal procurement channels." Howell favored Tangretti with a dark look. "You turn them into a law unto themselves and talk about letting them loose to win the war on their own. What are you going to ask for next? Artillery? Tanks? Air support? Why stop at a handful of SEALs when you can send over a whole mob of them? We'll just tell the Marines and the Army that it's time for them to go home and let our guys handle the mess, huh?"

Tangretti frowned. "I said we had to play to our strengths. That doesn't mean turning the SEALs into a bunch of ersatz soldiers. They're not cut out for heavy equipment . . . or for the kind of top-heavy supervision the regular services have, either. SEALs won't win the war alone, Lieutenant. But they'll make a hell of a difference if they're just allowed to do what they have to." He looked at Bucklew. "I know we can't get completely out from under MACV, Captain. But couldn't we get 'em to ease up a little? If they'd cut Baxter and his people a little slack, it would sure make things go more smoothly all the way around."

"What do you have in mind?" Bucklew asked. He didn't sound particularly encouraging . . . but neither had he cut Tangretti off out of hand.

"Just . . . a little more freedom for Baxter to come up with his own mission plans, instead of waiting for headquarters to decide what they want done. Maybe some more cooperation between departments." He held up the letter again. "Baxter seems pretty upset over this fuck-up . . . this mess with the South Vietnamese agent who got waxed by the SEAL patrol in the Rung Sat. SEPES never bothered to let our people know they were inserting operatives into the VC units in the area. And our liaison people haven't been going out of their way to keep the Vietnamese up to speed either. It's a crime, when you've got that kind of confusion between so-called allies. We never had that kind of problem working with the Brits before Normandy."

"The Brits weren't riddled with enemy agents," Bucklew said. "But I take your point. I don't know how much pull we'll have with the MACV staff, but we can see what kind of cooperation we can get. I don't know if it'll be enough, though. And I do *not* approve of your notion of encouraging the SEALs to ignore MACV directives."

"No, sir, I didn't really figure you would," Tangretti said with a rueful smile. "Thought I'd take a shot, though."

"Meanwhile, we still have the letter to deal with," Howell

said. "And particularly our Lieutenant Baxter. If he wants to be relieved so bad, maybe that's just what we should do. Yank him out of there now before he does something really stupid."

"That would be a big mistake, sir," Tangretti countered. "His tour's up in a couple of months anyway. Pulling him out early would be a real slap in the face. Or an admission that what he said here was right, that there really isn't a place for his outfit over there."

"Agreed. We can't have lieutenants deciding SEAL policies." Bucklew gave Tangretti a long, telling look. "But we could step up the rotation schedule, get his replacements over in July instead of early August. Maybe a new man can tackle things from a fresh perspective, get our operations over there back on track. What do you think, Mr. Tangretti?"

He nodded slowly. "That would help," he said thoughtfully. "That would help a lot. . . ."

"All right, then," Bucklew said, leaning back in his chair. "I'll get off a reply to our wayward Lieutenant Baxter and tell him he's stuck for the duration. He might as well try to see ways he can *use* the SEALs, instead of crouching in a corner and complaining of what he *can't* do. And we'll implement as many of these other ideas as we can. Thank you both, gentlemen. You've been a big help."

Back at his desk in the outer office, Tangretti picked up his phone and dialed the number for one of the SEAL barracks in the compound across the street. It took a few minutes to track down his quarry, but eventually a familiar voice came on the line.

"Talk to me. It's your nickel."

"Spence? This is Gator. Meet me in town tonight . . . nineteen hundred hours. At the . . . at Mickey's Place. We have to talk, buddy. . . ."

Mickey's Place
San Diego, California
2025 hours

Tangretti had been in the bar a few times before. It was smaller and quieter than the Anchorage, and there were no dark-haired complications among the waitresses. But he hadn't been out drinking with Spencer or any other SEALs since the night he'd ended up with Sheila Martin, and ordinarily he wouldn't have wanted to risk a repeat of that unfortunate binge.

But tonight he was on SEAL business, however unsanctioned and unofficial.

"Sounds pretty grim, Gator," Mike Spencer said as he wrapped up his account of the meeting with Bucklew and Howell. "I know Ed Baxter. He's not the kind to let shit get to him like that."

"Well, I should have known what he was going to be up against," Tangretti said, taking a sip from a glass of beer. "It never changes. The brass screw around, and the guys out on the line are the ones to pay for it."

"So why tell me about it?"

"You're the senior chief in your platoon, right?"

"Yeah." Spencer took a sip. "Can't say it ever did me much good."

"What's your platoon CO like?"

"Wilson? He's a pretty good guy . . . for an officer." Spencer grinned. "Likes to get down and dirty with the men. A lot like a guy I knew back in Korea once . . . except he's prettier than you ever were."

"Glad to hear it," Tangretti said. "Okay, look. If this Wilson's the kind of officer who listens to what his chiefs have to say . . ."

"He is," Spencer said.

"Then I think you'd be doing everyone a favor if you started to let him know how the real world works." Tangretti finished his glass and wiped his mouth with his sleeve. "If he goes in knowing the score, maybe he'll be smart enough to see he can't please everybody . . . and the only way he's going to get the job done is to ignore those fat-assed bastards in Saigon and concentrate on running his unit. Know what I mean?"

"Don't they call that 'inciting to mutiny'?"

"Only if they catch you, Spence," Tangretti said with a grin. "Only if they catch you. . . ."

Chapter 11

Friday, 10 June 1966

Virginia Beach, Virginia
1745 hours

"Hey, make way for a SEAL!" Torpedoman Second Class Henry Elliot Richardson, Jr., called out as he opened the front door and stepped into the foyer with the swagger he deemed appropriate for a Navy man on liberty. It wasn't until he'd closed the front door and muffled the street noises outside that he heard the sounds of a woman sobbing.

Richardson hurried into the living room. "Mom? What's the matter, Mom?" He swallowed uncertainly as he caught sight of his mother, dabbing at her eyes with a handkerchief. "Has something . . . Is it Dad?"

Veronica Tangretti looked up at him with a blank expression. Richardson found himself realizing how *old* she looked, as if she'd aged years in the time since his last weekend home. It wasn't so much a physical change, though. She was still slender without looking frail, and if her black hair was a little more streaked with gray than the last time he'd seen her, it still hadn't changed all that much. It was her attitude that made her seem older, a dullness in her eyes instead of the sparkle he remembered from his childhood years . . . the drab, faded dress . . . the air of a woman who was past caring about her looks or her life any longer.

He hated the thought. Richardson had never known his father, killed long before his birth. His mother had been the only stable thing in his life, and he didn't like to contemplate the changes in her these last few months.

Ever since the fight with Dad, he thought bitterly. His step-father had been a part of his life for so long that it was hard to think of him as anything but his real father. When his mother had started her long-distance fight with Steve Tangretti over his desire to have the family join him in California, Richardson had felt caught in the middle. Of course, he wouldn't have been directly involved, since he lived on base and would stay in Little Creek as long as the Navy wanted him there. But somehow his mother had managed to drag him into the middle of the fight by claiming she didn't want to move away and leave him behind. Richardson had done his best to hide it, but he'd resented his mother's stubbornness from the very begin-ning of the fight. She had used his half-brother Bill and Rich-ardson himself to gain an advantage over their father, and he didn't much care for that.

Particularly since Steve Tangretti had never treated Rich-ardson as a weapon in his personal arsenal. Tangretti had never tried to present himself as a substitute for Richardson's dead father, not even when family strains made things tough. His father's parents, particularly his grandfather, had insisted they wanted the family name to go on, and Tangretti had gone along with their wishes. He had never allowed their digs about his financial status or his Navy career to come between them and young Richardson, although his stubborn pride had made the pressure on him all the stronger. And as Richardson grew up Steve Tangretti had been as much a friend as a father, so much so that he'd decided to join the Navy as an enlisted man straight out of high school and try for a spot with the SEALs Tangretti had founded. It had meant turning his back on the fancy college his grandfather had picked out for him, and even risking the trust fund that would have made his life very com-fortable indeed, but Hank Richardson had wanted to show Tangretti how much he respected and loved him.

"Did something happen to Dad?" he repeated, feeling a knot in his stomach. Steve Tangretti had lived on the edge for a long time, especially since the creation of the SEALs. Since he'd joined the Teams himself Richardson knew better than most the risks his stepfather had been running all those years.

But he'd come back to the States safe and sound. . . .

"Your father's . . . fine. . . ." Richardson's mother looked away. "At least I haven't heard from him . . . not since that tape last week. *You* heard it. . . ."

"Then what's *wrong*?" Richardson demanded. "What's got you so upset, Mom?"

She still wouldn't meet his eyes. "It's . . . it's your brother." Her voice quavered, still on the edge of tears. "He . . . he's . . ."

Richardson knelt beside her chair. "Take it easy, Mom," he said softly. "What's wrong with Bill? How can I help?"

"You!" That was a whipcrack, angry and harsh. "You've done enough already! You and your father both!"

He recoiled from the sudden attack. "Mom, please . . . I don't understand what's wrong. What have we done? What's wrong with Bill?" Richardson was getting really worried now. It took a lot to break through Veronica Tangretti's control. She had been a Navy wife for more than twenty years, and Navy wives learned how to cope with almost anything.

"He went down to the Recruiting Office today," she said, her voice muffled by her handkerchief as she started to sob again. "Signed his enlistment papers . . . didn't say anything about it, not until it was too late. . . ."

"Bill signed up?" Richardson couldn't keep the puzzled note out of his voice. *That* was what had upset his mother so badly? He would have thought she'd be proud. . . . "What's wrong with that? He didn't . . . he didn't go for the Air Farce, or something shameful like that, did he?"

His joke didn't work. She turned angry, red-rimmed eyes on him. "Maybe you think it's funny," she said. "Maybe you're so caught up in the service that you don't know what it's been like for me . . . just like your father! The Navy took Hank away from me before I ever had a chance to get to know him. And it's been the only thing your father . . . your step-father . . . ever *really* loved. I put up with that . . . I didn't even speak up when you decided you had to join up, even though I hated the thought. But now Bill, too? Hasn't the Navy taken enough away from me? It isn't *fair*!"

"Mom . . ." Richardson hesitated, then took her hand. "Mom, I'm sorry. I didn't know you didn't want me in the Navy. But it was just something I had to do, you know? After everything Dad told me . . . about my real father, I mean. I thought it was . . . the right thing to do."

She jerked her hand away. "You made your decision," she said, her voice bleak. "I learned to live with it. But now Bill's going, too. And with that awful war in Vietnam getting worse all the time . . . you can see how bad it is, on the six o'clock news every night . . . I just know I'm going to lose one of you, sooner or later. You, or Bill, or Steve . . ."

"Mom . . . Dad's back in the States now. And Bill's always been the smart one in the family. Odds are he'll get posted to some really top-notch A school, end up in the Hospital Corps or Engineering or something like that. The odds are against him getting assigned to anything very dangerous. Even when he gets sea duty, he'll probably be on some nice, safe ship in the Med. And me . . . well, SEALs get some pretty rough jobs, sometimes, and there's a chance they'll start sending us to Nam out of Little Creek. But they trained me every way they knew how, to teach me how to stay alive. None of us is in all that much danger, Mom . . . really." He didn't add that most of the East Coast SEALs, himself included, had already put in for duty in Vietnam if the rumors about Team Two drawing duty in Southeast Asia turned out to be true. Richardson, like most SEALs, was eager to see action in a real war zone, but he knew better than to upset his mother further with such talk.

She shook her head. "You can't just put me off by saying I'm overreacting," she told him. "I've been a Navy wife too long. Your father's too damn stubborn to retire, and I just know he'll put in for more time overseas if they let him. And Bill . . . what makes you think he'll choose anything but the SEALs once he's in? He's as bad as you and your father, always talking about how exciting it must be to be a frogman. . . ."

"Bill? In the Teams?" Richardson laughed. "Mom, Bill's a good kid, but he wouldn't last ten minutes in Hell Week! I mean, he's the serious straight-A student, right? Hates gym class. Hardly dated all through high school, and never even *thought* about smoking or boozing. He'd never fit into an outfit like the SEALs, Mom. Believe me."

"Maybe you ought to tell him that," she said. "Because I heard him telling his buddies all about joining up, after he got back this afternoon, and I heard him say he wanted to be a SEAL . . . just like his brother."

Richardson frowned. "Oh, God . . . maybe he's not the smart one after all. Where is he?"

"Up in his room. He went up there and slammed the door on me because he thought I was treating him like a little kid. . . ." She looked away. "Maybe I did, a little. He's always been my baby. . . ."

Richardson stood up slowly, trying to keep from letting his emotions show on his face. He'd always had the sense that his mother disapproved of him somehow. It wasn't that she didn't love him . . . but sometimes it seemed as if she resented him at the same time. Maybe it was because he reminded her of the husband she'd lost in Normandy . . . or maybe it was because of the strain he had added to her marriage with Steve Tangretti. There had been a time, early on, when he'd been like a little ghost of the first marriage, and thanks to Richardson's grandparents and their insistence that he keep his name that ghost had never been completely exorcised.

Or perhaps she just had some natural mother's instinct to love the younger, more vulnerable child a little bit more . . . especially since Hank Richardson had grown up to be the kind of son his stepfather could really relate to, while Bill Tangretti had turned out quite a bit different.

"I'll talk to him, Mom," Richardson said quietly. He was out of the living room and halfway up the front stairs before his mother even stirred to look after him.

The door to the bedroom he'd shared with his half-brother was closed, but Richardson tried the knob and found it wasn't locked. He went in without knocking. "Well, Tadpole, looks like you really managed to screw up this time," he said.

Bill Tangretti sat up on his bed. Since Richardson had joined the Navy, he'd taken over the whole room for himself. Richardson still found it strange that the bunk beds were gone and his sports posters and memorabilia had been taken down and stored in the attic. "Don't you know how to knock?" Tangretti demanded. "And stop calling me Tadpole!"

Richardson had been using the nickname for years, and he wasn't about to give it up now. Not when it was the best way he knew for getting his younger brother's goat. Bill's father was a frogman, after all, and Tadpole was just such an apt name. . . .

"Sorry," Richardson said, not meaning it. "I forgot. Look, Tadpole, Mom's crying her eyes out down there. What the hell were you thinking of, to upset her like that? You know how it's been . . . ever since Dad went to Coronado."

Tangretti looked away. "It wasn't my fault." he said. "She overheard me talking to Tommy and Jeff, and it set her off. And once she got started, everything I said just made it worse. You know how it is, sometimes. . . ."

"Doesn't excuse you from what you did," he said, sitting on the edge of the bed. "What's all this about joining up, anyway?"

"Hey, look, my eighteenth birthday was last week. I'm out of high school and old enough to strike out on my own. *You* did."

"I told Mom and Dad about my plans first," Richardson countered. "I didn't sneak off and enlist and then let them find out because they heard me telling a bunch of my friends about it."

"And would it have helped if I'd told her?" Tangretti looked stubborn. Though he took after their mother in his appearance—small, slender, with features that could almost be described as delicate—at that moment Richardson could see a strong resemblance to his stepfather in the younger man's expression. "She'd have argued . . . and then she'd have cried . . . and I might not have been able to go through with it. And I *had* to, Hank. I just had to."

"Why? C'mon, Tadpole, with your brains you'd breeze through college. Why join the Navy?"

Tangretti looked at him with a sour gleam in his eye. "You're the one with the trust fund, not me, remember? I doubt the folks have enough money to send me to barber college. The Navy'll give me a shot at some G.I. Bill money."

"This isn't about money," Richardson said. "Dad told me he had a way figured to borrow money against the trust fund so you could go to school, and I okayed it. Quit kidding around, Tadpole, and tell me what's really going on."

"Can't I be as patriotic as you are?" Tangretti asked. "Just once? Can't I have good reasons of my own? Or are you the only one who's allowed to serve his country?" He shrugged, looking away. "Look, I've already made up my mind, and nobody's stopping me. Not Mom, not you . . . nobody."

Richardson studied him for a long moment before responding. "Still jealous . . . that's it, isn't it? You think I've got something going in the Navy, so you just have to have a piece of it yourself. Like that time you almost drowned yourself trying to get a seashell on the beach because you were jealous of the one I had.''

"The one Dad gave you," Tangretti said quietly. He wasn't bothering to hide the bitterness in his voice.

"God, Bill, are you still hung up on that? Dad loves you . . . you know he does. You're his real son, not me.''

"Then how is it he doesn't treat me that way, huh?" Tangretti shook his head slowly. "Yeah, he loves me. And Mom thinks I'm the baby who needs looking after . . . Sometimes I just can't stand it, Hank. When you turned sixteen, Dad took you to a strip joint, said it would help you turn into a real man. When I turned sixteen, I got fifty bucks and a card telling me to spend the money on whatever books I wanted . . . and *he* was overseas, couldn't even manage a phone call to say 'Happy Birthday.' Dad may love me, but he sure as hell doesn't *like* me . . . not the way he likes you. You're his buddy . . . I'm just his son, who reads too many books and spends all his time studying.''

Richardson gave him a twisted smile. "I'm his buddy, all right . . . his dead buddy, from the war. He thinks I'm a pocket edition of my real father, so he treats me that way. You've heard the stories about Good Ol' Hank Senior, the condom king. But you . . . you're his son. You're the one he's really proud of. You're just . . . not the kind of guy to take carousing. Some people would say that's a pretty good compliment, y'know?''

"Yeah. Maybe." Tangretti mustered a rueful grin. "But sometimes I wish I was more like you, Hank. I wish I could get just one 'attaboy' out of the Old Man. That's why I'm going Navy . . . and why I'm going to put in for SEALs first chance I get.''

Richardson frowned. "Mom said you were talking about that. Do you have any idea what you're getting into?''

"How could I live in this house and *not* know?" Tangretti asked with a shrug. "Yeah, it's tough to get in, and tougher to stay in . . . but it's something I have to do, Hank. It's either that or start growing a beard, 'cause I won't be able to look at myself in the mirror if I don't give it my best shot.''

"You're really serious about this, aren't you, Tadpole?" Richardson studied him closely. "Look, I think I know what you're going through . . . a little bit, at least. It ain't easy to live up to Dad's expectations, sometimes. At least it isn't easy to fit into his image of my father.''

''At least he *has* expectations *you* have to live up to,'' Tangretti responded. ''I just want to have him look at me the way he looks at you. Just one time, I'd like him to have the same *kind* of pride in me. Not that 'I'm proud of my son, the class brain' crap, either. You and I both know that what he respects is the SEALs, first, last, and always. So that's where I'm going.''

''You could be letting yourself in for a real disappointment, Bill,'' Richardson said softly. ''I've seen a bunch of guys who couldn't cut Hell Week, some of them a lot bigger and tougher than you. That's not a put-down. That's just the way it is. We're not all cut out to be SEALs.''

''Oh, I know the odds are against me. But at least I'll take a shot at it. Maybe that'll at least get Dad to look at me different. At least he'll know I tried for it.'' Tangretti looked stubborn. ''But I'll do a hell of a lot more than just try. I'll make it . . . you just watch me.''

Richardson clapped him on the shoulder. ''Whether you make it or not, kid, you're all right in my book. I hope you pull it off. . . .'' He looked away. ''But that still doesn't help square things with Mom, does it? She's convinced we're all going to end up in the middle of the war, and that's got her scared.''

''Yeah.'' Tangretti looked glum. ''God, I hate seeing her like that. But she just doesn't understand . . . not about me and Dad. Not about me and . . . myself. I have to see this through . . . but I sure wish I had her in my corner.''

''You want my advice, Tadpole?'' Richardson asked. ''Just cool things down a little. Don't try to argue with her, and don't try to convince her about how right you are. And by the same token, don't give her the chance to try to talk you into anything. It'll be tough, but if you can just give it some time without making things any worse, things are bound to get better. Mom's solid, and once she realizes you've made up your mind she won't stand in your way . . . even if she still doesn't like it.''

''That's a pretty tall order,'' Tangretti said. ''What am I supposed to do? Hide out up here until it's time to report to boot camp next month?''

''Just . . . don't be obvious.'' Richardson spread his hands and shrugged. "Hell, I don't know how you *do* it. But if you want to be a SEAL, you'd better start learning how to adapt your tactics to a changing battlefield situation, y'know what I mean? Otherwise you might as well chuck it now and go make peace."

"No surrender!" Tangretti said in his best imitation of his father's gruff voice.

"That's the spirit," Richardson said. He looked away. He'd come up promising his mother he'd talk Tangretti out of his decision, and he felt like a traitor to be encouraging him instead. But he understood something of his half-brother's feelings, maybe better than Bill did himself. The youngest Tangretti had been a pawn caught between his parents for too long now, and he needed to get out and prove himself once and for all . . . not just to earn his father's respect, but, far more important, to earn his own. "Tell you what, Tadpole. It's been a while since your sixteenth birthday . . . What say I take you to a little club my buddies and I hang out at sometimes? If you're gonna be a SEAL, you'd best start learning the ropes."

Tangretti gave him a half-hearted grin. "Mom'll have your scalp if she thought you were taking me to a strip joint. . . ."

"Yeah . . . but Dad would be all for it, wouldn't he? Make a man out of you." Richardson stood up. "I'll tell Mom the truth, though. I'm gonna take you out and tell you horror stories about the SEALs, and if you have the common sense God gave a potato it'll be enough to talk you out of this nonsense. Not that you're anywhere close to a potato in the common sense department, Tadpole."

"Thanks a lot . . . Junior," Tangretti replied, using Richardson's most common nickname. "But go easy on me. I'm not one of your SEAL buddies. Not yet."

Richardson watched him change his shirt and slap some after shave on his face. He wasn't sure Bill Tangretti would be up to the challenge of the SEALs . . . but he was damned proud of his younger brother for having the grit to try.

Chapter 12

HQ, Military Assistance Command, Vietnam
Saigon
1000 hours

Click-click.

Lieutenant Charles Wilson stood at a relaxed, not-quite attention, watching with mild interest as Captain Quinton Garland read the sheaf of closely typed orders. He held the bundle of papers in his left hand; his right hand, on which he wore the large, gold ring of a graduate of the U.S. Naval Academy, was resting on the polished desktop, palm down. From time to time, Garland would flick his ring finger twice, tapping the desk with the heavy gold. *Click-click.*

A ring-knocker, Wilson thought to himself. *This is going to be fun. . . .*

Wilson felt like part of a study in contrasts. Both he and Garland were wearing their Navy whites, but the uniform worn by the executive officer of the MACV's Navy Advisory Group in Vietnam was spotlessly crisp and pressed, the rows of colored ribbons on his left breast perfectly aligned, his face closely shaved, his shoes so brightly polished they flashed in the room's fluorescent lighting when he leaned back and crossed one leg over the other. Wilson's uniform, on the other hand, looked as though he'd slept in it—which, in fact, he had. He'd arrived in Saigon two hours ago, after a day-long series of flights aboard an Air Force C-130 transport, island-hopping from North Island Naval Air Station to Hawaii to Guam to Clark's Field in the Philippines, and finally in to Tan Son Nhut. He'd found orders waiting for him there directing him to report immediately to Captain Garland in Saigon. Wilson hadn't taken the time to shower or change or even shave after the long flight, and he imagined he must present a somewhat piratical picture just now. His bags were still waiting in the outer office.

Wilson had had the impression that Garland was drawing this ceremony out, pretending to go over the orders in meticulous detail just to keep him standing there. He'd already been kept waiting in the exec's outer office for nearly an hour, but Wilson wasn't particularly bothered. He considered himself to be a student of bureaucratic idiocy; he loved watching bureaucrats do what they did best, and he had the feeling that with Garland he was in the presence of a master.

At long last, Garland leaned forward in his comfortable swivel chair, uncrossing his legs and carefully replacing the orders atop the rest of the documents Wilson had brought in the string-tied manila envelope, straightening the corners of the stack with geometric precision. The sound of multiple typewriters clacking on a dozen desks floated through the thin door of Garland's office.

"I don't like this," Garland said.

The sentence appeared to be a simple statement of fact, and one that did not require a response. Wilson stood his ground in front of Garland's desk. An air conditioner clattered in the wall nearby. *Christ* the guy liked his office cold. Outside, on the streets of Saigon, it must be ninety degrees, with that steamy, tropical oppressiveness that was the sure forerunner of a downpour.

"I don't like this one damned bit," Garland continued. "If I had my way, Lieutenant, every one of you SEALs would be shipped the hell out of this country."

"Would the captain care to tell me why?" Wilson said, keeping his voice carefully neutral.

"Because everybody back stateside seems to think that you SEALs are some kind of *wünkerkind*, super-sailors who are going to win the war for us over here. But the SEALs *I've* seen and worked for are some of the most slovenly, lazy, no-good, no-account slackers it has been my misfortune to command since I left the Academy.'' Impatiently, he flicked his finger again, tapping the desktop. *Click-click-click.*

''I understand the officer I'm to relieve has not conducted many patrols recently. . . .''

''*No* patrols! None. Zip. For two weeks! If you ask me, Lieutenant, I think Baxter's got short-timer's disease.''

A short timer was someone who didn't have long to go before leaving the Navy or, in this case, before leaving Nam for the United States. A certain reluctance to risk getting killed or wounded scant days before you were scheduled to rotate home was understandable, perhaps . . . but SEALs were expected to show more initiative, and considerably more gumption, than that.

Baxter's slackness was hard to understand. Wilson had reviewed the man's service records and fitness reports carefully, and noted that he'd been an exemplary officer in all regards, at least up until the past month or two. His Quarterly Evaluation for June had been abysmal, a sure-fire career-wrecker if he'd had any plans to get beyond the rank of lieutenant: *Lieutenant j.g. Baxter shows less than perfect diligence in the performance of his duties as a naval officer. He has shown undue familiarity with the enlisted personnel under his command and has repeatedly questioned the orders of his superiors. . . .*

With a quarterly like that, Baxter most certainly needed no enemies. He would be lucky if he made full lieutenant with *that* in his record, and he would most assuredly never make lieutenant commander after that. Of course, the evaluator who'd written that little gem of understated career homicide had been Commander George White, and Wilson knew that there was a feud between those two men. Something about a letter Baxter had written last May to the CO-NOSGPAC.

So what had happened to the eager-beaver young j.g. who'd led the first SEAL direct-action group into to Vietnam five months ago?

Wilson had arrived from CONUS with eighteen others, four officers and fourteen men, formerly members of Platoons Golf and Hotel of SEAL Team One. One of the old Det Delta men had somehow wangled another tour, and he was joining the new unit, Detachment Golf, along with some other new arrivals. Det Golf would now number five officers and twenty enlisted men, operating out of Nha Be in the Rung Sat Special Zone. Wilson had accepted the assignment eagerly, but now he was wondering if he and his men hadn't just stepped into a war zone even worse than the Rung Sat itself.

"All of that's going to change now, sir," Wilson said. He gestured toward the stack of documents. "Det Delta's going home in a few weeks. From now on, Det Golf is going to be running patrols in the Rung Sat, and I promise you, things are going to be very different."

"So you say. I still find this entire concept of naval commandos just a bit ludicrous, Lieutenant. What the hell are *sailors* supposed to do miles inland from the sea? Sounds to me like the Navy's just trying to muscle in on the Marines' territory."

"Possibly, though there are plenty back in CONUS who would disagree. The Navy needs Special Warfare, to handle jobs ashore that you can't take care of with battleships or carrier strikes. I'm sure you've seen Commander Anderson's order."

Five days earlier, Lieutenant Commander Franklin Anderson had taken over command of SEAL Team One, and one of his first official acts had been to expand the scope of SEAL activities in Vietnam.

"I have. And it doesn't change a damned thing. Frankly, there's nothing I can do about this planned increase of SEAL forces in Vietnam, but I will tell you this. Me and every officer in the chain of command above you in NAVADVGRU and the MACV are going to have our eyes on you, Lieutenant." He tapped a warning forefinger on the stack of orders. "I've already had more than my share of trouble with your people. If you or they get out of line just once, if you fail to deliver, if you screw up, I personally am going to throw the lot of you on the first plane out of here. And the report I write and send off after you will set fire to desks from here to the Navy Department. You will be damned lucky to find yourself in command of a flotilla of kayaks operating out of Adak, Alaska. You read me, mister?"

"Loud and clear, sir."

"Where are your men now?"

"Already on their way to Nha Be. Your orders said you wanted to see me this morning, not them, and I thought it would be better if they went on ahead and got settled in.''

"Hmph. Very well. You'll be relieving Baxter, of course. He will be shipping out in a day or two. Back to the States.'' His tone of voice suggested he thought that the man was getting off too easily. "You'll be in command of the old Det Delta people at least for the next couple-three weeks, until their paperwork comes through. The idea is that they can pass on to your people whatever they've learned during their tour. Your NILO at Nha Be will be Lieutenant Blanding. He's a good officer. Pay attention to what he says, let him show you the ropes.''

In other words, Wilson thought, reading between the lines, *don't pay attention to whatever Baxter or his pirates have to say.* "Aye-aye, sir.''

"I'll give it to you straight, Lieutenant. From everything I've heard here, morale in the SEAL camp down at Nha Be is shot. I've had, shit, I don't even want to think about how many reports I've had come across my desk. Drunkenness. Fights. Disorderly conduct. A week ago, a couple of those kids stole two PBRs and were drag-racing them down the Soi Rap.''

"Stole them, sir?''

"Misappropriated. I can't prove it yet, but I think someone forged Commander White's signature on a requisition. Internal Security is still looking into that one.''

Wilson raised his eyebrows. "That's shocking!''

Garland's eyes narrowed, as though he wasn't quite certain whether Wilson's response was supposed to be straight or sarcastic. "Indeed it is.''

"Did you get them back?''

"One of them had to be towed off a mud bank by an LCM and was subsequently logged for fifteen hours of unscheduled maintenance. The jet intakes on those Jacuzzi units, you understand, are easily fouled, and plowing them through thirty yards of mud doesn't do them or the engines any good. Those new patrol boats draw nine inches, but I think that SEAL thought he could fly the thing. Hell, the guy probably *was* flying . . . on Thirty-Three.''

"Thirty-Three?''

"You'll find out. It's a brand of Vietnamese beer. I think the French introduced it, originally, but the locals have improved on the recipe.'' He shook his head, frowning disapproval. "Wicked stuff, worse than white lightning, worse than the worst home-brew you could imagine. Smells like embalming fluid. They say it kills you and pickles you with one jolt."

"You know, Captain," Wilson said, "it would help me tremendously if you could have one of your people type up a list for me."

"A list?" Garland's eyes narrowed suspiciously. "What kind of list?"

"A list of all of the irregularities, problems, reports, complaints . . . anything you feel that I, as the new commanding officer of this SEAL unit, should know. This is a completely new unit, Captain. New personnel. A new CO. We intend to deliver."

Garland studied Wilson for a moment, and the SEAL officer could almost see the interior walls coming down. That's what it took to handle fat-assed chair-warmers like this one: get them to vent their spleen for a bit, then make a proposal that actually seemed to go out of the way to accommodate the guy. Suggest something that added a bit to the workload of his own people—that was always a good touch, a way for him to justify his own position and improve his internal prestige. Bait the hook with the attitude that you really *cared* about what he cared about.

The key to a bureaucrat's heart, in Wilson's experience, was recognition of his power, and acknowledgment of the reach and scope of his personal empire.

"You might start with your uniform and personal appearance, Lieutenant. It sets a bad example for the men in your command to be seen in rumpled whites, no shave. . . ."

"I could not agree more, Captain. Your order, however, said immediately. I came here straight off the plane. If you would prefer that I come back in an hour or two, more presentable—"

"Oh, that will hardly be necessary," Garland said, giving a casual wave-off with his hand. "This is a war zone, after all. In future, though, you will note that proper dress is expected of all personnel in Saigon."

"Of *course,* sir."

Garland tapped the line of ribbons on his breast. "Appropriate ribbons and awards *are* to be worn. They are a proper part of the uniform and will be regarded as part of the uniform of the day."

Wilson read the man's ribbons, aligned in rows of three above his shirt pocket. Bronze Star. Navy Distinguished Service. Legion of Merit, Legionnaire. Navy and Marine Corps Medal. Armed Forces Expeditionary. National Defense. Vietnam Service. Joint Service Achievement. Good Conduct. A half-dozen or so others that he didn't even recognize. Shit, the only *combat* medal in the lot was the Bronze Star . . . and even that one, nowadays, could be awarded ''for heroic or meritorious achievement or service,'' meaning you didn't have to be shot at to get it.

''Particularly when you have such a proud rack to display,'' Wilson said. ''Um, I really could use that list of problems you've been having with the unit.''

''Well, ah, um,'' Garland said. ''That is, my office is extremely busy, just now. But perhaps I can have one of my yeomen run something off. I must say, though, that I'm delighted at your attitude, Mr. Wilson. My office has not been properly appreciated by Mr. Baxter or his people up to now. It will be a refreshing change to have some cooperation from the Nha Be SEAL detachment. Of course, if there's anything my people can do for you, be certain to requisition it.''

In triplicate, and with the proper counter signatures, Wilson added mentally. But he grinned. ''Absolutely, Captain Garland. You can bank on it!''

U.S. Naval Base
Nha Be
1245 hours

Wilson stepped off the bus into a muddy dirt road. The ruts were half full of brown rain water, and the air was still wet from the lingering freshening of the storm that had passed an hour earlier. Rather than making the air smell fresh, however, there was a distinct odor hanging over the camp of decay, the proximity, Wilson guessed—*hoped*—of the Rung Sat marshes.

The camp was dingy and dirty. Mud was everywhere, laundry was hung like white and olive-drab pennants from crisscrossing laundry lines. Garbage cans were full to overflowing. The debris extended beyond the fenced-in perimeters of the camp and into the village of Nha Be that rambled along the river bank nearby. The village was fairly modern, more up-to-date than Wilson had imagined it would be. There was a laundromat, a restaurant, and several buildings that looked like they were probably brothels. The streets were littered with trash and paper. Wilson wondered whether the filth of the base had contaminated the town, or if it had been the other way around.

Parts of the camp were well-ordered, he noted. A fair-sized river patrol boat facility had been set up here, and a number of the new PBRs were pulled up at the wooden piers and docks extending into the river. A large barn had been erected at the top of railroad tracks running down a concrete ramp into the water, where boats could be hauled out of the water and taken inside for inspection and maintenance. Craft at the piers or riding at anchor further out included a dozen PBRs and twice that many LCPLs, LCMs, and other landing craft, as well as an array of junks, sampans, and river coasters.

The small part of the base set aside for the SEALs, however, showed evidence of considerable decay . . . both in the discarded food on the ground and in the general atmosphere of the place that reflected the state of the occupants' morale. Things were bad here, that was certain, and they'd been getting that way for a long, long time. Wilson wondered why one of Baxter's superiors hadn't come in and taken things in hand. Then he remembered Garland's mirror-polished shoes and realized that the men in Saigon probably never got this far out in the boondocks . . . even when "this far out" was a matter of a few miles.

A high-pitched whine, like a subdued jet engine, caught his ear. Stopping and turning, he saw a small boat, a PBR, moving "on a step," its nose high and well out of the water as it balanced on a rooster tail of white spray. Some distance astern, a solitary figure trailed the patrol boat, kicking up his own wake from a single large water ski as he clung to a tow rope invisible at this range.

"Shit, Skipper," Chief Mike Spencer's voice said behind him. "What have we gotten ourselves into?"

Wilson turned. "Hi, Spence. Got the boys squared away?"

"Yes, sir. Getting there, anyway. The accommodations kind of leave something to be desired, you know?"

"We'll have it shipshape in no time."

"And those clowns?" Spencer nodded toward the PBR. The boat was making a broad turn in mid-river, pulling a crack-the-whip on the trailing skier. The man tried to navigate the turn, faltered, and vanished in a cloud of white spray.

"Those clowns are SEALs too," Wilson said. "They'll fall into line. I just hate to think of what's been *wasted*."

A wooden sign outside the door identified the hootch for junior officers. Walking inside, Wilson was assaulted by new odors, dirty laundry, old food, and sweat. Unshaven and wearing nothing but boxer shorts, Lieutenant j.g. Baxter lay on a cot in the corner, beneath a bamboo-framed window that had been propped open and screened off by mosquito netting.

"You're the new guy," Baxter said.

"That's right." Wilson looked Baxter up and down. He recognized the man from a photo he'd seen in Coronado, but this man lacked something that his photos had possessed, a fire, a drive that was no longer present. Beer cans had piled up around the man's cot . . . along with a collection of bottles that had once held bourbon, whiskey, and gin.

"If I were you," Baxter said, sitting up slowly on the cot, "I wouldn't even bother unpacking. They're going to be shipping all of us out before long. You included."

Wilson dropped his bag heavily on the floor of the hootch. "Maybe. But in the meantime, I'm going to do my job. As for you . . . you might start by remembering that I rank you."

"Aw, who the fuck are you trying to impress?" But the words were muttered, so low that Wilson almost hadn't caught them. He chose to ignore them . . . for now.

"I'll also point out that you have a job too, at least until your DEROS."

"DEROS," Baxter said, sighing. "What a beautiful, what a *wonderful* word."

Variously translated as "Date Eligible to Return from Overseas" or as "Date of Expected Return from Overseas," the word held a special fascination for every American serviceman in-country.

"Your job," Wilson said, pressing ahead, "is to help me and my men get settled in here."

"Mosquito repellent."

Wilson blinked. "I beg your pardon?"

"Mosquito repellent. For leeches. When you're out in the bush, wading around in muck up to your chin, when you crawl out you're going to find yourself covered with nice, fat, juicy leeches. All over. Inside your pants. Riding in your crotch. Tucked nice and neat up the crack of your ass. All the manuals say you use a cigarette to burn 'em off. You smoke?"

Wilson shook his head.

"Neither did I. I started, a couple months ago. Not because of the leeches, you understand. But because a man needs a hobby in a God-forsaken cesspool like this. Anyway, if you don't smoke, you're still supposed to burn the leeches off. Cigarette lighter goes snick-snick, though. Gives you away to Charlie, who's probably watching you from behind the nearest mangrove tree, laughing himself silly because you've got a leech this big"—he held up his thumb and forefinger, spread several inches apart—"this big stuck right up your ass. Or maybe he's riding on your pecker, giving you the ol' Rung Sat blow job. So, to get the bugger off, you can stick a cigarette lighter up your ass or set fire to your dick. But, in my expert experience, a dollop of the mosquito repellent they issue here does almost as good as sprinkling salt on a slug. Tell me, Lieutenant. You ever sprinkle salt on a slug? No? Neat stuff. You ought to try it on some of the monsters they grow down here. They start oozing yellow, like pus, and—"

"Mosquito repellent," Wilson said, not certain whether the man was putting him on or not. The way his mind was jumping around behind the rambling monologue was genuinely alarming. "I'll remember that. But I'm going to be depending on you for a hell of a lot more. You've been working these swamps for five months now. I need to know how you adapted. How you adjusted to the climate. The problems you've had."

Baxter, still sitting half-naked on the cot, blinked, then chuckled, a very dry, empty sound. "Problems, huh? Like the fact that we were sent here to do a job, then dumped?"

"If you like."

"Shit, there's nothing to like about it! Let me tell you about our last op. Couple of weeks ago, it was. We had intel come down through our NILO. You met Blanding yet?" Wilson shook his head. "Ah, you'll love him. Mr. Personality, though I guess he's better than Kellerman, the guy he replaced. We had intel from him that Charlie was using this particular trail, about four klicks in from the Soi Rap, sending heavy patrols back and forth. We went in after sunset, dropping off the PBRs. Waded ashore, then took the long way in. Eight klicks, at least, most of it through mangrove swamp and jungle. Got to the trail after midnight. Lay there all night. Nothing. Lay there all the next morning and into the afternoon. Nothing. Finally, three guys show up, one with an AK, one with an SKS, one with an M-1 carbine straight out of World War II. We open up on 'em. Well, hey. They were the best target we'd seen in better than twelve hours. Killed one, wounded one. The third ran off into the jungle. A couple of guys chased him, but he gave 'em the slip. So we gave the wounded guy first aid, dragged him to the river, and called for an extract.

"And the write-up for the op? We were out eighteen hours, all told, tying down the assets of four PBRs and two helos on ready-evac for two days. Lay in the mud watching that damned trail for thirteen, fourteen hours. Expended a couple of hundred rounds of ammo. And for what? One dead VC and one prisoner . . . and the prisoner turned out to be this scrawny little fifteen-year-old fucking *kid* who scooped up from some village west of here about a month ago and didn't know jack shit. Couldn't even tell us where his base camp was."

"What's the point of all this?"

"The point? The point is we expended all of that time and effort and got zilch. What's the fucking use of going through all of that, just to play truant officer to some kid who should've still been in school, instead of out playing with carbines?"

"Very touching, I'm sure. Are you through?"

"Yeah. Yeah, I'm through. I'm through with this whole fucking country. With this fucking war."

"No, mister. You are not. As the incoming CO of this unit, I am, formally calling an assembly of all hands. You, personally, will gather up your men . . . after you have made yourself presentable, of course. I believe you'll find some of them water skiing out back." Wilson checked his watch. "First, I am going to get something to eat, if the galley's still open. We will meet on the docks, down by the boats. Shall we say . . . 1400 hours?" He didn't wait for a reply. "Good. See you then."

Turning abruptly, he strode out of the hootch, before Baxter could gather his wits and utter a single word.

Chow, as Wilson had expected, was less than exciting, but it gave him time to think about the situation and, in particular, about how he was going to approach it. He almost headed back to the officer's hootch to shave and change into a clean uniform but decided against that approach for several reasons. These men had been fighting the neatly-pressed-and-starched battalions for months now. He preferred to approach them on their own ground.

His biggest fear, though, was that nobody would show . . . that Baxter wouldn't even bother to pass the word, as he'd been ordered. As Wilson walked out of the mess hall tent and proceeded toward the docks, however, he could see a small band of men gathering there. They were in two sharply defined groups, of course, his own men, the new-comers, and the old hands, some of them still dripping wet and smelling of river ooze after their water sports earlier. One of the men was in uniform. Baxter had pulled on a pair of cut-off blue jeans. The rest wore shorts or fatigue pants or dungarees. Most were bare-chested; those who weren't wore T-shirts, the tails dangling outside their pants.

"Good afternoon," he said. "I am Lieutenant Wilson." He waited until he had their attention, then pulled out the envelope he'd brought with him from MACV headquarters, unwrapped the string holding it closed, and extracted the neatly typed and stapled sheets inside. The document was only about seven pages long, but he'd contrived to staple an extra twenty sheets of typewriter paper to the bottom of the stack, to make it look thicker. Every eye was on him as he held the papers up for inspection. "This, gentlemen, was given to me by your friends and, um, admirers up at MACV. It is a list of all of your recent infractions, violations, and general homicidal disregard for the Uniform Code of Military Justice." Lowering the sheaf of paper, he thumbed through the first couple of pages. "Which one of you is Bosniak?"

A hand went up. "That would be me, sir."

"Um. Tell me, did you just not see that mudflat before you ran the PBR across it?"

"Well, sir, it's like this. That particular PBR had been given the regular crews a shitload of trouble for a long time. Running rough, y'know? They kept putting in for maintenance with HQ, but there wasn't anything really bad enough wrong with it to warrant taking it out of service. Some of us SEALs, well, those of us who know something about engines, anyway, have been helping the riverine boys with the maintenance, but we knew we needed a full engine overhaul for number three.''

"Ah. So you stole the boat.''

"No, sir. Temporarily appropriated. We *did* return it.''

Not under its own power, I see.''

"Well, no, sir. Not exactly. But we really revved up the engine there. When it overheated in the mud, well, we had excuse enough to send it in for a really thorough inspection and replacement.''

"I see. So stealing—I'm sorry—appropriating that PBR was just a means of getting around the lead-bottomed bureaucrats back in Saigon.''

"Yes, sir! Exactly, sir.''

"Which one of you is Luciano?''

"Here, sir.'' One of the wet and dripping SEALs raised his hand.

"Why'd you appropriate *your* PBR?''

"Oh, well, it was running rough too.''

"Ah. But you didn't run it into the mud.''

"Didn't need to. By the time I had her opened up, goin' twenty-five, twenty-six knots, man, that two-twenty was purring like a pussy cat. She just needed a good run, y'see, to clear out the carbs. Us SEALs, you see, gotta take good care of our equipment.''

"I see.'' Wilson appeared to consider this for a moment. Then, with solemn dignity, he walked toward the group, past them, and out onto the dock. The water, oily and brown, lapped at the pilings just below his feet. "Here's what we're going to do with these charges,'' he said. And he tore the sheaf of papers in half.

Now he really had their attention, as he tore the papers again, then again, and finally yet again. Even his considerable strength, however, honed by BUD/S and constant work-outs stateside, could not tear the pieces a fifth time. Turning, he tossed them out over the water, a white, fluttering cloud that descended like snow on the surface of the river. "So much for Saigon.''

The cheer was sudden and enthusiastic, and with that, the ice was broken. Wilson noticed how several of the old hands seemed to drift closer to the newcomers. Several talked among themselves, and he saw several of the Det Delta SEALs gesture in his direction.

Asking if this guy is for real, he thought.

Turning, he placed his hands on his hips and tried to strike a confident tone. "Okay, SEALs, listen up. Me and my boys are newbies here, and we need your help. I could give you the usual speech about what a pigsty this place is, what a shit-faced lot you are, but I'm not going to. You've obviously been through hell, and I'm not here to make it harder on you. I am going to require your cooperation in bringing us newcomers up to speed. We're grown-up enough to know that a lot of what they taught us back at Coronado is just flat wrong. You men have been here, in the thick of it. You know things about how SEALs should adapt to jungle fighting, that we need to know.

"While I will not comment on the condition of this camp or these quarters, I will say that I would prefer to have the area properly squared away, rather than being forced to call in an air strike, napalm the place, and require the tax payers to build me a new base . . . even though that course might be easier than what I propose. I am not being a hard-ass here, people. If you live in filth, well, I hate to think what your *weapons* look like. And God help any SEAL who doesn't take care of his weapon!

"You men are scheduled to rotate home, most of you, in another three weeks. You have that long to get this camp in order and to pass on what you've learned us newbies. One week from today, I will be leading the first patrol of Det Golf into the Rung Sat." He saw the alarmed glances several of the old hands shot to one another. "Don't worry. I know you're all coming up on the single-digit-fidgets. You've made it this far without taking a single casualty. None of you wants the honor of being the first combat casualty in SEAL Team One, and none of you wants to risk getting hurt or worse just a few days before you're on your way back to the land of the round-eyes."

That drew some appreciative chuckles. "Yeah, *female* round-eyes," one of the sailors called out.

"So none of you will have to go. Unless, of course, I have some volunteers. You see, my idea of cool would be for you men to go back home feeling like you'd accomplished something here. Go back with a solid win . . . not like you got whipped and had to slink home with your tails between your legs.

"We'll worry about that later. For right now, we've got plenty to worry about right here on base. I want every weapon, and I mean every weapon, brought out, stripped, laid out on tarps on the ground, inspected for corrosion, cleaned, oiled, reassembled, logged, and properly stowed. After that, we're going to start on the web gear, the SCUBA gear, ammunition, packs, boots, field gear, and every RBS in inventory.

"And after that, well, then we'll really get serious. . . . "

By the time he was finished and had dismissed the group, he knew that he'd gotten through to them. Some had even been showing a spark of life in eyes that had been dead at the start of his talk.

He just wondered if he'd said anything that would make a *difference. . . .*

Chapter 13

Wednesday, 27 July 1966

Long Thanh Peninsula
West of Can Gio, Rung Sat Special Zone
1520 hours

SEALs hated insertions in midday. If they'd learned one thing over the past few months, it was that the night could help them as much as it helped Charlie, providing a blanket over their movements that let them literally move anywhere, observe anything unseen, and withdraw again with the enemy never knowing they'd been there. Back in BUD/S training, their instructors had stressed that the water was the SEAL's best friend. If they were ambushed, they were to form a perimeter with a river or the sea at their back, an escape route over which the enemy would not or could not follow. Long swims in the open ocean, "drown-proofing" in swimming pools, endless drills in everything from freezing sea water to molasses-thick mud had convinced the SEAL trainees that they were indeed amphibious, creatures as at home in the water as on the land.

Now, however, Vietnam was teaching them that their *second* best friend was darkness. "The night belongs to Charlie" was a popular and oft-quoted aphorism among all Americans stationed in Vietnam. With SEAL One, however, that saying was no longer entirely true.

That was why Torpedoman Third Class Christopher Luciano particularly hated day ops. At night, things were pretty much even; if you couldn't see Charlie, he couldn't see you.

This time, however, they were going in by day. Long Thanh was the name both of the southernmost of the cluster of islands making up most of the Rung Sat and of the peninsula extending from the corner of that island into the South China Sea. At midday, three teams of six SEALs each had inserted from LCMs a few kilometers west of the village of Can Gio, at Long Thanh's southeastern tip. The three units had waded ashore on the same sandy beaches the Marines had hit back in March, at the beginning of Operation Jackstay. Plunging into the jungle, the three patrols had been moving north, their lines of march roughly parallel and close enough to one another that each could expect help from the other if it got into trouble. They were going in by day because Lieutenant Wilson wanted to take advantage of four Navy Seawolf helicopters that had been assigned to the SEALs. They were hovering on station a few miles to the south, available in case the SEALs ran into something they couldn't handle and needed a fast extraction. The patrol orders, written by Wilson just the night before, were delightfully simple: *Patrol until contact is made, or until 1630 hours. Kill as many enemy as possible. Extract upon completion of mission.*

And that suited Luciano just fine.

For weeks now, he'd been wondering if he'd made the right choice, pulling some highly unauthorized strings to stay on for a second six-month hitch in the Nam. His reasons for doing so had been uncomfortably vague and difficult to put into words but were centered around the realization that in the past five months he and the other SEALs of the old Det Delta had only just begun to get a handle on jungle warfare . . . and on the very special fieldcraft required to fight the VC in this hellish environment. For Luciano to quit and go home now would be an admission of personal defeat.

And, ever since his days growing up on the tough, Italian Southside of Chicago, Lucky Luciano had never admitted defeat to anyone.

Besides, he was finding that he *liked* Vietnam. The pumping of the heart when you were on point, the pounding of adrenaline through your system during a firefight, combined as nothing else to let you know that you were *alive*.

He was on point at the moment, never a popular position on patrol, but one he'd volunteered for simply because the other five men in his squad—Chief Mike Spencer, Franky Horowitz, Tim Radenaugh, Willy Marshall, and Lieutenant j.g. Toland—were all newbies. They'd been practicing the art and fieldcraft of walking point for a week now, but on hot patrols like this one, where the chances of enemy contact were good to excellent, a trained set of eyes, ears, and reflexes could make all the difference to the team.

Luciano waited for a long moment, crouched unmoving among the hanging curtains of leaves, reaching out with all of his senses to examine the wall of green and brown vegetation ahead. Boobies—booby traps—were one of Charlie's specialties, whether they consisted of hidden pits lined with shit-dipped pungi stakes, elaborate sapling-loaded spring traps bristling with spikes, or carefully hidden or thread-thin tripwires connected to mines or hand grenades. After enough hours spent walking point, a man developed something akin to a sixth sense, an almost supernatural awareness that something in the landscape of jumbled twigs, leaves, ferns, and branches ahead wasn't quite right. There were subtle differences to natural objects that had been recently disturbed by men . . . even men as closely in tune with the jungle as the VC seemed to be.

Nothing. Gently, scarcely moving at all, Luciano extended one mud-caked foot, taking another step into the jungle.

Except for the mud, he was bare-footed. Most SEALs still wore coral shoes or sneakers in the bush, but more and more were starting to shuck footwear all together. Boots or shoes could get uncomfortable on long marches, they could get sucked right off a man's foot in thick mud, they didn't add that much protection since most of the ground in the Rung Sat was soft anyway, and they left a hell of an imprint on open ground. Bare footprints in the mud told the enemy much less than the tread marks of American-made sneakers or, worse, combat boots.

Lieutenant Wilson's willingness to let his SEALs wear other than regulation dress was probably the number one reason Luciano liked him. Sometimes it seemed as though all officers did was supervise the uniforms their men wore, making certain their dress was regulation, their hair closely cropped, their facial hair removed or very neatly trimmed. Uniform regs had their place, certainly, and a lot of the stuff was of pretty good quality. His jacket was the tiger-stripe pattern favored by Vietnamese LLDB forces and authorized for use by American special forces in certain circumstances, and he wore a sturdy regulation combat vest over that, festooned with the usual load-out of grenades, ammo, and a SEAL knife in its sheath.

But below his web belt and its two dangling canteens was a different story. Not only was he barefoot, but he was wearing civilian jeans too, an unspeakable breach of military propriety that would have called down an immediate reprimand from any REMF officer who happened to see him.

REMF officers, however, were in very short supply out here in the Rung Sat. A month or two ago, several of the men in Det Delta had started wearing blue jeans on patrol. At the time, it had been a kind of mild rebellion against the military command authority that all of the SEALs felt was throttling them, but it had soon evolved into something more. Jeans were more comfortable than fatigues. They were tougher, too, less susceptible to tearing than even military-issue rip-stop trousers.

His headgear was unofficial and unapproved as well. By now, few SEALs wore the black berets favored by the riverine forces. They looked dangerous enough, certainly, but they weren't very practical for keeping a man's eyes either dry or shaded. Currently, the most popular headgear were the broad-brimmed, floppy bush hats known as "boonies" or "boonie hats," or a triangular length of olive-drab bandage material fashioned into either a headband or a scarf, pulled tight at the back and tied off like a pigtail. Luciano favored the latter style; with the bushy mustache he'd been cultivating over the past month, it gave him a piratical appearance that he rather liked and, together with the layers of black and green paint smeared over his face, it helped break up the headlike outline of his head, hid his black hair, making him look just a bit less human.

And that, after all, was the whole point of camouflage, to rob the wearer of enough human characteristics of shading, coloring, and patterning that he blended into his surroundings more easily. What had started as a mild form of protest had been embraced by the new skipper. "I don't give a fuck what you people want to wear out there," he'd said, a couple of days after his arrival. "Just so long as it works. Camo pattern, headgear, footgear, even choice of weapons, within certain mild limits, it's all up to you. After all, it's your life."

That common-sense approach had impressed Luciano. All too often, decisions about what a soldier should wear, what he should carry in the field, were made by REMFs way up on the chain of command who either had never had to carry a full combat load-out in their lives or else had done so in Korea or World War II, a simpler age that hadn't loaded its warriors down with so much ammo and high-tech gimmickry they could scarcely move.

Ammo, especially, was a real headache on a modern combat patrol. Back in World War II, the vast majority of U.S. troops had carried semiautomatic rifles like the M-1 Garand, which fired rounds loaded eight at a time from a clip inserted in the top of the receiver. Only a very few had packed weapons capable of full-auto fire, like the bulky BAR or the M3 "grease gun." In Vietnam, however, weapons capable of full-auto were the rule rather than the exception. The trouble was that with a cyclic rate of eight hundred rounds per minute, an M-16 blazing away on full-auto rock-and-roll would empty a twenty-round magazine in something like a second and a half. Survival in a firefight often meant dumping a *lot* of lead at an unseen enemy in a short period of time . . . which in turn meant that survival depended on lugging a lot of ammunition into the bush. Heavy load-outs were the order of the day. To have a skipper actually come in and tell the men that they could pretty much wear what they wanted in the name of comfort and practicality was, in Luciano's experience, nothing short of astonishing.

His ammo load-out on today's patrol was particularly unusual, with pouch after pouch each holding a single 40-mm grenade or shot canister. His weapon of choice was the M79 grenade launcher he held tightly in his black-gloved hands. Essentially, the M79 was a single-shot shotgun, a stubby, short-muzzled weapon only seventy-three centimeters long and weighing less than three kilos loaded. It had originally been designed to lob a 40-mm grenade up to four hundred meters, a lightweight and quickly reloaded replacement for the old Army rifle grenades, and it was still a reliable weapon in that role. The distinctive, hollow sound an M79 made when it fired a grenade had given it the nickname "bloop gun" or "blooper."

Early on in the fighting in Southeast Asia, however, SEALs and Army Special Forces using the blooper had identified a key problem. The high-explosive fragmentation grenades fired by the thing had a five-meter burst radius; to keep the bloop gunner from scoring own goals, the grenades armed themselves in flight, giving them a minimum range of fourteen meters. Most engagements in the jungle, however, were fought at extremely close quarters, ten meters or less, in some cases. Grenadiers needed a weapon they could use at damn near point-blank range.

Hence the M576E1 Multiple Projectile, a 40-mm antipersonnel round chambered and fired from the M79 exactly like a grenade. Instead of high explosives, however, the round packed twenty balls of number four buckshot riding in a cup and shrouded by a plastic sabot. The shot had a muzzle velocity of 885 feet per second—considerably less than that of a conventional shotgun—and was effective at any range out to forty meters, which made it perfect for combat within the close confines of the Rung Sat's mangrove forests. Though it had to be reloaded manually after each shot, an experienced gunner could get off a round every four or five seconds. The Navy SEALs, among others, had been testing the new ammo under field conditions; a round of M576E1 was chambered in Luciano's weapon now.

Three more steps . . . then pause, looking and listening, using *all* of the senses. The undergrowth was thinning out ahead; it looked to Luciano as though the SEALs were coming to a trail that ran east and west across their line of travel.

Turning, he signaled Lieutenant Toland, just visible in the brush ten meters behind him: *Trail! Wait!*

Toland flicked a handsign in reply. *Go ahead! Careful!*

The SEALs avoided trails when at all possible. Move along one of those narrow fire traps through the jungle and you were inviting ambush or an encounter with a booby trap. Charlie used trails though—most of the paths zigzagging through the Rung Sat were probably of his making—and the SEALs could use that against him, sometimes. Lieutenant Wilson had suggested that the SEALs start setting booby traps to catch the Cong, and Luciano was all in favor of that. Carefully edging forward, he reached a point where he could actually see the path, a muddy, red clay slash through the green. He waited, watched, listened, breathed a moment more, then cautiously stepped forward onto the trail.

It was narrow and well-hidden, winding to take advantage of the thickest portion of the forest canopy overhead. The ground was muddy, and a number of footprints were visible, some bare, some made by sandals, all heading west. Marking the heel of one distinctive sandal track with a pebble, Luciano then checked ahead until he found the matching track of the opposite foot, about eighteen inches ahead, and marked it at the instep. Next, he counted the prints between his two marks, including those overlapping others or extending outside of the lines, but counting only one of his two key prints.

Seventeen. Dividing by two gave him eight-and-a-half . . . call it nine people who'd left their footprints in the trail.

All of the tracks were smaller than those made by Luciano's feet, but large enough that they were probably made by Vietnamese men and certainly not by children or small women. Most of the prints had crisp, clean edges and, as he studied some of the deeper ones, he was aware that water was still very slowly seeping out of the surrounding mud. These prints were fresh . . . probably made within the last hour or so.

Not fuckin' bad for a kid hot off the streets of Chicago, he thought with a cocky grin. Turning again to face Toland, he signaled his find. *Nine men. Going that way. One hour.*

Carefully, he began following them.

Luciano liked following a trail less than he did moving in daylight, and he didn't intend to follow it for long. VC often doubled back on their own trails either to set booby traps or to arrange an ambush for anyone who might be following them.

In this case, though, it looked like Charlie didn't suspect a thing. Several of those prints were very deep in the mud, indicating that their owners had been heavily laden. This looked like moving day to Luciano. He decided to follow the trail long enough to get a good idea of where it was leading. The rest of the patrol would flank him left and right, providing cover in case he got into trouble.

He hadn't gone very far, however, when the VC appeared, walking around a bend in the trail just ahead. Obviously they weren't expecting danger, for they were walking quickly, taking no precautions to hide themselves or cover the noise they were making. One moment the trail was empty; the next, Luciano was just turning to look up its length when three Vietcong walked into full view, a scant three meters away.

The lead Cong looked up and his eyes grew big and round as he stared at the green-faced apparition blocking the trail. He stopped short; the man behind him collided with him. Luciano was already bringing his M79 up as the lead VC fumbled with the AK-47 dangling from its sling at his side.

Luciano fired first, loosing the shotgun blast from waist-level, the ringing *thoomp-crash* exploding above the background noises of birds and frogs. The packet of shot decapitated the Vietcong in the lead, dissolving his head in a sudden pink and red spray that painted both of his comrades and the leaves of the trees twenty feet beyond.

Both of the surviving VC turned and scrambled for safety before the body of their friend, arms flung wide, had landed on its back in the mud of the trail. Luciano smoothly broke open the breech of the M79, flicked out the smoking, spent cartridge, dropped home a 40-mm HE grenade plucked from his vest. Snapping the breech closed, he brought the thump gun to his shoulder and triggered the second round: *thump!* The grenade hurtled through the leaves at the bend in the trail, and an instant later the grenade's ringing crack erupted from fifty meters ahead.

He broke the breech open again, discarded the second cartridge, and reloaded with number four shot. There was no movement or sound from ahead, nothing out of the ordinary at all save for the dead soldier on the path, so he sidestepped into the brush. No sense making a better target of himself than he had to.

The rest of the patrol moved up; he could hear them slipping through the forest to either side.

Toland materialized at his side, as stealthily silent as a ghost. *How many?*

One down, Luciano signed back. *Two more running, that way.*

The patrol fanned out through the jungle, making a careful search of the area. Luciano and Toland knelt by the body of the Vietcong in the path.

"Nice shooting," Toland said, his voice just above a whisper. There was little left of the dead man's head, save the lower jaw and a bloody spill of shattered bone and tissue. He had a satchel slung over his shoulder, and Toland pulled it open. "Hello, what have we here?"

Inside the satchel, the SEALs found five Soviet-style RGD-5 fragmentation grenades and a roll of thin wire. "They must've been doubling back to set up some boobies," Luciano whispered.

"What say we return the favor?"

"Sounds good."

Luciano took the satchel, and the two SEALs explored further down the trail. A short search located the blast crater from the HE grenade Luciano had fired blindly after the fleeing VC, and the two SEALs checked the area carefully. Luciano hoped that his shot might have taken out the other VC, but, though Toland did find a streak of blood on the root of a tree a few yards away, there were no bodies, no dropped equipment. They would have to assume that the others had escaped . . . and that the group Luciano had been tracking now knew that the SEALs were here.

Before they moved on, however, Luciano performed a small ceremony. Reaching inside the left breast pocket of his tiger-striped shirt, he extracted a single playing card and tucked it into the dead man's hand, which he carefully positioned on the VC's chest. It looked for all the world as though the soldier had been looking at the card when his head had exploded.

The card was the ace of spades, and it was the latest twist in the growing psychological war between the communists and the SEALs. The SEALs had recently made the interesting discovery that many Vietnamese had an almost superstitious awe of the ace of spades, which they interpreted as a death mark. Lately, the SEALs had been begging, buying, or stealing the ace of spades out of every deck of cards they could find between Nha Be and Saigon, and leaving them as calling cards on the VC they killed.

They reasoned that a shaken enemy was an enemy who would make mistakes . . . possibly fatal ones.

Nearly a kilometer farther to the west, the trail entered a clearing nestled into the curve of a broad, swampy stream. The clearing looked natural—a blow-down, Luciano thought, from a storm some years ago, but someone had built a number of thatch-and-palm buildings within the shadows cast by the trees around the glade's perimeter, camouflaging the roofs with mud and still-living plants. The six SEALs watched the area for some time, until the other two six-man teams joined them. The camp looked deserted and, after using the team's PRC-22 to check with Wilson aboard one of the Seawolf helos, Toland gave the order for four men to go in and check it out.

Luciano, Spencer, Marshall, and Horowitz were the volunteers. They moved carefully, alert to the danger of possible booby traps, but everything they found suggested that the camp had been hastily abandoned. Some of the pits for cook-fires still held warm ashes. A scattering of brass on the ground marked where someone had dropped a handful of 7.62-mm cartridges as he'd left a building and not bothered to stop to pick them up.

It was the largest Vietcong facility the SEALs had seen yet. The mess hall was a long, thatch-roofed building with several broad tables, with places enough for eighty men. A bunker dug into the ground nearby had been designed as an armory. Obviously the place had been hurriedly emptied out, but in their haste the base's former tenants had abandoned a couple of ammo cans with over five hundred rounds of 7.62 x 39 mm ammunition, the same kind fired by the most common communist-made weapons. There were also five AK-47s, one SKS, and even a Czech Vz 58v assault rifle.

As soon as the entire camp had been swept, six of the SEALs took up lookout positions in a perimeter around the base, while the rest joined their fellows in searching for booby traps or anything of importance . . . particularly, anything that might be important to military intelligence. Luciano and Horowitz together explored a thatch-roofed, wood-frame building that had probably been a barracks, empty now, but with hooks driven into vertical posts that had probably supported hammocks. Some litter had been left behind, including a crumpled page from a letter, and one of the gourd-shaped canteens favored by the VC, with words and decorations scratched into the green-painted metal.

At one end of the room, a woven mat board had been erected on the wall, with a number of hand-written papers and gaudy posters tacked to it. Franky Horowitz began examining the writings.

"What's that, Franky?" Luciano asked him. "The target for tonight?"

"Poetry," Horowitz said. He tapped one of the pages. "This one, anyway."

"Poetry? What's it say?"

"Uh . . . can't make it all out. Its title is 'From the Rear Area to the Front Line,' and it looks like a love poem. Goes something like:

> *'Here is all my love offered to you.*
> *I hear marching music echoing somewhere.*
> *I miss you and send you my love. . . .'*

"Can't make out the rest of this. It gets a bit tangled. Something about the heroic soldier whose shoulders are bent with love for country and family."

"Shit," Luciano said. "Not much of a poem."

"I guess it loses something in the translation," Horowitz said. "Let's grab all that stuff and take it."

"Yeah," Luciano agreed. "We'll see if G2 can make anything of a love poem to a VC soldier."

After completing his assigned sweep, Luciano found Lieutenant j.g. Toland in the building that had probably been a platoon commander's office.

"Barracks are all checked out, sir," Luciano told him.

"Looks like room for forty-eight. We did find some papers and stuff for Intel."

Toland was seated behind a wooden desk, examining several papers. The filing cabinet in the corner, the map thumbtacked to one wall gave the place a shabby resemblance to the office of any U.S. military CO. There were posters on several walls, most showing Communist soldiers in various heroic postures, with slogans written in large, crude letters.

Toland glanced up at Luciano. "Hey, Lucky. Forty-eight, you say?"

"Yeah. That many spots for hammocks, anyway. No way of telling if they used all of them."

Toland held up several of the papers on the desk. "According to these, they only had one platoon, twenty-four men, based here permanently. Looks like they used the place as a major staging area, though. Possibly for attacks on the main shipping channel east of here."

"You read gook, Lieutenant?"

"Military symbols are pretty much the same, Lucky, here or stateside. A lot of their officers were trained under the French, remember. Man, oh, man, G2 is going to go into orbit when they see this stuff!"

Luciano came closer. A stack of papers, forms, and folders covered the desk. He saw the neatly stenciled words TOI-MAT on the outside of several manila folders. That had been one of the Vietnamese phrases taught to SEALs back at Coronado: *top secret*.

"Looks like a damned good haul, Lieutenant."

Toland laughed. "A splendid haul, Lucky. A *splendid* haul!"

Luciano licked his lips. "I was just wondering, sir. Before we, ah, turn this shit in to MACV-SOG, maybe it'd be an idea to let Franky have a look-see, y'know? He talks gook. Who knows? Maybe he could let us in on where Charlie's hanging out."

"Not a bad idea, Lucky. The brass at Coronado has been hot on us gathering our own intel anyway." Toland considered for a moment. "Okay. First, get Horowitz in here. Have him find a notebook . . . no. Belay that. I've got one here. Next, have Jerry crank up the Prick-twenty-two and call in the choppers."

"You got it, Skipper. Are we evacking this shit?"

"Yup. And I imagine Lieutenant Wilson is going to want to see this stuff for himself."

"Great!" And he meant it. Luciano hadn't been sure what to expect of the new SEAL One skipper in Vietnam at first, but the more he'd seen of Wilson, the happier he was that the guy was on board. Baxter had been okay, an all-right guy, not stuck-up like most officers he knew, but Charles Wilson really had it on the ball.

Maybe, he thought, with Wilson in command the SEALs were going to go somewhere in Nam after all.

Seawolf Golf-1
Long Thanh Peninsula
1610 hours

Wilson leaned past the door gunner to watch the treetops skimming past, only a scant few hundred feet below the UH-1B's runners. The clearing opened up just ahead, though from the air, the buildings described by the SEAL team were invisible, even from this low altitude.

The other Seawolf helicopter in the flight took up its station at a watchful distance, its rotor wash lashing the tree tops beneath its belly to a writhing frenzy. Wilson's machine, rotors thundering, drifted down into the center of the clearing, where a red smoke marker provided positive ID and the assurance that this wasn't an ambush.

The Seawolf was the Navy version of the Army's ubiquitous UH-1. Stripped down as a transport, it was known as the "Slick" and could carry either seven fully loaded troops or three stretchers and an attendant. The Navy's UH-1B Seawolf version, newly arrived in Vietnam at just about the same time as Det Golf, was among the first of a whole new family of helicopters, the helicopter gunship. Though it could serve as a transport like its Army counterpart, the Seawolf also mounted the M16 weapons system: four M60C machine-guns, each belt-fed with three thousand rounds; two M158 rocket pods packing seven 2.75-inch rockets each; and two M60 machine guns for the door gunners, who also had M79 grenade launchers and plenty of ammo within easy reach. Heavily armed, they still had room for a squad of four to six men. This time, however, they were serving another purpose than insertion or exfiltration.

For this patrol, Wilson had ordered four Seawolves to spell each other in groups of two throughout the afternoon. The helos had a loiter time of only about ninety minutes, so Wilson had been spending a lot of time during the past six hours shuttling back and forth between the loiter waypoint south of Long Thanh and Nha Be, where he would change over from an incoming chopper to an outgoing one. He'd decided not to attach himself to one of the three patrols on the ground because he'd wanted to follow the progress of all three; now that they'd hit paydirt, however, he was determined not to miss a thing.

Wilson leaped off the aft deck of the helicopter before it touched ground, stooping low to avoid the chattering rotors as he dashed across the clearing to the spot where Toland, Chief Spencer, and several other SEALs were waiting.

"Jackpot!" Toland told him as he got close enough to hear over the steady *whup-whup-whup* of the Seawolf's rotors. "We sure as hell didn't come up dry this time!"

"What did you get?"

"We're still cataloguing everything. So far, though, we've got six weapons, five hundred rounds-plus of seven-six-two, two hundred pounds of rice, a couple of sampans, and . . ."

"And?"

"Documents, skipper! Documents!"

"What documents? T and Os?"

"Wait'll you see!"

Toland led him to the wood frame building identified as the base headquarters. Franky Horowitz was sitting at the desk, going over several stacks of papers and making entries in a notebook.

"Hello, Franky," Wilson said as he walked in. "Whatcha got?"

"Hey, Lieutenant! We got some good stuff. Can't read it all, not by half, but I can give you some guesses."

"Go ahead."

"Okay. Mr. Toland has already found some rosters for the platoon that was based here. He can fill you in on that." He pulled out several large sheets with topographical lines drawn on them. "These, though, are maps of the area, mostly of

Long Thanh. This one shows defensive emplacements, bunkers, trenches, stuff like that. This one shows mine and booby trap emplacements. The VC based here were an engineering platoon, and it looks like they've been busy. Some of these mines are marked in the shipping channel. We'll have to pass this on to the riverine boys right away.''

"Affirmative," Wilson said, taking the map from Horowitz and studying it briefly. "What else?"

Horowitz held up a paper covered with columns of names. "We have a regimental order here. Names and ranks on several hundred VC. Also what looks like a list of contacts in the region, collaborators and such. I'm surprised they didn't burn these."

"Probably didn't have time," Chief Spencer suggested, coming up behind Wilson. "Looks like they evacked in a hurry."

"There's also a map here of bases like this one. Rice stores. Ammo depots.''

"It's party time," Toland said with a grin.

"Roger that," Wilson said, handing the map back.

"There's lots more," Horowitz said, "but I haven't had time to more than glance at most of it."

"You did just fine." Wilson was thinking furiously. "You know, with your help, bet we can put together our own translation of most of this stuff tonight. How about it, Franky? Feel up to pulling an all-nighter with me?"

"Sure, Lieutenant."

"What's the deal, sir?" Toland wanted to know.

Wilson tapped the pile of files and papers on the desk. "This stuff is all time-sensitive. I mean, a half-life measured in a few days, maybe hours."

"Sure," Toland said. "As soon as the VC realize we've got these maps and things, they'll change everything, move all the bases. . . .''

"Right. You also know how slow they move back in Saigon. When we turn this stuff in, half of it'll get lost or misfiled. The rest might get acted on . . . maybe a month or two after the VC finish moving it all anyway. I figure, with Franky here to help me pinpoint what's important, we can either make copies of some of these documents, or, ah, never find them in the first place, as far as Saigon knows. We'll start assembling our own little library of intelligence data.''

''About fuckin' time,'' Spencer said.

Wilson glanced at the SEAL chief. The man was grinning at him; they'd discussed this problem often enough in the past. Some of the NOSG brass back in Coronado had been trying to organize something of this sort for months now, recommending that the SEALs handle their own intel. The trouble was that the SEALs in the field were caught in a web of conflicting and overlapping bureaucracies, with jurisdiction claimed by CO-NAVADVGRU, by his bosses in MACV, and by the CO-NOSGPAC back in Coronado.

''Son of a bitch,'' Toland said. ''Withholding intel? You could get your ass kicked clear back to CONUS if they find out.''

''Maybe. That's why we're not going to tell them, right?''

''Right!''

''Okay, gentlemen,'' Wilson said, clapping his hands. ''You've all earned your government paycheck today. Start bundling this stuff and get it onto the helo,''

While several SEALs loaded the captured documents aboard the waiting Seawolf, others took cans of kerosene—fuel for lanterns and cook stoves—and began liberally sprinkling the stuff over the thatched roofs of the camp's buildings, throughout the interiors of the largest structures, across several bags of rice, inside two sampans drawn up on the bank of the stream, and anywhere else where they thought it might do some good. Then, as the Seawolf with Wilson aboard once more lifted into the air on a rising whine of rotors, the SEALs faded back into the woods, putting as much distance between themselves and the VC encampment as possible.

Moments later, as the other helo rode shotgun, the UH-1B lined up on the camp at a range of five hundred meters and an altitude that held it just above the treetops. At a command from Wilson, the 2.75-inch rockets were triggered, firing two at a time, one from each side of the aircraft. The rockets streaked down out of the sky on scrawling white trails of smoke; shrieking into the camp, they exploded in paired thunders, hurling mud and thatch and pine-log walls high into the air. Kerosene ignited, and in seconds the entire camp was blazing, sending up a roiling column of black smoke shot through with hungry tongues of flame. The Seawolves continued loosing rockets two by two. The mess hall exploded in a whirl of splinters. The office of the camp's commanding officer slumped to one side, burning furiously. The barracks collapsed, the roof aflame.

And when all fourteen rockets had been expended, the Seawolf peeled off and began circling the area as the other UH-1 moved in for some target practice. By the time its rocket tubes were empty, the entire VC camp had been engulfed in a raging inferno.

1745 hours

Later, after the flames had died down and the Seawolves had peeled off and departed toward the north, the SEALs returned. It was fully dark now, though the orange-glowing embers of the wreckage and isolated flickers of open flame continued to cast an eerie, hellish light across the clearing. The smoke was fog-thick, acrid and as bitter as war.

The SEALs made a final check of the encampment, performing damage assessment and making certain that nothing useful remained there for the enemy.

The SEALs left a parting gift before they faded back into the jungle and began their meandering hike through the darkness to the point on the river where patrol boats were waiting to take them off the island. The five Russian grenades they'd recovered earlier in the day from the soldier Luciano had killed were carefully wired to the trunks of saplings or bushes alongside the trails leading away from the clearing; their cotter pins were worked nearly free, then tied to lengths of gray thread that were strung across the trails at just about the height of a man's toenails.

Other grenades were added to the mix. Several were planted, their pins removed but their arming levers carefully retained against the pressure of the springs, beneath sheets of hot corrugated tin or other bits of debris lying in the smoldering heap of wreckage. When the Americans had gone, the VC would return to see what could be salvaged. As they started poking through the ruins, they should stumble across some of the SEALs' greetings. One of the booby traps was a white smoke grenade; when that went off, Charlie would either think it was a gas attack or assume that the Americans were about to launch another air attack targeting the smoke. Either way, he would panic and run and, just maybe, he would find some of the grenade traps that he might have missed going in.

And as a final touch, one of the AK-47s was left lying in the open, its firing pin removed but the weapon otherwise intact. A grenade was placed in a scooped-out hollow underneath, the cotter pin pulled and the grenade carefully positioned so that the weapon's weight held down the arming lever, with a playing card, the ace of spades, braced against the spoon. Some VC was almost certain to pick up what he would think was a weapon accidentally dropped by the departing Americans, and when he did . . .

The SEALs were learning to fight Charlie's kind of war.

Chapter 14

Thursday, 28 July 1966

The Pentagon
1425 hours

"What do you think it's all about, Hawk?" Hank Richardson asked. "I mean, what the hell does Captain Galloway want with us?"

"Damned if I know, Junior." Chief Gunner's Mate Bob Finnegan shrugged and yawned, but Richardson knew better than to believe his elaborate show of disinterest. It wasn't every day that ordinary sailors, even SEALs, were called in to a meeting with a senior officer on the staff of the Chief of Naval Operations. "Maybe they're going to give us good conduct medals or something."

"Yeah, right," QM/1 Jim Horner spoke up from his chair on the opposite side of the waiting room. "When they start handing out medals for the three Bs, I'll believe them giving one to you, Hawk." That sparked laughter. The three Bs—beer, bullets, and broads—were recognized as the SEAL's chief interests in life.

"Pipe down, you three." That growled order came from the fourth man in the little waiting room, Lieutenant Jack Kessler, who commanded Team Two's Second Platoon. "This isn't Vinny's Bar, and you guys aren't on liberty, so keep your mouths shut and try to remember what it's like to be a blackshoe, okay?"

"Yes, sir, Lieutenant, sir," Horner answered, grinning. There wasn't much hope that any of them would be mistaken for blackshoes—members of the regular Navy. In the SEALs, at least on the East Coast, informality between officers and enlisted men was the rule. And anyway Horner—his nickname in the Teams was "Badges" from all the special school qualification patches sewn onto his jumpsuit—was a plank owner in Team Two, one of the founding members of the unit. He could get away with even more than his comrades.

At that moment a civilian secretary appeared at the door. "Captain Galloway will see you now," she said. Her voice was a pleasant contralto, and she had long blonde hair and a pair of legs shown off to good advantage by her dark skirt. "Will you follow me, please?"

"To the ends of the Earth, beautiful," Richardson said, winking at her. He had a reputation as one of Team Two's leading Don Juans and tried hard to live up to that reputation wherever Second Platoon went.

"Down, boy," Finnegan said. "You'll have to excuse him, ma'am. Hasn't had all his shots yet."

The secretary gave them both a frosty look and then led the way down a long, nondescript corridor. "In there, *gentlemen*," she said with another look at Richardson. "The captain will be here in a moment."

"She wants me," Richardson said as she closed the door behind them. They were in a conference room, a spartan chamber dominated by a large wooden table. There were neither windows nor decorations on the walls. Richardson found a seat and looked around. "Nice to know our taxes aren't being wasted on frills, huh?"

Before anyone else could respond, the door swung open again. Two men entered, one a slender, fiftyish Navy captain with reddish hair starting to go gray, the other dressed in a business suit and carrying a briefcase. All four SEALs stood as they came in, but the captain quickly motioned them to sit again.

"I'm Captain Galloway," he said as he took a seat at the head of the table. His companion sat down next to him. "This is Mr. . . . Jones, from a government agency interested in Navy special warfare capabilities."

Richardson glanced over at the civilian, Jones. A government agency . . . that was usually code for the CIA, in SEAL circles. The Central Intelligence Agency often turned to the SEALs for special missions, such as the scouting his stepfather had done in Cuba.

"The four of you were brought here to discuss a somewhat . . . delicate matter," Galloway continued. "Your platoon is leaving for France next week to conduct joint training exercises, correct?"

"Yes, sir," Kessler replied. "We had a French unit over here last month working with us, so it seemed reasonable that we get the return engagement over there."

Galloway nodded. "Right. Well, that's a pretty standard mission. I gather all of you have been overseas before on NATO training exercises."

"Yes, sir," the others chorused.

Richardson cleared his throat. "I wasn't on any of the European exercises, sir," he said, feeling a little awkward at speaking up. "But I was in the Caribbean last year . . . Santo Domingo, and the Virgin Islands."

"Ah, yes. Now I remember the file entry. Your experience in Santo Domingo will stand you in good stead. You four have something extra to do while you're over in France." Galloway looked at each of them in turn, his eyes assessing each. "First off, let me warn you that this meeting and everything we discuss in it is to be considered classified. It is not to be discussed with anyone else. Is that understood?"

"Yes, sir," Kessler repeated. The other three, Richardson included, nodded.

"Good. While you are training in France, you will be at the main French naval base at Toulon. We would like you to obtain some information for us while you are there . . . without letting the rest of your platoon, or your hosts, know that you are doing so.''

"Sir?" Kessler's eyebrows had gone up. "We're supposed to spy . . . on the French?''

Galloway nodded. ''That's about the size of it. The information we want falls into two broad areas. First, beach reconnaissance . . . specifically, full-scale hydrographic surveys of the beaches closest to the base. You know the drill. Water depths, landmarks, bottom composition, obstacles . . . sand conditions above the water line, too. The whole nine yards, right out of the UDT handbook.''

"And the other area of interest, Captain?" Horner asked. "What about that?"

This time it was the man who called himself Jones who responded. "The base where you will be training is the main center for French missile testing," he said. "Virtually their entire missile program is run from facilities located there. The information we want you to obtain relates to these missile operations. We're looking for as much as you can bring back about the physical parameters of the test sites—dimensions of the facilities, the thickness of the concrete around their test beds, that sort of thing. Also, of course, the times and conditions of any launches they may make while you're there. You'll get details on what we're looking for in Paris, at the American embassy. Use my name, and you'll be referred to the proper office for your briefings. They'll be expecting you.'' The civilian glanced around the table. ''And let me stress again the need for absolute secrecy. It would not be . . . wise to let the French know about your actions.''

"I should think not," Finnegan muttered.

Kessler glared at him. "We understand . . . sir."

Jones just nodded. Galloway studied them for a long moment, then nodded approvingly. ''All right, then. You have your orders. You'll report back here when you get back from France. Any questions?''

"Just one thing, sir," Kessler responded. "If we're caught spying on the French? . . ." He left the question hanging in the air.

"Our government will deny any connection with this mission should you reveal it to the French authorities, Lieutenant,'' Jones told him. ''You will seem to be acting entirely on your own. I would . . . suggest that you not let that happen.''

''Don't worry, we won't,'' Finnegan said. ''SEALs don't break. Ever.'' That wasn't just an idle boast. Every SEAL went through an intensive Survival, Evasion, Resistance, and Escape course that simulated capture and interrogation by Communist forces. The school was so realistic some men who went through it found themselves wondering if they hadn't actually been captured. And anyone who violated Article V of the Code of Conduct by revealing any information, no matter how trivial, beyond name, rank, and serial number was bounced from the SEALs.

''We'll do the job, Captain,'' Kessler told Galloway.

''I know you will,'' the captain replied. ''Very well, then, you men may go. See you in about a month.''

No one spoke until they were in Horner's car in the Pentagon parking lot. As Horner maneuvered toward an exit, Richardson leaned forward from the back seat. ''What was that all about, anyway?'' he asked.

''Just what the man said, Junior,'' Kessler told him. ''The CIA strikes again. . . .''

''Yeah, Lieutenant,'' Richardson said. ''But . . . it just doesn't feel right, you know? The French are supposed to be our *allies*. Those swimmers they sent over last month . . . I liked those guys. Doesn't seem right to spy on them.''

Finnegan, sitting beside him, chuckled. ''The spooks'll spy on anybody, Junior,'' he said. ''Better learn it now.''

''Anyway,'' Kessler added. ''Think it through. French politics haven't been exactly stable, you know what I mean? They just announced they were pulling out of NATO at the beginning of the month, and that's got to make people pretty uncomfortable at Langley and Foggy Bottom. The Socialists are pretty powerful over there. Some day they could take over, in an election . . . even a coup. Especially with all the trouble de Gaulle stirred up when he gave up Algeria. Best we find out what their missile program can do now, before we're staring at those missiles and some Commie sympathizer has his finger on the button.''

''I guess you're right,'' Richardson said uncertainly. ''But it still seems like a pretty lousy thing to do. . . .''

Horner spoke up without taking his eyes off the road.

"Look at it this way, kid," he said. "We're SEALs. We carry out our orders. Even the stupid ones. But if you're gonna get squeamish on us, you don't have to take part. Just keep your trap shut and we'll do the work."

"No way, Badges," Richardson told him. "I carry my weight. If you guys are going to play James Bond, I'll be right there with you." He grinned. "After all, I want my share of all the broads you super-spies are going to get!"

Friday, 5 August 1966

Paris, France
1245 hours

"Well, Junior, how do you like Paris?" Jim Horner studied Hank Richardson's face as the younger man glanced around the crowded boulevard, the very image of an American tourist visiting the French capital for the first time.

"Man, oh, man, this place is something." Richardson gave him a grin. "I thought Washington was a pretty fancy place, but Paris . . ."

"What is it you like, kid?" Chief Radarman Simon Farnham asked with a broad grin. "The architecture, or the history . . . what?"

"The French broads," Horner said before Richardson could reply. "What else?" They all laughed, Richardson loudest of all.

Second Platoon—twelve enlisted men and two officers—had arrived at Orly Airport near Paris the day before aboard a commercial flight out of Washington National Airport. They were scheduled to leave Paris on Sunday, which gave the SEALs time for sightseeing and getting acclimated. Horner was uncomfortably aware of the fact that he and the other three who'd visited the Pentagon would also have to find time to finish their briefings at the U.S. embassy, but Kessler had scheduled that for Saturday. In the meantime, they were staying at a nice hotel, they had time on their hands, and the lures of Paris beckoned them onward.

So today they had time to goof off. Farnham had suggested the outing today. This was likely to be his last chance to travel overseas at Uncle Sam's expense; he was slated for retirement in another few months. He'd decided to make the trip to

France count and had invited Horner to join him. Horner, in turn, had extended the invitation to Junior Richardson as well. He had liked the younger SEAL from the very start and tried to offer him advice and encouragement whenever possible. Their relationship had a name—Horner was Richardson's "Sea Daddy"—and a long Navy tradition behind it. That was how continuity was maintained in the service, a senior man taking a young newcomer under his wing, showing him the ropes and passing on his wisdom. Not that Horner felt particularly wise. He just thought Richardson had the potential to be a damned fine SEAL and was determined to give him the chance to make good use of that potential.

They had already been through some of the usual tourist routines, with a visit to the top of the Eiffel Tower, to the Arc de Triomphe, and to the tomb of the Emperor Napoleon. At the last Farnham, a military history buff who frequently talked about Napoleonic history, had broken the other two up—drawing no small number of frowns from other visitors to the solemn and historic site—by commenting "If he was alive today, he'd want to be a SEAL, but he was too damned short to make the cut!"

It was mid-afternoon now, and they were walking back to their hotel along a pleasant little boulevard. Horner was idly watching a pretty French girl on a bicycle when Farnham spoke up. "God damn, I think I'm in love. . . ."

Without turning, Horner chuckled. "It's just hormones, Pete." Perhaps inevitably, Lieutenant Tangretti had bestowed the nickname on Simon Farnham, the ranking CPO in Team Two, in the early days of the unit, going on to intone solemnly, "Upon this rock I will build my SEALs."

"Not this time, guys," Farnham responded. "You gotta see this."

Horner and Richardson joined him at a small shop window. His gaze was riveted on a six-string banjo being put up on display by a clerk. It was obviously a handmade custom job, with a guitar neck. Farnham shook his head. "Man, that's just what I could use." Everyone in the platoon knew that Farnham, who already played guitar and mandolin, wanted to learn the banjo. The instrument in the shop window was ideal for him; it would give a banjo sound but could be played like a guitar.

The three men went into the music shop. Richardson spoke fair high-school French, and with his help Farnham persuaded the proprietor to let him see the banjo. He tried a few chords and they all agreed it sounded good, but Farnham wanted to compare it to a regular guitar. Horner, who also enjoyed playing guitar in his off-duty hours, suggested that they go back to their hotel and fetch their instruments. Inside of half an hour the three men were back, Farnham and Horner carrying their guitar cases.

They turned the rest of the afternoon into an impromptu country music concert in the tiny shop, with Richardson taking Farnham's Martin while Horner played his own Gibson. Farnham tried out the banjo and fell in love with it. The proprietor looked at them dubiously at first as they played a string of Patsy Cline and Hank Williams numbers, but the music drew a crowd and he soon was smiling his pleasure at the three Americans. When they finally stopped and put their instruments away, he sent a boy to a nearby shop for wine and bread and offered the SEALs refreshments.

While they were enjoying the last of the wine, Farnham grew depressed. "It's a hell of a nice instrument," he said morosely. "But did you see the price? I can't afford to spend six hundred bucks for a banjo . . . no way. Dottie would kill me."

Horner nodded in sympathy. Farnham had a wife and four kids at home, and they'd soon be facing college expenses. Moreover, with his retirement coming up, Farnham couldn't even be sure what kind of income he'd have after he left the Navy. Raiding his savings for something like this was out of the question. "That's a damn tough break, Pete," Horner told him, taking a last sip of wine.

Farnham nodded and got up, crossing over to the window display to look at the instrument again. When he was gone, Horner leaned close to Richardson. "Hey, Junior, you got enough on you to buy that banjo?"

"Me?" Richardson raised his eyebrows. "Yeah . . . sure. It'll pretty well wipe me out, but . . ."

"Look, we've all been trying to figure what to give Pete when he retires. The way I figure it, the whole platoon could chip in on that beauty, and you know he'd love it."

"Good idea, Jim," Richardson said. "Yeah . . . that'd be

perfect. A great way to send him off.''

"Well, you buy it today. Tell everybody you're getting it for yourself. Later on, though, we'll give it to Farnham. And everybody will chip in to reimburse you. Okay?''

"I'll be pretty short until you guys pay up. . . .''

"Yeah . . . right. Look, we all know you can wire your granddad for money, the way you did in St. Thomas last year. We'll help tide you over for a day or two until you can get your cash. Right?''

Richardson nodded. "Yeah . . . Yeah, sure. My grandfather likes to remind me where the inheritance is coming from. He likes rubbing my stepdad's nose in it. Might as well use it to someone else's advantage for a change. Okay, you're on.''

Farnham seemed surprised and a little hurt when Richardson went ahead and bought the banjo, but he was happier when the younger man offered to let him try it out any time he wanted. By the time the three returned to the hotel again, all of them carrying instrument cases this time, they were in high spirits. Horner was particularly happy. Farnham had always been a good mate, and the SEALs looked after their own.

Saturday, 6 August 1966

Paris, France
2015 hours

"How about a toast," Horner said, standing up a little unsteadily. "To our last night in Paris! May it be a memorable one!''

The other SEALs at the table echoed his sentiment, clinking their glasses together and laughing when Roger Reynolds missed Chief Finnegan's glass and sent wine spilling across the tabletop. There were eight of them in the restaurant, including Richardson, Farnham, and Harry Matthews, all members of Horner's squad. The others were from Second Platoon's Alfa Squad. It was the last night before they took the train to Toulon and got down to business, and they intended to make the most of it.

Wearing civilian clothes, they looked more like a bunch of tourists out on the town than one of the most deadly fighting forces in the world. The restaurant staff was starting to look askance at them, but they paid little attention to looks from either waiters or other patrons as they ate, drank, laughed, and talked. Their table was on the second floor of the restaurant, on a balcony that overlooked the street, giving them a spectacular view of the glittering lights that illuminated the banks of the Seine. Horner was struck again by the beauty of the city, so clean and pleasant, a peaceful contrast to the hustle and bustle of a typical American city.

He snatched a look at his watch. It was getting late, time to start thinking about the rest of the evening they'd mapped out back at the hotel. They were really just marking time here, until they could head over to the Crazy Horse Saloon to catch a late show.

Horner wondered if Lieutenant Kessler was sorry to be missing out on the evening, or relieved he didn't have to go out carousing with his motley crew. Kessler had been ordered to return to the American embassy tonight for some final briefings on their secret mission. All four of the SEAL spies had spent most of the day studying for the job, memorizing endless lists of information required and poring over old maps of the area to prepare for the beach survey they were supposed to perform. It had been a long day, spent under the steely eyes of a civilian in a dark suit who had offered neither name nor position. Although they looked nothing alike, the embassy man might have been created from the same basic CIA mold as Jones, the man who'd briefed them in Washington, humorless, quiet, watchful, and not a little bit disdainful in the way he treated the SEALs.

Horner felt sorry for Kessler, slaving away at the embassy in such dull company. The lieutenant was missing out on one hell of a party, but then he had always been the serious sort who didn't enjoy the night life nearly as much as his men. He wasn't anything like Steve Tangretti, Horner's first SEAL CO, one officer who really understood what it meant to get out and enjoy himself.

Chief Boatswain's Mate Ted Brubaker caught Horner's eye. He glanced toward Richardson, then at the door on the other side of the room. Horner nodded. It was time for the SEALs to make their move.

"Think I'd better hit the head," he said, standing. "That French wine goes right through you."

"Yeah, same here," Farnham chimed in. The two of them left the table, a little unsteady on their feet. In addition to plenty of wine with their meal, they'd already done some serious drinking at a bar near the hotel on their way over.

Neither man took the turn toward the door marked *Hommes*. Instead, they went downstairs and out the front door, throwing mock salutes to the big black man who acted as a combination maitre d' and bouncer, posted outside the front door just under the balcony table where they'd been eating. The two Americans were careful to turn up the street, staying out of the line of sight of their fellow SEALs until they'd reached the end of the block. Then they crossed to the mouth of an alley on the other side where they could keep an eye on the front of the restaurant.

Chief Finnegan joined them a few minutes later. "Doesn't suspect a thing," he said. "He's too busy eyeing that French chick at the next table. And Brubaker's started egging him on. That'll give the rest of the guys their chance to make a break."

"Poor old Junior," Horner said with a grin. "When's he going to learn to watch his back when he's chasing pussy?"

The others laughed. The SEALs of Team Two loved playing practical jokes on each other, and right now one of their favorites was just on the point of completion. By time-honored custom SEALs going out on the town would always invite all their buddies along, even the ones who were tapped out and couldn't pay their own tabs. One of the other guys would cover the one who was running short, and he'd do the same for another buddy some other time. It all evened out in the long run. But you had to keep a sharp eye out for the kind of scheme Finnegan, Brubaker, and Horner had hatched tonight. The SEALs were trying to sneak out of the restaurant, leaving the one man they knew didn't have any money to cover their bill holding the bag. Tonight it was Hank Richardson, who was still flat broke following the banjo purchase he'd made the day before.

They watched the front of the restaurant for a time, and soon the other four SEALs, led by Brubaker, appeared at the door. Finnegan showed himself at the mouth of the alley just long enough to attract their attention.

"He was right in the middle of making his move on the girl," Harry Matthews said as the others joined them. Finnegan was maintaining his lookout, keeping an eye on their balcony table. "Trouble was, her boyfriend showed up right in the middle of his pitch and made a scene. We slipped out while Junior was trying to smooth things over."

"This is better than the time we fixed him up with that hooker and didn't tell him he was expected to pay," Farnham said, grinning from ear to ear. He was still nursing a grudge at having Richardson buy the banjo he'd wanted so much, and he seemed to be enjoying himself even more than the rest of the group.

Horner could just imagine how Richardson must be feeling. He remembered the time he'd ended up stuck with the tab at a nightclub in North Carolina during training with the Army Special Forces at Fort Bragg. Right about now, he figured, Richardson would be realizing that none of the others were coming back. He would either have to ask for the check or keep right on ordering, postponing the inevitable. Because he certainly didn't have enough money on him to cover the bill eight hungry and thirsty SEALs had run up. Or he could try to make a run for it, somehow. . . .

"Hey, guys," Finnegan said from his lookout post. "I think the kid's getting ready to make a move. Better come and take a look."

They crowded around the CPO at the entrance to the alley. Richardson was standing by the balcony railing now, looking around as if trying to make up his mind what to do. Horner thought he could see a waiter approaching from behind, though it was hard to tell from his vantage point.

Suddenly Richardson was a blur of motion, grabbing at the railing and vaulting over it like it was a barrier on the obstacle course. He plunged downward, hitting the pavement below in a perfect Parachute Landing Fall. Horner grinned. It was a gutsy move, but could the young SEAL recover from the PLF before the bouncer closed in on him? It was going to be tight. . . .

Then all seven men in the alley mouth broke out laughing. The bouncer stared open-mouthed at the SEAL for a long moment as if unable to believe his eyes. Then he, too, was moving fast, but not toward the fugitive. The man turned and ran, screaming something incoherent in French. Richardson's reflexes were a credit to his training. As soon as he realized the man was running up the street, he took off at a fast trot the other way. Finnegan stepped out and waved him over, and the SEALs all clapped him on the back.

"You bastards," Richardson gasped. "You fucking, sneaky bastards. Just you guys wait. I'll get each and every one of you, some day. You won't know when, you won't know how, but I'll be waiting to get you all!"

"In your dreams, Junior," Brubaker told him. "What do you guys say? Did he pass?"

They chimed in with various opinions, ranging from complimentary to obscene. Still laughing, they started down the alley and away from the scene of the confusion. Horner remembered, though, to get the bill from Richardson. In the morning, he'd make sure to collect the money everyone owed and send it—together with a sizable tip—to the restaurant. Whatever the final cost came to, it would be well worth it. You didn't often get a night's entertainment to match a SEAL scaring a bouncer half to death.

Monday, 8 August 1966

Combat Swimmer's Compound, Naval Base Toulon, France 0630 hours

"Man, these Frenchies have it made. Wish we had a spread like this back home."

Hank Richardson nodded agreement at Horner's quiet observation. The French combat swimmers had their own separate compound outside of the main naval base near Toulon, located on a small peninsula and almost isolated from the other facilities. The American SEALs had arrived during the night, with little chance to see the facility that would be their home for the next few weeks.

"Yeah," Richardson said. "Just like Coronado. I'm starting to think our East Coast gang's been getting the shaft, you know?"

The SEALs were lined up along one side of an open parade

ground, casually dressed in shorts and T-shirts. The French combat swimmers were out in the middle of the field, sweating through physical therapy led by a set of tough-looking petty officers. There was one Frenchman, a second-class equivalent, who stood off to the side watching, as if far too superior to take part in the exercises. None of the Frenchmen seemed to find anything odd about this, but the Americans had exchanged a few comments among themselves. Back at Little Creek, morning PT duty was mandatory, under the harsh supervision of CPO Rudy Banner, and it was the chief aim of every SEAL to figure out ways to miss the workouts any time they could manage to. The thought of simply standing to one side and looking on made them wince; Banner's command of invective was popularly reputed to be able to flay a man to the bone at twenty paces.

Needless to say, in their exalted status as advisors and observers in France the SEALs had made it clear they weren't planning on taking part in the physical training alongside their hosts.

Looking at the sweating, straining line of men, clad in identical fashion to the SEALs, Richardson was struck by the similarities between the two groups. Both were the elite of their countries' naval forces, and they worked and trained and fought the same regardless of the differences in language and customs. His stepfather had made the same observation once about the Vietnamese LDNN trainees he had worked with in Southeast Asia. Perhaps war, and preparing for war, were universal constants.

"Nice to know we fit in here, at least," he said aloud. "Better than in Paris . . . or on that damned train."

Horner laughed. The Americans had played tourist in Paris, of course, and almost inevitably had drawn a lot of attention to themselves from the locals in the process. But for the train trip down to Toulon the day before they had intended to try to blend in with the French around them, so as not to call undue attention to themselves. The American embassy had thoughtfully provided each of the SEALs with a little pamphlet on French customs and etiquette to help them. But so far the results of their efforts had been more humorous than practical.

The pamphlet had advised that all French passengers traveling by train carried their own food; meals were not normally provided. According to the booklet, they carried bread, cheese, and wine in a little string bag. So the SEALs had dutifully equipped themselves with string bags and the appropriate contents for the trip to Toulon.

Unfortunately, as it turned out their fellow passengers were all carrying paper bags stocked with sandwiches and similar lunch foods. The SEALs, in fact, were the only ones with string bags on board . . . and thus had proclaimed themselves to be foreign tourists just as surely as if they'd worn loud sports shirts and carried cameras around their necks.

"I don't know, Junior," Horner said, still chuckling. "Didn't seem to me like you were having a whole lot of trouble fitting in last night . . . although I've got to say it sounded like a pretty tight fit from where I was!"

Richardson grinned at him. "Just doing my part for Franco-American relations, that's all," he said. He'd spotted a particularly attractive French girl on the platform at the station and struck up a conversation with her, using a blend of his halting high school French and her fairly good and beautifully accented English. She'd reminded him of the star attraction in the strip show his stepfather had taken him to see in New Orleans for his seventeenth birthday, and as it turned out he wasn't far off the mark. She danced at a club in Paris, not the famous Crazy Horse but another night spot nearby, and she was on her way to visit her family in Marseilles for a few days.

One thing had led to another, and by the time the train was pulling out of the station Richardson had maneuvered her into his upper berth and out of most of her clothes for an interlude of very intense foreign affairs.

No one spoke for a few minutes as they watched their hosts. Richardson couldn't get his mind off the feeling that the SEALs had more in common with these men than they did with civilians back home. "I still think it's a crying shame," he said quietly to Horner after a long silence.

"What's a shame?"

"That we're supposed to spy on these guys. Hell, we've got more in common with these Frenchies than we do with any of those spooks we talked to."

Horner's eyes darted left and right. "Can it, Junior," he growled. "You're supposed to keep your mouth shut." He hesitated. "But you're right. It is a damned, dirty shame. Trouble is, orders are orders, and that's all there is to it." He looked away, and the two men were silent thereafter.

The combat swimmers eventually finished their workout, and their instructors gave them the word to fall out for breakfast. Immediately several of the Frenchmen crossed over to join the SEALs. These were the same men who had formed the French contingent visiting Little Creek earlier in the summer. They had already formed friendships over there and now were assigned to help shepherd the Americans through their sojourn in Toulon. Richardson recognized one of them, a young, small, olive-skinned man he knew only as Jacques, who had been teamed as his swim buddy during some of the evolutions back at Little Creek. Jacques greeted him with a very American slap on the back and a warm handshake.

"*Mon ami!* I am pleased to see you again!"

Richardson smiled. "Yeah . . . same here, Jacques. Looks like we're right back where we were six weeks ago."

"Not quite, my friend," Jacques told him. "This time, you are, how do you say, on my turf, eh? Over here I can be sure that it is not the custom in the night clubs for the shortest man to buy the first round of drinks." He paused. "Here it is . . . the one with the worst French accent, no?"

"Well, then, I'm safe as long as old Badges here sticks close," Richardson said. "At least I get it right some of the time!"

They started walking toward the mess hall, passing within earshot of the Frenchman who had watched the PT session from the sidelines. One of the instructors, a dour, shaven-headed hulk who might have stepped out of a Foreign Legion movie, was talking volubly to him, with much waving of arms and pointing toward a nearby building. The second class gave him a long, withering look, said, "*Merde,*" and stalked off in the opposite direction. The bigger man looked after him, shrugged, and shook his head.

"What was *that* all about, Jacques?" Horner asked. "How does a second class get to be king of the roost like that?"

The Frenchman smiled. "Ah, that is just Pierre," he said, chuckling. "Pierre is very . . . secure . . . in his place here."

"How do you mean?" Richardson prompted.

"Ah, well, you must understand something about Pierre. He was an ordinary seaman during the troubles in Algeria a few years ago. During the fighting, he single-handedly took out a guerrilla machine-gun nest armed with nothing but a bayonet. An act of great bravery, no? President de Gaulle honored him with a direct Presidential appointment to the rank of second class petty officer in the combat swimmers, the posting he desired most.''

"Still doesn't explain how he gets away with acting like that,'' Horner said.

"No? Think on it. Pierre has no ambition of rising higher. Being a combat swimmer, and a great hero of the Algerian war, he gets his share of girls, you see? And his pay is all he wants or needs. So he does not care if he never rises higher . . . and of course no one would dream of demoting . . . busting, you would say? Busting the man who was given his rank by the President himself!''

The two Americans broke out laughing. "Well, I guess that shoots down any hope of learning his secrets and trying them back home,'' Horner said. "Damn. I thought he'd found the secret to real world-class goldbricking, too!''

"Ah, but he did, *mon ami.* Unfortunately, it requires a most powerful patron to carry it off. And I fear most of our kind will never match such a good choice in patrons.''

Richardson thought about how his stepfather had outmaneuvered the Navy's inquisition as a result of President Kennedy's support. "Oh, I don't know, Jacques. I think it's probably a hell of a lot more common than you might think.''

Chapter 15

Thursday, 18 August 1966

Long Thanh Peninsula
West of Can Gio, Rung Sat Special Zone
1920 hours

The SEALs were starting to hurt the VC everywhere within the Rung Sat.

Of course, Intelligence had been saying *that* from the very beginning, but by the middle of August the SEALs themselves were starting to believe it as well. They could *see* the difference.

Especially when a patrol turned up fresh meat . . . like this one.

Chief Mike Spencer stood in the burned-out clearing, watching as the other SEALs of his squad swept the target zone. His job at the moment was to provide cover for the rest of the team with his Stoner Commando light machine gun, but it didn't look as though he was going to be needed after all. There was no sign of Charlie, no sign of anything but that tortured and smoking, hellfire-torn patch of earth scarring the otherwise unbroken forest.

Early that morning, SEALs from Det Golf, working on the information provided by the documents captured three weeks ago, had located two carefully hidden silos here, containing an estimated 306,000 pounds of rice . . . the biggest haul taken so far in the war, and much too big a target for the SEALs to destroy by themselves and be certain of getting most of it. Instead, they'd extracted, reporting their find to MACV HQ. Within hours, the spot on Long Thanh Island pinpointed by the SEAL patrol became the focus of a blistering attack by air and naval units. Air strikes launched from a carrier group in the South China Sea, followed up by a massive bombardment by Navy warships, had transformed this part of the jungle from a dense forest of tropical mangroves to something more closely resembling the surface of an alien planet.

"Looks like a strip mine," Willy Marshall said, surveying the cratered terrain. Whole blocks of earth had been overturned, and mangrove trees two yards thick had been upended, splintered, and tossed about as though by some vengeful and furious giant.

"Put it down to urban renewal," Spencer said.

"Shoot, what urban? This is country."

"Okay. LBJ's War on Poverty. How's that?"

Marshall chuckled. "Nice to know we're doing our bit."

The SEALs were almost relaxed as they covered their teammates . . . *almost*. A careful sweep of the area had turned up nothing; chances were that any VC within ten miles of this spot had fled as the napalm started raining down on this one tiny swatch of jungle. Still, if the SEALs could make it back, even by helicopter, so could the VC. Spencer kept his eyes on the surrounding forest as he talked with Marshall.

"It *is* nice," Spencer agreed. "I've been getting sick and tired of chasing ghosts. Every once in a while, it's nice to find some tangible proof that there's an enemy out here."

"Yeah," Marshall said. "And blot it off the map!"

Already, the SEALs of Det Golf felt like they were starting to get somewhere after months of repeated failure and frustration. Det Delta had left for CONUS on August first, back *to the World* as troops in-country had started calling it. Four days later, a Det Golf patrol had captured three sampans on a river just sixteen miles southeast of Nha Be. They were big ones, too, two of them motorized, and they were laden to the gunwales with some three tons of rice. Two days later, the SEALs ambushed two more sampans and a large junk off Long Thanh and, in the firefight that followed, seven Vietcong were killed.

And finally, this morning, this monster cache had been located. The American SEALs were starting to hit the VC where it really hurt: in their stomachs.

There was an intense, grinding frustration to this type of warfare, a warfare that concentrated more on attrition of the enemy's will to fight than it did on actual numbers. But an army marched on its stomach, at least according to the military aphorism attributed to no less than Napoleon, and the destruction of the communists' stores of rice scored victories on several levels. Hungry soldiers were less likely to fight, more likely to desert. Hungry armies had to delay plans for attacks in order to secure additional food supplies. Villages already taxed by the VC for rice to supply the communist forces would have to be taxed again . . . and that would swiftly erode much of the popular support the Vietcong enjoyed in the Rung Sat. If the VC grew too demanding, too heavy of a burden on the local rice farmers, they would soon find they'd lost their safe havens and be forced to move elsewhere.

The loss of 153 tons of rice would be a crippling blow to VC logistics throughout the Rung Sat.

Spencer and Marshall watched quietly for a time as SEALs explored the ripped-open silos where the rice had been stored. Much of the rice had been scattered by explosions, burned by napalm, or ruined by the water that had seeped in afterward, but a good many tons remained inside the cement remnants of the silos. The SEAL force had been reinserted partly to assess damage, but also to make certain that all of the communist rice stores had been destroyed. A number of SEALs were plying the interiors of the silos with generous sloshes of liquid from five-gallon cans. Someone shouted warning, and the SEALs scattered for cover.

"There she goes!" Spencer said as orange flame billowed into the evening sky. "Rice Krispies!"

"Yeah," Marshall said. "What do you think, Chief? Think the VC'll pull out of the Rung Sat after this one?"

"I don't know, Willy," Spencer replied. "Depends on how many more silos they have buried in these swamps. And on what they can keep sneaking in from the Mekong Delta."

"Aw, we got their supply lines snipped. They want to hang around here, they're gonna starve to death!"

Spencer watched the flames mounting against the evening sky. "I sure as hell hope you're right, Willy."

Friday, 19 August 1966

Long Thanh Island
Thirteen miles southeast of Nha Be
1015 hours

Step . . . pause, studying the terrain ahead. Step . . . pause again. Willy Marshall moved slowly and with studied precision through the undergrowth, following the trail. He was crouched low, his M-16 tucked up beneath his arm with every shackle, every bit of loose metal carefully wrapped in black tape. Water dripped from the brim of his boonie hat, but his mouth was desert dry. Charlie was close, close enough that the young SEAL could damned near feel him. But where? Where?

Marshall had had the feeling all morning that the VC were up to something. Yesterday's strike on those rice silos must have made them yelp loud enough to be heard all the way back to Hanoi . . . and with a general effect that could probably be compared to finding a wasp's nest and kicking it over. His initial feeling that Charlie was going to have to abandon the Rung Sat after losing all of that rice had evaporated overnight. Now he was thinking that even if he was flat out of food,

Charlie could hang on a good many days before he finally had to move out. Besides, thinking that the SEALs had crippled Charlie's logistical network, or that Charlie couldn't keep getting more supplies from neighboring districts, was just a continuation of the dumb-ass wishful thinking that had kept American forces in Nam blundering around blind for all of these years now.

No, Charlie was definitely still here in the Rung Sat in plenty of force. If there was a difference today, it was that now he was *really* pissed off at the SEALs. . . .

The SEALs had inserted off of PBRs early that morning, two teams of six SEALs each pulling a recon sweep along the banks of the Dinh Ba River, thirteen miles from Nha Be. There'd been plenty of signs along the trails and near the river indicating that the VC were in the region, and in strength, but the climax had come with the discovery of a series of trenches, bunkers, and weapons positions above the river bank, positioned to sweep the Dinh Ba with rifle, machine-gun, and mortar fire.

Hurriedly, then, hoping to catch some of the VC who'd built that complex, the SEALs had extracted by PBR, then moved further upriver. Seawolf helicopters quartering the sector had reported two heavily camouflaged sampans pulled up on the shore, and Lieutenant Toland had decided to check it out. Reinserting once more, they couldn't find the sampans, but they found plenty of tracks in the mud beside the river, and a trail running west to east through the jungle. It looked like several dozen people at least had passed that way, probably within the past few hours.

Lieutenant Wilson had been bossing this operation personally from the deck of one of the PBRs. He'd ordered Toland to take seven men with him and follow the tracks, while the rest of the SEALs and the PBRs continued upstream. The seven included Marshall, Chief Spencer, Luciano, Tom Herrick, Frank Horowitz, Tim Radenaugh, and Randy Conway.

As the SEALs started to off-load their gear, Marshall had turned to Wilson. "Jeez, Lieutenant," he'd said. "I'm not real crazy about daylight patrolling."

He'd not meant it to sound like whining and he'd not meant it to sound scared, though now he was wondering if it had come across as both.

Step . . . pause. Study the terrain. Step . . . pause . . . step . . .

"You want out, son?" Wilson had asked.

"Hell, no! I just think it's stupid wandering around on those trails in broad daylight!"

Wilson had chuckled. "Well, you should be okay." He'd pointed toward the sky. "We've got two Seawolves up and covering you."

"Yeah, okay." He'd tried not to sound dubious.

He'd also offered to take point as soon as the eight SEALs reached solid ground. No special reason, exactly . . . except that he was feeling ashamed of what he'd said to the lieutenant.

They were well into the jungle when a radio call had come through from the PBRs. The sampans had been spotted less than five hundred meters east of Toland's team. They would close on them in a pincers movement, Toland and his seven SEALs coming in from the west, Wilson and the others moving up the river in the PBRs. If there were VC near the sampans, they would probably flee when the PBRs closed in . . . smack into Toland's patrol.

There'd been some disquieting news at the same time, however. The Seawolf helicopters had, at best, a ninety-minute loiter time; in fact, they'd been shuttling back and forth between their way point over the Rung Sat and Nha Be all morning and now, once again, they were running low on fuel and returning to Nha Be.

Which meant that the SEALs were on their own now, with no air cover at all.

Step . . . pause . . . listen. . . .

Somehow, Marshall didn't think the VC were fleeing. The jungle was entirely too still, with none of the usual bird and insect calls that made the Rung Sat such a continuously noisy place. That silence carried two messages: if the VC were running, Marshall was pretty sure he would have been able to hear them; more important, and more worrisome, the unnatural quiet meant that something, some*one* had startled the chorus to silence. Maybe it had been the SEALs themselves, but usually, the SEALs moved with such stealth that the animals scarcely noticed them at all.

He didn't like following this trail. A better approach would have been to split the team and move to either side of the path, avoiding possible tripwires in the road and getting behind any ambushers waiting in the forest, but the mangroves were thick back there. Taking the overland route would have been both noisy and excruciatingly slow. There were times when speed was preferable to stealth.

Even speed, however, was relative. They were moving faster than they would have had they avoided the path, but they were still taking their time to work their way back toward the river. Marshall was on point. Fifty meters behind him, Toland was crouching in the shadows with his M-16 covering him, and off to either side, tucked in among the trees bordering the trail, were Lucky, Chief Spence, and Franky, with the rest bringing up the rear. Plenty of support if he needed it. . . .

Step . . . carefully placing the ball of his foot on the ground, testing by feel to see if he'd come down on twigs or dry vegetation before daring to ease his full weight to that leg. His back and shoulders ached with the strain; he'd been doing this for an hour now, making painfully slow progress toward the sampans, and he was about ready to call it quits. Step . . . pause, carefully studying the ground ahead, the vegetation ahead. He was more certain than ever that something up there wasn't quite right.

Abruptly, the vegetation thinned out, and Marshall could see a clearing . . . actually more of a wide spot in the trail, where the trees stepped back far enough to admit a generous shaft of daylight all the way to the forest floor. Beyond and to his right, less than twenty meters away, now, he could see the river. Two long, low sampans, their deckhouses festooned with freshly cut clumps of shrubbery, were pulled up on the bank.

He smelled something . . . the sharp pungency of overripe fish. . . .

Possibly that was what had been nagging at him subconsciously for the past several minutes. The stink of *nuoc mam* hung over that clearing like an invisible cloud. Someone had been cooking with the stuff recently, probably at the river bank in or near the sampans.

Carefully, he raised his hand so that the SEALs following him could see. *Stop*, he signed. *Wait!* No sense in everybody blundering forward until he'd checked out this change in the terrain. He studied the clearing carefully, seeing nothing out of the ordinary, but noting too those parts of the landscape that were still blocked to view from this vantage point. He needed a closer, unobstructed view.

Dropping flat on his belly, he inched forward through the ferns and swamp grass bordering the path. He moved slowly, with the studied, coordinated precision and control of a stalking jungle cat. Emerging from the shelter of the overhanging trees and moving into daylight, he stopped again, his view now unobstructed. Concentrating hard on the random, almost abstract background of vegetation, Marshall systematically divided the wall of forest surrounding the clearing into sections, then analyzed each one by methodical one, willing himself to really *see*. . . .

Almost by magic, a face separated itself from the background of one of those search sections, a face almost invisible among the shadows of the forest, but distinguishing itself by being a blob of color not quite in tune with the abstract patterns of light and dark on the foliage around it. Once he'd spotted the face, Marshal could trace the other outlines of the man's body. He was wearing black pajamas or other dark clothing, squatting behind a log deep within the shadow of an overhanging bower of bamboo. The guy had a good position, too, as good as any SEAL ambush site Marshall had ever seen.

Knowing now what to look for, Marshall continued studying that wall of foliage. There! There was another ambusher, twenty meters from the first, his face partly hidden by the receiver of a heavy weapon of some kind, probably a Russian- or Chinese-made RPD machine gun. And next to the trail, close to where it emerged by the river . . . there was another. And another.

Marshall let out a long, carefully smothered exhalation. He was definitely looking at an ambush, with at least four men positioned on both sides of the narrow clearing. As he visualized a map of the area and placed the gunners and their probable fields of fire, he realized with a sudden, inner iciness that he'd already moved deep into the ambush kill zone.

The setting of an ambush is both science and art. Ideally, the ambushers place themselves in an L shape, with the long side parallel to the long side of a designated kill zone, and the short end at right angles to that, sweeping the entire zone with concentrated automatic fire. The idea is to give every man in the ambush team a specific field of fire overlapping the fire of his comrades to both left and right, and to reduce the chances of scoring own goals by keeping friendly forces out of the line of fire. One man in the ambush decides when to spring the trap, usually well after the point man in the target force has moved past his position . . . or at least after the main body has entered the kill zone too deeply to extract itself easily. The ambush team leader can decide to trigger the attack early, of course, if it appears that the target force has been alerted and is pulling back.

Marshall needed to think of none of this, of course. It was all there, the cumulative lore of many hours of BUD/S combat training and exercises, and he could react without having to stop and think things through. Judging from the position of the four men he could see, this appeared to be a carefully thought-out ambush. The only mistake the VC had made that Marshall could see was the fact that, once the trap was sprung, the SEALs would have their backs to the river . . . and the two PBRs were already motoring slowly up the stream, its crew manning its weapons as the second six-man SEAL team prepared to get into the water to investigate the sampans.

Shit! Charlie just never learns, does he? flashed through Marshall's thoughts. The SEALs always tried to place themselves with their backs toward water, providing a perfect escape route if things got too hot.

But as soon as that thought crossed his mind, Marshall questioned it. The hell with that noise. Charlie *always* learned . . . and was always getting better at what he did, using his mistakes to improve upon his tactics.

Now if I were setting this ambush . . .

Marshall's eyes widened. The long side of the ambush L extended south along the trail almost to the river itself, which left a very short base to provide the crossfire. If you wanted to extend that base, to set up a decent crossfire, you'd have to put more men . . . *there! Among the trees on the opposite bank of the river. . . .*

He couldn't see anyone over there, but suddenly, with an absolute conviction born of both training and experience, Marshall knew they were there. The VC in this area would have known SEALs would be the ones to respond to air reports of a couple of camouflaged sampans. And they'd be eager to strike back after the SEALs had hurt them so badly yesterday. They must have analyzed SEAL movements and attack patterns, and figured that the Americans might try a two-pronged approach on the bait, one group coming from the water, the other from the forest. When this trap was sprung, it would catch not only the SEALs of Toland's squad coming out of the jungle, but the PBRs and the SEALs moving toward the beach as well.

Twelve SEALs, eight PBR crewmen, two river boats . . . not a bad haul. The possible scope of the ambush, though, told Marshall something else. He'd spotted four men and assumed the presence of others. How many others there were would be determined by how many men the VC commander thought might be necessary to trap and kill two squads of SEALs backed up by the machine guns of a couple of PBRs.

How many might that be? A twenty-four-man platoon? Two platoons? How many men could that commander squeeze in among these trees and keep them hidden? Marshall could imagine several hundred men out there, especially if the VC followed proper small-unit tactical doctrine and maintained both a reserve and a rear security element.

The most astonishing aspect of the situation was that, so far as he could tell, the VC had not spotted him yet. Of course, that didn't mean that someone *hadn't* already seen him. The eight SEALs could have been under observation ever since they'd come ashore, and the lurking ambushers' lack of movement or excitement could simply be the result of very good discipline. Or, possibly they'd been tracking the squad from the river but hadn't yet seen him, out in the lead. With his green-painted skin and carefully camouflaged form, it was possible he'd managed to crawl into the target area without being noticed.

That might say a lot for his woodscraft, but not a great deal for his chances of getting out of this. Having spotted the ambush, he was now faced with the far more difficult question of what to do about it. Normally, if he discovered something like a booby trap or a waiting ambush or something else of interest to the squad, the point man would move back to the squad leader and communicate with him by signs or whispers. That approach just wasn't going to be possible here. Backing up with a stealthy tread was far more difficult than moving forward, and if he was spotted while trying to back away, or if the VC commander did already have him under observation, his movements would pinpoint exactly where the SEAL squad was coming from. If he took too long trying to back out or turn unobserved, sooner or later one of the other SEALs in the squad would come forward to investigate, possibly triggering the ambush. There was a sign, holding his fingers over his face like a mask, that meant "enemy in sight," but even that much of a movement could give him away . . . and it might also bring Toland and the rest forward to see what he'd run into.

In fact, no matter what he tried to do at this point, chances were that Toland and the others would move forward . . . and if they did, they would be walking smack into that kill zone.

As far as Willy Marshall could tell, there was one and only one thing he could do. . . .

Turning slightly, he brought the muzzle of his M-16, still tucked at the ready beneath his arm, to point at the nearest of the waiting, shadowed faces, then clamped down on the trigger, loosing a fusillade of full-auto fire into the jungle growth.

A flock of water birds, silent until now, sprang into the air with an unheard flutter of wings as gunfire barked and chattered. Immediately, the hidden VC returned fire, their bullets snicking through the vegetation and churning up the ground in sharp, spurting geysers of earth. One round slammed into Marshall's left shoulder, the shock brutally savage and numbing, but he kept holding down the trigger of his M-16 until the magazine ran dry and the receiver snapped empty. Rolling to one side, he dropped the empty mag, then fumbled one-handed for a reload. His hand was sick with blood, but he managed to snap the thirty-round banana clip home, then release the action, chambering the first round.

He was taking aim on another Vietcong gunner when a round slammed into his head, blasting out the back of his skull and killing him instantly.

1028 hours

The roar of gunfire crisscrossing the clearing ahead was deafening. "Willy!" Toland yelled. "Willy, are you all right?"

''He's down! He's down!'' Spencer yelled back. He was positioned ten meters off the trail to Toland's right, at the edge of the thickest part of the mangrove swamp. The CPO leaned into the recoil of his Mk 23 Stoner Commando, slamming round after round across the fire-torn clearing and into the trees beyond. Full-auto gunfire thundered through the forest, where seconds before there'd been complete silence. Nearby, Conway was on the radio. ''Bowman! Bowman! This is Archer One! Ambush, grid Alfa-three-five by Sierra-one-niner! We have a man down! Ambush!''

Radenaugh's M79 gave its characteristic hollow thump as it hurled a 40-mm grenade clear of the trees. Seconds later, an explosion erupted at the treeline opposite, hurling dirt, branches, and shredded vegetation into the air. Spencer kept firing his Commando, triggering short bursts aimed at the muzzle flashes that revealed each enemy gunman. Moving carefully, using the trees for cover, he worked his way to the edge of the clearing, ten yards from Marshall's body.

From here, he could see across the clearing, could see the river and the two sampans pulled up on the near shore. The PBRs were taking fire from the opposite bank, the south side of the river where more VC had been lying in wait, and were returning fire with rattling, full-auto enthusiasm. It was clear enough to Spencer what had happened. Marshall must have spotted the ambush before either the SEALs or the PBRs were fully into position for a clean hit. Rather than betraying the position of the rest of the SEALs in the squad, he'd elected to trigger the ambush early by opening fire himself . . . a gutsy decision, but one that might have just killed him. From Spencer's position, crouched behind a tree, it looked as though most of the back of Marshall's head was gone; his boonie hat, stained bright red with flecks of white and gray, lay upside down beside the trail just a couple of yards away.

As the other SEALs in the squad moved up to the treeline, the volume of fire sweeping the clearing doubled and redoubled in sheer, devastating fury. Leaves and stalks of bamboo, saplings, and branches were snapping free and falling to the ground as lead slashed through the thick vegetation. On the river, all eight machine guns aboard the two PBRs were in action, along with the concentrated weaponry of the other SEAL squad. Spencer saw two men in dark clothing suddenly break and run from the river bank, making a dash for the thicker part of the forest. He swung his Mark 23 to track them and squeezed the Stoner Commando's trigger, leading the running forms by a couple of feet. The figures, briefly silhouetted against the river, kept running, vanishing into the trees. *Shit!*

"Spence!" Toland yelled from Spencer's left. "Can you see Willy?"

Several rounds snapped through the foliage within a few feet of Spencer, and he jerked back behind the sheltering mangrove, his back against the wood. "He's down! I think he's dead!"

"Cover me! I'll make pickup!"

"Negative!" A bullet gouged a fist-sized furrow of wood out of the mangrove's trunk with a loud *thwock*, sending a spray of wet, pulpy splinters past his face. "Negative! He's bought it!"

"Cover me!"

Taking a deep breath, Spencer broke open the Commando's box magazine to make sure he still had plenty of rounds left from the 150-round belt, then shifted around to face back into the clearing. A VC round snickered a foot above his head, but he aimed at the general area where he thought the fire was coming from and held down the trigger. He saw his rounds lashing the earth in front of the treeline and walked his fire up. To his left, Toland broke from cover, firing his 16 from the hip as he dashed toward Marshall's body.

A VC appeared at the far end of the tree, standing up behind a fallen log to aim at the SEAL officer. Spencer shifted position, swinging his Stoner to cover this new threat. He didn't know if he'd managed to hit the guy, but he vanished as soon as Spencer fired. Toland dropped to the ground near the treeline as bullets snicked among the palm fronds and ferns curling above his head.

"Lieutenant!" Spencer called. "You okay?"

"Yeah! Don't think I can reach him."

"Maybe we should pull back."

"Not and leave him out there."

"Lieutenant, he's *dead!*"

"We don't leave our own!"

The gunfire from ahead increased in savagery and volume. If the SEALs had moved all the way out into the clearing before the VC had opened up, all eight would probably have gone down. *Shit!* Willy had probably managed to save all of them.

Spencer felt torn about recovering Marshall's body, though. He'd always considered himself to be a professional, a cold-blooded pragmatist when the situation warranted it. For months now, in bull sessions back at Nha Be, the SEALs of Det Golf had told one another that they would never leave a buddy behind, but that had always seemed to be a kind of bravado, a machismo swagger more in keeping with Wild West gunplay and John Wayne heroics than the cold art of war.

But at the same time, he knew Toland was right. They couldn't leave Willy out there.

The only problem was, how the hell were they supposed to reach him without getting cut to ribbons?

Conway moved closer, lugging the heavy PRC-22. "Lieutenant?" he said. "Bowman is telling us to pull back."

Toland aimed his M-16 into the clearing and began triggering quick, frenetic bursts of fire. "Can't hear you, Randy," he said. "Call Bowman and ask when the choppers'll be back!"

"Roger that!"

The uneven gun battle continued for several minutes more. Spencer had the feeling that some VC were trying to flank the SEALs to the north, so he kept leaning out and sending long bursts of fire from his Commando to the left, hoping to disabuse them of the idea. They were at a stalemate; the SEALs could pull back, but they didn't want to leave without Willy; the VC were relatively safe where they were, but they couldn't bring accurate fire to bear on the SEALs back in the jungle and, if they tried to rush them, they would be cut down in a bloody massacre.

"Lieutenant!" Conway called suddenly.

"What?"

"Choppers inbound!"

Smoke drifted in blue-white clots among the trees, as explosions continued to crash and thunder. Over that cacophony of raw noise, however, another sound intruded, the steady, blessed *whup-whup-whup* of an incoming helicopter heard long before the lean, black, insectlike machines themselves became visible. Then the first of the Seawolves heaved itself noisily above the trees on the far side of the river, its M16 system engaged, the four muzzles of its side-mounted machine guns flickering as it swept the VC positions south of the river with fire. A moment later, and the first pair of rockets hissed from the Seawolf's weapon pods, exploding among the trees on the river's south bank with savage twin concussions.

The second Seawolf roared low overhead, turning toward the VC positions along the trail. Machine-gun fire swept the forest, though it was clear the gunners were overshooting by quite a bit. The boys in the helos couldn't see the SEALs on the ground and were trying to avoid scoring against their own team. Spencer found himself thinking that he'd have been willing to accept a friendly strafing run if it would guarantee capping some of those bastards across the way.

An irrational thought . . . common enough in combat. He stopped firing because he no longer had even a suggestion of where the enemy might be hiding.

As the Seawolf thundered overhead, Toland yelled, "Cover me!"

Spencer leaned around the bullet-mangled tree trunk he was hiding behind and opened up on the hidden VC, firing wildly. Toland reached Marshall's body; Spencer stepped out from behind the tree, still firing, his body hunched over as though to make a smaller target, and dashed out into the smoky sunlight to join him.

Toland was short, only five-seven; Spencer was over six feet, while Marshall was in between the two. Awkwardly, they hoisted the downed SEAL between them and started backing toward the relative safety of the trees as Spencer continued loosing one-handed bursts from the Stoner. He doubted that he was hitting a damned thing with the cowboy gun slinging, but he sure as hell could scare the bastards into keeping their heads down for a critical few seconds. . . .

A grenade burst near the far treeline erupted in a fast-boiling cloud of gray and white. The first smoke grenade was followed by a second, as Radenaugh put down a blanket of smoke. Spencer and Toland dragged Marshall back in among the mangroves, then lay him down. The most cursory of inspections was all Spencer needed to confirm that Marshall was indeed dead; a round had entered his head just above and behind his right eye and gone out the back, taking with it half of the back of his skull and most of his brain tissue as well. Marshall's right eye was missing; the other stared up at Spencer with a curiously intense, blue gaze.

"We *always* bring back our own," Toland said at Spencer's side.

"Affirmative!" Spencer had known Marshall was dead, but the confirmation was a brutal shock nonetheless. With a sharp, bitten-off profanity, he moved back from Marshall's body, took up a firing position beneath the overhang of a fallen tree trunk, and resumed firing.

The Seawolves continued to circle overhead, pouring down fire on the VC positions. "Okay, people!" Toland yelled. "Time to get the hell out of Dodge! Lucky! Help me with Willy! Spence! Cover us!"

"Rog!"

He unclipped the box magazine on his Mark 23 and snapped home a fresh one. If Charlie was going to rally and counterattack, or if they'd managed to layer two ambushes on the trail against the possibility of the main body getting away from the first, this would be the time for them to make their move. . . .

But there was no counterattack. He opened fire again, hosing the trees along the clearing, but certain now that the VC, once again, had slipped away. Some shots followed them as they made their way back through the jungle; Spencer continued to cover the group's withdrawal, while Toby Bosniak carried Willy's body. After a while, it was clear that there was no longer any incoming fire, that the SEALs alone were responsible for the continuing crackle and bark of gunfire in the jungle.

Soon, those shots too had ceased, and a stunned, exhausted silence returned to the jungle. The VC, if there were any remaining in the area after the Seawolves had appeared, stayed under cover and silent as the seven SEALs, still carrying the body of their fallen comrade, rejoined the PBRs near their insertion point further downstream.

Chapter 16

Sunday, 21 August 1966

Toulon, France
1538 hours

"Eighteen feet."

"Eighteen ... three fathoms ... got it." Richardson scrawled a notation on his slate board while Harry Matthews reeled in the weighted line. "Looks like that wraps up this stretch. Shall we move on?"

"But of course," Matthews told him, removing his boonie hat with a flourish and giving a sitting bow. "Sou' by west, helmsman, and full speed ahead!"

It had to be one of the most bizarre hydrographic surveys ever conducted, Richardson thought as the two men began to pedal while he held the tiller bar hard over to steer the bobbing, awkward little craft. They had rented the paddle boat from a seaside concession stand on one of Toulon's crowded public beaches, two ordinary American tourists out for a quiet afternoon on the blue Mediterranean. The boat wasn't very stable or seaworthy, a precarious two-seat perch mounted atop a pontoon arrangement and driven by paddles connected to bicycle pedals. But it could get the two men almost anywhere along the beach, with a little sweat. And it was certainly not the kind of craft the French authorities would suspect of carrying two spies hard at work charting their beach approaches.

After a short time pedaling, Matthews raised his binoculars and started studying the shore while Richardson got his compass out of his pocket. Harry Matthews was a late addition to the spy team, authorized by their spook contacts at the American embassy. The SEALs needed to operate in two-man teams for much of their work, and it was hard for someone as conspicuous as Jack Kessler, the platoon CO, to get involved with the enlisted men. So Matthews and Richardson were a more-or-less permanent pair, while Horner and Chief Finnegan covered other aspects of their espionage mission as the other team.

"Well, do you have a landmark to take a bearing on, or don't you?" Richardson prompted after a moment.

"Oh . . . yeah. Sorry." Matthews lowered the glasses and grinned. "Spotted some French chick changing into her suit over there. You wouldn't believe what she was getting away with, right out in public. She was better'n that fan dancer at the Crazy Horse, you know?"

"Hey . . . don't I get a look?" Richardson demanded.

"Sorry, Junior, she's done by now. But I'll let you use the glasses the next time." Matthews raised the binoculars again, swept them along the beach. He found a church spire and the towering walls of an old fort to use as landmarks. The SEALs took bearings on each one, and then used the weighted line with its series of measured knots to take a depth reading. From a distance, they'd look like a couple of tourists idly fishing with a hand line. Richardson reached back and pulled a couple of bottles of beer from an ice chest behind the seat to complete the illusion.

So far, such methods had worked out perfectly. It was a far cry, he told himself, from the stories his stepfather told of UDT beach recons in World War II, but the mission was going surprisingly well. Another weekend would finish off the hydrographic survey entirely, just in time for the SEALs to head for home in early September.

As for the French missile base, it had turned out to be almost as easy. Early on, the SEALs in the spy detail had decided to go all-out to give Washington the information they had asked for . . . and more. As Kessler had pointed out, this was their chance to show just how much a team of real operators could bring back if they were turned loose on a scouting mission under their own initiative. Given some of the stories that had been coming out of the West Coast men returning from Det Delta's Vietnam assignment, every bit of proof the SEALs could produce to show the brass hats what they were capable of would be useful.

So they'd hit the ground running at Toulon. During regular duty hours, they worked and sweated alongside their combat swimmer counterparts on a variety of exercises. But in their free time, the five American spies went to work cracking the missile base security in the most unlikely fashion. The SEALs, after all, were welcome guests, trusted friends and allies. They were also Americans in a foreign land and behaved as such— brash, curious, rude and intrusive. Hawk Finnegan had been the one to suggest the obvious course for them. All they really had to do in order to get the job done, he'd maintained, was behave normally.

Horner and Richardson had taken to wearing cameras from the platoon's equipment locker everywhere they went off duty, and over the course of a few days their habit of taking pictures of almost everything in sight was written off as typical American enthusiasm run wild. The cameras became so much a part of their civilian garb that the French stopped noticing them entirely. And the four enlisted SEALs roamed everywhere, gaping at the scenery, pointing objects of interest out to one another, chattering about everything and nothing, snapping pictures of each other for souvenirs.

A lot of those pictures happened to be taken around the outskirts of the missile base. And before they went out on these expeditions, Matthews and Finnegan were carefully measured. The SEALs knew each man's height, the length of arms and legs, the distance between buttons on their clothes . . . everything that would serve as a useful yardstick. So when Matthews had his picture taken against the backdrop of a test bunker, it was easy enough to tell the thickness of the concrete based on the measurements they'd already taken of the man and his garb.

They'd virtually completed their work before a French sentry finally happened to notice Horner taking photos of Finnegan in a restricted area. He'd been very apologetic and polite. Perhaps it had not been explained fully, he suggested, but photographs were not allowed in certain portions of the naval base. The Americans had apologized profusely, and there the matter stood. No effort had been made to confiscate the offending cameras or to discover what else the SEALs might have photographed before. They couldn't use their cameras any more, of course, but the remaining bits of information they needed to finish out their observations were easily gathered by less brazen methods.

Richardson expected the CIA to be surprised when they received the SEAL report on Toulon. It wasn't often that a covert intelligence report was supported by full-color pictures featuring men in loud Hawaiian shirts mugging for the spy camera. . . .

They didn't move on right away from their position off the beach. There was no point in making their day's movements look too purposeful or patterned. Anyway, it was a warm Sunday afternoon, the beaches were crowded with pretty girls in the briefest swimsuits either man had ever seen, the beer was cold, and the motion of the water was relaxing. Their spy mission had turned into a real holiday, and now that they were so close to finishing, Richardson, for one, was glad to just kick back and relax for a while.

Tuesday, 23 August 1966

Off Cap Cepet
Toulon, France
0427 hours

Quartermaster's Mate First Class Jim Horner moved under the water with the smooth, easy strokes born of long practice and a natural affinity for the sea. He checked the compass on his wrist every so often to make sure of his bearings. Even the clear waters of the Mediterranean were murky under a pitch-black night sky. He couldn't even clearly make out the shape of his French swim buddy a few feet off to his right, though he could sense the man's presence as he moved.

Who would've thought a scrawny kid from Allentown would end up here? The thought struck him, now and again, whenever his Navy career led him to new experiences like this one. He'd wanted to be a Navy diver ever since he'd seen Richard Widmark in the movie *The Frogmen*, back when he was just a teenager dreaming of a future that would take him away from a dreary life in a dreary Pennsylvania town miles away from anywhere interesting or exciting.

So Jim Horner had applied himself, exercising, pushing himself to what he thought were the limits of his endurance, adding muscle and bulk until he thought he had a chance to be a frogman. He'd joined the Navy in '55, after a summer loading and unloading trucks for his father's shipping company. It had taken years to finally realize his dream and get accepted to UDT training, and when he'd finally made it Horner had quickly discovered that his childhood efforts were feeble by comparison with what his instructors had demanded of him in Little Creek. Horner and his classmates had been pushed well past the limits of endurance there, to a place where only sheer willpower and determination could keep the body going.

The UDT in the early sixties hadn't been much like the service depicted in that movie. There was no war on, and even if there had been one he'd soon found out that he shouldn't plan on fighting underwater battles with enemy swimmers or any of the other more improbable sequences from the film. The UDT's job was beach survey work, destruction of obstacles, and other essentially routine functions. Sometimes things got a little more interesting, like when divers got assigned to a space capsule recovery. Horner's one exotic experience in the Teams had come in 1961, when he was assigned to a UDT unit training in Greenland. Diving into icy waters from a hovering helicopter wasn't quite what he'd signed on for, but it was better than loading trucks on a New York City dock or hanging around Reading waiting for something, *anything*, to happen.

But the same determination that had earned him a spot in the UDT had attracted attention from his superiors, and when the first list of men assigned to the new SEAL Team Two had been posted in Little Creek, Horner's name had been on it. Since that time, things had started getting a lot more interesting. SEALs were always on the move, attending special schools, rotating overseas to train with European commando units . . . and always holding themselves ready for the call to action. Horner had missed out on the Cuba swim with Steve Tangretti, but he'd been on hand for a second recon mission in the middle of the Cuban Missile Crisis. And in 1964 Horner's SEAL platoon had been involved in the brief but intense guerrilla conflict in Santo Domingo, which had culminated in a running firefight through the streets of the capital city.

No one could claim he wasn't getting excitement now. And

there had been rumors back in Little Creek that Team Two was going to be tapped for service in Vietnam in the next few months, alongside their West Coast counterparts from Coronado. Horner hoped the rumors would turn out to be true. He enjoyed training, liked the chance to see new places . . . but those things palled next to the prospect of a real fight. Jim Horner had always given two hundred percent, and if his country was at war he wanted to be there, be part of it, the way his Uncle George had been there with the Marines in World War II.

He detected motion at his side and realized that André was reaching out to tap his shoulder. The French swimmer pointed toward the surface, and Horner nodded. Both men angled up, moving carefully to keep from making any tell-tale disruptions in the glassy water.

On the surface, starlight gave just enough illumination to pick out the rocks thrusting out of the water less than fifty yards away. Horner scanned the uneven, steep-sided shore until he spotted a familiar landmark. He touched André's arm and pointed, feeling smug. They'd come up less than a hundred yards from the tiny shelf of beach where they'd hidden their kayak a few hours earlier. Even by SEAL standards it had been a damned fine piece of navigation.

Still not speaking aloud, they dove under the surface again and struck out for shore.

Emerging from the water, Horner was glad to be able to push up his face mask and unstrap the Mark 57 closed-circuit diving rig across his chest. He liked the French rebreather system a lot better than any of the units in use in the States. Wearing it in front not only made it easier to check the oxygen bottle and the baralyme canister that absorbed CO_2, but it also freed up the back to carry other gear. And it didn't have a breathing bag like many other systems Horner had used. There was never a concern with CO_2 buildup. But even with all these advantages, he was glad he didn't have to use it any more tonight. It had been a long and difficult exercise, but now the two men were nearly done.

As they pulled back the brush that concealed their kayak among the rocks, André echoed Horner's unspoken sentiments. "It is good to have that done with, is it not?"

"I'll say," Horner agreed. "You think the guys on the *Colbert* are still on the lookout for us?"

André laughed. "If so, they are in for a long night, eh? I would like to see the look on Monsieur Bonaire's face when he finds out his boasts were empty."

The night's exercise had sprung out of a chance encounter at a Toulon bar a few nights earlier, when some regular French Navy men had suggested the combat swimmers and the SEALs with them were useless against the real Navy. It had nearly developed into a brawl then and there until a French lieutenant named Bonaire had challenged the commandos to do their best to prove their claims of superiority. So tonight Horner and his partner had turned a scheduled exercise in penetrating harbor defenses into the opportunity to make their point. They'd been dropped off from a patrol boat well out to sea in a kayak, which they'd brought ashore on the rocks of Cape Cepet. Then they'd gone the rest of the way in underwater to plant phony limpet mines on the bottom of the cruiser *Colbert*, Bonaire's ship.

They still had to make it back to the pickup point without being detected, of course, but the hard part of the exercise was over now. Horner decided they had a few minutes to celebrate, so he reached into the covered bow of the kayak and pulled out the two bottles of beer he'd hidden there before they'd left the swimmers' compound the evening before.

He turned to face André, extending one of the bottles, and broke into laughter when the French swimmer proved to be offering him a bottle as well. "Great minds think alike, I guess," Horner said as they both laughed.

With great ceremony they traded their bottles and pried them open, taking deep swigs of the warm brew. Horner studied his opposite number as they drank, thinking how much alike the two of them were. André was about his own size and build, though he was a few years older and rated as the equivalent of a CPO. He'd seen service with the French in Vietnam before Dien Bien Phu, and later in Algeria as well. That made him a combat veteran. Horner, despite his experiences in the SEALs, didn't feel he qualified as such yet, and he was faintly envious of the Frenchman as a result. But that didn't detract from the camaraderie the two men had built up, first at Little Creek and now here in France. André had "seen the elephant" by going into combat in Nam, but that was the only real difference between them.

They finished their beer without saying more than a few quiet words, then dragged the kayak down to the water's edge and climbed aboard. As he pushed off the rocks and began to wield his double-ended paddle with practiced skill, Horner told himself that it wouldn't be long before that remaining difference between them was erased. If the rumors were true, he'd have a shot at Nam soon, and he didn't intend to miss out on the action.

Friday, 26 August 1966

Submarine *Daphne*
Off Toulon, France
1045 hours

"Okay, people, let's keep in some kind of order here. There isn't much room, so try not to bump into anything."

" 'Isn't much room,' " Richardson muttered. "Thank you, Lieutenant. I never would have known . . . unless maybe having somebody's elbow in my eye might've tipped me off."

"Quit your griping, Junior," Jim Horner told him. "What's the matter with you, anyway? Feeling clausty today?"

"Fuck off," Richardson shot back. "I just don't think God intended this many people to crowd together in one place, okay?"

Horner's comment had touched a raw nerve. Even a mild fear of tight places or the total darkness of a night dive in deep water could be a SEAL's undoing, and no one would ever admit to being claustrophobic, "clausty" in SEAL slang, under any circumstances. Nonetheless Richardson wasn't fond of cramped quarters or close-packed crowds, and conditions aboard the French sub *Daphne* were making him edgy today.

It was a routine exercise, so the briefing the previous afternoon had assured them. Just a little ordinary practice locking in and out of a submerged submarine. He'd gone through the same sort of thing aboard the *Sea Lion* in the Caribbean the year before. But even though the procedure for using escape trunks for a quick undetected exit was old hat, Richardson was growing increasingly irritated. Any sub was too small by far for his taste in the first place. And as the SEALs and their French swim buddies had worked their way forward in the boat, he hadn't seen anything that looked like an escape trunk.

The sign over the compartment they were entering now translated as TORPEDO ROOM, and Richardson assumed that was at the very bow of the sub. It seemed pretty strange to put the emergency escape hatch this far forward. Wouldn't a more central location have been smarter? . . .

Inside, he looked around. The compartment was crowded, with four SEALs—Richardson, Horner, Kessler, and Brubaker—and their four French swim buddies, plus some sub crewmen who were looking at the swimmers in their underwater gear with curious, even envious expressions. But it wasn't so crowded that he couldn't see the fittings clearly . . . and he still didn't see anything that even remotely resembled an escape trunk.

Richardson turned to Jacques, his swim buddy. "Maybe I shouldn't be asking, but just how the hell are we supposed to get out of here?" he asked.

Jacques grinned and pointed toward the bank of torpedo tubes at the forward end of the compartment. One of the crewmen was undogging the hatch and swinging it open. The French swimmer didn't say anything, but his meaning was clear enough.

"Please . . . please say you're just shitting me," Richardson said. The sinking feeling in his stomach reminded him of the time when he was ten and he'd felt his bike sliding out from under him as he'd tried to swerve out of the way of an oncoming car. . . .

He swallowed. He'd survived that . . . and a hell of a lot worse, too. But he didn't have to enjoy the prospect.

"Er, Lieutenant," he said aloud. "I thought the Navy studied torpedo-tube lockouts and decided they weren't a real good idea?"

Kessler shrugged. "I guess our hosts have different ideas," he said. "That's what we're here for, isn't it? To compare the ways we handle different problems?"

Yeah, right, he thought. *We're getting ready to do something the Navy, God bless them, decided not to use. Wonderful.*

"Okay, here's the drill," Kessler said. "Each pair, one SEAL, one swimmer, will go out together. Each man gets a mini-lung, and each pair will have a flashlight and a hammer . . . use the hammer to tap on the tube if you get in trouble,

so the crew can pull you out, but don't forget how these submariners feel about people damaging their boats. Save that
hammer for a real emergency, people.'' He fixed a particularly
long look on Richardson. Ever since he'd run into trouble
qualifying on deep dives under a sub off Puerto Rico, his
reputation as a potential clausty had gone around the platoon,
and his comments hadn't helped his reputation any this time
around.

"It will take about eight minutes for the tube to flood and
the outer door to open up. Once you're out, swim for the
surface,'' Kessler went on. "There's a rescue boat waiting up
there. We'll be sending out the whole platoon in batches, so
you guys'll have a little bit of a wait on the surface, but don't
sweat that. The important thing is to show what we can do,
right?''

"Hoo-yah!'' Brubaker gave the conventional SEAL response, but even he didn't seem too happy about it.

"Right!'' Kessler said. "Okay, Junior, you're first up.''

"Me, sir?'' Richardson blinked. "Er . . . Chief Brubaker's
a lot better swimmer, sir. Maybe he should take the first
shot. . . .''

"You don't want to go, Richardson?'' Kessler said, frowning. "I don't want to have to downcheck you on this exercise.
It wouldn't look good. . . .''

"Look, Skipper, I'll jump out of an airplane, hike a hundred
miles, kill anything that moves, and skip breakfast if I have
to, and you'll never hear me gripe about it,'' Richardson said.
"But I'm telling you right now, I do not like the looks of that
thing.'' He jerked his thumb at the open tube.

Brubaker chuckled. "Neither do I, Junior,'' he said, forcing
a smile that didn't strike Richardson as being very convincing.
"But that's the drill for today. Think of it as an adventure . . .
like something Lloyd Bridges might have done on 'Sea
Hunt.' ''

"Look, Chief, I ain't no Lloyd Bridges, I ain't on no TV
show, and I ain't going,'' Richardson told him. He wasn't sure
himself whether he meant it as a joke or not.

Apparently Horner wasn't sure either. He moved close be-
side Richardson and bent to speak softly in his ear. "All right,
Junior, you've had your fun,'' he said. "But take my advice.
Don't push it. Kessler already has you figured as clausty, and

if you keep this up he'll have your hide. You get me? You could get dropped from the Team . . . especially if the orders for Nam come through. Your stepdad wouldn't like that.''

"Yeah . . ." Richardson gave Horner a glance. "Yeah, you're right. Thanks, man." He turned to Jacques. "Well, I guess nobody's going to be happy until we make like a couple of sardines," he said. "You want to lead the way?"

The French swimmer gave him a sardonic grin. "As you wish, *mon ami*."

"Unless, of course, you guys let broads into your combat swimmer outfit," Richardson went on, eyeing the tube again as he followed Jacques across the compartment. "Little cramped-up place like that would be a great place to take a date. . . ."

That made everyone, even Kessler, laugh. Jacques accepted his gear from a crewman, strapped on the mini-lung and tucked the flashlight into his belt. Then he grabbed a support above the tube opening and lifted himself feet-first into the tube. After a moment of squirming, he disappeared into the darkness. Richardson hesitated one last time, then stepped forward to collect his own mini-lung and the small hammer proffered by the French sailor. Once the lung was in place he clamped the mouthpiece in place and took a few experimental breaths, listening to the sound of air passing through the regulator. Unlike the Mark 57 unit they used for most dives, this one was a compact open-circuit rig, useless for undetected swims, but light and small. Richardson wasn't sure a full-sized rig would have fit in the narrow confines of the torpedo tube.

He entered the tube head-first, so that he lay head to head with Jacques. Behind him, a crewman swung the inner door shut with a clang that reminded Richardson unpleasantly of a tomb being sealed. It was pitch dark, and the sound of the two men breathing through their mini-lungs was an eerie rasp. Richardson fought to control his breathing.

It felt like being buried alive. The tube was little wider than a coffin, and it took all of Richardson's self-control to keep from betraying the rising waves of panic within him. He couldn't even talk to Jacques, thanks to the mouthpiece, but perhaps that was a blessing. He might have screamed aloud if it hadn't been for that hard lump of rubber between his teeth. He stiffened for a moment as a new, regular drumbeat sounded in his ears, the noise of pumps pulling seawater into the tube. It had already been cool, but now the temperature dropped as the chill water began to fill up the cramped space around the two swimmers.

A fleeting, almost hysterical thought crossed his mind. Maybe the French had discovered their spy efforts; if so, this was the very best revenge they could take. Kessler had said it would take eight minutes to flood the tube, but Richardson was beginning to think he'd been trapped inside far longer. Eight minutes . . . eight hours . . . eight years . . . the measurements were meaningless, there in the encroaching dark.

Richardson thought about pulling out the hammer and tapping on the steel to signal the crew and call it off, but he suppressed the impulse. He couldn't back down now, especially after his initial show of reluctance. Even if he wasn't dropped from the Team for giving in to his fears, he knew he'd never be able to face his stepfather again. Steve Tangretti believed Richardson, like his real father lost all those long years before, could do no wrong. He wouldn't shatter the illusion if he could help it. . . .

Besides, another irrational stray thought ran through his head . . . submariners *really* hated to have their boats banged up.

Jacques switched on the flashlight, and for a moment Richardson was blinded by the dazzle. After a few moments it cleared. He still couldn't see much, but he could make out the Frenchman's eyes by the faint light. The other man didn't look concerned. Richardson tried to draw some comfort from that as the waters rose around them, leeching out whatever heat was left in the tube. Richardson had to fight a yearning to keep his head above water as it rose higher. The unyielding steel above his head made it impossible anyway, but that didn't help stave off the impulse at all.

Then the water was over his head, and a crescent-shaped sliver of brightness appeared at the end of the tube, beyond the half-seen bulk of the French swimmer. Richardson forced himself to stay put until he was sure Jacques was clear, then slithered down the length of the torpedo tube and out into the open sea beyond.

Once outside the boat, he could function again. Jacques was waiting for him, and as he kicked clear of the outer tube door the Frenchman pointed toward the surface. Richardson nodded vigorously and the two men started upward.

The exercise was over. As Richardson's head broke water he knew a deep feeling of relief. After facing his fears today, he told himself, nothing else the SEALs threw at him would ever be as bad. Not even combat. Not even Vietnam. He could get the job done, like a good SEAL.

But he prayed he never had to go through another day like this one. . . .

Friday, 2 September 1966

Toulon, France
1740 hours

"Hey, Badges, congratulations!"

Jim Horner lifted a hand in acknowledgment of Ted Brubaker's call and went into his room before anyone could pin him down to talk. He was pleased, of course, that the French had seen fit to grant combat swimmer badges to Horner, Finnegan, and "Red" O'Malley, three men out of the entire SEAL contingent of fourteen. Not even Lieutenant Kessler had been awarded one, and Horner took it as a real mark of respect. But inevitably it was an honor that would bring up all the old jokes about his overabundance of school patches and his zealous pursuit of specialty training in every conceivable area of Navy service. After a while, the lines got old.

Anyway, he wanted to get packed. The SEALs would be leaving for Paris by train fairly early in the morning, and Horner planned to make one last bar-hopping pass through the waterfront district of Toulon before he left. If he was packed and ready to go, he could get thoroughly shit-faced tonight and still be able to get his act together when the time came to get up. Horner had some very strict notions of how to make a plan and then stick with it, and he wasn't going to let a lot of well-meaning buddies throw him off the track. . . .

He had just started to pack his sea bag when a knock came at the door. Horner sighed. Maybe he wasn't going to be able to stick with his plan so easily, after all. "Come on in," he said.

It wasn't one of the American SEALs, but André, his swim buddy. The Frenchman looked apologetic as he came in the room, holding a bundle under one arm. "Forgive the interruption, my friend," he said. "But since you are leaving tomorrow, I wanted to give you a little gift."

André's bundle proved to be a set of fatigues with the tiger-stripe camouflage pattern that had first been used by French units in Indochina a decade back. Since then the tiger stripes had been adopted by the Vietnamese armed forces, and by some American units as well.

"I know where you will be going," André said quietly. "And these blend in quite well."

Horner stared at the uniform, hardly knowing how to react. No one in the platoon had ever hinted to their French hosts at the possibility that they might be going to Vietnam. A unit's deployment options was one thing that wasn't shared even with allies. But André, a veteran of Indochina himself, must have realized that the SEALs would find a way to get into the war, one way or another.

It was quite a meaningful gift, one nation passing the torch to another. . . .

"Er . . . thanks," Horner said at last. "Thanks." He took the fatigues from his swim buddy.

"And do as I did, once you find yourself over there," André went on.

"What's that?"

"If you examine them closely, my friend, you will see no holes in them. I would hope you can keep them the same way when you wear them . . . in a far country."

"I'll do my best," Horner told him. "Believe me, I'll do my best."

Chapter 17

Tuesday, 6 September 1966

U.S. Naval Amphibious Base
Little Creek, Virginia

"All right, you squirrels, listen up! You might think that coming back from an all-expenses paid vacation to the south of France entitles you to a little time to readjust to the real world before you get down to work again. Well, I'm here to tell ya that ya thought wrong!"

Jim Horner tried to hide a smile as he listened to CPO Banner's familiar gravelly voice. The man was a legend in SEAL Team Two, a tough little fireplug who took it as his divine mission in life to turn extraordinary men into extraordinary SEALs, whatever the cost. Hearing his growled comments as he paced back and forth on the grinder in front of the platoon wearing a T-shirt and swim trunks was like the first real taste of home after the sojourn in Europe.

They'd made the trip back with a minimum of complications. On the train ride from Toulon to Paris, the Americans, wiser now, had come equipped with paper bags and ordinary lunches, so that this time they were hardly noticed at all. Kessler had called at the American embassy over the weekend, but his reception there had been low-key. The SEAL spy team had been curtly instructed to deliver their findings to Captain Galloway's office at the Pentagon, and then dismissed. After all the buildup, it seemed anticlimactic, but the SEALs had put it down to typical agency bureaucracy in action.

In Washington, though, after their plane had landed and the rest of the platoon had already departed for Norfolk, the orig-

inal four men, plus Harry Matthews, had found their welcome
far warmer. There was a certain amount of confusion at the
Pentagon—evidently word had just come through that Galloway had been promoted to rear admiral and was about to be
reassigned, which left his office in some disarray over the
coming changeover—but once they were back in the same
conference room where they'd received their orders in July, it
was plain they had scored some points. The debriefing had
been headed up by Jones, with a trio of business-suited col-
leagues who might have been cut from the same ''spook''
mold as their boss. All four men had been startled at the depth
and thoroughness of the SEAL report, complete with color
photographs. By the time the session had wrapped up, the
government men had made it plain they were pleasantly surprised at just how much the Navy commandos had been able
to accomplish. Galloway had made a point of seeing them
before they left, adding his congratulations and good wishes
and hinting that they had done the SEALs a genuine service.

So now they were back in Little Creek, back to the old
grind. It was almost as if the trip to France had never happened
at all. . . .

''In other words, ladies,'' Banner continued. ''Welcome
back to Banner's World, where we try to give you a little taste
of hell on Earth each and every day.'' He gave them an evil
grin. ''Before we get started, though, some announcements.
While you folks were working on your tans and learning to
parlez vous with all the good-looking French broads, Commander Teller got new orders. The new CO of Team Two is
Lieutenant Commander Hood, and he's got a few things to
say before we get started. Commander?''

Banner stepped aside to allow the officer, a slender man in
a well-pressed uniform, with his hat at a jaunty angle, to come
forward. ''Thank you, Chief,'' he said. ''I am Lieutenant
Commander Robert Hood. The first man who calls me 'Robin
Hood' gets two hours extra of PTs. The *second* man to do so
will get his butt kicked from here to Berlin.''

Some polite laughter in the ranks greeted his sally, and
Hood allowed himself a smile. ''While you were away, gentlemen, some decisions were made that affect your platoon.
First of all, Mr. Kessler has earned a well-deserved promotion
to lieutenant. He is being posted to a specialty school for the

next few months, which opens up an officer's slot in your outfit.'' He gestured toward Lieutenant j.g. Hechinger, who had been Kessler's second-in-command. ''Mr. Hechinger will take over the duties of platoon CO immediately. As your junior officer, I am assigning a very promising ensign, Daniel Mariacher.''

At Hood's sign, the ensign took a step forward from the cluster of officers behind the new Team Two commander. Horner examined him with interest. He looked a little old for an ensign, in his mid-twenties at a guess, with clean-cut features but calculating, knowing, dark eyes. Mariacher looked tough and ready to take on anything and anyone that got in his way.

''That's *My*-ocker,'' Hood said, grinning, ''not Merry-ocker, the way it's spelled. Mispronounce it at your own risk!

''Now I know a lot of you have been eager to learn if the rumors about Team Two and Nam are true,'' Hood continued. ''To tell you the truth, I kind of wish I knew myself. The fact is, we're waiting on word out of the Pentagon for a final answer. Things over in Vietnam have started heating up the last couple of months. Some of you may have heard we've taken the first SEAL combat casualty over there. It looks to me like Team One's going to need all the help they can get, especially as the powers that be keep widening SEAL responsibilities over there. So I'm guessing that sooner or later we're going to get our shot . . . and I expect all of my Team Two platoons to be in topnotch shape so that we're ready when the opportunity comes.'' His smile grew broader. ''That's why I'm turning you back over to the tender ministrations of Chief Banner, who has promised me that only genuine grade-A number-one SEALs will even survive his physical training program from here on out. So may God—and Chief Banner—have mercy on your souls! Chief, take over.'' The commander rejoined his staff officers, while Ensign Mariacher joined the ragged line, standing out from the others in his crisp khaki jacket and trousers.

Banner looked the ensign over. ''You want to change into something more comfortable, Mr. Mariacher?'' he asked.

The ensign shook his head. ''Never mind that, Chief,'' he said cheerfully. ''Do your worst! Nothing wrong with getting a little sweat on your clothes.''

''All right, then,'' Banner said. ''You asked for it. Let's start with push-ups. Down in the dirt, you squirrels!''

Banner led them through the mindless physical jerks, working them as hard as a batch of new recruits going through boot camp. It was a grueling workout, but as they finished the first phase of the exercises Horner had trouble suppressing a grin of anticipation.

"Right!" Banner called out at last. Though he had set the pace all through the workout, the chief wasn't even winded. "On your feet! Now it's time for a little run. It's down to the beach for the lot of you!"

Horner exchanged glances with Hawk Finnegan. That was the signal the platoon had been waiting for. Almost as one the SEALs of Second Platoon—all except the two officers, Hechinger and Mariacher—yanked down their swim trunks and stepped out of them, ready to follow Banner down to the beach. The CPO did a double-take but hid his surprise well.

They'd hatched the plan back in France. The combat swimmers in Toulon customarily wore skimpy briefs, rather than trunks, when they swam, and the SEALs had all acquired their own bikini-cut suits during their stay. They'd all worn their new suits under their regular trunks this morning, so Banner was suddenly confronted with the spectacle of twelve SEALs in the scanty attire of the beaches of France.

He looked them over for a moment and then shook his head. "Well, if you apes want to run in your skivvies, that's fine by me. We'll just take a couple of extra laps around the compound so that you can all show off those legs of yours. Let's move it! Double-time! *Hut*-two. *Hut*-two! *Go! Go! Go!*"

Horner was chuckling as the formation moved out. It took more than a simple practical joke to put Rudy Banner off his stride.

Monday, 26 September 1966

Norfolk Naval Air Station
Norfolk, Virginia
1447 hours

As the C-130 transport plane rolled to a stop on the tarmac, Ensign Daniel Mariacher studied the other men in his squad and smiled. They were a good crew, he told himself silently. Damned good. He'd been lucky to draw an assignment to Sec-

ond Platoon . . . and when the time came, he—and they—
would make a real mark.

Mariacher had been born in Perth Amboy, New Jersey, three
days before the Japanese attack on Pearl Harbor. His grandparents on both sides of the family had been immigrants; his
father and mother had broken up before he was born and the
"father" he remembered had been his mother's second husband. He'd grown up poor, and most of the stability in his life
had come from inside himself, not from family or friends or
even the Catholic school he'd attended as a child.

For a poor kid from New Jersey, there weren't many tickets
to a better life. College was out of the question, and most of
the work Mariacher could have landed were boring, dead-end
jobs. But he'd been raised on war movies and John Wayne
Westerns, and by the time he'd reached his seventeenth year
he'd already known that he wanted to be a military man. Mariacher had dropped out of high school and tried to join the
Marines but was turned away because he'd still been under
age. But a few months later, after his eighteenth birthday, he'd
joined the Navy as an enlisted man, a common sailor.

Mariacher hadn't taken well to Navy life, though. At first
he'd been ideal material, gung ho, the kind of sailor who
would spit-shine the bottoms of his shoes as well as the tops.
But he'd always had a stubborn streak that resisted authority,
and it hadn't taken long for Daniel Mariacher to realize that
he didn't often agree with those in authority above him. Restless, he'd put in for transfers to every post that sounded even
a little bit exciting or exotic, and to his surprise he'd been
accepted to Underwater Demolitions.

Posted to UDT-21 in Little Creek, Mariacher had fallen under the influence of a crusty chief petty officer named Broadhurst. The man had seen potential in Mariacher—not that he'd
ever admitted any such thing—and pushed him unmercifully.
Thanks to Broadhurst, he'd finally completed his high school
equivalency tests, learned the ins and outs of Navy administration and how to make them work in his own favor . . . and
he'd applied for Officer's Candidate School. Mariacher still
wasn't quite sure when or why he'd decided to become an
officer. It was just something Broadhurst seemed to expect of
him . . . and no one in his right mind failed to live up to Chief
Broadhurst's expectations.

He'd completed OCS just before Christmas of '65, and spent his first six-month tour as an ensign in the Engineering Department of a destroyer in the North Atlantic. That was the same kind of duty he'd rebelled against as an enlisted man, and Mariacher did everything in his power to get a posting back to the UDT . . . or, better yet, to the Navy SEALs, whose reputation for daring and independence struck a genuine chord in Mariacher. As it happened, he'd started his campaign to win acceptance to the SEALs at just the right moment, when the orders came down doubling the size of each of the two Teams. They needed officers, badly, and an ensign who already had experience as a UDT frogman was just the sort of officer they needed. Despite the fact that Mariacher hadn't been through all the phases of training he needed to qualify as a SEAL, he'd been accepted and transferred off the destroyer in June.

Mariacher had gone through the service schools he needed to round out his qualifications during the summer. Now, at last, he was a full-fledged SEAL, in command of Second Platoon's Bravo Squad. But that, he told himself, was only the beginning. All his life he'd managed to make things happen instead of just waiting for the luck of the draw. And he wasn't about to stop now. . . .

"Hey, Mr. Mariacher," QM/1 Horner spoke up from the other side of the transport. "Think they'll give us liberty before we have to go back to the grind?"

"Shit, Badges," Mariacher said with a grin. "You just got back from two fucking weeks in fucking Puerto Rico, for God's sake! Most people'd call that a fucking *vacation*, and you still want liberty? Un-fucking-believable."

The other men laughed, some a little nervously. They didn't really know what to make of Mariacher, who swore like an enlisted man and treated most of the Navy's sacred cows with undisguised contempt. It created a bond with some, but others seemed to be put off by it all. But if they expected Mariacher to act like some stiff, uptight, pencil-dicked little prig of a Regular Navy officer, they were sure to be disappointed. The sooner they got used to it, the better.

"That was Puerto Rico?" Richardson piped up. "All the walls were puke green, we spent the whole time swimming in circles around some damned island gunnery range, and I didn't lay an eye—or a hand—on a broad the whole time. If that's a vacation, I sure as hell don't want to see what it's like to get back to work!''

"Sorry, kiddies,'' Mariacher said. "I missed the chance to find some willing pussy just as much as you guys did. Maybe more. I know what to do with it when I find it. But them's the breaks sometimes. Ours not to reason why . . .''

"Ours but to make 'em die,'' Gunner's Mate Second Class Roger Reynolds finished. He gave a smile that was all startling white teeth in his dusky-complected face. Half-Cherokee, Reynolds was a big man who enjoyed every aspect of his life as a SEAL and excelled at everything from diving to knife-fighting to handling an M60 machine gun like it was a child's toy. "Don't worry about these guys, Mr. Mariacher. They're just afraid Old Lady Waverly's been thinking up some new way to get even. . . .''

That generated another laugh.

"Serve you bastards right if she did,'' Mariacher said with an expression of mock sternness on his face. " 'Oh, the *indecency* of it!' ''

The stunt Second Platoon had pulled with the French bikini swimwear at their first muster back in the States hadn't fazed Rudy Banner at all, but it had turned out to have some unexpected results nonetheless. While they were running on the beach, they'd been spotted by the wife of Captain Waverly, one of the senior officers at the Amphibious Base. Waverly, an old-time UDT man himself, would never have thought to wonder at the antics of the SEALs, but his wife had been another matter. Her complaints, long, loud, and strenuous, had resulted in disciplinary action for the unit, starting with orders that all PT evolutions would in future be performed in full sweats to avoid giving offense to any of the more sensitive ladies on the base. It was still a sore point with Second Platoon, who tended to feel that a civilian shouldn't try to impose her standards on Navy men while on a Navy base. If she was offended, let her look the other way! But such was not the case, not among the officers who had to deal with complaints like hers.

The transport's crew chief opened the door and waved the SEALs toward it with the air of a man who wanted the strangers out of his domain. Mariacher was the last man off, descending the steps outside with his seabag over one shoulder. As he reached the bottom, he caught sight of a cluster of SEAL officers near one of the buildings. One of them gestured him over. It was Commander Hood, looking like he was nearly bursting with good tidings.

"Ensign Mariacher!" he called over the hundred-decibel roar of a jet taking off. "Welcome back! I've got news all of you have been waiting to hear! We're authorized for Vietnam. Two reduced platoons, twenty-five men. Twenty enlisted and five of you guys!"

The words struck home with all of them. It was the word every man in Team Two had been waiting for. Mariacher didn't hesitate. Like a good officer, he reacted fast to get the tactical advantage, clamping a hand on Hood's arm, drawing him out of the circle and leading him off to the side. He wasn't as big as Hood, but his grip was strong and backed up by an unyielding determination to be the first to make his case for the duty every SEAL in Little Creek wanted.

"I want in, Skipper," Mariacher said urgently. "I've got one of the best squads in the Team, and I know we can do the job better than any of the other outfits in this whole damned unit." He went on, outlining all the reasons why Hood should grant the request. A few of his claims were even true, and he drew on every lesson he'd ever learned from CPO Broadhurst on the care and feeding of superior officers to make his case as watertight as possible.

Hood heard him out, never even trying to interrupt him. But when Mariacher finally paused, the commander shook free of his grip as if he hadn't even been trying to hold on and laughed in his face. "Mariacher, you are one obnoxious son-of-a-bitch, I'll give you that," Hood said. "Last time I heard the bullshit flying like that a matador showed up and put the poor beast out of its misery. But you should never try to shit a shitter, kid. I'd sooner buy swamp land in Florida than fall for a con job like that one."

Mariacher tried to hide a crestfallen look, but Hood wasn't done yet. "Mariacher, the reason I'm going to send you to Vietnam has nothing to do with logic, or with that pitiful excuse for begging you just pulled. I'm sending you over there to face those poor Vietcong bastards for two reasons. First, it'll deprive you of pussy. That'll make you one *really* mean mother, which will result in a high number of VC casualties, and that'll look good on the unit's record, and therefore on mine. Second, you're the junior guy in the outfit, and that means you're expendable. Cannon fodder. You get yourself killed stepping on a mine or getting sniped, we don't lose somebody with much experience, and the unit—and me—*still* looks good. So you can pack your bags. You're going to Vietnam."

Mariacher grinned. "Sir, I don't care *why* you're sending me. Just as long as I get to go. If you weren't a man, I'd kiss you . . . hell, I'd *marry* you, if I wasn't married already! Matter of fact, I think I could kiss you anyway, Skipper. . . ."

"What, and make your squadmates jealous?" Hood laughed. "All right, kid, you've had your fun. But we've got a lot of work to do, if we're going to get our people in shape for a tour in Nam. So let's get to it!"

"Aye-aye, *sir.*"

Mariacher had never meant those simple words more than he did now. He was going to Vietnam. . . .

Chapter 18

Saturday, 7 October 1966

Long Tau River
Rung Sat Special Zone
0540 hours

They'd been out most of the night, and now the sky was swiftly growing lighter, promising a bright and cloudless dawn. The fourteen SEALs, two reinforced squads out of Team One, were aboard an LCM moving up the Long Tau some twenty miles from Nha Be. First Squad was commanded by Lieutenant j.g. Toland; Second Squad was under the command of Lieutenant j.g. Ray Evans. The LCM's Navy crew consisted of one j.g. and three men. Lieutenant Pham Van Sinh, a Vietnamese LDNN liaison officer, rounded out the contingent.

The squads had inserted at several points on Long Thanh Island during the night, searching for any evidence of VC activity. By this time, the SEALs had established a fairly sound intelligence network based on information they themselves had gathered, both from captured documents translated before they were passed on to Saigon, and from friendly informants within the various villages along the rivers they patrolled. The SEALs, it turned out, were increasingly viewed with something approaching awe by the locals. Lieutenant Wilson had passed the word early on: anything the SEALs could do to establish closer ties with the people living in the SEALs' Area of Operation could help the team establish useful contacts. For instance, Golf Platoon's hospital corpsman, Gary Shaw, held sick call for the locals in several of the smaller riverside villages every other week, and other SEALs had spent whole days visiting some of the towns, getting to know the people, trying to pick up some of the language, and volunteering muscles for such diverse activities as helping to raise the roof on a new schoolhouse run by some Vietnamese Catholic nuns in the village of Ap Thanh, to helping to haul a junk out of the river in order to repair a hole below the waterline in Can Gio.

The outreach program was paying off, too, especially with contacts made with sick and wounded people helped by Shaw's ministrations, or by passing out antibiotics and clean bandages to local physicians. Villagers befriended by the SEALs regarded them with something like wonder, and they'd met plenty of people who were more than willing to tell everything they knew about VC movements in the region. It didn't really matter any longer that Saigon refused to sanction information gathered this way with the hallowed name *intelligence*. By living and working and talking with the villagers, the SEALs were beginning to develop a fairly clear idea of who could be trusted, who was just sounding off to ingratiate himself with the Americans, and who might be actively working against them.

At first, of course, even the friendliest of villagers had been afraid to tell the Americans anything. Terrible things happened to "collaborators with the Imperialists" and the SEALs had heard plenty of gruesome stories of villagers kidnapped, tortured, and killed by the VC. Lately, though, the VC had been more and more on the defensive. Terrorized villagers often fled rather than face more of the same, leaving fewer people behind to grow the rice the communist rebels needed to survive . . . the beginnings of a cycle that was definitely counterproductive. As Charlie eased up on the locals, more and more of the locals were willing to be seen talking with Americans, almost to the point that some areas of the Rung Sat could be considered "pacified," to use the jargon popular back in Saigon.

And friendly villagers meant more intelligence that the SEALs could use than ever.

The previous night's patrol had been launched on the strength of such locally provided information. According to some of the residents at Ap Thanh, near the mouth of the Long Tau, the VC were going to be crossing the Long Tau in force tonight, moving from Long Thanh Island to the next, smaller island to the east. The word was that Long Thanh had become too hot for Charlie and he was pulling out. The two SEAL squads had been deployed by LCM in the hope of blocking Charlie's exit. If the lead VC elements could be stopped from crossing, the rest of the unit might pile up behind, creating a traffic jam in the jungle large enough to be spotted—and attacked—from the air.

That was the idea, at any rate, as explained the day before by the team's NILO. Mike Spencer was dubious. The Long Tau stretched for a somewhat meandering twenty-five miles, all the way from its branching off from the Soi Rap opposite Nha Be down to Can Gio on the South China Sea. There was no way one LCM and fourteen SEALs could blanket that entire stretch of jungle-clad river. Hell, Navy riverine forces already patrolled the Long Tau regularly, and they hadn't been able to stop the enemy movements. He could picture the VC just squatting there among the reeds and ferns at the water's edge, watching the clumsy landing craft motor slowly past, then giving the go-ahead signal to their comrades: *All clear! Let's go!*

More effective by far were the hunter-killer patrols launched by small teams ashore. Four or six SEALs, stealthily moving for kilometers through thick jungle, could set up an ambush along a recently used trail, wait silently for twenty-four, even thirty-six hours, then strike at the first VC target of opportunity. The SEALs had racked up an impressive list of kills and captures that way. Perhaps the most telling proof that the SEALs were hurting the VC, however, came from stories told to them by friendly locals. According to the villagers, the VC knew the SEALs well. They called them "the men with green faces" and held them in an almost superstitious dread.

You knew the enemy was hurting when he started personalizing you with nicknames, especially names the SEALs could glory in.

Spencer leaned against the gunwale of the LCM, watching the massed blackness along the east bank slowly resolve itself into deeply shadowed trees. Dawn was less than thirty minutes away, and it was already bright enough to see both sides of the broad river easily, rather than try to pick details out of the uncertain darkness. The LCM was moving slowly, its twin diesels chugging valiantly as it labored against both a four-knot current and its own sheer bulk.

The Landing Craft, Mechanized, had originally been designed to land a single armored vehicle on the beach during World War II. Armed with a pair of .50-caliber machine guns, its only armor was quarter-inch steel plate around the control station aft, enough to stop shrapnel or small-arms fire, but not enough to more than slow a machine-gun bullet.

Since being pressed into duty in this new kind of war, however, LCMs serving on the rivers of South Vietnam had been heavily modified with an eye to increasing both their survivability and their offensive punch. This vessel, just fifty feet long and with a draft aft of four feet, had been festooned with jury-rigged armor, including steel plate scavenged from a Seabee construction site, mattresses, and discarded tires. The ugly little monsters with their makeshift armor and dangling fenders made the naval brass in Saigon despair and were the butt of jokes in the "real Navy" clear back to Subic Bay, but at least there was half a chance that they would actually survive a river ambush.

They had teeth, too. Besides the two fifties aft, the landing

craft now mounted an arsenal consisting of four .30-caliber
machine guns, a 20-mm cannon, and, mounted on the tank
deck just aft of the boat's bow ramp, emplaced on a deuce-
and-a-half's truck tire filled with sandbags to absorb the recoil,
a 60-mm mortar. Besides that rather impressive armament, the
SEALs had their own personal arsenals, including 40-mm grenade launchers and a pair of Stoner Commandos.

Now if only they could find Charlie. The trouble was, Charlie wasn't stupid, and he wasn't about to let himself get cor-
nered by big, slow bullies like a converted LCM.

Turning, Spencer surveyed the men gathered on the LCM's
well deck. They were quiet, not talking much, their green-
painted faces studies in grim seriousness. Some of the faces
were new, too, replacements from the States. There'd been a
distinct change in the character of the team, Spencer thought,
since Marshall's death. It was as though the SEALs had entered a whole new kind of war.

It had been two months since the ambush near Can Gio, but the
SEALs of Det Golf still hadn't entirely gotten over the death of
Radioman Second Class William Marshall. As week had followed week in Vietnam, the individual members of the unit had
drawn closer to one another, strengthening the bonds first formed
in BUD/S. Marshall's death had shaken them. They didn't discuss it, of course. Perhaps the biggest effect it had had on the
SEALs was the sure and certain knowledge, also unspoken, that
SEALs *always* brought back their own, dead or alive.

Spencer thought about the reports he'd seen on the action
since then. Intelligence had determined that the SEALs had
been ambushed by between thirty and forty VC that afternoon.
No one could say how many of the enemy the SEALs had
capped in return, though follow-up patrols had found blood
trails in the jungle. The VC, too, carried out their dead when
they could.

But a SEAL . . . dead? It still didn't seem possible. Most of the
men who volunteered for SEAL training in the first place thought
they were invincible . . . and having survived BUD/S they were
convinced of it. And as the SEALs had gone out on patrol after
patrol, engaging the enemy in sharp firefights, burning his supplies, hunting him like game and all without a single casualty,
that feeling of invincibility had been reinforced.

As Lieutenant Wilson had been careful to point out, Mar-

shall hadn't even been the first SEAL to die in the Nam; a
SEAL officer had been killed in a mortar attack on Da Nang
a year ago. But Willy was the first to go down in a firefight,
slugging it out with an enemy he could *see*. Given the type of
war the SEALs were fighting in the Rung Sat, it had been
inevitable that they should lose someone sooner or later, but
that knowledge hadn't helped.

Neither had the word that Marshall had been awarded a
posthumous Silver Star. So far as Chief Mike Spencer was
concerned, that snippet of red, white, and blue ribbon attached
to a bit of metal was designed more to assuage the guilt of
senior officers than anything else. Certainly, it was damned
precious little to send home to Willy's mom and dad in the
place of their son.

Sometimes, Spencer dreamed of Willy, dreamed he was sitting with the rest of the SEALs back in the rec hall at Nha
Be, or at the Hoa Bien in Saigon, and he'd be laughing and
drinking just as he always had. Then he would turn and look
at Spencer with that one remaining, vacant blue eye. . . .

Some of the SEALs had requested transfers out after that
. . . even a few old-timers, plank owners like Harvey Stewart.
As far as Spencer was concerned, it was an astonishing turn
of events. The individual members of most military units had
little choice in whether or not they were in combat, but the
SEALs had been designed from the beginning as something
else, as a professional unit of highly specialized warriors who
were doing what they were doing because they wanted to.
Lieutenant Wilson had accepted their requests to rotate home,
and he'd pulled some strings to get them sent stateside. There
was some question even yet as to whether those men would
be allowed to remain as SEALs, or if they'd be "sent back to
the fleet" as the old saying went. That had really hurt the
skipper, Spencer knew. Somehow it just didn't seem right that
they'd split as soon as one of their own was killed.

Spencer didn't really care, one way or the other. The men
were gone . . . and so far as he was concerned, plank owners
or not, they'd broken faith with the rest of the SEALs . . . and
with Willy Marshall.

The men who were left would keep the faith.

Doc Shaw walked up beside Spencer. "Hey, Chief. You
look thoughtful."

"There goes my reputation."

"Whatcha thinking about? From the smell of the smoke, it doesn't seem to be one of the Big Three."

A running gag in the enlisted barracks held that there were just three topics worthy of serious consideration or group discussion: sex, the perennial favorite, and the wilder and more unlikely the better; booze, a classification that could be extended to include various unlikely adventures, sexual and otherwise, enjoyed under the influence of alcohol; and home. That wasn't a hard and fast rule, of course, but it did seem that nearly every barracks bull session sooner or later devolved onto one or several of those sacred topics.

"Nah. Nothing, really." He turned his back on the east bank of the river and started stripping his Stoner Commando down. The Stoners had been in service for a year now and were the subject of frequent cursings and gripings by nearly everyone who used them . . . except the SEALs. The entire Stoner weapon system had proven notoriously sensitive to dirt and hard use . . . and there was plenty of both in Vietnam. Only the SEALs seemed to be able to use them effectively, and that seemed to be because they alone kept almost religious care of all of their weapons. Spencer's Mark 23 had never jammed on him. Never.

"Looks like a heavy nothing, Chief. Don't mean to pry, but—"

"Not prying. I was just thinking about them giving old Willy the Silver Star. I wonder what he would've thought about that?"

"Shit. He never cared for fruit salad. You know that."

"Fruit salad usually just means campaign ribbons, doesn't it?" Spencer asked. "He didn't have anything against real medals that I knew of."

"I thought it was two or more colorful rows of anything here." Shaw slapped the left breast of his tiger suit.

"I think that was more WW Two. Same idea, though. Most guys don't care much one way or the other for baubles. Even the fuckin' CM of H."

"Most SEALs, anyway."

Spencer shrugged. "That's what I meant. Of course, there's always the million-dollar medal."

"Purple Heart?"

"Fuckin'-A."

"Shit. Even that's getting to not mean much anymore."

Spencer gave him a hard, sidelong look. "What do you mean, Doc?"

"Ah, the whole medal bit is getting FUBARed, y'know? Sometimes I think all the brass does anymore is award each other medals for things they never did in places they've never been."

Spencer chuckled. "You know, that accusation goes back a long, long way." He thought a moment. "There was a song that was popular with American troops in France back in the First World War. Had a chorus that went, ah . . .

"Oh, the general, he got the Croix de Guerre," he sang, roughly approximating the tune of "Mademoiselle From Armentierres."

> *"Oh, the general, he got the Croix de Guerre.*
> *The general got the Croix de Guerre,*
> *But the son-of-a-bitch wasn't even there.*
> *Hinkey-dinkey parlez vous."*

"Hey, Chief Spence," Torpedoman Second Class John Furman said, joining the two of them. He was one of the newbies in the Team, a kid from Cincinnati who was wearing so much green paint on his face at the moment that you couldn't tell his skin was black. "I didn't know you could sing!"

"Ah, he's just remembering the good old days," Shaw put in. "Telling us about the Great War, 1918, and all that."

"Gee," Furman said with mock, wide-eyed innocence. "You were in World War One, Chief?"

"Can it, shitheads," Spencer growled. He looked at Shaw. "I want to know why you think even the Purple Heart doesn't mean anything anymore. It means something to *me,* and not for the million-dollar ticket home, either. It means some guy got wounded in the line of duty, that he put his life on the line for his buddies and his country, and the honor doesn't come any higher than that."

"Right on," Furman said.

"Yeah," Shaw said with a shrug. "Maybe that's what it's supposed to mean. I knew a guy, another Navy hospital corpsman, who was stationed in Saigon at MACV headquarters last year. He told me this story."

"Go on."

"Seems there was this Navy commander working a desk at NAVADVGRU. He showed up at sick call one morning, and this buddy of mine saw him. The guy'd been to breakfast at the Puzzle Heart."

Furman cocked his head to the side. "Puzzle Heart? What's that?"

"That's what the restaurant in the headquarters building is called."

"Shit," Spencer said, grinning. "What happened to the poor bastard? Food poisoning? I hope?"

"Nope. He'd had hard-boiled eggs for breakfast."

"Well, la-di-fuckin'-da!" Furman said, holding up a limp wrist. "All the comforts of the good life, huh?"

"Yeah. Well, the way my buddy told it, this guy went to crack the eggshell with his spoon and a little piece of it flipped up into his eye."

"Aw," Furman said. "The poor dear!"

"So this commander went up to sickbay, and the corpsman washed out his eye and dispensed a bottle of eyewash. When he went to write the guy's medical report up, at the blank that said 'describe treatment' he wrote 'Removed shell fragment from eye.' "

"Jesus H. Christ!" Spencer said, disgusted. "The guy got a Purple Heart for *that?*"

"Sure did. War is hell, right?"

"What, did the officer make the corpsman write it up that way?" Furman wanted to know.

"Nah. It was more of a services-rendered arrangement, y'know? Working at MACV, it never hurts to have some officer types up there who owe you."

"Shit," Spencer said. He suddenly felt tired and very heavy, almost as though he couldn't go on. *"Shit!"*

"Aw, don't let it get you down, Chief," Furman said, dropping a hand on his shoulder. "The officers have this war rigged. They get the medals. We get the shit."

"Yeah," Shaw said. "Back in the sailing navy days, you know? Wooden ships and iron men and all that. They kept the enlisted pukes quartered forward, packed in like sardines on the gun decks, while the officers had their own cabins aft. The men had a saying back then. 'Aft the honor, for'ard the better men.' Figures, huh?"

"The honor doesn't matter," Spencer said. "The medals don't matter. It's how we do our jobs, that's all. And how we look out for each other."

"Right on," Furman said.

There seemed to be nothing else that could be said about it.

Spencer had completed stripping down his Stoner and lovingly wiping each piece with an oiled cloth. Now he began snapping pieces back into place, checking their alignment, working the action. As he snapped a fresh box magazine home and chambered the first round of the 150-round belt, Lieutenant j.g. Toland came down the portside ladder from the control station and walked forward toward the small group.

"Of course, some officers are okay," Furman added.

"Yeah," Spencer said. "*SEAL* officers."

"Whatcha got here?" Toland asked. "Shriner's convention?"

"We got the funny hats," Shaw said, patting the green bandana he wore pulled tight over his skull.

"Well, keep a sharp eye out, gents," Toland said. He nodded toward the sky. "Getting light, and that means we've got a chance of actually seeing something out here."

"I hate daylight, man," Spencer said. He was thinking of Marshall.

"Can't say I'm crazy about it either, Chief. At least we know Charlie's less likely to hit us in broad daylight."

"Air cover, man!" Furman said. "The *only* way to fly!"

"Well," Toland said, looking at the glowing sky where a couple of planets continued to gleam brightly with predawn fervor. "It'll be a couple more—"

"Deck there!" a sailor on the raised fantail aft yelled. He leaned against the cockpit's plate armor, pointing forward. "We got dinks!"

Spencer was on his feet in an instant, leaning over the LCM's gunwale to peer past the view-obstructing fence of the craft's raised bow ramp. The LCM had just come around a bend in the river, and as she cleared the wall of forest on the western shore, a line of black dots could be seen scattered across the river further upstream. At first, Spencer thought the LCM sailor had been mistaken, that what they were seeing was a line of floats—or possibly mines—stretched across the stream, but as he stared hard into the gloom still shrouding the shadowed river, he realized that what he was seeing was a number of men clinging to a heavy, hemp cable. The Long Tau was deep here—this was Saigon's main shipping channel, after all—and the current ran a respectable four knots. They must have surprised a force of VC crossing the river by using a cable as a wet but serviceable bridge.

Almost immediately, the two fifties on the fantail opened up, slinging quick, hard bursts toward the river-crossers, hurling up sheets of spray as the rounds slammed into the water. Several SEALs leaned over the gunwale to either side and began taking potshots as well. Several of the heads vanished, either hit or ducking beneath the water.

And then the forest on both sides of the river erupted in a hailstorm of enemy fire.

Spencer and the other SEALs ducked below the level of the gunwale as rounds struck the LCM's makeshift armor with an ominous *dunk-dunk-dunk* sound; ricochets shrieked through the sky, and bits of metal hurled across the crowded well deck as some rounds either penetrated the armor or spalled pieces of debris from the LCM's inner bulkheads.

Spencer checked aft. The two fifties were both manned by SEALs, the one to starboard by Seaman Richard Denning, the one to port by Engineman Third Class Conway. Both men were gripping their weapons' handles, thumbs down on the butterfly trigger as they swept left and right, valiantly attempting to suppress the wave of gunfire from the hidden positions ashore.

Ambush! was Spencer's first thought. There were too damned many VC lined up in decent, well-hidden firing positions for this to be anything else. That line of men crossing upstream could have been bait for the trap.

Then, as the LCM's crew continued to pour fire into the jungle, he wondered if he might not be mistaken. They could have simply stumbled across a large Vietcong force, surprising them, smack in the middle of a river crossing. An infantry unit would be vulnerable at a time like that, especially with the Long Tau so well patrolled. The troops already across and those waiting to go would take positions to cover their comrades in the open.

He leaned against the LCM's bulwark and rattled off a long

volley toward a clump of fallen logs just visible above the river's eastern bank. Ambush or accident, it didn't much matter. The sheer volume of firepower coming from that lone LCM appeared to have startled the Vietcong, not silencing them, certainly, but suppressing their fire by quite a bit. As he pumped rounds into the tangle of fallen logs, he saw a dark shape suddenly leap up, arms spread wide, then flop back into the shadows.

Had he just killed a man?

He dismissed the thought and kept firing. Bullets thumped into the hull of the boat. A high-pitched whistle sounded overhead . . . and an instant later a pillar of white and brown water erupted thirty feet into the air close beside the LCM's port side. For a second or two afterward, it rained, buckets of water streaming down out of the deep blue sky and splashing across the men crowded in the landing craft's well deck.

"Mortar!" someone yelled.

"Here's one back at 'em!" Luciano yelled, holding a 60-mm mortar round above the sky-pointing barrel of the small mortar on the deck forward. "On the waaay!"

He dropped the round down the mouth of the tube; a second later, the mortar fired with a thump that hurt the ears and was transmitted through the LCM's deck like a swift, hard kick. Seconds after that, a crash echoed among the trees forward, just beyond the east end of the rope bridge. Luciano dropped another round down the spout. That round sent water geysering into the air fifty yards upstream of the bridge.

An incoming mortar round crashed to starboard, the plume of spray erupting halfway between the LCM and the shore, thirty or forty yards off. Another round exploded closer, less than ten yards from the boat's side, and the concussion slammed Spencer's body through the LCM's bulkhead and set his ears to ringing. Luciano fired again, the round lost in the trees. Spencer shook his head as he kept triggering bursts of gunfire into the jungle. Never in his wildest dreams had he imagined finding himself in the middle of a pitched artillery duel on the water.

Mortars were finicky beasts that required careful positioning and careful adjustments in order to aim them with even a prayer of accuracy. Luciano didn't have a chance in hell of hitting anything deliberately with indirect fire launched from the deck of a moving vessel, but he sure as hell could let Charlie know they were in the fight.

"On the waaaay!" Luciano yelled . . . and a second later he lived up to his nickname "Lucky" when the round detonated on the river bank close to where the cable bridge emerged from the water. From his firing position, Spencer could see one man in black pajamas flung headlong into the mud; the VC still in the river were waving and struggling as the cable, snapped by the LCM's mortar round, slid free from the bank and began moving downstream with the current. Vietcong were swimming in the river, struggling to reach the shore; others were visible on the banks to both sides now, emerging from shelter to fire at the LCM. Water leaped and spat and spouted all around the landing craft as light machine guns hidden in the jungle added their challenges to the banging and cracking of small arms fire.

And still the SEALs returned fire. The 20-mm cannon mounted close beside the armored cockpit was in action now, slamming round after screaming round into the woods, which echoed with thundering concussions now. Several SEALs had their thumpers going, adding 40-mm grenades to the destruction being wreaked beyond the treeline. Other SEALs manned the .30 calibers, two to port, two to starboard, while Spencer and Tom Herrick kept firing the team's two Stoners.

Lieutenant Toland turned aft, facing the boat's coxswain, pumping his fist up and down to signal him to goose it. With its load of armor and extra weapons, the LCM was lucky to make six knots, but the more speed they could crank out of her, the harder she would be to hit . . . especially with those mortar rounds. Toland grinned at Spencer, as though reading his mind. "And they call LSTs Large Slow Targets," he yelled, as another communist mortar round exploded twenty yards to port.

Lieutenant j.g. Montoya, the LCM's riverine Navy skipper, yelled down at Toland. "Whatcha want, SEALs? Straight ahead or back 'er up?"

Toland pulled the boonie hat off his head and waved toward the LCM's bow ramp. "That way! Go! Go!" He put his hat back on and grinned wildly at Spencer. "We'll take her straight through!"

"Roger that!" If this attack *was* a carefully laid ambush,

there was a very good chance that the enemy would have positioned more troops and more mortars somewhere downstream, waiting to catch them when they turned around to escape the ambush upriver. A safer course by far in a situation like this was to ram straight through, blazing away at anything that moved, breaking out upstream where they had the luxury of choosing whether to continue on to safety, or turn around and continue the fight. Spencer felt the throb of the boat's diesels increasing as the Navy crew urged her into what was for a heavily ladened LCM a headlong gallop.

With a sudden jolt, Spencer's Stoner jammed. "Shit!" Quickly, he tried to clear the weapon, but steam was pouring off the barrel, and he suspected that he'd let the weapon get too hot. He stepped back from the gunwale, turning inboard to concentrate on his weapon. Nearby, Toland was breaking open a wooden crate of twelve 60-mm M49A2E2 high explosive rounds for the mortar, which was piled with a dozen other ammunition cans aft, just forward of the LCM's cockpit. Carefully, the SEAL officer pulled two rounds out of their sleeves and, cradling them beneath his armpits, he made his way forward.

With a ratcheting clack, Spencer managed to clear the jam, sending a dented brass cartridge bouncing across the deck. A mortar round exploded to starboard, sending up a sheet of water, followed almost immediately by a second explosion to port. The twin concussions made the LCM lurch and pitch heavily and Toland, encumbered by the mortar rounds, staggered, bumping into Spencer.

"Watch it, Lieutenant!" Spencer said, reaching out to steady him. "Don't drop the eggs, okay?"

"Ah, no sweat, Chief," Toland said grinning. "Those bastards couldn't hit the broad side of a—"

Thunder engulfed Spencer from aft, picking him up, hurling him forward, viciously slamming him into the starboard bulkhead.

Around him, bloodied, badly wounded SEALs writhed shrieking on the deck. . . .

Chapter 19

Saturday, 7 October 1966

**Long Tau River
Rung Sat Special Zone
0605 hours**

Chief Spencer shook his head . . . and immediately wished he hadn't. Stunned, half-conscious, his ears ringing loudly from the detonation, he could barely move, and moving his head brought waves of dizziness and a thundering pain behind his eyes. Reaching up to touch his head, he felt something wet, hot, and sticky. He blinked at his hand; it was covered with blood.

But then, *everybody* aboard the LCM was covered with blood. In every direction that Spencer looked, SEALs were on the deck, blood streaming from wounds, from eyes, from ears. For a moment, Spencer thought the battle had ended because the thunderous roar of gunfire had ceased. Then he saw Tom Herrick, lying on the deck a few feet away with his hands cupped over his crotch, his eyes shut and his mouth wide open, and Spencer realized that he'd been deafened by the blast.

Spencer crawled toward Herrick. He found it difficult to coordinate his movements, but somehow he managed to reach the wounded man's side. Pulling Herrick's hands back from the wound, he winced. The SEAL's left leg and groin had been slashed open; bright arterial blood was gushing from deep inside the leg, and the man's severed penis was lying in a bloody smear on the deck. Herrick's fists pounded against Spencer's side and back, his good leg thrashed wildly. Turning sharply, Spencer slammed the heel of his hand into Herrick's jaw, the impact jarring his arm and knocking the wounded man out cold. Turning back to the leg, he ripped a long strip of cloth from the torn side of the trousers, looped it about Herrick's leg just above the pulsing artery, tied it, thrust a screwdriver lying on the deck close by through the knot, and began twisting it until the bright red spurts weakened, then faded away.

The muffling, empty silence was beginning to fill with a roaring sound like the thunder of a heavy California surf. The air was thick with the smell of smoke. Was the LCM burning? He looked around . . .

. . . and was chilled to see white smoke pouring from the stack of ammo cans and crates piled up against the well deck's aft bulkhead just below the cockpit. The machine-gun ammo was stored in metal cans, but the 60-mm M49A2E2 rounds came in wooden boxes, twelve to a case. A white-hot piece of shrapnel had fallen on the lid of the open crate and was swiftly burning its way down through the wood.

The wood around the glowing fragment was blackened and charred, and smoke was curling off as the blackened area swiftly spread. If the fire took hold, it would detonate the mortar rounds; two crates, one half-empty . . . eighteen or twenty of those things detonating together would blast the LCM into matchsticks. The smoke grew thicker.

In three swift steps, Spencer reached the piled-up ammo. He grabbed the smoking lid and tugged, but it was still attached to the storage crate which in turn was partly buried under several thirty-five-pound cans of 7.62 machine-gun ammo. The first flames flickered to life around the hot chunk of metal. He slapped them with his bare hand, then, not even stopping to think about what he was doing, grabbed the twisted piece of metal. Embedded in the charred wood, it didn't come free at once; Spencer thrust his fingers around the thing and pulled, feeling the wood crumble an instant before the pain hit him like an electric current searing up the nerves of his hand and arm. He could feel the skin of his hand sizzling . . . and then the pain grew so great he could feel nothing at all except the pain.

Pivoting, stiff-armed, he hurled the hot chunk of metal into the air, over the starboard gunwale, and into the river. New sounds were beginning to penetrate the roaring in his ears, though it took a moment to recognize his own screams among them; the palm and fingers of his right hand were badly blistered, and in one quarter-sized spot the skin was as charred as the lid of the ammo box. The charred spot felt dead; everything else still felt as though it was on fire. His left hand was burned too, but not nearly so bad as the right; he clutched his right wrist in his left hand and tried to squeeze away the searing, hellish pain radiating from the flesh around the third-degree burn on his palm.

"Easy, Chief!" a voice said, sounding very far away, and someone was holding his shoulders, guiding him to a seat against the portside bulkhead.

"Fire . . . in the ammo . . ." he said, rasping out the words against the pain.

"S'all right, man," Furman said, sitting him down. "Don't sweat it! They got it!"

He looked aft. Two SEALs, both bloodied, were smothering the last of the flames with a dark-colored blanket.

His hearing was definitely coming back, though he had to concentrate to make any sense out of the jumble of sounds buffeting him. Gunfire continued to bark and thunder all around, mortar bursts roared, sending up columns of white water and spray, men were screaming in pain or in battle-rage. He looked up at Furman and was startled by the mask of blood the man wore. His green face paint was nearly obscured by the red streaming from a savage cut in his forehead. "Furman! You okay? . . ."

"Jus' a scratch, man. You stay put!" The SEAL turned away to help another man, who was lying on the deck, clutching a shattered knee to his chest.

Hell . . . had *everyone* aboard been hit? Spencer scanned the deck. Of nineteen men aboard the LCM, nearly all had been wounded. As he pieced together what he was seeing, he realized that a mortar round must have struck the landing craft's fantail only a few feet from where he'd been standing.

Had it fallen into the well deck, where most of the SEALs were gathered, it probably would have left little of the team save a thin red jam on the well deck's interior bulkheads. By striking the fantail, most of the shrapnel had passed over their heads, though the stuff that had hit had done damage enough. Most of the people he could see had blood on their faces or shoulders. Luciano, up forward, appeared unhurt as he continued to drop rounds down the spout of his mortar. Crouched low on the deck, the blast had missed him entirely.

At least half of the SEALs were still on their feet, leaning over the gunwales to port and starboard, firing their weapons at the jungle to either side of the LCM and, moment by moment, more and more SEALs staggered up off the deck and moved to join them. Looking aft again, he saw that the starboard-side .50-caliber machine gun was silent, its muzzle pointing uselessly at the sky. Struggling to his feet, he made his way aft toward the starboard ladder and, one-handed, clambered up to the fantail.

As soon as he reached the top, he was a target. From here, he had a splendid view of the sweep of the river ahead and astern of the LCM . . . and the hidden gunners ashore had a splendid view of him. A bullet screamed off the top of the ladder inches from his left foot. Another struck the armored shell surrounding the coxswain's station; two more shrieked off the well serving as the gunner's station for the silent fifty. Ignoring the incoming fire, he crawled painfully aft until he reached the fifty's mount. Seaman Richard Denning was slumped in the bottom of the well, with a thick coating of blood on his back and on the back of his head. Carefully—as carefully as he could manage, anyway—Spencer hauled Denning out of the gun tub, dragged him out onto the deck, then carried him forward. At first he thought Denning was dead . . . but he could feel a pulse at the angle of his jaw. "Help me!" he yelled. "Help me here! Wounded man!"

Furman and two other SEALs reached up to lower Denning to the relative safety of the well deck; Spencer turned and retraced his steps. Bullets continued to spang off steel armor or crack as they passed overhead. He reached the gun position without being hit, however, and lowered himself inside. The LCM, he realized, was not moving, though he could feel the rumble of the diesels through the deck beneath his feet. Smoke blanketed the fantail, swirling off the vivid, jagged-edged gash where the mortar round had struck and partly cloaking the aft end of the LCM. To his left, the boat's coxswain was crouched low in the control station, working the LCM's throttles back

and forth with a patient desperation. Judging from the slight
cant to the LCM's deck, and the way the river's surface was
flowing alongside, Spencer thought that the landing craft must
have gone aground seconds after the mortar round had hit.
They were closer to the east bank than the west; if they were
kissing bottom, the water here must be only three or four feet
deep, shallow enough that the VC could easily wade right up
to the LCM and clamber aboard if they were given half a
chance.

Aground, half the crew disabled, the enemy swarming toward them from two sides. . . .

He had to reach across the weapon to drag the charging
lever back left-handed. Then, grasping the fifty's handles, he
pivoted the weapon to aim across the water forward and to
starboard, where several dark shapes were visible moving
swiftly along the shore about two hundred meters away. He
pressed the butterfly trigger between his hands and the gun
thundered; the jarring recoil of the weapon against its mount,
the jackhammering sound and vibration, sent fresh waves of
pain searing up his arm, but he kept the trigger clamped down
and kept firing. As the pain mounted, he screamed, but he kept
working the weapon, swinging the muzzle back and forth in
sweeping arcs. The group of shapes he'd fired at first was
gone, though whether they'd been killed, scattered, or sent to
ground, he couldn't tell.

"Hoo-yah!" Spencer yelled above the hammering of his
machine gun, turning the scream of pain that was rasping his
throat into the bellowed war cry SEALs learned in BUD/S.
"Hoo-*yah!*"

"*Hoo-yah!*" The cry was taken up by other SEALs
forward. Ten or twelve men had returned to their stations and
were blazing away, laying down a staggering volume of fire.
Spencer added the fifty's fury to that hail of gunfire, firing in
one long, continuous burst, hosing VC targets when he could
see them, sweeping the muzzle back and forth across the jungle above the river's east bank when he couldn't. He could
see a number of still, dark shapes now lying beside the water's
edge, and there were several bodies floating slowly downriver
past the LCM's position.

His weapon snapped empty. He fumbled with an ammo can
resting beside the mount, trying to figure out how to snap a

fresh belt into the weapon's receiver, when Gunner's Mate Second Class Phil Pettigrew flopped down next to him, snapped open the receiver, fed it the first round, and locked it tight. "Go!" Pettigrew yelled, and Spencer opened fire once more.

Seven VC burst from cover directly opposite, racing down the bank and into shallow water, firing wildly as they ran. Pivoting right, Spencer sent his fire slashing into the group, sending geysering splashes erupting one after the other in a steady line through their midst. Two staggered and fell, face down in the water; a third pitched backward, hands clawing at the sky; two more broke and tried to run but were cut down by other SEAL gunners firing from behind the LCM's starboard gunwale; the last two flopped down in the water, wounded or hiding, then vanished as a 40-mm grenade from a SEAL thump gun detonated squarely between them in a crashing eruption of water and mud.

The rusty, armor-draped little landing craft had become a tiny fortress in the river. After the VC charge was broken, the enemy faded back into the jungle, continuing a blistering fire on the grounded LCM but unwilling to expose themselves to the storm of SEAL counterfire. A mortar round exploded in the river, far out from the LCM's position. Spencer kept firing, watching the fall of his shots as they plowed up the mud and sand on the riverbank, then walking them into the tangled vegetation just beyond. He couldn't tell if he was hitting anyone, but in a shock-fuzzed way he realized that the team's only hope to get out of this was to send out so much fire that the enemy fire was suppressed. When he glanced forward again, he saw that only a handful of SEALs were still out of action; Luciano had left his mortar to man one of the starboard .30s, preferring the machine gun's precision to the mortar's relatively useless blind lobs. Pettigrew was crawling back and forth between his fifty mount and the port-side mount, still manned by the bloodily wounded EN/3 Conway, keeping both guns in action by helping both men reload. He spotted Toland crawling along the well deck, moving from one badly wounded man to another, bandaging wounds, passing up fresh magazines to the men on the gunwales.

Or perhaps the mortar tube had simply grown too hot. Spencer could tell he was going to have trouble with his own weapon soon. Firing steadily on full-auto, cycling at five hundred rounds per minute, the air-cooled barrel was swiftly overheating. As he sighted down its length, shimmering waves of heat were steaming off the barrel, causing his view of the shoreline to ripple and distort.

Another mortar burst erupted from the river, closer this time. A second hit would finish them, Spencer knew, but there wasn't a damned thing to do about the VC mortars, not a damned thing to do about anything except to keep the fifty firing. The barrel was actually glowing now, and he could feel the tempo of the shots slowing as he kept on firing. The rounds themselves were coming out of the barrel so hot he could follow their flight as tiny, dim white stars flicking like tracers across the dark water and into the jungle.

The weapon snapped empty. He looked back over his shoulder. Pettigrew was lying on the deck next to Conway, helping him reload his fifty. Spencer grabbed another case of five hundred rounds, popped the lid, and started trying to feed the end of the topmost belt into the weapon's receiver. He was having a hell of a time; his right hand wasn't hurting as much now, but each attempt to grab either the linked rounds or the hot, hot metal of the machine gun sent new jolts of pain clear to his shoulder. Suddenly, a hand grabbed his left arm. He looked up into the blood-streaked, soot-blackened face of Lieutenant j.g. Montoya, the LCM's skipper. "Okay, Chief! Get out of there! I'll take it!"

He didn't want to relinquish the gun; it was as though the weapon had somehow become a part of him during the past few, fire-shot moments, but he allowed the boat's skipper to help him out from behind the mount. Montoya's wounds were superficial, and his hands hadn't been hurt. In seconds, he accomplished what Spencer hadn't been able to manage, snapping in a fresh belt of linked .50-caliber rounds, snapping home the charging lever, and opening fire in a swift cascade of precisely choreographed movements.

Spencer slapped the man's shoulder twice with his left hand to say "thanks," then crawled forward, stumbling down the ladder and back into the well deck. Benny Fitzgerald had grabbed his Stoner and was banging away with it over the gunwale; he considered picking up one of the other weapons lying in the well deck but decided that his burns would keep him from handling it with any accuracy. Instead, he stooped next to the nearest badly wounded SEAL and started improvising a bandage to staunch the flow of blood from the wound in his side.

As he kneeled on the deck, he felt a shudder transmitted through the LCM's hull. At first he thought the landing craft had been hit by a shell; then he realized that they were moving again. The coxswain was standing again in the helm position, leaning over the rim of his armor plate and peering aft into the smoke as the LCM backed off the mudbar that had stranded it.

Rising, he made his way unsteadily toward the starboard side, crowding in between Furman and Seaman Frank Horowitz. Gunfire was continuing to probe after the LCM from the shore, sending up splashes or screeching off the armor, but it was coming much more slowly now as the SEALs continued to pour a devastating volume of fire toward both river banks. Every time a gunner revealed himself with the flicker of his muzzle flash winking deep within the shadows of the trees, half a dozen SEAL weapons swung to concentrate their fire on that one small stretch of jungle, hammering down one VC position after another by literally smothering it with lead.

Spencer felt momentarily dizzy and took a step back. Something needle-sharp jabbed his arm; he looked down in time to see Doc Shaw pulling a morphine syrette away from his shoulder. "You'd better sit down, Chief," Shaw told him. "You look like shit."

"You don't look so hot yourself, Doc." The SEAL corpsman's head had been gashed by a bit of flying metal; he'd stopped the bleeding by removing his bandana and folding it into a long narrow bandage that he'd wrapped tightly around his head, but enough blood had soaked through the cloth or trickled down his green-painted face to give him a truly horrific appearance.

The morphine didn't stop the pain, exactly, but Spencer began feeling a bit fuzzy, and the intensity of the ache in his hands receded, less demanding, less urgent. He sat down heavily, then found he couldn't get back to his feet. "You stay put," Shaw told him, clapping him on the shoulder. "You've done enough hero-type stuff for one day!"

The LCM's engines gave a throaty bellow, and the craft

lurched as the coxswain threw the throttles full forward. After backing down for several tens of meters, the LCM swung its nose slowly left, cancelled its aft drift, then began accelerating as the coxswain guided the ungainly craft past the mudbar, angling once again upstream. Rising as far as he could manage, Spencer peered over the starboard gunwale, studying the eastern shore carefully; the VC would have no trouble at all keeping pace with the slow-moving landing craft if they wanted to follow it, continuing to hammer at it with small arms and light machine guns, but the volume of incoming fire had already dwindled to a fraction of its initial strength. As the LCM proceeded up the river and passed the spot where the rope bridge had been positioned, the VC fire fell away to nothing.

It was almost as though they were just as happy to see their prey escape the trap.

Monday, 9 October 1966

SEAL Compound
Nha Be
0945 hours

Lieutenant Wilson read the intelligence report a second time before looking up at Blanding. "How solid is this?"

"Solid," the Team's NILO said. "A riverine group went down there yesterday to check the river, while a special forces team was landed by helo. They counted forty bodies on the banks up and down that stretch of the river, or a short way back into the jungle. Lots of blood trails, too. If the usual three- or four-to-one ratio holds, your boys capped forty VC and wounded well over a hundred more."

"My God. How many attacked them, anyway?"

"That's anyone's guess. MACV thinks your SEALs stumbled into at least a VC battalion in the middle of a river crossing. That would be something like six or seven hundred men, if they were at full strength."

"Three officers, 687 men," Wilson said automatically. By developing their own intel sources, the SEALs had managed to obtain a remarkably clear picture of the VC infrastructure within the Rung Sat.

"Uh, yeah. Right. So, G2 figures your boys may have handed that unit something like twenty-five percent casualties. That's enough to completely wreck a military unit, make it worthless for anything for months."

"Hmm. What about Det Golf, then?"

"What about 'em? They're heroes, my boy! MACV's eating this shit up!"

Wilson blinked. He'd meant the question ironically. Fourteen men out of the twenty-five of SEAL Team One's Vietnam detachment had been wounded in that river ambush, three of them seriously. Tom Herrick had lost his leg, and both Denning and Lieutenant j.g. Evans were still in serious condition. All three would be going home soon, if they lived, and chances were they were all bucking for civilian status with medical discharges. Some of the others would be on medical down time for quite a while; Mike Spencer might never recover full sensation in his right hand. Fourteen down out of twenty-five was a fifty-six-percent casualty rate . . . and Blanding didn't think *that* would wreck the SEALs of Det Golf?

"I mean," Wilson said quietly, "that Det Golf isn't going to be patrolling for a while. We can't. I have two officers and eight men who aren't in sick bay, and I don't dare send them out after what just happened to their buddies." He wasn't entirely sure what the result of such an order would be . . . screwups because they'd been shaken by having so many buddies hurt, or screw-ups because they were so damned mad at Charlie that they would take stupid risks to get back at him. All Wilson knew was that he wasn't ordering them out there again, not right away.

He could still remember Marshall looking up and telling him that he hated daylight ops.

"Not to worry, Chuck," Blanding said, using the one personal name that Wilson truly detested. "The wheels are turning. Admiral Hargreaves thinks you SEALs are the greatest thing since sliced bread. He's already talked to both the Pentagon and NOSG. The word is your team is going to be expanded."

"When? How much?"

"Damned fast. I heard by the end of the month. And as for how many, how does seven officers and thirty men sound?"

"Pretty good." With thirty-seven men, he could *really* start hitting the VC, hitting them where it hurt, hitting them until they stopped being a threat in the Rung Sat. . . .

"While we're at it, Captain Garland asked me to find out from you if there was anyone in particular you wanted to see decorated in that action."

"Decorated? Hell, they *all* deserve medals, and more. . . ."

"Well, that's not going to happen, except for the Purple Hearts, of course. The captain was wondering if you could pick out one guy for special distinction."

A showcase decoration, then, a way to point to one man and say, "Look at what a great unit he represents! I'm to be congratulated for supporting the SEAL deployment in Vietnam. . . ."

Yeah, right.

"If I had to choose one," Wilson said, "I suppose it would be Chief Spencer."

"The guy with the hands."

"Yeah. The guy with the hands." Wilson closed his eyes briefly, trying to picture the hell that must have been that LCM, and Mike Spencer grabbing a white hot piece of metal and throwing it overboard, saving the life of every man on that boat. To reduce all of that to "the guy with the hands" seemed obscene. "I've already written him up for a Silver Star."

"Betcha he gets it. The brass is feeling real generous after this one, Chuck."

"I'm submitting a list of several other decorations, Mr. Blanding. As I said, they all deserve recognition."

He was thinking about a story he'd heard once, about an action involving seventeen Navy personnel aboard a landing craft during the invasion of North Africa in World War II. Those men, the forerunners of the Underwater Demolition Teams and, by extension, of the SEALs themselves, had snuck in ahead of the landings to cut a barrier across a river, under fire and in heavy seas. Every single man in that boat had won the Navy Cross, the second highest decoration in the United States Navy's pyramid of honor. Of course, by today's standards, that was a bit extreme. . . .

"We'll have to see. You know, I'm sure, that there's a

pecking order being set up for military decorations. So many for officers, so many for enlisted . . .''

"Quotas, huh?"

"If you like."

"Well shit-fire. We'll just have to see if we can schedule future heroics to fit MACV's schedule of decoration availability."

But Blanding seemed to miss the sarcasm in Wilson's jibe completely.

Chapter 20

Thursday, 19 October 1966

North Island Naval Air Station
Coronado, California
1539 hours

Lieutenant Steve Tangretti watched the T-39D Sabreliner taxi to a halt without bothering to hide the frown that creased his face. It was somehow symbolic, he thought bitterly, that his role at NOSG-Pacific had been reduced to shepherding visiting VIPs. Over the past several months, he had felt himself being pushed increasingly to the side as the special warfare office had finally started to find its stride. Ironically, it seemed Tangretti had managed to do himself out of a job through the advice he'd given to Chief Spencer before Det Golf had left for Vietnam. In the months since then, SEAL operations in the Rung Sat had started yielding solid results . . . and complaints from higher brass in Saigon about SEALs ignoring procedures and striking out on their own had increased to a veritable flood. So it looked like his advice was being heeded, but as a result Bucklew had a lot less need for his input at the office.

Adding to the frustration he was feeling was the unresolved situation with Veronica. Ever since Bill had enlisted and reported to boot camp at Great Lakes Naval Center near Chicago, the tone of Veronica's letters had grown increasingly harsh. There was no hope that she'd ever join him in California now, and he was beginning to wonder if the marriage could hold together even if he capitulated and took the retirement she'd been urging for so long.

It felt as if the world was closing in on him, and all Tangretti wanted to do now was bury himself in real work again, *meaningful* work . . . preferably alongside the men he'd been trying to help from behind his NOSG desk, over in Vietnam. But instead he was the official greeter for some group of junketing Pentagon types. It was enough to make him start to wonder if Veronica wasn't right after all. Maybe it really was time to chuck it all.

The transport plane's hatch opened as the ground crew finished wheeling the steps into place. Tangretti stepped forward as the passengers emerged, snapping off a crisp salute and hoping his face wasn't showing too much of the contempt he felt for REMF officers everywhere.

The first man down the steps wore an admiral's uniform. He returned Tangretti's salute and then stepped toward him, grinning and extending his hand. It was only then that the man's identity registered.

"Captain Galloway . . . I mean, *Admiral* Galloway!" Tangretti took his hand and returned his smile. Here was one staff officer he'd always respected, a man who really cared about the people out on the front lines. Joseph Galloway had helped get the first naval combat demolition units and UDTs off the ground during the Second World War, and he'd been at Tangretti's side the day he met with President Kennedy to talk about forming the SEALs. And, of course, he had played a part in posting Tangretti to NOSG-Pacific . . . but Tangretti was prepared to forgive him that. "It's *good* to see you again, sir. Congratulations on your promotion. When did it come through? Last I heard you were still a captain on the CNO staff."

Rear Admiral Galloway shrugged. "Orders were sent out in

August," he said. "And the next thing I knew, it was goodbye Pentagon, hello world." He smiled again. "You know, for years I wanted nothing but a shot at getting free of that five-sided squirrel cage so I could go out in the field, where the action was. Last winter Ginny and I moved into a new house in Silver Spring, and *bam!* I get posted to duty overseas."

"Overseas?" Tangretti raised an eyebrow. "In Nam?"

The admiral nodded. "Another damned staff slot, but at least I'll be closer to the action. I'm supposed to be a liaison between USNAVFORV and MACV-SOG. We'll be over-seeing naval special warfare elements attached to Special Operations . . . spooky stuff, with the CIA looking over our shoulders. They're impressed with your SEALs, Lieutenant. Very impressed indeed."

"Thank you, sir. Good to know *someone* appreciates us. The regular Navy hasn't always been . . . supportive."

"Well, that could be changing," Galloway said. "And you owe a part of it to that stepson of yours, young Hank Richardson."

"Hank? How so?"

Galloway grinned again. "Over the summer the Agency decided to see just what kind of job SEALs could do gathering intelligence. So they set up this elaborate spy operation over in France, with SEALs visiting the French combat swimmers in Toulon ordered to bring back as much data as possible on the naval base and missile range over there without being de-tected by their hosts. It was all stuff they already knew from other sources, but of course they didn't tell the SEALs that. Your stepson was one of the team that drew the job. And they came through with flying colors, let me tell you. I never saw a bunch of agency guys so impressed before in my life. Rich-ardson and his buddies didn't just bring back measurements and soundings . . . they actually went in there and took *photos,* if you can believe it, photos of top-secret installations in broad daylight without drawing more than a casual reprimand from the French! It was one hell of a job."

Tangretti grinned. "I've always said Hank takes after his old man," he said.

"*And* his stepfather, too," Galloway added. He glanced around as the other passengers from the plane gathered behind him. "Ah, I've been rude. Lieutenant Tangretti, these are some of my new staff. Commander Manners, Commander Thomasson, Lieutenants Beeman, Harper, and Dahlgren. And Yeoman Espinoza. I hope we won't be straining your transportation capacity too much?"

"No problem, Admiral," Tangretti said. "We've got three cars. Do you want to settle in at the hotel first, or head straight over to the base?"

"Hotel will do for now," Galloway said. "Just lead the way, Lieutenant."

The conversation lagged until the staff cars were on their way. Galloway had placed Tangretti in the seat beside him, and once they were moving he turned toward him. "I'm glad you're still available here, Lieutenant," he said. "I was specifically hoping to see you on this trip, but I was afraid things would be all shook up by the time I could make it here."

"You mean the captain's transfer, sir?" Tangretti shrugged. "We've had word, but it doesn't take effect for a few more weeks. Things are a little bit up in the air, but we still generally know what we're doing. At least as much as we ever did."

The admiral chuckled. "Well, at any rate I'm glad I made it in time. Having just come out of an office in the middle of a major staff change, I know what kind of hell it can lead to."

Tangretti nodded. The rumors had started several months back, but they'd only been confirmed within the last week. Captain Bucklew wouldn't be heading up NOSG-Pacific for many more weeks. He was being transferred to a Pentagon post, another step up on the career ladder he had always been so concerned about. The fate of the rest of the NOSG staff was still up in the air, though. Howell had been talking about trying to wangle duty in Nam to get a few brownie points in a combat zone. As for Tangretti, he wasn't sure what he wanted any more. The odds were against the next head of NOSG being much of an improvement over the current administration, and anyway he was thoroughly sick of reports and analyses, files and projections.

What he really wanted was a chance to get back out in the field . . . except that a part of him was hoping to find a way to patch things up with Veronica, and that was sure to require a tour back at Little Creek . . . at the very least.

"Fact is, I can use you," Galloway continued. "None of my people have any firsthand experience of Vietnam, or of the SEALs, for that matter. If we're going to end up trying to be the bridge between the CIA and the Navy SEALs, we're going to need a better idea of just what we're talking about. I know all the stuff that's on paper, of course. You don't spend twenty years of your life dealing with special warfare without getting a pretty good idea of the theories behind it all. But the last time I saw navy commandos actually going out on an op, it was when we were launching Operation Torch. The last combat I saw—and that was from a distance—was at Tarawa, for God's sake. I need to get an idea of SEAL capabilities from someone who really knows what's going on . . . you. So I'm going to want you to set up a series of briefings for me and my men over the next couple of weeks. Think you're up to it?''

"I'd be glad to, sir,'' Tangretti said. "As long as Captain Bucklew doesn't have a problem with it. It'll be a pleasant change of pace to have someone over in Saigon who not only appreciates the SEALs but actually understands them. I think our boys have had more grief from the brass than from all the VC in Vietnam.''

"Same old Tangretti,'' Galloway said with a smile. "Still making waves, huh? I'll talk with Captain Bucklew and make the request through channels.'' He changed the subject. "So . . . how's life been treating the first SEAL? I saw Hank just last month . . . but how are Veronica and . . . Bill, wasn't it? It's been a long time. . . .''

Tangretti kept up his end of the conversation almost automatically. In his mind, though, he was turning over the possibilities that went with Galloway's new assignment in Saigon. Perhaps now the SEALs would really have a friend in high places over there. That was something they needed. Something he was glad to help make possible.

Friday, 20 October 1966

HQ, Naval Operations
Support Group, Pacific
Coronado, California
0945 hours

"Ah, Tangretti. Just the man I needed to see.''

Tangretti met Howell's eyes and gave a small shrug. "I'm not hard to find,'' he said. His gesture took in his work station. "Where would I hide, after all? What's up?''

The aide's expression was neutral, businesslike. "Admiral Galloway mentioned something about needing some briefings at dinner last night," he said. "I just wanted you to know that you won't have to bother with any of that. I'll take the job. After all, it's the kind of staff work I'm pretty well used to . . . and you've always made it clear where you stand on dealing with these Pentagon types." Howell showed his teeth in a fleeting smile, but his eyes remained flat, noncommittal.

"The admiral specifically wanted me on that," Tangretti said quietly. His mind was racing ahead of his words, trying to fathom Howell's motives. It certainly had nothing to do with altruism. "He told me so, yesterday. Best if I . . . if *we* stick with his program, don't you think?"

Howell looked to both sides, as if to see if anyone was in earshot. "Look, Tangretti, just for once, don't make waves on this, okay? Does it really matter who does the show-and-tell for the brass?"

"Apparently it does to *you*," Tangretti commented. "My question is, why?"

The aide didn't answer for a moment. "All right, look, here's how it is," he said at last. "I know one of the guys on the admiral's staff. Commander Manners. I worked under him in Procurement a few years back. Manners could be my ticket to getting a slot on the admiral's staff in Nam, but only if I can make an impression on them. Doing the briefings would give me a real leg up. I know you're not disposed to do me any favors, Tangretti, but I don't see why you'd care. You're not looking for a job with Admiral Galloway, are you?"

"I've had all the staff work I could deal with for the next twenty or thirty years," Tangretti told him. "You're welcome to it . . . if Galloway will have you. But the briefings . . . like I said, he asked for *me*."

"Can't you be reasonable about this? It's not like I'm asking you to give up something important, for God's sake. It's just a bunch of routine garbage about special warfare ops. They'll probably all sleep through it anyway."

"You think so, huh? Listen, Howell, I've known Admiral Galloway since back before the Normandy landings, and he's one man who always takes his work seriously. And it just so happens that this 'routine garbage' you want to brief him on is all about the whole future of the SEALs. I know how you really feel about special warfare, Lieutenant, and I don't happen to think that your views are the ones the admiral and his staff need to hear right now. If you want to play politics to get yourself a nice safe overseas staff slot you can put on your service record, fine. But you *don't* go playing politics with the SEALs. Not on my watch, anyway."

Howell drew himself up to his full height and gave Tangretti a steely stare. "Maybe you're forgetting, Lieutenant, that I rank you. I'm giving those briefings, and that's final." He turned and stalked away without waiting for Tangretti to respond.

"You think so, huh?" Tangretti said softly as the aide walked off. "Think again, Mr. Howell. Think again."

A yeoman appeared a few moments later with a stack of reports he needed to review in time for Bucklew to get them on his desk after lunch, so Tangretti couldn't get back to the problem of Howell for close to two hours. When he was finally able to put aside the last of the reports, he typed out a list of files and summoned an E-4 to his desk. "I'd like this material ASAP," he told the man. "Especially these items here—the barn dance cards from Nam, and the debriefings from Lieutenant Baxter's people. Get them to me before you break for lunch."

"Aye-aye, sir," the rating said.

It didn't take long for the man to return, though . . . empty-handed. "I'm sorry, Lieutenant, but everything on this list was checked out first thing this morning." He looked apologetic. "Clerk down in the records office said the order was signed by Lieutenant Howell."

"So . . ." Tangretti leaned back in his chair, frowning darkly. "All right, Lafferty. Thanks anyway. That'll be all." The enlisted man looked relieved as he left.

Tangretti looked across the office toward Howell's desk. Evidently the aide hadn't waited to see if he'd have Tangretti's agreement or not. He was determined to take over the briefings.

And Steve Tangretti was equally determined to stop him.

1328 hours

"Tell Lieutenant Howell I'd like to see him on his way in from lunch," Tangretti said. "About the admiral's briefing program."

"Aye-aye, sir," Yeoman Lafferty replied.

As the enlisted man headed back for his post by the front desk of the NOSG office, Tangretti opened his desk drawer and double-checked his arrangements. He knew he needed to act fast if he was going to keep Howell from winning their little duel, and he'd had to improvise quickly. A quick lunchtime visit to his BOQ berth—he'd finally left the Hotel de Coronado for base housing after it had become clear that Veronica really wasn't coming—had gained him a weapon of sorts. It wasn't exactly orthodox, but SEALs made the best of the tools that came to hand.

He heard Howell talking to Lafferty and looked up in time to see the enlisted man gesturing toward him. Tangretti reached inside the desk drawer and switched on the tape recorder he'd brought from his quarters, checked to be sure the spools were turning, then closed the drawer carefully. The mike was nestled between two stacks of papers on the desk top, hard to see unless someone knew what to look for. Hopefully, it would serve his purposes. . . .

"You had something more to say about the admiral, Tangretti?" Howell asked as he approached the desk.

"Only this," Tangretti told him. "That was a real cute move, freezing me out from all the files. Guess you figure I can't brief Admiral Galloway if I don't have access to the intel data, huh?"

"I already told you, Tangretti, that the question of who does the briefings is *settled*. I'll be needing those files to do my job. And I'll thank you to keep clear of it from here on out."

"Just tell me one thing, Lieutenant," Tangretti said. "Did Captain Bucklew approve this little power play of yours? Or does he even know about it?"

"Captain Bucklew agrees with me that you're not exactly the best man to handle staff briefings," Howell said coldly. "I would not suggest that you go behind my back and try to change his mind. You've already been warned about the consequences of stepping out of line, Tangretti. Don't make me take action against you for going outside the chain of command."

"I see. When you ignore an admiral's expressed preferences, that's okay, but if I try to carry out his orders that's going outside the chain of command. Really cute, Thurston. And does Big Stoop know your *real* reason for taking me off this assignment? Does he know about Commander Manners and the job on the admiral's staff?''

"That's none of your concern, Tangretti!" Howell said, flushing at the use of the hated nickname. "Get it through your thick skull, old man. I'm delivering those briefings next week, and nothing you can say or do is going to change that fact. You're *not* getting between me and that staff job in Saigon. Unlike you, Tangretti, I've got a worthwhile career ahead of me, and I'm not going to let some useless bastard who's way overdue to be put out to pasture screw up my whole future. You get me, mister?''

"Oh, yeah," Tangretti told him with a gentle smile. "I get you. I just wish you'd reconsider, Lieutenant. I really hate to be in the position of ignoring the admiral's preferences . . . and I think you should, too.''

"You'd be better off worrying about *me*, Tangretti," Howell said harshly. "Because if you cause me any more trouble, I'll see they haul your ass off to the brig when I bring you up on charges. Keep it in mind." Once again he strutted off, leaving Tangretti alone.

Still smiling, Tangretti switched off the tape recorder. His plan, hasty though it had been, couldn't have worked out better with a week of preparation. Howell had definitely said too much, and he had it on tape.

The question now was how to use it to the best possible advantage. And Tangretti already had a fairly good idea on that score.

Monday, 23 October 1966

HQ, Naval Operations Support Group, Pacific Coronado, California 1005 hours

"Shall we begin, gentlemen?" Tangretti asked, glancing around the conference room that had been appropriated for Admiral Galloway's staff briefings.

His presence in that room was testimony to the success of his tactical maneuver to neutralize Lieutenant Howell. He had considered how to use the tape he'd made for quite some time before he'd finally made his move. At first he'd turned over the idea of a little quiet blackmail but had rejected it as too uncertain. Howell might have found a way to use such an attempt to trap Tangretti in his own scheme, and that would have been unpleasant. At any rate, blackmail wasn't an approach Tangretti favored. He was a man of direct action, first and foremost.

He'd also considered letting Bucklew hear the tape, but that solution had been almost equally objectionable. After all, Big Stoop might well have decided that Howell had every right to act as he did . . . and, again, could make things sticky for Tangretti in the process.

In the end, the only option that had really seemed sound was to turn the tape over to Galloway himself.

He'd done it discreetly, of course. Tangretti had written out a brief note apologizing for being unable to handle the briefings as Galloway had requested, then wrapped it up together with the tape and given it to Commander Thomasson, one of Galloway's men. That had been Friday evening, just before the end of the work day. He'd heard nothing further all through the weekend.

But this morning he'd arrived in the office to find a tall stack of files on his desk and a note signed by Captain Bucklew authorizing him to carry out the briefing program as he saw fit. Any and all NOSG files were at his disposal, and any clerical staff he needed to handle the assignment.

There was no sign of Lieutenant Howell in the office. Apparently he had suddenly decided to take some accumulated leave and hadn't even come in to the headquarters building to tidy up his desk.

It was a SEALs kind of victory, Tangretti told himself as he looked around the room from Galloway to the rest of the assembled officers. Swift and decisive, gained by unorthodox tactics and against long odds. Maybe now Howell would have a little more respect for the potential of naval special warfare operations. . . .

"I . . . didn't have a lot of time to prepare," he said aloud. "So this morning I'm going to concentrate on an overview of SEAL activities in Vietnam. SEALs have been serving in an advisory capacity ever since 1962, especially at the naval base at Da Nang where they've been training and organizing South Vietnamese boat raids into northern territory. But the first direct action SEAL unit was dispatched in February of this year. Since that time we've continually expanded the scope of our operations.

"At the moment, SEAL Team One has two detachments incountry. Det Echo is the Da Nang advisor force, one officer and five enlisted men. It is still confined to a strictly noncombatant role. Det Golf, which operates in the Rung Sat Special Zone, consists of two understrength platoons, five officers, twenty men. Due to a fairly serious encounter last month, we've had to rotate new men in to Det Golf ahead of schedule, but despite this our men have been steadily improving their operational techniques and are starting to show some solid results. There are plans to increase the size of Det Golf next year, and to bring another unit in drawn from SEAL Team Two in Virginia. This new force will be designated Det Alfa and assigned to operate in the Mekong Delta area."

Galloway spoke up. "Tell me, Lieutenant, do you think either Team could provide an additional platoon for service in Southeast Asia without stretching themselves too thin? In addition to currently planned commitments, that is?"

Tangretti nodded. "Shouldn't be a problem, Admiral," he said. "Both Teams are expanding fast. We've established a training program for platoons destined for Vietnam, so you'll have a four-to-six-month delay before you can get a new unit ready for direct action, but aside from that, I'm sure there'd be no major difficulties."

"We might not need the same degree of direct-action training," Galloway said. "Though I'd imagine *some* advanced training would still be a good idea . . ."

"What sort of work are we talking about, Admiral?" Tangretti asked.

"Well . . . it's still in the planning stages yet, so don't take it as gospel. And don't spread it around in any event. But the head of CIA Asian operations, Bill Colby, has been trying to organize a counterterrorism force in Vietnam. It's made up of local troops, irregulars called Provincial Reconnaissance Units, set up to act independently in each province. Their job is gathering intelligence, carrying out kidnappings, even assassinating local VC infrastructure leaders. Colby's had good reports on the SEALs and has proposed we set up a program to provide each PRU with a SEAL advisor."

"Hmmm." Tangretti was thoughtful. "That would combine the ability to gather and process timely intel with larger re-action forces than we can field now with the SEAL detachments. A pretty good idea . . . as long as the intelligence got shared. We've had a lot of trouble with coordinating different commands and programs over there, and a hell of a lot of good opportunities have gone by the wayside because the trail was cold before we could get our people to act on intel that had taken too long to filter down to the local level."

"That will be one of my jobs over there," Galloway said. "Making sure the PRUs tie in with other operations we have going on over there."

"Then you might have a real winner on your hands, sir," Tangretti told him. "I wouldn't mind getting a piece of that action myself. It sounds a lot like what I was doing with the LDNN a while back, except we'd be able to go out on real combat ops instead of training hikes."

"From what I've heard, Lieutenant, your training hikes *were* combat ops," Galloway said with a smile. There was no trace here of the suspicion and outright horror that men like Bucklew and Howell had shown over his record with the LDNN. Galloway was a man who appreciated results over everything else. "Colby would be damned lucky to have you. If you want, I'll see about putting you in for assignment to the project. It'll be designated Det Bravo, and it should be off the ground in a few months. Maybe as early as late spring."

"Thank you, Admiral," Tangretti said with a grin. He was thinking of Howell and his quest for a staff job. Without even trying, Tangretti had landed an even better plum . . . a chance at a direct-action unit.

Of course, another tour overseas would mean putting off a chance at squaring things with Ronnie. He wasn't sure the marriage could survive another such blow. But on the other hand, Tangretti wasn't sure *he* could survive much more of life in the rear echelons. After the infighting with Howell, he was more convinced than ever that he preferred the life of a SEAL in the field, where the enemies didn't wear the uniform of the U.S. Navy.

He went on with the briefing in a contemplative frame of mind. Steve Tangretti had a lot to think about.

Chapter 21

BUD/S Training Center
Coronado, California
1418 hours

Steve Tangretti studied the big black man behind the desk for a few moments before stepping forward and clearing his throat. "Afternoon, Chief," he said casually. "I'm here to draw my berthing assignment and gear."

The CPO looked up from his paperwork and nodded. He started to speak and then did the most perfect double-take Tangretti had ever seen. "*You're* here for BUD/S?" he asked, unable to keep the skepticism out of his voice. After a moment he added "Sir?"

Tangretti smiled at him. "Don't get too many old-timers in here, huh, Chief? Well, don't worry about it. I can keep up with the young punks. Seems the powers-that-be want me to recertify before they'll give me another shot at active duty with the SEALs."

"Then you've already been through the course before, Lieutenant?"

"Chief, I went through Fort Pierce back in '43. *And* UDT training on Maui in '44 . . . and I helped set up the SEAL training program in Little Creek, too. I probably know more about training SEALs than an Eskimo with a bucket of fish."

The black man narrowed his eyes. "Training's gotten tougher, sir, the last few years. You're in for a pretty rough time of it."

"I can handle it, Chief," Tangretti told him. He noted the

257

name on the man's chest. "Connors, is it. That name rings a bell . . . You were in Det Delta over in Nam, weren't you?"

"Yes, sir," Connors said. "How'd you know that, Lieutenant? I don't remember you from over there. . . ."

"I wasn't over in Nam during your tour, Chief," Tangretti said. "I was stuck behind a desk here in Coronado at the time. Where one of my main jobs was reading over the barn dance cards that came out of Det Delta and trying to turn comments from the field into policy decisions. All in all, I think I would have liked it better if I'd been with you guys."

Connors shook his head. "Don't know as I'd agree, sir," he said quietly. "That place was hell on Earth, and no mistaking it. I watched a lot of pretty good SEALs learn the hard way that you can't really prepare for a war by training for it. Just doesn't work."

Tangretti remembered the beaches of Normandy on D-Day, the sheer overwhelming scope of thousands of men hitting the beaches under withering fire. He nodded. "Yeah, it's never quite what you think it'll be." Leaning over the desk, he lowered his voice. "Tell me something, Chief. Lieutenant Baxter, your CO. What happened with him? Everybody thought he was a hell of an officer . . . but it was like he just didn't give a damn by the time Delta was ready to pull out."

Connors didn't answer right away. "Lieutenant," he said at last. "Mr. Baxter was a damned good officer. No disrespect intended, but he just didn't get the kind of support he needed from headquarters . . . from the people who read the barn dance cards, if you get my drift." His look was challenging. "But he's *still* a good man, for all that. You'll probably get a chance to see that for yourself. He's on the training staff now, like me. I just wish he could've come back from the Nam with a little more of his self-respect intact."

"Hmmph." Tangretti hesitated. "For what it's worth, Chief, I always thought you guys should be given a hell of a lot more freedom, but my bosses didn't want to listen to it. I'm *still* trying, in fact. Things are getting better. Maybe it isn't even too late for Lieutenant Baxter."

"Maybe," Connors said. "Anyway, Lieutenant, if you're really sure you want to spend your vacation with us, I'll check you in. Name?"

"Tangretti. Steven Vincent . . ."

"What, another one? It ain't every day you get two Tangrettis, Lieutenant. But I just checked one through this morning. . . ."

"What? Not . . . not *Bill*?"

"William Wallace Tangretti," Connors said. He was frowning. "You related? It's not a real common name."

"Yeah . . . we're related." Tangretti swallowed. The news had shaken him to the core. The last he'd heard, Bill had graduated boot camp at Great Lakes and was waiting for orders to come through to an A school. How had he turned up at BUD/S training? "He's my son."

Connors whistled. "Whew, boy, that's gonna be one hell of a mess. Can you imagine a kid tackling Hell Week with his dad looking over his shoulder? Lieutenant, I sure as hell don't envy either one of you."

"Yeah." Tangretti looked away. "Yeah, it's going to be pretty damned tough. . . ."

Hut #5, BUD/S Training Center
Coronado, California
1508 hours

Seaman Bill Tangretti tucked his pen behind his ear and read over the last two paragraphs of his letter.

Fact is, Hank, I was starting to wonder if I'd ever get posted to BUD/S. They turned me down four times at Glakes, and I washed out on the aptitude test the first time I tried here. Maybe I'm not tough enough to be a SEAL, but I think you'll have to admit I'm stubborn enough. I just kept trying until they finally decided I was worth a look after all.

I'm already off to a rocky start, though. After I checked in this morning I asked a first class for directions to my hut, and he jumped all over me. "What do I look like, Information Central?" was the only printable thing he said the whole time. Later on one of the other guys pointed him out as one of our trainers, Ferraro. Turns out he's some kind of a legend in these parts, like Rudy Banner is in Little Creek. They say he's half-Spanish, half-Indian, and all mean . . . and wouldn't you know I'd manage to get on the wrong side of him even before training starts!

He looked up as the door to the Quonset hut banged open, expecting to see one of his bunkmates. His eyes widened as he recognized the tall, stocky figure of his father standing beside the doorway.

"Dad? What are you doing here? How'd you find out I was in BUD/S?" Bill Tangretti swung himself out of the top bunk and dropped to the floor, facing his father. He tried not to grin, but it was a losing battle.

"I found out about it from Chief Connors when I was checking in," his father told him. "Otherwise I never would have realized—"

"Checking in?" Bill interrupted. "Wait a minute, Dad. This is getting pretty weird. What are *you* doing *checking in* to BUD/S training . . . you, the original, number-one SEAL?"

Steve Tangretti showed his teeth. "Seems I need to prove that an old man can still cut it with the Teams if I'm going to get myself back into the field. Admiral Galloway's lined me up with a new project over in Nam, but nobody would okay it unless I showed 'em I was up to it."

Bill frowned. "Mom's gonna be pretty bummed out," he said. "I mean, she hit the ceiling when I enlisted, but I think she figured you'd start winding down pretty soon. When she hears you're going back to Nam . . ."

"Yeah. I know." His father looked away. "Don't you worry about it, son. I'll handle things with your mother and me." He paused for a moment before going on. "But how did you end up out here? When you joined up last summer I was surprised. I thought you'd want to try for college . . . or maybe see about wangling an Annapolis slot. Senator Forsythe would've been glad to sponsor you. But you went and enlisted . . . and now you turn up here for BUD/S! You didn't even get an A school assignment. . . ."

"Well, I knew I wanted SEALs right from the start, Dad," Bill told him. "But I didn't get accepted right away when I was in Great Lakes. After boot camp I ended up on a waiting list for Gunnery School, so they stuck me in Personnel for a while. I got fed up there and talked my CO into getting me transferred to Coronado. And right after I got here, I ran into

Chief Spencer. He just got back from a tour in Nam, you know. . . ."

"Yeah," his father nodded. "I saw him a couple of days ago. His hands are healing up pretty well. . . ." The elder Tangretti frowned at him. "He didn't mention anything about seeing you, though."

"I asked him not to," Bill admitted. "The chief and I got to talking, and he found out I wanted in the SEALs, so he arranged for me to take the test again, and I got accepted for Class 40." He didn't mention the rest of his saga—how many times he'd flunked the requirements for BUD/S training, first at Great Lakes and then here in California, or how Spencer had actually helped him fake his way through the last test by distracting the instructor assigned to evaluate him at a crucial moment. He didn't want his father to suspect just how poor his performance had been up until now.

Not that it mattered. If his father was going to be part of his training class, he'd soon be able to see every slip, every mistake.

It just wasn't *fair*.

"Dad," he said seriously. "Do you really have to take the training course again? I mean, couldn't you hold off and go through Class 41 or something. It's going to be real awkward to take on SEAL training with you in the same class."

"Afraid I'll try to pamper you? Or are you worried because I might show you up?" Steve Tangretti shook his head. "I know it's tough, Bill, but I can't pull out now. Not if I want to be ready in time for the deadline Admiral Galloway set for the new assignment in Nam."

"I just . . . I just don't like the idea of you being there if I crash and burn during Hell Week," Bill said. "I signed up because I wanted you to be proud of me, Dad . . . but now you could end up seeing me get in trouble, instead, and it really bugs me."

"Oh, come off it, Bill," his father said with a grin. "Shit, if an old fart like me can make it, you sure as hell can manage just fine! And I don't want to hear any more talk about you failing, either. You hear me?"

Bill bit back a bitter response. He squared his shoulders and drew himself up to attention. "Aye-aye, sir," he said.

"Good! You watch, Bill, it's a snap once you catch on. If you need any advice . . ."

"No!" Bill said. "Er . . . no, Dad. Please. I have to try to get through BUD/S on my own. If I have to lean on you to make it . . ."

That made his father smile again. "That's my boy. Stubborn as they come. All right, Seaman Tangretti, as of now you're just a classmate, nothing else. I'll be seeing you out on the grinder, come Monday morning." He paused. "Of course, if you want to acknowledge your old man long enough to have a beer or two in town over the weekend? . . ."

"Sure, Dad. Yeah. That'd be great."

"I'll stop back around nineteen hundred hours, then. I've already got all the best places spotted. See you later!" Steve Tangretti clapped his son on the shoulder and left, leaving Bill to stand and stare at the door after it had closed behind him.

He'd thought his luck had finally changed, but now he knew it hadn't. The next four months were likely to be nothing short of sheer hell. SEAL training was bad enough by itself, but Bill Tangretti had more to prove than most trainees.

He had to show his father he could cut it. And that wasn't going to be easy.

Monday, 4 December 1966

BUD/S Training Center
Coronado, California
0530 hours

Steve Tangretti stood in ranks, one man among over a hundred SEAL candidates in trousers, T-shirts, and helmets with green-colored liners, shivering in the cool California winter breeze as they waited for the start of a training program most of them couldn't even imagine. The odds were that less than forty of them would complete the course. SEAL training was designed to push the men to their very limits and beyond, to weed out the weak links early and prepare the ones who did make it for the realities of combat.

Tangretti had no fear of failure. He was middle-aged, and it was true that his joints creaked a little more and he couldn't go without sleep quite as long as he'd been able to back in World War II, when he'd first faced training alongside Hank Richardson, Sr., at Fort Pierce. But he'd learned a valuable lesson over the years that put him ahead of the young kids who surrounded him. The real secret of SEAL training wasn't so much physical as it was mental. Willpower, discipline, and the ability to think ahead of the game were far more important to coping with the training program than sheer physical stamina.

That was why he had no doubts about his son, either. Bill Tangretti was no athlete, but he was smart and he was stubborn, and those two traits would stand him in good stead in the weeks ahead. Steve couldn't see his son from where he stood now, but he knew Bill Tangretti would be standing near him the day the class graduated. His son had what it took, all right. He hadn't even been looking for a lot of fatherly reassurances when they'd been together over the weekend. Clearly he was a young man who knew his own mind and didn't need to hear anyone say what a great job he was doing. That made Steve all the more proud of his son, to know he didn't depend on anyone outside himself to give him confidence and strength.

There was a slight stir in the ranks as a cluster of officers and senior petty officers put in an appearance. One man broke off from the rest, a swarthy figure wearing a ball cap, aviator sunglasses, and a windbreaker emblazoned with the single word GOD across the chest. The man paused in front of the lines of trainees and pulled out a pouch from under his belt. He took a large wad of chewing tobacco and put it in his mouth, then produced a cigar, made an elaborate show of lighting it up, and took a puff without displacing the chaw. After a moment he spit out an arcing stream of dark fluid and ran his eyes over the ranks.

"Well, well," the man said, shaking his head slowly. "What a sorry-looking bunch of bananas." He jabbed the cigar towards one of the rigid trainees. "You know why I call you a banana, banana?"

"Sir, no sir!" the trainee replied crisply.

The instructor took three quick steps up to the trainee, so that they were eye to eye. "Don't you *ever* call me 'sir' again, banana!" he shouted. "Do I look like a puke-soaked officer to be called 'sir'? Do I look like I don't work for a living? My name is Petty Officer First Class Ferraro, banana, and around here my rank is God! It's my job to see that *none* of you sorry rejects from the blackshoe Navy ever become

SEALs or frogmen. You pukes are all going to drop out before this course is over, and I'm going to make it easy on you!''

He stepped back from the luckless trainee again and lowered his voice. "You trainees are bananas. That's because you're all soft on the outside, but even more soft and mushy inside. Bananas don't finish this course. They either learn how to toughen up, or they drop out. When you decide it's time to drop this course and go back to the blackshoes where you belong, all you have to do is go over to that side of the grinder.'' He gestured with his cigar again. "You just ring that bell over there, and you'll be on your way home to Mommy in no time flat.'' He gave them an evil grin. "Or if you don't think you can make it to the bell, just take off your helmet and drop the liner on the ground. We'll understand the message just as well. And I'm betting there ain't one of you can make it through without ringing that bell or dropping that liner. So . . . the sooner we get started, the sooner you bananas can give up and drop out!''

Ferraro waved forward a trio of other petty officers, CPO Connors among them. Within a few minutes, the trainees had counted off into sixteen groups of seven men each. Steve Tangretti was an "eight.'' Each group was one boat crew, the basic unit in training—seven men who would work together in all aspects of the tortures Ferraro and his cohorts would be throwing at them in the days and weeks ahead. As the only officer in his boat crew, Steve Tangretti was in charge of the unit . . . which was no advantage at all. He'd be drawing more than his share of attention from the instructors, since he was responsible for everything his teammates said and did for the foreseeable future.

He mildly regretted the fact that his son had ended up in boat crew number thirteen, but Bill was probably glad not to be in the Old Man's shadow.

Once the boat crews had been sorted out, Connors led them in physical training, gruelling calisthenics followed by a four-mile run along the beach. Running over soft sand was a particularly nasty brand of torture, since the grit ended up coating the trainees from head to toe and working its way under their clothes and into their boots. And coarse sand that found its way into a man's underpants would chafe and abrade until the trainee was bleeding around the groin and his private parts felt like ground hamburger.

By the time the run was over and they were making their painful way back to the mess hall for breakfast, most of the trainees were wincing and flinching with every step they took.

One of Steve Tangretti's boat crew, a towering hulk of a man named Woods, watched Tangretti walking across the grinder with a look that mixed envy and amazement. "How the fuck do you do it, Lieutenant?" he demanded. "I feel like I just got a blow job from a meat grinder, and you're walkin' along like nothing ever touched you out there."

Tangretti smiled at him. "Just a little advance preparation, that's all," he told the big man. "Over the weekend I went shopping downtown and got myself some silk skivvies."

"Silk? What are you, some kind of fag?" Woods drew back with a look of contempt.

"Hardly," Tangretti said, still smiling. "But I found out a long time back that silk undies keep the sand out. You might want to give it a try, some time. Today was the easy run ... four miles. They'll have us going four times that by the time Hell Week rolls around, and I guarantee the sand doesn't get any softer as time goes by."

"Well, I'll be dipped in shit," Woods said slowly. "Silk, huh? Hey, Lieutenant, what other bright ideas you got for beating the odds, huh?"

"Now, now, that would be giving away my edge," he told Woods with a grin. He thought of the extra pairs of boots he'd laid in, so he would always have a clean, dry, well-shined pair even after running through salt water. Or the extra T-shirts in his foot locker. Tangretti had learned a lot of tricks of the trade over the years, ways to stay ahead of the curve so he could concentrate on the real demands of training without being distracted by the kinds of petty harassment that made life so much harder for most trainees. It wouldn't do Woods any good to have all the best dodges handed to him on a silver platter. Let him show a little initiative and come up with ideas on his own. That was a big part of being a SEAL, learning how to cope with any new environment.

Still, the man was part of his boat crew, and teamwork was essential if the trainees were to survive and prosper as SEALs. Tangretti shrugged. "Tell you what, though. I'll let you in on the most important secret you'll ever need to know to get through BUD/S, okay?"

"Yeah . . . sure. What is it?"

"Well, the instructors will never say this out loud, but here's the scoop. They don't care if you lie, cheat, or steal to get through the training . . . in fact, they *expect* it. It's a pretty dumb SEAL who tries to tackle everything by the book when there's an easier way. Just don't let 'em catch you at it. You remember that, and look for all the angles, and you'll do just fine."

Friday, 8 December 1966

BUD/S Training Center
Coronado, California
1448 hours

"Up boat!"

At the shouted order from Chief Boatswain's Mate Fred Archer, each boat crew hoisted their 250-pound Inflatable Boat, Small, into the air and balanced it on top of their heads. Bill Tangretti heaved with all his strength but quickly realized he had a real problem to overcome.

The other six men on his boat crew all stood over six feet tall, while he was almost half a foot shorter. There was no way he could bear his part of the load.

"What's the matter, Shortie?" Archer demanded, approaching Tangretti's boat crew with a malicious grin on his square-jawed face. "Can't play with the big boys? Well, don't worry about it. You can carry all the paddles. Fall in behind your crewmates! Move it!"

Tangretti gathered up the paddles as ordered. He noticed some of his crewmates giving him dirty looks; without him, they had to shoulder more of a burden now. "Sorry, guys," he said as he stooped to pick up the paddles, but the muttered curses that answered him weren't very reassuring. Not for the first time, he wished he was built like his father . . . or like Hank Richardson, with his athletic frame and broad shoulders.

They were only a few days into the training process and Bill Tangretti already knew he was in trouble. The training was every bit as demanding as Richardson had promised him it would be, and there were a lot of things his half brother had never told him about that made life even more miserable for the trainees. Like the sand which got into everything and made moving after a beachfront run sheer agony. And sandblasting, another torment that might have come straight out of Dante's vision of hell. Trainees would have to sit in the sand along the waterline as the surf rolled in, holding their trouser legs open. The water would stir up wet sand and send it right up their legs. It was supposed to make them indifferent to the conditions they might encounter while crawling up onto an enemy-held beach, but Bill Tangretti was starting to wonder if he'd ever be able to get past the pain.

Today they were doing boat drills, with each team carrying an IBS across the beach, launching it, paddling through roaring surf, then starting the process all over again. They were being timed, each crew against the others, and the losing crew had been promised an extra mile's run on the beach before chow.

All too often, whether it was running, swimming, or calisthenics, Bill had found himself among the slowest and least able of the trainees, the so-called "goon squad." And the goon squad was generally given "encouragement" in the form of extra exercises, additional laps, or other kinds of harassment designed to break their spirits. It was working, too . . . Bill Tangretti's spirit hadn't broken, yet, but he knew it was starting to bend a long way out of shape.

The real killer, though, was the knowledge that his father was breezing through these early days of training. Nearly fifty, the man seemed able to tackle it all in stride. And that just made Bill Tangretti feel that much worse. He couldn't even keep up with a man more than twice his age. . . .

As he trotted after the rest of the boat crew, clutching the paddles and feeling his cheeks burning with the shame of not pulling his own weight, Bill Tangretti vowed he would keep at it. He was going to show his father that he wasn't a quitter, no matter what it cost him.

Thursday, 14 December 1966

BUD/S Training Center
Coronado, California
0932 hours

Basic Underwater Demolition/SEAL training was divided into three distinct phases. Phase One was a nine-week program of basic physical toughening, designed principally to weed out the unfit and to turn those who stuck with the program into disciplined, hardened fighting men. The second phase, also nine weeks long, concentrated on techniques of demolitions and land combat, while the third phase was a seven-week course in underwater warfare.

For the moment Bill Tangretti wasn't thinking in terms of phases or weeks. It was enough for him to cope with the day-to-day trials of Phase One.

This was the part of the training where the instructors bore down the hardest. Bill could remember his father describing the training program and the reasons behind it, but nothing in those descriptions had prepared him for the reality of it all. It cost a great deal of money to train a frogman or a SEAL, and Phase One was supposed to drive away those who were unfit before the Navy had invested too much time and money in an individual who turned out to be unprepared for it all.

He understood it, but it didn't make things any easier.

Still, he was starting to learn. After the first fiasco with the IBS where he'd earned his boat crew's scorn by not being able to carry his part of the load, he'd come up with a solution. The next time the "Up Boats" call had gone out he'd produced a coffee can, fit it over the top of his helmet, and balanced his part of the load on that. A SEAL had to be resourceful . . . and a SEAL had to work as part of a team. After that, Tangretti had been accepted by the rest of the boat crew. But the challenges went on, a little more difficult each time, and not all of them could be solved so easily.

Today, for instance, they were performing a "Log Run"— carrying a shortened telephone pole on their shoulders as they ran a fourteen-mile course. At the halfway point, they'd been ordered to dump the pole into the water, dive in, swim through the booming surf until the instructors called them back in to shore, and then retrieve the now thoroughly soaked pole for the return trip. Wet, it was a massive weight on Tangretti's shoulders, even though he had five other men to split the load.

Five others . . . the boat crew had already suffered its first casualty.

Slogging through the sand, Tangretti could still picture Machinist's Mate Third Class Harold Evans, the tall, skinny black trainee from Chicago. Two days earlier, the instructors had set their charges to a particularly silly exercise, sitting in a circle facing outward and scooping up handfuls of sand to hurl up in the air while shouting "I'm a volcano!" at the tops of their lungs. It was supposed to get the bananas used to being in an environment where there was a lot of flying sand, like a beachhead under fire, but it was so patently inane that it had made more than one of the trainees break down laughing.

Evans had been one of them. Connors had given him a curt order to wipe the smile off his face and resume the exercise, and then Evans had made his fatal mistake. "Ah, c'mon, Chief," he'd said. "Cut me some slack. With all these honkeys around, us brothers gotta stick together, man! Gotta look after each other—"

Connors had grabbed him by the T-shirt and hauled him to his feet, standing nose to nose with the trainee and bellowing his response. "Boy, you are no brother of mine until the day you graduate from BUD/S, and I'm here to tell you I'm gonna run your ass out of this outfit long before that!"

Stunned, Evans had resumed the exercise, but a few hours later, with Connors riding him hard during PTs on the grinder, he'd given up and rung the bell.

Tangretti had taken the lesson to heart. Men like Connors didn't think in terms of class or skin color or religion. You were either a SEAL, who had been through the training like every other man in the Teams, or you were nothing at all. The only "brother" CPO Connors would acknowledge was a brother at arms, a fellow frogman.

He knew he was still near the bottom of the class in terms of most of the exercises they were expected to perform, but Tangretti didn't plan to give in the way Evans had. He'd stick out the training.

He had to. The alternative was to drop out with his father watching, and that was something he couldn't face. Not as long as he was able to draw breath.

Chapter 22

Friday, 22 December 1966

U.S. Naval Amphibious Base
Little Creek, Virginia
1822 hours

Ensign Daniel Mariacher looked up from the desk as he heard footsteps pause in the hall outside his open office door. Lieutenant j.g. Hechinger was looking in at him with a frown creasing his long horse-face.

"You still here, Mariacher?" the lieutenant demanded. "Good God, man, do you know what time it is?"

"Yeah," Mariacher grunted. "So what?"

"So it's the Friday before Christmas, you dumb shit, that's what," Hechinger told him. "You should be home with Susie and the kids, not hanging around this dump."

"Just going over the evaluations from Camp Pickett one more time," Mariacher said. "Trying to figure if I should schedule some more training exercises for the squad before we ship out for the West Coast."

"Can't it wait, man?" The lieutenant shook his head. "Anyway, you've already got those guys fine-tuned pretty damned well, if you ask me. Instead of worrying about whether you can squeeze a couple of extra percentage points out of their scores, you should be worrying about what's really important. Like your family. Or has it dawned on you yet that you won't be seeing the wife and kids for six months or so? Or that you might not be coming back to see them at all? That's what you should be worrying about now. Especially since it's Christmas."

Mariacher shrugged. "Yeah, maybe you're right," he said without enthusiasm. "Okay, just let me get wrapped up here. A few more minutes. Then I'll head for home."

"Good," Hechinger said, turning away. He paused. "Oh, yeah, Merry Christmas!"

"Merry Christmas," Mariacher echoed dutifully. He waited until the sound of the lieutenant's footsteps had receded down the hall, then turned back to the reports and plunged back into them.

It wasn't that he had anything against Christmas, and God knew he loved his wife, and his young son and infant daughter. But for Dan Mariacher, the last four months had centered entirely upon his squad and on the upcoming tour in Vietnam. He was determined to show just what he could do over there, to make an indelible mark on the Navy that would keep them talking about Daniel Mariacher as long as SEALs sat down together in a bar for a drink and a yarn.

So he had thrown himself into the work of preparing for Southeast Asia, not just himself but the men of Bravo Squad as well. The Team Two platoons slated for Nam didn't have any of the direct experience of Vietnam that their counterparts at Coronado enjoyed, so they'd been forced to put together a Vietnam training program almost from scratch. They'd heard of Team One doing exercises in a marshy stretch of California river land that simulated conditions in the Rung Sat region, so Hawk Finnegan had poured over maps and recon photos trying to find a place the East Coast SEALs could get in the same kind of practice. They'd finally picked the Black River in North Carolina and negotiated with Union Camp Corporation, which owned the land in the chosen area, to let the SEALs perform their maneuvers there.

Finnegan had also been invaluable in helping the unit to sharpen its marksmanship skills at Camp Pickett in Virginia. The first time Bravo Squad had gone out on the range, their performance had been terrible, with everyone pouring massive amounts of ammunition downrange without doing anything in the way of real damage. And Mariacher still winced at the memory of how Finnegan and Badges Horner had actually come to blows that day after Horner—who should have known better—had taken up the wrong position and let hot brass from his M-16 fall on Finnegan's back. Mariacher had waded in to separate them, jettisoning all the rules about the niceties of leadership and the dignity of command to swear a blue streak at both of them until he'd shamed them into realizing just how bad they'd been. After that, things had started to improve, but it had worried Mariacher that even good, experienced SEALs like the two of them could get slack. He didn't want the rot to eat away at his unit, not when it held the key to success or failure in Southeast Asia.

But through hard work and constant training he'd brought them up to snuff at last. On Halloween the unit had visited Camp Lejeune, the Marine base in North Carolina, and gone through a simulation of combat conditions in Vietnam with Marines who had actually been in-country playing the part of VC and NVA regulars. Bravo Squad had acquitted itself well down there, out-thinking and out-fighting the Marines at every turn and earning grudging words of praise from the "enemy" CO himself.

Even so, Mariacher wasn't ready to let his guard down yet. He'd run them back through Camp Pickett a few weeks ago, just to check their marksmanship and ambush skills one more time, and he'd been serious when he told Hechinger he was thinking of doing it again before they left Little Creek in mid-January. Daniel Mariacher wasn't leaving anything to chance. The SEALs needed to know they could rely on themselves over there, since from everything he'd heard and seen it was pretty goddamned clear that the fat-ass, pus-nuts, pencil-dicked paper-pushers running the war over in Nam weren't going to lift a finger to support an outfit like the SEALs that actually got things done without filing a request in triplicate ahead of time.

He leaned back in his chair. For all of that, he did have to admit that Hechinger had a point. A six-month tour in Nam was a long time to be away from wife and children, especially since he'd spent four of the last five months away from Norfolk on a variety of training missions. And even though Mariacher had every intention of coming back safe and sound and covered with glory, he'd be a fool to avoid thinking about the chance that he might not make it home at all. The Navy had made that clear enough these last few weeks, first taking all the SEALs bound for Nam over to the base hospital for in-oculations against a host of diseases few of them had ever even heard of, and then turning them over to legal eagles from BUPERS who sat down with each man to help him draw up a will before he left. It had been a sobering day.

Mariacher made no great pretense of being a faithful husband; he didn't even make much of an effort to conceal his casual affairs from Susie. But she was special to him, the hometown sweetheart who'd been his first sexual conquest and who was still the best of them all. And he genuinely adored three-year-old Danny and little Sally, who'd been born while he was stuck in the North Atlantic as a brand-new ensign. Maybe he'd been letting his drive to excel in Nam push aside these three people who meant the world to him, for all his act of gruff indifference to anything that smacked of sentimentality.

He abruptly stood up, closing the folder on his desk and putting it into the olive-green file cabinet alongside. It was Christmas, he decided, and time he reminded himself what it was that made his life worth fighting for.

Saturday, 23 December 1966

Washington, D.C.
1710 hours

The streets of Washington blazed with lights in the darkness of an early winter evening, bringing together the ordinary lights of buildings, houses, and street lamps with the softer glow around the monuments and public buildings in the heart of town and then capping it all with gay Christmas lights twinkling in red and green and white. Paris was known as the City of Lights, Hank Richardson thought as he walked aimlessly down Independence Avenue, but tonight the American capital easily outshone the French one.

He tried to shut out the traffic noises and the blaring Christmas songs alike as he walked. Richardson was feeling depressed tonight, at odds with the spirit of the season, and the sights and sounds around him did little to help him out of his sour mood.

Christmas. It was supposed to be about family and friends, about hope for the future. But this year Richardson was short on all three.

Take family . . . His stepfather and Bill were both in Coronado. He'd received letters from both of them describing their experiences in BUD/S training, but from the sound of things they certainly didn't seem to be talking about the same place or events. Bill was struggling hard just to keep from failing, but their father seemed totally oblivious to it all as he breezed through the program. And Richardson's mother had surprised him last week by suddenly announcing plans to go home to Milwaukee for the holidays, to see her brother and his family for the first time in several years. This would be the first Christmas that there hadn't been some kind of family gathering in the house in Little Creek, and that bothered Richardson more than he was willing to admit to anyone. It was the end of a long tradition . . . and seemed like an omen of things to come.

As for friends, Second Platoon had scattered to the four winds for the holidays, taking advantage of their last chance to see loved ones before they shipped out for Vietnam in three weeks' time. The empty barracks at Little Creek had been so depressing that Richardson, restless and bored, had decided to drive up to Washington to do some sightseeing just to get away from the place.

And what about hope for the future? He made a wry face at the thought. He was going to Vietnam, and while he'd been looking forward to the prospect for months now, the chance to finally put his training and skills to use, he couldn't help but feel a measure of uncertainty as he contemplated the next six months. Sure, he was a SEAL, trained to handle any contingency. But he remembered how scared he'd been in that torpedo tube in France, despite all his training and all the mystique of being one of the Navy's chosen few.

It didn't help to remember that his father had been killed in combat without ever even knowing he would have a son. Stories Steve Tangretti had told him in years past about the fighting in World War Two kept coming back to haunt his dreams at night. SEAL or not, Hank Richardson was afraid . . . not so much of being killed or wounded as he was afraid that when the time came he might not be able to meet the challenges of combat head-on, the way his father had done so many years ago.

So here he was in Washington on the weekend before Christmas, on his own and feeling sorry for himself. He'd spent the afternoon at the Smithsonian Museum of Natural History, wandering from one exhibit to the next but hardly seeing any of them. His car was parked a good three blocks away, so he had a walk ahead of him through the chill evening air. It hadn't been cold enough for snow, but there'd been a bleak, bone-chilling drizzle all day that was threatening to turn to a more substantial rain shower.

Up ahead Richardson spotted a Salvation Army band at the corner, complete with a bell-ringing Santa. He fished in the back pocket of his pants—he was in civvies tonight, rather than his blues—and found his wallet, stopping long enough to slip a dollar into the collection pot. It earned him a hearty "Merry Christmas" from Santa, but Richardson hardly noticed. His eye had been drawn to another group on the sidewalk beyond the band.

They were about his own age or a little younger, but had the long-haired, unkempt look that was starting to get popular among the college crowd. A couple of them waved signs in the air that demanded the U.S. withdraw from Vietnam, and they were chanting words that seemed to blend in with the competition from the Salvation Army Santa. He strained to hear better. . . .

"Ho, Ho, Ho Chi Minh!" When Richardson finally heard it clearly, he felt his jaw clenching in anger. *Damned Commie sympathizers!* he thought angrily. *How can they go around promoting the leader of a country where Americans were fighting and dying?*

He started to push past them but found his path blocked by a girl holding out a pamphlet in one hand and wrestling to keep hold of the rest of the stack under the other arm. She was bundled up in a long coat and a wool cap, but he couldn't help but notice her pretty face, the strands of auburn hair that had escaped from her hat and the intensity in her startling green eyes.

"Stop the war in Vietnam!" she said, holding out the pamphlet. "Learn the truth about Ho Chi Minh, the George Washington of his country! Stop the war!"

For a moment Richardson thought of telling her exactly what he thought of Ho Chi Minh and the war, but something stopped him. What was the use in starting trouble here? And two days before Christmas . . . hell, he might as well live and let live. He took the pamphlet with a muttered "Thanks" and kept on going, but something about the look in the girl's eyes stayed with him even after he'd deposited the booklet, unread, in the first available trash can.

Under other circumstances, he might have been tempted to try to seduce the girl. But pretty as she was, she just didn't interest him. Richardson couldn't see himself getting involved with anyone who chanted Ho Chi Minh's name and compared him to George Washington, not even for a one-night stand. Maybe, he told himself with a smile, he was finally developing a set of standards after all.

The SEALs in Second Platoon would never believe it, of course. Just as they wouldn't believe that Richardson would be spending Christmas alone with a good book.

Monday, 25 December 1966

Allentown, Pennsylvania
1955 hours

> *"Hark, the herald angels sing,*
> *Glory to the newborn King,*
> *Peace on Earth, and mercy mild,*
> *God and sinners reconciled. . . ."*

Peace on Earth, Jim Horner thought wryly as he joined the rest of his family in the traditional Christmas carol. *That's some strange kind of sentiment to be coming from a Navy SEAL on his way to Vietnam!* He tried not to let his cynicism show on his face. The family was upset enough, knowing he'd soon be heading for Southeast Asia. He didn't want to fan the flames any further.

They finished the carol, and Katherine Horner got up from the battered old piano and announced that she needed to take a break before playing or singing anything else. "Meanwhile, who wants eggnog?" she asked with a gentle smile.

"Can I give you a hand, Mom?" Horner asked her.

She shook her head. "It's under control, Jimmy. You just enjoy yourself."

He watched her heading for the kitchen, her back straight, her bearing graceful and serene. Horner's father had died five years back, but somehow his mother had always managed to carry on with a quiet strength he genuinely admired. He knew she must be dreading his upcoming tour in Vietnam, but she never showed her fears.

His orders hung like a cloud over the little family gathering, though. Horner had brought his wife Lucy and their daughter Debbie for the Christmas weekend, but they were having trouble getting into the holiday spirit as long as the prospect of a six-month separation loomed so near. His brother Ed and his family looked at Horner a little askance at the best of times; Edward Horner, a Protestant minister, had been speaking out against the Vietnam war since the very beginning and had been part of a huge peace march to the Pentagon just two months back. He didn't quite blame Jim for his choice of career, but neither brother really understood the other's commitment.

The other couple at the old Horner home in Allentown, Uncle George Drake and his wife Mariko, were probably the only two Jim felt really comfortable being around. His mother's brother, Drake had served in World War Two and understood the call of duty. He, at least, approved of Horner's determination to serve in Vietnam.

But it was Christmas, and everyone was making an effort to ignore the undercurrents of tension as they celebrated the season. Ed's son David, nine, and Jim's daughter Debbie, seven, had gleefully opened their presents and played with their toys while the older members of the family exchanged gifts and talked about old times in the Horner home. Horner's mother had served them up a wonderful Christmas spread, and now they were singing, even laughing a little, holding thoughts of war and loss at arm's length for a few more hours.

After the eggnog, they gathered around the fireplace and read the Christmas story from Luke, passing the family Bible around so that each of them, the children included, could read a short passage aloud. Then it was time for the children to get ready for bed, a task Ed and Lucy took in hand while Ed's wife Ann helped her mother-in-law in the kitchen. George

Drake drew Horner aside and led him to the study, closing the door behind them.

"Something wrong, Uncle George?" Horner asked.

Drake shook his head. He still wore his hair in a close-cropped crewcut, and it was hard to guess his age. His leathery face and square-cut jaw made him look every inch the Marine gunnery sergeant who had served his country through the long years of the Second World War. "Nothing's wrong, Jim," he said, his voice like the rasp of a sword being drawn from its scabbard. "No, I just wanted to let you know how proud I am that you decided to serve your country. Maybe your brother has his reasons for what he does, but I sure as hell can't understand how he can go around speaking out against the country . . . and against the military, too. It just ain't right."

Horner shrugged. "Ed's just . . . Ed. He really does hate war . . . any kind of violence. At least he's sincere about it. I've seen kids out waving protest signs and chanting for Ho Chi Minh who probably don't know where Vietnam is, much less understand any of the moral issues the way Ed does. For most of these kids, protesting the war's just a way to stage sit-ins instead of going to class . . . or to give themselves a legitimate reason to duck military service without letting people think they're just plain old cowards. Ed's not like that, thank God."

"Well, you're a lot more tolerant than I am, I guess," Drake growled. "Anyway, Jim, I just wanted you to know how I felt. And I wanted to give you something . . . a little extra Christmas gift I couldn't put under the tree, for fear of stirring up all sorts of grief neither of us really needs right now." He pointed to a package on the desk. "That's for you, Jim. I hope you never have to use it for anything but a paperweight . . . but if you need it, it'll serve you well."

Horner hefted the heavy, oblong package and unwrapped it. Nestled inside a plain cardboard box was a knife and scabbard. The well-worn leather showed that they weren't new, but both were in excellent condition. Horner drew the blade, testing its feel in his hand.

"A genuine Sykes-Fairbairn," Drake said proudly. "Matter of fact, you can't get a whole lot more genuine than that one. You know, I was stationed at Fort Pierce with the Marine Scouts and Raiders through most of the war, and they recruited me for old Dave Coffer's training program . . . the Demolitioneers, the ancestors to your SEALs. I trained a bunch of those guys, let me tell you, before I finally got my orders for the Pacific and Okinawa. And while I was at Pierce we had a visit from Major Fairbairn himself, the Brit that designed that knife. He was in the States teaching us how the British commandos did things, and before he left he gave me that knife as a gift. I carried it through Okinawa and Korea . . . and now I'm turning it over to you. It's your turn to carry on the tradition, Jim. I always meant for Frankie to have it, but . . .''

"Yeah," Horner said quietly. Drake's son Frank had been killed by a drunk driver three years back. "Look, Uncle George, I don't think I should take this. I mean, there's a lot of history in this thing. Memories. You don't want to give them all up, do you?"

"You better believe I want you to have it. And don't just stash it in your attic somewhere, either. You take that knife with you when you go overseas next month, Jim. It might just save your life. It sure as hell saved mine a time or two.''

"I . . . Thanks, Uncle George. I'll . . . I'll try to measure up to it." Horner replaced the knife in the scabbard. For a moment his thoughts strayed to the tiger-stripe uniform André had given him in France. There was a bond between fighting men that people like Ed could never really understand. The warrior breed, the ones who served their country in peace and in war alike, accepted sacrifice as a necessary part of their lives, so that others would never need to make those same sacrifices themselves.

"One more thing, Jim," Drake said. "A piece of advice from an old-timer. When you get over there, you get into combat for the first time, remember that it won't be like anything you've ever trained for. It won't be what you expect. You keep yourself alert and ready for anything, Jim. And if you have to kill somebody, don't hesitate, not for a second. Just do it! Because it's either you or him, out there. Make sure it's him.''

"I'll try, Uncle George," Horner said. "I'll try."

Chapter 23

Friday, 5 January 1967

**Mess Hall, BUD/S Training Center
Coronado, California
1815 hours**

Lieutenant Edward Charles Baxter paused by the door of the mess hall and casually returned a salute from Mannie Ferraro. "God" was wearing his usual windbreaker and baseball cap and had a cigar clamped between his teeth. Baxter thought back to Vietnam, to bull sessions where some of the old-timers had maintained they'd given up smoking because it hurt their wind and made them cough when they were out on patrol. Ferraro didn't have any trouble, though. He could outrun any instructor in the unit when he was putting the trainees through their paces, and Baxter had never heard the man hacking the way so many smokers did. Of course, there was a legend of sorts around North Island that held that Ferraro never actually smoked his cigar for more than a puff or two before he let it go out. There were those who claimed he'd been "smoking" the same cigar for two years straight. He was the kind of man who inspired tall tales, that much was certain.

Though Manuel Ferraro wasn't the ranking petty officer in SEAL Team One's training cadre, he was one of the best. And in typical SEAL fashion, rank mattered a lot less than competence when it came to dividing up responsibilities to get the job done. Chiefs like Connors and Archer followed his lead gladly when planning out training exercises. They all could recognize genius when they saw it.

If only we could have had a few more people who understood the concept in the chain of command over in Nam! The bitter thought made Baxter wince inwardly. He didn't like to think of what had happened to him over there.

He'd come close to requesting that he be returned to the fleet, or at least allowed to transfer to a UDT after Det Delta returned to the World. But something inside Baxter had refused to go that far. He didn't want to face another tour like the one in Vietnam, but neither was he willing to give up everything and opt out of the SEALs entirely. He'd made the best compromise possible, instead: a position with the training cadre at Coronado, where he might at least be able to pass on the experience he'd picked up over there. That was one thing he'd learned from Wilson, the man who had relieved him in the Rung Sat. Wilson had shown him that his knowledge and experience really did count for something, despite his personal failures at the head of Delta.

"How's it going, Mannie?" he asked casually. "I don't see your flock anywhere around. Don't tell me you killed them all off already?"

Ferraro grinned. "Nah, that's next week, Lieutenant," he said. "Most of them are inside trying to shovel in enough chow to get 'em back on their feet. They just finished the IB run, and they need all the calories they can get. A few of their mates are still out there . . . the goon squad."

"Ah, the IB run. I remember it well. I'm still working out some of the leg cramps from when I went through it." The Imperial Beach run was a milestone in the first phase of BUD/S, a ten-mile run straight down the beach from Coronado to the Imperial Beach pier. The run itself was bad enough, but the instructors usually took the opportunity to add a few refinements to the torture for the goon squad, the ones who were hovering on the edge of dropping out already. They might be ordered to sit along the surf line and endure a sandblasting from the rolling breakers, or broken out to do an extra few hundred yards of running over broken ground. Once they made it to Imperial Beach, the whole class had to do calisthenics before turning right around and heading back, with more torments facing the laggards on the way home. It was a brutal test of endurance.

But there was method behind the madness. The IB run was

the last big exercise before Hell Week, where real frogmen were separated from the ones who just couldn't make the cut. If a trainee in the goon squad couldn't overcome the rigors of the IB run, it was sure he wasn't going to see it through to the end of Hell Week. Better if he dropped out early.

"Who's bringing in the tail-end Charlies today?" Baxter asked. "Connors?"

"Archer," Ferraro told him. "He's decided to be a special friend to some of the goon squad crew."

"Poor devils," Baxter commented. "What do you think of your class this time around, Mannie?"

Ferraro shrugged. "Good enough, I guess. Won't really know until we get through Hell Week. I figure that'll take out the weak sisters who haven't rung the bell already."

"Well, that's what you're there for," Baxter said. "You going in for some chow too?"

"Cup of coffee. I need to wash the sand out of my mouth. How 'bout you, Lieutenant?"

"I think I'll join you in a cup . . . if God has no objection."

"None, my son." Ferraro grinned again as he held the door open for the officer.

Inside was a cacophony of noise. There had to be three or four hundred men crowded into the large mess area, mostly SEALs and trainees from Class 40. You could tell the trainees instantly even without their helmets with the color-coded liners, which were piled up just inside the door. The trainees were the ones who were gulping down milk and juice without wasting any effort on chatter. Most of them looked like they'd been through the ringer—"Rode hard and put away wet," as Gil Chalker would have put it.

Baxter's eyes were drawn to one man, though, who stood out from the others. He was seated among a group of officers who were obviously trainees, but he didn't seem to be quite as overcome with sheer fatigue as the others. The man was laughing, his hands pantomiming in support of a story that must have been dirty and possibly biologically impossible as well. If he was a trainee, he was in damned good shape.

And he was no youngster, either. Baxter guessed him to be around forty, old for a lieutenant . . . ancient for a SEAL, especially a trainee.

He touched Ferraro on the arm and pointed the man out.

"Is he one of your trainees, Mannie? He looks like he sailed with John Paul Jones."

"Ah, yes, the infamous Lieutenant Tangretti." Ferraro shook his head. "I'm telling you, Mr. Baxter, that one's a real phenomenon. Man's service record says he's forty-eight. But he's been at the head of the class ever since the training started. Knows all the tricks, how to pace himself, how to get around the hassles like sand in his pants or wet boots. Connors says he's been a SEAL for a while now . . . plank owner in Team Two, in fact . . . but the brass ordered him to requalify before they'd authorize him for another tour in the Nam."

"*Another* tour? I didn't think any of the East Coast pukes had been over there yet."

"Mr. Tangretti has," Ferraro said. "Worked as an advisor. He's been over there on, I don't know, three, maybe four different tours, setting up training programs for the Saigon government. He's a real character, I'll give him that much."

"Tangretti . . . Yeah, I heard about him when I was over." Baxter remembered Doc Randolph's story now, about the SEAL advisor who'd been friends with a VC battalion commander and took his LDNN trainees out on patrols that were deliberately intended to provoke firefights. "Shit, what's he doing going through training so he can go back over to that hell-hole, anyway? He could retire . . . or wangle damn near any stateside job he wanted, with his record and seniority."

"Word is the man hates it here in the World," Ferraro told him. "All he wants is another crack at the action over in the Nam. Guess he figures he can make a difference over there. From what I've seen, a few dozen like him could win the whole damned war in a few months, with or without help from the brass. He ain't afraid to get things done . . . and he sure as hell ain't afraid to cheat, either."

"Sounds like a real dynamo," Baxter commented. "I'm surprised he can keep up with the physical side of things."

"Well, he ain't the fastest, or the strongest, but he makes up for it by being one of the smartest." Ferraro smiled. "Strange thing is, his son's in the class too. But Bill Tangretti's really been struggling. He's been pretty consistently in the goon squad, and it doesn't look like he's even going to make it *into* Hell Week, much less last through it. Kid's eighteen, but his old man runs rings around him."

Baxter shook his head. "Hard to believe, Mannie," he said. "Hard to believe. . . ."

He thought about Ferraro's description of the elder Tangretti and about the story Doc had told him back in Saigon that time. Here was a man who had dedicated his entire life to the SEALs, it seemed, a man who felt more at home in Vietnam than in the States. Tangretti had shown a cheerful disregard for accepted procedures, for the entire blackshoe Navy, and somehow he'd managed to get away with it. What was it Ferraro had said? *He ain't afraid to cheat.*

The door opened behind him, and Baxter glanced around in time to see a trainee with a green helmet-liner leaning wearily against the door frame. His face was red and dripping with sweat, his eyes were bloodshot, and his uniform was stained with salt water and crusted with sand. He would have had to improve his looks quite a bit to appear half-dead with fatigue.

With a clear effort of will the trainee staggered through the door, stumbling and going down on his hands and knees inside. Baxter was about to go to help him, but Ferraro shook his head. "Hold off a minute, sir," he said softly. "I want to see how Seaman Tangretti handles himself."

Tangretti . . . so this was the son Ferraro had mentioned, the one in the goon squad who was having trouble keeping up with his father's intense pace. The trainee didn't even try to stand up. Instead he took off his helmet and tossed it onto the pile with the others, then crawled on hands and knees toward the water cooler, thirty feet away.

The chow hall fell silent as the assembled sailors gaped at the trainee. Only the other SEALs continued as before, still drinking and eating as fast as they could, barely noticing the new arrival. A sailor tried to help the younger Tangretti, but he waved the man away and kept on his course. CPO Connors was standing near the water cooler, and when Tangretti finally reached him his voice was surprisingly loud in the quiet room.

"Chief," he croaked. "Do me a favor, would you? Pour some water over me, please . . . at least until I revive enough to get my own."

Connors shrugged and filled a cup from the cooler, splashing it over Tangretti's head and face, then repeating the process. After a time Tangretti shook his head and slowly, painfully got to his feet. "Thanks, Chief," he said, taking the cup from Connors's hand. "I'll take it from here." He filled the cup one more time and gulped the water down.

Across the room, a chair scraped. Baxter looked across to see Lieutenant Tangretti standing up, looking toward his son with a hint of a smile on his craggy features. "Hoo-yah, Bill!" he called, the rallying cry of the SEALs.

"Hoo-yah!" the cry was taken up by a score or more of the other trainees. Bill Tangretti seemed to draw strength from the shout, straightening slowly and walking stiffly to a nearby table.

Baxter looked from father to son, and back again. Steve Tangretti was impressive enough, tackling SEAL training at an age when most military men were already retiring from active service. And his son, goon squad or not, was clearly cut from the same cloth. Stubborn, determined, pugnacious men, they were the very essence of the SEAL spirit.

If men like these could overcome so many obstacles and keep coming back for more, how could Edward Charles Baxter let himself be defeated? He shook his head slowly. Vietnam had robbed him of his enthusiasm, his energy . . . his fighting spirit. He'd come home a beaten man, with barely enough pride to cling to his position in the Teams. The one way to get back those things he'd lost was to face the demons he'd left behind.

Baxter followed Ferraro across the room with his back a little straighter, with more of a spring in his step. He was going back, first chance he got. And he would live up to the example provided by men like the two Tangrettis.

Tuesday, 9 January 1967

BUD/S Training Center
Coronado, California
1054 hours

Hell Week. It was still officially known as "Motivation Week," but as far back as the early days at Fort Pierce Steve Tangretti had never heard a trainee refer to it as anything other than Hell Week. Originally, it had been an intense program distilled from the eight-week Scouts and Raiders course into a single frantic week that pushed a prospective Navy Demolitioneer to his limits. Since then there had been plenty of refinements, but the basic concept remained. Trainees who went through Hell Week had to survive the closest thing to combat conditions a man could face outside a war zone.

Once, Hell Week had been the first week of training, but now it didn't come until the sixth week. The new restructuring of BUD/S training allowed the trainees a chance to build themselves up physically and mentally before they had to face the overpowering pressures of "Motivation Week." Not that anything could really prepare them. . . .

Officially, Hell Week started on Monday morning, but Ferraro and the other instructors chose to interpret that as starting just after midnight. The trainees had been roused from their bunks by explosions and automatic weapons fire to fall out for moonlight calisthenics, a run to the beach, and a swim in water that couldn't have been warmer than fifty degrees. And that was just the beginning. It continued with hardly any let-up, hour after hour.

It was only the second full day of Hell Week, but already Steve Tangretti felt as if he'd been at it for an eternity. Tuesday was traditionally the day set aside for demolition harassment. Tangretti remembered it as So Solly Day from Fort Pierce, when it had been the last and most difficult day of Hell Week. Every exercise and evolution the class undertook on Tuesday would be accompanied by near-constant explosions set off around the trainees. The idea was to get the men so thoroughly accustomed to detonations that they could ignore them in battlefield conditions.

Tangretti looked around as another explosion went off to his left. This was one part of the test that didn't bother him much. No matter how taxing Hell Week might be, it couldn't come close to a real combat zone. He'd been through heavy fighting at Normandy and Okinawa and had witnessed the naval bombardment before the Inchon landings. Even a sharp firefight in Nam produced more of a "pucker factor" than demolition harassment; at least here he knew the charges had been set and triggered by experts, and none of them was *trying* to inflict casualties on the trainees.

There were others in the outfit who weren't doing as well, though. The constant noise battering them from all sides made some men flinch, and one trainee, an ensign named Barbour, had ended up crouched beside a low wall with his arms wrapped around his head, refusing to move until the explosions had let up for a few minutes. As soon as they'd slacked off for a time Barbour had stood up with every appearance of calm and coolly removed his helmet, throwing his colored liner to the ground and stalking away toward the grinder with exaggerated dignity.

He hadn't been the first to give up, and he wasn't likely to be the last.

Right now, the object of the exercise they were engaged in was to cross a narrow wooden suspension bridge built over a mud pit. Each trainee had to cross while instructors shook the rickety structure from either end and the blasts went off one after another. Anyone who landed in the mud had to go to the end of the line and try again. So far, there hadn't been many who'd made it across the first time out.

A whistle shrilled. "Next up!" Ferraro shouted. "Tangretti! Move your ass, Lieutenant! Go! Go! Go!"

He was up and running before the instructor had finished his shout, running for the bridge. Tangretti crouched low as he started across, to keep his center of gravity down. He grabbed the rope lines on either side with both hands, clinging stubbornly as the bridge began to shake. It took a fair sense of balance to stay on the bridge, but Tangretti managed to keep moving without being distracted by explosions, the wild bucking under his feet, or the taunts of the instructors shouting at him as he tried to pull himself across.

He made it, but not without drawing a glare from Fred Archer. "We'll get you next time, old man," the CPO growled.

"Not fucking likely," Tangretti shot back.

They didn't give him any time to rest. Another instructor waved him on and ordered him to run for the beach for the next part of the day's exercises.

He found time to wonder, as he ran, how Bill was holding up. His son had been struggling almost from the start of the training course, and Hell Week was that much more for him to deal with. But he'd met every challenge with the same determination as he'd shown after the Imperial Beach run, driving himself right past the limits imposed by his body. Bill Tangretti had all the makings of a SEAL . . . if only he could manage to hold on.

His father was sure he'd make it.

Friday, 12 January 1967

BUD/S Training Center
Coronado, California
1228 hours

Bill Tangretti was chest-deep in cold, squishy mud, wishing the torture could end.

It was the last day of Hell Week—barring some arbitrary decision by the instructors, that is—and the younger Tangretti had never been so completely exhausted in his life. In five days the trainees had been granted no more than two hours of sleep, plus whatever they managed to snatch when no one was watching. They'd been put through running, swimming, long-distance boat trips, passing telephone poles back and forth, demolition harassment, and heavy calisthenics, at all hours of the day and night and under conditions that should have been banned as cruel and unusual punishment. Eighteen men had rung the bell since the start of Hell Week . . . though according to some of the instructors that wasn't any particularly noteworthy number.

Bill Tangretti had come close to dropping out himself on more than one occasion, but always he'd forced himself to hang on. Now they only had a few more hours to go. But those last hours weren't likely to get any easier.

The day at the mud flats was one of the most notorious parts of Hell Week. The trainees had been herded to the marshy plain on the southern end of Coronado early in the day and told to wade out into the mud. For hours on end they'd been standing there, soaked to the skin, shivering as the mud leached away every bit of body heat. Instructors kept them on their toes by devising various extra hassles, like when Ferraro had decided to walk across the flats by stepping from one set of shoulders to the next so that he wouldn't get his boots muddy, or when Connors had strolled up and down the grassy slope above them barking out questions on everything from hydrographic survey techniques to the General Orders they'd all been forced to memorize back in boot camp.

After five days virtually without sleep, Tangretti had been hard-pressed to remember his name, much less the First General Order. But somehow he'd dredged it up when Connors singled him out.

Fatigue was taking its toll other ways. Hallucinations, for instance. The night before, they'd gone on an exercise paddling their inflatable boats down San Diego Bay almost to the Mexican border at Tijuana and back. Twice on the trip, Bill Tangretti had been certain he'd seen flying saucers skimming low over the harbor, and once he carried on a prolonged and quite lucid conversation with his mother, who had unaccountably replaced Ensign Harriman in the boat crew.

Now he had to fight to stay awake. Falling asleep here in the mud flats would probably drown him, and he wasn't sure any of the other trainees would notice if his head slipped below the surface.

They had just finished lunch, if you could call it that. Eating a meal while standing in the mud, with hands and body and face caked in the sticky stuff and a cloying stench all around, with mud in your mouth that you couldn't clear away and no fresh water to rinse with or drink, was an experience Tangretti had never pictured when he'd dreamed about becoming a SEAL. The very idea would have made him sick a few months ago, but today he'd wolfed down the meal. From the way the others gulped and grunted, they might have been a pack of wild animals worrying over their prey.

Up on the hillside above them, the instructors were looking pleased with themselves, as well they might. They were clean and warm and dry, and just as lunch was starting a station wagon had pulled off the road nearby and disgorged a bevy of women, some of the girlfriends and wives of the instructors carrying coolers with sandwiches, beers, and thermoses of hot coffee and soup. They were up there living like kings, watching the animals grunting in the mud for their amusement.

He shook his head. Even fuzzed out on a week of fatigue and adrenaline, he knew it was just another ploy. Ferraro, Connors, Archer, and the rest just wanted to push them over the line, and they didn't care how. Tangretti glanced across the flats to where his father was standing, hardly recognizable with all the mud on his face and body. As long as Steve Tangretti was there, Bill wasn't going to give in, no matter what. All he had to do was hold on. . . .

"Fuck," the man next to him muttered. It was Meadows,

one of his boat crew. "Goddamn it, I don't fucking *believe* her. . . ." He trailed off, staring up at the hillside.

Tangretti followed his look. He recognized Archer's girlfriend up there, sitting beside the chief and sipping a beer. She'd been around the compound a time or two, always giving the trainees the eye, deliberately provocative any time there was an audience. Today was no exception.

She raised the bottle to her lips and ran her tongue around the rim, taunting, teasing. Beside her, Archer gave a laugh and pointed down at the trainees in the mud, toward Tangretti and Meadows. The woman, laughed, too, and set aside the bottle. Quite deliberately she toyed with the with the buttons of her blouse, knowing their eyes were on her. Then, all at once, she opened it up, revealing pale white breasts with rose-tipped nipples unhampered by a bra. She held the pose for an instant, then covered up again, laughing. Archer kissed her and slipped a hand under the blouse before she could finish buttoning it up again.

Tangretti blinked. Had she flashed them? Or was it just another fatigue hallucination? . . .

Beside him, Meadows was moving. Growling wordlessly, the trainee surged out of the mud and ran up the slope, whether in the grip of lust or anger or some other emotion, Tangretti couldn't tell.

Archer was ready for him, though. In a smooth motion, the chief was on his feet as Meadows reached them, laying the trainee out with a well-placed uppercut. He hauled Meadows to his feet and faced him back toward the mud. "Back in the pool, banana!" he yelled. "Back in the pool, unless you want to ring the bell! C'mon, Meadows, what's it going to be? You can quit any time! So pack it in or haul your sorry ass back down into the mud!"

Meadows shook his head like an angry bull. Then, slowly, he slogged back down to join the rest of Class Forty. "Goddamn prick-teasing bitch," he muttered.

"Easy, Meadows," Tangretti told him. "Don't give Archer the satisfaction. Best way to get him back is to make it through Hell Week."

He repeated the words to himself and resolved to hold on a little while longer.

BUD/S Training Center
Coronado, California
2052 hours

"Class Forty, secure from Hell Week!"

They were the six sweetest words Lieutenant Steve Tangretti had ever heard. The sudden sense of relief among the ranks of trainees assembled on the Grinder was almost palpable. One or two men even collapsed in a dead faint as they finally relaxed their rigid control over bodies pushed too far and too long.

Hell Week was over at last.

Tangretti had to admit, now, that it had almost been more than he could handle. The one advantage of youth over experience was in strength and stamina. There had been times in the past few days when Tangretti had realized that he just wasn't quite as capable as he'd been once. His only edge was his ability to sleep anywhere, any time, allowing him to catch a quick catnap under the most unlikely circumstances. He was fairly sure, for instance, that he'd done the two-mile ocean swim largely in his sleep.

Or maybe that was another of his hallucinations. He'd managed a few real dandies, the last couple of days, including the one where the obstacle course had briefly become the beach at Normandy and he'd relived the moments just before old Hank Richardson had died in his arms. CPO Connors had roused him from his waking dream, and he'd found himself cradling a boat paddle instead of his dead friend's head. That one had nearly broken his resolve, but Steve Tangretti had refused to quit. With tears streaming down his face he'd plunged back into the drill.

Now it was finally over. He'd made it to the end . . . and so had Bill. All told, twenty-three men had dropped out during Hell Week, but none of them had been named Tangretti.

The whole class staggered toward their barracks huts. Tangretti's bleary eyes noted the presence of sentries outside the buildings. That was a fairly recent wrinkle. With the trainees so utterly exhausted, there was no telling what they'd do under the influence of more hallucinations, so they'd be locked into their huts until they had a chance to get some sleep and rejoin the ranks of the human race.

He didn't much care, as long as nobody tried to get between him and his rack. Steve Tangretti felt ready to sleep for a month. Pity he'd only get the weekend. . . .

Monday morning they'd be right back at it. Hell Week might be the psychological climax of BUD/S, but it didn't even mark the end of Phase One of the training. They still had three more weeks of basics, followed by the land and underwater warfare phases of the school. Another nineteen weeks, all told, before they were pronounced ready to become part of a UDT or SEAL outfit.

But the class had gone over the hump, as it were. Few people who survived Hell Week dropped out afterward unless they were injured, and then they usually just rolled back to the next available class to try again. Hell Week was intended to weed out the weaklings. From here on out, the instructors wouldn't be focusing on how to run the trainees out of the program, but on how to mold them into the best possible men for naval special warfare.

He looked around for a moment, trying to spot Bill so he could congratulate him, but his son was nowhere in sight and he was too tired to waste any energy looking for him. Tangretti turned back toward his own hut, staggering a little, and bumped into someone. " 'Scuse . . .'' he muttered.

"No problem, Lieutenant." The voice was vaguely familiar, and Tangretti forced himself to focus on the man's face. It was Lieutenant Baxter. "Look, Lieutenant, after you've had a chance to get some sleep, I hope you'll stop by my office sometime," the younger officer was saying. "I've, uh . . . decided to put in for another tour in Nam, but I thought you might have some advice for how I can make it really work this time out."

Tangretti nodded, not entirely registering the words. "Sure, sure, Lieutenant," he mumbled. "Glad to help. But not tonight . . . oh, God, not tonight. . . ."

He stumbled away, feeling more dead than alive. But under the fatigue, a part of him was feeling triumphant. The Tangrettis, father and son, had survived Hell Week.

Chapter 24

Ensign Daniel Mariacher stood at attention with the rest of his SEAL platoon on the grinder behind the SEAL Team One headquarters building at Coronado. Despite the fact that it was the middle of January, the weather was warm, almost balmy, and the enlisted uniform of the day was whites, while the officers and the chief petty officers sweltered in their dress blue jackets.

"... and on the morning of 7 October 1966, while serving with Det Golf at Nha Be in the Rung Sat Special Zone of the Republic of Vietnam ..."

Mariacher sighed, eager to get this crap over with. It was hot, he was fed up with pencil-dicked bureaucrats and asshole regulations, and there were bars to hit and girls to lay ...

... and miles to go before I get laid. ...

The misquotation of that fragment of Robert Frost made his face crease with a wry grin. On the bunting-draped podium in front of the gathered SEAL platoons, Captain Halley seemed to sense the less than military expression in the ranks and glanced up from the paper he was reading. Mariacher kept his face carefully frozen in neutral as the officer looked back to his paper and continued.

"... the LCM at that time came under heavy and sustained attack by a full battalion of communist insurrectionists. Early

293

in the combat, a mortar round exploded on the LCM's fantail, wounding sixteen of the nineteen men aboard, including all fourteen of the SEALs present. Chief Petty Officer Spencer, though stunned and barely conscious, noticed that a piece of hot shrapnel had landed in a stack of crated mortar ammunition piled on the LCM's well deck. With complete and utter disregard for his personal safety, Chief Petty Officer Spencer grabbed the hot piece of metal with his bare hands, sustaining second- and third-degree burns before he was able to throw the fragment over the rail and into the water. . . . ''

Bright, Chief, Mariacher thought to himself with a barely suppressed grin. *Real bright. Those twelve-round mortar cases only weigh, what? Thirty, thirty-five pounds? How come you didn't chuck the whole thing overboard and save yourself a shitload of grief?*

Mariacher had no patience at all with the Team One people, not the ones he'd met so far, anyway. They didn't seem like such hot shots out here; this nonsense about a two-week course for the East Coast SEALs to prove they were up to West Coast SEAL standards . . . what a crock of shit! Any day that SEAL Two couldn't run rings around a bunch of pus-gutted beach boys, in the sand, in full gear, with RBS and full load overhead, that was the day that Dan Mariacher would look for another job. One with some zip in it, maybe!

''. . . though he had sustained serious burns, Chief Spencer then carried a wounded squadmate to safety, then took over the wounded man's station at a fifty-caliber machine-gun mount aft, and for several minutes thereafter laid down a heavy, sustained, and highly accurate fire that broke at least one Vietcong charge. . . .''

Charlie tried to charge one of those overgunned LCMs? In broad daylight? Shit, the poor skinny bastards probably got lost and ran the wrong way. From everything he'd heard so far, Charlie wasn't so tough. Clever, maybe. Adaptable to really shitty conditions, but then, that's what being a SEAL was all about.

''. . . and even after being relieved, Chief Spencer continued to administer first aid to more seriously injured shipmates. Throughout his ordeal, Chief Petty Officer Spencer continued to reflect the outstanding valor, dedication, and team spirit which has become the hallmark of the officers and men of the

United States Navy SEALs. It is, therefore, my very great pleasure and honor to present to Chief Petty Officer Michael Spencer both the Silver Star of the Armed Forces of the United States of America, and the Purple Heart. Chief Michael Spencer! Front and center!''

Chief Spencer was standing at attention with his own platoon, several ranks down from Mariacher's position. Resplendent in full dress blues, his uniform jacket's left lower sleeve heavy with gold hashmarks, each signifying four years of honorable service, Spencer marched around squared-off corners to the stand, mounted the white steps, and approached the podium. He saluted, and Captain Halley returned the salute, crisp and formally proper. Mariacher narrowed his eyes, trying to see if there was any sign of those burns Spencer was supposed to have suffered, but he couldn't see any scars. He'd have to see if he could talk the old boy into a drink later on, maybe swap some war stories. He really had his doubts that things had been as tight out there that day last October as the after-action reports made them out to be.

''Chief Petty Officer Michael Spencer, for wounds suffered while engaged in action against an enemy of the United States of America, on or about 7 October 1966, you are hereby awarded the Purple Heart.'' Turning to an aide, a beribboned commander, Captain Halley plucked the heart-shaped medal from a grey, velvet box, reached out, and pinned the deep, blue-purple ribbon with its white border stripes to Spencer's chest. The chief, Mariacher noted, already had quite a heavy rack of medals on his breast, each one overlapping the one next to it in military-perfect formation.

Fucking crackerjack trinkets. . . .

''Chief Michael Spencer,'' Halley began once again. ''For distinguished gallantry in action against an enemy of the United States of America, I present you with the Silver Star, and the sincere thanks of a grateful nation.''

The medal he removed from the second box was a five-pointed silver star bearing a laurel wreath with a smaller star inside. The ribbon had a single red stripe down the center, flanked left and right by thick white and blue stripes, and with a thinner white stripe on the outer part of the blue. He pinned the second medal on with, Mariacher thought, more of a flourish than he'd shown with the first. Then, taking one step back, he saluted the chief, who returned the salute sharply.

By the time I'm done over in the Nam, Mariacher thought with a wry, upward twist to the corner of his mouth, *I'll have me a pocketful of those little baubles. But the only one I really want is the old CM of H. Bag* that *baby, and the admirals have to salute* me! . . .

The idea of wearing an itty-bitty blue ribbon that made the brass—hell, that made the President of the United LBJ States—all snap right up to toy-soldier attention and render the first salute tickled Mariacher. It was the only use he could think of for the damned things. As for Spencer's ribbons, well, hell's bells, everyone knew the Star was political nowadays. And as for the Purple Heart, well, some of Chief Spencer's wounds had been caused by a mortar burst . . . and he hadn't had a bit of control over that. The rest had been caused when he picked up that hot chunk, and that was just plain stupid. Shit, he'd heard that another West Coast SEAL had also won both the Silver Star and the Purple Heart . . . that kid, what was his name? Marshall. Willy Marshall. He'd picked up both ribbons . . . or rather, his parents had, when he'd gone and gotten himself killed while out on patrol.

Now *that* was fucking stupid!

No, Dan Mariacher was not impressed.

The speeches continued for another half hour, and Mariacher sweltered in his blue jacket. He was aching to strip down and take an afternoon swim, and maybe go for a run down the beach. Getting hot and sweaty while exercising was one thing. Standing here melting like the witch in *The Wizard of Oz* while listening to kiss-ass speeches and play-soldier silliness was sheer torture.

"Comp-*nee*, dis-*missed*!"

It was over. At fucking long last, it was over.

The assembly broke up, though individuals lingered, clotting into small clumps of white and blue. The two groups, SEAL One and SEAL Two, still hadn't started mingling much yet. The two platoons from the East Coast SEAL Two had only arrived three days before and were hardly settled in yet. Hell, Mariacher figured he still had to get himself laid. He'd heard that California pussy was something extra-special but tended to dismiss the claim as more West Coast propaganda. If he could get into San Diego tonight, though, he just might be able to put it to the test.

"Well, Ensign," a rough voice said at his back. He turned and found himself facing a big, hard-muscled chief, a black man who looked as mean as anyone Mariacher had ever encountered. "You ready to hit the surf tomorrow?"

Mariacher's eyes skipped to the man's chest. Bronze Star. Purple Heart. A Meritorious Unit Citation. Meritorious Service. Several Vietnamese medals Mariacher didn't recognize, other than to know they meant he'd been *there*.

"Sure thing, Chief Connors," Mariacher said, smiling easily. "I figure the surf out here in sunny California can't be half as cold as the Atlantic."

The chief smiled at that, and several other West Coast SEALs standing nearby burst into laughter. "Shit, Ensign," one of them said, laughing. He was a big, brawny first class gunner's mate. "You don't *know* cold until you've hit the Big P! You're gonna freeze your balls off."

"No problem, pencil-dick," Mariacher said. "Long as I've got you to warm 'em up!"

The man's smile vanished, and Mariacher could damn near read the thoughts behind those hard eyes. A first class couldn't deck an officer, even a lowly ensign, not without getting kicked clear out of the unit and back to the fleet, just for starters. But there were other ways a know-it-all jerk of an ensign could be made plenty uncomfortable.

Screw it on, shithead, Mariacher thought, continuing to hold his most pleasant and disarming smile in place. *Screw it on! We'll see who the better man is! . . .*

Mariacher thought he was going to enjoy this.

Friday, 19 January 1967

Mickey's Place
San Diego, California
2020 hours

". . . so then Ferraro climbs up on his back and just stands there, puffing on his cigar, while poor old Woods has to start the push-ups all over again."

Hank Richardson emptied the last of the Seagram's into the glass in front of him and lounged back in his chair, smiling.

It was hard to believe that Bill Tangretti had changed so much in just a year of Navy life. His half-brother sounded more alive than Richardson had ever heard him before, and he looked tanned, fit, and ready for anything. He looked, in short, like a Hell Week survivor.

The BUD/S class where the two Tangrettis were training had wrapped up Hell Week the day after the East Coast SEALs had arrived in Coronado, and on that first weekend Richardson had avoided looking them up so they could catch up on their rest after the ordeal. Then he'd been tied up with the rest of the Team Two force on the series of exercises their West Coast counterparts had cooked up to test their skills. *That* hadn't lasted long, though. By the middle of the week the West Coast pukes had been forced to grudgingly admit that the East Coast SEALs knew their stuff and were routinely running through evolutions they claimed would take hours in mere minutes instead.

This morning Team One had finally given up in defeat, agreeing with Ensign Mariacher that they'd get just as much use—and a hell of a lot more fun—out of dedicated survey of San Diego bars, strip clubs, and whorehouses.

So there'd been nothing to keep Richardson from planning an evening with his brother and his stepfather, to celebrate their completion of Hell Week and catch up on each other. A number of other SEALs, from both Teams, had attached themselves to the party, and every time another batch drifted in to the bar they gravitated toward the group of tables the early arrivals had appropriated and pushed together in one end of the room. All of them wore casual civilian clothing, though their short haircuts tended to mark them as military men, and the other patrons kept their distance as they started to get rowdy.

The place was dimly lit and smoky; Paul McCartney was singing "Yesterday" in sad tones over the sound system, but it was difficult to hear the words over the clatter and clink of glasses and the ongoing buzz of conversation. The waitresses wore short leather miniskirts and brief halter tops, and he thought he'd seen a couple of them giving him the eye as they passed. All in all, Richardson thought with a contented smile, it was turning into quite a party.

"Sounds like this Ferraro would give old Rudy Banner a run for his money," he said aloud.

Harry Matthews and Roger Reynolds both chuckled at that, but his father shook his head. "No way, Junior," he said. "Chief Ferraro's a good man, don't get me wrong, but Rudy's still the best thing in torture since the Spanish Inquisition. When Rudy finally passes on and goes to hell, Old Nick's got a job reserved for him modernizing things so the damned'll know they're *really* paying for their sins!"

That drew general laughter, and Richardson grinned. "Yeah, I guess you're right, Dad," he said. "I still remember when I went through BUD/S back in '64. Rudy was doing a stint as an instructor then, and he was running us through the Kennedy Bridge problem."

That drew groans from a few of the East Coast men. One of the Coronado SEALs, Diver First Class Frank Horowitz, raised an eyebrow. "What's that?" he asked.

"It's a bridge out in the middle of nowhere, where a pretty big highway crosses over the Nataway River. Miles away from Camp Pickett . . . and from damned near everything else, too." Richardson drained his glass. "Every class gets a variation of the Kennedy Bridge problem. Basically, you get to hike all night over hill and dale with forty-pound packs on your back. You get close to the bridge, set up camp, and then do a quick sneak-and-peek. The instructors are defending the bridge, playing the enemy, and the idea is to mount an assault just at dawn, clear away the bad guys, and then plant fake charges on the thing and simulate blowing it up. A real fun night's work, y'know?"

A waitress went by, and Richardson reached out and deftly snagged the hem of her miniskirt just below her buttocks and gave two sharp tugs. The woman whirled, eyes narrowing with anger, but he tossed her his sexiest smile and held up his empty bottle. "Hey, gorgeous! How about another one of these?"

"In a minute," she said curtly.

"I think she loves me," Richardson said dreamily as she strode away. "Okay, anyway, when my bunch did the Kennedy Bridge problem, nothing went right. Part of the way you're navigating right up the Nataway, in the river bed, and we got really bogged down. Delayed us so that we didn't even get *to* the bridge before dawn, let alone do the recon. So we did a real hurry-up job and launched our attack without much of a plan. Worked real good, too. When we'd done the pre-mission briefing, we talked about going in from the north side, and of course the instructors had listened it and set up their defenses accordingly. But we didn't have time to stick to the original scheme and came in from the south. Faked 'em out completely. Afterwards, they told us we'd done a brilliant job and ordered us to hike back to camp. They said we could use the roads this time, 'cause we'd been such good little boys.

"Well, we started back, and we all knew what was going to come next. Every class always got hit by an ambush on their way back from the Kennedy Bridge. The instructors always hit at this same place, a little bridge about ten miles down the road. So we were slogging along, talking about it, and one of the other guys—Rick Davis, I think it was—he spotted an army truck coming up behind us and had the bright idea to flag it down. We talked the Army guys into letting us hitch a ride in the back of the six-by. We buttoned up the canvas in back so nobody saw us riding and had 'em dump us a little ways from the ambush site. Hell, we were there long before the instructors! Got ourselves a real nice sleep for ten, eleven hours, then we set up an ambush of our own and just waxed those guys when they showed up and started to set their trap. And that really blew 'em away, too! They were really impressed that we'd covered the ground so fast and hit 'em before they were ready."

The waitress chose that moment to show up, a fresh bottle of Seagram's on her platter.

"Hey, thanks, honey," Richardson said. Reaching behind her, he slipped his hand in between her black-stockinged legs, caressing her thigh. Angrily she spun and slapped him across the face. "Keep your hands off me, you creep!"

"Whoa!" Richardson said, holding both hands up. "Sorry, babe! Hold your fire!"

"Don't pay him no mind," Harry Matthews told the woman. "He never grew up."

She gave them an appraising look. "You guys are SEALs, aren't you?"

"That's classified," Richardson said, rubbing his cheek.

"Can't talk about it in public. But if you'd like to get together later . . ."

"Never mind, hero," she said. "Just keep your mitts to yourself, okay?"

"She's definitely interested," Richardson said as the woman stalked away. "You can tell by her voice. . . ."

"Aw, knock it off, lover-boy," Torpedoman Third Class Luciano growled. "What about Kennedy Bridge?"

"Well, they were so happy with us they gave us the day off, and we were sure feeling proud of ourselves. That is, until Rudy Banner got to drinking over at a bar outside Pickett and ran into the WO4 who drove the truck we hitched with. He got to telling Rudy about giving a ride to a bunch of SEALs, and Banner got really pissed. He was more than half-drunk anyway, and so was Chief Farnham. So they decided then and there to teach us a lesson. Hauled us out of our racks in the middle of the night, issued us full combat gear, and drove us back out to that damned Kennedy Bridge. Told us we'd walk back to camp this time, and they'd watch us every step of the way, and told us we had to make it back in two hours and twenty-two minutes or we'd have to turn around and do it all over again, until we made the schedule. And the previous class record for hiking from Pickett to Kennedy Bridge was two and half hours, so they figured they had us for sure."

"So what happened?" Toby Bosniak asked. "How many times did you have to try it?"

"That was the best part of all," Richardson told it. "Don't ask me how we managed it, but we made the hike back in two hours, nineteen minutes . . . first time. I thought old Rudy would blow a gasket!"

"The way I heard it," his father put in, "Rudy got out of BUD/S training after that 'cause he was sick and tired of smart-assed young punks making him look bad!"

"Yeah? Well, Dad, you know how it is." Richardson grinned. "Us young kids are starting to move in on your turf. Simon Farnham retired last month, did you know? You should have seen the look on his face when we gave him the guitar I bought over in Paris. Rudy Banner'll be next . . . all the old guard."

"Now hang on just a minute, Hank," Jim Horner spoke up. "I'm a plank owner in Team Two, just like Rudy and Pete.

And I'm not on the way out yet, not by a long shot!''

"Neither am I," Steve Tangretti said, glowering at his stepson. "You watch your mouth, Junior, around your betters. This is one SEALie who ain't ready to hang up the old swim fins yet."

Before Richardson could respond he was distracted by another conversation that had broken out on his other side between Harry Matthews and Randolph, the hospital corpsman. "All I'm saying is that somebody screwed up somewhere," Randolph said, sounding intense. "I mean, sure, they use this transporter thingamabob to beam people back and forth. It sounds pretty farfetched, but I'll buy it. But they did a whole episode where the transporter was on the fritz and a bunch of people are freezing to death down on this ice planet, and yet two, three weeks later we find out the ship carries shuttles that could've gone down, rescued the guys, and solved the whole problem. I just think they oughta try to be consistent, that's all!''

"Well, hey, what do you expect from a show where the captain of the ship keeps leading the landing parties and takes his bridge officers down with him?" Richardson chimed in, grinning. "How many cruiser skippers have you seen who'd do something like that, huh?"

"Yeah," Randolph agreed. "Yeah, those Hollywood types are nuts. This 'Star Trek' thing's never gonna go anywhere."

"Give me 'Combat' any time," Roger Reynolds added. "Vic Morrow . . . now there's a guy who's got his shit in his seabag. Should've been a SEAL."

After a time, the party started to break up. Eventually, it was down to the Tangretti family again, and Richardson found the chance to get serious with his stepfather. "Dad . . . I'm glad you got your shot at this new assignment," he said. "I know it's what you want, after that fucked-up NOSG gig. But . . . have you talked to Mom about it at all? She's really been bummed out, ever since the Tadpole here signed up."

His father looked into his beer for a long moment. "I've tried to talk with her, Junior," he said slowly. "I really have. But I can't make her understand how important this life has been to me. I'm just not ready to retire and settle down to fight crabgrass and play checkers. Not yet. There's still a hell of a lot I can do that's worthwhile, that'll help the SEALs. She won't look at it my way.''

Richardson gave him a long penetrating look. ''Maybe you haven't tried to see it her way, either, Dad,'' he said quietly. ''Think how she must feel. I'm going over for my first tour at the end of the month. You're going back for . . . what is it? Number three? Four? Now the Tadpole here is training for it, too, and he'll end up with the West Coast pukes. They're still sending most of the SEALs who go over. It's got to be hell for her, Dad.''

Steve Tangretti nodded. ''I know it, Hank. God knows I know it. I'm the one who had to tell her how your father died, don't forget, so I know how she must be feeling. But this ain't something I can just switch on and off. I want to work things out with her . . . but she's got to be willing to meet me partway.'' He frowned. ''You know as well as I do, Junior, that a SEAL doesn't surrender. Not even to your mother.''

Chapter 25

Tuesday, 31 January 1967

Over the South China Sea
1310 hours

The deep, rumbling drone of the C-130's engines filled the cavernous cargo deck of the aircraft, as it had for the past several hours since leaving Clark's Field in the Philippines. Lieutenant j.g. Fred Hechinger was sitting in one of the aircraft's bonebreaker seats, a torture-chamber contraption of metal pipes and canvas temporarily mounted to the bulkheads. The windows were small and high and difficult to see out

of . . . not that there was much to see, yet. The South China
Sea looked like any other tropical ocean seen from thirty thousand feet, flat, blue, and featureless.

"Hey, Lieutenant?"

He looked up from the detective novel he'd been reading.
The C-130's cargo master, a twenty-year-veteran senior master
sergeant, was standing over him. "Yeah?"

He jerked a thumb over his shoulder. "The major says you
can come up front. You might like a look."

"On my way."

Dropping the novel on his seat, he hauled himself upright
and followed the Air Force man forward. The enormous cargo
deck of the Hercules transport was filled—packed, really—
with crate upon crate of weapons, of ammunition, of food, of
clothing and radios and special equipment, with seabags carrying personal gear, with batteries, with explosives, even with
SCUBA tanks and garb, all carefully packed and riding on
cargo pallets, lashed down with web straps secured to deck-
mounted belaying rings.

Bulkiest in that small mountain of SEAL gear were the
Team's two STABs, Seal Team Assault Boats, strapped down
on their trailers and with their bulky, twin outboards shrouded
in plastic and hanging off their sterns. He gave STAB One a
loving pat as he passed. These babies were going to be real
innovations in riverine warfare, and the SEALs were looking
forward to giving them a good workout under combat conditions.

Now, though, both STABs were serving as cargo carriers,
piled high with ammo, weapons, and gear. Getting everything
aboard the Herky-bird back at North Island NAS had been a
near thing, not because it was difficult to load, not even because the tonnage exceeded published safety limits, but because the bureaucratic mind-set of the Air Force had insisted
that so much gear would *never* fit aboard a Hercules.

The SEALs had proven otherwise. Horner had once been
an aircraft loadmaster—sometimes Hechinger thought there
was *nothing* that guy hadn't done at some point in his military
career—and he and the other senior team members had gone
over the SEALs' gear piece by piece before they'd even
shipped out of Little Creek, determining the mass and center
of gravity for each and laying them all out on the floor of a

hangar, mapping out where everything would be stowed, and how. Back at North Island, Major Ball, the aircraft's skipper, had been blunt in his assessment that the SEALs would never get that much gear aboard, let alone themselves, but he'd been willing to let them try. It had been a close thing; the last trailer load of equipment had been lashed to the C-130's tail ramp and drawn up into the aircraft's belly when the ramp had been raised, but they'd made it and the major had been impressed.

For their part, the SEALs had maintained a stoic, business-as-usual attitude, ignoring the crowding on the cargo deck that left twenty-eight men with scarcely room to turn around in for the long hours of the trans-Pacific flight. Some had taken to sleeping on top of the tarp-covered bundles and cases in the center of the bay; most stayed in their seats to either side of the aircraft, reading, talking quietly, or just sitting. Hechinger stopped briefly beside Chief Ted Brubaker, who was hunched over in a corner petting Max. The big German Shepherd, trained back in the States to follow scent trails, looked up at Hechinger and gave a playful whine, and he reached down to rub the dog's head. "How's he holding, Chief?"

"No sweat, Lieutenant," Brubaker replied, grinning. "This here's Max the Wonder Dog. *Told* ya he was aircraft-broken."

The long flight had been a matter of some concern, since the cargo chief had told them pointedly what he would do if Max made a mess on *his* deck.

"Hang in there, guys."

Hechinger made his way up the starboard side of the aircraft, following the Air Force cargo master forward. Access to the cockpit was over on the port side, past the aircraft's nose access door, then hard right up a set of steps so steep they nearly constituted a ladder, and left into the cockpit. "You wanted to see me, Major?"

Major Ball, seated in the left-hand seat, gestured ahead through the Herky-bird's windshield. Ahead, the azure of the South China Sea gave way abruptly to a flat quiltwork of brown and green.

"We're about to go feet dry, Lieutenant," the aircraft's commander said. "Thought you might like a look."

Leaning between the pilot's and copilot's seats, Hechinger stared at South Vietnam. He could see the waves on a beach, frozen, as though in a photograph, by distance and altitude.

To the right, further up the coast, a broad river flowed around
a huge, teardrop-shaped island; the water was yellow-brown,
staining the blue of the ocean with a gradually fading smear
of color that stretched for miles out to sea.

"What's that river?"

"The Bassac," Ball replied. The sun flashed brightly off
the ocean to the southwest, and Hechinger understood why
both the pilot and the copilot were wearing sunglasses. The
intensity of the sun was dazzling, especially after the semi-
darkness of the cargo deck. "Binh Thuy's up river, about fifty
miles."

"Where's the jungle?" he asked, squinting against the glare
off the water. "I thought this area was all jungle."

"Used t' be," the copilot said with a dry, down-East twang.
"Until the B-52s came through."

"And defoliants," Ball added. "I get the idea MACV won't
be satisfied until there's not one damned tree left growing in
the whole damned country."

As the Hercules drew closer to the coast, and Hechinger's
eyes grew more accustomed to the light, he could see the pattern of immense, overlapping craters that dotted the landscape
and turned it into something more like the surface of the moon
than tropical southeast Asia. Many were bull's-eyed by cir-
cular pools of water, creating the impression of hundreds of
round, unevenly spaced swimming pools.

"Carpet bombing," the copilot added, talking around a
piece of gum. "Y'see, the idea is to make it so Charlie doesn't
have anywhere t'hide."

Hechinger didn't reply. He was rather forcibly reminded of
the old doctor's joke about how the operation was a success
but the patient died. There'd been a lot in the papers lately
about the notion of winning the war by "winning hearts and
minds." Well, MACV was certainly making an impression on
the hearts and minds of the Vietnamese people, but he wasn't
sure that the message they were getting was the one MACV
originally had in mind.

The politics of the message wasn't the SEALs' responsibility, however. All the SEALs had to do was deliver it . . . with
STABs, with Stoner Commandos, with all of the knowledge
and skill and combat instinct their training programs could
pass on to them.

Somewhere in the back of his mind, however, was a lingering question. How would the SEALs—how would he personally handle combat? He'd heard stories enough from vets back stateside to know that all of the field maneuvers and training in the world weren't enough to demonstrate whether a man would carry out his mission or fold and break when real bullets, fired by a real enemy, started flying.

Vietnam, he knew, would be a test of far more than newly evolved combat tactics and gear.

"That's feet dry," Ball said as the Hercules swept across the beach and over the desolate patchwork of craters below. In the distance, Hechinger could see patches of thick forest—evidently the defoliators hadn't managed to kill all of the trees just yet—and sunglint off of a maze of canals and narrow waterways. Ball reached out and pulled back on the throttles slightly, and the C-130 gave a bump as it settled lower in the sky. "How're your people holding up back there?"

"Just fine, Major."

"How's the dog?"

"No accidents yet."

"Used t' have a dog," the copilot said around his gum. "Hell of a note, sending an innocent dog to Vietnam."

"He'll earn his keep," Hechinger said. "We're going to use him to follow trails, track VC suspects, stuff like that."

"Well, you can tell your boys that we'll be touching down in about fifteen minutes," Ball told him. "I imagine Senior Master Sergeant Godfrey would appreciate a hand unloading your stuff. I want to have the aircraft cleared out and airborne again before dark."

"Yes, sir."

"And, when we touch down, move it fast, okay? We nearly always take a round or two once we're on the ground. I don't like being a target any longer than I have to be."

"I'll pass the word."

Ball grinned at him. "Welcome to Vietnam, Lieutenant!"

1345 hours

Ensign Daniel Mariacher leaned back against the tarp-covered sled loaded with ammunition and demolition equipment trying to catch some sleep, but he'd not been having much success. Usually he was able to sleep anywhere, any-time, a talent acquired during his BUD/S training that had served him well countless times since, but on this occasion the talent had abandoned him, driven away by the pounding of his pulse, the surge of adrenaline in his veins.

The Nam. I'm going to the Nam . . . at last!

Vietnam was where it was happening, where a trained, pro-fessional warrior could put his training to the real test. It was something Mariacher wanted, something he wanted so badly he could taste it.

Though he knew some of the Det Alpha SEALs were won-dering how they would perform under fire, Mariacher had no doubts on that score, either about himself or the others. He'd faced plenty of tests along the way and met every one; he would meet this one as well. If he had any worries at all about going to Vietnam, they were rooted in his conviction that the brass was bound and determined to screw things up for the SEALs if they could find a way to do so. There was a built-in perversity to the universe: if something could go wrong it would. There was a similar perversity behind the functionings of bureaucrats and the brass: if it's a good idea, tinker with it until it isn't.

He fully expected to have to face narrow-minded brass-hatted stupidity in Vietnam; but he also expected that he'd be able to find some room to swing freely. Mariacher considered himself to be a operator, a free-thinking and free-acting indi-vidualist who knew where the corners could be cut and which rules could be bent or broken.

"Fifteen minutes, people!"

Mariacher opened one eye. Lieutenant Hechinger was emerging from the passageway leading up to the cockpit, and the cargo chief was with him. "About time," he said, loud enough to be heard above the rumble of the engines. "The service on this here airline sucks, the in-flight movie stinks, and these are some of the *ugliest* stews I've seen in a long time!"

"We'll take your complaints up with the travel agency, Mr. Mariacher," Hechinger said. "Now listen up, people. The plane's captain says they take some fire from time to time when they're landing. So let's keep our heads up, and no lark-ing around."

"What," Roger Reynolds said, looking up sharply. "We're going into a *hot* LZ?"

"Lukewarm," Hechinger replied. "We're going to help the crew offload our gear, so let's have some hustle out there."

Preparations started at once. Mariacher and Horner began breaking out M-16s and passing them out. Each man took a .38 Smith and Wesson automatic and strapped it on. Another locker held banana-clip magazines, loaded weeks ago in Little Creek with thirty rounds apiece. Each man took three of them, snapping one home into the receiver of his rifle.

Mariacher waited until the cargo chief turned and left the area before reaching down and yanking back the charging lever, chambering the first round.

"Hey, Myok," Hechinger called. "What the devil are you doing?"

"Hey, Mr. Myok," Brubaker added. "That's a no-no."

Mariacher grinned. "What's your point? If we're hitting a hot LZ, I'd just as soon have something ready to protect myself with besides my charming personality and outgoing manner."

Richardson chambered a round, the *snick-snick* loud even with the roar of the aircraft's engines. He was standing below Mariacher's perch. "The man's right," Richardson said. "Always prepared."

"Boy Scout," someone said, but in moments the rest of the SEALs were chambering their weapons as well, checking to make certain that the safeties were on. Regulations prohibited carrying weapons locked and loaded, with rounds chambered, aboard an aircraft, but the entire team had just tacitly agreed that regulations had their place . . . and that that place was subordinate to tactical common sense. There was a definite feeling of being part of an elitist fraternity, running from man to man like an electric current. Maybe ordinary grunts weren't allowed to carry loaded weapons on a plane, but these were *SEALs*.

The cargo chief returned with an airman a few minutes later. If he noticed all of the weapons, he kept his opinions to himself. The Herky-bird was turning now, the deck slanting sharply beneath their feet as it circled around to approach Binh Thuy from the north. The landing gear went down with a thump; there was a breathless, how-much-longer pause . . . and then they kissed the runway with a heavy bump, the turbo-props shrieking as the pilot reversed the engines. Moments later, they'd taxied to a halt and the cargo ramp started going down. Mariacher, standing next to one of the STABs, braced himself. *Vietnam! Vietnam!* The name raced through his brain like a litany.

The SEALs trotted down the ramp in a double column, M-16s held at the ready. Mariacher blinked in the sudden day-light, trying to absorb it all. Binh Thuy was a huge airbase, all endless tarmac and concrete buildings, Quonset huts and row upon row of aircraft. The smell was almost overpowering, a mix of jet fuel and rotting vegetation. A UH-1 helicopter clattered past; somewhere, a jet was revving its engine, pre-paratory to takeoff.

Mariacher hadn't been certain what to expect. Jungle, cer-tainly, and he couldn't see anything here but concrete, even though he was certain that he was smelling it. The air was thick with strange and spicy odors, still heavy behind the more familiar stink of diesel fuel, avgas, and kerosene. There were plenty of people in view, Air Force, Army, and lots of Viet-namese too, wearing tiger-stripe camouflaged uniforms exactly like those given to the SEAL Two men in France months before. Vietnamese Special Forces, he decided, the *Luc Long Duc Biet.*

Binh Thuy Air Force Base
1340 hours

Where the hell was the enemy?

A jeep drove up toward the rear of the aircraft. In the ve-hicle were two familiar faces, Chief Gunner's Mate Bob Fin-negan and Boatswain's Mate First Class Carl Estrada. Two long-time members of SEAL Two—Finnegan was a Team Two plank owner, and both men had been UDT for years before the creation of the SEALs. They'd been sent to Binh Thuy ahead of the rest of the unit, along with Lieutenant Kes-sler, the Team's CO, to make the necessary berthing arrange-ments and generally check the lay of the land.

"Hey, Hawk!" Mariacher called to Finnegan. "You seen any action?"

"What the fuck are you guys play-acting at?" Estrada said

laughing. "The war don't start around here till sundown."

"Yeah," Finnegan said. He reached into the back of the jeep and extracted a beer, dripping wet. "Incoming!"

He tossed the beer and Mariacher caught it. It was *cold*.

"The aircraft commander said he gets shot at sometimes."

"Sea stories," Finnegan said. "Oh, Charlie takes a potshot now and again, but he don't mean nothing serious by it. The real fun starts at nightfall."

"Come on, guys," Estrada said. "Grab your beers and relax a sec. We'll give you a hand offloading and show you where to stow your shit."

"So where's this place we're going to be holed up?" Horner wanted to know as he accepted his beer.

"Tre Noc. It's on the river a mile or two from here. We'll have to move to get squared away by sundown. Of course, there's time to finish your brews first."

"War fought on a schedule," Hechinger said, shaking his head. "Must be nice. . . ."

Chapter 26

Tuesday, 31 January 1967

SEAL Team Two, Base Det Alpha
Tre Noc, Mekong Delta

In Tibet, the river is called *Dza-Chu*, the Water of the Rocks. The eleventh-longest river in the world, it changes name each time it crosses another national boundary on its twenty-six-hundred-mile march to the sea. It is the Turbulent River, *Lan-Ts'ang Chiang*, as it cascades through the steep-walled gorges of China's Yunnan Province. In Thailand it is the *Mae Nam*

Khong; in Laos the *Me Nam Khong*; in Cambodia the *Mekongk*. At Phnom Penh, it branches in two, flowing across the Cambodian border into Vietnam as the *Tien Giang* to the northeast, and the *Hau Giang* to the southwest, though Westerners usually referred to the Hau Giang by its French name, *Bassac*. Between the towns of Vinh Long and My Tho, the Tien Giang splits into three more rivers, the *Co Chien*, the *Ham Luong*, and the *My Tho*. Spreading across the land to form a vast, alluvial plain—one of the largest in the world— these four branches of the great Mekong empty into the South China Sea through eight separate mouths. Since eight is an unlucky number to the Vietnamese, however, their name for the Mekong Delta and its snakelike tangle of rivers and tributaries is the *Cuu Long Giang*, the River of the *Nine* Dragons.

Binh Thuy and the mammoth U.S. air base there were located a few miles back from the river. Several miles away, perched on the south bank of the Bassac River about halfway between Chau Doc on the Cambodian border and the two mouths of the Bassac on the South China Sea was the village of Tre Noc. The next nearest fair-sized town was Can Tho, about five miles downstream.

As they rode into Tre Noc in the open back of a two and a half-ton truck, Richardson perched himself atop the truck's cab, trying to see everything in every direction at once. Vietnam! This was what he'd been training for, working for, for all of these months. Once they were outside the air base perimeter, they were surrounded by Vietnamese people, a blurred confusion of Oriental faces and costumes, old women stooping in rice paddies, young girls in flowing white gowns, young men and boys driving cyclo pedal cabs, old men carrying bundles of goods like small mountains on their backs. Most of the men, Richardson noticed, were armed. He saw AK-47s, M-16s, and a variety of weapons of World War II vintage, Garands and M-1 carbines, mostly. Remembering discussions and training sessions both back in the States that had warned of the difficulties in telling VCs from friendlies, he gripped his M-16 just a little more tightly.

Tre Noc was a pleasant surprise. The SEALs had been expecting tents pitched in a jungle clearing; what they found waiting for them was a large and well-established military camp, with row upon row of concrete buildings that looked more like cheap and rather spartan stateside motels than traditional barracks. There were air conditioners in the windows, sidewalks lining the roads, a huge and solidly built mess hall, and an impressive concrete-block headquarters building. The entire camp was surrounded by a double row of concertina wire, topped off by strands of razor wire that glittered in the late afternoon sun. Watchtowers, each with batteries of searchlights and machine guns, rose above perimeter fortifications, sandbag bunkers, and prepared firing positions that gave the place the atmosphere of a fortress. How many men did they have stationed here to defend the place, anyway, Richardson wondered? He saw plenty of Vietnamese inside the perimeter, most of them civilians, but some military men as well. Perhaps Tre Noc was defended by a battalion or two of LLDBs.

Past the main gate and turning sharply south, they had their first view of the Bassac River, a mile or more wide and looking more like thin mud than water. There were extensive dockyard facilities for the riverine forces, with dozens of small craft tied up to the piers, PBRs, LCMs, patrol boats of various types and sizes, and a big APL anchored offshore. That last, the SEALs were told, had been a barracks barge before being converted into a floating machine shop for the riverine boats.

"Welcome to the riverine force's Bassac River command center," Estrada said, waving a hand to take in the entire stretch of river, dock facilities, and fortifications. "Task Force 116."

"Operation Game Warden," Finnegan added. "It started about a year ago, with U.S. Navy forces taking responsibility for certain parts of the Mekong Delta and the Rung Sat Special Zone, over near Saigon. We're going to be helping the riverine boys patrol the Bassac, track down VC couriers, check sampans . . ."

"Oh, yeah," Estrada said. "We're also responsible for the defense of this base."

Richardson looked at Estrada sharply. "Say what, Chief? They're using us as *infantry*? On *static point defense*?"

Estrada shrugged. "Hey, somebody's got to do it. Who'd you expect, the goddamned U.S. Marines?"

"What about the riverboat guys?"

"Shit. They don't have the combat training we do." He

shook his head. "Welcome to the real world, boys. It ain't as nice and neat here as it was in training."

The next several hours were spent getting squared away with the local red tape. The SEAL officers reported in at the headquarters building to turn in the unit's orders and records, while the men grabbed their sea bags and filed into one of the barracks to check in.

There was a seemingly endless round of lectures required for all newly arrived personnel, lectures on hygiene and on how to deal with the natives, the VNs as they were called; lectures on which bunkers had been assigned to the SEALs in case they had to fight off a large-scale attack, and lectures on the local economy. In the interest of keeping the South Vietnamese economy strong—and U.S. dollars out of the black market—all new American servicemen in-country had to turn in their money, receiving instead Military Pay Certificates, paper scrip representing everything from nickels and dimes to five-dollar bills. Scrip could be exchanged for piasters, at least up to a certain limit, for paying the VNs. To Richardson, the whole system smacked of the typical big-government, big-military answer to any problem, a system so unwieldy that it probably aided and abetted the very black market forces it was designed to fight.

"At least," Ensign Mariacher said as a paymaster counted out stacks of folding small change for him, "the fucking nickels and dimes won't jingle in our pockets when we're on silent routine!"

The most important lesson, however, was delivered by a serious-faced, blond-haired Navy lieutenant named Yates. "Remember, gentlemen," Yates had said, raising a finger in admonishment. "The night here belongs to Charlie. No one is to go outside the wire after dark."

"Come on, Lieutenant," Mariacher had said. "That's what us SEALs're here to do, for Chrissakes. Take the fuckin' night back from the VC! You can't keep us penned up like animals!"

Yates had given Mariacher an expression like that of a man sucking lemons. "Ensign, the precise status of your unit, and the capacity in which it will be used to support riverine operations, are still to be determined. I repeat, no one is to go outside the wire after dark."

After chow, all of the SEALs, enlisted and officers, gathered in one of the barracks lounge areas to smoke, knock back a couple of beers, and talk. It was a fairly large and comfortable room, as such facilities went, air-conditioned and spacious, with a small refrigerator, several large tables, plenty of chairs, some battered-looking sofas, and even a television set.

"All the comforts," Richardson said, patting the top of the TV. "Don't even have to miss 'Star Trek.' "

"What gets me is the maid service," Reynolds said, grinning. The unit had been assigned so-called "hootch maids" to do their laundry. "Hey, duty stateside was never like this!"

"So what's on the schedule, Lieutenant?" Horner asked Hechinger. "When do we get to kick some VC ass?"

"Not immediately," Hechinger replied. Several voices sounded in protest and he held up his hand. "Whoa, there, hold it! We just got here, okay? We've got six months to kill things. The program calls for some of us to head up to the Rung Sat and see how Team One has been doing business for the past year or so."

"Team One?" Mariacher said with a snort. "Those pussies. . . ."

"Those SEALs have accumulated a lot of info, Mr. Mariacher. Info on how to work in the jungle, on how Charlie thinks, on how to get the most effective use out of limited assets, information we need unless we want to spend the next six months reinventing the wheel. Clear?"

"Affirmative," Mariacher said, though he still didn't look convinced.

"The rest of us will stay here and start getting acquainted with Task Force 116. Some of these people have been here a long time already. We're going to want to pick their brains." He nodded toward Estrada and Finnegan. "Our point guys, too. I'm sure you two have some ideas already."

"Yeah," Richardson said. "How about it, guys? Where can we go to find some action?"

"Well," Estrada began, "the Task Force commodore is going to want you guys to familiarize yourselves first. There are some free-fire zones down the river a ways. Maybe we can ride along with the PBRs some evening and check those out."

"Hold it," Richardson said. He didn't like the sound of that. " 'Free-fire zones'? As in, we're allowed to use our weapons in some places, but we can't anyplace else?"

"Something like that," Finnegan said. "Free-fire zones are places that are supposed to be uninhabited. If you see someone moving in a free-fire zone, you can take immediate action. For the rest, well, you're going to have to receive your rules of engagement first."

"Rules of engagement," Mariacher said. "You can't have fucking Marquis of Queensbury rules in a fucking war!"

Finnegan sighed. "As Commander DuPont will no doubt explain to you, Ensign, this is *not* a war."

"Yeah? What the fuck is it?" Roger Reynolds wanted to know.

"A fucking police action," Mariacher said. "Like Korea."

"Nope," Estrada said. "Not even that."

"He's right, gentlemen," Hechinger said. "We are here as part of the U.S. Military Assistance Command. We're here at the request of the South Vietnamese government to assist their military in the suppression of Communist insurgents."

"Tell it to the Marines," Horner said. He sounded bitter.

"Don't you worry none," Finnegan said with a smile. "There's war enough for everyone, no matter what the REMFs choose to call it. You see, the truth of the matter is, there isn't a—" He broke off suddenly, listening.

The others heard it too, a high-pitched whistle sounding from somewhere high overhead and outside the building.

"What the—" Matthews began.

"*Incoming!*" Richardson yelled. He dove for the nearest table, scrambling beneath for cover. Every other SEAL in the room had the same idea, excluding only Finnegan and Estrada. A savage ka-*WHUMP* sounded outside, the blast strong enough to rattle windows. The first blast was swiftly followed by another . . . and another.

Still sitting on the sofa with his legs crossed, Estrada looked at his watch. "Right on time," he said.

Lieutenant Hechinger crawled back out from under the table. "What the hell?"

"Zero-thirty, Lieutenant," Finnegan said. He took a pull from his beer. "Time to start the fuckin' war."

"Aren't we supposed to go man a bunker or something?" Richardson wanted to know.

"Nah. That's just if Charlie launches a major attack. This piddling shit goes on every night." Another explosion rocked

the barracks. "This is light stuff. Mortars. Sometimes they
throw in a rocket or two. Nothing to worry about."

Ka-*WHUMP*!

"Well fuck this!" Mariacher said, rising and brushing off
his utilities. His eyes were wide, and a little crazy. "I'm
fucked if I'm going to hide under a fucking table while the
fucking VC use the fucking building for fucking target practice! C'mon, guys. Let's go get the bastards!"

"I'm with you, Mr. Myok," Richardson said.

"Me too!" Brubaker called. Half a dozen other men scrambled out from beneath tables or off the floor to join the impromptu hunting expedition.

"Hey, hey," Estrada said. "You guys can't just go running
around out there during a mortar attack!"

"Watch us!" Mariacher said.

Richardson wasn't entirely sure why he followed the pugnacious ensign out the door.

It was dark outside, though spotlights in the perimeter towers swept back and forth, casting brilliant white pools along
the wire and across the clear-fire zones outside the base. The
mortaring appeared to have let up, at least for the moment. A
siren was wailing in the distance, and several base personnel
were running past.

"Hey, sailor!" Mariacher called to a man in dungarees who
was trotting past. "What's the skinny?"

"Alert," the man called back. "Sappers inside the wire!"

"Sappers?" Reynolds asked. "What the fuck is a sapper?"

"VC," the sailor replied. "They sneak in under the wire
sometimes. What's the matter, you guys cherries or some-
thin'?"

As he ran off into the darkness, Matthews looked at Mariacher. "Jeez, Mr. Myok. Our barracks are right by the wire.
Guess who gets buggered if the bastards are sneaking in?"

"We could find the SOB," Brubaker pointed out.

"Max!" Richardson cried. "Where is he?"

"Got a kennel set up for him behind the barracks. Let me
go get him."

"Yeah," Mariacher said. "We could run the wire, see if he
picks up a scent."

"I think you should get the guys organized, Mr. Myok,"
Brubaker said. "If this is an attack, we want to be ready."

Mariacher considered this. "Okay. I'll talk to the lieutenant about it, maybe see about breaking out weapons for everybody. But you get Max working fast. If there's a trail out there, we don't want it to get cold."

"I'll go with him," Matthews said.

"Me too," Richardson volunteered. "We'll cover Bear and Max."

"Do it."

Minutes later, Richardson was moving along the wire on the south side of the base, his M-16 gripped in sweaty hands, following Brubaker and Matthews and the German Shepherd, Max. His heart was pounding, his mouth dry. It was impossible to shake the feeling that somewhere out there, maybe in the darkness beyond the wire, maybe among the shadows of buildings or structures right here inside the Tre Noc camp, a VC sniper was already drawing a bead on him.

Richardson was delighted to find that fear kept him moving and alert and aware of every part of his surroundings. His biggest concern about going into combat had always been that he would freeze up.

Once, when he'd been about seven or eight, his mother had taken him and Bill to visit her family in Wisconsin. It had been memorable because it was just the three of them—his father had been in some faraway place called Korea—and because that was where he'd seen his first snow and, led on by a pack of neighborhood kids, gotten into his first snowball fight.

It had proven to be a rather inglorious disaster personally. After spending half an hour making plans with the kids on his team, he'd led them toward the enemy in a valiant charge . . . until the first snowballs started flying.

He'd hidden behind the corner of a house while his playmates exchanged volleys of snowballs at close and gleefully vicious range. He'd lied to them later on, claiming he'd been trying to work his way behind the other kids to attack them from the rear, but he'd always known, deep down inside, that he'd simply been afraid. There'd been something about the vivid imagery of a missile of ice and packed snow hurtling straight for his face that had paralyzed him with fear.

Funny. He'd not thought about that incident for years and years. He thought about it now, however, as he imagined that

VC sniper taking aim, with his head in the crosshairs. He found himself walking with a distinct stoop, as though trying to pull his head down inside his shoulders for protection. The hairs on the back of his neck prickled; each shadow seemed to have a life of its own. His surroundings felt ominously silent with the end of the mortar barrage, despite the sounds of men shouting at one another in the distance. He tucked the reassuringly heavy, sweat-slicked plastic of his M-16 in tighter beneath his arm and kept moving forward. Training took over as fear threatened to blur his thinking. *Face it*! he thought. *Face the fear! It'll only hurt you if you give in to it!*

Somehow, he kept moving.

Brubaker was in the lead . . . or, rather, Max was in the lead, with Brubaker in tow on the end of a leash. Matthews and Richardson followed, their M-16s at the ready. Max, nose to the ground, suddenly let out a sharp bark, then lunged forward. "Hey!" Brubaker called. "He's got something!"

Max was clearly excited, following a definite trace on the soft ground. He led them to a particular spot at the wire, where he paced back and forth, yowling and whining with eager impatience. "What is it, boy?" Brubaker called. Max put his nose to the earth in front of the wire and pawed at the ground. He barked.

Richardson had the light. Shining it across the ground between the two rolls of wire, he could see imperfections and marks in the soil, made clear by their long-cast shadows.

The two rolls of concertina wire marked out a clear space between them that was theoretically a death trap for anyone trying to cross it. There were alarms of various kinds, ranging from sophisticated sensors to strings attached to tin cans filled with pebbles. There were mines of various types. There were claymores, shaped charges set to fire titanic shotgun blasts of solid lead pellets in deadly sprays across preplanned killing zones if an intruder touched their tripwires.

But clearly, someone had made it across without triggering any of the alarms or detonating the mines. That alone seemed suspicious to Richardson; Tre Noc was a big camp with a long perimeter, and obviously its builders had elected not to mine every yard of the wire. That meant there were places where an intruder could sneak through—if he'd had a chance to inspect the crossing area carefully, in daylight.

Someone *inside* the camp, perhaps?

The marks on the ground suggested that, whoever it had been, he'd been going out. The flashlight clearly showed the ridges in the dirt where his feet had dug in as he'd wriggled beneath the wire, probably on his back so he could move the wire up and out of the way. Richardson pointed that out to the others.

"Okay," Brubaker said, picking up some soil and crumbling it. "I'm betting these tracks are damned fresh."

"Like . . . using the mortar barrage for cover?" Richardson asked.

"Yeah. It was a clear, sunny day today. No rain. These tracks would've dried out a lot more if they'd been made, say, *last* night. This guy just went through a few minutes ago."

Richardson nodded. "What say we go outside the wire and see if Max can find the bad guy?"

"You heard what they said about going outside at night," Matthews said.

"Sure," Richardson told him. "You also know the SEALs are supposed to be defending this camp, right? Well, seems to me tracking down a guy that's been sneaking in and out under the wire might be a good place to start."

"I'd like to know what he was doing in here," Matthews said. "You know, we have lot of gear that could be pretty readily sabotaged if someone got to it."

"Yeah," Richardson said. He pointed through the double layer of concertina wire, toward the clear-cut zone outside. "Let's see if Max can pick up the trail out there."

It took some fast talking to get past the Navy personnel standing security watch at the main gate . . . but the three must have looked pretty dangerous, Richardson thought, armed with assault rifles and trotting along after a German Shepherd. "We're tracking a sapper who got through the wire!" Matthews told them. "You wanna take it up with HQ and let the bastard get away?"

The sailors, with no orders to the contrary and unwilling to challenge three heavily armed men and their dog, waved them on through. After all, it was their job to keep bad guys out, not presumably friendly forces in.

Ten minutes later, the three SEALs were outside the south perimeter of the camp, with Max lunging out ahead on his leash as he looked for the trail. He picked it up almost at once just opposite the spot where they'd lost it under the wire inside; with a joyful bark, Max tugged Brubaker along at a brisk clip, moving diagonally away from the wire, across the one-hundred-yard defensive zone, then through a line of trees and onto a highway.

We have got to be fuckin' nuts, Richardson thought, shaking his head. *The first thing they warn us about is to stay inside the camp after dark. And what do we do?* ...

Richardson hadn't been this scared since that time in the torpedo tube, but he was pleased to find himself moving more freely now. If he thought about it, he still half-expected a bullet to come sizzling in out of the darkness, but as he kept on moving, the moving became easier. *Just don't think about it*, he told himself. *Look at the others*. They're *not scared*.

Or were they simply hiding their fear, as he was?

There were lots of Vietnamese civilians on the highway, some on bicycle, some on foot. They gave the Americans and their dog curious looks but kept their distance as the men charged along the road after Max. The dog seemed definitely to have a particular scent to home in on; he ignored all of the civilians, not even giving them a glance, but kept bounding ahead with his nose to the ground.

Suddenly, the dog looked up, growled, and nearly tore the leash from Brubaker's hand. He started barking, and the object of his attention appeared to be a Vietnamese civilian walking down the road a few yards ahead. The man turned at the bark; Richardson turned his flashlight on the guy's face.

"Hold it right there!" Matthews warned, raising his M-16. "Hands up!"

"I no do anything!" the man protested. "I no do anything!"

"Uh-huh," Brubaker said. "Hold it, Max, hold it! Heel, damn it!"

Max was going insane, barking and jumping as though he wanted nothing less than the VN's throat between his jaws. The man, for his part, was clearly terrified. He kept his hands up and his eyes riveted on the dog.

"Keep him covered!" Richardson snapped. He reached the man, grabbed his arm, forced him to the ground. A rough search turned up nothing in the way of weapons, but that proved little. Out of all of these civilians, Max had picked out this one man as the one who'd snuck out under the wire.

Richardson rolled him over onto his stomach to secure his hands with a plastic binder strip. Before he let the prisoner up, though, he brushed at the back of his shirt.

"You been crawling around in the dirt, Jack?" Richardson asked. The shirt was sweat-soaked and stained in several places with mud.

"Me no Jack! Me no do anything!"

"Okay, okay," Matthews said. "Let's get this guy in to Security."

The man lunged, trying to get away, but Richardson extended a foot and swept his feet neatly out from under him. He landed heavily on the pavement, blood drooling from his nose.

"Team Two's first VC prisoner!" Brubaker chortled as Richardson pulled him to his feet.

"Me no VC!" the man said, plainly terrified. "Me no VC!"

"Uh-huh," Richardson said. "We'll let you tell that to Security."

The fear was gone, lost in the adrenaline rush of the confrontation.

On the way back to the front gate, Richardson felt about ten feet tall.

Chapter 27

Monday, 6 February 1967

**SEAL Team Two, Base Det Alpha
Tre Noc, Mekong Delta
0845 hours**

"Try," Lieutenant Hechinger said with a distinct air of long-suffering, "*please* try to stay out of trouble while we're gone!"

"Hey, Lieutenant," Mariacher said with a grin. "It's *us* you're talking to!"

"That, Ensign, is precisely what I'm afraid of."

"Aw, listen, Lieutenant," Richardson said. "Isn't there some way around this numb-nuts Mickey Mouse? It isn't going to be any fun around here without you guys."

"That's probably the general idea," Estrada observed. "You've been bad boys. You don't get to come out and play."

Most of Det Alpha was on its way to the Rung Sat, there to participate in a two-week indoctrination and training session with members of SEAL Team One. "Myok's Marauders," however, were staying behind at Tre Noc.

It was obviously a punishment detail, at least so far as Richardson was concerned. All fourteen men of First Platoon plus the seven men of Alpha Squad in Second Platoon were on their way to the Rung Sat and, training mission or not, they were going to be with other SEALs and they were going to be having fun. Patrols. Ambushes. Fun and sun with Charlie in the romantic Rung Sat.

It was discrimination, pure and simple, against the misfits of Second Platoon's Bravo Squad.

The squad had been under a cloud—a dark and ominous storm cloud—ever since the capture of that suspected VC infiltrator the first night they'd come aboard at Tre Noc. The suspect had remained in custody for exactly forty minutes that night; the OOD had called up to TF 116 Admin, rousting the duty officer from a warm rack, and the word had come back in seconds. Ha Xuan Hung, the young man captured by the SEALs just outside the base, turned out to be a clerical worker and translator in Admin. His ID and papers checked out and he was allowed to leave.

The SEALs responsible—and Hechinger, their commanding officer—had been roundly chewed out the next morning by none other than Lieutenant Commander Harry Benson, the operations commander of Tre Noc. Benson, the SEALs had been told in no uncertain terms, would not tolerate mavericks or cowboys in his command. Rushing off into the darkness, leaving the protection of the base in pursuit of shadows, chasing down and terrorizing innocent civilians . . . these had been utterly irresponsible acts and a repetition would not be tolerated.

Brubaker had pointed out how Max had followed the man's

scent off of the base, how he'd picked Ha out from among dozens of other Vietnamese, but the argument had carried no weight with Benson. "You men are trusting the word of a *dog*?" he'd asked incredulously.

"Actually it was his nose, sir," Brubaker had pointed out.

"What I want to know is what the hell was that guy doing crawling out under the wire?" Hechinger had demanded, coming to his men's defense.

"Lieutenant, at this point we have not determined that Mr. Ha *did* go out under the wire. We only have your word for that . . . or perhaps I should say, the word of a mutt. Good God, people, maybe your dog picked up the scent of *nuoc mam*, you ever think of that? Maybe all VNs smell the same to him."

"With respect, sir," Brubaker said, "that's not what happened. As Chief Brubaker pointed out, Max trailed that SOB and picked him out from among all those other people on the road. He knew that was the right guy. You could tell, the way he was going after him."

Benson looked at Brubaker with an expression that wavered between disbelief and amazement. "Chief, how the hell do you know what a *dog* thinks?"

"Commander—"

"Look, if it *was* Mr. Ha, well, maybe he forgot something after leaving the camp, and he wanted to go back and attend to it without the embarrassment of checking through the front gate after hours. These people are tremendously sensitive to losing face, you know." He'd rapped the knuckles of his hand on his desk, holding Hechinger's eyes with his own. "The issue here, Lieutenant, is not Mr. Ha's behavior, but the behavior of the men under your command. I don't care what kind of elite supersoldiers you people are supposed to be, I will not tolerate this sort of hooliganism on my base!"

Bravo Squad was confined to the base for five days, a relatively benign punishment, as it turned out. There was plenty of work to do, including stripping down every weapon, cleaning it, and stowing it carefully against the omnipresent tropical humidity.

In the meantime, however, Lieutenant Hechinger and the three other officers, along with twenty-one of the men, were on their way to the Rung Sat, while Myok's Marauders stayed home.

Mariacher watched as the last of the First Platoon people scrambled aboard one of the helicopters on the pad at Tre Noc's small landing zone. Possibly Hechinger had read some of the disgust and hurt visible on his face. "Don't worry, Dan," he said cheerfully. "You've got toys to play with. Take it easy. Enjoy the rest. You can all catch up on your sun tans."

The reference to sun tans—a running joke among the East Coast SEALs at the expense of their Californian comrades— made Mariacher grin.

"Don't you worry, Lieutenant," Mariacher said at last. "We'll take good care of the base while you're gone."

Hechinger nodded glumly. "I suppose you will. Try to be gentle, won't you? Remember, my career's at stake here."

"The base'll still be here when you get back, sir," Richardson said. "I'm just not entirely sure that son of a bitch Yates will be."

"Ride it out, SEAL," Hechinger said. "He can't be any worse than Hell Week."

Minutes later, the seven SEALs remaining at Tre Noc watched as the last of the Hueys lurched into the sky, went nose-down, and roared off into the eastern sky.

Two weeks . . . and an injunction against any and all military operations until after Hechinger's return.

"You men!" a sharp, nasal voice snapped. "What are you doing there?"

Mariacher turned, slowly. Lieutenant Gordon Yates was a royal pain in the ass, one of those eager beaver junior officers with connections enough to ensure his political climb to the top of the Navy's totem pole, given enough years in and enough of the right assignments. Chief among those, of course, was that precious line in his personnel file that indicated service in a combat zone; Yates, Mariacher was pretty sure, was a ticket puncher, an officer who'd wangled an assignment to Vietnam in order to ensure that his career stayed on track and that his next promotion was assured. He was relatively junior officer on Benson's Ops staff, and the man who would be in charge of the remaining SEALs in Hechinger's absence.

"Why, Mr. Yates," Mariacher said, a grin fixed in place as though painted there. "We were just thinking about you."

"Get your men together, Mariacher," he ordered, mispronouncing the name. "And I mean now. If you'd bothered to check the daily order, you'd see you and your pirates are scheduled for thirty minutes of PT every morning at oh-eight hundred. It's nearly nine-hundred hours now. You'd better get your ass in gear, mister!"

"So why are we doing calisthenics?" Brubaker wanted to know. He let a second or two pass before adding the word "sir."

"Yeah," Matthews added. "You don't see the riverboaters doing jumping jacks."

"The riverine crews do not do calisthenics," Yates said. "Admin and logistics personnel do not do calisthenics. You, however, are combat personnel, at least by reputation, and therefore you will do the requisite PT. Or is everything I've heard about the big, bad SEALs just eyewash?"

"Sir," Mariacher said reasonably. "The point is that we like to remain inconspicuous. Look. Nobody on this fuckin' base does push-ups every morning. Then a bunch of new guys shows up, and they do push-ups. If you're a VC scout, taking a look-see, what does that tell you?"

"It tells me that the commander of this base isn't going to put up with your nonsense any longer, Mariacher. Now! Back to your barracks, change into shorts and T-shirts, and back on the grinder behind the barracks in five minutes, or every man jack of you is on report!"

"C'mon," Mariacher said quietly as the men looked to him. "Let's not give the fucker the satisfaction."

He deliberately said it just loudly enough that Yates could hear.

Tuesday, 7 February 1967

Base Det Alpha
Tre Noc, Mekong Delta
2010 hours

The seven of them were sitting around a table in the barracks lounge, poring over a map Mariacher had conned off of a buddy up in Admin. The map showed the Bassac, and the checkerboard pattern of canals and rice paddies to either side.

SEAL Team Two's AO—their Area of Operations—was going to be a long section of the Bassac, including a lot of the canal and swamp areas both up- and down-river of Tre Noc.

Richardson studied the other men around the table. Mariacher still had that school boy's confidence, a foul-mouthed optimism that was infectious. QM/1 Horner, GMC Finnegan, EM/1 Matthews, TM/1 Reynolds, BMC Brubaker, Richardson himself, all of them had attached themselves to Mariacher's train. The man was unstoppable, never losing his drive or his energy, no matter what the obstacle might be.

"I've had it with the vacation, guys," Mariacher said as he smoothed the map out on the table. "I figure we need a little cruise to get away from it all."

"I'm with you there," Brubaker said.

"You know, we could get around the restrictions down here," Matthews said, pointing to an island several miles downstream from Tre Noc. The name was listed as Cu Chau Moi.

"Free-fire zone," Horner said, nodding.

"Yeah," Brubaker said. "If someone shoots at us, we could shoot back. I like it."

"How do you know anybody's there, though?" Richardson asked.

"We don't, my boy," Mariacher said. "Maybe there's nobody on that island, like they say. But shit fire, since when has anything anybody with any responsibility in this fucking war said turned out to be the straight shit, huh?"

"The man has a point," Richardson said, grinning at the others.

"The best part is getting out from under Yates," Reynolds said. He shuddered. "Christ, I hate that man."

"Do you guys have any idea how badly I want to *salute* him?" Richardson said.

The others laughed. There was no saluting at Tre Noc, not when the assumption was that Charlie was watching the camp from a distance. There'd been several people hit by snipers early on, and an important lesson learned was that the VC liked to pick out who the officers were by noting who saluted who.

"Now, now, none of that," Mariacher said. "I wouldn't mind capping the little SOB myself, save Charlie the effort, but we're professionals, right?"

"Right, Dan," several of the others chorused.

Richardson took a swallow from his beer. The various members of Myok's Marauders had very swiftly melded themselves into a closely interlocked brotherhood that outsiders found impossible to fathom. *Tight* was how he thought of that relationship, seven men who were closer to one another in some ways than any family Richardson had ever seen, closer, certainly, than the members of his own family. Any military unit where the men could freely call their commanding officer by his first name . . .

It was a good feeling. These guys would *die* for him if they had to, though they'd likely call him a stupid son of a bitch as they went out.

If anything, Yates had brought them even closer together. Ruefully, Richardson rubbed his shoulder up close by the base of his neck, where his skin had been abraded almost raw that morning. The . . . disagreement over whether or not the SEALs should do morning calisthenics had evolved that morning into a quiet protest. Alpha Squad had done the exercises, but they'd showed up on the grinder wearing heavy Kevlar flak vests.

If Yates even noticed the voiceless protest, he said nothing. Exercising under the weight of that vest had been tough, but certainly no tougher than most of what the SEALs had endured in BUD/S. Mostly it had just been damned uncomfortable . . . and the vest had chafed Richardson's skin in several spots.

"Okay, so what's our excuse gonna be?" Finnegan asked.

"Training and familiarization, of course," Brubaker replied. "We're supposed to be here learning the ropes, right? That means having a look at the AO."

"Chief Davenport says he'll come along," Mariacher said. "I talked to him this afternoon. He'll be our tour guide, kind of point out the sights, y'know?"

"You got *Davenport* to talk to you?" Brubaker said, his eyebrows rising. "I thought that old guy didn't talk to anybody!"

Master Chief Richard Davenport was something of a minor legend at Tre Noc. With no family back in the World—at least, none that he was willing to talk about—he'd come to Tre Noc almost three years before and simply kept extending his tour. By now, the man knew the Bassac as well as he knew his own Penobscot River down East. He also knew the people.

The scuttlebutt was that he had something going with his hootch maid but that was impossible to confirm; the man never seemed to get close enough to anybody to open up.

Mariacher grinned. "Well, turns out we were on the same ship together a few years back. The old *George Clymer*. Back before I went SEAL and I was a scroungy E3 striker."

"What, you knew him?"

"Nah. I was a snipe and he was deck division. But we knew a lot of the same people. As soon as he found out I wasn't just another smart-ass pup of an ensign, that I used to *work* for a living, well . . ."

"He'll help legitimize our run," Richardson pointed out.

"Shit," Mariacher said. "I just don't want to go out on that mud river out there without having someone along who knows where the sand bars are. It'd be embarrassing if we lost a very expensive STAB by running her aground our first time out!"

"It'd be even more embarrassing if the VC got her," Finnegan said.

"You know, we could have one other small problem," Horner pointed out. "Ammo. They guard that stuff pretty close. Make you account for it damned near round by round."

"Well, I have an idea or two about that," Mariacher said. "Here's what we're gonna do. . . ."

Wednesday, 8 February 1967

Base Det Alpha
Tre Noc, Mekong Delta
1030 hours

Getting ammunition for the planned excursion was probably the largest single problem the SEALs faced. All ammo had to be checked out of the base armory, and it took requisition forms in triplicate to get past the supply officer who held the keys. Mariacher had considered forging the necessary papers but hit upon a simpler plan instead.

It was mid-morning, and various riverine crews were at work on their boats tied up to the Tre Noc piers. The dock area was a beehive of activity, as men patched, painted, and otherwise readied their craft for another day in the Mekong

Delta . . . and that included arming their boats and stowing ammunition.

Richardson struck first. Wearing dungarees like any other working sailor, he walked down the line of LCMs and PBRs, stopped to chat and share a smoke with a couple of sailors on a break, then casually walked on. A two and a half-ton truck was backed up to the pier, and its bed was piled high with all kinds of ammunition—7.62, .50 caliber, 5.56 . . . everything a SEAL had ever dreamed of. Reaching up, he grabbed two cans of fifty-caliber, slid them off the bed, and kept walking . . . one more sailor among hundreds on a work detail.

A few minutes later, Brubaker acquired one case of 7.62 ammo and a box of 40-mm grenade rounds the same way. Then it was Horner's turn, then Matthews's, then Finnegan's. The scam ran all through the rest of the morning and well into the afternoon, with the ammo-hungry SEALs acquiring what they needed two ammo cases at a time. While one SEAL was out foraging, the others worked on the STABs under Finnegan's sharp eye. Those sleek and deadly looking boats were his babies, and not even Ensign Mariacher could open up an access hatch or stow a can of .50 caliber without his express say-so.

It was late afternoon when Finnegan checked over the two STABs one final time, then reported them ready for duty to Mariacher. Both boats were bursting to the gunwales with ammo and the weapons had been mounted—one .50-caliber Ma Deuce on the pedestal mount amidships, one M60 on a gunwale mount.

"Well, me hearties," Mariacher said in a pirate's rough and gravelly voice, "let's hoist sail and get these tubs under way!"

The designated coxswain for each craft, Finnegan in STAB Two and Horner in STAB One, climbed into their craft and started up the engines. Richardson cast off the bow lines, then scrambled into STAB One along with Mariacher, Matthews, and Chief Davenport. Brubaker and Reynolds would be riding with Finnegan in Two.

With the powerful twin 325-horsepower outboards barely purring, the two STABs slipped away from the dock and swung out into the river. With the skill of an Indian scout, Horner pulled the lead boat around and under the lee of the big APL moored offshore, placing the floating machine shop directly between the two STABs and the headquarters building ashore until they were well out toward the middle of the river.

Then, with Davenport pointing out a couple of barely submerged but invisible mud banks off to starboard, they swung right, following the Bassac downstream. Each STAB was twenty-six feet long and had a draft of about four feet—more, actually, when they were this fully loaded.

"You know, sir," Richardson called to Mariacher as Horner opened up the throttle and put the STAB onto a step, racing down-river at better than thirty knots. With Davenport within earshot, he didn't use the officer's first name. "This is really a dumb-ass stunt, you know that? No one back at Tre Noc even knows we're out here!"

"Shit, it's just a training run, right?" Mariacher replied with a boyish grin. "Piece of cake."

"Sure!" Horner put in, calling back over his shoulder from the STAB's helm. "What could possibly go wrong?"

Minutes passed as the STABs moved in formation. Richardson was standing by the .50-caliber mount, enjoying the blast of fresh air hitting him full in his face. At this point, the Bassac ran northwest to southeast and was over a mile wide. Ahead, the island of Cu Chau Moi was a low, green smear lying closer to the southeastern bank, with a space of only a couple of hundred yards between the island and the mainland.

Horner throttled back as they approached the narrow passage. Davenport was pointing to the right side of the island. "You can get through up there," he told Mariacher. "To hit it, you line up on that water tank on the south shore . . . see it? As soon as you have the western point of the island coming off your starboard bow, bring your heading up twelve degrees the left of that tower. Hold that heading until the island's point is off your port beam. Most river traffic passes north of Cu Chau Moi, of course, through the main shipping channel, but it's navigable through here. You can squeeze up to within, oh, fifty yards or so of the island, but watch the south side. You've got a mud bank that comes almost two hundred yards out. The water's two foot deep there or less. See those tree limbs sticking up out of the water? That's your clue that the water's getting real shallow in through there. You can make it in a PBR no sweat, almost up to the south bank, but these heavy beasts of yours'll hang up on the mud, sure as shit. . . ."

Richardson was only listening to the lecture with half of his mind. Even throttled back, the STAB was moving fast enough to create a fresh breeze that was thoroughly delightful after the hot and humid claustrophobia of Tre Noc, and he was enjoying every moment of it. The island was thickly forested—not jungle, exactly, in the scientific sense of the word, but tangled and murky and impenetrable. The island wasn't large; it probably measured less than a thousand meters from east to west, but the vegetation was thick enough to hide a battalion of VC. It looked peaceful, though the thunder of the STAB's twin Mercuries drowned out any of the usual bird and frog noises that might be expected in such a scene.

There was plenty of river life, though. A splash erupted from the water between the STAB and the island . . . a fish jumping, he thought. There was another . . . and two more.

"Hey, Chief!" he called. "You got your rod and reel? The fish're sure jumpin' today!"

Davenport cocked an eye toward the island, and his weathered face split in an out-of-character grin. "Shit, son," he said. "Those ain't fish. That's automatic weapons fire! Someone's shootin' at us from the beach!"

A chain of splashes stitched its way across the water between the island and the boat's port side. Richardson felt a sharp thrill, a jolt of energy like he'd never experienced before in his life. It wasn't fear, exactly, but it was an intense, almost vibrant sense of being very much alive. He racked back the charging lever of the .50 caliber and swung its muzzle to aim at the featureless blur of green vegetation some two hundred meters abeam. "That qualify as provocation, Mr. Myok?" he yelled.

"Shit, it's a free-fire zone!" Mariacher yelled back. "Shoot the fucker! Shoot!"

Richardson clamped down on the butterfly trigger, and the fifty bucked and thundered in his grip. Hot brass spun from the breech, most spilling onto the deck at his feet, but some caught by the wind of the STAB's motion and flipped back into his face. He ignored the distraction and kept firing, sweeping the muzzle back and forth in tight, precisely controlled arcs as he loosed short bursts, just the way he'd been taught back in support-weapons training in Phase Two of BUD/S.

Then he realized that he couldn't see his target at all, that he couldn't even take a guess as to where the enemy might be hiding in that whole, half-mile-long stretch of island. *Fuck it*! he told himself, and he clamped down the trigger, loosing one long, continuous volley of full rock and roll, the bolt on the right side snapping back and forth so fast it turned into a blur.

The other SEALs were firing too. Matthews was on the M60 mounted on the port gunwale just in front of and below Richardson's fifty. Horner was steering the boat with his right hand, while he gripped an M79 grenade launcher in his left. As he brought the STAB hard left, he aimed the launcher up and over the windshield and pulled the trigger. The hollow thump was loud enough to be heard above the roar of the engines; seconds later, the 40-mm grenade landed in the water just short of the island, sending up a towering white geyser of spray. Mariacher and Davenport both had M-16s and were alternating between watching the position of the two STABs in the channel and firing their weapons blindly at the shore.

Richardson concentrated on firing the fifty caliber. It was loaded with ball ammo, with tracers linked in one for every ten rounds. He could see the white-glowing tracers as they whipped toward the island, one following the next in a deadly necklace. They moved in pretty much of a straight line for the first couple of hundred yards, but then he could see them starting to fall; with a little practice, he soon was able to elevate the weapon just enough to let the tracer stream plunge into the shore, walking the fire through the forest. As he hosed his fire across the shoreline, he noted one spot where the tracers vanished into the trees, then leaped high into the air like startled quail. He wasn't sure whether he'd found a rock or something more valuable, like a VC gun emplacement or bunker, but he decided to concentrate on that spot for a time. He might be doing some damage to some hidden equipment, and at the least, whatever his bullets were bouncing off of must be hard enough to shatter the incoming rounds and spray the whole area with deadly shrapnel.

The STABs had come about almost as soon as they'd been taken under fire, presenting the smallest possible aspect—their ten-foot beams—to the unseen marksmen ashore. As they drew closer to the beach, however, Horner swung the STAB sharply to port. Richardson waltzed around the fifty's standing mount, reacquiring the island and renewing the steady, hammering thunder of the weapon's fire.

They were closer now, less than seventy yards from the beach. As Richardson continued firing, he could see great tufts of weed and marsh grass being hurled into the air, branches snapping, leaves spinning to the ground as the volume of fire from the STAB scythed across the water and into the forest. Mariacher was standing next to the helm, shouting into the radio's microphone. "I'm sorry!" he yelled. "Your transmission weak! I do not copy!" He reached out and clicked over the channel selector. "Shitheads!" he said. "Call 'em for support and they want to know what we're doing in a firefight. What the fuck do they think we're doing, dancing?"

"What, they want us to go back?" Matthews asked.

"Yeah, the assholes want us to go home. But hey, we got plenty of ammo, nobody's hurt. I say, now that we got his attention, let's kick us some Charlie ass!"

Horner took the STAB west along the island's south shore. Matthews shifted the M60 to the starboard mount and continued firing; the other STAB was in the lead now, pouring round after round into the jungle in an unending fusillade of sheer destructive power.

Mariacher was on the radio again. "I say again! We are taking fire from Cu Chau Moi Island, just above Can Tho! Request air strike soonest! Repeat! Request air strike soonest!"

For fifteen minutes after that, the two STABs continued to weave a complex pattern back and forth in the channel between the island and the shore, as spent brass bounced and scattered in the crafts' well decks until it was impossible to take a step without treading on them. The SEALs had practiced this sort of combat plenty of times before back at Little Creek when they'd first taken delivery of the STABs. When one boat passed inshore of the other, the offshore boat ceased fire with a perfect coordination that made the passage less a military maneuver than it was an artfully choreographed dance. Whole trees were beginning to topple now on the island as the steady rain of lead smashed through trunks in splinter-spraying bursts.

Gunfire continued to probe toward the STABs from the shore. One bullet slammed through STAB One's fiberglass hull just aft of Richardson's position with a loud crack. A moment later, a bullet skipped on the water between boat and shore; Richardson saw the splash as it hit, and an instant later Matthews jerked back from his M60, his boonie hat flying clear, a bloody gash opened in his scalp from just above his right eye clear back into his hairline.

"I'm hit!" he screamed. "God, I'm hit!"

Richardson caught his arm as he staggered back from the gunwale, then helped him sit down. Mariacher was with him an instant later, probing the nasty wound with a finger. Matthews's face was nearly obscured behind a mask of blood, and Richardson was astonished that he was even still alive.

"Ah," Mariacher said, clapping Matthews hard on the shoulder. "You're lucky you've got a thick skull! That bullet just skidded right up along the bone. You're fine!"

"Now get back behind that sixty!" Horner yelled back at him. "Get the hell back in the war!"

"R-right. . . ."

Matthews looked shaken, and the bloody scalp wound looked far worse than it actually was, but he got back up and returned to the M60, shouldering the weapon's stock and beginning to hammer away once more at the jungle.

Horner, meanwhile, continued to pump 40-mm grenades into the forest, as did Finnegan in the Number Two STAB, and each thunderous blast added to the mayhem ashore, until it seemed impossible that anything could live through that maelstrom of fire and lead.

Throughout the battle, Richardson never once actually saw the enemy, not so much as a muzzle flash or a silhouette. Eventually, though, he realized that there were no more rounds incoming, that the only shooting going on was coming from the two STABs.

"That's it for the fifty!" he yelled as the last round fired and the bolt clacked back.

"I've got maybe eighty rounds left," Matthews reported.

"I'm dry," Horner said, breaking open the breech on his M79 and shaking out the empty cartridge.

Mariacher was consulting with the SEALs in STAB Two. "Okay," he said. "Those guys say they're about dry too. I think maybe it's time we moseyed on back to the ranch."

"Head 'em up!" Davenport replied, grinning. He looked like he'd been having a wonderful time. "Move 'em out!"

The cruise back to Tre Noc was uneventful. Richardson and

Mariacher worked together to bandage up Matthews's head wound. Halfway back, a growing, rumbling thunder sounded out of the west. Seconds later, four aircraft howled low overhead, a flight of F-4C Phantom IIs out of Binh Thuy, and they were hurtling toward the island with blood in their figurative eyes. Each of those aircraft, Richardson knew, when fully loaded for air-to-ground ops could carry twice the bomb load of World War II–era B-17. As the STABs motored slowly into the anchorage at Tre Noc, the distant, muffled thunder of the air strikes floated across the water from the east.

Lieutenant Commander Benson was standing on the dock as they approached, his features just visible in the gathering gloom of the evening.

"That man," Richardson said slowly, "looks mad enough to spit nails."

"Don't sweat it, guys," Mariacher said, grinning. His face was smoke-smudged and dirty, his hair tousled and disarrayed when he pulled off his boonie hat. "I'll handle this guy. Piece of cake. . . ."

Chapter 28

Wednesday, 19 April 1967

SEAL Team Two Base
My Tho, Mekong Delta
1325 hours

Ensign Daniel Mariacher often thought about that first STAB raid and the furor Bravo Squad's return had caused. He would think about it and laugh, sometimes, remembering Lieutenant Commander Benson standing on the pier at Tre Noc, alternating between furious, red-faced, foot-stamping rages and a cold, hard, sarcastic fury that had convinced Mariacher that he was about to be court martialed.

Other times, he would think about it and his fist would clench in frustration and disbelief. *How* could supposedly intelligent and well-trained personnel be such pus-gutted, shit-for-brains assholes?

The resolution of that confrontation with Benson had turned out to be anticlimax in the end. Mariacher had been put on report, along with all six of his men, and only his insistence that he'd lied and told the riverine forces chief that the SEALs had clearance to go on a training run down the river, had saved Davenport from the same.

And all the while, as Benson alternately raged and turned sarcastic, Lieutenant Yates had stood nearby, smiling idiotically.

Bravo Squad was restricted to quarters, not allowed to even leave their own cubes inside the barracks save to go to the head down the passageway or to the mess hall across the grinder.

In truth, things didn't look good. Benson had already written up the report which would be submitted to the base's commodore at mast . . . and to the court martial board, if it came to that. Unauthorized absence. Theft of government property, including controlled munitions and sensitive equipment—meaning the two SEAL Team Assault Boats which were still classified. Unauthorized use of weapons. Engaging the enemy without authorization. Requesting air support without proper identification or authorization. Richardson had laughed when he'd read the list and noted that gun-running and drug-smuggling on the Bassac were about the only crimes not listed.

Matthews, his head bandaged in white gauze, had grinned and told him "Not so loud, guy. They can still append pages to that thing, you know."

The days dragged by without anyone telling the SEALs anything whatsoever. According to Davenport, who came over to the SEAL barracks from time to time with a duffel bag full of smuggled six-packs, Benson was waiting only for the return of Kessler and the other SEAL Two officers before deciding just how vengeance was going to fall.

Then the intelligence reports had started coming through.

On 6 February, a large VC force had begun moving south across the Bassac in the vicinity of Cu Chau Moi. The south bank of the Bassac, between Binh Thuy and Can Tho, was heavily patrolled by both RVN and American troops, so the VC had holed up on the island, which they evidently knew was supposed to be deserted. More communist troops had come across each night, until well over two hundred men had been hiding on the island.

Documents recovered by teams sent to search the place showed that the VC strike force had been at very nearly full strength. Evidently, they'd planned to cross the final few hundred meters of the Bassac on the night of the eighth. Their target had been no less than the American air base at Binh Thuy.

Opening fire on the SEALs in the two STABs had obviously been a mistake—probably the result of panic fire by inexperienced or shaken men. The SEAL counterfire, however, had broken the VC unit . . . and the heavy bombing that had followed from the Phantom IIs, including a napalm strike, had finished them. Twenty bodies had been recovered in the jungle, though it was likely that there'd been lots more, destroyed later by the bombing or drifting away on the river. Dozens of VC had fled south across the narrows; some had drowned, others had been killed in firefights with ARVN troops or security forces, and fifteen had been captured.

Every one of those prisoners had spoken in awe of the incredible, the unbelievable fire coming from the two tiny speed boats patrolling down the river. Even now, over two months later, Military Intelligence was reaping the benefits of Myok's Marauder's unauthorized raid.

After that, of course, there'd been no way that Benson could put the seven SEALs before a court-martial board. SEALs were expected to be aggressive, to set their own agendas, to seek out the enemy and destroy him; any attempt to censor them for being *too* aggressive would work only if they'd tried and failed. In military operations, success brought its own justification. The fact that the encounter with the VC just as they'd been trying to cross the river had been the result of pure chance was immaterial; Mariacher was of the opinion that ninety percent of everything in combat was chance, and that the guy who was best prepared to take advantage of the opportunities presented to him was the guy who would successfully complete his mission.

Still, it had been clear that the SEALs—Mariacher's squad, at any rate—were no longer welcome at Tre Noc. They'd been kept out of several ops and assigned to the reserves—providing backup for another squad—for several others. Requisitioning equipment, ammo, even filing "float plans" for training runs aboard PBRs or STABs had suddenly become a constant struggle against the bureaucratic mentality. In March, then, the entire Second Platoon of SEAL Team Two had been reassigned to a different base.

My Tho—pronounced "me-toe"—was a fair-sized village located on the banks of the My Tho River, northernmost of the three major branches of the Mekong in Vietnam. Commander Vincent Douglass, the CO of the PBR base at My Tho, had requested that a SEAL platoon be assigned to him on what amounted to a trial basis and was eager to try them out in his AO. Benson had been only too happy to get rid of Myok's Marauders . . . and Lieutenant Kessler had felt that there were definite advantages to getting Second Platoon out from under the bureaucratic scrutiny at Tre Noc. If the SEALs worked out at My Tho, the force could well be expanded. Commander Douglass was a sharp officer who was aware of the necessity of adapting to the demands of jungle warfare; more important, he wasn't afraid to try a new approach. His PBRs had been taking fire, sometimes within sight of the base, and his requests for more infantry support had been ignored or lost in the bureaucratic shuffle somewhere upstairs. After hearing a divisional report on the success of SEAL Team One in the Rung Sat, he'd requested that SEALs be assigned to him in the hope that they might be able to do something about the situation.

Mariacher, for his part, had been delighted with the opportunity. *This* was the chance he'd been hoping for, a chance to operate with a free hand and decent support.

As he walked toward the main gate of the base, Mariacher thought about the operations of the past two months. Much of the time had been spent in familiarization with the area, but the SEALs had carried off a number of patrols and operations, and with a fair amount of success. He credited Bravo Squad's morale for a lot of that. They'd arrived at My Tho hot, feeling sharp, lean, and mean. Hell, they'd twisted Authority's tail and gotten away with it—always a good feeling for mavericks like these. They'd been in combat, *real* combat this time, and not just chasing down an unarmed suspect. In the language of another war, they'd "seen the elephant," and now they would never be the same. They'd even just picked up SEAL Team Two's first combat decoration—Matthews's Purple Heart—and they'd done it without losing a man.

And now they'd been assigned to a CO who wasn't afraid to use them the way Mariacher thought they ought to be used.

Yeah, he thought. They had a right to feel cocky.

The entrance to the PBR base was a short walk from the villa-resort that was the team's temporary quarters. The place was more like a hotel than a barracks—definitely comfortable living, with big ceiling fans and a comfortable downstairs sitting room. They'd already nicknamed it the SEAL Hilton. The base, which squatted on the banks of the yellow-brown river, was practically next door. It was a primitive place compared to Tre Noc; piers were boards laid across fifty-five-gallon drums serving as impromptu pontoons. The machine shops were small wooden or sheet-metal sheds by the water. Instead of the concrete block structures of Tre Noc, the buildings were either rounded Quonset huts or the newer, aluminum-sided Butler prefabs. One building had been set aside as the SEALs' ready room, complete with their own stores of weapons and ammo; hell, Mariacher thought, Douglass had even arranged for the SEALs to have an ammo allowance that they could draw as necessary from the base munitions stores. No more stealing ammo; now *that* was the way to win a war!

The rest of the platoon, along with the unit's NILO, was waiting for Mariacher as he walked into the ready room. "Sorry I'm late, guys," he told them as he dropped into one of the folding wooden chairs. He held up the clipboard he'd been carrying. "Had some message traffic I had to take care of."

"No problem, Dan," Lieutenant j.g. Fred Hechinger said. "While you were out, we went ahead and volunteered you for this next mission."

"Fuck you, sir."

"Fuck you very much."

Lieutenant Paul Cox, the prim and somewhat prissy NILO,

frowned disapproval. Not that his approval was necessary here; he'd not heard the nickname the SEALs had hung on him behind his back. "Ah, if we could get on with the briefing," he said.

"Of course! Of course!" Mariacher said. "Go right ahead! Don't mind me!"

"Ahem, yes." He had a map spread out on the table in front of him, along with several aerial reconnaissance photos and a stack of manila folders containing more photos and several thick files. "As I was saying, this will be a very large and complicated operation. However, our confidence in the intel is high. You men have an excellent chance of success."

"Never mind the sugar coating," Horner said. "We're big boys now."

Cox frowned again. Mariacher had the man pegged as one of those military types who insists on being addressed formally, by proper rank or title, and the informality of the SEALs, both officers and enlisted, could be unnerving at times.

"Myok," Hechinger said. "Maybe you should go ahead and give the rundown on the mission. We've got it pretty well scoped out."

"Sure thing, Heck." Rising, Mariacher walked up to the table, accepting the pointer from Cox. Operation Five-Star had been in the works for almost a week now, with Hechinger and Mariacher choreographing most of the details with both Cox and Douglass's ops staff. Now it was time to cut the men in on the mission details.

"This will be a full platoon op," Mariacher said. "Alfa as backup, Bravo on point." Several of the Alfa Squad SEALs groaned or booed at that, but Mariacher held up his hand. "Ah! None of that! Remember, they stuck Bravo on reserve after the mess back at Tre Noc. Now it's our turn. Right, Heck?"

"You're on deck, Myok," Hechinger said, arms folded and a grin on his young face.

"As I'm sure Lieutenant Cox has already explained, we have five targets, including a VC security chief, a unit paymaster, a civilian political advisor, and two guys we think are NVA big-wigs."

There was a stir at that. Most SEAL operations so far, both

in the Rung Sat and throughout the Mekong Delta, had been against the Vietcong, essentially local rebels fighting against the Saigon government with plenty of help from North Vietnam and elsewhere smuggled down the Ho Chi Minh Trail in Cambodia and Laos. North Vietnamese Army, though, meant regular soldiers—well-trained, well-armed, superbly motivated troops . . . definitely the other side's first-string team. It was an open secret, of course, that NVA units were operating in South Vietnam in much the same capacity that American units were working with the RVN troops. So far, however, direct combat between NVA and U.S. forces had been relatively rare. Having located these two NVA "advisors," U.S. military Intelligence was eager to find out what they were doing, who they were working with, what units they had in the South.

The objective was a village called Xa Tan Khai, located some three kilometers north of the river and about twenty klicks downstream. The targets tended to move around a lot, but intelligence had all five pegged as living—at least for now—in the ville or in hootches close by.

"Insertion will be by PBR," Mariacher went on. He used the pointer to lay out the planned route on the map. "We'll proceed overland here, through the jungle. There's a more direct route through this canal, but, frankly, Heck and I think that's a little bit too close to knocking on the front door. Five gets you ten they've got the canal covered by fire and booby-trapped to boot. We've marked the specific hootches that Intel has identified as where our targets are staying. The two NVAs are reportedly visiting with the political officer, here, in this house close to the center of the town. The paymaster is here, on the edge. The security chief is over here, in this isolated group of huts."

"Um, if I may, Ensign?" Cox said.

"Of course."

"Gentlemen, if possible, we want all five alive. However, you will make your own determinations at the time as to what is or is not feasible. MACV-SOG is extremely interested in interrogating these people, but they've also given the go-ahead to terminate them if that is your only option."

"And I will add," Mariacher said, "that I don't want any of you to risk your own lives unnecessarily. If you have to take the son of a bitch down hard, do it. It will hurt the enemy just as bad if we knock off the VC big wigs . . . kind of an up-close-and-personal demonstration that they don't have this jungle all to themselves anymore, right?''

''That's a roger!'' Brubaker said.

''Ay-firmative!'' Reynolds added. The other SEALs nodded enthusiastic affirmation.

''Enemy patrol activity is expected to be heavy. No word on exact numbers, but we can expect at least a battalion-level concentration within this district, and a lot of those boys will be close enough to come running once they know there's trouble.

''Mission support will be a Mike Boat. No STABs. Seems they've got a rep in town already.''

The others chuckled. According to intelligence, the STABs, with their distinctive silhouettes, had been attracting a lot of attention lately. Charlie knew that when the STABs were on the river, ''the men with green faces'' were about to do something unpleasant. The team would have a better chance finding their targets if the STABs were kept in the barn this time around. The Mike boat, an LCM-8 converted to carry armor, an 81-mm mortar, and plenty of machine guns for fire support, would serve as mother hen to the PBRs and be available to lay down one hell of a bombardment if the SEALs needed it. They were slow, but the good thing about LCM-8s was that lots of them had been operating up and down the My Tho River as monitors, as transports, even as repair craft lately, and the appearance of one making its way down the river in the company of a couple of PBRs should raise no unusual comment.

''What about air support?'' Finnegan wanted to know.

''We'll have Seawolves for emergency extraction if we need it, but we won't have them loitering nearby. This op is going to take all night.''

Mariacher continued the briefing, describing the team's approach, their marching order, and their weapons. Because of the likelihood of strong opposition, he wanted to go heavy on support weapons. Though weapon choice among SEALs tended to be a somewhat personal decision, the team as a whole often talked it out in sessions such as this one, to make certain the overall balance of firepower on an op was what the mission required. In this case, there would be two support weapons; Finnegan would carry a Stoner Mk23, while Brubaker would be humping an M60.

Besides that selection of full-auto mayhem, Richardson volunteered to carry a new weapon only recently arrived in Vietnam, the XM-148. This was a 40-mm grenade launcher similar to the popular M79 "thumper" but designed to be mounted beneath the barrel of an M-16, with the trigger set inside a guard just in front of the assault rifle's magazine. As good a weapon as it was, the M79 had two serious disadvantages: it was a single-shot weapon, requiring a sweaty-handed, adrenaline-trembling reload after each shot; and with an arming range of fifteen meters, it was decidedly *not* a close-range weapon unless you were loaded with number four buckshot or one of the new flechette-packed 40-mm cartridges. The XM-148 still fired only one shot between reloads, but the gunner had the M-16 with either a twenty- or a thirty-round mag as backup, an added piece of security that made the SEALs eager to try it out. Headquarters wanted a report on the XM-148 after field testing, and the SEALs were more than happy to oblige.

Matthews would be carrying an Ithaca combat shotgun; the rest had M-16s.

They spent almost another hour discussing alternate approaches, LZs in case they needed to call for an emergency pickup of a wounded man, and alternate plans in case of ambush or just plain bad luck. Aerial reconnaissance photos gave them images of the target hootches from the air, and a good idea of possible hazards to a silent approach—a chicken coop, a spindly legged rack for drying palm fronds, a slit trench that might be either a latrine or something more sinister. They also spent some time going over intelligence photos provided by the NILO. Often, on such ops, Intelligence would provide a Kit Carson—a former VC who'd been turned and was now helping the government—to go along and identify specific targets, but this time around they had photos, from what source, Mariacher had no idea. The SEALs memorized the faces carefully.

"Just one more thing," Mariacher said at last, keeping his voice even, his expression as grim as death. Walking back to his seat, he picked up the message board he'd been carrying. "Horner? I think you'd better have a look at this."

Handing the board to Horner, he watched the man's face run through a gamut of expressions, from surprise through concern through worry through determination; nobody liked being given a telegram, and most official messages within the Navy are worse than that.

EFFECTIVE 22 FEBRUARY, 1967

HORNER, JAMES D. IS HEREBY ADVANCED TO QUARTERMASTER CHIEF
BY DIRECTION,
E. F. HALLEY, CAPT USN
CO-NOSGPAC
CORONADO, CALIFORNIA

"Son of a bitch . . ." Horner said, staring at the message.

"What is it, Badges?" Richardson wanted to know.

"I'm a chief. I've been a chief for two months and didn't even know it!"

"No shit?" Finnegan said, his leathery face creasing in a wide smile. He looked at Brubaker. "Me and the Teddy Bear're gonna have to throw you a rocker party! Right, Bear?"

"Abso-fuckin'-lutely!"

"How come it's so late?" Richardson wanted to know.

"Maybe those bastards at Tre Noc've been sitting on it," Reynolds suggested.

"Nah," Mariacher said, shaking his head. "Lieutenant Kessler's a good guy. He would've put it through as soon as he knew."

"Yeah," Brubaker said, his expression guarded. "But maybe they didn't tell him until just now. Those guys really wanted us screwed."

"Well, you got your rocker now anyway, Chief," Reynolds said, referring to the curved bar that turned the chevrons of a first class's rank insignia into a chief's.

"You guys're going to have to treat me with more respect from now on," Horner said, grinning.

"You're right," Matthews said, nodding. "Remember, guys! From now on, it's *Chief* Horny, not 'you horny bastard!' "

He laughed. "Sorry about that op tonight, Mr. Myok."

Mariacher blinked. "What do you mean?"

"Hey, I just made chief! I can't go on an op tonight!"

"The fuck you're not! Everybody works together in this outfit. Everybody plays together. You're going!"

"Negative!" He shook his head. Lieutenant Cox's eyes widened at the sight of an enlisted man refusing a direct order. "Hey, I'd be out of uniform! My ID still says I'm a QM/1. If I'm gonna get killed out there, I want to get killed as a chief, not as a first class!"

"I got news for you, son," Mariacher said, a sarcastic note edging his voice. "You just made chief petty officer, not chief of naval operations. The day you make four-star admiral, I'll let you off the hook. In the meantime, you've got the point tonight, and you're going!"

"Shit!"

"Don't worry, Chief," Richardson said. "We'll take good care of you out there."

"Why do I feel like some clown just walked on my grave?"

"Lighten up, Chief," Finnegan said.

"I think," Horner said, "that I need a beer."

Chapter 29

Wednesday, 19 April 1967

Bravo Squad
My Tho River, Mekong Delta
2220 hours

After making several false insertions up and down the river, the PBR had dropped them off a kilometer or so above the canal that led inland toward Xa Tan Khai. Clad in tiger-stripe camies, a variety of headgear, and green paint, they'd slipped silently into the warm, muddy water at just past 2200 hours, then begun wading upstream, hugging the shore to their right. The sky was clear and star-filled, the air alive with chirping, creaking, peeping frogs and insects. Reaching a landmark identified earlier, they turned inland, slipping as stealthily as shadows through the deeper shadows of the night.

Jim Horner had point.

Chief Jim Horner had point; it was still a little hard to believe. He'd passed his test for chief the previous fall and knew he was on the promotions list, but promotions had been coming slowly of late. There was only room in the Navy for so many chief petty officers, and the new ones coming up from below had to wait their turn until those at the top died or retired or moved on up to master chief.

A twig snapped beneath his boot, as loud as a rifle shot. *Damn it! Keep your mind on your work!*

Briefly, he considered removing his boots and going barefoot. Lots of SEALs did, claiming they didn't leave behind the big, rubber-tread-soled prints that declared that Americans had been here, but Horner still felt a bit finicky about that. He'd heard there were worms here that could get at you by burrowing through the skin of your foot, and in its own small way, that thought was almost more unpleasant than the idea of being shot.

Besides, he wasn't going to wear his boots around his neck, and leaving the things for the VC to find tomorrow would be worse than letting them find his tracks. Pausing to listen to the chirps and singsongs of the night, he waited a moment, then pressed ahead, step by painstaking step.

He really didn't want to be here.

Jim Horner had always had a rather fatalistic attitude about life, a feeling that things were going to happen or not and that very little he did would change them, one way or the other. Still, it was impossible to be posted to a combat zone, especially while serving with a high-risk unit like the SEALs, and not develop a certain superstitious dread of *anything* that might jinx your chances for coming out of the deployment alive. Making chief was like tempting the gods; going out on this op tonight was the same as pulling a really hairy mission the night before you were scheduled to rotate back to the States.

Yet he'd not been able to refuse Mariacher . . . hadn't even been able to give him a decent line of bullshit. SEALs were an independent bunch of mavericks for the most part, and Myok's Marauders were more so than most. If it had been Lieutenant Yates ordering him out tonight—or Lieutenant Commander Benson—he could have, he *would* have found a way out.

But not when the officer was Mariacher. The mustang ensign was too much a fellow soldier for someone like Horner to deny him anything. Shit, if Myok had ordered Bravo Squad to march into hell, chances are every one of his men would have followed, and cheerfully.

Damn. He didn't want to die tonight, not after finally making chief!

The first target hootch should be just ahead and, as they drew closer, he could smell smoke . . . and the unmistakable odor of *nuoc mam*. Stopping, he gave the SEALs behind him the hand signs for *danger* and *I smell something*, then, dropping to his belly, he slithered forward across wet moss and humus until he'd reached the edge of a clearing.

As expected, there were five hootches clustered together; a fire was going in the clearing, tended by a woman. Two other women were sitting in the doorway of one of the hootches, talking. One laughed, a magical, chimelike sound tinkling against the sounds of the jungle.

The thatched hut to the right of the building with the two women was the one identified as belonging to the local Vietcong security chief, but the interior was dark and there was no sign of life.

Where were the men? Inside sleeping? That didn't seem likely with the women awake and outside. In fact, the whole set-up was a little strange; Vietnamese living in the country tended to go to bed soon after sunset. Seeing those women out and awake seemed to bode . . . not evil, exactly, but something different, something outside the normal course of events.

In combat, the unexpected is what usually kills you.

He waited there for twenty minutes, watching, careful not to look into the clearing itself or at the fire since he needed to keep his night vision intact. He was pretty sure the fire might be a signal of some kind, for the woman tending it didn't appear to be cooking anything. Possibly, too, it was just a way to keep the night and the jungle at bay for a time. There was no sign of any men. Possibly they were all away in the nearby town. The fire might be a beacon to guide them home in the darkness.

There were crates and fuel drums about, but not really enough to excite suspicion. Had there been a large stockpile of fuel or supplies of any kind, even rice, the SEALs would have investigated more closely, but so far as Horner could tell, there was nothing threatening or out of the ordinary about this place at all.

Carefully, he slipped back from the edge of the clearing, moving back to confer in mouth-to-ear whispers with Mariacher. There were two ways to do this that Horner could see: rush into the clearing and smash into the target hootch, looking for the suspect . . . or try to move in on him in a somewhat more circumspect manner. Horner was opting for circumspect; it was too early in this game yet to tip the locals off that the men with green faces were in the area, which was exactly what they would do if they rushed the place. If the security chief was inside the hootch, there was another way to verify it.

Nodding, Mariacher agreed, then turned to deploy the rest of the squad. Slipping his M-16 over his shoulder, Horner reached up to his combat vest and unsheathed his knife, the sleek and deadly black Sykes-Fairbairn his uncle had given him at Christmas. Blade in hand, he worked his way on his belly around the clearing, moving to a new position where he was facing the back of the target hootch. Throughout that maneuver, he avoided looking into the fire, or even into the glow backlighting the hootches; night vision was more critical than ever now, in an area where there might well be tripwires to booby traps or alarms.

At last he was able to slip out of the jungle and into the clearing itself, staying inside the shadow cast by the target hootch. The building was typical of many in Vietnam, a lightweight frame of wood posts filled in with boards or rusty sheet tin and roofed over with thatch. Carefully, he used his knife to work one of the boards loose and pull it back. He was looking into the small building's main room.

There were sleeping mats on the floor . . . but no men. In one corner were two children, two boys aged about eight or nine, both naked and asleep.

This was crazy. Technically, this entire area was a free-fire zone, a place where no one was supposed to be living at all . . . a place where there were no restrictions and the Americans could open fire indiscriminately, on the assumption that anyone here was VC.

But Horner wasn't here to make war on women and children. Oh, he'd heard plenty of stories about eight-year-olds with hand grenades, but he wasn't about to start killing kids just on the chance that some of them might be the VC's youngest recruits. Possibly—even probably—the women outside were VC, or at least VC sympathizers, the wives or girl-friends of Vietcong soldiers.

But he wasn't about to make war on them either. Carefully, silently, he slipped the board back into place, then worked his way back to the jungle. Ten minutes later, he rejoined Mariacher, whispering softly to him that the target was a dry hole.

Mariacher accepted this with his typical calm equanimity. "Fuck. Okay. Let's hit the next one."

Next was the paymaster's house, located in a larger wood frame structure on the outskirts of the village itself. After reporting by radio that the first prisoner snatch had come up empty, the SEAL team set off once more, moving through the jungle to approach Xa Tan Khai from the north rather than from the direction of the river. The VC knew how important river traffic was to the Americans and to the Vietnamese government, and they tended to place their heaviest defenses facing in that direction.

The village itself was fair-sized as such villes went, though considerably smaller and dingier-looking than My Tho. The few stone or cement buildings, colonial structures such as the villa where the SEALs were housed, all contributed to give My Tho the feeling of civilization. This place, with its mud streets and thatch buildings, looked about as civilized as the native village in *King Kong*, though even here some of the houses were obviously the property of wealthy people.

Evidently the paymaster, a powerful member of the VCI— the local Vietcong Infrastructure—named Nhoi Da was one of the wealthier members of the community. Horner wondered how the man reconciled the relative opulence of his dwelling with his Communist principles . . . or if he even tried.

The building was close enough to the shelter of the woods

that the SEALs had elected to try to rush it, despite the proximity of other hootches and buildings in the ville. Brubaker maintained his position at the edge of the woods with the M60, covering the team and the approaches from the rest of the town, as well as keeping the unit's radio safe and out of the way.

The other six SEALs split into two-man fireteams: Mariacher and Finnegan, Richardson and Matthews, Horner and Reynolds. Taking advantage of the shadows, they closed in swiftly, leapfrogging ahead three at a time as their partners covered them.

They'd almost reached the covered porch when a sudden motion at the doorway made them all drop and freeze. A man stepped out into the night, a Vietnamese in civilian clothing. He paused on the bamboo-railed veranda, pulled out a cigarette, and lit it.

It was the paymaster. In the brief glow that flared from his cigarette lighter, Horner could see the mustache, the dark eyes, the jug-handle ears. It was their man, Nhoi. Horner looked back at Mariacher and gave an interrogative sign. Mariacher pursed his lips, then returned a thumbs-up. *Do it*!

There might be others inside the house. There might even be soldiers, bodyguards, inside, but there was no way to deal with that save make a move and see what developed. Mariacher signaled, a finger pointing forward. Horner rose to his feet and sprinted ahead covering thirty meters in seconds, with Richardson sprinting along behind. The approach was silent . . . but the target must have heard or sensed something. He whirled, eyes widening, just before Horner vaulted over the railing and onto the porch.

"*Dung lai!*" Horner snapped, thrusting the muzzle of his M-16 forward, threatening.

The man stumbled backward, tripping over a rattan chair on the porch and sprawling on his back with a crash of splintering furniture. "*Cuu toi voi!*" Nhoi shouted, the words twisting into a scream. Fear clawed at his features. "*Mat mau xanh la cay!*"

Horner advanced on the man, passing the open doorway. Someone else burst out of the door at the same moment, a man, a very young man wearing shorts and a T-shirt and carrying an AK-47 that looked three times too big for him.

Horner pivoted, shifting the aim of his M-16, but a sharp, short burst of gunshots rang out from the darkness, staining the boy's T-shirt with a rich splatter of blood. The man lying on the porch shrieked, the fear on his face turning to anguish. A relative? His son, possible? . . .

No time to think or question. Horner spun as the man tried to rise, smashing the heavy plastic stock of his M-16 into his face.

The VC went down hard, arms outstretched. Horner pounced on him immediately, rolling Nhoi over onto his stomach, kneeling on his buttocks as he pulled his hands to the small of his back. Using a plastic restraining strap from his prisoner collection kit, he swiftly bound Nhoi's wrists together. Richardson knelt beside the body of the boy, searching his pockets, then retrieving the AK. A woman's voice cried out from inside the house, questioning . . . and terrified.

"Time to get the fuck out of Dodge!" Richardson whispered, grabbing the dropped weapon and rising. He pulled a playing card—the ace of spades—from a belt pouch and dropped it on the dead man's body.

"I'm with you!" Someone would have heard the gunshots besides the woman in the house. Hoisting the prisoner up over his shoulder, Horner jogged away from the house as the other SEALs covered him. Swiftly, still silently, they moved away from the house, Richardson taking the tail gunner position and backing away as the team filed off into the jungle. They could hear shouts from elsewhere in the village now, and one random gunshot that might have been a warning or simply an accidental discharge.

The jungle, however, was beginning to look a lot more dangerous than it had before.

Half an hour later, the SEALs crouched with their captive deep in the jungle, the noise from the village muffled now by distance. Matthews, Finnegan, Brubaker, and Reynolds dropped into position in an outer perimeter, crouching as they watched in all directions. The others gathered by the prisoner. The spot was identical to a million other points in the tangle of jungle growth north of the My Tho, but it had been plotted on the SEALs maps as Rally Two, one of several rendezvous points set in case the squad was forced to break into smaller fireteams, or if members of the unit found themselves separated from the main body.

"Okay," Mariacher said. Nhoi had nothing in his pockets but cigarettes and his lighter, but the man himself would be an important intelligence coup if they could get him back to My Tho. "So far we've got one for five. I'm for going back and trying to nail those NVAs as well. What do you guys think?"

"Go for it," Richardson said. His teeth flashed white in the dim light behind the horridly painted mask of his face.

"Roger that," Matthews said from a few feet away. "We can take 'em!"

"Hoo-yah!" Finnegan said, whispering the SEAL war cry, and Brubaker and Reynolds both gave silent thumbs-up.

"Jim?"

Horner caught his lower lip between his teeth, hesitating. He'd pushed his luck this far and was still alive . . . an exhilarating feeling. If they extracted now, he might even live to celebrate that chief's party and get his new ID.

Reluctantly, though, Horner nodded. "Go," he said.

"All right!"

Quietly, Mariacher issued orders. The prisoner was tightly tied to a convenient tree at Rally Two, his mouth gagged with gauze and tape from a medical kit. The SEALs would come back for him, if and when they could, but they couldn't be burdened with a prisoner now. By midnight, they were moving once more, slipping through the black forest like wraiths, invisible and silent.

The intelligence reports had pinpointed the two visiting NVA advisors at the house of the regional political officer, a high-ranking member of the local Communist party. As with Nhoi Da, the political officer occupied a relatively large wood-frame house considerably roomier and more comfortable than the majority of the hootches and huts that made up the village of Xa Tan Khai.

This was a much more dangerous area to approach, more built-up, with more people living close by. The target house was not as accessible, and if gunfire was exchanged, if somebody shouted for help, the SEALs might easily find themselves cut off from the safety of the jungle. They'd not expected that they would be able to rush the house as they had with the paymaster. Instead, they positioned themselves in the forest overlooking the approach to the house.

And then they settled down to wait.

Xa Tan Khai, Mekong Delta
0605 hours

Well over six hours had passed since they'd left the rally point. It would be light within another hour or so, with sunrise this morning scheduled for 0749 hours. The SEALs could remain in place throughout the daylight hours, of course, hoping to try for the remaining targets the following night, but that would mean taking the chance of losing the one prisoner they already had. Their attack on the house at the edge of town had already stirred things up as effectively as thrusting a stick into a hornet's nest; they could hear small groups of VC moving around in the jungle nearby, sometimes calling to one another, occasionally taking shots at imagined enemies in the darkness. If the SEALs tried to wait out the day, they were vastly increasing the risk that someone would find their captive; likely there were search parties out now, to judge by the noise; come full daylight and this jungle was going to be as bustling as Manhattan at rush hour.

At the moment, it was clear that the main body of the enemy force was gone, and that worried Mariacher as he lay on the soft forest humus and watched the targets' house. This village, Intelligence had estimated, was large enough to be home to anywhere from twenty to forty VC, assuming all of the men and boys older than about fifteen or so were members of the local cadre. At night, however, it was generally the case that the active VC troops left, vanishing into the night to rendezvous with other insurgents from other villages to train, carry out ambushes, or whatever else was on the agenda for the evening. By dawn, the men would return; it was a topic of constant speculation among the SEALs that the men they were trying to kill—and who were trying to kill them—each night were the men cheerfully waving at Americans from the side of the road during the day. These same VC soldiers who were lobbing rockets, mortar shells, and sniper rounds at them during the night would simply hide their weapons and go back home the next morning, there to mingle with the rest of the populace, invisible, undetectable. Mariacher was well aware that many of the friendly and helpful VNs he ran into during the day, even some of those working inside the My Tho base, were Vietcong . . . transformed, like monsters of legend, by the setting of the sun.

And there was no way to tell the difference between a VN civilian and a VC insurgent unless you were able to catch the man with a weapon.

Mariacher reared a little higher, studying the target house. There'd been no sign of life throughout the night. The targets *could* be asleep, of course, but that seemed unlikely, given the VC's nocturnal preferences. He was going to have to decide quickly, now, whether to extract with one prisoner, or wait a bit longer in the hope of bagging three more. The SEAL squad was spread out along the edge of the woods, four men concentrating on the house with overlapping fields of fire, and with Matthews and Reynolds watching both flanks and the rear. If necessary, they would ambush the targets, trying for a clean kill rather than attempting a capture. He was beginning to think reaching for a five-target capture had been a really bad idea, one that had put the squad in considerable jeopardy. Saigon had overreached itself a bit this time; his recommendation for the future was certainly going to be that the teams exercise a bit more patience, taking down their targets one at a time.

Patience *always* paid off in an ambush.

He heard voices.

Gently lowering himself once more, he watched as a line of men materialized out of the darkness twenty meters away, walking single-file into the village. At first Mariacher thought it was one of the search patrols returning, but as the shadowy figures kept coming, he realized that this could well be the village's entire VC contingent. Most of them were armed . . . and that was a disturbing break in the routine. Mariacher wondered if someone here in the village had called for more searchers after the paymaster's abduction.

Whatever the reason, they hadn't hidden their weapons but had brought them along. Mariacher saw a few AK-47s—those ubiquitous Soviet- or Chinese-made assault rifles were generally carried by the more experienced or the more important of VC personnel—and numerous older weapons, M1 Garands and carbines, SKS rifles, and even some old French rifles and submachine guns. Some wore camouflage fatigues, but most wore the traditional black pajama peasant costume. There were no reports of any pro-Saigon militias in this area, so it was a sure bet that these were VC.

"Shit," Horner mouthed in a near-silent whisper against Mariacher's ear. They lay side by side in the forest, studying the town. "I make it . . . maybe twenty guys."

"Looks like a damned party," Mariacher replied, just as quietly. "I think maybe our guy at the first target must be here. Maybe they're all here."

It was very nearly daylight now, and a decision had to be made.

Mariacher made it. If the SEALs pulled out at once, they might be dodging enemy patrols all the way back to the extraction point. If they attacked, if they hit the VC patrol now, hard, they might confuse and scatter the enemy enough to give the SEALs a decent chance to get out.

This, Mariacher thought, was definitely one of those situations where the safest call was to take the most direct action.

The incoming patrol had halted not far from the target house, several of their leaders talking to one another. It was light enough now to make out details of faces, uniforms, and weapons. The door of the house opened and another man joined them. It wasn't one of the suspects, so Mariacher was glad he hadn't let his impatience goad him into investigating the place up close during the night. It was distinctly possible, he thought, that he was actually looking at some kind of elaborate trap, an attempt to draw the SEALs out.

Well, if these folks wanted SEALs, he was happy to oblige. Sighting down the barrel of his M-16, he aimed at the group of VC talking—officers, he guessed—and squeezed the trigger.

Gunfire roared from the jungle, first Mariacher's M-16, then close behind his opening shot, a fusillade from Richardson, Horner, Brubaker, and Finnegan. Each SEAL was responsible for a forty-five-degree swath extending in front of him and overlapping slightly with the kill zones of the SEALs to either side. The hammering of Brubaker's M60 on the right flank was particularly insistent, and at a range of only a few tens of meters it carved a bloody swath through the VC soldiers and sent them toppling to the ground. Finnegan's Commando was firing from the left, catching the VC who ran in that direction to flee the M60's destructive thunder. Richardson's XM-148 gave a full-throat thump, and seconds later, the grenade roared, throwing up a clump of earth and caving in the front of the target house.

Several VC were down, unmoving. Others were down, writhing on the ground and screaming. Some of the VC unhit by that initial barrage simply stood where they were, staring at the jungle in gape-mouthed astonishment until they were mown down by the SEALs' full-auto rock-n-roll. Others jumped and ran, with or without their weapons. A few tried to return fire where they were but were rapidly cut down.

An absolute rule of ambush warfare, however, had been proven once again. Someone in the ambushed party *always* manages to get away, and with the SEALs so badly outnumbered, the survivors this time around were quite numerous. Several had ducked behind the house, while others had thrown themselves flat right where they were, using the ground or the bodies of their comrades for shelter. A fair number were still running, and it was a good bet that they would be back soon, with plenty of reinforcements.

"Reynolds!" Mariacher yelled back over his shoulder. "Get on the horn! Tell 'em we need that air support, fast as they can get it here!"

"Roger that!"

As Reynolds began talking urgently on the squad's PRC-22, Mariacher turned his full attention back to the ambush. He fired at a running VC, missed, and then his weapon was empty. He thumbed the magazine release and snapped in a fresh mag.

To the left, several VC suddenly sprang up and rushed toward the jungle, weapons blazing. "Shit!" Finnegan shouted. "On the left!" He cut loose with his Stoner Mk23 Commando, rattling off a series of bursts that sent the oncoming VC diving for cover. Richardson shifted the aim of his M-16, reached in front of the magazine, and triggered his XM-148. The weapon thumped, the recoil jerking it in his hands. A moment later, the high explosive grenade detonated inside the village, about 150 meters away.

The enemy's counterattack had been broken . . . but only for the moment. There were probably other troops already in the forest, trying to work their way around behind the SEALs.

"Okay, Myok!" Reynolds told him. "My Tho says two Seawolves are on the way. They want confirmation that the town is a free-fire zone."

"Shit!" Mariacher yelled. "Tell him it don't get no freer than this!"

The VC were organizing again, over at the far side of the village. The light was still poor, the sun not yet up, but Mariacher thought they must be trying to put together a flanking party. "That's it!" he told the others. "We're not getting anywhere with that mob in there. Pull back! Pull back!"

"Did we get the guys we were supposed to get?" Horner called to him.

"Fuck it. We got one alive and a shitload of dead 'uns. It'll have to do."

Another grenade burst at the edge of the village, spilling dense white smoke in a low-lying fog across the sprawled, still forms of the dead. "Let's go!" Mariacher yelled to the others. "Rally Point One!"

Two by two, the SEALs began dropping back into the jungle.

Chapter 30

Thursday, 20 April 1967

Xa Tan Khai, Mekong Delta
0652 hours

Richardson and Horner were the last two SEALs to hold the line at the edge of the village after the others had fallen back. Richardson continued firing high explosive grenades until several VC tried to rush the forest treeline again. Then he reloaded with number four buckshot, and the blast slashed through the running Vietcong and tumbled them to the ground in a bloody, kicking shambles.

He was angry. Mariacher was the squad leader, and it was his decision to trigger the ambush by opening fire. But Richardson knew he never would have given that order.

Ambushes such as that one worked best when there were four or five or six VC, not a whole damned platoon. What's more, there was now no way to tell whether they'd hit any of the other men who were their targets. In Richardson's opinion, the attack had been cowboyed, a shoot-from-the-hip decision made more on the basis of ego than of measured and rational thought.

Breaking open the breach of the grenade launcher, he slipped in a smoke cartridge. He glanced at Horner. "Let's scoot."

"Affirmative!"

"You first."

Horner hesitated. "I don't—"

"Shit, Badges," Richardson said. "I'm not being gallant. I've got the grenade launcher, okay? Now move!"

Rising to his knees, he braced the butt of his assault rifle against his thigh and triggered the XM-148. Seconds later, more white smoke burst near the target house, thick and comfortingly opaque.

Horner was gone. Richardson reloaded the grenade launcher with another shotgun shell, then began moving slowly backward through the trees.

Rally One, South of Xa Tan Khai
0658 hours

Mariacher crouched on the embankment above a small stream, an unmarked patch of jungle designated "Rally One" during their planning of the op yesterday. Beside him, Reynolds was talking on the radio. Brubaker, Finnegan, and Matthews were crouched in the brush nearby. Horner and Richardson were missing.

Fuck, fuck, *fuck!* He tried to blot some of the sweat trickling down his face with one hand. *Daniel, you shit-for-brains walking clusterfuck*, he thought to himself angrily, *you've really gone and put your foot in it this time.*

He should have waited, should have let the VC column go without attacking it, should have ordered the squad to pull a fast, silent fade and come back to hit the mission's targets another night. He should have realized that something big was up, probably maneuvers of some sort; that fire they'd seen at the first cluster of hootches, the one being tended by a woman, that could have been a waypoint beacon for trainees . . . or it might have been a signal fire to guide a large force of Communist troops, troops who didn't know the area because they were coming from some distance away.

Shit, what had Bravo Squad stumbled into here? Whatever it was, it was something big.

Too big for seven SEALs.

And now, two members of his team were missing. Normally, SEAL squads were supremely proficient in the art of moving through even the thickest jungle terrain without their individual members becoming separated, but they'd had to break contact with the VC in a hurry, and in the rush and the darkness and the difficult terrain, the last two SEALs at the ambush site must have gotten separated.

Damn it. SEALs never left their own, alive or dead. Mariacher wasn't about to become the first SEAL Team squad leader to abandon two of his men in combat.

"Anything?" he asked Reynolds.

"Negative, Mr. Myok," Reynolds said, looking up from the radio. "Of course, they *could* have their Motorolas turned off."

Mariacher nodded. It was a good assumption. Each of the SEALs carried a small tactical radio, called a "Motorola" for the manufacturer, for communications within the squad. There were times, however, when the burst of static preceding a transmission could be deadly—when the SEAL was lying quietly in concealment a few feet away from an enemy patrol, for example—so the SEALs usually kept the devices switched off. Hand signs and mouth-to-ear whispers were all the squad members usually needed to coordinate their actions anyway.

"We're not gonna be able to wait for 'em long," Brubaker said, not taking his eyes from the encircling wall of jungle growth. "Somebody out there's got damned heavy feet."

Mariacher could hear it, the sounds of someone crashing through undergrowth toward the east. The corner of his mouth quirked upward. Charlie had a rep for being a master both of night and of jungle warfare, deadly, skilled, and silent. While that might be the case for some units, however, and while it was true that most of their operations took place at night, the VC were only as good at operating in this environment as their training . . . and the majority of the Vietcong were draftees with little practical experience in specialized warfare.

He heard someone sbout, the words unintelligible but carrying the singsong tones of Vietnamese. SEALs would *never* make that much noise, even if they were moving at a flat-out run. From the sound of things, the VC they'd ambushed were getting reorganized. They would be meticulously searching the forest by now, and they would be hungry for blood.

"Hey, Myok," Reynolds said, whispering. "Call for you!"

"You got them?"

Reynolds shook his head as he passed Mariacher the radio's handset. "Nope. But we got air-to-ground!"

He accepted the handset. "This is Sierra Bravo One-one," he said. "Go ahead."

A low-voiced *whup-whup-whup* sounded toward the northeast, swiftly growing to a clattering roar filled the forest. Pressing the handset against his ear, Mariacher looked up, trying to glimpse the incoming choppers through the trees.

"This is Skylark One, Skylark One," a voice said in his ear. "Calling Sierra Bravo One-one. We are coming in on the ville. What is your posit, over?"

"Skylark, this is Sierra Bravo One-one," Mariacher said, holding the radio's microphone to his lips. "We are east of the target village, about one kilometer. It sounds like you're pretty close to us right now, northeast of our position. Over!"

"Sierra Bravo, do we have clearance to fire, over?"

"That is affirmative, Skylark. Burn that fucker to the ground! Over!"

"Ah, roger. Will comply. Keep your heads down there, fellas."

"Roger that!"

"Skylark One, out!"

One of the Seawolves howled low overhead, its shape momentarily glimpsed through the canopy of the forest against the dawn-graying sky, its glowering, glassy face like the visage of some huge and furiously angry insect. Seconds later, the SEALs heard the swoosh-swoosh . . . ka-*vham!* of 2.5-inch rockets firing two by two. If the Vietnamese had been worried about the SEALs in their backyard before, they had one hell of a lot more to worry about now.

Mariacher considered the situation a moment more. Brubaker was right. They *couldn't* stay here for long . . . and they still had to retrieve the prisoner they'd left tied to a tree further north. It was also possible that if Horner and Richardson had been unable to get through to Rally One, if they'd found themselves cut off by those unseen VC crashing around in the underbrush near the village, they would double back toward Rally Two, where they'd left the prisoner nearly six hours ago. Horner and Richardson could be there already.

If the VC hadn't found the prisoner and set up an ambush or booby trapped the area. If the two SEALs weren't lying dead or wounded somewhere near the village. If, if, if . . .

"Pack up," he told the others. "Bear, you take point. We're heading for Rally Two."

East of Xa Tan Khai
0703 hours

Machine-gun fire chattered in the near distance as the Seawolves' 60-gunners strafed the village. Horner could hear someone yelling in shrill Vietnamese not far away, and once in a while he heard someone thrashing about in the underbrush, just a few tens of meters behind them.

Horner and Richardson continued slipping through the jungle, using their compasses to maintain a more or less straight-line bearing toward Rally Two. They'd found themselves cut off as they'd broken contact at the village; a squad of VC had been trying to get around behind the SEAL ambush; they'd moved too slowly to catch the whole squad, but they'd managed to cut off the two tail-enders. Horner had made the decision to give up trying to reach Rally One and move to Rally Two instead. The rest of the guys would show up there sooner or later, no matter what, if only because they would want to try to retrieve the prisoner they'd left there.

A helicopter roared overhead, low enough that the downdraft from its rotors setting the highest branches of the forest canopy slapping and whipping back and forth. Rocket fire hissed. Explosions detonated to the west, a thumping, rumbling thunder punctuated by the *pop-pop-pop* of small arms fire as VC shot at their airborne tormentors.

The VC resistance felt scattered and disorganized to Horner, who'd been trying to gauge its effectiveness by listening to the sounds of gunfire. He was pretty sure that the VC contingent the SEALs had ambushed had been thoroughly broken, that most of its members were scattering, running through the jungle in every direction. The greatest danger now was that the two SEALs might collide with some of the panicked fugitives by accident.

Richardson touched him lightly on the shoulder, then touched the Motorola unit hooked to his combat vest, his green-painted face asking the question. Call the others?

Horner shook his head, then touched his ear. *No. The VC might hear.* He didn't want to risk an inopportune hiss of static revealing their position. Besides, with so many Vietcong blundering around in the woods, the rest of the squad could be in a similar situation. He consulted his compass once more, then pointed toward the west. *That way.*

Near Rally Two, East of Xa Tan Khai
0712 hours

In the swiftly growing early-morning light, Horner examined the forest in all directions, trying to get his bearings. The two SEALs were close to Rally Two—he was certain of that—but their navigation had been by dead reckoning: "If we moved so many paces south, then our objective to the west must be this many paces northeast. . . ." And when pace counts were thrown off by the necessity of constantly detouring around trees, impassable sections of swamp and mud, or noisy parties of VC, the accuracy of any overland navigation was always thrown into considerable doubt. They were *probably* within a hundred yards of the spot, but it was impossible to see more than twenty yards in any direction, and most parts of this jungle looked exactly like most other parts.

Why am I doing this shit? Horner asked himself suddenly. It wasn't hard to imagine missing the rally point and wandering around lost out here for hours. The squads' fail-safe fallback rendezvous was the extraction point, a stretch of the My

Tho River several hundred meters downstream from the canal. He was not seriously worried about being left behind; the PBRs would wait as long as they could, and others would come by periodically if the boats were forced to leave before the entire squad showed up.

But he was worried about what would happen to him and Richardson if they encountered a powerful enemy force. It was almost full daylight now, and it would be damned difficult to hide unless the two SEALs went to ground, finding a hard-to-reach stronghold where they could hole up, unmoving and well camouflaged, for the rest of the day. There was no possibility of fighting back, not with just the two of them and with limited ammunition. And if one or the other was killed or wounded, it would be damned hard for the other one to make it out on his own, harder still if he had to lug his partner's dead or unconscious body.

SEALs never left their own . . . but it was beginning to look like there might be a first time for everything.

Horner banished the thought. If something happened to Richardson, *he* wasn't going to be the first SEAL to abandon his buddy. And he knew with an unshakable, rock-solid conviction that Richardson wouldn't leave him behind either. *Don't even think about it! Concentrate on finding the damned rally point!*

Maybe *that* way . . .

Silently, he signaled Richardson to hold his position, then starting slipping forward through the underbrush. To avoid simply circling around blindly in the jungle, one man would become the anchor for a methodical search by the other. Horner would move away from Richardson until the two SEALs were out of visual contact, but still close enough to find one another easily; he would search a short arc ahead, then return to within visual range of the anchor and try again. The process slowed their movement but gave them a much better chance of consistently searching the area, avoiding what would otherwise be a largely random, hit-or-miss stumbling through the woods.

A trail opened up in the forest ahead, the surface hardpacked and solid through an area of soft, damp, almost muddy ground. He wasn't positive, but he thought it was probably the path that connected those first five outlying hootches southeast of Xa Tan Khai with the main village. Carefully, he checked all around, looking for signs of ambush, and spent some time listening as well. The nearest sounds of pursuit were behind them, to the west. If it was the same path, then Rally Two was *that* way, across the path and slightly toward the north.

He stepped out into the trail, heard a noise, and spun. A man was there, an *armed* man standing in the trail to his left less than twenty feet away.

If you have to kill somebody, don't hesitate. . . .

The encounter lasted for an instant, for an eye's blink . . . yet it seemed to be dragging on in slow motion, to take an eternity of seconds as the two men stared, reacted, moved. The other man was a Vietnamese in black pajamas and a French-style army helmet . . . and the expression on his face was swiftly changing from surprise to pure, black hatred. He was holding an AK-47, and as Horner watched with an ice-cold clarity of vision and awareness, the man snapped off his weapon's safety as he dragged the muzzle around to point at Horner's head and pulled the trigger.

Horner had been moving as soon as he'd seen the other man, but he'd had to turn in place as well as raise his weapon, and the VC had a split second's lead. A single shot barked and something snapped in the air inches from Horner's right ear, while the muzzle of his M-16 was still pointed at the ground halfway between him and the enemy, but he was already dragging back the trigger, and his weapon cut loose with a long burst of rock-and-roll fire that plowed into the ground at the soldier's feet, then walked up the target with the recoil. Bright scarlet splatters erupted from the legs of the man's loose-fitting black trousers, then from his stomach, then his chest. Hatred shifting to astonishment on his face, the Vietnamese man toppled backward and collapsed on the ground, his assault rifle clattering on the path beside him.

Moving closer to the man, Horner felt himself starting to shake and had to clamp down hard to stop the adrenaline-rush reaction. If that guy had cut loose at him on full auto instead of trying to take him with a single shot, Horner knew, it would be that VC was standing over *his* body right now, not the other way around.

As he knelt beside the body and checked it first for life,

then for documents or anything else of use, another thought touched him, dark and slightly chilling. Horner had never killed another man before . . . not up close and personal, like this.

His uncle had told him that the first one was the hardest, that it got easier after that. He'd assumed that he was over any psychological reaction he might have had to making his first kill. After all, he'd been in combat plenty of times already, starting with that wild shooting spree at Tre Noc. Chances were, in fact, that he'd killed several men.

But not like *this*.

When he and Richardson had closed in to make the snatch on the paymaster and that kid had come bursting out of the doorway, he'd been about to fire without even thinking about it . . . but someone else had nailed the guy first. Later, when Mariacher had initiated the ambush, Horner had been blazing away at the massed human targets in front of him, but even that hadn't been the same as killing this man. It was, he thought, something like the old idea of a ten-man firing squad having only nine loaded rifles, so that no one in the detail would know positively that his weapon had killed the prisoner. Hell, when he'd been one of five SEALs firing into that village, he'd not been able to tell for sure if he was hitting anyone or not. He'd been part of a group, functioning as one of many, and that had taken him a step back from this one-on-one, him-against-me feeling of combat at knife-fighting range.

All of those thoughts flickered through his mind in an instant, were drowned by the excitement of finding two waterproof pouches on the body, tucked into a pack slung from the man's web belt. Those pouches, as well as the fact that he'd been carrying an AK-47, suggested that this man might have been important or fairly high-ranking.

Richardson materialized out of the shadows next to the trail, drawn from the anchor point by the gunfire. "You okay, Badges?"

"Okay." He glanced up and down the path. Others might have heard the shots as well, but it was possible that this guy had been by himself. How far off were his buddies? There was no way to tell. "Help me with this guy, will you?" He wanted to get the body off the path, get it someplace where he could search the guy thoroughly.

Then other figures materialized in the woods . . . Brubaker, closely followed by Mariacher and the rest of the SEALs.

"Man, are we glad to see you guys!" Richardson said, visibly sagging a bit with relief.

"Same here," Mariacher said. "Heard your 16 and thought we'd come give you a hand."

"Shit, you tore this guy apart, Badger," Finnegan said, kneeling by the body. "How close were you?"

"Six yards."

"Son of a bitch." He shook his head. "Next time, try a chainsaw."

"You okay, Badges?" Mariacher said, looking at him.

"Fine. I'm fine." He took a deep breath. He *was* fine, and that discovery was just a little startling. He'd expected to feel . . . more.

Finnegan was examining the AK that the enemy soldier had dropped. "Hey, Jim," he said. "Have a look."

Horner walked over and leaned over Finnegan's shoulder. The SEAL was pointing to the AK-47's fire selector switch, a design reversed from that of most American weapons where the lever clicked from safe to semiautomatic to full-auto, in that order. On the AK, when the lever was up, the weapon was on safe; when thumbed down, it went first to full-auto, *then* to semiauto.

Horner called up that crystalline image still in his mind of the VC snapping off his safety an instant before he fired. The guy must have clicked the lever all the way down through full-auto to semi in the excitement of that instant, a mistake that helped explain the surprised look on his face. If he'd snapped the selector to full-auto, as he'd no doubt intended to, his burst would have chewed through Horner's body at point-blank range an instant before he'd been able to fire.

A tiny mistake, caused by the confusion and terror of a firefight . . . and it had cost the man his life.

Mariacher knelt beside Finnegan, looking at the body. "Hey!" he said suddenly. He reached down and turned the man's head from side to side with one hand. "This's one of our targets, one of the NVA guys!"

"Shit!" Horner said, looking more closely. "You're right!" In the excitement, he'd not recognized the man, not looked closely at his features after the firefight.

Mariacher began going through the guy's pockets. There was a wallet in his pants, as well as a small, red case of some kind. "I think we'd better take this stiff with us," he said. "Don't know who he is, but he's got a lot of shit on him. C'mon. Day's half over already, and we still have to pick up our POW. Let's move out!"

Horner turned, slowly scanning the forest. The sounds of pursuit heard earlier had faded away. The sounds of the Seawolf attack were absent as well, and he wasn't sure how long it had been since they'd ceased. Several minutes, certainly.

He began to allow himself to think that he might actually get out of this nightmare mission alive.

My Tho River
Five kilometers east of My Tho
0855 hours

The LCM-8 chugged slowly up the river as the new day dawned bright and clear. Richardson sat in the well deck, trying to push back the exhaustion that threatened each moment to overwhelm him. The exfiltration back to the extraction point had been carried off without any further problems, with one of the SEALs packing the still-unconscious prisoner, and another the bloody body of the man Chief Horner had killed. At the river, they'd found the PBRs waiting offshore for them, and moments later they'd transferred to the LCM for the passage back upriver to My Tho.

This fight had been nothing like the battle on the STABs back at Tre Noc, nor had it been like the several raids, ambushes, and minor ops the platoon had carried out so far in the area around My Tho. This time, the enemy had been right *there*, a few feet away; he'd never been so scared as he'd been at the VC paymaster's house when that kid had come at them with the AK.

The prisoner they'd picked up was aft in the well deck, already being questioned by Mariacher, Hechinger, and a Vietnamese LLDB interpreter. The body was on the deck at his feet. Richardson had already seen most of the stuff he'd been carrying on his person when he'd been shot. Maps. Documents in typewritten Vietnamese. Official-looking papers. A real treasure trove that would make the Intelligence boys happy.

That red case turned out to hold a military medal of some kind, an ornate gold star with lots of red enamel. There'd also been personal papers, handwritten, and a number of photographs in the man's European-style wallet . . . a young, pretty Vietnamese woman. An old man and woman. Two kids, both girls, aged eight, maybe ten.

Richardson wished he hadn't seen those. Shit . . . it was a lot harder when you realized that the guy you were shooting at was someone just like you, with a family, loved ones, and a life somewhere beyond this stinking jungle. It was so much easier when the enemy was simply a faceless target.

He found himself thinking about home, about Mom and Dad. . . .

He wished he could see them again.

SEAL Team Two Base
My Tho, Mekong Delta
1035 hours

Horner was sitting in the SEAL ready room at My Tho, slumped in a chair as he enjoyed a beer. It was a bit early in the day for alcohol, of course, if you kept a normal schedule, but he'd been up all night and much of the day before and so far as his body was concerned it was late in the evening.

The SEALs had returned to My Tho with their trophies, including the corpse of the man he'd killed. He'd had time to shower, go through an initial and rather cursory debriefing with the NILO and several bigshot intelligence-types who'd heloed in from Saigon, and grab a quick bite of late breakfast at the mess hall.

Now he was going to have one beer before he headed back to the SEAL Hotel and hit the rack. Several of the other SEALs who'd already completed their debriefings were in the room, but everyone was dead tired and the conversation so far had been less than sparkling. It was often like that after a firefight, a few moments of almost electric excitement and rapid-fire exchanges as the men swapped stories, followed very swiftly by a long period of silent introspection mingled with utter exhaustion.

He'd been thinking a lot about the photos in that dead soldier's wallet. His uncle had never told him about that part of the equation, about what it felt like afterward when you realized the man you'd shot had had a family somewhere, and it had left Horner feeling a little depressed.

Shit. Maybe it wasn't even worth it being a SEAL. He hated that thought, but there was no escaping it. What good was he *really* doing out here, anyway?

Mariacher and Hechinger entered the ready room. "Hey! Chief Horner!" They looked tired too, Myok especially, but they had grins on their faces.

"Yeah?"

"Thought you might like to hear a bit of news. You know the guy you capped?"

"I was not personally acquainted with the gentleman, no, sir."

"You know damned well what I mean. Seems he was a bit more of a bigwig than we knew."

Horner's eyebrows crept up his forehead. "What, I bagged a general?"

"Better. The guy was an NVA commando. One of the packets we picked up had his records. Special training in North Korea and in the Soviet Union. *Spetsnaz* training."

Horner's eyebrows moved up another notch. Soviet *spetsialnoye nazhacheniye* troops—the name meant "special purpose"—were roughly the equivalent of America's Special Forces—the Army's Green Berets—and the Navy SEALs rolled into one. In the same way that the Green Berets trained Vietnamese forces like the LLDB, the spetsnaz trained agents and commandos from the militaries of Soviet allies.

Mariacher chuckled. "Okay. Remember that big mother of a harbor dredge that got taken out in Cam Ranh Bay last year?"

"Sure."

"Third largest dredge in the world," Hechinger said, "and a dozen North Vietnamese combat swimmers snuck in, planted Soviet-made limpet mines, and sunk the fucker right in the middle of a supposedly impregnable harbor."

"What's your point?"

"Guess who was in command of that detachment?"

"Oh, shit . . ."

"His name was Vinh Do Thu. He was a SEAL, Badges . . . a SEAL on *their* side."

BUSINESS REPLY MAIL

FIRST-CLASS MAIL   PERMIT #128   HARLAN, IOWA

POSTAGE WILL BE PAID BY ADDRESSEE

GolfWorld®
A GOLF DIGEST PUBLICATION

SUBSCRIBER SERVICES DEPT
P O BOX 3300
HARLAN IA 51593-2057

"It gets better," Mariacher added. "My friend, that man you capped this morning was a winner of what amounts to a North Vietnamese medal of honor. He even had his medal on him. That was the one in that red case we found."

"Congratulations, Badges," Hechinger said. "You done real good!"

Later, though, back in his quarters in the SEAL Hilton, Horner wondered. The exchange of fire had been such a damned close-run thing; he was alive only because Vinh had made a mistake, a very, very *small* mistake. Horner had made a mistake too; he shouldn't have been running blindly like that, or he wouldn't have nearly run into the guy. Maybe victory in combat was just a matter of comparing two ordinary guys and seeing who made the fewest mistakes.

He wished he could talk about it with his uncle. Why did he feel so bad?

Chapter 31

Saturday, 3 June 1967

Virginia Beach, Virginia
1450 hours

"You're going to Vietnam."

Veronica Tangretti had known the moment Steve had walked in the door. This was what she'd been afraid of for so long, but now she just felt dead inside.

"That's right," Steve told her. "Admiral Galloway offered it to me . . . you remember Joe Galloway? Looks like I'll have my orders in another week or two." He was smiling . . . the bastard was actually *smiling*, as though he'd just told her he'd won the grand prize in a sweepstakes giveaway. Veronica's hands closed into tight, painful fists and she battled not to cry.

Each time Steve had come home, on leave or literally en route from one damned duty station to another, it had been getting more difficult. This time was the worst she could remember. The man was becoming more and more a stranger who occasionally showed up on the doorstep, luggage in hand.

"Why?" she asked him. "Why do you have to go? It's not like they, they drafted you or something. My God, Steve . . . what about that training assignment I told you about? Here at Little Creek? You want to pass that up for another trip to Vietnam?"

"Look" he said, all trace of smiles gone. "Vietnam is where the action is right now. It's what's happening."

"Damn it, Steve. You make it sound like a love-in. A *happening*. It's a war, damn it. And people get killed in wars. Or have you forgotten that?"

Tangretti's lips tightened, a thin, hard line. "No. No, I haven't forgotten."

Veronica knew immediately that she'd said the wrong thing. *Again.* Sometimes . . . sometimes it seemed like Hank Richardson, Sr., was still present, a part of them, a part of their relationship, despite his death on Omaha Beach twenty-three years before. Steve was sensitive, even yet, to the fact that he'd come second, that he'd stepped into the role—and the bed—of his best friend.

She'd been thinking about that a lot these past few days, especially. June sixth was coming up, the anniversary of the Normandy invasion, and such anniversaries tended to make her introspective . . . and a little bitter. She loved Steve, loved him more than anything in this world save, just possibly, her sons . . . but the Navy, the damned Navy and its damned UDT program had stolen Steve from her just as surely as the UDT/ NCDUs had stolen Hank from her twenty-three years ago.

She was willing to grant that most of the past two decades had been okay, even fun, but the separations—frequent and often unannounced—had been brutal. Sometimes, like when Steve had been stationed at Yokosuka, in Japan, she'd been able to go along, living on base housing and sharing, in some small way, at least, in what he was doing. At other times, though, and for the vast majority of his deployments, she'd lived either in the San Diego area or here, in or near Virginia Beach, the two places where the Underwater Demolition Teams maintained their principal stateside bases, while Steve deployed to the Arctic, or to Lebanon, or to places where he wasn't even allowed to tell that he'd been to.

And since the SEAL Teams had been created—since Steve had helped create them, rather—it had been worse. She knew he'd been to Cuba during the Missile Crisis; he wasn't supposed to tell her, of course, and he hadn't, not directly . . . but she'd known. And there'd been other times when his work with the SEALs had sent him off at a moment's notice or less. There'd been that time, back in '63, in the goddamn middle of the night, when they'd literally been in each other's arms, in bed making love, when the phone had rung. Steve had answered, and fifteen minutes later he'd been gone. Someone had sent a car and driver to pick him up, and he'd been gone for three weeks after that . . . and not a word of where he'd gone or why or even whether or not he was still alive.

The SEALs hadn't killed him like the NCDU had killed Hank . . . not yet. But when the *idiot* got so damned puppy-dog happy at the prospect of going to another world hot spot, to a *war* of all goddamned things . . .

And the worst part of all was that the SEALs—thanks to Steve—had also stolen both of her sons.

"Steve," she said, suddenly very tired. "I'm sorry. I didn't mean that. It's just . . . it's the not knowing. Not knowing what's happening to you night after night after night when you're off on some secret mission or other. And you, you had to push both boys into the SEALs—"

"Now wait a minute, Veronica. I didn't push anybody—"

"Of course you did. Just by, by *being*. They see you come home in your uniform with row upon row of pretty colored ribbons on your chest, and they hear you talking about things you've done and places you've been, about meeting with the president that time, and, well, what do you expect? God, Steve, do you know what it does to me to have *three* of you gone in the SEALs?"

She was shaking, and it was all she could do to remain standing. The odds against SEALs in the kinds of missions they took part in were not good, not good at all. With the three of them in the same unit, what were the odds that she would lose one or more, sooner or later? Odds. She hated figuring the odds, but it was impossible to be a SEAL wife and not think that way sometimes.

Lately, she'd found herself regarding the possibility as something almost inevitable. Which one was it going to be? Which one would be first, Hank? Bill?

Or Steve?

"What is it you want?" he demanded, frowning. "Huh? What do you want, for me to drop the program?"

"What is so great about the program that you can't treat your wife like a human being once in a while?"

"Veronica, you know I can't just . . . just turn my back on the program. On my friends. On everything I've built. It's my career. It's more than my career. It's my *life*."

"You're almost *fifty*, for God's sake! You should be thinking about retiring, not running around in swamps playing soldier!"

He snorted. "That again! I'm not ready to be put out to pasture, Veronica. I'm a *SEAL*!"

"And what about your wife?"

"Veronica, we've had this discussion before. You can't expect me to choose between you and the Teams."

"The *Teams*! The *Teams*! I wish I'd never heard about the Teams!"

"Veronica, you're getting upset over nothing. Really! Maybe you should . . . I don't know. Go see your folks for a few days. Get out of the house, maybe . . ."

"Maybe . . . I should. And maybe I won't be back!"

"Veronica!"

"Did Hank tell you about Christmas?"

"He said . . . something about it. You left. Didn't tell anyone."

"Because I'd had it up to here with the fucking *Teams*!" The obscenity was shocking on her lips, and she saw Steve wince at the word. *Good!*

"Veronica, look . . ." He reached out to take her arm.

She slapped his hand away, and when he reached for her again, she slapped his face so hard that her hand stung. "You bastard!" she screamed through the pain and the tears. "You bastard, the Teams have taken my husband and they've taken my sons and I don't want to hear about the Teams ever again!''

"Please, honey . . .''

"Don't you touch me! You can sleep on the couch tonight, damn it!''

He hesitated, about to say something. Then she saw him reconsider and shake his head. "I don't think so,'' he said. "I'll stay on the base tonight. And until you, I mean, until we decide what to do.''

He left the house an hour later, his clothes and personal belongings in two small suitcases. She didn't say goodbye because ignoring him was one more small way to get back at him, to *hurt* him for what he'd done to her.

But she watched through parted curtains as he backed the car out of the drive and turned it . . . not toward the base, but toward the town.

Veronica knew he saw other women, knew it without having to be told. Somehow, that didn't hurt as much as knowing that the whole SEAL idea, the tough-guy image of hard men and fast women and sexy guns, had helped make him what he was now. She'd seen it in Hank. How long would it be before Bill was corrupted too?

She wondered if she even still loved him at all.

Veronica wondered if she would ever see him again, and the pain and the loss and the loneliness hit her then, and she cried as though Steve Tangretti were already dead. . . .

Friday, 30 June 1966

HQ, Military Assistance Command, Vietnam
Saigon
1205 hours

"Good talk, Steve. I knew all along you were the right man for the job.''

"Thanks, Admiral,'' Steve Tangretti said. He took a sip from the glass in his hand and tried not to make a face. No doubt it was some fancy vintage stocked to impress the VIPs, but he preferred beer. "You really pulled out the stops, sir," he went on to cover his distaste for the drink.

Rear Admiral Joseph Galloway smiled. "You know Ginny came from a real political family," he said. "I used to hate those Washington parties, back during the war, but I always seemed to end up getting dragged to the damned things. Matter of fact, Captain Metzel dragged me to one of them, and that's where we first talked seriously about Naval Combat Demolitions. I finally got it through my thick skull that the best way to expose politicians and high-ranking officers to new ideas is to get them together at a party, stuff them with good food and fine wine, and then find a way to sneak in the real agenda when they're least expecting it."

Tangretti chuckled. "Hope it works, sir. We sure as hell could use some cooperation out of some of these . . . folks." He showed his teeth in a humorless smile, and the admiral laughed.

"Don't tell me you're learning diplomacy, Mr. Tangretti," he said. "That would be too much!"

Tangretti had been in-country for less than two weeks, but things were moving fast . . . so fast that the interlude back home with Veronica had faded from his mind, though it still hung somewhere in his subconscious like a bad tooth that might flare up if probed too closely. His assignment was to take command of the unit being referred to as Det Echo, a platoon-sized unit of SEALs drawn from Team One in Coronado but scattered across a dozen different provinces as advisors to individual Provincial Reconnaissance Units. But he'd hardly had time to come to grips with that job—and the conflicts sparked by placing an old East Coast officer in charge of a bunch of West Coast pukes—before Galloway had approached him to help with another, more immediate concern, the Naval Special Warfare Symposium.

It was a pet project of Galloway's, one the admiral had been trying to organize ever since his arrival in Vietnam just after Christmas. Worried by the tales Tangretti had shared with his staff regarding the problems of getting the regular Navy—and virtually every other service in Nam—to utilize SEAL capabilities properly, Galloway had decided to tackle the problem head-on. So nobody knew what to do with the SEALs? Then teach them what SEALs could do . . . and hope they'd pick up enough of an idea of what special warfare was capable of that they'd start thinking about using the SEALs the way they would any other combat asset. Hence the symposium, scheduled to extend through the coming weekend.

And Tangretti, once again, was the man Galloway had entrusted with the task of sharing his experience . . . and his ideas. It was a flattering request, but Tangretti wasn't sure how much good it would really do. The officers attending the symposium included staffers from Saigon, base commanders, riverine force skippers, even a few Army and Air Force men and a handful of men who were probably part of Colby's CIA operation, a broad spectrum indeed. But how many of them would really care enough to retain what they heard in the lectures once they got back to their own comfortable little offices cut off from the realities of the war?

Precious few of them, he thought bitterly.

The whole problem was the way the American military mind worked these days. There were, Tangretti was convinced, two ways to wage war. One way, the traditional way, he had worked in World War II . . . outproducing the enemy, throwing army after army at him until he broke, overwhelmed by force of numbers and quantity of equipment. Bomb his cities to rubble, wear down his battalions by attrition, smash every road center, every railway, every bridge, every factory until he had nothing left with which to fight. Nuclear warfare was an extension of such tactics; the final act of World War II had been to annihilate two Japanese cities, convincing Tokyo that the Allies had the will to reduce one city after another to rubble until there was literally nothing remaining to fight for.

But there was a new type of warfare in the world, and there was a lot of evidence to suggest that this might be the way wars were going to be fought in the future, more often than not. So Tangretti had believed ever since he'd seen what the old UDTs could accomplish, back during the last years of World War II. Small teams of highly trained professionals, operating covertly behind enemy lines, possibly deep within his home territory, assassinating key leaders, blowing up key supply dumps or command-control-communications facilities or transport centers, *that* was what the SEALs were all about.

It was at once an old and a radically new kind of warfare, old because partisans and guerrillas had played a part in waging more traditional wars for centuries, new because technology was becoming more and more important, a decisive factor that could give a handful of men the firepower of a regiment with the precision of a surgeon slicing out a cancer.

Back in the early days, right after the Teams had first been put together, the SEALs had often discussed the idea in late-night bull sessions over a six-pack or three of beer. You didn't have to reduce an entire country to smoldering ruins to save it. How long would North Vietnam continue supporting the Vietcong insurgents in the south if Ho Chi Minh was capped one morning by a sniper . . . as was the guy who followed him, and the guy who followed him, and so on, leader after leader, general after general, politician after politician. Sooner or later, someone up in Hanoi would get the message, especially if he got the idea that he was next in the crosshairs.

Of course, the United States was publicly committed to the idea that assassination was murder, and not a *proper* way to wage war at all. But which, Tangretti wondered, was the more immoral: targeting a few hundred or even a few thousand enemy leaders for death, the men who made the political decisions and sent their nations' armies off to war in the first place . . . or having to fight those armies in the field while smashing their cities to rubble, burning their villages, killing their civilian relatives, defoliating their forests, starving whole populations, and visiting upon their families all of the other horrors attendant on traditional warfare? . . .

Now that he had seen the results of large-scale warfare in person—in the form of burnt-out, defoliated valleys swept clean of life by carpet bombing—Tangretti was more convinced than ever that the SEALs would be able to prove themselves here, as an alternative to mass destruction. The Army and the Air Force were seeking to win the war by hurling indiscriminate and overwhelming firepower at an enemy that most of the time they couldn't even see; how much more effective might a handful of SEALs be, given halfway decent intelligence and the freedom to operate on their own?

The biggest challenge the SEALs would be facing, Tangretti knew, was the hidebound resistance of the more conservative elements of the military high command to *anything* new or unusual. Many of the senior officers had received their baptism of fire in World War II or Korea, and tended to think in terms of massed battalions, massed artillery bombardments, massed air strikes, and infantry tactics developed in World War I or before. Territory was basic to this kind of thinking; how many villages did the enemy control, versus how many villages do we control? Lines of supply, lines of communication, lines of retreat, all nice and neat when laid out on a DOD 1:250,000 Joint Operations Graphic.

But JOG maps couldn't possibly show the reality of this war. Back in World War II it had been possible to point to a town or an island on a map and say "this place is enemy held," or "the front line is here." That kind of thinking just didn't work any more, and the military's old guard was only just beginning to realize that.

SEALs didn't need to worry about front lines. Intelligence. Insertion. Ambush. Extraction. And overwhelming firepower brought to bear on one tiny and precisely defined target . . . not whole cities. Those were the focus for modern, small-unit tactics.

Tangretti was looking forward to applying them to warfare in Vietnam. The PRU program, now, was an obvious place to start. Colby's project envisioned the irregular Vietnamese units functioning both as intelligence-gathering networks on a countrywide scale, and as a quick-reaction force that could take advantage of that information and strike quickly, while it was still valid. *Exactly* what Tangretti had been urging as the best way to use the SEALs in the Rung Sat when he was locked up in Bucklew's NOSG office back at Coronado. With SEALs acting as advisors to the native PRUs, the same principle could be applied on a vastly greater scale.

Of course, the idea was likely to meet plenty of opposition. It relied on Vietnamese forces rather than good old American firepower . . . and on the same unconventional tactics the SEALs had been baffling their more hidebound superiors with for over a year now. And there were rumors that the CIA was actively planning to use the project to start mounting kidnappings and assassinations of Vietcong political and military leaders—the VCI, or Vietcong Infrastructure, as the agency called them—on a wide scale. If it worked, they'd be heroes. If not . . . things could get dicey for the Americans involved in the new project. The war was already unpopular back home, and once questions of morality got mixed in with those of national policy, anything could happen.

And Steve Tangretti's Det Echo would be squarely in the middle of the controversy.

He looked around the room again, taking in the assortment of officers decked out in dress uniforms with row after row of fancy ribbons that mostly signified skill at brown-nosing in the line of duty. If a few days of talks could get any of this crowd to see the SEALs and their role as vital, it might just be worth the effort.

The Teams needed all the help they could get, these days.

An admiral, looking like a rumpled bear in whites about a size too small for his massive frame, raised a hand and hailed Galloway in a voice that reminded Tangretti of a California earthquake. "Joe, you old dog! Don't tell me you finally got out of that damned Pentagon office you used to gripe about so much?"

Galloway smiled as the admiral came up. "Yes, sir," he said. "I think I finally understood the Emancipation Proclamation the day the orders came through. I didn't even wait to see if I was getting forty acres and a mule!"

The big admiral guffawed. "Hell, boy, they had you buried in that place longer than some of the classified files. What're you up to in these parts?"

"Mostly running shows like this one, sir," Galloway said. "And trying to persuade officers like Lieutenant Tangretti here to get on the lecture circuit a little more often. Have you met Admiral Bledsoe, Lieutenant?"

"No, sir," Tangretti said.

"Ah. Well, George Bledsoe was a commander on the planning staff for Operation Torch back when I was a loud-mouthed lieutenant with screwy ideas and a big mouth."

"They turned out to be pretty good ideas, Joe," Bledsoe said. "But you have to admit you went out on a limb pitching them in front of the brass instead of keeping quiet and making sure the coffee cups were all topped off."

Galloway shrugged. "What did I know? I was a reservist back then. I figured the worst they'd do is put me on a destroyer fighting U-boats, or something. Instead they exiled me to the Pentagon!"

Bledsoe studied Tangretti for a moment. "Heard your talk this morning, Lieutenant," he said. "You're not one of these new kids pitching a lot of fancy bells and whistles. Seems to me you've been at this for a while . . . and you really believe all this about special warfare and commando tactics and whatnot.''

"Yes, sir," Tangretti said. "I certainly do."

"Hmph. I wasn't too sure about your SEALs when I got here. The guy who had my slot at USNAVFORV before I got here, Captain Garland, he said your lot were nothing but trouble. My aide tells me the same thing. But I've seen some of the summaries of what your boys have been doing in the Rung Sat, and down in the Mekong. And after your little talk today . . . well, maybe I'll have to rethink a few things."

"I hope you do, sir," Tangretti said. "Properly used, SEALs represent the best bang for your buck. . . ."

He trailed off as Bledsoe turned away, distracted by the approach of another officer in crisp dress whites. "Admiral . . . I've lined up the dinner reservations you wanted with the ambassador for next week. . . ."

The voice was jarringly familiar, and Tangretti turned to stare at the newcomer with undisguised hostility.

Peter Howell.

He'd known that Howell had managed to wangle a staff assignment in Saigon despite his setback at NOSG with Galloway, but Tangretti hadn't given him any thought since the day he'd left the office at Coronado to report to BUD/S training. It seemed the younger lieutenant always landed on his feet. A slot as aide to the COMUSNAVFORV would look good on the man's resume when it came under scrutiny by a promotion board.

Tangretti met the man's eyes, but Howell didn't even acknowledge his existence. That was fine by him. . . .

Bledsoe had mentioned an aide who had argued against relying on the SEALs. So Howell still had the same old chip on his shoulder. Fortunately his boss had enough of an open mind to listen to the truth.

There was hope for the SEALs after all, if a few more like Bledsoe were willing to give them a chance to prove themselves.

Victoria Hotel
Saigon
2312 Hours

The pool had the same familiar greenish tinge to the water, and the bar girls still had the same predatory smiles and calculating giggles. *Ah, the old Victoria*, Tangretti thought as he sipped his beer. *Nice to know some things never change*.

Back when he'd been working with the LDNN he'd lived at the hotel full time, and it had become a popular hangout for SEALs in Saigon since his day. Tangretti had booked a room on the sixth floor for the duration of the symposium, but when he'd returned from MACV headquarters after a full day's lecturing, he'd been reluctant to face that tiny, lonely room.

It had been a long time since he'd missed Veronica this much.

Oh, he'd *missed* her, all during the stay at Coronado, especially when their long-distance quarrel had started to turn ugly, right after Bill's enlistment. Had the boy really only been in a year now? It seemed so much longer.

But even during the worst times, he'd always been sure he would be able to win her back if he could just *talk* to her, face to face. There had always been that feeling that the old Tangretti charm could fix anything, from a three-day pass to a tottering marriage. It had never let him down before.

But now it had. He'd cut short his leave in Virginia and reported in to Saigon early, after that last fight. And for the first time in a long, long time Steve Tangretti really wasn't sure he'd be able to put the pieces back together. That left an empty place inside him.

He'd known that place before, during the war, after Hank Richardson had died on Omaha Beach. It was that empty spot that had turned him into a wild man, bent on drinking and brawling and screwing and doing anything and everything he could to forget the emptiness, but none of it had worked. After he'd come close to actually raping a nurse during a stupid UDT prank in the South Pacific, Tangretti had realized just how far out of control he'd slipped, and somehow he'd managed to take charge of his life again. The Teams had helped him then, and the feeling of camaraderie and shared dangers that made those combat swimmers his brothers. But that had faded after the war, with the UDTs cut to the bare bones and the realities of peacetime service changing everything but the hole that still gaped in his life.

Veronica had changed that. He'd kept in touch with her after Hank's death, of course, and tried to help with Hank Junior even though the Richardson family was rich and eager to claim their new grandson. The trouble was, they'd been less willing to accept Veronica, who was hardly their idea of a proper bride for their dead son. *She* had needed him then, to help her cope with things . . . and, in return, he'd found out that *he* had needed her to fill up that empty spot and make him whole again.

Now she might be gone for good . . . gone, because he'd wanted her and the Teams both, but he'd started taking her for granted. And that empty spot was staring at him again, a darkness in his mind and in his heart.

He didn't want to go back down that path again.

Tangretti finished his beer. Hank Junior had finished his tour in Nam and was back in the States, posted to Vietnamese Language School. He was already talking about putting in another tour as soon as the chance presented itself. And Bill had graduated out of BUD/S into Team One. His new unit, Bravo Platoon, had drawn orders to get ready for a tour in Vietnam starting the end of this year. So all of Veronica's fears were bound to keep feeding on themselves. There was nothing he could do about any of that. Nothing . . . except maybe agree to leave the service, the way she wanted him to.

But now he had to wonder: would she take him back if he retired? Or would he give up the Teams only to find out that she still wouldn't have him?

Tangretti couldn't lose *both*. And there were no guarantees where Ronnie was concerned, not any more. That didn't leave him with too many options.

He drained the glass and slammed it on the table, then stood slowly. One way or the other, he had at least six months before this tour would be over, maybe longer depending on the vagaries of the war. And until the tour was up he had to focus all his attention on his duty.

But he had to find an answer. . . .

A pretty Vietnamese bar girl in a miniskirt and halter top caught his eye and gave him a suggestive wink. For a moment, Tangretti was tempted. But then he shook his head.

He knew the only one who could fill the empty place in his life was back in Virginia, and this time there was no cheap substitute that could take her place. Not even for a night.

Chapter 32

Saturday, 9 December, 1967

**Bravo Platoon, SEAL Team One
Nha Be, Rung Sat Special Zone
1000 hours**

Lieutenant Edward Charles Baxter stood just inside the gate leading to the Nha Be SEAL compound and laughed.

WELCOME TO THE NHA BE SUMMER RESORT.
FOR YOUR PLEASURE WE PROVIDE
    SWIMMING FACILITIES: DELIGHTFUL FROLICS UN-
    DER THE SHIPS IN THE HARBOR.
    BOATING EXCURSIONS: TRY ONE OF OUR FAMOUS
    MOONLIGHT CRUISES DOWN THE RIVER.
    CAMPING TRIPS: ENJOY A NIGHT OUT IN THE
    OPEN AIR AS YOU SIT COMFORTABLY AND COM-
    PANIONABLY BESIDE A TRAIL OR A STREAM.

The sign had elements of the same humor that had led to the UDT tradition of erecting their ''Welcome Marines'' banner on enemy beaches just ahead of a Marine landing. It was encouraging, he thought . . . *very* encouraging, for it suggested that morale among the Team One SEALs was considerably higher now than it had been during his first tour.

Lots more had changed besides morale, too. The SEALs had a mission now, and it was being supported, albeit reluctantly sometimes, by the Navy command.

Baxter thought back to the way things had been almost two years ago—his constant battles with the brass, the piss-poor intelligence, the knowledge that sooner or later one of his boys was going to die because they weren't being used for operations they'd been trained to handle—and he wondered how they'd managed to get anything done at all. Hell, he'd recommended that the SEALs pull out of Vietnam entirely. From what he'd seen and heard, particularly from other SEALs returning from Vietnam, the situation was still far from perfect—especially in the area of intelligence—but things were getting better. In AOs where the SEALs were allowed to fully develop their own intelligence sources, they were scoring success after success.

And the word was that the Men with Green Faces had become every VC's blackest personal nightmare, high-tech boogeymen who might be behind any tree, inside any shadow, beneath any stretch of placid water in canal or stream, silent killers who struck out of the night suddenly, invisibly, and with deadly accuracy.

When there were SEALs about, the night no longer belonged to Charlie.

"All the comforts, eh, Lieutenant?"

Baxter turned from his study of the sign and grinned at Chief Mike Spencer. "They forgot to mention water skiing on the placid waters of the exotic Soi Rap River, Chief."

Twelve more men clustered around the sign—the other members of Bravo Platoon, SEAL Team One.

"Okay, people," Baxter called. "Let's let 'em know the SEALs have arrived."

"Hoo-yah!" several shouted in concert.

Spencer's eyes narrowed. "What do you think, sir? March 'em?"

"Shit, Chief," Baxter replied. "Since when do SEALs *march*?"

Spencer seemed to relax a bit and nodded. "Not after they're out of BUD/S, anyway." Turning, he addressed the platoon. "Okay, men. We straggle . . . but I want it to be a proper *military* straggle."

Several in the group laughed at that. "Yeah, leave marching to the Marines," Lucky Luciano sang out.

"Boot camp chicken shit," Doc Randolph added. A chorus of agreement punctuated the statement.

Baxter surveyed his new command with mingled pride and expectation. A number of them, including Spencer, Luciano, and Randolph, had been in Nam before. The newbies—over half of the men had come out of BUD/S just six months ago—would learn the ropes real fast with the old hands to show them.

Turning from the sign, Baxter squared his shoulders and strode into the camp with a feeling both of homecoming and of renewal. It seemed strange to be once more on the riverine base where he had commanded the first direct action SEAL Team in Vietnam almost two full years before. If the SEALs had changed in that time, well, so had he. Some of the rough edges had been knocked off during the past couple of years, both by his experiences during his first tour of duty in Vietnam and afterward.

As he walked toward Nha Be's administration building at the head of his platoon, he took the time to examine the base. Beyond the perimeter, the silt-brown waters of the river were much the same as they'd been two years ago, as was the smear of poisonous green on the horizon to the southeast, the edge of the Rung Sat.

The base itself, however, had changed quite a bit. The dock area had been expanded and upgraded and both the piers and the anchorage were now crowded with ships and small craft of bewildering variety. The PBRs were still there, in greater numbers now. There were dozens of armored LCMs and converted landing craft of various types, including a huge, shaggy-looking river monitor that looked more like something out of the American Civil War than a twentieth-century naval combat support vessel. Nearby, the low, jet-black lines of several STABs moored to the pier provided a sharp contrast to those of their larger, slower and clumsier neighbors.

Ashore, new buildings had been added, including a barracks that looked like a block of apartment buildings. When he'd been stationed here before, the place had seemed sleepy, isolated, and remote, despite the fact that it was only a few miles from the swarming mobs of Saigon. It was a lot busier now, with lots more people, more noise, and more bustle.

He'd read the reports and seen the numbers, so the changes weren't a complete surprise, but actually seeing the place was quite different from going over columns of figures. The Navy's presence in Vietnam, like that of the other services, had swelled enormously, especially during the past year. If the war in Vietnam could be won by sheer military muscle and by a dogged determination to get things done, then victory was damn near assured.

Now all that remained was to convince Charlie of the fact.

The SEALs were a large and powerful part of the argument.

The Navy was expanding the SEAL program with dizzying speed, increasing the number of BUD/S classes for both SEAL Teams One and Two, as well as boosting the size of individual classes. There was even talk now of initiating a SEAL draft, in essence snagging recruits on their way to the UDT and putting them in the SEALs.

The SEAL program, it appeared, had at long last received the both the financial backing and the official approval that it needed, thanks primarily to the successes both Teams had eked out for themselves under grim and difficult conditions. No less a celebrity than General William C. Westmoreland, the commanding officer of MACV, had said of the SEALs earlier that year, "I would like to have a thousand more like them." And for the past year, BUD/S had been trying to oblige.

"Hey, Lieutenant?" Seaman Bill Tangretti said, looking around as they reached the grinder in front of Admin. "This doesn't look as primitive as you were saying it was."

"Yeah," RM/2 Bob Gordon said, grinning. "Or was all that stuff you were handing us back at school just sea stories?"

"It's true, youngster," Chief Spencer growled. "And you can believe me that fancy buildings aren't going to make things one bit easier."

"Heads up."

A young, muscular-looking lieutenant wearing SEAL tiger-stripe camies came through the Admin door and walked up to the group, accompanied by a stocky, weathered-faced chief. "Jeff Phillips," the officer said. "Echo Platoon. I gather you're our relief?"

"Ed Baxter." He neither saluted nor offered to shake hands. VC snipers not only knew American saluting protocol, but they were smart enough to pick the senior people out of a group by watching to see who shook hands with whom. "Bravo Platoon, Team One."

"Welcome aboard. Chief Guthries here'll show you men to your quarters and get you fixed up. Lieutenant, if you'd come with me? We'll get you checked in with Admin."

"We were just commenting on the improvements you guys've made around here," he said to Phillips as they walked together into Admin.

"You were here before, right?"

"That's right. Det Delta, February through August, '66."

"Old timers, huh?"

"Some of us."

"You'll find it's a whole new war over here. You guys look out for yourselves, okay?"

Baxter found the warning disquieting, but it wasn't enough to overturn his feeling of quiet optimism and determination.

"We'll do that," he said. "But Charlie and the REMFs had better watch out themselves."

Sunday, 17 December, 1967

SEAL Compound
Tre Noc, Mekong Delta
1330 hours

Lieutenant j.g. Daniel Mariacher climbed off the bus and took a look around. Yup . . . same old place, not much changed since his last tour here. The rest of his men were gathering behind him, seabags slung over their shoulders, the old hands like Richardson and Finnegan joking about the last time they'd been here.

A Navy lieutenant commander was waiting there to greet them. "You guys our new SEALs? Replacements for Fifth Platoon?"

"That's right," Mariacher replied. "Eighth Platoon, SEAL Team Two, reporting for duty."

"I'm Lieutenant Commander Schwartz," the officer said.

"Welcome to Tre Noc, Lieutenant. And Merry Christmas!"

Mariacher's eyes widened slightly. He'd been so busy for the last several weeks, getting his team ready for the deployment to Vietnam, that he'd completely forgotten the approaching holiday. "Hadn't even thought about that, sir. Merry Christmas yourself."

"Not much of a Christmas present, I must say, getting stationed in this rat hole."

"Ah, it's not so bad."

"Well, I'll be damned glad to see the last of it, let me tell you!"

"I gather Captain Benson's gone now."

"Yup. Captain Voight is CO of TF 116 now."

"How is he?" Mariacher was wondering if the chicken shit and the Mickey Mouse were as thick here as they'd been last year. "What's he like?"

"Good man," Schwartz said, nodding approval. "Career officer. Annapolis."

The corner of Mariacher's mouth twitched upward ever so slightly. "I'm sure we'll get on splendidly."

But he knew differently. Annapolis? Hell, chicken shit city, with no room for mustangs or individualists, no room at all for innovation. Well, he already had some ideas about how to get along with the brass hats this time around and still carry out some useful missions.

After he and his men had checked in with the base admin office, they made their way back to the Tre Noc barracks. There was a new SEAL ready room now, and cold beer waiting in the refrigerator. A small, potted palm tree had been decorated with spent brass, ranging from empty 9-mm cartridges to big .50-caliber machine-gun shell casings. SEAL Team Two's Fifth Platoon, it seemed, had gone to some lengths to make Eighth Platoon feel welcome. On one wall was posted a large, hand-lettered sign:

PEOPLE WHO KILL FOR MONEY
   ARE PROFESSIONALS.
PEOPLE WHO KILL FOR FUN ARE SADISTS.
PEOPLE WHO KILL FOR MONEY AND FUN
   ARE SEALS.

The incoming SEALs got a chuckle out of that. It was a sign that had already received a certain amount of notoriety, ever since the *New York Times* had quoted it in an article.

It was articles like that, Mariacher thought, that were probably responsible for the Navy sending him out on that damned PR tour.

For the past year, Mariacher had been a kind of good-will ambassador for the SEALs. Beginning in June, shortly after his return from his first deployment to Nam, the Navy had had him out on public relations tours, crisscrossing the country and talking about the SEALs . . . an attempt, at least in part, to undo damage to the SEAL image caused by articles like the one in the *Times*.

It was not an assignment he'd been particularly happy with. What the hell did SEALs need with public relations, anyway? Whether on an op or between missions, SEALs thrived on secrecy, thrived on the cloak of night and the invisibility it provided. He didn't like being in the public eye, and he didn't like putting the program there either . . . especially with the public climate the way it was right now back in the States.

Mariacher grimaced with distaste at the memory of one luncheon . . . a press club do at a hotel in downtown Chicago that had been open to the public, a chance, he'd been told, to let the public know what was really going on in Vietnam, to let them know the importance of supporting the military's policies there.

That in itself had probably been a mistake. Mariacher wasn't personally convinced that American involvement in Nam in the first place had been a bright idea, though he knew better than to make an issue of that. His feeling, though, his very strong feeling, was that since America was involved in that nasty little war the only course of action that made any sense at all was to *finish* the damned thing, to stop pissing away resources, money, and men in this endless series of step-by-step build-ups and good-money-after-bad escalations.

So far as the military's policies in Vietnam were concerned, he was convinced the Pentagon had it all exactly bass-ackwards. What was needed was not more B-52 raids on Hanoi, but a small and secret army of SEALs to slip in all along the North Vietnamese coast. Inside of a month, there wouldn't be a single Russian or Chinese cargo ship left afloat, not a single bridge still standing, not a single command post left to direct NVA and VC activities in the south. A small and elite team of well-trained SEALs could go places, see things, and carry out surgically precise missions that B-52s simply could not manage.

But he'd played the good soldier, had tried to carry out his orders and do what they'd told him. In Chicago, he'd stood up to give his spiel, resplendent in his dress uniform with the shiny new lieutenant's bars, and begun talking, describing the SEALs as modern, high-tech warriors who could make a real difference in the way the war was being fought. A young man—one of the new counterculture types, long-haired, bearded, wearing beads, various bits of ironmongery, and a big peace symbol sewn to the back of his denim jacket—had stood up in the front row. "Isn't it true that you are a member of a top secret commando organization trained to assassinate citizens of foreign powers?" the kid had demanded, his voice strident, and powerful enough to carry to every corner of the room "Isn't it true that you and your so-called elite commando unit are guilty of butchering innocent civilians, of burning their towns, of destroying their crops and fishing boats and livelihoods? Isn't it true—"

Mariacher had leaned forward and grasped the mike at the podium. It was clear that the speaker in the audience was simply looking for a chance to spout off and maybe grab some publicity for himself and his cause; if Mariacher hesitated, the guy might go on all night. "Isn't it true," Mariacher had said, using the room's sound system to drown the guy's words out with a full-volume blast from the speakers. There was a harsh squeal of feedback from the amps, and he moved his lips back from the mike just a little. "Isn't it true that *you* are a strutting, puffed-up, pompous little dumb-fuck of an asshole?"

The guy had gaped at Mariacher, thunderstruck. The rest of the audience, many of them reporters, the rest businessmen and women who'd received invitations, sat in still, stunned silence.

"You want to hear about butchered civilians, dipshit?" he'd gone on, relentless. "Let me tell you about what Charlie likes to do to the civilians in villages that don't share his political persuasion. . . ."

"You can't do that!" the man had screamed, lunging out

of his seat and running toward the podium. The silence in the room suddenly dissolved into babbling pandemonium. Two hotel security people had intercepted the guy.

"Can't do what, shit head?" Mariacher had asked, genuinely perplexed. What was this guy on, anyway?

"You can't call me names like that! . . .*"*

The security men had hustled the kid out . . . but at the same time several of the naval personnel in charge of his PR tour— he thought of them as his handlers—came onstage and led him away. His speech had been summarily canceled.

Later, he'd received a stiff lecture from Lieutenant Commander Dennison, his boss handler. "Jeez, Mariacher," Dennison had told him, more exasperated than angry. "You and Patton!"

"What? What about me and Patton?"

"General Patton used, ah, colorful language, and it got him into a world of shit."

"I thought he just punched out one of his men."

"Maybe that too, I don't know. But I do know that you've got to watch your mouth."

"What about my mouth?"

"Mariacher, you *don't* use the F-word in public, okay? Not in front of women. Not in front of the press. Not in front of civilians, even if you disagree with them, you got that? This is the *real* world, Mariacher, not the jungle, okay?"

And what the fuck do you know about the real world? Mariacher had wondered, looking into the spectacled, skinny face of the PR officer. Dennison was a kid, younger than Mariacher by at least five years, despite being the senior officer. College educated, an officer by the grace of NROTC, his tours of duty so far, Mariacher had learned, had included the Navy Yards in Washington, across the Potomac at the Pentagon, and Roosevelt Roads, Puerto Rico. The two of them, Mariacher and Dennison, were from radically different worlds. Hell, in some ways, ignoring the fact that the PR officer at least was willing to wear his country's uniform, Dennison probably had more in common with the protester than he did with Mariacher.

All things considered, Mariacher decided that he'd have been happier back in Vietnam. It was sometimes difficult to tell friend from foe there, but at least they weren't his own people, his own countrymen. To Mariacher, that protester's attack had smelled a lot like treason. Sure, he understood well that Vietnam was not a popular war back home, not in the sense that World War II had been a "good war" against tyranny and foreign dictators. Hell, most Americans could care less about who governed Vietnam, north *or* south, and Mariacher himself was of the opinion that people got the government they deserved.

But Mariacher was also used to the ethic that said that men in uniform should be respected for what they stood for, for what they did, for the fact that they were willing to fight for their country and their flag.

Of course, sentiments like that were fast becoming old-fashioned back in the World. Students were burning their draft cards and holding mass rallies, attacking the government, the military, and the establishment in an accelerating tempo of protest and demonstration. It was beginning to look like a revolution . . . a civil war as divisive as Vietnam's, if not nearly so bloody.

Mariacher didn't begrudge the demonstrators their free speech. Hell, everyone ought to be able to sound off about how he or she felt. But since when, he wondered, had *rudeness* become an integral part of the common culture?

In another town, during his PR tour of the country, kids in love beads and long hair had picketed the theater where he was to deliver his presentation. As he'd walked through the line, wearing his uniform, several had jeered at him: "Fascist! Butcher! Pig!" The line suddenly took on the appearance of a gauntlet, and Mariacher had almost reached for the holstered sidearm that wasn't there.

Then one long-haired youth had gotten close enough to spit on his uniform.

Swiftly, before his handlers could stop him, Mariacher had spun, reached out, and grabbed the kid by the hair. The kid had yelled, face red with fury, and thrown a punch; Mariacher had deftly snagged the incoming wrist with his free hand and applied a practiced touch to the ulnar nerve, a martial arts control grip that transformed the kid's yell into a shriek of pain. Gently levering the hand back, controlling the protester with a steady, rocking pressure on that nerve, Mariacher had guided him to his knees on the sidewalk, then used a handful of dirty blond hair to wipe the spit off his jacket.

Mariacher smiled at the memory. He was pretty sure that the theater incident was what had finally gotten him off of that particular shit detail. That speech had been cancelled too . . . and Mariacher had been chewed out afterward in no uncertain terms. "Mariacher, if you don't learn how to control yourself, they're gonna ship you back to Vietnam! Shit, that was assault you pulled out there tonight! The cops could heave your ass into jail and the Navy would never be able to save you! Hell, you damned near started a riot at that theater!"

"That punk attacked me. I was simply defending myself."

"That 'punk,' as you call him, was a citizen exercising his right of free speech."

"By slobbering on me? Shit, Lieutenant, that scraggle-faced asshole should get down on his knees and thank me! He's lucky I was in a mellow mood tonight. I could have killed him!"

The man shuddered, as though he believed Mariacher might actually have done such a thing. "Well, thank God for small favors, Mariacher, and thank you especially for your restraint. But damn it, man, stop behaving like an animal in public!"

Mariacher had thought about that incident for a long time. Who was the animal . . . the SEAL back from war, or the college student with the manners of a chimp at the zoo?

When they'd finally offered him command of the new-formed Eighth Platoon, and a free hand in picking men to fill it out, he'd leaped at the chance. Mariacher had had quite enough of peace demonstrators, hippies, and protests against the immoral war in Vietnam.

An immoral war? He shook his head at the thought, disgusted. Looked at one way, no war was moral, not when you thought about what it did to the ordinary people, the civilians caught in the middle. But like it or not, war was a part of human nature and human history, and all of the protests, all of the feely-grabby love-ins and smoke-ins and peace rallies in the world weren't going to change that.

War was the SEALs' profession, was Mariacher's profession.

And both were very good at what they did.

Chapter 33

Tuesday, 9 January 1968

Eighth Platoon, SEAL Team Two
SEAL Team Two Barracks
Tre Noc
1330 hours

"Rise and shine, night owls, rise and shine! Drop your cocks and grab your socks. Let's *go*! Let's *go*! Let's *go*!"

Richardson groaned and opened his eyes. Reveille already? He squinted at his watch. Early afternoon . . . the middle of the night for SEALs.

Chief Horner went to each of the other three racks in the cube. "All right, you squirrels, out of your trees! Move it! Move it!"

"Just like fucking boot camp," RN/3 James Patterson said, rolling out of his top rack.

"Nah," GM/3 Tony Huerra said. "The CPOs were prettier in boot camp. I remember. I was just dreaming I was there."

Horner kicked his rack. "This is a mission alert, people," Horner growled at them when he was sure he had their attention. "Grab your gear. Briefing at 1530 hours. Let's get hot!"

"Let's go kill things!" TM/2 Craig Selby shouted, and the others laughed.

Richardson was fully awake now. Since Mariacher had taken over planning the SEAL ops up and down the Bassac, missions tended to materialize out of nowhere, as quick-paced as the hammer of your pulse in combat, as sudden and as unexpected as a SEAL ambush. Security in the camp was tight, so tight that no one knew about an impending mission save Mariacher and one or two others until the actual day of the op.

Two hours. Time enough to shave and shower and grab a cup of battery acid before heading down to the arms locker and drawing his gear.

Richardson got up and began getting dressed.

SEAL Team Two Briefing Room
Tre Noc
1541 hours

"*Unless otherwise directed*," Mariacher said, stressing the words as he read from the copy of the mission orders on the clipboard in his hand, "Alpha Squad of Eighth Platoon, SEAL Team Two, will proceed down the Bassac to the general vicinity of Juliet Crossing, and there set an ambush for expected VC traffic operating on the Phu Non Canal, just inside the U-Minh Forest opposite Cu Lao May Island."

The six enlisted men gathered in the platoon's briefing room, "the bull pen," chuckled. The orders Mariacher had written, known now as "UNODIRs" because they started with the words "unless otherwise directed," had become famous at Tre Noc, a classic piece of misdirection that actually took advantage of the ponderous, molasses-slow nature of the military bureaucracy. By writing the orders with that heading, by submitting them to the Ops Staff just hours before the SEALs were scheduled to leave the base to carry out the mission, Mariacher all but insured that the SEALs would have a free hand because they would be gone before anyone back at headquarters got around to rewriting or vetoing them. Few junior officers—and not that many senior ones, either—would call a halt to a mission already underway unless they had a damned good reason to do so. In any bureaucracy it was always simpler to go with the flow, to ride events rather than to try to direct them.

So long as the SEALs continued to bring home successes that the brass at Tre Noc could crow about to Saigon, no one was going to interfere too much in the Teams' efforts. Success was its own justification.

And the SEALs of Eighth Platoon had scored plenty of

successes since their arrival just a month before. The entire platoon had raided Tan Dinh Island on the day after Christmas, their first op since arriving in Vietnam, and the first of Mariacher's UODs. They'd carried out several more raids and ambushes during the next week, bagging a total of six Vietcong, and Alpha Squad had killed five more in one engagement on 4 January. They were bringing in prisoners too, as well as plenty of confiscated weapons, captured documents, and first-hand intelligence about the entire AO.

Mariacher was intensely proud of his boys. By now, they knew each other so well, knew each other's moods and thoughts and pains and ways of doing things, that they could almost read one anothers' minds. Anything as clumsy as spoken language was damned near superfluous.

As he spoke, he took the time to study each man in the squad, making mental notes to himself. He'd been lucky enough to land four old hands of his original Second Platoon bunch—two good chiefs, Horner and Brubaker, plus Roger Reynolds and Hank Richardson. In setting up Eight Platoon's two squads, he'd decided to split up his experienced assets, placing Brubaker and Reynolds in Bravo Squad, while Horner and Richardson went to Alpha. Those experienced personnel—in particular the chiefs—had become the heart and soul of the two squads, steady men who would get the job done, no matter what.

Alpha Squad's newbies were settling in well. "Pit-pat" Patterson, "Hairball" Huerra, and "Slinger" Gunn were all three former UDT men. The only one Mariacher had any doubts at all about was Craig Selby, the squad's new Stoner man who'd come to the SEAL program straight out of boot camp. He was a quiet guy, not really the physical type, but in one way or another he seemed obsessed with the need to prove himself in combat.

The others had all proven themselves more than capable, and Mariacher had no worry that any of them was going to pull some bone-headed John Wayne stunt; Selby, though, was still largely an unknown quantity, even though he'd seen plenty of action already just in the past few weeks. His BUD/S scores were good; more to the point, he showed an engaging enthusiasm, an almost puppylike eagerness to please. But Mariacher feared that at least part of that enthusiasm arose from Selby's determination to prove himself . . . whether to himself or to someone else, Mariacher wasn't yet sure.

The trouble was that combat was a bad place to deliberately try proving anything. The proving either happened or it didn't; trying to force it was a great way of getting yourself killed.

Richardson seemed to have adopted the new guy, maybe because they were both from military families. That was fine with Mariacher. SEAL recruits were introduced to the buddy system in BUD/S, and in his opinion there was no better way to steady a new guy until he'd shaken down in a few firefights.

They'd seen firefights in plenty on this deployment already and would see plenty more. Selby had acquitted himself well under fire, and Mariacher was beginning to believe he was going to work out just fine.

The kid just needed a bit more seasoning.

Swiftly, Mariacher continued running through the pre-mission brief. Met claimed the sky would be overcast tonight . . . well, they might be right *some* day. Air temp. Water temp. No moon. They'd be operating at slack tide. The river current would be running at about five knots. Terrain types: heavy jungle, thick brush, and the river itself. Nothing new there. No special terrain features or obstacles. Their insertion craft would be a PBR, with a second to provide fire support if they needed it.

Their target had been fingered by Intelligence, a sampan convoy coming down the maze of canals south of the Bassac. Army Intel had passed the word to expect three to five sampans carrying ten to fifteen armed VC, ammunition, and other supplies.

Tonight, however, the run would not be going through as scheduled.

SEAL Team Two Barracks
Tre Noc
1715 hours

Torpedoman Second Class Craig Selby gave his gear a final check. The SEALs were gathering their gear for that night's mission, drawing ammunition, and giving their weapons a final strip-down and cleaning. He paid particular attention to his Stoner, wiping and oiling each part with loving care, then hand-checking the rolls of linked 5.56-mm cartridges.

He would leave nothing to chance . . . *nothing*.

Craig Selby was the son of Conrad Selby . . . *Colonel* Conrad Selby who, as a lieutenant in command of a Marine rifle company during the long march back from Pusan, had blown up two ChiCom machine-gun nests with hand grenades, then carried one of his wounded men to safety on his back. His exploits had won him a promotion, a Purple Heart, and eventually the Congressional Medal of Honor, and had made him the hometown hero of Delmont, Iowa.

Craig had been seven when his father had come home from Korea, just old enough to have been afflicted with a serious case of hero worship. Naturally enough, everyone in the family had always known that Craig would be joining the Marines. When he'd failed the physical—high blood pressure, they'd said—it had felt like the end of the world. The fact that the Navy had accepted him hadn't helped. If anything, that had almost made things worse.

For his father, too. The idea that his oldest son hadn't been good enough for the Marines had gnawed at him like a cancer and made an already distant relationship with Craig more strained and distant still. The colonel had always had a problem relating with his three kids in anything like a normal family relationship. The kids had been brought up calling him "sir" and had stood at attention while delivering their daily reports on what they'd learned in school.

Craig wanted desperately to please his father. For him, that blue ribbon with the white stars his father wore perched atop all the rest of the colored bars on his dress uniform had become the unattainable Holy Grail of his own career. Winning the coveted CMH might finally be the way to get his father to notice him, to give him a sincere "well done!"

When the Navy had accepted him, Selby had immediately volunteered for the SEALs, a way, he thought, to make up for the shame of being a Marine reject. His father had scarcely acknowledged the fact, however, and ever since BUD/S, Selby had been striving to push himself harder . . . and harder.

Mariacher, his new CO, had warned him about taking risks. For Craig Selby, though, the chances he took in firefights weren't chances so much as they were opportunities, *testings* of his own mettle. Once, when he was fifteen, he'd deliberately held his hand in a fire to see how much pain he could stand without flinching or showing emotion and had gotten a nasty second-degree burn on his palm and wrist. Combat was like that, the ultimate testing of body, mind, and spirit.

The receiver group of his Mk 23 Commando snapped smoothly into place, the action working with a sweet, clean *snick-snack.* Gunfire banged and clattered outside; the last of the SEALs were test-firing their weapons on the range overlooking the river. It was taken for granted that VC observers were watching the base, but since the SEALs spent a fair amount of time on the range every day anyway, the testing wouldn't attract undue notice.

Patterson entered the barracks, unslinging his M60. "Hey, Craig," he called. "Five gets ya ten it's a no-show for the gooks tonight!"

"You're on," Selby replied, grinning back at the other SEAL. "Tonight we're gonna kick ass and take names. I feel it in my bones, man."

"Shit," Patterson said, laughing. "If they show, we're gonna kick ass and take initials, 'cause—"

". . . we'll be moving too fast to take names," Selby finished, chorusing the old joke's punchline with Patterson. He snapped a full magazine into his M-16, slapping it home on the palm of his hand. The blow stung. "They'll show."

SEAL Team Two Mess Hall
Tre Noc
1840 hours

Jim Horner set his tray on the table in the mess hall and dropped into the seat next to Hank Richardson. His meal, as usual, consisted of rice and fish, a trick he'd learned from Chief Brubaker on their previous tour. The VC claimed to be able to smell Imperialist beef-eating Americans from kilometers away; that claim might be propaganda, but many of the SEALs took it seriously enough to have adopted diets as close to what the native Vietnamese ate as possible. For Horner, that didn't extend to generous dollops of *nuoc mam* on his food; as he liked to put it, the idea was *not* to be smelled a mile off.

For some SEALs, the diet had adopted an almost mystical

aura, a means of helping them somehow adopt the psychic personas of their enemies. Roger Reynolds, for instance, over in Bravo Squad. Reynolds was part Indian, and eating Vietnamese food had become a way to capture their spirits, as he liked to say with a dark and menacing grin. Others rejected the whole notion as unscientific mush . . . but even they ate LRRP rations instead of fresh meat.

Horner's attitude fell somewhere between the two. He knew for a fact it was possible to smell fresh meat on an American's breath in the same way a nonsmoker could smell cigarettes on a smoker's breath and clothes. Somehow, too, eating fish and rice seemed to help him get in tune with the way the locals thought, as though it made him, in some way utterly beyond rational analysis, become one of them.

"You still eating that gook shit, Chief?" Richardson asked, eying Horner's dinner with an unpleasant grimace. "You pull out the nuke mom, man, an' I'm outta here!"

"It's cool," Horner replied. "Negative on the nuke shit." He glanced at Richardson's dinner, an unappetizing, half-eaten LRRP. "But man, I'm not even gonna *think* about what you're eatin'!"

"Yeah," Richardson agreed. "Now, if we could just convince the gooks to eat this shit, we wouldn't have any more problem with 'em. They'd all go belly up."

"Yeah, I guess only SEALs're tough enough to eat LRRPs. SEALs and gyrines."

"Tough enough? Or dumb enough?"

"That too."

They spent the rest of the meal discussing the mission.

Pier Two
Tre Noc
2130 hours

After evening chow, the SEALs had spent more time going over the mission, rehearsing one another in the positions each would take, and the silent hand gestures they would use. Most of those, like the finger-to-eye "I see something" were automatic now, as much a part of their vocabulary as anything spoken in English, but the rehearsals were carried out nonetheless. Afterward, most of the SEALs had opted for a nap.

Like most men who faced combat from day to day, they'd learned the art of grabbing what sleep they could, anywhere, anytime.

Now, however, they were loading aboard the PBR, shouldering their weapons and satchels or canisters filled with ammo as they clambered into the craft's well deck. It was dark, and the lights of Tre Noc sparkled on the waters of the Bassac, while, to the west, a pale glow against the sky marked the runway lights of Binh Thuy.

Mariacher watched his men, observing each detail of equipment, of demeanor, of bearing. The SEALs had painted their faces with their trademark green and black camouflage paint; the men with green faces were on the prowl again this night. As always, they wore a ragtag mix of uniform pieces and equipment. None wore dogtags; SEALs always bring out their own, and dogtags were both superfluous and an unnecessary security risk. Most were wearing civilian jeans; several were barefoot; Huerra wore black pajamas instead of fatigues. Headgear was pretty evenly divided between scarves and floppy-brimmed boonie hats. Gone were the old black berets, even among the PBR's crew. The eleven men crowding onto the PBR—seven SEALs and four riverine sailors—looked more like heavily armed pirates than members of the world's largest and most powerful navy.

They looked great.

While Mariacher stood with Chief Wagoner, the PBR's skipper, in the craft's cockpit, the enlisted SEALs crowded into the recesses to either side of the forward gun tub. Charlie had added a new twist recently to the science of riverine warfare, setting traps for the SEAL PBRs. The most common consisted of a pair of RPG-2 rocket launchers wired to tree trunks and aiming out across the water at one another, their trigger mechanisms linked by a tripwire stretched just at or beneath the water's surface. When the patrol boat fouled the wire, the rockets would fire; generally the weapons were positioned to send two rockets squarely into the PBR's midships area. Since the first couple of attacks like that, SEALs had started riding far forward, working on the theory that they were better off in the bow portion of a sinking PBR than aft with the flaming diesel fuel and ammunition.

Adaptation to this new type of warfare was proving to be a

continuing evolution, a literal survival of the fittest.

"Cast off," Mariacher called in a low voice, and Selby, standing forward, tossed the PBR's bow line to a sailor on the pier, while the PBR's aft .50 gunner undid the stern line. Chief Wagoner eased the throttles forward and back, walking the PBR gently clear of the dock before bringing the helm over and applying a bit more power. Astern, the second PBR fell into line, the boats cruising downstream so slowly they barely left a ripple in the black waters of the Bassac. In the darkness, VC observers across the river might be aware of the departure, but since PBRs were patrolling up and down the river almost all the time, they wouldn't know whether these two carried a payload of SEALs or not.

Mariacher never, *never* took for granted the security at Tre Noc, not after that episode with Max the Wonder Dog during his first night at the riverine base a year ago. It was more than probable that VC agents were still working on base, likely even that they would have access to the orders he'd written that morning.

So every possible precaution was taken. During briefings in the bull pen, an armed SEAL stood watch outside the door, and at the end of the session, the blackboard was carefully washed down, the maps and reconnaissance photos were locked in the SEALs' own safe, and anything else that might give a clue to the mission objective was either secured or destroyed. Mariacher detested the necessity of putting the mission on paper, but the brass both at Tre Noc and back in Saigon would have large and squalling litters of kittens if he proceeded without the required paperwork, so he took steps to insure that those orders didn't reveal too much, too soon. The UNODIR label and the orders' late submission to HQ was as much for Charlie's benefit as for that of Mariacher's bosses, the details comfortably vague, the landmarks mentioned subject to random change in order to maintain the team's operational security.

Besides, the PBRs' actual destination could only be conjecture so far as any enemy agents were concerned; the Bassac, its tributaries, and its associated labyrinth of canals formed an astonishingly large and difficult chessboard. The SEALs had learned how to make the complexity of the terrain work for them as well as it had always worked for the Cong.

North of Juliet Crossing
Bassac River
2248 hours

Richardson crouched in the PBR's bows, trying to make out some identifiable feature of the shoreline to the right. There was little to see but black, though the sounds of the jungle carried easily above the throaty, low-voiced purr of the PBR's diesels. It was close, a universe of night and sharp, piercing cries. Richardson could smell the jungle too, could almost taste that rich and earthy mingling of stagnant water, decay, and lush vegetation that was part of every breath drawn in Vietnam, but which tended to fade behind the kerosene, diesel fuel, and latrine smells of the camp.

Imperceptibly, the PBR slowed. "Time, ladies," Mariacher called softly. "Another day at the office."

They were pulling a fast one this time, dropping off at the *first* stop along the way instead of the third or fourth . . . and well north of the Juliet Crossing specified in Mariacher's op orders. The PBRs would continue downstream for several kilometers, stopping periodically in order to confuse VC river outposts and observers, and if enemy agents working on the base at Tre Noc had picked up on Juliet Crossing as the site of the SEALs' activity tonight, they would be disappointed. With scarcely a splash or a ripple, Richardson rolled off the side of the PBR away from the shore, dropping into warm, silty water that was just less than chest-deep. By the time the PBR had moved past his position and he was wading toward the shore, the other six men had gotten wet as well, moving slowly through the river, weapons held above the flowing black water.

From now on, conversation would be nonexistent, communication limited to hand signs or mouth-to-ear whispers. When the SEALs reached the south bank of the river, they quietly crawled ashore, moving ten meters into the jungle before dropping to earth, spread out in a circle that gave them a three-sixty view, and waited, silent and unmoving, for ten full minutes.

They heard nothing throughout that time save the normal and familiar sounds of the jungle. Just minutes after 2300 hours, Mariacher held up his hand, then signaled. Horner took point, moving south, deeper into the jungle as silently as a wraith. Richardson had the number two position, ten meters behind. Huerra was tail-gunner, bringing up the rear, walking backward as often as forward as he watched and listened for VC who might be following the SEALs.

Their path through the jungle covered nearly four kilometers in a broad quarter-circle that took them first south, then southeast, then east, a route that took them over an hour to cover. At each stop along the way, they took time to listen to the jungle, to smell it, to use all of their senses as they became part of their surroundings. Twice, they swung back wide on their own trail, watching and waiting, checking to make sure that Charlie wasn't tracking them.

At last, however, they reached the chosen ambush site . . . not the Phu Non Canal, as Mariacher had described in his orders, but another canal nearby, and also on the VC supply convoy's expected route. If Communist agents back at Tre Noc had managed to see those orders and warn the VC convoy, the enemy might not show.

If they *did* show, however, the ambush would be a surprise no matter what information they might have learned ahead of time.

They deployed for the ambush in perfect silence, with no need for spoken orders. The canal—actually little more than a deep, broad stream through the jungle—narrowed to about forty meters' width at this point, providing an excellent kill zone. RD/2 Carl Gunn, "Slinger" to his mates, took the extreme right flank with the squad's M60, positioning himself on the shore with the sixty-gun sited to sweep down stream, almost at right angles to the fire from the rest of the team. Horner, Huerra, Richardson, and Selby strung themselves along the bank of the canal in that order, wading out a short distance and crouching until only their heads and weapons were above the black water. Hunkering down in the water gave them an added combat advantage; the enemy, once he came under fire, would expect the ambushers to be ashore, up on the bank among the tangle of trees and fallen logs, not right at the water's surface, and his fire would tend to climb a bit anyway, especially if he went full-auto. Each man had an assigned field of fire extending straight out from the shore and slightly overlapping the fire zones of the men to either side. Horner and Selby both had Stoner Commandos, while Richardson carried an M-16 with the under-the-barrel grenade launcher that had only been recently redesignated as the M203. Huerra was packing an AK-47 tonight. While the SEALs' favorite weapon, arguably, was the Stoner for its high volume of fire, more and more SEALs were beginning to acquire AKs from their enemies; the rugged automatic weapons had proven damned near indestructible in the mud and metal-eating climate of Vietnam, and the flat and distinctive crack they made when fired would keep the communists guessing.

Mariacher remained ashore at the center of the line, lying flat on his belly and keeping his eye close to the rubber eyepiece of the Starlight scope mounted on his M-16. Patterson, with the radio and an AK-47, also stayed ashore, positioned about ten meters behind Mariacher where he could provide rear security for the ambush.

They waited, hour following hour in peeping, rustling, chirping monotony.

The SEALs had learned to be very good at waiting. Mosquitoes swarmed about their faces and hands, but the men didn't move. The most serious problem they faced at this point was staying awake; the warm water of the canal, the long hours passing with nothing to break the soporific chirping of frogs and insects, dragged at the men's minds and bodies. Their experiences in Hell Week during BUD/S, when each man had only a handful of hours of sleep for six full days, actually worked against them since their bodies knew how to drift off no matter how uncomfortable the surroundings, if only they had a moment's peace. . . .

Richardson chewed gum to help stay awake; some of the others were working on wads of tobacco or a bit of beef jerky. All knew the trick of alternating among various sets of uncomfortable positions, allowing the aches and cramps to jab them to full alertness. None of them smoked, of course. What had begun as common-sense preference for individual SEALs was now firm operational policy; the SEALs would be able to smell Charlie long before he was able to smell them.

And still they waited. Richardson spent a lot of time thinking about his mom and dad . . . and about young Bill, out here now on his first deployment. He knew Bill was at Nha Be right now, but he hadn't been able to make contact yet. The team had been so hellishly busy ever since they'd gotten back in-country....

He felt the sound before he actually heard it, a gentle put-put-putting coming from the left. Instantly, Richardson's mouth went cotton dry. No matter how many ambushes he managed to spring, these last few moments took a man's guts and wound them tight as a mainspring. What if the enemy had been tipped off and reinforced? What if this wasn't the target? What if, what if . . .

It was so dark beneath the overcast sky he couldn't see more than a few feet across the water. Rigidly, he held himself in control, not allowing himself to turn toward the noise. His field of fire was already set; he would not deviate from the plan, not and risk getting turned around and putting his teammates at risk.

The noise grew louder . . . a blending now of several small outboard motors.

To Richardson, it seemed as though the hammering of his heart was loud enough to be heard even above the noise of the engines. . . .

Ambush site
U-Minh Forest
0352 hours

Mariacher glanced at the luminous dial of his watch, mentally recording the time before re-covering the dial with a loose strip of electrical tape. Raising the Starlight scope to his eye once more, he carefully studied the convoy. The scope's electronics cast a small green light against his eye, but he kept his face close enough to the eyepiece to keep the gleam blocked and invisible from the river. In some night ops he preferred not to use the Starlight scope at all for fear that the light would give him away, but tonight, the ambush set-up required it, with darkness so deep that the men probably couldn't see the targets at all.

From his vantage point ashore, sheltered behind a moss-covered log beneath a curtain of hanging vines, Mariacher scanned each of the sampans as they rounded the bend up-stream and began threading their way into the narrow part of the canal. There were four of them painted in the starlight scope's ghostly greens and whites, long, low-to-the-water shapes, each with a number of armed men crouched low in the narrow vessels. They appeared watchful but unworried.

That wouldn't last for long.

He waited . . . waited . . . His shot would be the signal to spring the trap, and he had to gauge exactly when the convoy was fully inside the overlapping ambush fire zones.

When the lead sampan was nearly even with his position, Mariacher squeezed his M-16's trigger.

The weapon hammered out a full-auto clatter, snapping bright green tracer rounds across the water and into the lead sampan. The tracers were both firing command and guide to the other waiting SEALs; a fraction of a second after he opened fire, the four men in the water to either side added their rock-and-roll mayhem to his, and Gunn's sixty opened up on the right with a deep, thundering chain of detonations that swept the convoy from front to rear. Mariacher kept his fire on the lead sampan, which appeared to stagger at that deadly caress and hesitate in the middle of the river. The water around the sampans erupted in splashes as bullets swept the surface of the canal or chewed through the sampan's hulls in hurtling clouds of splinters, as men pitched over the sampans' low freeboards and vanished in thrashing white foam.

In the water, men were dying. . . .

Ambush site
U-Minh Forest
0353 hours

Richardson's M203 coughed; seconds later, an M583 white parachute flare exploded in the sky well beyond and above the sampans, drifting slowly toward the water and casting the line of VC watercraft in sharp, impossible-to-miss silhouettes against the glare of that light. He immediately lowered his aim and opened fire with his M-16, sweeping the number three sampan, which was now less than twenty yards away and directly in the middle of his fire zone. After two quick bursts, he took the time to chamber a 40-mm high explosive round in his M203, take aim, and fire. With a thump, the grenade streaked toward the target, which was just far enough off to let the fuze arm itself in the short flight. It struck amidships, detonating with a thunderous eruption of mud, water, spray,

and hurtling chips of wood and canvas. The two halves of the
sampan drifted apart. Someone out there was screaming.

Reload . . . this time with a 40-mm shotgun shell. Aim . . .
fire! Number four shot swept across the water, sweeping a
standing VC from the bow of the last sampan in line and cata-
pulting him into the water. Reload . . . but this time he dropped
his finger back to the M-16's trigger and began stroking off
short, accurately placed bursts of fire, selecting targets inside
his fire zone. The VC were in total disarray; one managed to
loose a burst toward the shore behind the SEAL positions, but
he was cut down almost at once by a long, savage thunder from
Gunn's sixty. One stray round from the sampans struck the river
a few yards to Richardson's left; he scarcely noticed the slap-
splash as it hit. Someone—he thought it was Huerra—hurled an
M26A1 fragmentation grenade; it struck the water and exploded with a sharp, wet concussion that hammered through the
water and thudded heavily against Richardson's body.

The firing died out very nearly as swiftly as it had begun. The
flare, still drifting beneath its brilliantly illuminated parachute,
was nearing the water, beginning to gutter out as it fell and casting weirdly shifting shadows through the blue-white haze of
gunsmoke that hung above the scene. M583s had a burn time of
forty seconds; less than that time had passed since the beginning
of the ambush, and already the SEALs had ceased firing, as if by
shouted command. There was nothing left in the target area now
but the drifting shapes of the sampans themselves, and a few
scattered lumps of flotsam knocked into the water by the ambush firestorm. As the flare hit the river and its brilliant light
faded, the SEALs in the water began wading out to see what
their ambush had snared.

A man splashed a few yards to the right; Richardson lunged
forward, grabbed him by the collar, and yanked him up and
back. *"Cuu voi!"* the man gibbered at him. *"Cuu voi!"*

Help me.

As he dragged the VC ashore, the stink of human feces hit
Richardson; he glanced down and saw intestines spilling from
the man's abdomen. He was still trying to decide whether a
shot of morphine would help the man or not when the VC
died, arms and legs shuddering in a final, fatal convulsion.

Richardson returned to the water, helping to retrieve the
sampans before they drifted away. His eyes met Selby's above

the drifting hulk of the tail-end boat; the new SEAL looked hard and grim but was functioning well, despite the sight of a severed, bloody arm and several unidentifiable lumps of flesh floating in the water in the bottom of the craft.

He gave Selby a thumbs up as they dragged the craft ashore and got a weak smile in reply.

It was always rough the first few times. Richardson thought Selby was going to be okay.

Ambush Site
U-Minh Forest
0354 hours

Mariacher watched as his men secured the catch. Huerra was shepherding two wounded VC ashore, while Horner collared a third who appeared ashen-faced and dazed but otherwise unhurt. All three were stripped to their shorts and their wrists strapped behind their backs with plastic ties. Carefully the SEALs began going through everything, the sampans, the prisoners' clothing, even the clothing of the bodies that they'd managed to drag from the river.

"Hey, Boss?" Horner said, standing above one of the sampans. "Have a look at this."

"Whatcha got?"

For answer, Horner merely pointed into the well deck of the sampan. Peering in, Mariacher saw what looked like a bale of clothing. It was hard to tell in the darkness, but the material looked green.

Uniforms. *Lots* of uniforms. The sampan was full of them. He picked up a tunic and fingered the collar tabs. Horner picked up a green pith helmet, hefting it speculatively.

Mariacher looked up at Horner. "NVA," he said, his voice scarcely above a whisper despite the fact that the ambush would have alerted listeners for miles around. SEALs found it difficult to break the habits ingrained by combat.

"Yeah," Horner said. "What the fuck are VC doing smuggling NVA uniforms into the South?"

"I'm afraid to ask."

Another sampan held more uniforms . . . as well as a dozen cases filled with AK-47s still packed in oilskins. Selby recovered a case of 7.62 ammo from the spot where the third sampan had been sunk . . . and another bale of uniforms. Still more bales were recovered floating down the river.

North Vietnamese Army uniforms. The thought stirred the hairs at the back of Mariacher's neck.

"Boss?" Selby appeared out of the night, a folded sheet of paper in his hand. "Found this on one of the prisoners. Thought you'd like a look."

Mariacher pulled out a penlight with a red filter, unfolded the paper, and studied it closely.

A map. A fascinating map, for he recognized the area it covered, smack astride the Vietnamese-Cambodian border in the region around the Tien Giang and Bassac Rivers. It appeared to show troop concentrations . . . and possibly a supply depot of some kind, positioned between the two rivers not far from the town of Chau Doc. Dots plainly showed routes coming down across the border along both rivers. Someone had made precise notations in Vietnamese in one margin of the map. Intel was going to have a ball with this. . . .

He looked back at the pile of North Vietnamese Army uniforms, and a low, quiet whistle escaped his pursed lips.

Chau Doc . . .

Chapter 34

Monday, 15 January 1968

Eighth Platoon, SEAL Team Two
Nearing Chau Doc
On the Cambodian border
0925 hours

"Can't get no . . . satisfaction! . . ."

The SEALs had to sing loud to hear themselves above the thuttering, clattering thunder of the rotors, but they managed, belting out the Rolling Stones' song with the Seawolf's turbines hammering out the percussion. The helo's crew members were getting into the spirit of things, the door gunners doing a little go-go dance as they leaned against their safety tethers, the pilot forward laughing as he skimmed inches above the calm brown water of the Bassac.

Mariacher sat in the Seawolf's crowded cargo space, shoulder to shoulder with the other men of Alpha Squad. Glancing left out the helo's open side door, he could see the second Seawolf a hundred meters to port, maintaining station on the first as it carried Eighth Platoon's Bravo Squad north.

This, he thought ruefully, *is one shit-headed, hairy-assed idea.* . . .

The ambush they'd launched early on the morning of 10 January had started it . . . or rather, it had been started by the intel that ambush had secured. After using thermite grenades to destroy the cargo found aboard those sampans, Alpha Squad had withdrawn four hundred meters through the jungle, dragging their prisoners with them, to their primary extraction site on the Bassac River. Chief Wagoner's PBR had been waiting there off shore, as promised, and less than an hour after the ambush had been initiated, the SEALs had been on their way back to Tre Noc.

And then the debriefings had begun.

Much of Intel's interest in the SEAL ambush had centered around those NVA uniforms. To Mariacher, the explanation for the contents of a small uniform shop floating down a tributary of the Bassac was simple: the enemy was planning something big, something that involved smuggling large numbers of North Vietnamese troops into South Vietnam. The soldiers would have an easier time infiltrating down out of the myriad branches of the Ho Chi Minh Trail if they were dressed as peasants; their uniforms and equipment could be more securely smuggled in separately.

There were plenty of NVA troops in South Vietnam already, of course. The SEALs had tangled with regular units more than once. But to Mariacher, this had the smell, the stink, really, of something much larger.

And he was pretty sure it had to do with the upcoming Tet New Year.

Tet was the major holiday of the year throughout Vietnam,

a four-day celebration marking the beginning of the Chinese Lunar New Year. The date was set by the first new moon over China between 21 January and 19 February; this year, Tet would begin on 31 January.

In years past, there'd been repeated attempts to set up a ceasefire throughout the holiday period, and plans were underway for a similar truce this year. Everyone knew that the Communists used those periods of relative calm to build up their forces for a renewed offensive after the holiday, but that could be ignored in light of the good press appearing back home: TET TRUCE HOLDING!

Mariacher snorted. From what he'd heard, from what he'd seen on his last rotation back to the World, the peace movement was taking on near-hysterical overtones back there . . . and the government was bending itself into knots trying to accommodate them, or at least to play down the conflict. Increasingly, the only good intelligence—so far as MACV-SOG HQ in Saigon was concerned—was intelligence that proved that America and the Saigon government were winning the war.

It was a piss-poor way to run a war, about like squeezing your eyes shut and listening only to the advice you *wanted* to hear as you tried to thread your way through a maze. The emphasis now was on body counts . . . as if the VC or their NVA sponsors gave a shit about how many of their own they lost in exchange for scoring one solid propaganda victory. The war, the American people were being told each evening on the six o'clock news, was very nearly won, was *already* won in every way that counted. All that was needed was patience and a bit more firepower. . . .

Alpha Squad's find in the U-Minh Forest was being discounted.

His team had made a careful tally of the goods they'd snatched that night. Thirty-one bales, each with four complete uniforms in them; that was 124 uniforms, not counting the ones that had floated away or been destroyed in the firefight. Eight cases of AK-47 assault rifles, five rifles to a case. Forty weapons . . . and more had probably been lost when that grenade had nailed the number three sampan.

The significance of the numbers wasn't the fact that ambushes carried out against sampans usually netted only a handful of weapons being smuggled in threes or fours along the Mekong waterways; it was the fact that, if the enemy had risked shipping so many weapons and uniforms in this one convoy, it was because he *had* to in order to move a much larger quantity in a short period of time. Mariacher often wondered just what percentage of supplies the SEALs were intercepting on their raids and patrols. Five percent? Given the level of VC activity throughout the Bassac AO, that was probably wildly optimistic ... but even that inflated figure suggested that eight hundred assault rifles had been smuggled into the area during the same general period, and Mariacher had a gut feeling that the actual number must be much higher.

During his debriefing, Mariacher had told the Military Intelligence people who'd flown in from Saigon that he was pretty sure the communists were planning something big, and that it would be going down soon. Since they were obviously scrambling to get their supplies in place before Tet—their usual resupply window—it seemed logical that whatever they were doing was geared to take place during Tet.

Military Intelligence. The best oxymoron Mariacher knew. The grave-faced Army men from Saigon, including two captains, a major, and a light colonel, had smiled and pursed their lips and shaken their heads. Obviously, Mariacher had been assured, his estimate of the situation was in error. G2's assessment proved that VC activity was down throughout the region, that interdiction efforts along the Ho Chi Minh Trail had reduced military shipments to the south by over thirty percent, and that local civilian sympathy for the Communist insurgents was definitely on the wane.

There would be no Communist offensive during the Tet holiday ... and quite likely none afterward either. The enemy was beaten, *finished*.

Three times, the Army officers had tried to get him to downsize his figures. Wasn't it possible that his men had been confused, that there hadn't been *forty* AKs, but only thirty? Or twenty? ...

And as for the uniforms ... "Lieutenant, I don't think you saw that many uniforms," the major had said with quiet confidence. "It was dark, there'd been a battle—"

"I know what I saw, damn it! I had thirty-one packages—"

"Precisely," the lieutenant colonel had interrupted. "You *had* those packages. But you burned them, didn't you? Makes verification a bit harder for everyone."

"We couldn't drag all that shit back to the extraction site!"

"Of course not. You did quite right. I merely suggest that your numbers would carry more weight if they could be verified. Under the circumstances, we simply cannot accurately assess your claims."

The capper had come late in the briefing, when the Army officers had withdrawn for a few moments to discuss something out of Mariacher's hearing. The major, who'd been making notes for the past hour on a legal pad, had carefully torn off the top sheet and locked it away in his briefcase, which he'd taken with him . . . but Mariacher had taken the opportunity to liberate the new top sheet of that legal pad, which had been carelessly left on the desk. Later, he'd "developed" the impressions left in the paper by lightly shading it with a pencil, bringing out enough to see the words "uniform bales," together with the number 31, crossed out and replaced by a 20. Underneath that had been written "20 uniforms, poss NVA."

The shit-for-brains REMFs were literally rewriting the war, turning 124 North Vietnamese uniforms into 20 *possible* NVA uniforms with a stroke or two of the pencil.

Mariacher's first response had been a blind, blood-red rage. What kind of a dreamworld were these assholes living in, anyway? Mariacher and six of his people had risked *everything* to bring back good, solid intel, and these Army G2 REMFs were pissing it all away, rewriting it in order to make somebody's theories or assessments or goatfucking guesses look good.

For just a moment, Mariacher had stood in his quarters, precariously balanced between driving his fist through a wall and going back across the compound, finding those pus-sucking bastards, and pounding them into the mud until they saw things from his point of view.

Then, slowly, the cold rationality that embraced him during combat ops reasserted itself. This *was* combat of a kind, even if the enemy swore allegiance to the same flag he did, and acting in a rage was a great way to end up dead.

Besides, these four Army pricks were only the tiniest possible sliver of the whole, vaster problem. Mariacher thought about those four, then multiplied them by the wholesale ass-covering and number-crunching and outright lying that must be taking place all over Vietnam right now. Shit . . . other teams, other SEALs must be finding similar evidence of a big Communist push, if this thing was as big as Mariacher thought it was, and that meant a wholesale cover-up, one that might reach all the way back to CONUS and into the Pentagon, or even the White House basement. Pounding the shit out of four Army pencil-pushers—however personally satisfying—would do nothing save end Mariacher's career.

But there might, just possibly, be another way to go about this.

And so, five days later, Mariacher was flying north with his platoon. *Unless otherwise directed*, the orders he'd left with the riverine command at Tre Noc had read, *Eighth Platoon, SEAL Team Two, will proceed by means of available transport to Chau Doc in order to coordinate operations aimed at severing VC/NVA supply lines terminating in the Binh Thuy AO. . . .*

As usual, the UNODIR was considerably less informative than it could have been. It told the TF 116 command staff where Team Two was going to be for the next day or two but was less than candid on the purpose for this strange, even unprecedented excursion to the Cambodian border.

The maps and other hard intel the SEALs had recovered were gone, vanished into the maw of MACV after that so-called debriefing, but Mariacher had had plenty of time to study them before he'd turned them over, and he was pretty sure he knew what they represented. If Uncle Ho was engaged in some big-time smuggling of uniforms, men, and equipment across the Cambodian border in time for some New Year's fireworks, it looked like a fair amount of the stuff was coming through past Chau Doc. Mariacher had decided that the only way to get brass-hatted officialdom to notice the real numbers would be to come up with something so big that when he rubbed their noses in it, they *couldn't* ignore it.

Chau Doc was the provincial capital of An Giang District, and a long way outside the SEAL's usual Area of Operations. The place was 120 kilometers north of Tre Noc, squatting on the Bassac less than five kilometers from the Cambodian border. There was no riverine base there, much to Mariacher's disgust; in fact, the Navy had no official interest in the place at all. Chau Doc belonged to the Army's Special Forces, the Green Beanies, and anything that could be construed as Navy interference would not be tolerated.

He had an idea, however, and one that had been enthusiastically received by the other SEALs of Eighth Platoon. Chau Doc was a half hour's helicopter flight from Tre Noc, no more, and despite all of the double talk and mil-speak about AOs and assigned theaters, there was no reason why Eighth Platoon couldn't extend its intelligence-gathering activities as far north as was necessary to get the job done. His plan was to make contact with the U.S. forces in the area and set up a listening post along the Cambodian border. He wanted to get hard intel suggesting a big communist push during Tet, intel so large and so in-your-face, kick-in-the-ass blatant that the REMFs *couldn't* sweep it under the carpet, no matter how hard they tried. His reasoning was that by the time the goods made it to the area around Binh Thuy, the stuff would have already been dispersed, scattered across the countryside to hundreds of different villages and VC meeting sites and NVA staging areas. Up at Chau Doc, though, they must be driving the stuff across the border by the truck load. If the SEALs could reveal the magnitude of that pipeline, the bastards would *have* to listen.

"Lieutenant!" the Seawolf's skipper yelled back. Mariacher unstrapped himself from the safety harness and made his way forward, leaning against the side-by-side seats in the cockpit.

"Whatcha got?"

The pilot pointed upriver. "Chau Doc!" he said, raising his voice to make himself heard above the thunder of the rotors. "Thought you'd like to see."

The Seawolves passed over the city, then circled sharply south, careful not to cross the invisible "Red Line" that marked the border between Vietnam and Cambodia. From the air, Chau Doc was fairly impressive as Vietnamese cities went, an old-world sprawl of French architecture surrounded by the more traditional and primitive huts, hootches, and palm-frond-and-bamboo shacks. The center of town looked almost European. On the south side, close to the river, a small Catholic church and a whitewashed, cement-block hospital gave the place a decidedly Western flavor.

Mariacher studied the area with an experienced eye. There was an army post south of the city, Camp 510, a geometric fortress of ditches, towers, sandbagged walls, and coil upon coil upon tangled coil of concertina wire. The city's dock area, on the downtown stretch of the waterfront, was at least four klicks from the Army camp, and therefore well outside any protection it could offer.

In fact, the tactical set-up didn't look good at all. Chau Doc was on the southwest bank of the Bassac; Cambodia lay to the northwest, just beyond the zigzaggings of a canal, the Vinh Te, that usually paralleled the border but, in some instances, crossed it. The Special Forces Camp that theoretically protected the town and watched for smugglers coming across the border was positioned to do neither, too far from Chau Doc to offer more than moral support, too far from the river to control water traffic slipping south from the border. The camp didn't look very large, either; the helipad had been set up outside the wire, which would make things damned inconvenient if they needed resupply or medevac during an attack.

"Where do you want to set down?" the Seawolf pilot called.

"The Army base," Mariacher decided, pointing. "Just outside the front gate. We'd better do this one by the book."

"Roger that." The Seawolf flared out, nose-high, for a landing.

"You boys trot on into town," Mariacher told them as they gathered beside the helipad. "Scout out the lay of the land. See what we're up against."

"Hot damn!" Richardson said, grinning. "Liberty call!"

Selby laughed. "We know what kind of lay *he* wants to scout."

"Where are you off to, Boss?" Horner wanted to know.

Mariacher jerked his thumb over his shoulder, toward the camp. "Checking in. I'll meet you guys in front of the church ... make it eleven hundred hours."

Thirty minutes later, he was in the office of Colonel Thadeus Perry, a chisel-faced, silver-haired, somewhat overweight career Army officer who examined the SEAL with the barely suppressed repugnance one might feel for some newly discovered and extraordinarily loathsome insect.

Mariacher was enjoying the confrontation hugely. Like the

other SEALs, he'd come north decked out for war; his war-
paint was in place, he was wearing an olive-green bandana
instead of a more traditional cover, and his "uniform" consisted of Levis and a black tunic, the "black pajamas" af-
fected by Vietnamese peasants . . . and the enemy. His
weapon, a Swedish K submachine gun casually slung beneath
his arm, wasn't regulation either, though it was favored by
many covert operations groups, from the CIA to the Army
special forces themselves.

All in all, Mariacher's costume couldn't have been better
designed to shock the Army officer now facing him from the
far side of that big, brightly polished desk. Perry's uniform
was spotless, the creases as sharp and as crisp as the edge of
a ceremonial sword. Mariacher's sudden and unannounced appearance on his doorstep had clearly ruined his whole day.

"What the hell," Colonel Perry said slowly, his disbelief
showing in the way he lingered over the phrase, "are Navy
personnel doing up here?"

Mariacher glanced pointedly at the other man in the room,
a Vietnamese soldier in the uniform of a Regional Force/Pro-
vincial Force lieutenant. The RF/PF appeared to be on Perry's
staff; he'd ushered Mariacher into the colonel's office as
though he'd been doing the SEAL a tremendous favor, then
remained in the room at quiet parade rest.

Perry hesitated, then waved at the VN lieutenant. "If you
please, Vanh."

The man gave Mariacher a cold look, then left, closing the
door quietly behind him.

"Vanh is one of my best locals," Perry explained. "But I
can understand a little paranoia. I gather things aren't as . . .
secure in your region as they are up here."

Mariacher refused to rise to the jibe. "We are here under
orders," he said, ignoring the fact that he'd been the one to
write those orders less than twenty-four hours ago, "to set up
a listening post near the Cambodian border."

"I thought you . . . *people* only operated near the water."

Mariacher shrugged, and patted the two canteens hanging
from his web gear. "Shit, Colonel. I figure as long as we carry
our water with us, we're always close to it, right?"

The man didn't appear to appreciate the joke. "I'll ask you
to watch your language, Lieutenant," Perry said. "We're not

in the field here, do you understand me?''

Five fucking kilometers from fucking Cambodia, Mariacher thought viciously, *and this is the fucking rear*? He almost—*almost*—said the words aloud but restrained himself. ''Of course.'' He paused, letting the hesitation grow uncomfortably long. ''Sir.''

Perry's scowl deepened, but he didn't comment on what had been perilously close to insubordination. ''I'll ask you just once more, Lieutenant. What do you expect to accomplish up here?''

''Intelligence believes that the Communists are stepping up their efforts to bring weapons, equipment, and troops down the Ho Chi Minh Trail from the north,'' Mariacher replied, carefully not saying just whose intelligence he was referring to. ''It is possible that they're building up for a major offensive, possibly timed with the Tet New Year. The numbers suggest something very big. Sir.''

Perry looked puzzled. ''Well, I'll tell you, son,'' he said, his voice taking a puzzled and somewhat more fatherly tone, ''I've seen some of those numbers, and I'd have to say they suggest the exact opposite. VC activity is down, trail activity is down. If I was asked, I'd have to say that the enemy is on the run.''

''That's not the way we see it down around Binh Thuy. Sir. We have evidence of a massive stores buildup close to Chau Doc, just across the river.''

Perry chuckled. ''Well, son, I hate to disabuse your intel sources, but this sector is quiet. And secure. We haven't heard a peep out of Charlie in weeks, and that's with my command aggressively patrolling both sides of the Bassac all the way up to the border.''

Mariacher glanced again at the colored ribbons on Perry's chest and suppressed a grimace. Bronze Star. Army Meritorious Unit Citation. Army/Air Force Presidential Unit Citation. Army Commendation. Armed Forces Expeditionary. National Defense. Vietnam Service. Joint Service Achievement. Army Good Conduct.

Mariacher was willing to bet everything he had that Perry's Bronze Star had not been a combat award. Shit, if this pencil-pushing desk jockey had ever seen real combat, he'd have been so scared the crease would have come out of his trousers.

As a whole, Mariacher respected the Army Special Forces. Their training was good, their tactical doctrine stressed mobile infiltration and ambush over more traditional, hold-the-high-ground tactics, and, at least until relatively recently, they'd had superb esprit de corps. The mere fact that you couldn't even apply for Special Forces until you were an NCO meant that only men with experience would get to wear the green beanie. In some ways, they were almost as good as SEALs.

Almost.

Individually, however, as in any military unit, SEALs included, there were men good and bad within the Army Special Forces. That unevenness was especially noticeable among the officers, who usually didn't have the same level of experience as the noncoms they commanded. It had been getting worse lately, too. The Green Berets had once been damned tough three-percenters, a unit that accepted only three percent of the men who applied. That had changed of late, however, as the ongoing hell of Vietnam forced the Army to lower standards in order to insure a steady stream of new men.

You couldn't maintain high standards when some bureaucrat told you you *had* to meet your recruitment quota, and never mind the fact that there just weren't enough good men to go around.

Mariacher had known some damned fine Green Beret officers; he'd also known some real assholes, brown-nosing ticket punchers who'd arranged for a tour in the Nam at some nice, cushy post that would look splendid on their service records a few years down the pike when they were being considered for general.

That's how he'd pegged Perry, at least on first whiff. To be fair, Mariacher would have to talk with some of the guy's men, but so far he'd seen nothing in the man to be impressed about.

Somehow, Mariacher managed a smile. "Well, Colonel, and with all *due* respect, you wouldn't mind if my boys and I set up that OP for ourselves up here, would you?"

Perry's expression suggested that he might be worried about the SEALs messing up his nice, tidy battlefield. "Hardly necessary, Lieutenant, I assure you. We are quite on top of the situation here."

Time to play the trump card. "Well, you see, Colonel, I *am* operating under orders. Maybe you'd like to explain, in writing, why we're not permitted to operate in your AO. . . ."

That swung it. Perry grimaced, fussed, and scowled, but in

the end he gave his reluctant permission for SEAL ops to proceed in his backyard. Bureaucrats never wanted to commit themselves, especially if they weren't sure whose orders they were crossing with orders of their own.

"I'll want daily reports," Perry had demanded, shaking a querulous finger in Mariacher's direction. "I'll want a regular update on your ops and patrol destinations, so we can establish fire plans and opsec passwords. We do things by the book up here, Mr. Mariacher."

You've got to be shitting me, Mariacher thought, but he managed to look grave and nod his assent.

"But I must say, in all honesty," Perry continued, "that your presence here is neither necessary nor desirable. We have excellent relations with the regional forces. We have this entire district sewn up *tight,* tight as a drum. Nobody comes through here without my knowing about it. The region under my command is *pacified.* Completely secure."

Mariacher smiled, a rictus that simply exposed teeth in his green face. "Well, sir, you never know when you might need some extra help. That's what we SEALs are here for. If things got hot, well, we're only half an hour away by air, right?"

Perry's expression said it all as he gave Mariacher another up-and-down look, as though he feared some of that skin paint was about to drip on his spotless linoleum floor. "I think, Lieutenant," he said coldly, "that we have the situation well in hand. *Your* assistance will not be necessary."

"Well, there shouldn't be any problem, then. My boys'll carry out their mission, we'll set up an OP up north of the city, maybe run a patrol or two, and I'll be able to satisfy my bosses back in Binh Thuy that everything up here is, as you say, secure."

Perry's fingers drummed briefly on his desk top. "You will, of course, have your report cleared through my office." It was not a request, but a demand. Perry was not about to allow any report to be published that made him or his work look bad.

"Of course. Sir."

"Then I suppose I have no choice. Just keep my office posted on your deployments. Dismissed."

Vanh opened the door to show Mariacher out; clearly, he'd been listening at the door, for Perry's dismissal had been no louder than a conversational tone.

Yup, he thought to himself, giving Vanh a cold grin as he passed, and picking up an answering flicker of fear behind the man's emotionless gaze. *This place is really secure.*

But which side had secured it?

Chapter 35

Monday, 15 January 1968

Eighth Platoon, SEAL Team Two
Market Square, Chau Doc
1005 hours

Richardson, Patterson, Selby, and Horner had found Chau Doc to be quiet, charming, and postcard-pretty. Though there were armed Vietnamese men about, Regional Force/Provincial Force militia, from the look of them, the place was so peaceful it was hard to think of it as part of a country at war. As the SEALs strolled the streets, dodging traffic that ranged from cyclos to Fords, the men felt uncomfortably out of place in their camo fatigues and black pajamas, their face paint and weapons. The townspeople, for the most part, were wary of the newcomers, unwilling to lose face by fleeing the strange apparitions in the center of their waterfront marketplace, but obviously unsure of what to make of these green-faced and heavily armed men.

"Wonder where the war is?" Richardson asked, standing at the corner and eyeing a pretty Vietnamese woman holding a baby a few yards away. The woman looked him up and down, then turned and hurried away. Nearby, an RF/PF militiaman looked at the SEALs uncertainly, but didn't unsling his M-1 carbine.

"I feel like I'm at a friggin' costume party," Selby said. He hefted his Stoner. "We don't seem to be attracting all that much attention, though."

"You spoke too soon, son," Horner said, turning slightly and bringing his AK-47 up to the ready. "I think we've attracted some attention over here."

It was all Richardson could do to suppress a start when he turned and saw the group walking up the street toward the four SEALs. There were six of them, very large, piratical-looking men wearing expressions impossible to read but obviously less than friendly. They carried AK-47s; their clothing—too mismatched to be called uniforms—seemed drawn from several different issues, North, South, French, and American. In fact, they looked a lot like the SEALs themselves, though they weren't decked out in camo paint. Several wore what looked like necklaces of human ears, some still freshly bloody, others black and rotten.

One barked an obvious challenge.

"*Chung toi den tu Hoa-ky,*" Richardson said, watching their narrowed eyes for some sign of recognition or reaction. "We are Americans."

Several of the newcomers tensed, their fingers tightening perceptibly on the triggers of their AKs. Others looked less certain and glanced back and forth among themselves. For a long and deadly second or two, the two groups faced one another, weapons at the ready, a blazing firefight a heartbeat away.

"Who the fuck *are* these guys?" Selby said quietly.

"They sure as hell don't look like Ruff-Puffs," Patterson said, using the derogatory Americanism for the RF/PF militias.

"These aren't Vietnamese," Chief Horner said.

"Montagnards?" Richardson asked, referring to one of the hill tribes living in Vietnam, Cambodia, and Laos.

"They're Nung," a new voice said. "Mercenaries. And they don't like VC."

The man stepped out of a building off the side of the street. He wore civilian clothing, including a tan safari jacket, like a uniform, and his silver-gray hair was closely trimmed. "Well, well," Horner said, relaxing slightly. "Christians In Action."

The newcomer barked a few words of what sounded like Chinese at the Nung mercenaries, and the confrontation evaporated as swiftly as it had begun. The biggest Nung, with the biggest collection of ears, looked at Richardson and smiled—a cold showing of teeth.

"Loi just welcomed you to Chau Doc," the man said. He extended his hand. "Kenneth Aimes," he said. "I'm the local CORDS advisor."

Half an hour later, the five of them were seated in an outdoor cafe next to the Hong Fat Restaurant, sipping beers and sampling a fiery-hot, pepper-laced concoction that Aimes said was a local Nung delicacy.

"The Nung are damned good people to have on your side," Aimes told them. "That bunch you ran into are some CIDGs who've been working for me for almost a year now. They hate the VC, hate *all* Vietnamese, in fact. If they don't like you, they kill you . . . a very small piece at a time. The NVA are terrified of them."

"My kind of people," Horner said, grinning. From their table, they could see several Nung on the street beyond the low, white-painted fence around the patio, keeping watch. "The ear necklaces are a cute touch."

"What's the matter?" Richardson laughed. "Doesn't the agency like working with the Green Beanies down the street anymore?"

Aimes frowned. The man, in true agency fashion, had neither confirmed nor denied any connection with the CIA—the "Christians In Action," as some SEALs called them. CORDS, the Civil Operations and Revolutionary Development Support group, was theoretically a civilian-oriented and -run pacification program, but according to the SEALs' intel, the agency frequently used it for its own intelligence-gathering activities. Aimes had said he was an Army Special Forces staff sergeant on loan to CORDS, and from the way he talked, from his manner and bearing, Richardson was pretty sure that he was telling the truth.

But like the SEALs, the Special Forces had pulled more than one covert op on behalf of the CIA, a fact that gave them something in common. The Agency and the SEALs had a working relationship that went back at least as far as Cuba, a relationship that worked pretty well so long as the bureaucrats stayed out of it and let the professional warriors and the field agents handle things themselves.

"If you mean," Aimes said carefully, "that you're wondering why the local CORDS program relies on Nung CIDGs rather than on the Ruff Puffs, let's just say it's a matter of both survival and efficiency." He jerked a thumb over his shoulder in the general direction of the Special Forces camp to the south. "And if we had to rely on old Pus-Guts, we'd never get anything done."

"Pus-Guts?" Patterson asked.

"Colonel Thadeus Blood-'n'-Pus-Guts Perry," Aimes said with evident distaste. "For six months now, my organization has been feeding him intel, good, *solid* intel, on the build-up of VC and NVA forces in this district. Shit, the Bassac is Highway 101. Skip a stone across the water and you'd be hard-pressed *not* to hit a communist boat, chock full of arms, munitions, the works."

"I thought the Special Forces boys were better than that," Selby said.

"They *are*, damn it," Aimes said. This was clearly a sore point with him. "Theoretically, Camp Five-and-Dime supports a Mike Force—that's three rifle platoons and a weapons platoon, about 185 men. Perry has this idea of holding territory, however, and he generally has two platoons at a time scattered all over the countryside. He also puts too damned much reliance on the Ruff-Puffs and CIDGs." He pronounced it "sid-jeez," an acronym for Civilian Irregular Defense Group. "I think he forgets this is still a civil war."

"Friendlies passing info on to the enemy?"

"There's some of that, certainly. There's also a lot of, well, call 'em *arrangements*. The VC are planning to move a convoy through, the word gets to the Ruff-Puffs, who stage an ambush. Both sides shoot over each other's heads, no one gets hurt. A report gets filed with Pus-Guts concerning 'light enemy activity suppressed by RF/PF action.' The VC get their supplies through. And if there's ever a really big push by the enemy, well, somehow how our patrols never seem to turn up anything at all. It's like our patrols always go to the exact area where the enemy isn't, if you know what I mean."

"Cozy," Horner said.

"Fucking criminal," Aimes said. He tossed off the last of his beer. "So why do you boys want to get involved in this silly dance?"

"Part of why we're here, Sergeant," Horner told him, "is to assess the area's security. Our intel indicates the VC have a major supply and staging area up here, and a lot of their shit is ending up near Binh Thuy."

"I'm not surprised."

"We hope to set up an OP in the area, maybe see about stinging Charlie next time he tries smuggling a big load through. From what we've seen down in our neck of the woods, we think Charlie's getting ready for something big."

"Tet," Aimes said.

"Yeah. What do you know about it?"

Aimes shrugged. "Not a lot, but I can say our intel matches yours pretty well. My guess is that Hanoi thinks the South Vietnamese populace is just about ready to rise up and kick the bastards in Saigon out. Maybe another mutiny in the ARVN, like the one back in early '66. They're thinking that a big demonstration, something to show that Saigon and the Americans aren't as in control as they think, might be all that's necessary to bring down the government. They could be right, too."

"We've been finding NVA uniforms near Binh Thuy," Richardson said. "Lots of 'em. Enough to make us think that a lot of NVAs might be sneaking down from the North and slipping across the Cambodian border. They could have a whole damned army in place and ready to jump. We were sort of wondering if we can cut the bastards off at the knees up here, before they're able to get things rolling."

A twinkle worked its way into Aimes's eye. "If you're looking for targets, son, there're plenty of them. I know I wouldn't object to you boys pulling a patrol or an ambush or two."

Horner chuckled. "Maybe we could sort of, you know, share intel?"

"Maybe we could at that."

For the next few minutes, they discussed possibilities. The tactical situation in the Chau Doc region was worse than Richardson or the other SEALs could have imagined. Though Colonel Perry made a great show of running patrols of both Special Forces troops and his pet CIDGs, Aimes believed that the countryside was almost totally under communist control. Communist supplies weren't trickling across the border; they were flooding in, and only a fraction—perhaps twenty percent—were coming by way of the famous Ho Chi Minh Trail.

"I've been screaming my head off to my supervisors," Aimes told them. "Forget all that shit you've heard about the Ho Chi Minh Trail. Oh, there's stuff coming down from the North that way, sure. But most of the supplies are being offloaded from North Vietnamese, Chinese, and Russian ships over at Sihanoukville." That was a Cambodian port on the Gulf of Thailand less than forty kilometers from the South Vietnamese border. "Then it's an easy two-hundred-klick drive by truck to Xom Khanh Hoa, right up the road from Chau Doc. While the Air Force goes nuts trying to obliterate the Ho Chi Minh, most of the supplies are coming through untouched."

"You said you've been screaming your head off to your bosses," Horner said. "What's the matter, they don't believe you?"

"It's not so much that they don't believe," Aimes said. "It's that they have too much political capital tied up in other theories. Some of my bosses, well, they need to *look* right more than they need to *be* right, if you take my meaning."

Richardson smiled. It was the closest Aimes had come yet to admitting to who his bosses really were. "I know the feeling, Sergeant," he said. "We've seen our intel deliberately distorted, because it didn't fit the official version."

"Hell of a way to run a war."

"I think," Horner said, "that our boss is gonna want to talk to you. He's checking in with your colonel now, but maybe later we can sit down and work this out."

"Love to meet him."

"Speaking of someone I'd love to meet," Richardson said suddenly. He was staring past Aimes's shoulder at a woman who'd just walked up along the street past the restaurant, a tall, slim blonde in the starched whites of a nurse. "Oh, mama!" he said. "I've died and gone to heaven!"

"Not military," Horner said. "She must be a civilian."

Aimes glanced at the woman and smiled. "That's Lisa Moore," he said. "And yes, she *is* a civilian, though she's working with a government-sponsored relief agency. USAID. One of those hands-across-the-seas foreign relation things." He made a face. "I still think it's stupid letting American women work over here, but then, this area *is* pacified. Pus-'n'-Guts says so, right?"

"What," Selby said, eyes widening. "She's American?"

"Blond hair? Blue eyes? What'd you think, Navy, that she was Vietnamese?"

"I dunno," Selby said, shaking his head as he stared at the woman. "French . . . Dutch, maybe . . . but American?"

"Stop drooling, Selby," Horner said. "You're getting the table wet."

"I heard she's from California," Aimes offered.

"Hey, a California girl!" Selby said.

"Look at her tits move as she walks!" Richardson said. "No bra!"

"All nurses wear bras," Horner said.

"How would you know, Chief?" Patterson said.

"I checked, Pit-pat. I checked."

The woman had stopped beside a table, where another, plainer woman was sitting. The two were talking earnestly together, the blonde's back turned partly toward the SEALs.

"Who's the other woman?" Selby wanted to know. "The one at the table."

"Mary Guilford," Aimes replied. "School teacher. She's one of a couple of American teachers working over here." He didn't sound as though he approved of that, either.

"She married?" Richardson said, happily letting his gaze rove up and down her legs and backside. The sight of that one beautiful woman after weeks of living like a monk in Tre Noc had shaken him more than he would have thought possible.

"Who, Mary?"

"No, shit-head. That knock-out blonde."

"Not that I know of," Aimes said. He chuckled. "But you should know that every Army officer and enlisted man for thirty klicks in every direction has tried to score with her, and failed."

"Maybe she's a dyke," Patterson said.

"That?" Selby replied. "No way!"

"I think she's just choosy," Aimes said.

"She just hasn't seen the full range of the field," Richardson said, rising from his chair. "I mean, with nothing but Army to choose from." Pretending to straighten the lapel of his fatigue shirt, he walked toward her.

He wasn't entirely sure how he was going to approach her, but he knew he had to talk to her. Maybe the old "Hey, do you remember me?" line. Chances were, she'd been in Saigon before coming up here, and he could pretend to have met her there. His face paint would keep her guessing for a moment or two, wondering if she *had* met him already. At least it would give him a chance to impress her, maybe to get a conversation started.

Casually, he walked up behind her. "Hey, Lisa, sweet thing," he began. He dropped his hand to rest on her left buttock. "Remember me—"

At his touch, she whirled, her hand coming up and connecting with his cheek in a meaty, stinging smack. Her eyes widened when she saw his painted face, then dropped to the palm of her hand which was smeared with greasepaint. "Christ!" she said, picking up a linen handkerchief off of the table and trying to wipe the paint off her hand. "I had no idea the clown show was in town."

"Who is *that*?" Mary Guilford said, peering up at him over the tops of her glasses.

"I'm not quite sure, Mary. They have some strange things in the bush out here. Snakes . . . reptiles . . . you name it."

"I think you must have me confused with someone else, Lisa," Richardson said, rubbing his face. "I'm, ah, sure we met in Saigon—"

"I don't know what the get-up is for, mister," she said coldly, dropping the stained napkin. "But we have *not* met and you have no right to use my first name. I hardly ever meet with either clowns or reptiles socially, and when I do, they are better mannered than you are." She turned away, took several steps down the street, then stopped, looking back over her shoulder. She glanced once at the paint still on her hand. "You know, fella, that's a really cruddy skin condition you have. I'd have that treated, if I were you. See you, Mary."

Then she was gone. Mary, still sitting at the table, giggled loudly.

Richardson tried to be nonchalant as he walked back to the table, but it was difficult with the hilarity of his fellow SEALs. "Oooh!" Selby said, waggling his hand back and forth. "And the Don Juan of Eighth Platoon is down for the count!"

"Hey," Richardson said. "Cut me some slack, okay?" He rubbed his cheek again, grateful that the paint covered any lingering red mark. Jesus, but that woman could *hit*! "I think she likes me!"

Chapter 36

Monday, 22 January 1968

Bravo Platoon, SEAL Team One
Twelve kilometers southeast of Nha Be
Rung Sat Special Zone
1425 hours

Lucky Luciano clutched his M-16 a little tighter as he walked point through the jungle. He'd walked point a thousand times before, it seemed; there was nothing different, nothing special about this time.

But something was wrong.

He'd known something was different about today when Chief Spencer had rousted him that morning for a mission alert. "Showtime, SEALs," Spencer had growled. "All you squirrels, out of your trees! Time to be up and at 'em."

"Right," Luciano had said, rolling out of the rack.

Spencer's eyes had narrowed. "What's the matter, Lucky? You feeling okay?"

"Sure, Chief. No problems."

"Your mouth's not running overtime like it usually is. Thought maybe you were sick."

"I'm fine, Chief. Let's go kick the shit out of the gooks. . . ."

That's when he'd known something was wrong with today. The feeling had grown stronger as he and the other members of Golf Detachment's Bravo Platoon had listened to Lieutenant Baxter give them a run-down on this op, and stronger still as he and the other members of his squad had boarded a Seawolf helicopter at Nha Be, then lifted off in a swirl of dust and angled southeast across the river toward the Rung Sat.

There were times when he got these feelings. . . .

There were no atheists in foxholes, or so the old saying went. Luciano had been raised Catholic, even gone to a Catholic school for three years until they kicked him out for that incident in the john with that tenth of a dynamite stick Mario had snatched for him, but, as he liked to put it, he and religion had never really gotten along. Still, there were times when he could damn near feel someone or some*thing* breathing over his shoulder, and it set the hairs on the back of his neck to standing on end, prickling their warning.

He called it, at least in his own mind, his angel . . . though he still wasn't sure whose side the thing was on. The last time he'd felt it had been just before the ambush of the LCM over a year ago, moments before those VC mortar rounds had come crashing down and damned near everyone aboard except for him had been wounded.

His angel was trying to tell him something now.

What, damn it? he thought fiercely. *What are you trying to tell me?*

The platoon had split into two squads. Lieutenant Baxter was in charge of Second Squad, while Ensign Dorsey ran First Squad a kilometer or two to the east. They'd been inserted into the jungle by helo an hour ago, rappelling down through the treetops on nylon lines as the Seawolves hovered just above the forest canopy. West was a third squad of five Aussie Special Forces troops. The ANZACs had been in-country for several weeks now, exchanging training tips and war stories with their SEAL hosts and going on joint patrols like this one. Their mission today was to conduct a sweep south, then east through the forest in this part of the Rung Sat. The Team's NILO had reported a buildup of enemy activity in the area during the past weeks, nothing clear-cut or definable, but a definite sense that something was in the offing.

The SEALs wanted to know what it was.

At first, Luciano had wondered if the presence of outsiders—the ANZACs—had been what was causing his funk, but that didn't make sense. The SEALs had gone on ops with the Aussies before; they were good people, more in tune with the realities of combat in the bush than most non-SEAL Americans he knew, and they were the sort you liked to have at your back during a firefight.

He'd also wondered if it was the new guy on the team. New guys—the FNGs—made old hands like Luciano nervous. They made more noise than was necessary and weren't careful about where they put their hands or feet. Luciano had long ago come to the conclusion that you never knew about a guy, *any* guy, until you'd seen him in combat.

But Bill Tangretti was okay. A little green about the gills when he'd first shipped aboard, like they all were, but okay. Luciano liked him, liked him enough to have helped Doc put a harmless, three-foot bush snake in his rack at Nha Be a few weeks ago. Tangretti had pulled back the covers, snatched up the reptile by the neck, then loudly announced to the rest of the barracks, "Aw, *shit!* I don't care if this thing is poisonous or not, but he'd *damn* well better be housebroken!"

Better yet, Tangretti had received his baptism of fire, two days before Christmas, and he'd come through just fine, calm and ice-cold under fire. They'd been engaged in several firefights since, and Tangretti had proven himself to be as good as any other SEAL on the team. Scuttlebutt had it that Tangretti was the son of the guy who'd helped found the SEALs, the Tangretti who'd started off with the UDTs back in the Second World War. Luciano didn't know if that was true or not, and Bill hadn't volunteered anything about it, one way or the other.

Yeah, Tangretti was going to work out just fine. Damn it, though! Luciano's sweat-slicked grip tightened on the M-16 he was carrying, a weapon made bulky by the big M203 barrel slung beneath the foregrip. What was it that was setting off all of his danger alarms?

1428 hours

It was a long, long way from Hospital Corps School at Great Lakes and farther still from the sanitized, squeaky-clean world where medics were forbidden to carry weapons and had to wear big red crosses on helmets and armbands.

When John Randolph had joined the Navy, he'd done so planning on using the G.I. Bill to give him a boost toward medical school, and it had seemed a logical choice to choose the Hospital Corps as a way to begin his education. He'd volunteered for the SEAL program to stay with a best friend, one of the first hospital corpsmen to go through BUD/S at a time when most corpsmen in the Teams were simply assigned to a platoon without the benefit of SEAL training.

The friend had washed out in Hell Week; Randolph, however, had found new inner reserves of strength and will he'd never known he'd possessed. Ever since BUD/S, he'd been more SEAL than corpsman, and he rarely thought anymore about someday being a doctor.

Still, his gear included an extra canvas pouch with an M1 medkit and a small field surgical pack. His SEAL role in the mission was emphasized by his M-16, a prisoner-handling kit, and a pair of M26A1 fragmentation grenades. Like the other SEALs, he was wearing a specially designed buoyant vest over his tiger-stripe camouflaged shirt and Levi blue jeans; the vest had capacious pockets capable of carrying extra ammunition, as well as the survival kit, flares, a sheathed Randal Model 2 knife, plastic bags for securing captured documents or maps, and a couple of personal first aid kits, and included an inflatable life jacket as well. Unlike a number of other SEALs that he knew, Johnson always wore black coral shoes rather than going barefoot; his Corps School training had laid too much emphasis on the variety of tropical parasites infesting the area to make him comfortable with the idea of wading barefoot in teeming, fetid Vietnamese mud. He'd recently abandoned the SEAL-trademark broad-brimmed boonie hat for an olive-drab bandana pulled tight over his head and knotted at the back.

Looking at Randolph, no one could have mistaken him for a doctor . . . or even for a pre-med student. He looked every inch the deadly killer, the professional warrior, that he was.

At the moment, he was walking in line behind the new kid, Bill Tangretti, and just ahead of Chief Spencer. Tangretti was fitting in pretty well, so far. He wasn't using his father's name to wangle any special privileges or notice, and that was definitely something in the kid's favor. Randolph liked him, liked what he'd seen of him, anyway. It would be good to sit down with him sometime, have a few drinks, and maybe swap some stories.

Randolph had met the kid's father years before. Steve Tangretti was quite a character and on his way to becoming an honest-to-God legend both in the SEAL Teams and in the UDT. He wondered where the old man was now.

1432 hours

Bill Tangretti had never felt more alive than he did right here, right now. The very air around him felt as though it were electrically charged; he could feel his heartbeat hammering away beneath his vest, see every leaf, every stalk of grass, every fern and vine with a crystalline clarity he'd never known before. All of it, the training, the suffering of Hell Week, even the tears of his mother seemed to have come together, blending, becoming part of the thrust that had propelled him to this place, this world. For perhaps the first time in his life, he felt like he was genuinely a part of something much larger than himself, that he'd been fully accepted into a fraternity of the elite, part of the best combat unit in the greatest navy in the world.

It was a heady feeling.

He was well aware that the others in the squad still thought of him as the newbie, the cherry, the FNG . . . but he'd come through his first few firefights okay, and now both he and they knew that he truly was one of them, a SEAL. The training they'd all shared together had actually made that acceptance easier. Everyone knew that whether you were an officer, a twenty-year lifer chief, or an eighteen-year-old kid still wet behind the ears, if you'd survived Hell Week, you had what it took. At this point, the watching, the kidding and insults and name-calling, the light hazing, all were just part of the routine, a way of gentling him into his new, extended family.

He wondered where his dad and Hank were, right now. Last he'd heard, Hank was still with SEAL Team Two over at Binh Thuy. His dad was in the Nam somewhere, but he didn't know where. Saigon, most likely. Tangretti suppressed a grin. If he knew his father, he'd be running a hustle of some kind, working favors to get better recognition for the Teams, maybe wining and dining a staff bigwig in some hot Saigon nightspot.

Great duty, if you could pull it.

Ahead, Luciano stopped, his hand coming up, clenched in a fist. *Hold!*

Tangretti froze in place, trying to penetrate the surrounding jungle growth with his every sense. He couldn't see whatever it was that had made Luciano stop, but he knew better than to question the point; something was up ahead, something Lucky didn't like one bit, if the way he was holding his body, crouched, as if ready to spring, was any indication.

Luciano's hand moved again, forming a new sign. *Booby trap!* Then he signaled Tangretti to come ahead, slowly.

Gently, Tangretti moved forward, joining Luciano in a place where the brush and ground cover had thinned in a fern-shrouded gully until it was almost clear. Luciano reached forward with one finger and lightly touched something; it took Tangretti a second to focus his eyes on the nearly invisible thread . . . and when he did, he recognized it as a strand of transparent, plastic fishing line.

The sight of fishing line in the jungle was incongruous, almost humorous. He'd thought the VC went in for string or narrow-gauge wire or even jungle vines for their booby traps, not something you could pick up in the sporting goods section at Sears back home.

Carefully, Luciano tracked the line to the left, into a clump of ferns at the base of a moss-shaggy tree trunk. Tangretti checked in the other direction, tracing the nylon thread through some ferns and around behind another tree trunk. As he gently pushed a spray of ferns aside, he saw the grenade—an M26A1, an American-made fragmentation grenade. The pin had been pulled, the fishing line wrapped twice around the spherical body and tied in a granny knot, clamping the arming lever in place. The grenade itself was nestled down against the soft earth of the embankment, loosely tied to an exposed root; a careless boot dragging at the nylon line would have loosed the arming lever and flipped the live grenade out into the open, a few meters behind the luckless man who'd triggered it.

Luciano returned to Tangretti's side, signaling that the other end of the line was clear, an anchor only. He gestured toward the grenade, indicating that Tangretti should disarm it.

Tangretti was tempted to argue; it was easy enough to go around the thing, after all, but he knew better than to challenge Luciano. And, now that he thought about it, it made sense to take care of it right away, rather than risk blundering into it

later, maybe while they were trying to E&E from the area
under fire. Glancing around, he saw Doc and Chief Spencer
all watching from a distance, twenty meters away. Doc saw
his look and gave him a thumbs up.

Better get on with it, then.

His mouth was dry, his pulse racing. Part of his SEAL training had included instruction on booby traps, including quite a
bit of time spent learning to create them. They didn't hold the
same pitch of terror for SEALs that they held for others. Even
so . . .

As he began looking around on the ground for a twig or
something he could use, Luciano tapped him on the shoulder
and, with a disgusted look on his face, reached into a combat
vest pocket and produced a grenade cotter pin. Leaning forward, he put his lips close to Tangretti's ear. "Never, *never*
go out on an op without a few of these as spares," the SEAL
whispered.

OK, Tangretti signaled as he accepted the pin. His heart was
hammering, loud enough now that he was sure that the other
SEAL must hear it. Sweat beaded on his forehead beneath his
boonie hat. Carefully, aware that Luciano was watching his
every move for some betrayal of his fear, he reached down
and gently, gently, gently worked the end of the cotter pin into
the tiny hole that anchored the arming lever to the head of the
grenade. When the end of the pin popped through the hole at
the other side, locking the arming lever in place, he slowly
allowed himself to relax, then take a deep breath.

Piece of cake. Reaching to his sheath on his vest, he pulled
out his knife, snicked the fishing line anchoring the grenade
to the root. He grasped the grenade, picked it up. . . .

Another grenade had been positioned in a shallow hole immediately behind and beneath the first. As he picked up the
one grenade, a foot-long length of fishing line dragged the
second one clear, its arming lever popping high into the air as
its spring released it, a faint wisp of smoke sizzling from the
grenade's burning fuze. . . .

Tangretti heard the sharp ping of the arming lever, felt the
tug as he dragged the hand grenade free, saw it bouncing
across the ground; for an instant, he thought of scooping the
thing up and hurling it, but a fumble would kill both him and
Luciano, and so instead he lunged sideways into the other

SEAL, slamming against him, shoulder on shoulder, driving him over and down. The two men crashed to the ground, Tangretti on top, and then the grenade detonated just a few feet away, the blast slamming him in the back like a jackbooted kick and rolling him off of Luciano. Something cracked hard against his combat vest, and at the same time it felt like someone had just driven a fist into his thigh. The air stank and tasted of cordite; his ears were ringing so loudly he couldn't hear Luciano shouting at him, could only see the SEAL bending over him, his mouth working furiously. Doc was next to him, touching his throat, his side.

He started to sit up. "I'm fine," he said. His voice sounded strange, and he realized it was because he was at least partly deaf. "I'm fine. . . ."

But Luciano pushed him back down, still shouting something, then turning to grab his M-16/M203 combo lying nearby, his eyes wild. Tangretti couldn't tell what he was saying until something ripped splinters out of the side of a tree towering over his head. Rolling over onto his side and raising himself a bit, he could see a long line of flashes winking and flickering against the underbrush fifty meters off. Ambush! That booby trap had been the trigger of an ambush . . . and the SEALs had just walked straight into it.

1433 hours

Lieutenant Baxter flicked his hand left and right, deploying the squad. *Randolph . . . move up to support Luciano and Tangretti. Spencer and Jenkins, shift right. Pettigrew! Radio!*

It looked like the new kid was down; Luciano was returning fire but needed support, and fast. From the number of flashes he could see in the shadows beneath the trees, Baxter guessed there were thirty or forty bad guys up ahead, deploying in a long, straight line that capped the SEALs' T. The booby trap had been the tripwire, literally and figuratively; the enemy had opened fire within seconds of the grenade's detonation.

The cardinal rule if you are caught in an ambush is to *not* simply go to ground. It's a lot harder for troops who've lost their momentum to get moving again than it is to keep moving in the first place, and the cold equations of battle guarantee that you'll take fewer casualties fighting your way out of a firetrap than you will if you hunker down and take it.

Usually. Nothing is ever certain in combat.

The first thing to do, though, was find out how the enemy was sited. All of the fire so far was coming from a single front, parallel to the gully where Luciano and the new kid triggered that booby trap . . . not very inspired as traps went. It suggested that this was a hasty ambush, that the booby trap had been a kind of back-door burglar alarm to alert Charlie that the men with green faces had come calling.

If the VC hadn't been laid out waiting for them with a carefully prepared trap, then maybe the SEAL squad had stumbled into something important, something worth guarding with thirty or forty men.

Phil Pettigrew, who was humping the squad's PRC-74, passed Baxter the handset.

"Zulu Two! Zulu Two!" he called. "This is Red Fox. Do you copy, over?"

"Red Fox," Dorsey's voice replied. "Zulu Two. We copy. Talk to me."

"Zulu, we have heavy contact at map coords King-three-one by Bravo-niner-seven. . . ."

Baxter began rattling off the information that would allow Zulu Two, to the west, and Zed Three, the ANZAC contingent to the east, to close on the enemy position from both flanks. If this was a hasty ambush protecting a VC camp, they wouldn't be expecting a coordinated assault from three directions at once. His final call was to Overwatch One and Two, the Seawolf contingent that was providing air cover for the patrol.

That taken care of, Baxter ordered Pettigrew to stay put, providing rear security for the squad in case Charlie was up to something cute. Then he took his AK-47 and crawled forward, determined to get into the fight.

1435 hours

Tangretti's head was clearing as he shoved Randolph away. "I'm okay!" he said through gritted teeth. "I'm *okay!*"

"Shit, Tangretti!" the corpsman shot back. He'd just put a compress on the wound in Tangretti's leg and bandaged it tight. Now he was checking for other injuries. "You're hit! Shut up and lay down!"

" 'S'nothing." His entire right thigh felt numb, with a kind of throbbing beneath the numbness that told him the thing was going to hurt like hell soon . . . but it wasn't bleeding all that badly and he could still put a lot of weight on the leg so he didn't think the bone was broken.

He also felt numb in his right side and back, where he thought a piece of that grenade must have whacked him a good one, but that just felt bruised, as though someone had given him a swift, hard punch. His vest had probably saved him there. It didn't interfere with his movement, much, and he was damned if he was going to lie here in the mud and let Doc fuss over him like this. He shoved the other SEAL away again. "Look, you can check me at sick call tomorrow, okay?" Rolling away, he scooped up his M-16 and moved toward the embankment. *Damn*, his leg was starting to hurt now, but he could ignore it. He'd managed with worse in Hell Week. He *knew*, with complete confidence, what his body could endure.

He wasn't anywhere near the outside of his performance envelope yet.

The ringing was mostly gone now. In its place was the crack and clatter of automatic weapons. As he peered over the edge of the embankment, he could see a line of winking muzzle flashes, a pretty display curiously detached from the somehow alien concept that there were *people* over there trying their best to kill him. Taking aim at the tightest grouping of flashes, he squeezed the trigger, loosing a long burst of full-auto fire in reply.

Where were the other SEALs?

He pushed the brief, nagging sense of loneliness aside; Randolph was on his right, firing his M-16; Luciano was on his left, taking aim with his M203. The other SEALs would be deploying to meet the ambush. He *wasn't* alone.

Luciano's weapon gave its deep-throated thump; a moment later, the explosion shredded the underbrush a hundred meters ahead. Moments later, a new thundering opened up well to the right, the characteristic rattle of a Stoner Commando. A moment later, the sharp hiss of a LAW rocket launcher seared through the woods, also from the right . . . followed a moment later by the heavy *whoomp* of an explosion and a shrill cacophony of screams. That told Tangretti where Spencer and Jenkins were; Spencer was packing his beloved Stoner, while

Jenkins, in addition to his combat shotgun, had been carrying a couple of the disposable LAW portable rocket launchers. Then the lieutenant was there, dropping behind the embankment to Randolph's right, adding his AK's flat crack to the chatter of the sixteens.

Tangretti closed his mind to all of that, shutting out the noise, the confusion, the throbbing pain in his leg and side, and concentrated on pouring fire into the enemy positions. When his magazine ran dry, he dropped it with a touch of the release button and slapped a fresh mag into place. Jenkins's shotgun boomed to the right, a savage blast of raw thunder that momentarily drowned the cracking rattle of the Stoner. Luciano's M203 cut loose again to the left; the grenade's blast rang among the trees and elicited fresh screams.

Baxter slapped his shoulder, pointing left. *That way! Move!* Tangretti obeyed, though his leg nearly gave out beneath him. Clearly, the lieutenant didn't want them to stay pinned down here; it made too easy of a target for the enemy. The five of them, Luciano in the lead and Pettigrew bringing up the rear, began working their way west down the gully, circling to the left.

Several running shapes appeared, darting among the trees ahead, moving to get behind the SEALs' position. Luciano dropped, fired, and missed; aiming above Luciano, Tangretti triggered his M-16, sending a burst into one black-pajama-clad shape just as it scrambled up and over a log forty yards down the gully. A second shape appeared behind, this one wearing light tan or khaki. Tangretti fired again and the shape went down. A third kept moving, until Luciano lobbed a 40-mm grenade into the brush in front of it; the blast was deafening, powerful enough to pluck the running man from the ground and hurl him backward into the trunk of a tree.

The four kept moving, alert to other flankers, but saw nothing. Tangretti felt a chill, though, as they moved past the torn and bloodied bodies of the three they'd taken down; the man in khaki was wearing the uniform of the North Vietnamese Army. So far, the NVA hadn't been bothering with the Rung Sat. This was a first, and a deadly one.

Only a handful of minutes had passed since the beginning of the ambush ... two or three at most, when a new roar joined the battlefield, the piercing thunder of a helicopter's rotors, the whine of turbines, the shrill hiss of rockets firing two by two, followed by the crack-*wham* of warheads detonating in the forest. Tangretti looked up, then cheered with the other SEALs as the big, bug-faced shape of a Seawolf howled low overhead. Two by two, the 2.5-inch rockets shrilled from their launch tubes, arrowing into the forest to the north, and the rattle of their M60s was added to the cacophony of gunfire on the ground.

Feeling a bit cold and dizzy, Tangretti slumped to the ground, grateful for the respite. The SEALs would have to watch for enemy troops who might break and run in their direction, but the main part of the battle had just been taken out of the SEALs' hands.

The gunfire from the forest up ahead had ceased.

Tangretti was glad. He was feeling very, very tired.

1446 hours

They emerged in a village, a small and ramshackle collection of huts grouped not far from a large, earthen bunker. Two of the huts had collapsed and were burning; smoke boiled from the open bunker where a rocket had set off a chain of secondary explosions, probably fuel drums. Baxter gave hand signs, and the SEAL squad spread out, moving cautiously, alert for snipers or stay-behinds.

The two Seawolves continued to drone and circle, ready to pounce on the first sign of enemy resistance, but it looked as though Charlie had given up and fled north.

And not just Charlie, either. Half a dozen bodies lay sprawled in the clearing in front of the bunker and among the huts. Two of the six wore NVA uniforms, like the one they'd encountered in the woods.

Beyond the bunker, to the north, he could see the gleam of sunlight on water filtering through the smoke that continued to linger over the site—a river or broad stream. A couple of sampans were drawn up on the shore, and there were more bodies lying in the shallows. The gunships must have had a field day sniping at the enemy's panicked retreat.

"Fuck me," Spencer said softly, examining one of the khaki-clad bodies. Only half of the face was left, but it looked like a kid, eighteen, maybe nineteen years old. "This is the first we've seen NVAs in this area. I wonder what's up?''

"How about this, Chief?" Luciano said, walking from the river. He was holding a khaki-colored tunic. "There's a sampan over there and it's loaded with these uniforms."

"North Vietnamese. Damn, we've got an NVA army here."

"Regimental headquarters is my guess, Chief," Randolph said. He jerked a thumb at the bunker. "There are maps in there. And papers. Some good intel, looks like."

"Okay," Baxter said. He was worried about an enemy counterattack, though that was unlikely with the gunships overhead. "For now, secure the area, set up a perimeter. Zulu and Zed are going to be here in a few minutes. We'll tear the place apart when they get here." He turned, checking his men. Tangretti was standing ten yards away, leaning against a bullet-splintered post.

"Hey, Tangretti," Luciano called. "You okay? You ain't lookin' so hot."

"Doc!" Baxter yelled. He felt a cold stab of mingled fear and premonition. "Doc! Check Tangretti!"

1448 hours

Randolph reached Tangretti just as the SEAL's legs buckled beneath him. He supported the man as he slumped, easing him to the ground. Reaching up, he probed for a pulse at the angle of the jaw. There it was . . . thready and damned weak, and the skin felt as cold and as damp as a dead fish in the market. With all of that green paint covering Tangretti's face, it was impossible to judge skin color, but it looked to Randolph as though the man was quickly going into shock.

He checked the leg, but there was no fresh blood. The compress he'd tied on earlier was holding. Damn it, had Tangretti been hit somewhere else?

Quickly, he unfastened the SEAL's web gear and vest; as he pulled the black nylon vest away, he saw and felt that the black pajama shirt beneath was drenched with blood.

Working furiously, Randolph ripped the tunic open. There it was . . . a dime-sized hole in Tangretti's side, just in front of and above the right kidney. There was a hell of a lot of blood, and the skin that wasn't crusted over with blood was a cold, clammy white. Palpating the belly and abdomen, he could feel some swelling over the liver. Leaning close, he could detect a whiff of fecal odor as well, a sure sign that the kid's intestines had been pierced.

Shit! Shit! *Shit!*

Tangretti had taken internal injuries, big time, and hadn't even known it. *Randolph* hadn't known it, hadn't checked him thoroughly enough when he'd rendered first aid before, and that was damned unforgivable. Breaking open his field surgery, he used gauze and a forceps to probe the wound, trying to staunch the upwelling blood. He could only carry that so far, though. By packing the wound he might stop the bleeding, or most of it . . . but he might not, either, especially if the shrapnel had ripped through the hepatic vein or even the aorta.

No . . . no . . . if that had happened, Tangretti would be dead by now. The hell of it was, Randolph couldn't tell just how badly the kid had been holed, not without opening him up right here on the field, and that just wasn't practical. No, all Randolph could do—and it was so pathetically little!—was try to keep him going until they could get him on his way to a hospital. He was carrying one bottle of Ringer's Lactate in his kit, a field-expedient BVE—a blood-volume expander— that might keep Tangretti going until they got him aboard a medevac chopper.

Swiftly, working automatically, he cracked an iodine capsule over Tangretti's arm, prepping it, broke open an IV kit, and swiftly threaded the needle into an anticubital vein. "Lieutenant!" he yelled, but Baxter was close by his shoulder. "Lieutenant, we need an emergency medevac. Stat!"

"Already on the way. How is he?"

"Not good." He lifted the bottle of Ringer's, checked for bubbles in the plastic tubing, then opened the valve. Tangretti had already lost so much blood—most of it to internal bleeding—that this one bottle wasn't going to go very far.

If *only* he'd checked Tangretti more carefully when he'd been hit, fifteen minutes ago. Still holding the Ringer's aloft, he peeled back one of Tangretti's eyelids, checking pupil size. "Damn it, you dumb, stupid fuck!" he whispered fiercely into the SEAL's ear. "Don't you *dare* die on me!"

Damn it, how long would it be before the medevac arrived?

1451 hours

Damn it, you dumb, stupid fuck! Don't you dare die on me!
The words dragged at the raged edge of Tangretti's consciousness, pulling him back from warmth and peace to a death-cold chill.

For a moment, Tangretti was in a waking nightmare. It was Hell Week, and he was lying in that cold, cold sticky mud on the tidal flat behind Coronado. The rest of his BUD/S class was lying in the mud with him, all of them too exhausted to move, with sleep deprivation playing serious tricks on their eyes and ears and thoughts. God he was tired. And all he had to do was stagger out of the mud, shout "I quit," ring the bell three times, and toss his helmet liner down with all the other abandoned helmet liners, the silent record of all those would-be SEALs who'd realized when they'd had enough, who knew when to come in out of the rain, who were smart enough to quit before the routine broke them down completely....

It would be so easy to quit....

"Tangretti! Tangretti, you son of a bitch!"

Damn it, that bastard Ferraro wouldn't quit riding him, wouldn't let up.

"Why'd you ever think you had what it takes to be a SEAL, you dumb fuck? ..."

It would be so damned easy to go and ring that damned bell....

Give it up. Give it up.

Except that Dad was watching, and all of the other guys were watching, and there was strength in knowing that all of them were right down there in the mud with you, strength that you could draw on, strength that would help pull you through even when you knew, knew in your heart that you couldn't take another step, and damn he hated this mud, hated the cold, hated the day he'd decided to try to be a SEAL like his father and his brother, but somehow hanging on and toughing it out wouldn't be as hard as getting up and ringing the bell with all of them watching, all of them knowing he'd betrayed them, that he'd let them all down....

"...not gonna ... ring ... bell ..."

"Easy, there," Doc told him. "Just lay quiet, okay? We're

gonna get you out of here!''

What was Doc doing here? Where was Chief Ferraro? There he . . . no, that was Lieutenant Baxter. But there's Chief Spence. And Lucky . . . but they weren't at Coronado. Where was he? He could hear a helicopter coming in low and fast, its roar filling the universe.

"Where . . . what happened? . . ."

He felt so cold . . . so cold. . . .

"You just rest easy, Bill!" Doc told him. "You got a million-dollar wound there, guy! You're goin' home!"

But he didn't want to go home. He'd fought to become a SEAL, fought to win this place on the teams, fought for the chance to prove he was as good as Dad, as good as Hank. He *hadn't* rung the bell! He *hadn't*!

Damn it, it wasn't fair! . . .

The helicopter was touching down close by. He could feel the other SEALs placing him on a blanket and carrying him toward the *whop-whop-whopping* windstorm of the rotors. . . .

Chapter 37

Tuesday, 30 January 1968

Tran Van Kieu Street, Cholon
2205 hours

In one sense, the ancient city of Saigon was two cities nestled side by side. To the east, nestled against the curve of the Sai Gon River was Saigon proper, the bustling, cosmopolitan, and thoroughly westernized capital of the Republic of Vietnam. To the west, north of the merging of the reeking Kinh Ben Nghe and Kinh Tau Hu canals, was a city that might have been from another time, another world entirely. Cholon was predominantly Chinese. In fact, most Americans thought that the name meant "Chinatown" in Vietnamese. Actually, it meant "Big Market," an indication of just how important the ethnic Chinese minority was in Vietnam's economy.

Cholon was eerily and uncharacteristically quiet tonight, as Steve Tangretti drove the MACV motor pool jeep down Tran Van Kieu Street, then left across the bridge over the canal. Normally, especially on the eve of the Tet holiday, the streets would have been crowded, even this long after sunset, with merrymakers beginning the New Year's festivities, but it seemed the local population did not trust the promise of a ceasefire this year . . . or perhaps they simply felt there was nothing worthwhile to celebrate.

And Tangretti didn't blame them, not one bit, not after the reports that he'd seen . . . reports riding inside the locked briefcase on the seat beside him. There was a storm gathering, a damned big one. A storm that could sweep across the Americans in Vietnam and their Saigon government allies and sweep them both away.

Damn it, when was the command bureaucracy going to wake up and realize that its own damned, lethargic, selfserving incompetence was as much of an enemy as the Communists?

He was furiously angry, angry enough to commit the ultimate sin insofar as military form and protocol were concerned.

He was going over his bosses' heads.

On the south side of the bridge, he was passed through a checkpoint manned by ARVN security forces, the "White Mice," so named for the color of their helmets and gloves. South of the canal, the country opened up as he headed south on the Can Giuoc Road, giving way to scattered houses and occasional larger buildings, most with the distinctive Chinese flavor of old Cholon. His destination was about five kilometers south of the bridge.

Tangretti wasn't paying attention to the architecture as he drove, however. He was going over his arguments in his mind, rehashing them again and again. Damn it, the admiral *had* to listen to him! He *had* to!

His job running Det Echo and working with the South Vietnamese Provincial Reconnaissance Units had turned out even better than he'd hoped all those months ago. The PRU network idea had been a good one, providing good intel. But recently, in his day-to-day work with the information being sent up the line from various friendly sources, he'd been piecing together an ominous pattern. Something was brewing on the enemy's side, something very big, very nasty. Captures of supplies, especially arms and ammo, were way up this month over last; a number of units had reported capturing quantities of NVA uniforms . . . and the number of action reports recounting contact with North Vietnamese regulars was sharply up as well, often in areas like the Rung Sat where NVA troops had never been encountered before. The patterns of VC activity were shifting, too, moving out of the countryside and in closer toward all of the big cities, including My Tho, Chau Doc, and Saigon itself.

The changes weren't just occurring in the Delta, either. He'd seen reports from other PRU intel groups near Hue, Da Nang, and Nha Trang that all said the same thing.

Whatever was going to happen was going to happen all over this goddamn country at once.

For days, now, Tangretti had been trying to get a clear picture of the overall pattern and failing. But then it had started falling into place, and all because of the news about Bill.

Five days ago, he'd received official notification that his son had been seriously wounded in the line of duty and had already been flown back to the United States.

It was a screwy situation; Bill had been medevacked out of Nha Be, just a few miles south of Saigon; Steve had gotten the word by way of the National Naval Medical Center—NNMC—in Bethesda, Maryland, where Bill had been transferred for intestinal surgery.

His son had been close to dying just a few miles away, and he'd never known it.

The terse lack of information in the official notification had prompted Tangretti to try to learn more. Short of grabbing a helo and flying down to talk to Bill's CO at Nha Be in person—something that he knew would endear him neither to his bosses nor to Lieutenant Baxter—there wasn't a lot he could do save go through some of the intelligence reports being filed by Team One in order to find an after-action report or intelligence brief.

Getting at those, however, when you weren't supposed to see them, could take some doing. As usual the bureaucracy had seemed determined to stop Tangretti cold; as usual, when faced with such an obstacle, Tangretti had found a way around it.

This afternoon, he'd gone into MACV HQ and looked up an old buddy of his, a chief he'd served with aboard the same ship back in the late fifties who was now working with the naval intelligence spooks in Puzzle Palace East. He'd had to call in one hell of a lot of markers this time; he'd ended up owing that chief a case of bourbon on top of the traditional "Look, if you ever need anything from me, no matter what. . . ."

His friend hadn't been able to disclose anything classified, of course—and that Tangretti had gotten anything at all had been thanks mostly to his own security classification. All SEALs were cleared for handling a certain level of secure material, and Tangretti's level had been bumped several notches when he'd come to Vietnam to start working with the PRUs and native intelligence sources.

Still, it could have meant real trouble for his friend if it became known that he'd let Tangretti—who had no official "need to know," as the spooks' vernacular put it—see those particular files.

What he'd learned had told him little about Bill, save the fact that he'd been wounded by a booby trap, given emergency first aid in the field, then put on a medevac chopper for Saigon. After emergency surgery to stop the bleeding from a nicked hepatic vein, he'd been immediately triaged for a flight back to NNMC, where he'd undergone further surgery to repair his torn bowel. One interesting sidelight: Bill apparently had been wounded while knocking a fellow SEAL down to protect him from the booby trap. Lieutenant Baxter had put him in for a Silver Star, though it appeared that MACV-SOG was going to downgrade that to a Bronze Star instead.

That notation had made Tangretti laugh aloud, raising a curious glance from his friend, sitting across the room. Some things never changed; during the final year of World War II, Tangretti remembered quite well, an order had made its way down through the command structure of the Underwater Demolition Teams, directing that all UDT officers who swam up to an enemy-held beach would receive the Silver Star for the act, while all enlisted men who did the same would receive the Bronze.

The REMFs were still at it, all these years later.

Intrigued more than angered at that point, Tangretti had continued reading, tracking down at last the after-action report on the battle in which Bill had been wounded. The mission, it appeared, had been a routine patrol by Team One carried out in conjunction with a small group of Australian Special Forces. They'd encountered VC and NVA forces and had turned up an NVA regimental headquarters besides. A list of captured documents, letters, weapons, consumables, and other contraband was appended.

Mentioned on the list were fifteen NVA uniforms, including one with the rank insignia for the North Vietnamese equivalent of a colonel. . . .

Another haul of NVA uniforms. Strange, though, that he'd not heard any mention of this at MACV-SOG. This fit perfectly with the picture he'd been getting from the PRUs, that the enemy was smuggling large numbers of uniforms into the south, probably so that a very large number of NVA troops and officers could slip across the border from Cambodia disguised as civilians. The brass at MACV, however, had so far been oblivious to Tangretti's PRU reports.

Were they oblivious to this as well? Or to others?

With his friend growing irritated and glancing pointedly and frequently at his watch, Tangretti had begun digging through other records. He found a report filed on 10 January by Eighth Platoon, Team Two—Hank's unit!—that included a find of twenty NVA uniforms.

Unless somebody was planning on opening up a chain of uniform shops across South Vietnam, the area was going to be crawling in uniformed NVA troops any day now. The proximity of the Tet holiday was too obvious a deadline. The VC/NVA were getting ready for a big strike, and it was going to start on Tet.

Tomorrow!

His jeep's headlights carved a narrow swath out of the unfathomable darkness ahead. He was crazy, he knew, driving alone in an open vehicle through what was quite possibly enemy territory at night, but he had no other alternative open to him. He had to talk to someone with some real authority tonight and this was the only way he knew to do it.

He'd tried to get in touch with Hank at Tre Noc, partly to get his impression of the uniform capture, partly to see if he'd been informed about Bill, but he'd been told that Eighth Platoon had already left the area—his informant thought they'd flown up to Chau Doc, on the Cambodian border, a couple of days before, but he wasn't sure. Hell, maybe they knew something as well; SEALs were supposed to develop their own lines of intel and act on them. Tangretti had decided to drop that line of inquiry; there were enough reports of uniform captures to convince him that he was right. Instead, he'd spent the rest of the afternoon and much of the evening talking to higher and higher ranks within the hierarchy at MACV headquarters, trying to convince them that a major offensive was imminent, that someone was accidentally or deliberately overlooking some extraordinarily crucial intelligence.

He'd gotten exactly nowhere. "Oh, we've heard reports, but they don't amount to much," he'd been told by one major.

"Shit, if we jumped every time one of you SEALs spotted a gook," a Navy captain had said, "we'd never get any sleep."

"The VC are a spent force, Lieutenant," an army colonel assured him. "Even the North Vietnamese can't help them much at this stage. I wouldn't worry about it."

"This does not mesh well with our current official assessment of enemy capabilities," was the word from a civilian who, in Tangretti's estimation was probably CIA and most certainly an asshole. He had great respect for the Agency personnel who worked in the field; those who shuffled papers in the rear areas, though, were chair-warming ticket-punchers at best and REMFs at worst, and Tangretti had no patience with them at all.

It was after talking to the CIA man that he'd decided to take this drive in the country tonight. If he couldn't get anywhere with MACV-SOG, he might be able to sidestep that monster and get word to someone willing and able to act. The trouble with a bureaucracy like MACV was that it tended to formulate nice, neat theories about how the world worked and then, since people's careers and reputations were riding on the success of those theories, stick to them, even as more and more contrary evidence piled up, until they were literally living in a dream world, isolated from reality. So far as Tangretti was concerned, the bastards were welcome to any version of reality they cared to pick; where he drew the line was when their deliberate and self-serving blindness endangered American boys, *his* boys among them.

Then Tangretti had thought of Admiral Galloway. He was still on the job at MACV-SOG in Saigon, though the rumor mill said he was due to rotate home again soon. If anybody could get the intelligence to the place where it would do the most good, it was Joe Galloway.

If he could get through to him in time.

According to a harried second class personnelman at headquarters, Galloway was spending that evening at a New Year's Eve party hosted by Tran Dui Tho, an undersecretary in Saigon's Ministry of Defense. Mr. Tran reportedly lived on an immense and sprawling multimillionaire's villa just off the Can Giuoc Road. The trouble was, that function would be invitation only and with tight, tight security. There wasn't a chance in hell that they'd let a brash, middle-aged SEAL—and a mere lieutenant at that—crash the party.

Well, even a middle-aged SEAL still had a few tricks up his sleeve.

There was the turn-off, just ahead. Hauling the jeep's wheel over, he careened onto a narrow dirt road that plunged through thickening trees for perhaps two kilometers.

The guards appeared out of nowhere, a duo of White Mice in gleaming full dress, one standing imperiously at parade rest as the other gestured for Tangretti to stop. Behind them, a nine-foot stone wall topped by shards of broken glass and a coil of barbed wire rose up against the night. The gate was tall and imposing, constructed of wrought iron, and two more White Mice looked on from a guard shack, both armed with M-16s. Beyond, another kilometer distant, a blaze of colored lights marked the party at the Tran mansion.

"Yes, sir?" the senior White Mouse said in perfect English. He looked Tangretti up and down with only the slightest distaste evident in the curl of his upper lip. The SEAL wasn't exactly dressed for a party. He was wearing green Marine ODs and a fatigue cap, not exactly proper formal wear.

At least, Tangretti thought with a wry grin, he wasn't wearing green paint.

He showed his ID. "I am Lieutenant Steven Tangretti," he said. Pocketing the ID, he patted the briefcase beside him. "I have important papers for Rear Admiral Galloway, who is visiting here tonight. I must see him immediately. It's urgent."

"Do you have an invitation, sir?"

"Shit, do I look like I have an invitation? I'm not here to party, fella, I'm here to see *Admiral* Galloway!"

He'd hoped that stressing Galloway's rank would open the gate, but the White Mice appeared unmoved. Evidently, working for a ministry undersecretary took some of the awe from the exalted rank of admiral. From their unusual spit and polish, Tangretti guessed that these security people were on permanent assignment to Tran's retinue.

"I am most sorry, sir," the head Mouse said. "But this is a full dress party."

"Look, you must have a phone in that guard shack over there. Call the house, will you? Let me talk to Admiral Galloway!"

"I am most sorry, sir, but my instructions are that Mr. Tran and his guests are not to be disturbed. If you would care to leave a message in writing, I will see that it is delivered at an appropriate time." Meaning, Tangretti interpreted, never . . . or perhaps it would be delivered with an appropriate cash inducement. Unfortunately, Tangretti had only a couple of hundred piasters in his pocket—small change that wouldn't do to bribe a drink out of a bartender, much less cause this loyal servant of the government to waver in his duty to keep riffraff off the premises.

Well, there were other ways to do this.

Gunning the jeep's engine, he slapped the stick into reverse, spun about, and spat gravel as he raced back up the road.

He hoped he'd caught his Mouse friends with some of the spray.

Near the junction with the main road, he pulled the jeep hard left and off the road. Reaching down onto the floor behind the front seats, he produced a dark blue, moth-eaten blanket, a web belt with holstered sidearm, and a deadly looking Swedish K submachine gun, with three extra clips, all fully loaded. He'd been afraid it might come to this.

Leaving the jeep, with his briefcase in one hand and the folded blanket in the other, Tangretti sprinted through the woods back toward the Tran residence. He angled away from the road so that he would hit the property's encircling wall well clear of the sentry post at the main gate. He'd not had time to assess any special defenses or safeguards Tran might have in place, but he suspected that the man, like many of the rich, took a particular comfort in the number of his employees. Chances were he trusted in White Mice and Marvin ARVN rather than in minefields or electronic alarms.

Tangretti hoped that was the case. People were always easier to fool than electronics.

He reached the wall and stood there for a moment, listening. There was no sign of guards; the ground outside the wall was soft but showed no footprints, no indication of the beaten-down path a regular patrol would have left. Christ, didn't this guy care if someone snuck up on him at night? Or did he really think a little barbed wire and broken glass would keep a determined intruder out?

Standing in the wall's shadow, he unfolded the blanket, then gently whipped the free end up and over the wire at the top. There was a crisp rattling as the blanket snagged on the wire; he gave a tug, felt something give slightly . . . and then felt the blanket grab hold. Swiftly, he used a length of line to tie the briefcase to his belt and then, his Swedish K slung over his back, he grabbed the blanket in both hands and swarmed up to the top.

Wire and broken glass together were no obstacle. The blanket protected him from the wire and shielded his hands as he snapped off several of the shards. Keeping low to avoid providing an easy target to a sniper with a nightscope, he rolled over the gap he'd made and dropped lightly to the ground on the inside of the compound.

Dogs barking . . . and the swift pad of numerous feet. So *that* was Tran's backup security. With a muttered curse, Tangretti drew his sidearm and chambered a round in a single, smooth motion, The weapon was a 9-mm Smith & Wesson automatic with a bulky sound suppressor, a weapon designed to SEAL specifications for cases exactly like this.

SEALs called it the "Hush Puppy," for obvious reasons.

One dark black-and-tan shape loomed out of the darkness. Tangretti tracked the shape with a two-handed grip and tapped the trigger once . . . then again, eliciting two harsh coughs that were hardly silent but sounded nothing like the sharp crack of a pistol. The shape gave a loud yelp, then tumbled to the ground at his feet. A second shape was closing from the right; Tangretti pivoted and fired once more.

"Sorry, fella," Tangretti said as the second German Shepherd collapsed in a tumble of fur and bent legs. He didn't like shooting dogs, but there was no faster way to get through to Galloway. It briefly occurred to him that he'd just left a chink in Tran's defenses, but he dismissed it. If the dogs couldn't stop one renegade SEAL, they sure as hell wouldn't stop a VC kidnap or assassination team. Holstering his pistol, Tangretti broke into a ground-eating lope and headed for the house.

It griped him to be mounting a covert penetration of a presumably friendly target. He certainly wasn't planning to dispatch any of Tran's men the way he'd dispatched the dogs, but he was going to get through to see Galloway, and not hell or high water or all the ARVN White Mice in South Vietnam were going to stop him.

Perched atop a low and gently sloped hill, Tran's mansion was a surreal cross between a Chinese pagoda and something out of *Gone With the Wind*, a three-story affair with turrets and verandas and an enormous wooden patio deck brightly lit beneath the soft-glowing pastels of Chinese lanterns. The deck was crowded with men and a very few women; civilians were in formal evening wear complete with cummerbunds, while the military officers stood about in peacock displays of gold braid and dangling medals. Rock music thumped from large speakers; a stage on the deck near the house displayed two young Vietnamese women dancing topless more or less in time to the beat. The scene was at once opulent, decadent, and somewhat embarrassing. The American men, the older ones, at any rate, looked as though they would have been more at ease with Rachmaninoff than rock-and-roll; Tran, however, was notorious for his bizarre taste in things Western.

"*Ngung lai!*" someone shouted nearby. "Halt!"

Spinning, Tangretti faced an ARVN soldier, approaching him with an M-16 at the *en garde* position. It was a foolish move, for Tangretti had no trouble at all sweeping the weapon's muzzle aside with a blocking right, stepping close inside, and slamming the heel of his left hand into the side of the surprised soldier's head. The man collapsed without another sound.

"You! Stop where you are!"

"Shit!" Tangretti muttered, turning. "This is getting monotonous."

"*You!*"

Lieutenant Peter Howell stared at him, white-faced, from a few feet away, a Colt .45 gripped in unsteady hands.

"Howell!" Tangretti said. "What the fuck are you doing here!"

"I . . . think that I'm the one who should be asking that of you, Tangretti." Several more ARVN soldiers and a couple of White Mice appeared, all with weapons at the ready, but Tangretti was less concerned about them than the trembling Howell.

"Thurston, put that thing down!" Tangretti said, sharp sarcasm in his voice. "Before you hurt someone with it!"

"You're under arrest," Howell said. "You can't come in here like a wild man knocking people over the head."

Tangretti ignored the pistol in his face. "I want to see Galloway," he said. "Now. And if you play your usual paper-shuffling, swivel-chair, dick-jerking, pus-brained games with me, I swear I'll blow you away right here and now!"

"What's going on here, Lieutenant?" A large shape in dress whites loomed up behind Howell, resolving into Admiral Bledsoe.

"Admiral, I want to put this man under arrest," Howell said.

Bringing himself under control, Tangretti turned to the admiral. "Sir, I need to get in to speak with Admiral Galloway. I've got some urgent documents for the admiral that can't wait, sir . . ."

"For the love of Christ, man, it can wait until morning," Howell said, lowering his pistol.

"Lieutenant Tangretti, isn't it? Didn't we meet at the Special Warfare symposium last summer?" Bledsoe asked.

"Yes, sir."

"This is a rather novel way to crash a party, isn't it?"

"Admiral, I wouldn't be here if this wasn't crucial."

"It damned well better be, Lieutenant," the admiral replied. "It damned well better be."

Chapter 38

Tuesday, 30 January 1968

Tran Mansion
South of Cholon
2320 hours

Fifteen minutes later, a tired and dirty Tangretti slumped back in a sofa that might have cost half a year of the SEAL's normal pay, as Rear Admiral Galloway, resplendent in his full-dress whites, stood on the other side of the room, drink in one hand, an open file folder in the other. "You took one hell of a risk barging in here like that, Steve," the older man said, reading. "You could have been shot."

"Only way I could get in to see you, Admiral. They, ah, weren't exactly making it easy."

"Mmph. Those people out there are suggesting that I put you under arrest. What am I supposed to tell them?"

"Admiral, you can *put* me under arrest, for all I care. Pack me off to the brig at Portsmouth! But for God's sake do something about this intel. The REMFs are ignoring it, deliberately hiding it, and it's going to turn around and bite us!"

"I'm not sure that arresting you would do any good." Galloway grinned suddenly. "You've looked at the possibility of prison before, right? For, um, 'contravening established channels of procurement'? Somehow, I don't think I can scare you with the threat of a court martial."

"The point, Admiral, is what's in that briefcase. Not what happens to me."

"Lieutenant, are you really that sure that the VC are going to launch a big attack tomorrow?"

"Shit, Admiral, it could be tonight for all I know. Or maybe not for another couple of days. But it is going to happen, it will be big, and it will be timed to coincide with the Tet holiday." He grinned suddenly. "Judging from the really superb security Mr. Tran maintains here at his villa, I'd have to say that the VC would be idiots to pass up on the chance to snatch at least one Undersecretary of Defense."

"Mmm. I've been hearing some of this at headquarters," Galloway said, still reading. "But not about the NVA infiltration. This is verified, you say? By other sources than the locals?"

Like most Americans, Galloway had a low opinion of the reliability of VN intelligence sources. "Two different SEAL Teams, sir, One and Two, have both captured substantial numbers of NVA uniforms within the past couple of weeks. That verifies dozens of reports I've had through the PRUs and other sources. Damn it, Admiral, what does it take to convince people that this thing *is* going to happen?"

Galloway sighed, closing the folder and dropping it back into the briefcase. "Damfino, Steve. The official feeling is that the increase in activity has all been related to Khe Sanh."

"Shit, Admiral, that's clear on the other end of the goddamn country! What does Khe Sanh have to do with the Mekong or Saigon?"

Khe Sanh was a nondescript firebase twenty-five kilometers from the Demilitarized Zone between North and South Vietnam and perhaps fifteen from the Laotian border. Once a Special Forces camp, it had been taken over by the U.S. Marines late in 1966. Since April of '67, a series of sharp hill fights and skirmishes had been fought between the Marines and NVA units filtering down past the DMZ; since the previous fall, however, intelligence reports had been warning of a monumental NVA buildup in the area, possibly aimed at generating another Dien Bien Phu, a catastrophic defeat for the foreigners that would convince them, as the French had been convinced after their mass surrender in 1954, to pull out.

Just over a week ago, on 21 January, NVA regulars had launched an assault against Khe Sanh. The assault had been repulsed . . . but since that time the enemy had been closing in, cutting off the base's highway links with the coast and Hue, launching near constant harassing strikes and raids designed to wear down the defenders. Khe Sanh was turning into a siege, and many in the high command were convinced that *that* was Hanoi's objective, a single, isolated and near-useless Marine firebase, not some nebulous and ill-defined mass uprising throughout South Vietnam.

"The thinking in Washington," Galloway said carefully, "is that all seeming increase in enemy activity throughout the south is a diversion. An attempt to pull our attention away from Khe Sanh."

"What if it's the other way around?"

"Eh? What do you mean?"

"What if Khe Sanh's the diversion? Diversionary actions, as I understand the term, generally happen *before* the real show goes down, right? To give the target a chance to turn and meet what he thinks is the real threat. Then he can be sucker-punched from behind."

"You're assuming that the people running this show are rational." Galloway sighed. "I tell you straight, Steve, I agree with you. In my mind there's no question that we're about to be hit. I just don't know if there's any damned thing I can do about it."

Tangretti sagged, the drive, the will to keep pressing forward draining from him between one breath and the next. "What a clusterfuck," he said, his voice scarcely above a whisper. "A lot of damned good boys put it all on the line to get that intel, Admiral. Some of them got shot up bad, one of my kids among them. I hate to think of it being . . . just thrown away. *Ignored.*"

"Damn. Steve, I'm sorry about your son. Which one? Hank?"

He shook his head. "Bill."

"I didn't know he was in Nam yet."

"He just arrived last month. Booby trap." He pointed at the briefcase. "On a recon patrol that picked up some of those diversionary uniforms."

"I'm sorry. Damned bad luck."

"Yes, sir."

Galloway took a sip of his drink, rocking back on his heels. "It would be nice to have some independent verification of this."

"Just wait, Admiral. Charlie will give you all the independent verification you could ask for."

"Mmm. You may have a point." He thought for a moment more. "Okay, I'll tell you what." He gestured at the briefcase. "Let me have these. I'll get on the horn to the Pentagon . . . um." He looked at his watch. "Twenty-three-thirty hours Tuesday in Saigon is eleven-thirty Monday morning in Washington. Perfect. I'll see if I can use Tran's radio downstairs to call now and interrupt their two-martini lunch."

"What are you going to tell them, sir?"

"Well, I—" He broke off, listening. "Did you hear that?"

Tangretti cocked his head, listening. It sounded like a faint, far-off rattle.

Automatic gunfire, short, sharp, and insistent.

Standing, he went to a nearby door leading to a veranda outside and pushed it open. The sound was louder now . . . then suddenly cut off.

"That could be coming from the front gate," Galloway said. He picked up a telephone and listened for a moment. He dropped the receiver. "Line's cut. We're the target all right."

"Shit." Tangretti picked up his Swedish K, which he'd dropped on the sofa, and chambered a round. "Maybe before you call Washington, sir, you'd better call up to Tan Son Nhut and see if they can spare you some air assets. Helicopter gunships, if you can get 'em."

"I can do better than that." Galloway grinned. "There are a couple of Seawolves parked over at Nha Be, if I remember right. That's less than five miles away."

The figure jolted Tangretti. He'd not realized how close he was to the SEAL Team One base on the Rung Sat. "Great," he said. "I'll see if I can slow them up a few minutes."

"Be careful, Steve. One man can't stop an army, and *that* bunch—" He jerked his head, indicating the party guests outside. "They won't be much help."

"I'll manage. Watch your back, sir!"

"You too."

Tangretti pushed through the open door and into the night. As he jogged down the gentle slope of the house grounds toward the gate, he heard another burst of gunfire, followed by an ominous silence. He moved swiftly, sticking to the shadows of the trees. He wished now that he'd taken the time to blacken his face and hands; he felt damn near as naked as those two go-go dancers out there, and a lot more vulnerable.

Halfway to the gate, he saw movement, a cluster of shadows crouched beyond the iron bars across the driveway. A jeep was standing on the driveway, its lights casting a pool of radiance across the gate. In their glare, Tangretti could see four sprawled forms in white gloves and helmets on the ground—the four White Mice on gate guard detail—and at least five men in black pajamas attaching something to the gate's lock.

Inside the gate, another man, all in white, was down on the ground beside the jeep, still moving but obviously hurt. As Tangretti approached, one of the VC outside fired through the bars at the wounded man, a quick stuttering burst from an AK. The wounded man yelped, then dragged himself farther behind the cover provided by the jeep. One of the vehicle's headlamps flared and went out, cutting the light sharply.

Throwing himself flat, Tangretti aimed his Swedish K and fired, sending a burst into the gate. One of the black-clad figures screamed, flopping backward; two more returned fire with long, ragged volleys. Using the jeep's light to mark his targets, Tangretti fired three more tight, precise bursts; bullets screamed off stone or iron bars, sparking in the night, but others passed through, striking flesh. Two VC were down now, possibly three. The others pulled hastily back.

It looked to Tangretti as if the would-be invaders had been trying to attach an explosive charge to the gate. That seemed like the hard way to go about it . . . unless they were looking for a lot of noise and obvious damage to drive home some political point. Still, if they were blocked here, it wouldn't take them long to find their way over the wall at some other spot. Tangretti raced for the jeep, crouched low and staying clear of the glare from the headlight beam.

Gunfire barked from the top of the wall to the left. Bullets sprayed clumps of turf near his feet and he dove for the ground, coming up with his subgun nestled against his shoulder. He emptied a magazine, unable to tell whether he'd hit anything or not. A babble of voices, sing-song Vietnamese, sounded from close by in the darkness, and Tangretti swiftly slapped a fresh mag into his weapon. He was about to fire at the voices when he hesitated; something in the sound of those voices carried panic rather than any determination to press an attack.

An instant later, a gaggle of ARVN troops burst from the cover of some trees near the wall, fleeing toward the house. He realized that they *could* be VC dressed in government uniforms . . . but more likely they were troops in Tran's employ who'd been patrolling the grounds and been caught by the attack.

"Ngung lai!" he shouted, standing again and brandishing the Swedish K. The soldiers stopped, gawking at him. Several started to break and run again when they saw he was only one American, but he triggered his subgun, spraying a burst into the grass in front of them. *"Ngung lai!"* he shouted again. *"That* way!" He gestured with the K. *"That* way, damn it! Now!"

They blinked at him, uncertain, their weapons shifting nervously in their hands. From outside the wall, shouts could be heard, and the patter of running, sandaled feet.

He pointed at the biggest of the ARVN soldiers. "You! You speak English?"

The man nodded. "Affirmative, sir! I speak!"

"You're in command! Take these people down there and secure that gate!"

Comprehension, surprise, and fear struggled for a moment behind the man's eyes. Then he gave a stiff nod. "Yes, sir!" He brandished his M-16 and shouted to the half-dozen men behind him. *"Den!"*

Two of the ARVNs broke away from the group and kept running; Tangretti let them go. The others, steadied perhaps by a leader's clear-cut orders—or by Tangretti's menacing presence in their rear—charged the gate. Tangretti turned toward the jeep and the wounded man in white beside it.

The white was a U.S. Navy dress white uniform, with the billed cap of an officer lying nearby. The black shoulder boards carried the two gold stripes of a lieutenant. With an oddly cold feeling of premonition, Tangretti dropped to one knee beside the man and rolled him over onto his back.

Peter Howell.

He was still alive, too; his eyelids fluttered open. "Trouble . . . at front gate . . ." he mumbled. There was no sign that he recognized Tangretti.

Howell's white trousers were stained with blood, glistening and black in the poor light. Another stain had spread across his jacket over his upper right shoulder. He needed medical attention, but the wounds didn't look like they were immediately life-threatening. He seemed to be breathing okay, and his pulse was strong.

"Take it easy, Howell," Tangretti said. "We'll get you out of this."

The jeep was finished, the radiator riddled by gunfire from the gate, though the battery continued to power the one remaining headlight. He would have to carry the man out.

Gunshots banged from the front gate. Tangretti's impromptu army was taking cover behind the wall, exchanging fire with VC outside the gate. Carefully, he picked Howell up in a fireman's carry, turning to haul him back up the hill toward the house.

A sharp hiss sounded from the direction of the gate; he turned his head just in time to see a white contrail streak in from the night beyond and slam into the iron bars with a bright flash and the crack of a high explosive. Two of the ARVN troops behind the gate went down, one still, the other writhing and twisting on the ground. The other three wavered a moment, then broke and ran.

A second rocket-propelled grenade struck the gate, already twisted by the first explosion. The lock gave way and the two halves of the gate flew back into the compound. Debris was still falling as a stream of men in black pajamas burst through the opening, haloed in blue smoke and light, weapons firing wildly. Still standing with Howell draped over his back and shoulders, Tangretti aimed his Swedish K one-handed, snapping off burst after burst as the attackers fanned out into the Tran compound. At a range of thirty yards, firing on full-auto one-handed, it was virtually impossible to hit anything, but the sudden fire from immediately in front of them momentarily checked the VC's forward rush.

Something thumped on the ground a few yards away just in front of the jeep—a bright apple-green object, egg-shaped with a handle. Tangretti dove to the ground, dragging Howell with him. The Russian RGD-5 grenade exploded a second later, shattering the jeep's remaining headlight, smashing back the hood, and rocking the vehicle on its tires.

As the smoke cleared, Tangretti, lying full length on the ground beside the wounded Howell, opened fire. With the jeep's lights gone, the compound's perimeter was now in almost total darkness, though a haze of light continued to spill down the hill from the Tran mansion at his back. He could still dimly see the advancing VC, shadows slightly darker and more solid than the night behind them and occasionally given sharper form by the intermittent flashes from their weapons.

Able to brace his submachine gun in both hands now, Tangretti took careful aim and kept firing. One of the advancing shapes went down before his magazine ran dry. He snicked home another, the third of a total of five, and kept firing. He got another . . . and another . . . then reloaded again with his fourth magazine.

As though encouraged by Tangretti's stand in front of the gate, scattered shots were cracking from the top of the hill, where some of Tran's security forces were organizing for a stand. The VC were returning fire, but sporadically. It was hard to tell in the darkness, but Tangretti thought they were working their way left and right inside the compound walls. It was time to get the hell out of Dodge, before he was out of ammo and cut off. Picking up Howell once more, he started lugging the wounded man up the hill.

He was less than halfway up the slope when several dark shapes rushed toward him from the left. A shot barked, and a bullet cracked close behind his head. Spinning, he aimed his K one-handed and fired. At a range of less than five meters it was hard to miss; the lead VC caught a burst of five rounds squarely in his face and upper chest. Several more VC opened up on full auto; something struck Tangretti like a sledge hammer blow in his left side . . . then again in his leg, spinning him around. Overbalanced by Howell's weight across his shoulder, he went down, falling on his back. Two VC rushed forward out of the night; he triggered a long burst from flat on his back, letting the weapon's recoil drag the muzzle up and across the charging communists. Both staggered and fell as more bore down on Tangretti from the right, but as he shifted aim, the Swedish K's receiver snapped on empty. No time to reload; he dropped the subgun and fumbled at his web belt's holster for his Hush Puppy. The lead VC was carrying a Hungarian-model AK with an integral folding bayonet. With a shrill scream, he ran up to Tangretti and lifted the rifle high, ready to pin the SEAL to the earth; Tangretti dragged his pistol free of the holster and fired, a difficult shot upward, from the hip, but the 9-mm round smashed into the soldier's left arm and staggered him back a step. Tangretti fired again . . . and again . . . the harsh coughs of the sound-suppressed Smith & Wesson nearly lost beneath the crack and bang of the gunfire all around. The VC with the bayonet flopped back. Three more VC closed in. Tangretti fired twice at the new leader . . . and then the slide of his Smith & Wesson locked open, the eight-round magazine empty.

Tangretti knew in that moment that he was about to die.

Light exploded in the night sky above and behind Tangretti; thunder roared. For a frozen moment, a half dozen VC stood just a few feet down the hill from him, paralyzed, staring upward into that dazzling glare from the heavens.

The thunder grew louder, a pulsing, hammering *whop-whop-whop* as the helicopter gunship bore down on the cluster of figures pinned in the shaft of blue-white illumination cast by its spotlight. Behind it, a second Seawolf gunship hoisted itself above the treeline beyond the Tran mansion.

One of the VC threw down his AK, turned, and fled. In seconds, the rest broke and ran as well as the helicopter roared low overhead, buffeting Tangretti with the miniature hurricane of its rotor wash. He heard the sharp chatter of its M60s. The Seawolf banked sharply as it swooped over the compound wall, skewing sideways, then circling back. He could see the flashes from its paired machine guns as the aircraft, like an immense, black carnivorous insect, tracked down its prey and slashed it down.

Somewhere up the hill, people were cheering.

Tangretti tried to get up and found he couldn't. His leg was throbbing—not hurting, exactly, but pulsing with a dull, heavy numbness and refusing to support his weight. He was bleeding from his side, too; when he touched his side, his hand came away slick with blood.

One of the Seawolves was hovering nearby now, its landing skids a foot above the grass. Several SEALs—Tangretti recognized them from their green faces and dangerous-looking garb—leaped from the open side door and fanned out across the hillside. Gunfire continued to bark, but in isolated bursts.

"Steve!" a familiar voice called. "Steve, damn it, are you okay?"

Galloway was there, bending over him, holding him.

"Guess . . . there were too many of 'em."

"Shit," Galloway said. There was blood staining his white uniform. At first, Tangretti feared the admiral had been wounded too, until he realized that the blood was his. *"Shit, you stupid, dumb son of a bitch! I know one SEAL's more than a match for a hundred VC, but you just tried to take on two hundred. What's the matter . . . can't you count?"*

Tangretti could feel the darkness of the encircling night growing closer. He was very tired and wanted nothing more than to just let go and float away.

"Count?" he managed to say. "Shit, Admiral. They . . . never taught us how . . . in BUD/S."

Chapter 39

Wednesday, 31 January 1968

Eighth Platoon, SEAL Team Two
Waterfront, Chau Doc
0615 hours

Mariacher stood in the PBR's well deck, leaning over the starboard gunwale as he listened to the crump and rumble of distant explosions. "Shit, Lieutenant," Richardson told him. "It sounds like they're shellacking the place."

"Wonder if it's theirs or ours?" Selby wondered, cleaning his Stoner.

"Theirs, I think," Mariacher said. "Those explosions are all light stuff. I don't hear any heavy arty yet."

It was still dark, though the eastern sky was showing some sign of graying with the slow approach of the tropical winter dawn, with sunrise scheduled for 0723 hours. Flares hung above the horizon to the south, giving the sky in that direction an eerie, silver glow that back-lit the sharp black edge of the horizon. More light was coming from the city, where flashes from mortar rounds and exploding rockets intermittently pulsed and strobed among the buildings, and the overcast sky showed the sullen red glow from numerous fires.

The two PBRs were cruising downstream on the Bassac, the stone and concrete buildings of Chau Doc rising to their right as they slowly approached the town's waterfront. Eleven of Eighth Platoon's SEALs were divided between the two patrol boats; the men were keyed up but outwardly calm. In the past several hours, it seemed, the entire world had gone to hell.

It had begun the evening before, when the platoon had deployed north to the Vinh Te Canal on the Cambodian border, planning to set up a listening post and maybe, if they were lucky, snag some Communists humping contraband south. After several false insertions, they'd slipped off the PBRs and made their way ashore, actually circling across the forbidden Red Line into Cambodia in order to come down on their planned objective from the north. The maneuver, Mariacher had thought, would catch the enemy off-guard; Americans, after all, were the good guys and never, *never* broke the rules. . . .

The maneuver had been a surprise, all right, but for both sides. The SEALs had practically stumbled into the middle of an NVA camp, where troops were off-loading bags of supplies and crates of weapons and ammo from Russian-built trucks. Their approach had been stealthy, covered by the noise the enemy was making, but as they'd been pulling back, someone had seen them—or perhaps a nervous sentry had simply opened fire on shadows.

In a quick, sharp, running firefight, the SEALs had fallen back toward the canal; SEAL doctrine taught that the Teams *always* put water at their backs, that water was a natural escape route. With enemy bullets cracking through the trees above their heads, the SEALs had slipped into the canal, waded a hundred meters downstream, then clambered aboard the waiting PBRs as the riverine crews poured .50-caliber fire into the tree-lined banks at their backs. A radio call to Camp 510, warning them of the heavy concentration of enemy forces, revealed a new turn in the situation: at just past 0300 hours, the VC had launched a massive attack on both the Special Forces Camp and on the city the camp was defending. Chau Doc was now swarming with VC, the Army radio operator said, and the SEALs were on their own.

The announcement had not surprised Mariacher. SEALs fought best on their own in any case . . . but he had told the two PBRs' skippers to take it back to the city slowly. Though SEALs preferred fighting at night, Chau Doc was still unknown territory, and the handful of Americans could get chewed up real fast blundering through an enemy-held town at night.

A fresh round of explosions ripped through the early morning darkness, lighting up the sky to the west in vivid oranges and yellows. That would be Chau Doc's fuel farm ablaze. The sullen, wavering glow transformed the river and the fire-torn city on its banks into a panorama of hell.

Mariacher looked at his watch. An hour left until dawn . . . but the light was good enough now that the SEALs could at least see where they were going. He clapped the PBR skipper on the shoulder and pointed downstream. "Let's take 'er in," he said. The Navy chief nodded and turned the wheel.

The SEALs did have a base of sorts to return to—or at least, they did if the VC hadn't already found it and blown it up. They'd had several days now to prepare for this op. After their first visit to Chau Doc two weeks earlier, Eighth Platoon had returned to Tre Noc and mapped out a campaign. Ensign Crane and two Alpha Squad SEALs would stay at Tre Noc and keep a lid on things with the bureaucracy there, as well as work at coordinating air and other assets with the detachment in the north. Mariacher and the other ten SEALs had returned to Chau Doc early on 28 January, cruising north the long way this time aboard two PBRs on loan from the TF 116 base at Tre Noc.

The next two days had been spent getting settled in. Their official quarters were at Camp 510, outside of town, but they'd been spending more time in a cleaned-out storehouse on the waterfront that they were converting, with Sergeant Aimes's help, into a temporary docking and supply facility for the

PBRs. They'd brought most of what they would need—fuel, ammo, food—up from Tre Noc, but Mariacher had wanted a base they could operate from without being constantly under Colonel Perry's thumb. Aimes had turned up a real prize— two rusty and pothole-battered jeeps that looked like they were of World War II vintage. Horner and Brubaker had worked together to jury-rig pintel mounts in the backs of both vehicles that would accept the .50-caliber machine guns off the PBRs. That way, the Ma Deuces would be carried along on the patrol boats to provide covering fire from river or canal but could be remounted on the jeeps if they needed to patrol inland.

Besides, it was good to have the jeeps handy to cover all the ground between various points in Chau Doc and Camp 510, and the extra firepower was a good thing to have along in Injun country.

The PBRs nosed in toward the dock area. Gunfire cracked from a rooftop overlooking the waterfront, and gouts of water splashed from the river's surface nearby. The PBR's fifty-gunners returned fire, slamming twin streams of glowing tracers into the building's roof. A moment later, the vessel's bow thumped along the wooden pier, and the SEALs leaped over the gunwale and onto the shore.

Despite occasional incoming fire from snipers, it appeared the VC hadn't discovered the unofficial SEAL base in this part of town. The storage sheds were still locked and secure—not that they'd left behind much in the way of weapons or ammo. The jeeps were safe, however, and Mariacher ordered Brubaker and Gil Franklin to transfer the PBR's fifties to the jury-rigged jeep pintel mounts.

As autofire continued to rattle across the streets of Chau Doc, Mariacher returned to the lead PBR with several SEALs, accepting a radio handset from the boat's skipper. "We got the Special Forces camp on the line, Lieutenant," he said. "Call sign 'Fox Sierra.'"

"Right, Chief." He took the handset. "Fox Sierra, Fox Sierra," he said. "This is White Shark. Do you copy? Over."

"White Shark, Fox Sierra. Roger, we copy. What is your posit? Over."

"Fox Sierra, we're on the waterfront downtown. Looks like fairly light VC activity in the center of town. We were wondering if you wanted to coordinate a break-out with us. We can hit 'em in the rear, while you come out the gate. Over."

"Ah . . . that's a negative, White Shark. Our orders are to hold position. Over."

Mariacher struggled against a surge of anger. "Fox Sierra, how the hell can you protect the goddamn town if you're holed up in your bunkers? If we catch Charlie from two directions, he's going to break. Over!"

There was a static-ridden pause, presumably while unseen officers discussed things on the other end. Then, "Ah, White Shark, Fox Sierra. Our orders are to hold position. No personnel are to leave this compound. However, we will coordinate our fire so you can make it in through the gate. Over."

He thought about that. How many men, he wondered, did Colonel Perry have inside the camp? If what he'd heard from Aimes were true, half of the Mike Force could be deployed elsewhere in the district—and was probably getting the same loving treatment from Charlie that the town was right now.

If the eleven SEALs and eight riverine sailors entered that fortress, they would be under orders to stay and help defend it.

"Negative, Fox Sierra. We'll tough it out here. Over."

"White Shark, that was not a suggestion. Colonel Perry has ordered you and your men to return to Camp 510. Intelligence reports indicate that a large body of enemy troops have moved into the area, possibly as many as fourteen hundred VC and NVA regulars. You are directed to report to 510 immediately. Over!"

"No shit, Sherlock," Mariacher said, but his thumb was off the transmit key. The SEALs' reports had been part of that intelligence. He thought a moment, then pressed the transmit key again. Instead of speaking, however, he blew heavily into the mouthpiece.

"White Shark, White Shark, this is Fox Sierra," the voice said in his ear, sounding excited. "Say again last transmission. You are breaking up."

Mariacher blew into the mouthpiece once more. "Are breaking up," he said suddenly. "Fox Sierra, I did not copy last. Over."

"White Shark. White Shark. Come in, White Shark. White—"

Mariacher snicked off the switch. "I'll be damned if I'm

going to learn trench warfare at *my* age," he said, and the listening SEALs laughed.

"We should probably keep the frequency open though," the boat's skipper pointed out. "We've got other friendlies in the AO, and we might want to listen for air strike warnings."

"You've got that right," Mariacher said. He switched on the radio again. A voice was calling from now, but not the same as before.

"White Shark, White Shark, this is Ripcord. Do you copy? Over."

Ripcord was the call sign for Aimes and CORDS, worked out with the SEALs during their previous visit to Chau Doc. Mariacher was more than happy to talk to him.

"Ripcord, White Shark. I read you. Go ahead."

"White Shark," Aimes's voice said, "we intercepted your exchange with 510. Can you provide us with assistance, over?"

The way Mariacher was feeling at the moment, Perry and his green beanies could look out for themselves. Sergeant Aimes and his Nungs, however, were a different matter, especially if they weren't hunkered down safe in Camp 510's bunkers. "Ain't got nothing better to do at the moment," Mariacher said. "What's your sit? Over!"

"We're fine. We're okay for the moment at CORDS HQ. We're planning a little party for Charlie, and we'll advise you of our movements. But there's something else. Over." Aimes sounded worried.

"Let's have it."

"There are three American civilians unaccounted for in Chau Doc. They may have been trapped in the town when the communists attacked. We need someone to go in and pick them up. Over."

"Ripcord, you've got yourself a deal. Tell us what we need to know. Over."

Tersely, Aimes filled the SEALs in. Two American women, both school teachers, were believed to be at the school compound not far from Chau Doc's small Catholic Church, on the waterfront and south of the central part of town. Another woman, a nurse, was probably still at her house, in a block development next to Chau Doc's hospital further north. Richardson nodded confirmation as Mariacher repeated the information. "We met the nurse and one of the teachers when we were here two weeks ago, Lieutenant," he said.

Mariacher nodded back. "Okay, Ripcord," he said. "We'll get them. Over."

"Thank you, White Shark. Bring them to the CORDS compound. I'll tell my people to be expecting you." His people would be the Nungs. Mariacher had met some of them two weeks ago and been impressed. They were definitely a cut or two above the usual Vietnamese RF/PF or militia forces.

"Roger that, Ripcord. Tell 'em the cavalry's on the way."

"We're gonna need transport," Horner said as Mariacher replaced the handset. "More than two jeeps, anyway."

"How about that?" Brubaker said, pointing. Across the street on the far side of the street paralleling the waterfront, was a Ford station wagon, looking as innocuous as if it had been parked at a curb in downtown Virginia Beach.

"You think someone was stupid enough to have left the keys in the ignition?" Selby asked.

Brubaker looked pained. "Fuck the keys. Come on!"

Climbing out of the PBR once more, the SEALs trotted across the street. Brubaker used the butt-end of his diving knife to smash the driver's side window and pulled open the lock. Slipping behind the steering wheel, he used the knife's hilt once more to crack open the ignition block and extracted several wires. A quick strip of the wires with the knife . . . a twist . . . and the Ford's engine gunned to life.

"Hope you know you just shot the warranty on this thing to hell," Horner told him as he pumped the gas.

"Okay," Mariacher told Brubaker. "You see if you can go find those teachers. Take three men with you. If you need help, double back to the CORDS compound and talk to Aimes. Maybe he can loan you some Nungs."

"Roger that."

"Patterson!" he called. "Zale! Franklin! You three go with Bear. You've just been appointed cavalry-to-the-rescue for those teachers."

"Hey, maybe you can get laid," Richardson added. "Girls can be real grateful to the guys rescuing 'em."

"Fuck you, Richardson," Brubaker snapped back. "I don't want to hear your shit. This is serious."

"The rest of you, with me," Mariacher continued, ignoring the exchange. "We'll split up in the jeeps. One will provide cover for Bear, the other'll head up and find the nurse. Badges? See if you can break out some LAWs and divvy 'em up."

"Aye-aye, boss," Horner replied.

"How about the PBRs?" Brubaker wanted to know. "We pulled their fifties."

"They still have their sixties and their Gats," Mariacher replied. "They'll pull back into the river and give us fire support from the water. Okay? Let's do it!"

A mortar round landed nearby, punctuating the order with a dull *crump*.

Le Loi Street, Chau Doc
0720 hours

Half an hour later, the jeep carrying Richardson, Selby, and Horner careened around a corner and onto the street where the nurse, Lisa Moore, was supposed to have her quarters. With Horner at the wheel, Richardson stood in the rear of the jeep, bracing himself with the hand grips of the fifty as the vehicle clattered and bumped through streets littered with spills of debris and random potholes. Striking a pile of rubble and a fair-sized log tumbled across the curb, the vehicle jolted violently and momentarily became airborne. "Yee-hah!" Richardson yelled from the back. "Just like the 'Rat Patrol'!"

That pseudo-historical TV series had always amused him with its machine-gun jeeps flying over African sand dunes like low-level fighters, but the SEALs were bringing it to life now in the shattered streets of Chau Doc.

It was fully light now, and the center of the city reminded Richardson forcefully of the World War II movies he'd seen set in battle-torn French towns. The enemy was definitely inside the city, but not in major force. Twice, the jeep came under automatic weapons fire, but both times a thunderous reply from the fifty discouraged the enemy from getting involved in a major firefight. They'd seen only a few bodies along the way, but those had been grisly discoveries. All had been VC; the Nung, it seemed, liked to mutilate their victims.

Aimes's mercenaries had been busy in the early morning hours.

Lisa Moore's house was a small, concrete-block dwelling not far from the hospital, one of numerous houses constructed through various U.S. helping-hands programs according to the kind of institutional-style blueprints that contrived to make the structure look completely out of synch with the rest of the architecture in the area. As the SEALs pulled up across the street, they heard a woman's scream from inside, muffled by the thick walls.

"Shit!" Richardson called, grabbing his M-16 and vaulting from the jeep. "Chief! Give us some cover!" He raced up the walkway to the front door and took a position to the right, back to the wall; Selby moved in close behind, shifting left. Horner clambered into the back of the jeep and took over the fifty. Richardson checked his weapon, then nodded to Selby; they'd practiced room-clearing before, during weapons training in BUD/S, and in special combat courses afterward; Selby would kick in the door, Richardson would roll through and move into the room beyond toward the left, and Selby would follow, clearing right. Ideally, the maneuver would be executed with four men or more, but the SEALs didn't have time to gather an army. A second scream from inside, louder and more desperate, underscored the need for haste.

Richardson nodded to Selby, who stepped in front of the door, raised his foot and kicked hard. Thin plyboard shattered, hinges flying; Richardson pivoted on his shoulder and lunged through the opening while the shards were still falling.

The door opened directly into a living room with unpainted concrete block walls and bright, plastic-covered furniture. A standing clothes cupboard had been opened, its contents scattered, and Lisa Moore lay in front of it on her back, one VC astride her hips, pinning her down as he tore with two hands at her blouse. A second man with a Vietnamese K-50 submachine gun stood a few feet away, a comically surprised look on his face as Richardson burst in on the scene.

Richardson immediately sighted on the man with the SMG as the primary threat; the first VC definitely had his hands full as Lisa thrashed and kicked and he tried to hold her down. The SEAL fired his M-16 on full-auto, the burst of rounds slashing the surprised soldier across his chest and shoulders and striking sparks from the wall behind him. Richardson shifted aim . . . but Selby was in the room too, and his nearly simultaneous burst from his Stoner smashed the top of the VC's head in a gory spray of blood and bone, toppling him back and away from the struggling American nurse.

The weight gone from her hips, Lisa lunged to her feet and ran toward the SEALs; behind her, from a hallway leading to an open door in the back of the house, more black-pajama-clad men rushed forward, a scant ten feet behind her. For a moment, Lisa blocked the SEAL's fire; then she stumbled and fell headlong, tripped by a crumpled throw rug, and both SEALs opened fire together, sending a hail of 5.56-mm rounds slamming down the concrete-walled corridor, cutting down several pursuers in mid-stride.

Richardson dragged Lisa to her feet. Her face was bleeding—possibly a cut from ricocheting fragments. "You okay?"

She nodded, eyes wild, pushing back a matted handful of blond hair.

"Then move it!" he yelled. He could hear more VC approaching from the back of the house. "Move your ass!"

He practically launched the woman through the shattered door with a shove, then turned to back out of the house. Selby loosed another burst down the hallway to keep the surviving hunters cautious, then backed out himself. Horner signaled from the street. "Let's get the fuck out of Dodge!" he yelled at them. "The cavalry's on the way, and this time it ain't ours!"

Selby leaped into the jeep; Richardson grabbed Lisa by the waist and bodily threw her in on top of him. Gunfire banged from the front of the house. Horner leaned into the bucking recoil as he returned fire with the fifty, hammering away at the front door and windows of the building. Two VC burst through the open frame of the front door and were cut down the instant they appeared and tore fist-sized craters in the concrete block. Glass shattered. Richardson paused long enough to pitch a grenade through the living room window, then slid into the driver's seat. The explosion rained debris onto the street as the jeep squealed its tires in a burned-rubber getaway.

In the back of the jeep, Lisa—white-faced and with her hair in a wild disarray—struggled to get up off of Selby and out from under Horner's feet. Pulling the torn remnants of her blouse together, she managed a small grin. "You guys sure do know how to show a girl a good time," she said.

Richardson, however, was shaking inside; the rescue had been so tight, so *damned* tight . . . not because the VC had almost raped the woman or because they could have killed her, but because the SEALs had come in shooting, moving fast, assessing a confused situation on the fly. *They* could have killed her, and that realization was making Richardson's stomach turn. Contrary to the image routinely presented by Hollywood, the good guys do not always hit the right targets, handguns and submachine guns cannot be fired by running men with any real accuracy, and lumps of steel-jacketed lead travelling at 3280 feet per second do not simply *stop* when they hit nine-inch concrete block. They bounce, usually in razor-edged pieces still moving at high speed in different directions, and they take fragments of wall with them. Judging from the bloody scratch on Lisa's face, she'd literally come within an inch or two of being killed by that rescue, and Richardson was having a hard time dealing with that.

When Lisa made her joke, then, several jaunty replies were possible . . . but he merely shook his head. "We're just glad you're okay, Miss," was all he said.

Later, at the sandbag-ringed compound that was the headquarters for Chau Doc's CORDS facility, they turned Lisa over to Aimes and his staff. Selby dug an elbow into Richardson's side. "Hey, I gotta thank you, Hank!" he said with a lecher's grin. "I got a real eyeful when you tossed that chick in on top of me! Felt her up, too, while we were bouncing down the street! Man, what a great pair of tits!"

Richardson felt cold inside. "Selby, just shut the fuck up," he said.

Brubaker had been right. This business was too serious for that kind of shit.

Chapter 40

Wednesday, 31 January 1968

Quang Trung Street, Chau Doc
1145 hours

A little more than nine hours after the initial VC attack, the Battle for Chau Doc was finally turning in favor of the joint American-Nung-ARVN forces in the area. With the American civilians all accounted for and safely inside the CORDS compound, the SEALs had returned to the streets of Chau Doc. Coordinating their sweeps with the CORDS Nung, Mariacher's handful of SEALs had moved slowly through the central part of the city, fighting street by street and block by block to root out each VC hardpoint and stronghold as they found it.

From what the CORDS people had been able to determine, there were probably only about two hundred or so VC actually inside the city. The problem was that those enemy troops had divided into small groups holding isolated, dug-in positions scattered across the entire city, and each and every one of those positions had to be separately found and destroyed.

To break Charlie's hold on the town, the eleven SEALs worked with about fifty Nung and their U.S. advisors, coordinating their efforts by radio. Time after time they were taken under fire from hidden sniper or machine-gun nests. Sometimes they were able to knock the enemy position out with machine-gun fire; when the enemy was barricaded behind concrete or sandbags, however, the SEALs used their LAWS, disposable shoulder-fired Light Antitank Weapons that swiftly proved to be both deadly and effective in this kind of close, house-to-house fighting.

Mariacher broke his platoon into two-man teams, each with a portable radio provided by CORDS HQ, and with the machine-gun jeeps as mobile fire support. By late morning, he and Chief Horner were working up one side of Quang Trung Street, three blocks west of the waterfront, while Richardson and Selby worked the other side. They moved in tandem, one fireteam covering the other in a leapfrog advance. When they took fire from a storefront or first floor door or window, the team on the opposite side would pin the enemy down with gunfire, while the other two would move in close, kick down the door, and toss in a grenade or two. When they took fire from a stronger position, or one up high above the street, they would radio for help from one of the jeeps patrolling the area.

It was slow. It was grueling.

But they were winning, at God-damned last. . . .

1146 hours

Selby had been stung by Richardson's outburst back at the CORDS HQ. Shit . . . the guys were always talking about women or getting laid, and nine times out of ten during the past year it had been Richardson who'd picked the topic. *Something* was bugging the guy, and Selby didn't know what it was.

Still, as he moved up the street with Richardson as his partner, Selby gloried in the knowledge that *this* was what he'd been born for. Individual SEALs might get pissed at each other, but the *team* was as tight and as close as any secret brotherhood.

It made you . . . invincible.

Gunfire barked from a doorway on their side of the street, twenty yards ahead. Across the street, Mariacher and Horner dropped to cover and returned fire, sending a long, rolling volley into the open doorway and the windows to either side. Richardson signaled, then gestured to Selby. The SEALs across the street ceased fire as Selby raced up to the door, planted his back against the concrete wall, and pulled an M26A1 fragmentation grenade from a pouch heavy with the deadly baseballs slung over his hip. In true, John Wayne fashion, he yanked out the cotter pin, flipped off the arming lever, and counted off a *one second . . . two seconds . . . throw! . . .*

The grenade clattered down a hallway, then exploded, the blast ringing in Selby's ears and hurling smoke and chunks of debris past his face and into the street. Someone screamed inside; Stoner Commando at the ready, he rolled around the corner and into the smoky near-darkness inside.

Two men lay on the floor, one lying motionless with an AK still in his hands, the other screaming and writhing, clutching at the intestines spilled from his gut. The first man moved as Selby approached the second, jerking the AK-47 into firing position. Selby fired first, stitching the VC from groin to face, then walking the burst across the floor to the wounded man as well. The noise of his weapon was shockingly loud inside that room; the silence afterward seemed louder.

"First aid?" Richardson asked from the doorway. He looked angry.

"Shit, Hank, what's your problem? Two up, two down, and no prizes for second place, all right? What'd you want, for me to nurse the son of a bitch back to health?"

Richardson shrugged. "Hell, if you hadn't gotten him, the Nung would've. Let's get the fuck out of here."

"No way can we manage prisoners anyway, man," Selby said. He still didn't understand what was gnawing at Richardson. They stepped out into the street.

Gunfire chattered from down the street. A long, two-story building marked the end of Quang Trung Street, where it made a T with Trung Nu Vuong Street.

"Cover!" Mariacher yelled from the other side of the street. The two SEALs there ducked back into an open doorway, returning fire. Richardson, still in the doorway behind him, ducked as a bullet struck the door's frame.

"Down!" Richardson yelled. He aimed his M-16 out of the door.

Selby laughed. Shit, the VC couldn't hit the broad side of a barn, not at that range, not with the licking they'd been taking from the SEALs all morning. They were finished, and Selby was helping to finish them.

The Stoner bucked in his hands as he loosed a burst toward the rooftop. Bits of shingle or ridgepole flew in the air; one black, human silhouette rose for a moment, clawing the air, then tumbled down the front slope of the roof and dropped to the street.

Selby laughed again. Man! If *only* his Marine Corps hero father could see him now! . . .

It was traveling faster than sound, so he never heard the bullet that drilled into his skull. . . .

1148 hours

"No!"

Richardson lunged from cover, dropping to all fours in the dusty street at Selby's side. The SEAL lay on his back, eyes open, the left side of his head oddly crumpled. Bubbles of blood expanded and popped at his nostrils; Richardson felt for a pulse and found one . . . but thready and very, very weak. Selby was still alive, but he wouldn't be for long if they didn't get him some decent treatment fast.

Another shot cracked down the street and screamed off the face of the building at his back; a sniper was posted to the left of the site that Selby had taken out. Richardson saw the guy move as he ducked back in the window, high up in the third story of a shop overlooking the street seventy yards away.

"Where is the bastard?" Mariacher yelled.

"There!" Richardson took aim with his M-16 and opened fire, triggering short bursts both to drive the sniper under cover and to show Mariacher and Horner where he was. Horner dropped his rifle and took one of the LAWs tubes he'd been carrying over his shoulder and dashed into the center of the street, where he had a clear shot. Richardson continued bracketing the window with fire as Horner took a stance and triggered his weapon. The LAW gave a shrill hiss, and the rocket shrieked up the street, dragging a white contrail behind. It slammed into the building just below the window; the explosion obliterated the wall and left a gaping hole in the building's facade.

There was no way to tell whether the sniper had been hit or not.

Richardson laid his rifle down and cradled Selby's head. "Damn it, Sel," he whispered harshly. "Don't you die on me! *Don't* you die on me!"

Shit, he hadn't meant to come down so hard on the guy. He was still upset about nearly killing the American woman that morning, and his head wasn't together yet. *Damn it . . . me and my big mouth . . .*

Mariacher was there, leaning over them both. "Oh, shit!"

"He's alive, Lieutenant," Richardson said, still cradling him, rocking him slightly as he moved his body back and forth. "He's still alive!"

"Badges!" Mariacher snapped. "Call in the jeep. And have Aimes call a medevac. Move!"

Selby, somehow, was still conscious. He tried to say something, but the words weren't forming. His breathing was ragged and shallow, and his eyes were glazing over.

It was impossible to be teamed with a guy, to fight beside a guy, to live and joke and breathe and eat and sleep with a guy in conditions like this and not feel closer to him than any brother. Right now, Richardson felt far closer to Craig Selby than he did to Bill.

Or to his stepdad. Or Mom. His whole world was centered here inside the shattered head he held in his lap.

Chau Doc's streets were too narrow for a medevac chopper to touch down in. Gil Franklin drove up in one of the jeeps a few moments later, and the SEALs crowded aboard, with Selby lying across Richardson's and Mariacher's laps in the back, with Richardson holding a compress against the hole in Selby's head and wincing each time he felt the shattered fragments of the man's skull shift and grind with the vehicle's jolts. Minutes later, they screeched into the CORDS compound, where dark-eyed Nung watched impassively from atop sandbag walls, and an Army Huey with a red cross emblazoned on its nose gentled in out of the south for touchdown.

The woman was there—Lisa. She moved Richardson's hand aside and looked under the compress; a splatter of gray and white was oozing from the hole, and there was a lot of blood. Selby's head looked more misshapen than ever. By this time, his eyes had gone vacant, as though he were staring at something else, very far away.

Lisa touched Richardson's shoulder, ignoring the tears streaming down his face. "I'm sorry," she told him. "I don't think he's going to make it."

Craig Selby was probably already dead by the time they strapped him into a Stokes stretcher and lifted him aboard the chopper.

CORDS Compound
Chau Doc
1745 hours

The battle was won. Mariacher could feel that as he stood in front of CORDS headquarters and listened to the rattle of automatic weapons fire in the distance.

Somehow, though, it no longer felt like a victory.

For most of the morning, anyway, it had felt as though the SEALs were working almost completely on their own, an illusion fostered by the sheer size of the city and the tenaciousness of the enemy. But Aimes's Nungs had been moving like black shadows through the streets, and the VC appeared to be less willing to face those accomplished guerrilla fighters than they were to fight SEALs. By noon, Army Special Forces had entered the south side of the city as well, along with a large contingent of ARVN troops.

Fucking hurray, he thought bitterly. Mariacher still had a poor opinion of the Vietnamese; they were great at mopping up but had not been in evidence during the heaviest fighting. Nonetheless, he was glad when they did finally make their appearance.

And when the Green Berets left their fort, it was with helicopter gunships in support, plus mortars and a recoilless rifle with the Mike Force's weapons platoon. Two particularly stubborn VC strongholds—the hospital and the Catholic Church—were reduced to shattered, rubble-strewn hulks, but by mid-afternoon, the enemy was definitely on the run. By sundown, many of the civilians were beginning to emerge from basements and from makeshift bunkers behind beds and piled-up furniture in back rooms.

It was chilling to realize that some, at least, of the civilians watching the American and Vietnamese troops on their streets had been armed VC just a few hours ago; as the tide had turned, they'd simply ditched their uniforms and weapons and donned civilian clothing. Now, they stood on the scarred and littered streets of Chau Doc, happily waving at the Americans and the valiant, liberating forces of the Saigon government as they walked past.

It was, Mariacher thought, one hell of a way to fight a war. . . .

He saw Richardson slumped against a sandbag rampart, his M-16 across his lap. His pants and camo fatigue shirt were still stained by Selby's blood. Selby's death had hit Richardson hard, he knew.

He walked over to him. "Hey, kid. You okay?"

"Yeah. I guess so. Feels kind of numb right now, y'know?"

Mariacher nodded. "I feel the same way."

"It would help if it *meant* something."

"What do you mean?"

Richardson shrugged. "My dad died on Omaha Beach. Did you know that?"

Mariacher was surprised. "I thought I heard your dad was alive and in the Navy now. A SEAL."

"That's Lieutenant Tangretti. My stepfather."

"Lieutenant *Tangretti* is your father?" That surprised Mariacher even more. Most SEALs, certainly most SEAL officers, had heard of Steve Tangretti's original work at starting the Teams in the first place. And about his marvelous quick-step requisitioning M-16s for the Teams a few years back. It was a small Navy. . . .

"My *step*father," Richardson repeated woodenly. "My real father was Henry Elliot Richardson and he was in both the UDTs and the NCDUs during World War II. He was killed on D-day while helping Army engineers blast through a barricade in a defile leading up off of the beach. He won the Silver Star." He sighed. "That was before I was even born. My family has the medal, of course. They keep it on the mantelpiece. Kind of like a keepsake piece of bric-a-brac, y'know?"

Mariacher nodded. The kid needed to talk. He could feel that. He eased himself onto the ground at Richardson's side.

"Of course," Richardson went on, "I never knew him, of course. He died before I was born. My mom and my stepdad told me all about him, though." He snorted. "My grandparents insisted that I still have his name, even when my mom married my dad's best friend. I always got the feeling I was some kind of a fucking memorial to this, this total stranger.

"Today, though, I kind of feel like I know him a little better. He believed in what he was doing. So do I. He probably had buddies who died. Hell, maybe I understand my, my stepdad a little better, too. He was with my father when he died. Like I was today, with Craig.''

"So what's your point? Why did he die? Selby died because he was stupid.'' The words were hard and bitter in Mariacher's throat. He'd not meant them to be critical, but they came out that way nonetheless. More gently, he added, "I think Craig just kind of forgot where he was. If he'd gone to cover like he was supposed to—''

"That's not it. I think I'm looking for why he died. It's not right, long-haired sons of bitches protesting and picketing and moaning about U.S. war crimes over here, and good, decent kids like Craig get blown away and it's not even like he's dying for them or anything. My dad was fighting against Hitler and protecting democracy and all that. What the hell are *we* fighting for?''

Mariacher shook his head. "Shit, Hank. The good old patriotic flag-waving just doesn't apply here, you know that. We're not fighting for God or country over here. We're fighting because a bunch of fucked-in-the-head politicians in Washington decided it would be a neat thing to help out a bunch of other fucked-in-the-head politicians in Saigon. This is supposed to make sense?''

"It's not right.''

"Nobody ever promised that the world would be fair.''

"No, I mean it's all so stupid and futile!'' Richardson waved, taking in the shattered city beyond the compound walls. "We had intel, good solid intel weeks ago! Maybe months ago! What are those REMF bastards doing with it, back in Saigon and Washington and wherever REMFs crawl to breed, huh? What were we doing today, crawling through this damned city a building at a time, fighting like ordinary grunts when we could have snuck in and iced the VC offensive before it even got started!''

Mariacher felt cold. He'd not thought about it in quite that way, not since Selby had been killed. It had been *his* decision to turn his platoon into infantry today, and he still wasn't sure why he'd done it. Maybe the SEALs should have stuck to gathering intel—and to specific missions like rescuing those trapped Americans.

In that sense, it was his fault that Selby was dead. He'd been so damned anxious to smash an enemy that had finally come out of hiding and tried to make it a stand-up fight. That . . . and to show up Perry, and maybe rub a few REMF noses in the fact that his boys had called this assault with the intel they'd gathered in their Bassac operations.

But he knew he would do it again. If America was to win this fucking war, they *had* to make the enemy stand and fight, then kick him silly when he did.

"You think the SEALs could've stopped it?" Mariacher asked Richardson. "You know, Aimes is saying now we were up against fourteen hundred VC in this area. Two hundred in the city, but a lot more out in the country. And the word is, the bastards are hitting everywhere since last night. Hue. Da Nang. Binh Thuy. Saigon. I heard a report a little while ago that VC busted into the American embassy in Saigon at zero-three hundred this morning. Son, this shit load wasn't just aimed at us, at Chau Doc. It landed *everywhere.*"

Richardson looked up sharply. "God. You haven't, I mean . . ." He broke off. "My dad and my brother are both in Nam too. Both SEALs."

"If they're SEALs," Mariacher said, "they're with good people, right?"

"The best."

"That's it, then. They'll be okay, if their buddies have anything to say about it."

"That didn't help Craig, did it?"

"Sometimes nothing helps."

"I guess not."

"If you want to know what we're fighting for," Mariacher told him, "all I can tell you is that we're fighting for each other. Craig died for you, man. Just like you would've died for him. Right?"

"Yeah. Yeah, I guess so." He smiled. "You know, Lieutenant, it's a little weird. We've been trying to get Charlie to come out of the jungle and fight us ever since we got into this war. I guess he finally did."

"And we kicked his ass."

"Yeah. But you know, if the brass doesn't let us fight this war pretty soon, let us fight it *our* way, we're gonna lose it."

And there was nothing Mariacher could say to that at all.

Epilogue

Saturday, 3 February 1968

National Naval Medical Center
Bethesda, Maryland
1330 hours

Veronica Tangretti left her Plymouth in the visitor's parking lot, then walked across the pavement toward the looming gray tower that was the centerpiece of the naval hospital at Bethesda. She'd never been here before, and she found it a bit intimidating as she hurried up the broad marble steps. She clearly remembered seeing pictures of this building on the news, of course; they'd brought Kennedy's body here four years and some ago, hours after he'd been shot in Dallas, and the TV had been filled with images of that familiar, stark tower.

Veronica always associated the place with presidents, somehow; she knew that Bethesda was where the President went for physicals and such. Steve, in his characteristically easy, irreverently mocking way, had told her that the nickname for the hospital within the Navy was "Roosevelt's Erection," since it had been built under that president's administration, and the blatantly phallic imagery had managed to pop any reverence she might once have felt for the place.

But it was *still* a hospital, and like most people, Veronica disliked hospitals . . . places associated always with pain, sickness, and death. The only two times she'd ever been a patient inside a hospital had been when she'd had her sons, Hank and Bill; she thought that she really *ought* to be able to associate such places with new life and healing.

But those memories had been blurred by pain and drugs and time. Both her mother and her father had died in hospitals, and in both cases the dying had taken several months, a lot of pain, and many tears. She didn't like the clean asepsis, didn't like the smell of disinfectants and rubbing alcohol and starched linen.

Through the double set of heavy, brass-trimmed doors and into the building's rotunda. A Navy HM/3 in dress blues sat behind the information booth.

"Bill Tangretti?" she asked him.

The corpsman consulted a Rolodex file. "That would be Ward C, ma'am."

"And where is that? . . ."

He pointed past her shoulder. "Down that passageway to the right. Just follow the signs."

"Oh. He isn't up in the tower?"

He smiled. "No, ma'am. Except for places like peds and the psych wards, it's mostly just officers and big wigs up there."

"I see. Thank you."

"You'll need a pass. . . ."

He'd written her a pass and sent her on her way. She followed the signs, entering at last a long, broad room filled with hospital beds.

The ward nurse took her to Bill.

He was asleep, and she didn't want to wake him. Instead, she sat down in one of the stiff, metal chairs provided for visitors on the open ward, her back to a privacy curtain as she stared at her youngest son. He was wearing pajamas, but someone had pinned two medals on his chest side by side.

She recognized both, of course. A Navy wife knew these things. The red one was the Bronze Star, for heroism. The deep purple with the silhouette of George Washington was the Purple Heart, awarded for wounds suffered in the line of duty.

Noble awards, with long traditions, and a lot of valor and ideals and blood to back them up.

She would have traded any number of ideals, not to mention her own blood, if Bill could be whole and well again.

"They tell me he's going to be okay."

She started, rising from the chair. Steve was there, in pajamas and a thin robe, leaning on a cane.

"Steve!"

"He's had some extensive abdominal surgery, but they brought him out of intensive care a couple of days ago and put him on the ward. I was down earlier, when they pinned the medals on him. It was quite a ceremony, with the captain in command of NNMC, and a lot of junior brass. Our son's a real hero, Veronica. He pushed a buddy out of the way when a booby trap went off, then refused treatment until he collapsed after a firefight."

She faced him, ignoring his prattle. "What the hell are you *doing* here?" she demanded. "I heard, they told me you were in California!"

He smiled, and it was that damnable endearing smile she remembered so well . . . and still responded to. "I'd had word they sent Bill here," he said. "I ended up at Oceanside Naval Hospital, in California. I managed to wangle things, though. There was this corpsman at Oceanside who I did some favors for, and he let me write myself a set of orders to get me transferred here. They have me up on Tower Nine with—"

She held up her hand. "Damn it, Steve. I don't want to hear about how clever you are!"

"But—"

"I *know* you know the system! I know you can make it sit up and beg and probably get it to give you anything you want! Don't you see? I *hate* the system. *Hate* it! It took Hank, twenty-four years ago. It came *this* close to taking Bill. It damn near took you! It could take Hank Junior any time. Oh, God, maybe it *has*, and the telegram hasn't arrived yet. . . ."

She was crying. She didn't want to cry, didn't want to lose control, but she couldn't help it. The tears kept coming and she wanted to strike out at Steve, wanted to *hurt* him damn it for what he'd done, done to her and done to her kids, and at the same time . . .

At the same time . . .

He took her in his arms. She saw him wince as he moved and she felt as though she'd been touched by that pain herself, but she made herself ignore it and let herself be drawn in close. God, she *did* still love him. She *did*.

For a while there, she'd not been sure of that.

"I was just telling you that I wanted to be here," he said, whispering in her ear. "With him." She felt his grip on her shoulders and back tighten. "And with you. Damn it, Veronica, I can't lose you. Don't make me choose between you and the Teams! You're my life, my only love . . . but the Teams, they're . . . they're me. My soul. Can you see that?"

"Steve . . ."

"Please!" He was crying now as well. She felt his tears, wet on her ear and cheek. "I . . . love . . . you. . . ."

She squeezed him back. "I . . . I love you."

She wondered. Could she have chosen between Steve and Bill and Hank? Could she? She wanted them all, could never deny any of them anything.

But to have them *die* like Hank Senior. . . .

"I don't know if I can take this," she said. "I'm so . . . so torn up inside. Damn it, Steve. I don't want to lose any of you! And I nearly did. I so very nearly did. . . ."

He pulled her back to arm's length. For a moment, she stared up into his glistening eyes, her vision blurred by her own tears. "We'll *do* it, Veronica," he told her. "If we hold on to each other. If we stick *close*. Like SEALs."

And she believed him.